"This book has everything I love: Clean, crisp worldbuilding. Characters that live and breathe. A story that teases and surprises me. I like *Master Assassins* so much I wish I'd written it, but deep down, I know I couldn't have written it this well."

—*New York Times* bestselling author Patrick Rothfuss

"The prose is spectacularly good. Your adrenaline will flow. Your emotions will be toyed with. You will find yourself drawn in, turning the pages and worrying that fewer and fewer remain. I read a lot of good books. Quite a few very good books. This is one of the rare 6-star series openers I've encountered."

—Mark Lawrence, author of *Prince of Thorns* and *Red Sister*

"Robert Redick really nailed this one. What a great story! Fascinating plot and characters, and all of the author's formidable skills at play. I cannot wait to read the next one."

—*New York Times* bestselling author Terry Brooks

"An exquisitely written mix of heart-stopping action, masterful storytelling, and enchantment. Redick is a gifted wordsmith with a ferocious imagination. *Master Assassins* will produce many sleepless nights. I guarantee it."

—*New York Times* bestselling author Mira Bartók

"A blazingly smart thrill-ride of an adventure. The world of *Master Assassins* is deep, mysterious, terrifying, and utterly real, and I'll follow Redick's heroes, the mismatched brothers Kandri and Mektu, wherever they go in it. I can't recommend this book highly enough."

—Daryl Gregory, author of *Spoonbenders*

"With spare, sharp-edged prose, Redick balances his rollicking adventure story against a tale of love and uneasy brotherhood, offering a thrilling glimpse into a world both haunting and haunted. His finest work to date."

—Jedediah Berry, author of *The Manual of Detection*

SIDEWINDERS

BOOK TWO OF THE FIRE SACRAMENTS

SIDEWINDERS

ROBERT V.S. REDICK

Talos Press
New York

10 9 8 7 6 5 4 3 2 1

Library of Congress Cataloging-in-Publication Data is available on file.

Hardcover ISBN: 978-1-945863-60-8
Paperback ISBN: 978-1-945863-61-5
Ebook ISBN: 978-1-945863-62-2

Cover artwork by Mack Sztaba
Cover design by Shawn T. King
Map illustration by Thomas Rey

Printed in the United States of America

AUTHOR'S NOTE

Sidewinders is the second book of The Fire Sacraments epic fantasy trilogy. While the three books add up to a single tale, it is also my hope that each will offer a satisfying standalone read.

If you have not read Book One, *Master Assassins*, it may be helpful to know that it is the story of an accidental murder and the world-shattering consequences of the same. Our heroes, Kandri and Mektu Hinjuman, are half-brothers conscripted into the army of Her Radiance the Prophet and the terrible War of Revelation she is prosecuting. They are not assassins, "master" or otherwise, but have the grave misfortune to be mistaken for such by nearly everyone.

The first book follows the brothers' adventures from the night of the murder into hunted exile, and from deep ignorance about the wider world to the beginnings of understanding. *Sidewinders* greatly enlarges the canvas and the cast, although the brothers remain our anchor-point. The story will conclude—you have my promise—with Book Three.

Like Urrath, our own world is plague-ridden, and the deadliest of these plagues are racism, prejudice, and belligerent nationalism. This book is dedicated to those who reach across borders, who cut fences and clasp hands, undeterred by the fanatics and the fearful.

Urrath

Nebusul

(The Scarlet Kingdom)

Pavad Churi

Mostuc

Thrukkun Marshes

Orheym

Panzcanthyr Reef

Alapnysh

R. Thask

Gap of Orheym

Yusa Sara
(Nightfire Range)

Praman Hills

Thyl

Martyrs
Plateau

Necropolis

R. Sill

R. Ghef

Cebiru

The

Kasralys

Datibuc Hills

Sacred Plain

Perec Station

Kasrai

Naiuma

Nralaport

Twelve Hearts
Valley

Bandritramal

Dresheng

Fehinj

Font of Lupriz

Jekka's
Grave

Curtain Rift

Shefetsi

Famine's Table

rt Basin

The Kelde

Blackwind Mtns

Sumuridath Jal

(The Ravenous Lands)

And though they hide themselves in the top of Carmel, I will search and take them out thence; and though they be hid from my sight in the bottom of the sea, thence will I command the serpent, and he shall bite them.

AMOS 9:3

You'd better not invite me to be my natural self. Don't risk it.

DOSTOEVSKY, *THE BROTHERS KARAMAZOV*

PROLOGUE: KANDRI'S PEOPLE

The weight of his deed, and what must follow from it, are clear to him before the blood soaks through his trousers and begins to cool against his legs. But what is plain to the intellect is often shunned by the heart, and denied outright by the imagination. So it happens that he is far from the dead man, from the crooked shack and slumbering army, before he truly grasps what he has done.

His people understand the Gods. Knowledge wearies them, even of the smallest of lives. Mortal pain is sharp and certain, mortal error constant as the dawn. No one could endure a perpetual view of our stumbles, our bruised shins and broken crockery, our cities put to the torch.

A rich man walls off his garden, hiding views of squalor: the Gods placed a mountain between heaven and earth. We may never see it, but it towers above us, transparent against the firmament, icy peak higher than the moon. Sometimes the Gods visit the mountain, the better to spy on their imperfect children. Otherwise it stands deserted, a quiet and a sacred place.

On many nights after the killing, he finds himself on this mountain, seeing as the Gods alone are meant to see. Blackness, stars, and the great world spread below, cold and beautiful and weathered like buckskin, desiccated, torn. Canyons, rifts, fossil forests, seas of sand. And directly beneath him, two men fleeing for their lives.

They have emerged from an enormous war-camp, a sleeping city almost. They are young men and run swiftly, due east, straight for the world's desert heart. One tall and lean but erratic in his movements; the other stronger, steadier, laboring to *keep up. Fear deforms their expressions. Knives and machetes dangle from their belts.*

They do not speak. They rarely look at each other. They are brothers, but severed; even in their manner of running one can see the broken trust.

For a time nothing else in the wide world moves. Then a small commotion, a pinprick, disturbs the camp. Someone has poked the ant nest. Soldiers trickle from the wound.

A handful light upon the brothers' trail and set off in pursuit. They are horsemen, much faster than the brothers, but the watcher on the mountain keeps his eyes on the camp. The pinprick has grown into a sore. Lamps are lit, men spill from their hammocks. A second, larger party sets off behind the first. The brothers are well ahead but the gap is shrinking. The third posse is two hundred strong.

Always at this point he thinks he will turn away, drift to the far side of the mountain, gaze on some other, greener world. But that is forbidden. He must see it all, the savage earth, the fury of his comrades, the burning temples, laughter and necromancy, love flung at the desert like fistfuls of seed.

Matters pass beyond reason. The whole camp shudders awake. Three thousand set off after the brothers, wailing for vengeance, blades held high. He sends the fugitives a prayer. You're not fiends. Don't believe them. Run, run, until you've left this hate behind.

Lightning crackles, the skies convulse. The camp itself tears free of the earth and roars eastward, overtaking, devouring its soldiers.

Then the whole plain. Then the country, rabid and unforgiving. The brothers are estranged but have only each other to rely on, to point fingers at, to redeem or denounce. They must outrun their country, that million-eyed monster, the people whose Gods they have slain.

I. THE CARAVAN

When the river ascends the mountain,
And the earthquake mends the arch,
And the desert toad swallows the rattlesnake,
And the children of evil are redeemed by love,

Then shall we lay down this burden of memory
And live as others do.

WALKING SONG OF THE MISTAJAV CLAN
FROM *PARTHAN TESTIMONY AND DEMEANOR* BY THEREL AGATHAR

1. THE WASP

The pit had appalled him even before he learned what it contained.

From the plateau above it was merely a round hole in the earth, but as they descended it took on a quality of menace. Broad, black, dry as a desert tomb. Here on the canyon floor it gaped at him, promising nothing but disaster, a chill wind moaning across its mouth. He had no wish to approach it. Who in their right mind would?

Come, urged the camel drivers, breath blooming white through chattering teeth. Visit with us, a special place, the Well of Riphelundra, once only, mandatory.

"What's down there?" he asked.

Smiling at his unease but nervous themselves, they took his arms and led him straight for the pit. Fourteen men, nudging, hustling. You have to look, Mr. Kandri, they murmured. Don't you want good luck in the desert? Who knows if you will pass this way again? What if you die?

"That's just what I was thinking," he said.

Dawn had come; jackals sobbed in the hills. The camels stood immense and obdurate and the sun etched their sawtooth shadows on the canyon floor. The mercenaries lurched among the animals, blinking and grimacing; the Caravan Master was trimming his beard. Kandri's toes were numb and his hands cramped with cold. *Why me?* he wanted to shout at the camel men. I'm a coward, see? I don't even like basements.

Why us? their fixed smiles replied. We have just entered the desert, this great killer who dispatches even the best of us, the most sage and seasoned, indifferent as the rag that wipes the soot from the kettle. Now you appear and we must accept you, share our camels and our water and our way. They are rationed, life is rationed, why should we die that you might live?

"Aren't we leaving?" he tried, more anxious with each step. "The saddle-bags, my gear. I'm not ready for the march."

First things first, Mr. Kandri. Spurn a blessing and you may not arrive at all.

CB

The caravan had descended the ridge in darkness: ninety drivers, forty fighting men and women, a threadbare Prince and his lone retainer, a surgeon, a cook, a dour desert veteran bringing up the rear. One hundred fifty camels. A dozen goats to be eaten in stages. A crate of pigeons and a pocket owl, whatever that was. Two hairless dogs.

They were in mortal need of haste, but only a few of them knew why. The Caravan Master had forbidden Kandri and his companions to reveal the truth of their situation. When Kandri's half-brother Mektu observed that the truth would encourage speed in just about anyone, the Master had given him a stern rebuke:

"I set the pace, and the rest comply. They need no further motivation. And you know nothing of the desert or its people to suggest such a thing."

All the same they had set out before midnight; this daybreak pause was their first. As they marched him to the pit, Kandri glanced at the bleary-eyed company. One soldier sharpening her dagger, another limbering up against the cold. Two men burying the camel dung lest it give them away. Four figures hunched over a dying cookfire, and one pair of small, nimble hands, toasting flatbread on the blade of someone's machete.

The owner of those hands looked up suddenly and met his gaze. Eshett, desert woman, quietest and most mysterious of his circle of travelers. She was to leave them at sunset tomorrow, when the caravan passed the turnoff to her people's village.

Kandri rolled his eyes: *Harmless game. They want to show me so badly.*

Eshett's face was inscrutable. Her eyes moved to the pit and back again and she shook her head almost invisibly. They were newly lovers. In the night they had crept away from the caravan, made love standing up in a cleft between boulders, the wind howling about them like a beast in pain, laughing at themselves, at the cold and discomfort, the shooting stars that kept bursting overhead as if in mock congratulations, knowing that her departure was certain, that to indulge in talk of some other ending would be to wound themselves with fantasy, that two days and one night remained to them and must not be lost to grief.

Besides, there were entanglements. Mektu himself loved Eshett, however boorish his attempts to show it. And the brothers were already divided, had nearly become enemies for a time, over a woman from their own clan.

"Never tell him about us," Eshett had said the night before, as they held each other in the wind. "Promise me that before I go. You'll win back the heart of that other, if she's truly out there. And that will hurt Mektu enough."

"What if I come looking for you instead? What if I take you home?"

She had laughed; the idea was preposterous. Neither Kandri nor his brother nor their Uncle Chindilan could ever go home. They could only run, evading as many of the Prophet's servants as they could and killing the rest. The desert in its soul-swallowing vastness might yet save them, if they could lose their pursuers here, and emerge alive on its far shores.

In that abstract country beyond the sands, a city awaited them: Kasralys, ancient and eternal. They could dream of safety within its walls, and even, in time, some new path in life. But home? Never. Home was lost to them; all that remained of it was each other.

Kasralys. The city haunted him in dreams. Safety was the first reason they had to find it. But Kandri had a second, hidden reason, and he felt it more keenly than survival itself.

5

"Her name is Ariqina," he'd said to Eshett, not knowing why.

"She's waiting there, is she?"

Waiting. He could have laughed: when had Ari ever waited for anyone? But—

"She's there, in Kasralys. She has to be."

"Tell me something about her," said Eshett.

Kandri held up his hand, showed her the worthless copper ring from the neck of a fever-syrup bottle he wore on his thumb. "She gave me this—"

"And made a joke about it being a love charm," said Eshett. "That's sweet, and boring, and you've talked about it before. Something else."

Kandri thought for a moment, then smiled. "She told me once that if you saw an odd number of shooting stars it meant good luck for love or friendship, but an even number was terrible luck, because it could always be split in two. And that wasn't like her, believing such nonsense. She's a doctor. She knows how things work."

"And Mektu loves this woman?"

"Mektu loves *you,* Eshett."

They both knew he had dodged her question. "What about her own feelings?" asked Eshett.

Silence, alas, was not among his options. "She cared for us both," he admitted. "But she cared for Mek the way you do for a brother. A very *little* brother. But with the two of us—"

"That's why he resents you," said Eshett, laughing. "Because you always get the girl."

"What do you mean, always?" Kandri demanded. "Before you there was Ari. Before Ari there was no one."

Eshett reached up and gripped his chin.

"Never a word about us," she said again. "Promise me. Right now."

Kandri drew a deep breath. He promised. But he added that his brother already suspected the truth. Mektu was jealous if they walked within six feet of each other, shared a biscuit, exchanged a glance. "How lucky for everyone," said Eshett, "that I'll soon disappear."

CB

The mouth of the pit was fringed with button cacti and dead grass. Radiant cracks gave it the likeness of a window pierced by a stone. He could have bolted when he saw Eshett's reaction, that small but unmistakable *No*. He could have fought out of their grip and fled back to the main company. Safe for the moment. And branded spineless, craven, incapable of trust.

Closer, they urged him. This is a holy place. Do not refuse us please.

Kandri chuckled, a fly wallowing in tar. He had such fine, such *excellent* reasons to refuse. It was late. Soon the shadows would vanish and the heat would search them out. And the death squads on the road behind them: they would be searching too.

Don't fear, Mr. Kandri, said an older man with one cataract-clouded eye. No danger unless you disturb it. Otherwise, it sleeps.

Kandri blinked at him. The language they shared was neither the drivers' mother tongue nor his own. "What sleeps?" he demanded. "Are you telling me something *lives* in there? I thought you called this thing a well."

Yes, yes! they all assured him. A mighty well, an Imperial well, the very life of the district in earlier times. With stairs, landings, carvings of the Gods, alcoves for the storage of tubers and grain. Broad here at the surface, but narrowing to a bottleneck in the depths, above the water source.

"There's still water in that hole?"

Oh no—yes—maybe, gabbled the drivers, before arguing their way to a consensus. The world was drier now; the desert had advanced. Maybe water still flowed in the depths, but only a fool would seek it. The well had passed out of human hands. It belonged to the Wasp.

"Wasps, did you say?"

"*The* Wasp," repeated the camel drivers.

They considered him warily, as though alarmed by the extent of his ignorance. Then Kandri saw his brother standing at the back of the crowd. Mektu's long-fingered hands squirmed at his sides. His lips were puckered in bewilderment.

"*The* Wasp," he said. "That makes no Gods-damned sense. How big is *the* Wasp?"

Some of the men threw their arms wide. Others *tssk'd* and pinched the air. The Wasp was tiny, unless it was huge. "I have a great idea," said Mektu. "Let's leave."

Kandri nodded. The break was over; the Master's aide was waving his red kerchief. But the camel drivers stood their ground. Eyes closed, fists pressed together beneath their chins. The oldest among them chanting in a whisper.

"Thanks for this, everyone," said Mektu, overloud. "I mean it. We're honored to have seen this dead, cold, creepy—"

"Mektu," said Kandri, "they're praying."

Startled, Mektu uttered an obscenity, and the drivers flinched. Kandri glared at him, and Mektu hid his face in the crook of his elbow, as he did when overcome with shame. The drivers chanted—

Seedlings our people,
Flowering in dust,
Life where there was no life,
Brief mornings of green.

—and everyone crouched down to rub a little of the dry earth against their foreheads. Everyone save Mektu, who could not see what was happening.

Kandri considered a prayer of his own, for good behavior from Mektu. His brother had yet to insult the drivers in any ghastly way, but it would come. They had caught up with the caravan just three days before.

But what of your own behavior, Kandri? How close did you come to that worst of insults, spitting on an outstretched hand?

For it was suddenly clear to him that the camel drivers meant no harm at all. In their odd, alien way they had tried to befriend him, include him in a sacred moment. Him, and not his lout of a brother. And yet he had imagined the worst. A sacrifice! Madness, mutiny, the stranger flung into a hole! In the chilly morning his face began to burn.

He knew nothing of these people. They sewed gold and silver beads into the skin above their eyebrows. They smoked cheroots that smelled of savory and brine. The men were clean shaven. The women tied their hair up in complex piles each morning and shook them free after sundown. Men and women mingled only at night; by day they hardly seemed to speak.

Where did they come from? What country, what clan? Eshett had told him to mind his own business. They'll let you know if they wish to, she said. And if not, you of all people should understand why someone might want to hide.

The prayer ended; the crowd stood straight. Mektu lowered his arm. One of the elders offered him a pinch of dust and mimed the ritual gesture.

"Oh Gods, sorry, shit."

Mektu tried to rub the old man's forehead. Kandri turned away—*Hopeless, don't torture yourself*—and then the lunatic attacked.

ଔ

He was just one of the camel men, a dusty face in the crowd. He struck Kandri in a flying tackle and knocked him right off his feet. They landed together, grappling, barely a yard from the pit. His attacker clawed at him, seeking his eyeballs, howling the Prophet's name. His face awash with sweat and tears. Missing teeth, black gouging fingernails.

Then a knife. In Kandri's mind something leaped. He caught the man's wrist as the blade descended and the knife bit the earth beside his chin. He raised his head and seized the man's whole ear in his jaws and hugged the man and rolled. The first snap was the blade breaking, the second his attacker's thumb. A spasm of agony, a howl. He bucked to his feet in one motion and kicked the man in the stomach and drew his machete from its sheath.

"Kandri Hinjuman!" bellowed Mektu, triumphant. "That's my brother! You do not fuck with this man!"

No other attackers. Twenty faces, staring, abashed. He could have brought the machete down for the kill but did not need to, the man had fainted from the pain. But—

The letter!

His hand flew to his chest. The calfskin pouch was still there; he could feel its rawhide stitching through his robe. He had not dared to part with it when they joined the caravan, and their slight possessions placed in saddle-bags. He had sewn the pouch to his old army belt and wore it sidelong across his chest. Now it never left his person, or his thoughts. How could it possibly exist, that letter more precious than his own life, than all their lives together? And how was he able to sleep at night, to walk or run or fight or breathe? Its few pages weighed no more than one of Eshett's flatbreads, but it was crushing him, crushing him with its weight—

Kandri turned his head—and reeled. He stood just inches from the pit. He swayed, caught his toe on something, the black hole spun beneath him—

Mektu's hand closed on his arm.

"Bleeding?"

"Don't think so." He wanted to vomit, but it was only nerves, cowardice, his mortal fear of being buried alive. The camel drivers, looking guilty, began to back away.

"Thank you, Mek," Kandri whispered.

"Just a fucking minute," shouted Mektu, freezing the camel drivers in their tracks. He pointed at the fallen man. "Who is this shit? What's the Prophet to him? You sand rats have your own religion, don't you? What do you need ours for? Are you trying to become Chilotos? If you are, you're cracked. I'm a Chiloto. It's not a clan you want to join."

The camel drivers inched backward, studying them with more than a little horror.

"Not all believers are Chilotos," growled Kandri, steadying himself. "And we're unbelievers anyway now, you fool."

"I know that," snapped Mektu. "I forget, now and then I forget. Answer my question, somebody! What are you staring at me for?"

"Stop clowning," said Kandri, "and speak Common if you want them to understand."

Mektu obliged, unfortunately: "I'm not possessed, you know."

Oh fuck.

Kandri tried to throttle him, but Mektu held him at arm's length. "So what if I'm not like other men? That doesn't mean I have a *thing* in my head. Don't spread rumors, it's a nasty habit."

"There *were* no fucking rumors," Kandri growled. "Ang's blood, we just met them, get me *out of here*."

But Mektu was no longer listening. "You worship the Prophet, eh? Some of you, any of you? Listen: we know all about her. We killed for her, we carried her flag. And she's not what she claims, do you hear me? She's no favorite of the Gods, she's not invincible, she can't listen to your thoughts or punish you from a distance, that's nonsense, and anyway she's a mess, all warts and wrinkles and bits of food in her teeth, and there's this smell sometimes, it's revolting, you'd think the woman dined on—*help!*"

The ground collapsed into the pit.

First Interlude

Typical. The wise brother undone by the idiot, the idiot saying what no one else dares to say. And the madman, the believer in he knows not what: flailing, falling, drawn to death like a salt lick. Knives, fists, fury. And talk, always talk, unavoidable and inane. Arguments over Gods who don't care, mates who won't return, offenses never to be settled in this world or the next.

I'll come clean. I don't like human beings. And I'll ask you not to judge me unless you've done as I've done. Unless you've lived among them, worn their skin, dwelt in their sternums, felt the constant stabbing signals that race from brain to stomach to fingertips, listened to the gurgling advance of waste gasses down the coiled tubes in their abdomens, learned their names, sipped their terrors, attempted that bludgeoning exchange they call *communicating*, glimpsed the lake of fire they call love.

Go ahead. Try one of them on. I'll bet you won't last a day.

Mektu Hinjuman, now: a man so riven by self-doubt that he must bellow to strangers that his mind is his own. *I'm not possessed.* True enough, but is that something to brag about? Why should I wish to possess you? Given a choice of shirts, do you take the one with missing buttons, ragged cuffs, a loose patch dangling from one elbow?

Don't answer, you just might. But we yatras are fastidious creatures: we pull on the shirt least likely to come apart at the seams. I will not say that that my choice of a host was perfect. I had but seconds, after all. This same fool Mektu put a dagger in the chest of the one I'd inhabited for a profitable year. The man may have survived—the blade grazed a lung but missed the artery—but how could I chance it? He was unconscious, bleeding out, and the cold was flooding me.

Without a host, we yatras are corks on the psychic seas. For a matter of seconds, perhaps a minute at most, we can fight the current, hold our position, paddle furiously in place. And then exhaustion claims us, and we drift. Months, years may pass before we wash into the harbor of another soul. If we are caught in a riptide we may end up anywhere—another world, a dead world, a world of blind invertebrates in caves. That will never be my fate.

So I leaped. I considered the few humans at hand and chose one, slipping in through the eye, knowing before I reached the brain what an earth-shaking choice I had made. No, my host is not ideal. But neither is it—perish the thought—a Mektu Hinjuman.

Shelter is mine again. But safety? That is far from assured. For what hope is there for this caravan? One hundred thirty-one scared, shuffling bipeds marching into a furnace: you'd be forgiven if you thought them *all* possessed. It is an inescapable fact that human bodies wither in deserts: they simply dry up and cease to function. Yet in they must go, chins lowered, backs bent, even the survivors of previous journeys throwing off little droplets of thought that taste of sugar water. Optimistic thoughts. *This won't be so bad.*

The camels know better (why not a planet of camels? Why not make *them* the talkers, the tool users, the lords of the earth?). Made for the desert, those exquisite animals. And yet when the dawn broke on the summit yesterday, and they beheld the endless wastes that lay ahead, did they lie to their human keepers, to themselves? No, the camels remembered. They erupted in long wails of misery at the sight.

Of course the humans know the truth as well, in their hearts. It wasn't a camel who named the desert *Sumuridath Jal,* the Ravenous Lands—or in the more gruesome parlance, "the Land that Eats Men," though in point of fact it eats everything and everyone. Splendid monster! Silent and beautiful it beckons, mouth wide as the world. Its fangs are gravel, its molars mountains, its smooth inquisitive tongue the seas of sand that boil quietly over wells, villages, caravans, civilizations. Dig deep, and you will find your ancestors entombed, shocked expressions on their skulls, still dreaming of conquests to come. It is your museum, your archive, your ossuary. It is your past as a species, and very possibly your future.

In all fairness (you see, I do think of fairness), these camel drivers have no better alternative: none, that is, save the summary slaying of the Brothers Hinjuman. Ahead lie the tomb lands, Famine's Table, the Marastiin Floor. Yet behind them, mere hours probably, is a greater danger than the desert itself: namely, other humans. Death squadrons, worshippers of Her Radiance the Prophet, eager to crush and to crucify, to slash and hammer and gouge holes in the flesh of their human brethren, in a frenzy that always seems to me sexual, an ecstatic grappling with flesh, agonies created with the same abandon they reach for when creating life.

What am I doing with these people?

When did concern for them infect me?

Why, by all the swarming stars, did I chain my fate to their own?

The brothers and the maniac rode a torrent of sand and dust into the darkness. Scraping along a wall they could not see, a wall that yielded like tissue paper to their hands. They choked, spun, tried to shield their faces. Along with the noise of the landslide there was a second noise, a strange sudden thunder approaching from every direction at once.

Blackness, pain. A cry from the maniac as his body caught on some protrusion, stopping him cold. They fell away from his voice, away from the dwindling light. Then the shaft angled inward and they rolled to a stop.

Filth poured down, burying them. The thunder increased. Kandri began to struggle; Mektu groaned at his side. They had not reached the floor of the pit, only a bottleneck through which Kandri's legs protruded, dangling free.

"Kandri! *Jeshar*, I'm sorry—"

"I'm all right. Can you move?"

"Fucking sand in my eyes. I'm not dead, though. What's that noise?"

The thunder had become a vast, fluid roaring. It filled the shaft, filled the unseen warrens and galleries above them, and suddenly Kandri knew exactly what it was.

"Mektu," he whispered, "don't move. Please, please. Don't make a blessed sound."

"The Wasp?"

"Shut up."

It was the noise of ten million wings. The dim light vanished. Somewhere above the maniac was howling at them: *Abominations! Traitors to their Chiloto blood! Lord Jekka, rise and take their souls! Mine own for Her Radiance the Prophet, mine own for the one true—*

Nothing then but a scream, short and brutally snuffed, as though the man's throat had filled with ash. The brothers lay gripping each other, still as corpses in their cloaks of dust and sand.

Kandri could not see the swarm descend, but he felt it. The air grew heavy with the weight of hovering bodies, pressing down like a plunger.

Ten feet above them. Dust in his ears, eyes, nostrils. *Gods, let the dust hide us, let it blot us out.*

Two feet. Could they sense his horror, the scream inside him, the violent thumping of his heart?

Inches. A draft teased the skin of his forehead: the air churned by their wings. His brother miraculously still, and the scream inside Kandri rising, fighting to escape. *Always the darkness waiting, salivating, the starved earth spreading its jaws—*

The swarm rose. As one body, it geysered from the pit into the morning sky and was gone. Kandri twisted, retching; Mektu sneezed. And through the mouth of the pit, like a blade of amber, a single perfect sunbeam probed the depths.

2. A CHAT BY THE RIVER

"You know I've always liked you."

She met his eye as she spoke. It was the simple truth, but her glance forgave him for not believing a word.

"And dislike?" he asked. "What would that resemble?"

"Don't find out."

They spoke in the same wry tones they used at court. And indeed his posture in the high-backed chair was fit for dinner with the lords of the realm: spine straight, chin high, dark eyes level upon her. But they were a long way from court. When he blinked, the man's eyes sparkled in the morning sun, but it was only because tears had frozen at the tips of his lashes. He twitched at wrists and ankles, where the ropes were tightest.

The chair itself was lashed upright upon a raft.

From the shore, the woman in the white fur coat watched the motions of the prisoner's wrists. She had oval cheeks below bright tapering eyes, olive-brown skin, black hair straight as a curtain, long braid tucked away inside her hood. A sober face, and thoughtful, the expression attained not at all by accident: a face befitting the youngest Chancellor of Kasralys in six centuries, which is what she was.

The thaw had come early; across the wild river, chunks of ice like broken battlements were gliding downstream. But here by the banks among the cottony reeds, a delicate crystal skin had frozen anew overnight, and now blazed, perishing, in the morning sun. The raft's nearest edge was beached in mud, but the rest was afloat. Heaving and shifting. Eager to be off.

"Shooting stars last night, did you see them?" asked the prisoner. "Quite extraordinary. Even portentous, if you believe in that sort of thing. I counted twenty-one."

An odd number, thought the woman. *Good luck for friendship. Who was it told me that?*

Somewhere downstream a horse nickered, impatient. The man lifted gray eyes to the forest behind her. The woman waited in silence.

"You expect me to say something, Lady Kosuda," said the man, "but you must know I have nothing to say. If I did, those hellish dogs would have gotten it out of me by now."

"They're wolves, Ursad," she said.

"Wolves, then. What do I care? Demons at your beck and call is what they are."

"You were not harmed, I trust."

"I was brutalized, precisely as you intended. Scared out of my mind. This is nothing by comparison."

The woman, Kosuda Sarika Serr, glanced meaningfully downriver, where the spray of the great falls rose in a cloud.

"Nothing?"

"I do not work for the Kingdom of Shôlupur," he said, "nor for any foreign power. Unlike you, I was born in Kasralys, and my parents before me. Like you, I'm a proud servant of the realm."

A cough racked his body. The blanket she had brought for him slipped from his knees.

"Ursad Ramu," she said, "how is it that you can waste your last minutes on a charade? I've always imagined that as death approached I would lose all tolerance for lies, my own first and foremost."

"Will you kill me, then?" Ramu asked. "I would not put it past you, mind. I'm not one of those fools who consider you an exalted clerk."

She bowed her head, appreciative.

"But neither would I doubt your readiness to stage all this—two days riding, my left ear dead of frostbite, wolves snapping at my scrotum—just to prove some sort of point."

"No," said Kosuda, "to save Kasralys from those who would destroy her from within. A city unassailable by force—"

"No such thing," said Ramu.

"A city that has shrugged off assaults for thirty centuries," she pressed on, "behind walls the Gods would envy, and with the world's tallest cliff at its back. Such a city has but one thing to fear: corruption, daggers drawn against ourselves. You know this. You know that the Shôl, and others, dream that it shall one day come to pass. And hence you know that I cannot allow this Plateau to become a corridor of whispers. If the Shôl must forever be trying to worm out our secrets—and I suppose they must—let them use the front door, like other spies. The Plateau is too much trouble for all concerned."

She stepped nearer the water. "But I am sorry about your ear. You're still good looking, if you care to know."

He smiled. "Wasted on your kind, more's the pity."

She placed her boot on the raft and pushed. It glided backward, revolving, shattering the reeds and their corsets of ice. The sun swept the man's dark face like a searchlight. The raft began to slide downstream.

Kosuda walked beside him, hands in pockets. "There's a name I keep hearing," she said. "Thruko."

"Eyelash Thruko," said Ramu. "Yes, I've heard of him."

"When and where?"

"Palace chatter. Over a year ago, it was."

"Is he your cell commander?"

"My—" Ramu checked himself, visibly struggling for calm. He took a deep breath before he spoke again.

"Eyelash Thruko is a name—a nickname I presume—for some oddball visitor from the north. Or the west, I don't recall. Talk of him surfaced here and there about the city for a number of weeks, and then dried up. I never met him, nor learned his business with the Realm. Why? For the highly suspect reason that I made no attempt to learn. Why? Because no one ever suggested that he mattered. Next question."

Kosuda did not at first respond. She had bungled her question about Thruko, who mattered very much. *Timing. Timing.* Her old master had whispered the word, shouted it, threatened to brand it on her palm.

"All right," she said at last. "Explain your visits to this place. Five times in two years."

Ramu rolled his eyes. "What is there to explain? The Martyrs' Plateau is beautiful; I come here to recover from the noise and filth of Kasralys. And to hunt."

"That bow we took off you was laughable."

"It's what I could afford."

"You could afford a sablewood masterpiece by Rabhanu himself," said Kosuda. "The one you chose is ill-made, and brittle from lack of use. It's a prop, my friend. You're no hunter. You collect wind chimes and books about the War of the Alchemists."

The raft spun, a lazy leaf. His fine dark coat was torn at the shoulder.

"Since you *will* have a confession out of me, take this one," he said. "Every woman in Kasralys who I fancy—really fancy, open my heart to—sooner or later gives me to know that she prefers the attentions of women. Can you explain that to me, Chancellor? Do you go about recruiting them to your side?"

"It doesn't work that way," said Kosuda, smiling. "And if it did, I couldn't help you. I have the opposite problem."

He laughed aloud. "Now I know you mean to kill me. You've never been so frank before."

The raft shuddered, scraping over some hidden log or stone, and a surge of water bathed his feet. He gasped, trying helplessly to stamp them.

"I'd rather not," she said, almost in a whisper. "Kill you, I mean."

From his face she knew he'd not caught a word.

"By my age," he declared through chattering teeth, "I thought I'd be long done with courting. I wanted children, you know. I wanted to see them grow up to serve the city you think I've betrayed."

"It's still possible," said Kosuda. "Tell me what the Shôl want to know."

"Gods of the Last March!" he shouted. "I do not serve the Shôl—not today, not yesterday, not ever in my fifty years! I've never even set foot in the Scarlet Kingdom. And you, Lady Kosuda, are a less gifted inspector than I supposed. Look up my ancestry in the Manual of Sages. You'll find no hidden Shôl grandmother. No hidden anything."

"Did they ask you to report on His Excellency's health?" asked Kosuda, "or perhaps the feuds in the Chamber of Forty?"

"What feuds? No, hush, don't tell me. I care nothing for your politics, squabbles between generals, all that chaff in the wind. Just bring me ashore, will you please? My feet—"

"I'm also told," she interrupted, "that beyond the desert, a crisis has seized the whole of the Chiloto clan. An assassination within the family of the Prophet, to be precise."

"I give you my word as a gentleman," said Ramu, "that that is the dullest news I've heard in years."

"Did the Shôl dispatch assassins to the Prophet's domain? Are the clans going to war?"

"Why don't you think a moment, Chancellor?" he said. "Even if I were a spy, how could I predict what the Chilotos, with their mystical drivel, would do next?"

"Orthodox Revelation may be madness," said Kosuda, "but it is not drivel. It is a faith, the creed of their liberator, however distasteful we may find it. There are even adherents in Kasralys."

"It is a cult," he said, "and a bloody-minded one at that. You really do have a problem if such gibberish is catching on."

"You?"

"I mean we, of course. Don't play games. It's your headache to remedy, as the one who does the city's housekeeping. Because at the close of day—yes, you *are* a glorified clerk. And head butler, accountant, groundskeeper—"

"Rat catcher."

"The lords of the Realm must be pleased with you," he said. "Their talented pup, their little low-born terrier. So very efficient, cleaning up their messes, not leaving a trace. You asked for honesty, milady."

"I'm still waiting for it," said Kosuda.

He shook his head, musing. "The *Darsunuk*, the Time of Madness. It's coming, if you listen to the servants, the sailors, the old grandfathers in the park. There's some gossip for you—good Kasraji gossip, though I suppose you might hear it anywhere. But Orthodox Revelation! Why, it's hardly credible. There's scarcely a Chiloto to be found in the city—"

A sly look came over him. "Ah, but there's one, isn't there? That young thing at the School of Medicine. The prodigy. Who means to rid the world of Plague."

"Ariqina Nawhal," said Kosuda. "She's a Chiloto, yes."

"There you are," said Ramu. "Ask *her* what has riled her Prophet."

"Dr. Nawhal's no believer."

"What if she is, though? You're not infallible. Perhaps she's the one you should have tied to this chair."

"Perhaps you should answer my questions."

"I remember," he said. "She came to that summer banquet at the Sartaph's estate. In your coach, at your side. One of your projects, is she? And her beauty a mere coincidence?"

"Give me something, fool," said Kosuda. "Give me an option besides watching you drown."

The falls grew louder still. Kosuda took a deep breath, trying to calm her jangling nerves. The raft turned, the man revolved like a figure on a music box. His cough began again.

"Forgive my teasing," he said. "The truth is, I admire your taste. Persons like us, we only fall for the most difficult of conquests. Tortured artists, brilliant minds. Those who cherish and suffer for ideals. You're a misfit in Kasralys. Why not love another misfit? Why not a Chiloto?"

"You are babbling, Ramu."

"But there is gossip about your Ariqina Nawhal," he went on. "Others have tried for her. Even a Sky Lord tried to sweep her off her feet. She would not so much as flirt. Dr. Nawhal is spoken for, Chancellor. She has a hidden lover in the city, or someone exceptional back home."

"Speaking of homes," said Kosuda, "who is to inherit yours? If the paper-work's awry, I'll gladly see to it. Just name the beneficiary."

He straightened. "The Imperial Trust," he said, "and my books to the Indigents' Library. Put that in your report."

"How noble. And your sister?"

Ramu shook his head. "We had a falling out," he said. "Fortunately she wants for nothing. You could let her know that I forgive her, however. I'd be grateful for that. I mean if this isn't a bluff, if you're truly murdering a citizen, murdering me. Are you, incidentally?"

She faced him, speaking as gently as she could. "What was your assignment? Help me, I'm begging you. What message were you taking to the Shôl?"

"Lady Kosuda, I am innocent."

She gave a defeated shrug. Aren't we all, in our hearts?

They walked together in companionable silence. A raven leaped from a branch in a shower of snow. The falls became a thunder she could feel through the frozen ground.

And there, just ahead: her patient valet, shivering beside the coal-black stallion.

"This is where I leave you," she said. "There are two more bends before—well, you understand. I thought you might want to pray."

Ramu caught her eye once more as the raft revolved. His lips moved, toying with words he could not speak. Even now it would be a simple matter to retrieve him, dry him off, whisk him home to the city, to wind chimes and tea.

He shifted his gaze to the billowing spray, the four-hundred-foot plunge into a cauldron of foam. The sunlight caught him again and he was beautiful, one of the martyrs of the First Realm, a doomed saint in bronze. She turned to the valet and gestured with her chin.

"Let's be going," she said.

☙

The pines stood low and dense: in twenty yards the river was gone from sight. Kosuda lifted a finger to her lips, and the valet saw her and nodded. They would take no chances yet.

Another precious minute, leading the horse in silence through the trackless snow. They pressed through a holly thicket, up a steep embankment, along a wall of moss-gnawed stones that were, it was commonly thought, all that remained of Emperor Kavalismur's summer palace, and the grand fêtes of nine centuries before. Ahead, figures loomed through the trees.

When they stepped into the clearing everyone sprang to their tasks. The guards who had brought Ramu from the city were already mounted. First Marshal Lisrand, her chief aide, was conveying orders with grumbles and gestures, snowdrops glittering in his woolly gray moustache. He turned to look at her in that startling way of his, mild and piercing at once.

"He knows something about the Prophet," said Kosuda.

"The Chiloto Prophet?" Lisrand's eyes widened. "What does she have to do with Ramu's masters in Shôlupur?"

"Ask his nephew, once we're back in the city."

"I might," said Lisrand. "Young Palachim is proving quite the asset. Still, you were right to leave him behind. No good could come of him seeing his uncle in such a state."

"Is everyone in position?" asked Kosuda.

"Everyone," said Lisrand, "but the river is in flood, milady. Sunny days. This early thaw."

Kosuda felt a tightness in the back of her neck. "The shallows—"

"Not so shallow as we'd like," said the First Marshal. "I measured a rise of fourteen inches since—"

"Piss of the great bitch of Hell!"

Lisrand shook his head. "Just melted snow."

Kosuda drew a deep breath, picturing the river, the double bend, the woods on the opposite shore. *Fourteen inches.* Enough to drown the shallows ahead, speeding the raft toward the falls. How could she have failed to notice? What was happening to her?

She blinked: her people stood frozen, looking carefully at nothing. "Get on!" she fairly snarled. "What, did you think we'd fold?"

They sprinted to comply. Kosuda stood in the center of it all, directing with her eyes. Now that their doubts were answered, her people were calm and efficient; she had drilled them for days. One brought her the telescope, another pointed out the oak she was to climb. Then Lisrand cleared his throat.

She turned. Before them stood a woman of her own height, her own color, her own thick braided hair. Sappu Clan, like Kosuda herself, their ancestors brought to Urrath at spear point and trapped here forever by the Quarantine. Odds were that they were distant cousins—very distant, or Kosuda's research would have yielded the fact. She was twelve years younger than Kosuda, poised and smooth of skin. Her lips formed an enigmatic smile.

Kosuda did not return it. *You can earn my smiles, girl.*

She tore off the woman's hood. "That braid is sloppy. Tie it again."

Alarmed, the woman tugged at her hair.

"Don't arch your spine in the saddle, either: that isn't like me, is it?"

"No, Chancellor. I'm sorry."

"And don't look back once you're moving. They will expect no second thoughts."

"I understand, Lady Kosuda."

"If you don't, we've made this journey in vain."

They traded coats. Kosuda removed her own cap and placed it on the woman's head at the proper angle. Then she clapped her on the shoulder.

"Mount up, and be swift."

The woman put her foot in the stirrup and vaulted onto the stallion. With a last glance at Kosuda (that smile again, damn her insolence) she shortened the reins and nudged the beast forward. The other riders fell in behind her. Kosuda watched her double with concern.

"Too young for the part, really," she said aloud. "I don't have an ass like that."

The First Marshal dropped his eyes, not saying a word.

"What of our forest friends?" asked Kosuda.

"Everyone's in place, milady. Everyone but us."

They walked to the oak. About its trunk, a thin rope was tied at shoulder level. Fiddle-string tight, it vanished into the trees, angling back toward the river at a point upstream from where she had left Ursad Ramu.

Lisrand plucked the rope with two fingers. Someone in the distance plucked back.

"Try not to fall on me, Mistress," said Lisrand.

She smiled—this man had earned it, twenty times over—and pulled herself lightly into the tree.

The climb was sheer pleasure: no maddening choices, just this branch or that one, her good strong arms, ice-kisses of melting snow. Memories flew at her like splintered glass: the lake house at Auprinu, the soaring willows, her sister crawling ahead of her along a limb, laughing, teasing, their secret place in the sun.

Three decades ago. How's that possible? Why do we sit festering in cities, year upon year?

She eased out along a limb. The spot was perfect: hidden by the surrounding pines, she could nonetheless see everything that mattered. The river's serpentine. The falls, grinding like the devil's own mill. The dark wood on the far shore. The raft, thumping along to its destruction, lofting its blunt human mast.

Ramu, you great idiot! Why wouldn't you help me, why wouldn't you turn? The Shôl would have killed you themselves, soon enough. What would you have been to them, after you spilled your secrets? What but a loose thread in need of trimming?

She glanced to her left: there was the party, charging uphill, feigning a return to Kasralys. The black and buckskin horses magnificent against the snow, and Kosuda's double at the center, square-shouldered, proud. Exposed to all the world, or at least to the eyes across the river. The eyes that wanted to see her city burn.

Don't fail us, girl. Don't panic if the horse shies. Don't let them study your face.

She held her breath. There was another way this game could end: in grand betrayal, ambush, slaughter. A trap prepared so well, so early, that she and her people never dreamed they had walked into it, crawled into it, lain down at their ease on jaws of iron. If she could devote her life to such stratagems, why not her enemies?

She shuddered. After so much preparation it was unthinkable. *And therein, always, the danger.*

The party crested the hill. The morning silent, the stallion steady as a God. Slowed by the broken hilltop, they picked out a path. Kosuda watched, oaths frozen on her tongue. Then they were descending; then they were gone.

Kosuda glanced down, gestured. Lisrand set his hand on the rope.

On the river, Ramu's raft had wallowed into the shallows—or what had been the shallows. Despite the higher water, it slowed, dragging over submerged rocks. Ramu was writhing: another coughing fit, or perhaps sheer terror. Only some ninety feet remained before the falls.

But it wasn't a cough, was it? The man was struggling with his ropes, making a last, doomed effort to escape. This was better than she hoped for. The Ursad was quite visibly alive.

Seventy feet. Lisrand was gazing up at her from the base of the tree, making nervous motions with his hands. Ramu thrashed against the ropes with growing violence. Kosuda held the telescope at the ready but did not use it: she needed to take in the whole theater now, not the face of the fool at center stage. His suffering no longer mattered.

Sixty feet. Lisrand hissed her name. Kosuda raised her hand—slowly, slowly.

A boulder of ice struck the raft, jolting Ramu, splintering logs. Kosuda narrowed her eyes. Her hand still hovered in the air.

Then, from the trees on the far shore, men came sprinting. Four in all, shedding clothes and weapons and crying out to Ramu. *We're coming. Hold on you bastard, you misbegotten dog.*

Lisrand chuckled by the foot of the tree. He'd heard them too.

The men plunged into the water. They flailed, sputtered, roared at the cold. But they reached the raft, and three of them slowed its drift while a fourth crawled aboard with a knife in his teeth. Shaking all over, he moved to Ramu and began to saw at his bindings.

Kosuda dropped her hand.

Lisrand jerked the rope.

From their own side of the river, five wolves exploded from hiding. They flung themselves into the torrent, massive predators, leaping with the grace of seals. They swam in tight formation, with the huge pack leader the mountain hermits called Grayflame at the lead, weaving swift and smooth through the rushing ice. Kosuda wished Lisrand could see them: the wolves were so beautiful it hurt.

For ten or fifteen seconds the men at the raft saw nothing. Then Ramu, still bound at the ankles, jabbed a finger across the water and screamed.

Utter panic ensued. The men in the river let go of the raft and fled for land. The one aboard made to follow, but Ramu seized him in a death grip and fought him for the knife. When they separated, Ramu's hands were scarlet, but the blade was his and he used it, cutting the last of the ropes and leaping like a boy into the flood.

His motions were stiff and awkward, and Grayflame closed on him with ease. Ramu vanished below the surface; the wolf followed, and when they rose a moment later, Grayflame had him by the nape of the neck.

Three of his would-be rescuers fell in similar fashion. The last made it to dry land and lunged for his sword, but even as his hand closed on the weapon a wolf was on him; he fell under the huge black form and did not rise.

Ang's love, you perfect creatures. Where would I be without your help?

Flicker of motion. She swung the telescope, cursing already: a fifth man was sliding down from a tree. A lookout. Of course there was a lookout. He'd not seen through the deception, not given them away. But she had no one within a mile of his position.

He'll have a horse in the trees, same as we did. He'll get away, he'll talk—

The man's boots touched the ground.

A mile downriver, Grayflame looked up and saw the man and hurled himself into the chase. Kosuda's breath caught in her throat. The man was gone already into the trees. Grayflame flew like an arrow, but the distance, the distance was simply—

Archers. You should have lined the bank with archers. Bungling fool.

The other wolves hauled their quarry ashore. Ramu lay as if dead; the rest sat dazed in a circle. Kosuda signaled to Lisrand again, but her eyes went quickly back to the telescope. The forest's edge was still.

He never spoke to Ramu, she told herself. *But he saw us all, this whole operation. They will know Kasralys is at work here, and the next time it will be us who are ambushed.*

A full minute passed. On her side of the river, the rest of her team dragged the long boat into the water and started across. Well, it was time. Ramu was bleeding; if she delayed any longer he could die.

There came a cry of horror from the captured men. Grayflame was padding out of the woods. From his jaws, a human head dangled by a flap of skin.

୧

"Those voices," said Lisrand as he rowed them across. "Shôl accents, or I'm a cuttlefish. Your Ramu was lying through his teeth."

"He was," said Kosuda, studying the shore through the telescope, "but I don't want him to die for it. Can you row any faster?"

The First Marshal grunted, fighting the current. He tried to look over his shoulder, but could not twist far enough to see.

"One of them's talking?"

"Crying," said Kosuda. "Bleeding too. Get me ashore."

The man in question lay on his back. The wolf's front feet were on his chest and its jaws hovered inches from his throat. Heedless, the man wept and shouted and flapped a despairing hand. Kosuda hissed through her teeth: the hand was scarlet. Two fingers gone.

Knife work. He's the one who fought with Ramu. You're less helpless than you pretend, Ursad.

The man's voice rose to a delirious shriek. The wolf reared back, startled, then pounced and seized the man's neck in its jaws.

"Pitfire." Kosuda leaped into the water. The cold was so shocking she might have been in the jaws of some beast herself, but she struggled ashore, shouting at the wolf. The animal released the man and sat back, placid and unconcerned. Kosuda dropped to her knees before the captive.

His throat was bruised but not punctured. The wolves knew the accord: none of these men were to be harmed unless they resisted; this one had held the captive as it might a naughty cub. So why that smear of blood beside his hand? Kosuda moved the captive's arm with care.

Ach, shit. The knife had severed the veins in his wrist. It was a wonder he had made it to shore.

She tied a tourniquet quick as thought, but many a thought arrives too late. For a moment she considered plying him with questions: political questions, military questions, the ones that had brought her to this place. Then she loathed herself for the idea.

"Stars."

The word came clear from his slowing lips, but it was a discharge more than a breath. She bent low, sheltering him from the wind.

"The shooting stars?" she said. "You saw them too? Of course you did. You were here all night, like us."

The man's eyes swam in a hazy circle.

"Do you want absolution?" she asked. "Is there a God you follow, or a saint? What name will bring you peace?"

His mouth curved into a tortured grin. He could not speak, never would again, and so she tried to read his lips.

Ag . . . aath . . . thr . . .

"Agretu?" she tried, naming the Shôl God of mercy.

That smile again. Derisive, almost mocking, and then the light left his eyes. Kosuda sat back, making room for death. She felt a rage that seemed to have no object, until she realized it was directed at herself. She did not kill gladly. Today she had not expected to kill at all.

The dead man's smile faded as his muscles relaxed. She closed his eyes, whispered a quick intercession—*Let the quiet beyond worlds receive this traveler*—then rose and surveyed the scene.

The second skiff had landed; her full team swarmed about the captives, who made no move to resist. Lisrand was kneeling, striking sparks with flint and steel even as another agent assembled the firewood. The wolves had withdrawn into a huddle by the shore. The two surviving Shôl rose to their knees, crossed their wrists behind their backs as ordered.

What name will bring you peace? Not Agretu; the guess had sparked only amusement in the dying man. She resisted the urge to nudge the corpse with her toe. Once more, you. Speak up.

Ach . . . ahh . . . thaa

Ah . . . gahh . . . thra

It would plague her, like a half-remembered tune. She would wake in the night and toy with the syllables, see again the motions of those lips.

Lips that were cooling now, that would dry and shrink in the cold. The lips of a corpse, not a man with dreams, plans, hobbies, a sense of humor, a place in the world. Perhaps a wife, perhaps a little boy or girl he'd fed with a spoon in the wee hours a month ago, before setting out on the long road south to meet a spy.

One of her younger agents was approaching from the riverbank. She could see his smile from the corner of her eye: an eager smile above a short black beard.

"Victory, Chancellor," he said. "Ten months of shadowing that swine of an Ursad, reading his letters, picking through his trash."

Kosuda nodded curtly, hands in fists.

"And now we have the proof," the young man continued. "Proof positive of his betrayal, and of the true intentions of the Shôl. I hope the Grand Illim himself rewards you—"

"For what?" she asked, cutting him off. "We knew about Ramu already, and we've known for a century that the Shôl wish us harm. Don't start the celebrations just yet. There is no victory until one of them speaks."

The young man's smile faded like a mirage. He lifted something, offering it for her inspection. It was the severed head.

She made herself look. Disgust could wait, sorrow could wait, this was what it meant to serve the Seventh Realm. The neck was a snarl of gore, but the face looked merely sleepy and distracted, like a boyish drunk.

"He was no one special, I think," she said. "Show Lisrand, just to be sure."

31

There: the oil-soaked firewood was aflame. She moved to it and warmed herself for a silent minute. Then she turned and walked upriver. The five wolves flowed around her, knowing what came next. Kosuda chose a flat stone and sat cross-legged; the great predators dropped in the snow in attitudes of indifference. All save Grayflame, who circled once about his pack and came to sit before Kosuda.

Blue sapphire eyes. The smell of him came like a kick: wet fur and dander and rank human blood.

"I've never known just what you understand," said Kosuda, "but I thank you, wild brother. Our compact holds: all this land is yours, so long as I am Chancellor and His Serenity the Illim rules the Seventh Realm of the Kasraj. As you serve me in my need, so I serve you. Only go to the hermit who dwells in Ormscleft. He will send word to me. I will come."

Grayflame's eyelids lowered once. His lips retracted, revealing four-inch fangs. Then he stood and brought his muzzle—the jaws that had ripped flesh and shattered bones minutes before—close to her face. He sniffed with fierce attention.

"May the elk always be many," whispered Kosuda, "and your cubs grow fat."

Grayflame grazed her cheek with his fang—a thing he had never done; she sat terrified and amazed. Then he wheeled to face his pack. The other wolves rose, and all five loped with casual grace into the trees.

Kosuda watched them vanish, then returned to her people. Taking Lisrand aside, she said, "Drag the corpse into the forest. The head as well."

"Right you are, milady. We'll leave no scrap of them here. And Ramu's out of danger—long as we keep his would-be rescuers at bay. They blame him as much as us for how this ended."

"Did you check his mouth?"

"I'm not a trainee, am I?" growled Lisrand. "No poison pill, no hidden blades. In fact he's got nothing but the clothes we provided."

"Good," said Kosuda. "I want no further surprises today."

"Couldn't agree more."

Lisrand glanced upriver, and Kosuda felt a renewed stab of guilt. Grayflame had understood her error as well: the touch of that tooth had been no accident. He could have bitten her, scarred her, as the head wolf will do to one who strays from the established order, endangering the pack.

And perhaps he should have, you blundering fool.

If the scout had escaped to report the operation, Grayflame and his pack would never again have known peace. Like Kosuda's agents, they would have become targets of the Shôl—and perhaps of other enemies of Kasralys. Perhaps of that most hidden enemy, that cypher.

Thruko. She glanced at Ramu's shivering form. *By the beast in the pit, you will speak to me of Eyelash Thruko.*

"I didn't like the grin on that dying man," said Lisrand. "A grin of hatred, and a taunt. He knew something, or wanted you to think he did. What was it he said at the end?"

"I'm still trying to work it out," said Kosuda. "I asked what name would bring him peace. He answered with that wicked look. And a word, a name I think. Agretu, Agrator—"

"Not—"

"Hush!" whispered Kosuda. "No, not Eyelash Thruko. That man doesn't show himself to foot soldiers."

"Or anyone else," said Lisrand. "A poor guess, forgive me."

"I wish you'd make another. It's driving me rather mad."

When her aide said nothing, she turned and studied his face. "You *do* have another guess, don't you?"

Lisrand's eyes grew evasive. "Come," she said, "spit it out. It can't be as bad as your first."

"It's mad, but—Agathar."

She nearly laughed. Therel Agathar. Magnus General of Shôlupur. The miracle worker, who saved his country in the last war, routing the Važeks to the west and Kasralys itself to the southeast. The military genius of the age. But—

"You're trying my patience now," said Kosuda. "Agathar's old as the hills. He retired before I kissed my first girl."

"As recently as that?"

"Shut up. You're whistling in the dark. We get reports on that old man. He visits his garden in a wheelchair. He . . ."

"Milady?"

33

The prisoner's face swam up in memory; his lips deliberate and precise. *Agathar*. It was a closer match than any of her own guesses—and had been mouthed by a man who hated Kasralys enough to join this team, to wait in misery and mortal danger for the arrival of a spy. A man who had flung the name at her with a sneer of triumph. And died in peace.

Therel Agathar. Every military mind in Urrath had once lost sleep about the man. Every soldier in Shôlupur had breathed easier when he left the field.

Could the old general have moved on to spycraft? Could he have faked his retirement, the better to escape her notice, the better to undermine a city no army could overcome?

Could General Agathar be the force behind this shadow-enemy she had chased in circles around the realm, this Eyelash Thruko? Or did Thruko even exist? Two years, and she had never glimpsed the man. Was he only a diversion, a rumor, spoon-fed to credulous Kasrajis like herself? A shadow to keep her busy, keep her eyes averted, while the true enemy prepared to strike?

General Agathar. Eyelash Thruko. *Could they be one and the same?*

"It isn't possible," she said.

"You ordered me to spit it out," said Lisrand.

Kosuda shook herself. "My next orders," she said, "are to bring the prisoners across the river, and yourself down from the clouds."

Lisrand raised an eyebrow. It was as close as he ever came to telling her off.

❧

Ursad Ramu, bandaged and tied once more, was already seated in the boat. No saint now: only a traitor, purchased by their enemies. A canker on the body of the realm.

"Lovely excursion," he said. "We should make this a regular thing."

"You'll want to forget you ever took that tone with me," said Kosuda.

Ramu flinched, as if she'd passed him a cup of something foul, something best not examined too closely. The remainder of his life.

"Two deaths today," she said. "Shôl boys, your comrades. Here at your instigation."

One of the captives gave a violent start, straining against the guards that held him.

"No comrade of mine," he snarled. "Those men were my brothers, dog."

"I'm truly sorry," said Ramu, gazing at the river.

"Sorry!" said the fugitive. "You can go rot in hell. What are you worth, you old stinking turncoat, that we should kill ourselves to save you? What's the prize we're here to collect?" He spat in the snow. "The deep secrets of Kasralys. Horse shit, I say. The city's not been a threat to us since my great-grandfather's time. And the Gods know we can't threaten *her.*"

"The Gods know all," said Ramu. "Soldiers in the field, rather less."

"I know a fool's bleeding errand!"

Kosuda bent and fussed with her boots, careful not to glance at Lisrand. There was something unnatural about this argument. Was it staged for their benefit, rehearsed?

"Kasralys is more than a city," said Ramu, turning to face the captive. "It is a state, and a malignancy. It is the last live coal of the empire that beggared this continent and enslaved us all."

"Fuck off, that's ancient history."

One argues for destroying us, the other calls him a fool, thought Kosuda. *Definitely a performance. But who is performing, who sincere?*

"A single coal can light the fire afresh," said Ramu. "If we leave it smoldering, we may awake one day to find Kasralys marching again over this continent, and ourselves under the heel of a second empire, more terrible, more final than the first. The coal must be snuffed, don't you see?"

"I see a madman talking rot."

"Your friends died for the freedom of their countryfolk," said Ramu. "They died for all the people of Urrath."

"They died for nothing!" spat the captive, writhing. "Your mission's shit, Kasralys is impregnable, any child could tell you that. She's stood there like the Gods' own fortress for three thousand years!"

Ramu glanced sidelong at Kosuda. "There's a first time for everything," he said.

3. BROTHERS IN THE DARK

"So you're not?"

"What, possessed? I had to say that, Kandri. I had to calm those fuckers down."

"Calm them down?"

"I had to say *something*. Those camel drivers, they're dullards. They'd murder me if they thought I was carrying a yatra."

"So you're not."

"I know what you're thinking, Kandri. That I'm dangerous. Some animal you're stuck with forever."

"Mektu, why are you avoiding the question?"

"Am I a host. To a demonic fucking spirit, chewing me up from the inside like a worm. You try admitting that. See if a girl ever smiles at you again."

"I'm not a girl, Mek."

"But you talk about me with Eshett, don't you? And then you expect me to share my deepest secrets."

"So you *have* a secret? Does that mean—"

"Who cares, who cares, if we die down here?"

ରେ

By the lone beam of sunlight Kandri saw why they had not been crushed: the landslide was mostly an accretion of hive material, like airy plaster, which the wasps had glued to the stone walls across unfathomable years. Sticky, rancid, sweet. The brothers hung suspended in this mass, along with a well-churned mixture of sand, earth, cacti, snakeskins, dead wasps, skeletons of birds and rats and lizards, broken crockery, pilgrims' sandals. It was surprisingly comfortable.

But it was also sifting, hourglass-like, through the narrows beneath their feet. Kandri couldn't tell how wide the bottleneck was, but he guessed it would prove wide enough for them to be swept through with the next collapse.

And at some point the swarm would return.

"You're right," he said. "Let's get out of here."

But how, exactly? They had slid sixty feet or more into the earth. Where the hive material had shorn away he saw the ancient stonework: walls, pillars, landings. All intact, and every inch of it carved. Peacocks, flowers, children. Monsters with the bodies of spiders and the heads of snakes.

But six or eight feet above their heads the carvings gave way to sheer walls.

"A crack," said Kandri. "That's what we need. Just a toe-hold. If we can reach those carvings, we're free."

Mektu turned his head sharply. "Kandri, the letter! You haven't—"

"It's right here," said Kandri, feeling the calfskin pouch against his chest. "*Harach*, do you think I'd be talking about escape if I'd lost the letter?"

"I guess not. I guess we'd stay, search all this, no matter—"

"You're damn right. No matter what."

A plague had been savaging the lands beyond Urrath's shores for centuries, where it was said to be a greater killer than all wars, famines, and lesser diseases combined. The Plague did not much worry Urrathis, however, for the simple fact that most were immune. Such amazing luck did not endear them to the people of the Outer World, who claimed that the Plague lay dormant in the lungs of every single Urrathi, and so enforced a quarantine on the whole of the continent.

In the calfskin pouch Kandri carried a few scribbled pages that would transform the world: a cure for the Plague. The only mystery, an appalling mystery, was why its discoverer had wanted no one to learn the nature of that cure. No one anywhere, save the doctor in far-off Kasralys City to whom the letter was addressed.

"What if it's not just a cure?"

"Some other time, Kandri."

"What if it's a poison, a weapon?"

"Stop talking," said Mektu. "You're sounding like me."

"Use it one way and it frees the world from Plague, and us from Quarantine," said Kandri. "Use it another and it kills us all."

"Pitfire," said Mektu, "look at him."

The maniac dangled fifty feet overhead, shirt caught on some jagged beam or spike. Every bit of the corpse, even the mouth and eyelids, had swollen grotesquely. It seemed less the remains of a man than a weird doll made of sausage skin. Four taut red strings descended from heels and fingertips. No, not string: that was draining blood.

"What if the Wasp attacked the caravan, Mek?"

"What if, what if," growled Mektu. "Then they're dead, that's what. Uncle Chindilan, Eshett, Talupéké. And all those camel bastards. What were they *thinking*? Good luck in the desert, can you believe—" He broke off, eyes narrowing, then cried aloud: "Gods, we're saved, there's a staircase!"

Kandri turned only his neck—what a fine, what a beautiful staircase. But it was a good ten feet from them across the pit, and the lowest step was about at the level of their chins.

"Just sidle over," he said. "Slowly, slowly—*no!*"

Mektu gave a wild lurch. The whole mass of detritus sank by a foot.

"What the hell are you doing?"

"It's gone."

"Stop that! It's not gone, I told you, it's right here on my chest."

"Not the letter." Mektu twisted in place, scooping armfuls of debris. "The blade. It's gone!"

"Stop, fool, before you kill us!" Kandri hissed. "Forget your blade, I've lost mine too. There are spares in the caravan."

"Not my machete, Kandri. *The* blade. The mattoglin."

"No."

"Well, yes."

"You shit, Mek. You absolute shit."

The mattoglin. The great golden knife, jewel-encrusted, ancient. Eshett had taken it from the body of Ojulan, the Prophet's depraved and blood-thirsty son, minutes after Kandri had cut the man to pieces.

"Why in five heavenly fucks do you have the mattoglin?" said Kandri. "It belongs to Eshett, we agreed. Did she give it to you?"

"Yes!" cried Mektu. "I mean, give? Of course. But not the way you or I might—"

"Did she give you the mattoglin?"

"Give? No."

"You stole it. And now you've lost it down this sewer pipe."

"I only borrowed it, Kandri. I had to."

"You're the filthiest hog in the wallow, you know that?"

"She hates that knife," said Mektu. "She told me, it frightens her, worries her night and day, and it does the same to me you know, I can't sleep, not at all, I was even thinking that I ought to just—oh, *there* it is."

The handle of the mattoglin protruded from the debris some six feet to Kandri's left. The enormous blue jewel in the pommel winked in the half-light. Blood from the maniac above was spattering the grip.

For a moment the brothers held still, gazing at the knife. Then they lunged for the blade.

Which was sheer madness. How could it matter less who held the mattoglin, that priceless, useless, thing? Neither wanted it, and in any case their lives were inseparable. Yet somehow Kandri knew that he, not Mektu, had to reach it first.

The same lunacy had seized his brother. Lurching, swimming in the debris, they made for the knife. Kandri felt the rubble falling, thinning around his feet. They shoved each other, clawed. But it was Kandri's hand that closed on the hilt.

His brother cried out as if in pain. And in that moment the debris fell in a rush.

Panic took them. Both brothers kicked and pulled for the staircase, but the refuse was pouring like rain through a sluice. Kandri flung the mattoglin, heard it strike the wall above the stairs. They felt the funnel-shaped wall against their fingers, slick and featureless. They scrabbled and swore, unable to help each other, choking on filth.

Kandri found his grip as the last of the detritus vanished. He heaved himself seal-like onto the bottommost stair. He rolled. Mektu was sliding. His arm shot out and just managed to seize a flailing hand, and seconds later his brother was safe beside him, gasping.

Three steps above them, the mattoglin lay unscathed.

ଓ

"What happened? Why did we do that?"

"*Jeshar*, Kandri. I don't know."

"Why the hell did you take the knife from Eshett, anyway? What were you planning to do with it?"

"Nothing. It's like I told you: she hates the knife. She says it weighs her down."

"Liar. She doesn't even carry the damn thing. She keeps it in her pack on the camel."

"Why don't you let me take it, Kandri?"

"Because I'm not a fool, that's why. Now get up."

"I'll give it to back to her, I'll explain, I'll—"

"Mektu."

"Brother?"

"You're never touching it again."

ଓ

The climb to the surface was easy. Passing the body was not. Kandri looked with horror at the man who had tried to kill him. A balloon of pockmarked flesh. A froth of blood and chewed wasps filling the swollen mouth.

How many of you are there?

They stepped out into morning brilliance. The red earth was aglow. Dust hung in the air where the men and camels had rested, but there was no other sign of the caravan. Relief washed over Kandri: he had imagined bodies scattered like fallen fruit.

"They must have been running for their lives," he said. "Uncle and Eshett wouldn't have left us if they had any choice."

"How are we going to find them?" said Mektu, squinting into the sun. "I see four—no, five—trails leading out of here."

"They were north of the pit," said Kandri, "but they'd have turned east as soon as possible." He pointed. "We'll take that second trail, right over the ridgetop. It's steep but much shorter."

"How do you know it's shorter?"

"Eshett. Her people hunt in this country."

Mektu's cheek twitched. "You talk with her a lot."

"Do I?"

"You're not falling for her, are you, Kan?"

"Go to hell."

"You'd never do that to me, right? You know how I feel about her."

"I only know what you tell me."

Mektu glared at him. The look might have been unnerving if not for the bits of wasp hive stuck in his hair like crusts of bread.

"I found her first, Kandri."

"And then forgot all about it. About her."

"That was different," said Mektu.

"Can't argue with you there."

Months ago, Eshett had been kidnapped by flesh traders and brought to Eternity Camp, the sprawling central base of the Prophet's army. The kidnappers sold her to a brothel, and one night Mektu bought her services—"for the price of a chicken leg," she told Kandri later. When they met again after the killing of Ojulan, Mektu had no idea who she was.

Eshett's disgust with Mektu could hardly have run deeper. It was almost miraculous that she thought well of him now. Their escape from the west, the battles and blight fighting and murder and fear, had left much that came before indistinct, a landscape under fog. They had been one thing; they were becoming something else.

"Let's just go and find them," said Kandri.

Mektu did not move. "Are you lovers?" he asked.

Kandri turned to face him again. "Yes," he said. "We can't keep our hands off each other. We do it every chance we get."

A moment's pause. Then Mektu burst out laughing. He cuffed Kandri on the cheek, playfully. Or almost playfully. "Glad you still have a dream life," he said.

&#x03;

They ran uphill. It was a shortcut, but now that they were taking it, the danger of their position was suddenly all too plain. Full sunlight. A barren ridge spread open like a scroll to anyone approaching from the west. Once they reached the hill's opposite side they would be hidden again, but the summit looked far away. And the ridge behind them—that was not far enough. Kandri imagined the storm of arrows that would follow their discovery. The faint whines, the thunk and clatter of shafts among the rocks. The last sounds they would ever hear. They had slain the Prophet's favorite son, one of the future kings of Urrath decreed by Revelation. She had branded them with her curse, named them the Twin Abominations. No matter the cost or the distance, she would see them dead.

"Brother!"

Kandri whirled, unsheathing the mattoglin—the only weapon left to him—but his brother was pointing far up the gorge.

From a narrow side canyon, an animal came running. It was a goat, one of the caravan's by its markings, with a few yards of rope trailing from its neck. Blind speed, reckless terror. The creature was running for its life.

Moments later, a black shape flowed from the side canyon. Swift and dense, it raced along the gorge, barely a yard above the earth. The Wasp. At last Kandri understood the singular: the cloud of insects moved as one body, a shark gliding between reefs. It formed an oval at first, but as it neared the goat it spread two arms like giant pincers. The goat careened from left to right, but the black arms surged ahead of it and began to close from either side. The goat panicked, skidding, bleating. Then the body of the Wasp passed over it, and silence fell.

Kandri felt a sudden, explosive fury at the camel men. Never mind a lone maniac, seduced by some confused fascination with the Prophet. What about the rest of them? He'd trusted these people, put himself in their hands. Had they really brought him to the pit for good luck, a blessing on the journey? Or had they meant to dispose of him?

The swarm was hovering in place. As they watched, revolted, it changed shape once again and began to ooze across the valley floor. When it reached the rim of the pit, the whole mass poured into the black hole like molasses down a drain.

The body of the goat was already starting to swell.

ఇ

They resumed the climb, scrambling hand over foot. The danger now was the spectacle they had created—or rather, who might have observed it. For thirty minutes they climbed in desperate haste. At last, drawing close to the summit, they found a protruding boulder to hide behind and catch their breath.

"Why do you keep looking back?" said Mektu sharply.

Kandri started. "The pit," he said. "I saw something, you wouldn't believe—"

"When Terek deserted—" Mektu seemed to have forgotten his question. "—they brought him back to Eternity Camp and gave him his old boots and sent him marching around the drill yard. Remember? Around and around, hands on his head, forbidden to stop on pain of death."

"That's enough, Mek."

"Twelve times around, in boots with long nails driven up through the soles. Later they tried to strip him for the blackworm torture, but the boots wouldn't come off. It took two men, one to hold his leg, the other to—"

"Stop it!"

"And all *he* did was run," said Mektu. "Quit loving the Prophet, and run."

"The camel drivers," said Kandri, frantic to change the subject. "How did they talk you into visiting the pit?"

"They—didn't have to," said Mektu awkwardly. "I saw them leading you that way and just—"

Followed. Like a dog. Kandri closed his eyes. Mektu had followed him the same way into the army, into exile, into the hell-holes of the earth. On good days he saw the trait as loyalty. On bad days he was sure that Mektu couldn't stand the thought of Kandri having anything—a slice of bread, an army jacket, a lover, a glance into a well—that he himself was denied.

"She's got to them, hasn't she?" said Mektu.

Kandri shook his head. "That's the real question. How many believers in the caravan?"

"Fourteen for starters," said Mektu. "That mob who brought you to the pit."

"Maybe not, though," said Kandri. "That prayer they sang felt sincere. And if they all wanted me dead, why use the maniac? They could have cracked my skull with a stone and chucked me in that hole, and told the others it was an accident."

"Not after I showed up," said Mektu. "No one would have believed we *both* just happened to stumble. They got cold feet. And the crazy one, he couldn't stand it. He was all set to kill for Her Radiance, and we were denying him the chance."

"So he just attacked me? Alone?"

"That's where 'crazy' comes in. But don't fool yourself: the rest of that mob felt the same. Remember their faces? They detest us."

"They fear us," said Kandri, "because we're green and the desert's cruel, and small mistakes can kill. And at least a few, obviously, have heard a rumor that we're enemies of the Prophet. But that doesn't mean they're killers."

"The caravan," Mektu declared, "is rotten with converts. Maybe *all* of them are secret believers."

"What absolute rubbish."

Mektu shook his head. "Someone's selling it to them, whispering about Orthodox Revelation. And do you know who I think it is?"

"Just slow down," said Kandri. "We don't even know if—"

"That silent fucker at the back, that's who. With the earring and the staring eyes."

That one: the dour warrior, always stationed at the rear. "I hadn't noticed the earring," said Kandri, "but you're right, he does stare."

"So you agree. He's their leader."

"I don't agree. You should see *your* expression; you stare like a ghoul. And you'll make a mess of everything with your half-assed suspicions. For all we know, it ended with this poor idiot who attacked me, a lost soul who'd fallen for the Prophet."

Mektu glanced at him, alarmed. "Was that a joke?" he said. "Fallen for the Prophet? Kandri, did you just make a *joke?*"

"No. You're sick."

"Never be funny," said Mektu. "Not you, it's just wrong. But listen: there's one thing we've learned for certain."

He waited. Kandri heaved a sigh. "Well?" he said at last.

"However many they are—five, ten, fifty—they're willing to defy the Caravan Master."

Kandri looked up sharply, gave a reluctant nod. "And that," said Mektu, "is the worst news of all, don't you think?"

ଔ

His name was Ifimar Jód. A large man of formal courtesy and iron rules. Like Eshett he was some manner of Parthan, desert-born and raised. Unlike Eshett, his face was cold and unreadable. He was older than their Uncle Chindilan and his beard reached his ribs, but he had the vigor of a man in his twenties. He marched with his arms slightly raised before him, as though preparing to seize whatever or whomever he faced. Eshett had warned the brothers not to provoke him: in the ethos of the desert, to cross the Caravan Master was unforgiveable. Survival meant absolute order. The caravan's fighting men and women answered only to Jód. And Jód had guaranteed the brothers' safety.

Such at least were the formal arrangements; the reality was far less clear.

There were in fact two fighting companies, and they loathed each other. The caravan had set out with thirty mercenaries: hulking hired swords, all men, nursing a bottomless resentment of whatever had condemned them to this expedition. The other nine warriors had arrived with Kandri and his companions: an escort, and a personal guard. The nine were all volunteers, and yet the most disciplined soldiers Kandri had ever known. Five men, four women. A unit that fought not for money but honor—as their captain had informed Jód in the artless manner of someone stating his own height or weight.

"Honor is the marrow of the soul," Jód had replied, "but while you travel with us, both honor and oath must bind you to me. You will fight at my command, and exhibit perfect obedience in all other matters as well. Such are my terms. Swear to them or leave us now."

The confrontation had occurred in a wide, wind-scoured valley east of the Arig Hills. Kandri's party had caught up with the caravan just minutes before, after an eight-hour run from the high peak where they had spotted them, far off and getting farther. When they reached the camel train at last they had stood apart, bent over and gasping, unsure of their welcome.

At Jód's remark about "perfect obedience" the nine soldiers had glanced at one another. Their captain—a soft-spoken, lonely-eyed warrior named Utarif—cleared his throat and reminded Jód that they were already pledged to another master.

"And any pledge to our general is binding until death," he added, "as I believe you're aware."

Jód's fury had reached a nearly audible sizzle. For reasons no one had disclosed, he too answered to General Tebassa, infamous scoundrel and secret lord of the Lutaral.

"We can swear this much," said Utarif. "To obey you in all matters, large and small, save those in plain conflict with our general's orders."

To Kandri's surprise, Jód had accepted the compromise with no more than an irritable nod. He moved on to the rest of the newcomers, studying them like horses at auction. He did not appear to like what he saw.

But his response to the brothers, last in line, was altogether different. Jód looked at them as though they were the confirmation of something glimpsed in a repulsive dream.

"You are the sons of the inventor, Lantor Hinjuman?"

Kandri was thunderstruck. "Yes, yes we are. Do you know him, Master Ifimar?"

"I do."

A blinding elation filled Kandri's mind. Beside him, Mektu went rigid, eyes wide with hope. "When did you last see him?" asked Kandri. "Is he even alive? Please, sir, it's been years. Tell us anything you—"

The Master raised a hand for silence.

"One day," he said, closing his eyes. "An earlier start by *one single day*, and I should have been spared this doom. We would have been too far ahead; you would never have found our path. Between your fate and ours a mountain should have risen, impassable as the Mountain of the Gods."

"Sorry to disappoint you," said Mektu.

Jód inclined his head; apparently he took the remark as sincere. "When the Gods choose to speak, their decisions are binding even for the deaf." His eyes snapped open again. "But let us consider where things stand for the Brothers Hinjuman—and for that matter, their uncle, by all accounts a man distinguished in loyalty."

"He is that," Kandri agreed. But he was thinking, *By whose account? By our father's?*

"You are condemned," said Jód. "You killed the Prophet's favorite son. You left a second son bleeding his life out on the ground. Her killers are close behind you—perhaps less than a day. You carry something priceless, some talisman of hope, but the Prophet cares nothing for this. She wants revenge and she will have it; she will never, ever, give up the hunt. Therefore you must disappear—into the desert, or into her chambers of pain and oblivion. No third way exists. Have I forgotten anything?"

It was horrible, the way he named these facts. Kandri had long since learned to hold them at a distance in order to breathe and eat and cling to sanity.

"This thing we're carrying," he said. "It's not just priceless."

"Not *just*?"

"It's more important than riches," said Mektu.

"Name it then."

Mektu glanced at him sharply. Kandri swallowed. "We can't do that, Master Ifimar," he said.

Jód brought his fingertips together before his face as if he were praying, but it was nothing of the kind. He moved his feet slightly. His eyes were fixed on a point near Kandri's collarbone. And suddenly Kandri knew—as surely as he knew his own name—that in a matter of seconds both he and Mektu would be dead.

Do something! Speak!

"It's not up to me," he blurted. "If I knew you, if I could be certain—"

"Certain of what, you wretched animal?"

"Master Ifimar, this thing is more important than our lives. And the truth is I don't know why it's a secret—"

"Exactly!" said Mektu. "What could be more *stupid*? We should tell him, tell everyone. We should share it, scream it, paint it on walls—"

"Mektu," Kandri hissed.

His brother recoiled. "But we can't," he said. "Of course we can't. Not a word."

"Master Ifimar, the one who trusted us with this object—"

"Was born a fool."

"—was stabbed in the chest, before he could explain. But we know he believed that *everything* depended on secrecy, at least for now."

Jód studied him then. His fury had not abated, but alongside it something else appeared: a kind of burning fascination.

"You are honor bound to this dead man?"

"We don't know that he's dead," said Kandri, "but yes, we are."

"And it was his will that you carry this nameless treasure to Kasralys?"

"Yes."

"And surely you were trained in Chiloto battle-dance?"

"We were, Master. We're excellent fighters, truth be told."

"And you will swear obedience to me in all things?"

Silence. Kandri's jaw tightened; Mektu hid his face in his arm. Ifimar Jód looked from brother to brother, narrowing his eyes.

ೞ

Three years before, they taken just such an oath at the feet of Her Radiance the Prophet. A day of glorious madness, mind and body singing with the drug of faith. When they and the other new recruits completed the oath, a thousand soldiers pounced on them with feral howls. Doused them with wine. Cheered their recitations from *The Five Atrocities*, the book that explained the justice of the War of Revelation. Paraded them through Eternity Camp on their shoulders. The joy of it, the clarity. Brothers forever to the end of time.

A month later he was fighting, killing, in a mist made greasy by fire. No cheers, only mindless roaring and high shrieks of pain. Thatched roofs burning, a village burning. A charge after the routed enemy into a black bog that engulfed him to his thighs, the dead around him sinking in the ooze. The arrow-slain man with the stump of an arm still burning. The child lost beneath the muck save for a chin, a cheek, a lifeless eye.

And there was that one, of course—

And that other one, with—

And the one he dreamed of, every five or six—

And the one he would forever—

The first horror was what he had seen and done and lived in that campaign. The second was that he had continued as a Soldier of Revelation, a good Chiloto, a believer, for over two more years.

Now his faith was gone and his promise broken, and he was glad of both. Nothing good could come of such promises. Only enslavement, or condemnation if one tried to escape. In dreams he squirmed under the vulture eye of the Prophet, heard her voice of torn iron, screaming for his death.

Mektu suddenly dropped his arm. "I swear obedience," he announced.

Kandri's nails bit into his palm. No way out. No honorable way. "I swear as well," he lied.

Jód studied them as though reading a message inscribed in glyphs upon their faces. At last he turned to face the caravan.

"These men are in my keeping," he said. "You shall honor them and make them welcome, and teach them what you can of our ways. If any man shall harm them it shall be as if you raised your hand against my person. Take no liberties. I will know."

ଓଷ

The command could hardly have been clearer, but in the days that followed Jód himself had shown no great inclination to welcome the newcomers. He confiscated their food, and a faska of water from each. He ordered them not to smoke, although the camel drivers smoked both clay pipes and sweet-smelling cheroots. He had yet to invite them to an evening tea, a fact that scandalized Eshett. And on their first night with the caravan, after the tents were erected and a cold meal dispatched, the Master had appeared once more before them and issued his most startling decree:

"You newcomers shall not lie with anyone. You are forbidden all favors of the flesh."

Not bothering to observe their reaction, he withdrew into the dark, a phantom judge. Mektu, somehow certain that the order was directed at him, took Eshett's hand and began to explain to everyone present that there were oaths and oaths, a realm of practical things and a realm of the heart.

"And everyone knows that rules change when you cross borders. Customs change, languages change. Some clans have no word for snow."

"Every clan has a word for liar," said Chindilan. "You promised to obey him in all things."

"All things, exactly!" said Mektu. "All things. But not this."

Chindilan shook his head. Captain Utarif put on a philosophical smile.

Eshett, who had sat stunned since Jód's pronouncement, pulled her hand from Mektu's grip and shot a blazing look at Kandri. Their eyes met for the briefest instant, but it was enough. Kandri knew they would ignore the command, no matter the danger. And so, of course, they had.

But each night was a mortal risk. They tiptoed away in opposite directions, groped together around the edges of the camp, listening for sniggers or jeers. Once Eshett had arched up against his mouth and a cry had escaped her, and both of them had turned to stone. *This will end badly*, he thought, starting to kiss her again.

He did not want to believe that Jód could condemn them for lovemaking, but a deeper part of him knew very well that he could. Jód's contempt for the brothers was unmistakable. He would prefer them in irons, in the depths of the Prophet's torture vaults, in unmarked graves.

So why not kill them and be done with it? Jód knew nothing of the Letter of Cure, that short secret message which, Gods willing, a certain doctor in Kasralys might decode, freeing Urrath from the Quarantine, redeeming the world. Jód did not know, and might not care. He was merely indebted to their mutual friend, General Tebassa. His hand, for the moment, was forced.

And he loathed the obligation. Would relish any excuse to be free of it, of them. The brothers' lives, and the fate of a letter so much more vital than their lives, rested on an unknown debt to a single warlord—aging, lame, diminished in power—in a land that had vanished behind them.

ങ

They gained the hill's bald summit and scurried across it, rabbits under the falcon's eye. The world was bright, motionless, petrified. Kandri could hear each footfall on the rocks. Before them stretched a vast, burnt-orange plain, wide open, flat as an iron pan.

Mektu pointed, appalled. "Is *that* where we're—"

"Yes. Obviously."

But Kandri shared his alarm. Due north the land was mild; he even discerned a hint of green, as though new grass were sprouting here at winter's end. In the south, miles-long outcroppings of sawtoothed rocks erupted from the flats. But their path lay east, and he could see no shelter there, only countless miles of emptiness and pain. Bleak expanses of earth and gravel; meandering scars of dead rivers, clots of dead-looking brush. Round depressions that might have been sinkholes or empty lakes. One strange white basin that glittered like snow. And farthest of all, a tattered crust along the horizon: the next line of hills. To Kandri they looked as distant as the moon.

"You heard Jód, didn't you?" said his brother. "There's an oasis beyond those hills. An oasis with a thousand palms."

"I did hear him," said Kandri. "I heard him say that beyond those hills there's another plain, and another range of hills, and *then* an oasis with a thousand palms."

"Then we'll die," said Mektu, cheerfully enough.

Kandri glanced over his shoulder. "If we stand here it's certain," he said.

The summit was blade-narrow; in two minutes they had crossed it and were descending, hidden from any eyes to the west. This side of the hill glowed yellow in the morning light. And there, climbing laboriously up to meet them, was Uncle Chindilan.

"You daft bastards," he said.

He leaned on his war-axe, gasping. His beard, trimmed barely less than a week ago, was bleached white by the sun. He scowled at them, terrible, their own private God of wrath.

And far below him, the caravan appeared.

Kandri had never seen it like this, in full sun, emerging from around the hill like a strand of multicolored beads. The dark and light camels, burnt sugar and buttermilk. The cloud of biting flies nothing could disperse or discourage. The camel drivers in their robes of dilute indigo. The trim volunteer soldiers, the slouching mercenaries. And in front as always, leaning into the march, the tall, urgent figure of Ifimar Jód.

"Is everyone—"

"Alive, yes," said Chindilan. "No thanks to you. We had to stampede the camels out of the canyon; it's a miracle there were no falls, no broken bones. And what about our hearts, eh? We saw that hellish swarm. Eshett is just destroyed, and Tal's not much better, although she'd hate for you to see it. We thought you were dead, that you'd pinched the devil's ass one too many times."

"What about Jód?" asked Kandri.

"He mentioned impaling the both of you on stakes."

Mektu waved his hands. "But those camel drivers, the pit—"

"Ah, so it's down to them now," growled the smith. "Tell me: did they pick you up and carry you?"

Reluctantly, the brothers shook their heads. Chindilan had a way of turning them back into boys.

The smith gestured over his shoulder. "There are riders out there, north by northeast. On horseback, not camels. Jód spotted them right away."

Kandri caught his breath. He squinted, and thought he saw faint gray shapes near the horizon. Shapes vaguely in motion. "Are they Rasanga?" he asked.

The word made the others twitch.

"Too far to say," said Chindilan. "I had a look through your telescope and could barely count heads. Jód himself pulled out a scope as long as my leg, but I don't think he could be certain either. Of course he said nothing. Never does. But we know that there's a lot of them—and that they're between us and Eshett's village."

"Then she can't go," said Mektu instantly. "That's obvious. She'll have to carry on with us, there's no other—"

"Don't get excited," said his uncle. "Let's see what Jód has in mind."

"She can't leave," Mektu insisted. "As for us, we should wait right here. Wait and hide, and watch those bastards. If we're lucky they'll head off in the wrong direction, and we'll never see them again."

"Look over your shoulder," said Chindilan.

The brothers turned. High over the hilltop, a large bird was circling. It was a raptor, bright yellow talons, wings of tarnished bronze.

"That's a steppe eagle," said Chindilan. "Rare these days. The Kasraji emperors bred them for hunting. Did I ever tell you when I learned my birds?"

"No, Uncle," said Kandri.

"Never, that's when," snapped Chindilan. "But I sure as hell know a steppe eagle. Her Radiance the Prophet gave one to Jihalkra. She wanted her holy Firstborn to start playing the part. Future King of Kings and all that."

"Oh," said Mektu.

"He hates to talk, Jihalkra," said the smith, "but one thing he would talk about was his eagle. How clever it was. How he could just *think* what he wanted, and the bird would fly off to hunt it down. Small prey it would kill and carry back in its claws. For larger game, Jihalkra would saddle up and follow."

Kandri's skin had gone cold. The eagle stopped its circling and headed west, its long wings rising and falling, gathering speed.

"Those riders to the north could be anyone," said Chindilan, "but the shits following behind us? They're damned well servants of our blessed, bloodthirsty Mother-Of-All-Chilotos. And I'd bet my lungs and liver they know where we are. 'Wait and hide' is out of the question."

"Don't tell Jód," said Mektu. "He hates us already, Uncle. If you mention the bird, he'll—"

"Shut up."

Mektu hid his face in his elbow.

"Not one day of peace on this journey—not one," said Chindilan. "Your father called me his best friend. But part of him must have hated me, to name me your guardian. Better if he'd tied stones to my ankles and chucked me in a lake."

The brothers said nothing. How could they possibly disagree?

Their uncle straightened, frowning at the sun. Then he lumbered forward, scowling, and wrapped his arms around them both.

4. A SUMMONS

T he messenger did not like to wait.

The old man watched him through the iron fence and a skein of flowering vines. He was arguing with the chamberlain, sweating in his tasseled, tight-buttoned uniform, brandishing a scroll case of lacquered wood. Thirty, probably. At least they'd stopped sending babes. But the chamberlain had twenty years on him, and the old man another twenty beyond that. Let him wait. The old man's children were hungry.

They were lizards, his children. Red iguanas, chameleons, lion geckos longer than his forearm. The old man's gardens bordered the rainforest that swept up the mountain and down the other side, a last fragment of the jungles that had once blanketed central Shôlupur. He had let the jungle reclaim three-quarters of the land he owned, including two acres of the mansion grounds, so fond of these reptiles he had become. Every morning he walked to this wild corner with offerings of dates and melon and sweetened gruel. Down from the trees they clacked and clattered, a voiceless battalion, following his movements with eyes that rolled like the marbles he had flicked across these stones as a boy, marbles that still surfaced now and then when he wielded a spade.

He lifted the tray from the breakfast table. The messenger noticed his movement but turned away, disinterested. The old man smiled. Mistaken for his own gardener. There was something to be said for turning seventy.

Other peeping eyes, though, had surely been more discerning. *Some-one has seen me without the wheelchair. Perhaps riding, perhaps rambling in the mountains afoot. A good ruse while it lasted. How will I keep them away now?*

"I am not to leave unanswered!" He was shouting, the fool. "Those are my explicit instructions, from a higher master than your own."

The chamberlain straightened his spine. "There are few who meet *that* description between the desert and the sea."

"There is one," said the messenger.

The old man sighed. A phoenix lizard brushed his ankle, red scales raised like feathers about its neck. Others were approaching, belly-sliding through brush and leaves. He tossed the food widely, dispersing them. Beautiful as they were, they would fight to the death over a scrap of melon rind. A matter of instinct, nothing more.

"My good fellow," said the chamberlain, "if you would simply allow me—"

"No and no again!" cried the messenger. "I am to surrender this missive in one manner only, and that is to the hand of Therel Agathar."

"In that case, I can offer you no satisfaction but to wait in the foyer," said the chamberlain. "His Excellency is not yet dressed."

"When is he likely to *dress?*"

"Now see here, you brazen—"

"Never mind," called the old man, startling them both. "I'm as dressed as I plan to be. Show him in."

ભ

His accomplice the wheelchair stood proud beneath the almond tree, unaware that it would never fool anyone again. The general brushed off the leaves and sat, and the real gardener brought a second chair and set it facing his own. Moments later the messenger appeared, striding well ahead of the chamberlain, gripping the scroll case like a relay baton. The man flung himself down on one knee, bowed his head so low he might have been inspecting his genitals for lice.

"River Dragon—"

"That's not me," said the old man sharply. "That man retired ten years ago. My name is Therel Agathar."

"My apologies, Magnus General. I was told—my master quite insisted—"

"Have a seat. There's tea on the way."

He pried the scroll case from the man's death grip, gestured with it at the chair. The messenger continued to kneel, raising his head just high enough to see what the general might be doing with the scroll.

Agathar waited. The messenger opened his mouth, shut his mouth, blinked, swayed, grimaced, swallowed. A fly crawled across his forehead. He rose and took the chair.

"Welcome to Cauldron Farm," said Agathar. "You're our first guest this year."

"Alas, sir! My tenure as guest must be brief—not brief, less than that. Momentary."

"I'll provide a fresh horse for your return," said Agathar.

"Very kind, Your Excellency. The message—"

"Have the rains begun in Nebusul?"

"The rains?" The messenger looked ready to explode. "Magnus General, the letter I bring you is from the hand of our beloved King."

"That's plain enough from the seal. How is he, by the way? I've not clapped eyes on him since his divorce—his third divorce, from that cousin who paints. Now and then he threatens to visit, but I'm not holding my breath."

The messenger froze. "King Grapahir is a gift to all the people of Shôlupur," he said.

"This isn't a test, you know. We're just talking."

"He inspires us as much with his vigor as with his mind. He is our voice, our defender. Indeed he *is* the nation, as many say: the Scarlet Kingdom in human form."

"Does he still hold public executions?"

The messenger's jaw fell open.

"No?" said Agathar. "Well, perhaps it's for the best. In his grandfather's day, when executions were a private entertainment, they used a pool on the castle grounds built for the purpose. Round, sheer-sided, deep—twenty feet deep, and filled to within five feet of the rim. Placing that rim just out of reach, you understand, for a swimmer below. Have you heard this tale before?"

"Your excellency, I—"

"The prisoner would be stripped, branded with a symbol corresponding to the crime—murder, theft, kidnapping—and forced down a ladder into the pool, after which the ladder was withdrawn. Chairs were set around the pool, and they'd serve tea and cloudberry pudding. Not to us children, of course: that part of the grounds was off limits to us. Still, the adults must have known we spied on them. I think my father secretly approved."

"General Agathar—"

"They floated a good inch of oil atop the water, you see. Ballistics oil, fast-burning stuff. And upon the oil floated a dozen or more wooden saucers with lighted candles. The sport of it was to guess how long the prisoner could tread water without disturbing the candles. Once he started thrashing it was hopeless, of course. You can imagine, the waves in that pool—"

"Magnus General! The King commands me to seek your *immediate* reply, and to depart the very moment it is written."

"Yes," said Agathar, "but if I delay out of obstinacy and you gain the few minutes' rest any man should be afforded, that can't be held against you, can it? Here's your refreshment."

"River—that is, General, I—"

"Just eat, man. And drink your tea slowly, we serve it blistering here."

ଓ

He read the letter twice. Then a third time. He cracked his knuckles, stalling.

The messenger's eyes betrayed a hint of vindication.

For several minutes no one spoke but the querulous raven in the wood beyond his estate. *Krakaah,* it said, which happened to be a word in the Važek tongue. *Krakaah*. How the ravens had screamed it on the banks of the Brophin, one silent morning after carnage. Krakaah, stab wound. The only word it appeared to require.

The letter was full of chattering nonsense. *All of us recall with delight how you. Several years since we had the pleasure of. My niece has developed quite a fondness for.* But the blot of ink by the salutation announced a coded letter. The King had embedded certain telltale words—from the old list in his day-book, surely; the man could hold nothing in his head—which conveyed an altogether different meaning. An emergency summons. A threat of some sort to the very life of the Kingdom of Shôlupur. And no time whatsoever to waste.

Agathar lowered the parchment, ashamed of himself, and frightened. Listen to that, will you. Old man's heart in an old man's chest. Thump-thump-flutter-bump. Captive bird in a crate.

The messenger must have decided that he was a fool, chattering on about old horrors, with new ones close enough to touch.

"But what is it?" he demanded of the messenger. "War? Rebellion? Some new disease? Don't hide behind protocol. If you know, I command you to speak."

"Magnus General, all I know I have conveyed already."

Agathar let out a sharp sigh and rubbed his forehead. "Of course you have. I alone am to blame. Forgive me."

The messenger dropped his gaze, embarrassed. *Stab wound,* said the raven, delighted. *Stab wound! Stab wound!* As though it had invented such wounds and were celebrating.

He sprang to his feet, dry gristle of his knees protesting, and shouted for the chamberlain. "Pen and paper. And my riding clothes from the parlor. Bring Hesbur in from the east field and get him saddled. Provisions, standard road kit. Departure in twenty."

He pointed at the gaping messenger, who had not yet risen himself. "Pack this man a meal for his journey. And make it better than my own, as he's the finer servant of Shôlupur."

5. LOVERS AND GHOSTS

T he brothers' return left the camel drivers speechless.

No one stopped walking, of course. The caravan's forward motion had to be sustained, like some great stone ball to which they'd all put their shoulders. But their astonishment was plain. They watched the brothers' approach in silent awe, walking-songs dead on their lips.

It was an older woman who broke the silence at last, almost shrieking the obvious: "*Tufani*, alive, alive! Both of them! Not dead but alive!" The nearest drivers hushed her, walled her off behind their bodies. *We're always disappointing someone*, Kandri thought.

"Jód's changed direction," said Chindilan, squinting at the hills. "He's veering south. Those riders must have spooked him."

"We should apologize to Jód," said Kandri.

"You should do no such thing," hissed Chindilan. "Give him time to cool down. And for Ang's sake, don't cause another scene. Just shut your mouths and walk."

His advice proved impossible to take, for now the camel drivers had recovered from their shock. Men and women alike rushed forward to press the brothers' hands, making that fluid half-bow Kandri had come to recognize as standard courtesy. He bowed too, with less elegance. Mektu's efforts were like the bobbing of a crow.

"The Well gives you up!" said Kandri's friend with the cataract-clouded eye, almost tearful. "You are blessed, Mr. Kandri, and your brother alike." He looked at his fellow drivers. "*Kiben damrha:* are they not blessed?"

None dissented. They were blessed. Kandri thanked them, wondering which, if any, had murder in their hearts.

The more the drivers discussed their survival, the more animated they became. Heaven has a task for you! they declared. A special purpose! And we stand in your light, in the warmth of your fire. Then they spat out the name of the dead man and cursed his attempt on Kandri's life. Such a man was their brother no longer.

"He's not *anything* any longer," said Mektu. "He's not even watertight. Some reward for faith in Her Radiance, eh? Hanging there in the dark like a bag of fermented curd? Maybe the rest of you will listen to me now, she's not worth it, loving the Prophet will bring you nothing but—"

He broke off. A striking figure had stepped from the crowd. She was a girl in her teens, muscled like a wrestler, armed head to toe. Her eyes, haunted as always, flickered from Kandri to Mektu and back again.

"You stupid fuckers," she said. "How many lives do you have?"

"Love you too," said Kandri.

The girl cackled. Her arms rose, as though she would embrace them as Chindilan had done, but then her face clenched in a spasm and she glanced away. She was a soldier, one of General Tebassa's nine. The brothers and their company had found her in a wasteland, lone survivor of a decimated squadron. Lost, drugged, damaged. Her name was Talupéké.

"I'm sorry we worried you," said Kandri.

"Shut up. Here's a riddle." Talupéké looked at them sidelong. "These drivers: what's their new favorite word?"

"That's no riddle, that's just a question," said Mektu. "Give me a hint."

"You can't see it, but you think about it all the time."

"A woman's—"

"No."

"A sugar pudding. A stuffed chicken. A rump roast. A leg of lamb."

"One word," said Talupéké.

"Wasp!"

"No, fool! It's something *no one* can see."

"Wind. Love. Music."

Chindilan growled something in his ear, and Mektu's face fell. "Oh," he said. "I'm sorry."

The smith turned to Kandri. "*Yatra*," he murmured. "They believe in the creatures. Entirely."

"And now they've decided he must be carrying one," said Talupéké. "So have I, for that matter."

"Don't joke about such things," said Chindilan.

"Who the fuck says I'm joking?"

Mektu shook his head. "They have no reason to think that. Why would they?"

"Why?" Chindilan counted off on his fingers. "You babble about possession. The pit swallows you and spits you out unharmed. The swarm passes you by. So yes, the idea's taken hold that you're carrying a yatra, that you're protected by it, and Kandri as well I suppose, as long as he's at your side."

"In short," said Mektu, "they're blithering fools."

"That's not what Eshett says," said Talupéké. "She told me to imitate them, after she's gone. They may not be Parthans, but they've crossed the desert before."

At the mention of Eshett, Kandri felt a stab of longing. "Where is she, anyway?" he asked, trying not to betray his urgency.

"Up ahead with Jód," said Talupéké. "She and my grandmother are trying to explain why he shouldn't have you strangled." She laughed again. "You'll keep your distance if you know what's good for you. That man's face could make a bull run for the hills."

C3

Mektu, who had never known what was good for him, started forward at once. Kandri reached for his arm, but another stopped Mektu first. It was the surgeon, a small, plump man with graying sideburns. He stepped into Mektu's path, frowning over his eyeglasses.

"The daredevils," he said with some disdain. "You look a fright, both of you. Shall I start with your heads?"

The brothers glanced at each other. Back home they had worked in Ariqina's clinic for the poor. The army had taken their medical knowledge somewhat further. Both experiences had left Kandri suspicious of rural quacks.

"Don't trouble yourself," he said.

"Trouble? They say you fell ninety feet!"

"We got lucky, doctor. We're all right."

"I'll be the judge of that." He turned to Mektu. "You had a prior wound as well, I understand. Recent infection? Nearly killed you?"

Mektu shot an uneasy glance at Kandri. One hand rose instinctively to his left side, just above the hip.

The little man knocked Mektu's hand away and tugged up his shirt. There was the scar from the Rasanga arrow, closed and healed, though still slightly discolored.

The surgeon's eyes grew wide. "I'm floored, young man. That's Xavasindran work, or I'm a magpie." He snapped his fingers. "You have the luck of the Gods. The Outworlders almost never treat common battlefield wounds. They're not interesting enough."

"Don't feel lucky," said Mektu, like a bashful schoolboy.

The little man snapped his fingers. "Black Hat Tebassa! The General snuck you into the clinic at Mab Makkutin, didn't he?"

"He helped," Kandri admitted.

"Well, well. The old fox. Now bend over and show me your pupils."

"Next time, doctor," said Kandri. "We're all right, I promise."

The surgeon's face hardened, as though he were not used to being refused. "With that attitude," he said, "I doubt you'll live to see many next times."

He stepped away, still muttering to himself. But some of the camel drivers had understood the exchange, and the murmurs of awe redoubled. *They are not even wounded. The madman—the fall—the Wasp itself. None of it has touched them.*

Neither did their whispers, at least in Mektu's case. His fears and his glances were directed to the north. "What do you think?" he asked no one in particular. "Are the horsemen from *her*?"

"Oh, I'd put money on it," said Talupéké.

"Sons of bitches," said Mektu. "They're going to see us."

"Not without a telescope."

"Of course they'll have telescopes, girl," said Mektu. "We should turn due south, Jód's not thinking. Pitfire, it's almost as if he *wants* to be seen. And maybe he does. We're just an obligation, aren't we? One he'd be damned glad—"

Chindilan reached out and squeezed the back of his neck, not at all gently. "You will *desist* from such talk," he said. "You're deep enough in the latrine as it is."

"But Uncle—"

"Go check on your camel, boy. You'll look less idle that way."

Mektu obeyed—or seemed to. When he reached his cargo-camel, he merely patted the beast and kept walking. "He's going to pester Eshett, right in front of Ifimar Jód!" said Chindilan. "Damn the bastard! If there's a sore toe anywhere in the schoolyard, that fool has to find it and stomp."

Kandri nodded, but for once he envied his brother's recklessness. His own need to be close to Eshett was becoming unbearable. They had so little time left. And what would his brother do when she departed? Collapse, go mad—or simply forget her, as he'd done before?

Look at his loping figure. Whiplash-strong, fearless in battle, dangerous to himself. A gifted man, an idiot. A cruel and spiteful ass. A man who'd give his life for Kandri or Uncle or any of them. Somehow it all added up to Mek.

"He is the one, you know," said Talupéké. "The one with the yatra inside."

"Hush," hissed Chindilan, "that's nonsense talk. And dangerous."

"I saw him," said Talupéké. "On the mountain, on Alibat S'Ang. Grandmother saw him too. And we heard what came out of his mouth."

"That was a parlor trick," said Chindilan. "You throw knives, he throws voices. And it worked, didn't it? Our enemies thought they were facing a man possessed, and it rattled them. Made them hesitate until you lot arrived. If he'd kept quiet, we'd be dead."

"You're telling me it was an act?"

"What else?" said Chindilan.

Talupéké turned him a scathing look. She quickened her pace, leaving the two of them behind. "Never lie to me, old man," she called over her shoulder.

Kandri and his uncle exchanged a glance. She was right, of course. Mektu's eruption on Alibat S'Ang was much more than a parlor trick. But what *was* it, then? Madness, possession, some other kind of spell?

Mektu, for his part, dodged every question. His "trick" had bought them several precious minutes, enough time for Talupéké and her fellow soldiers to arrive. He had saved them. What more did they want?

Answers, thought Kandri. Some straight answers. Would that kill you?

Muffled shouts from the front of the caravan. Three mercenaries were dragging his brother back along the camel train.

Chindilan sighed. "Eshett's influence with Jód must have its limits."

Mektu was writhing, a weasel in a snare. The mercenaries swore at him. At last, judging the distance from the Master sufficient, they flung him face-first to the ground.

☙

Late morning. The plain blazed and shimmered. Already the heat was like solid barrier, a wall they pushed before them with their chests and faces. But much worse was the roaring in Kandri's mind.

Look back.

I will not look back.

Look north, then.

What's the point? What good could it possibly do?

You know they're coming. You know how close those killers are.

It lied, that voice of fear. All he knew for certain was what he saw out ahead: the next hills, impossibly distant, and farther yet thanks to Jód's swerve to the south. Kandri looked for Eshett in vain. She was among the women, where he would not be welcome until sundown.

Look back.

Why should I? Tell me that, or shut up.

Because you like to look at me.

Kandri almost laughed aloud. He was conversing with a ghost—he knew that now—and whether it was real or fancy or sudden madness, it was good to know that the dead could be as wrong, as plain stump-stupid, as the living.

C3

The dead had appeared to him before. In the wastes of the Yskralem he had seen whole fleets of drowned fisherfolk and war galleys, plying a sea drained dry centuries before. And just yesterday, he had watched files of ghost-women making their way up the same mountain trail the caravan was descending. Women in sarongs and kanuts, bearing casks, jugs, faskas, the water no less heavy for being ghost-water; women whose eyes searched the cold hills for home. Desert women, strong and severe. Women with Eshett's cheekbones. No one else had seen them: no one but the hairless dogs, who had growled and trembled. Kandri wondered if they saw what he did: the women glowing like marsh candles in the darkness, flickering out as they neared the caravan, springing to life again once they passed.

Three months ago that vision would have flooded him with horror. But since their flight from the army his sense of the nature of the world had been knocked off the table—shattered, like the dull bit of village crockery it was, against the strange stone floor of Urrath. Ghosts, all right. Tip your hat and keep moving. Weirder things had assaulted him. Darker burdens—the Prophet's curse, the hatred of his own people—had swamped his life.

But this new ghost was not like the women, or the fisherfolk before them. For starters it appeared by daylight, though it clearly preferred the darkness. It was also pursuing them. Sometimes it wandered or lost the way; sometimes it raised an arm and braced itself against a wind the living could not feel. Under the noon sun it became so transparent that it almost disappeared. But as dusk approached it solidified anew, half a mile behind them, matching their pace.

The ghost was different in one other respect: Kandri had seen its birth—or at least its birth into death. It had occurred as he and Mektu stepped away from the pit. Feeling an obscure sorrow for the man who tried to kill him, Kandri had glanced a last time at the bloated corpse and seen the ghost peel away from it like a rind. All in one fluid motion, save for its left hand, which remained snagged in the corpse's own. The ghost tugged at it, vexed. When at last the hand popped free the ghost winced and cradled its thumb—the thumb Kandri had broken against the earth.

The ghost was otherwise pristine. The numberless stings of the Wasp were nowhere evident. But the thumb, quite obviously, still gave it pain.

Look back, urged the believer. *Look back, come back to me.*

There were no limits to the Prophet's hunger for revenge. Not even her dead servants were exempt from its call.

ೞ

A yip. Kandri jumped and saw one of the caravan's hairless dogs trotting at his side. It was a lovely creature, gazelle-thin, its foxlike ears too large for its head. It looked earnestly at Kandri and yipped again.

"You're a charmer," said Kandri, "but you can't have my food."

"Tana-Dog is not begging, Chiloto."

He raised his glance. Ulren, Jód's second in command, was watching him with a sneer. He was a thin man with a rough, bulbous head, like a squash to which a narrow face had been grafted. Although he looked rather starved and sickly, he possessed a freakish energy that never seemed to wane. He spent much of the day trotting from consultations with the Master down the length of the train, repeating Jód's orders a dozen times, until he reached the dour Submaster who brought up the rear. "Don't whine, milksops," he told the brothers upon their arrival. "I won't take kindly to whining. Remember that for every mile you walk, I walk three."

It soon became clear that "Don't whine, milksops" was Ulren's message for all persons and circumstances, and yet he treated the brothers with special contempt. Something about their clan, the Chiloto clan, provoked him irresistibly. More than once, Kandri had caught Ulren pointing at them as he scowled and whispered to Ifimar Jód.

"Tana-Dog and her brother are pureblood Shefetsis," he told Kandri now. "They are desert-bred, desert strong. They do not beg like your fat western bitches."

You even hate our dogs. Kandri was more amused than irritated; Chiloto dogs tended to be thin and hungry. Like their owners.

"What are you waiting for?" snapped Ulren. "Follow her. Master Ifimar wishes to speak with you."

"The dogs are his messengers?"

"*I* am his messenger; the dogs are his servants. And so are you and your brother. Remember that, little man. In the desert, nothing is more important than—are you *laughing?*"

"No, no, it's just—" *Little man.* Kandri turned away, biting his lips.

Ulren barked at him: "Get on, you excrescence of a maggot! Now!"

Kandri trotted forward with "Tana-Dog," keeping in the shade of the camels. Ulren put such effort into rudeness and yet it was so badly done.

ও

He paused just long enough to greet his own camel, Alahari-Rana—not truly his, but the beast Jód had made him responsible for feeding, brushing, saddling, and the like. She was a beautiful animal—a "Sparavith," Eshett had told him, one of just a handful in the caravan. As a breed, the Sparaviths were more slender and fine-boned than other camels, which meant they could carry slightly less. "But they're born to run," she had added. "You've not known speed until you've galloped a Sparavith."

Kandri thought his camel's name well chosen. Alahari-Rana ("Princess of the Golden Heart") was the daughter of Samitra the Sun Goddess. It was she who walked ahead of Samitra in the darkness before dawn, trailing a knotted rope that lost souls could find by touch and follow to her mother, to the light. His own Alahari was strong but gentle. Her black eyes beneath their five-inch lashes took the measure of him swiftly. *This one*, they seemed to say, *will need all the help he can get.*

He passed Mektu's camel next: also a Sparavith, but if the beast ever had a name no one remembered it. Mektu, indignant at being assigned a nameless beast, declared that he would call it Fish. Kandri had thought he misheard.

"Fish?"

"Why not? It's the perfect name."

"It's idiotic."

"He gapes at you with his mouth open. You'll see."

೦೩

Up ahead, Jód was gazing as usual at the horizon, as if some treasure waited there, long promised, long withheld. Kandri considered the broad black sword lashed across the Master's back. The grip in easy reach of his hand.

It sobered him, that weapon. Jód was presumably still enraged. His debt to General Tebassa was old and deep: Talupéké had dropped hints about a prison raid, and Captain Utarif too had spoken of the Caravan Master's time in jail. But after years in the army Kandri could spot a readiness for violence, and Jód all but glowed with it. Kereqa—oldest soldier of Tebassa's nine—had confirmed this yesterday in Kandri's hearing, when she warned her granddaughter Talupéké not to provoke the man. *You know well*, she said, *all the graves Master Ifimar has filled.*

೦೩

He was ten feet from Jód when a hand touched his shoulder.

It was Prince Nirabha. Kandri was startled; he had never spoken to the mysterious Prince, three years his junior and somehow indebted, like Kandri himself, to General Tebassa. The youth's eyes were bright against his dark

69

olive skin. His full lips were pressed tightly together, as if he was still considering his words. An enormous manservant lumbered beside him like a circus bear, watching Kandri from the corner of one bulging eye.

How did you break the silence with a prince? *Did* you break the silence?

"It's up to you, my good man," said Nirabha, almost in a whisper.

"What is?"

"But at the very least, I thought you should know."

"What, know what?"

The servant growled in his throat. Nirabha looked pained, and Kandri understood that he'd been far too loud. "Merely this," whispered Nirabha. "That whomsoever you name shall be executed."

Without another word, Prince and servant turned and dropped back along the line of the caravan. Kandri was shocked, and then quite angry. To offer murder the way you might offer a smoke! Why did the fool think he'd want it? Kandri was leaving killing behind—for the rest of his life if he could manage it. He was sick to death of death.

Why, for that matter, was Nirabha part of this caravan? Kandri knew nothing of his clan or country. He had a vague idea that the Prince was going home, but home might be Kasralys or some other, unknown land in the east. When Kandri had first glimpsed him, in General Tebassa's bunker, the young man had been every inch a royal: dark silk shirt, gold thread at cuffs and collar, buttons of mother-of-pearl. But two days later Tebassa had joked about his poverty—how Prince and manservant were bedding down among the camels, and lucky for as much shelter as that. Now his finery was gone, save for one magnificent ring. Had he lost a fortune in a matter of days?

Whomsoever you name shall be executed. Not killed, *executed.* Perhaps royals saw the murders they committed as acts performed by their country, not merely their hands.

Well, he could burn in the Pits. Who was this threadbare Prince to be making such an offer? And who did he think Kandri might want to kill?

CS

He stepped up beside Jód and matched his pace. "Ang's love to you, Master Ifimar," he said. Eshett had been drilling him in courtesies.

"And to you, Kandri Hinjuman. You are not troubled in body or heart?"

No hint of the expected fury. Kandri wondered if he was being mocked. *Am I troubled? What the hell do you think?*

"I'm recovering, thank you."

"We are pursued by killers," said Jód. "Of that I have no doubt. But what ill fortune to find another threat waiting upon the plain."

"The riders," said Kandri.

Jód gestured to the north. "Seventy riders, beyond the Hasthu Rocks. They may be Soldiers of Revelation, or they may have nothing to do with the Prophet— or with you. But we are ill prepared to fight so many, should it come to fighting."

"Have they seen us?"

"Yes," said the Master, "but let us hope they have no telescope to rival my own, and cannot be sure what they have seen. And the Gods have blessed us with a second advantage. Between us and those riders there is a glass drift. Perhaps you noticed—a bright lake it would have seemed to you."

Kandri recalled the glittering white basin he had glimpsed from the ridge top. *A glass drift?*

"They will not approach such a hazard," said Jód, "but they could ride around it, if they grow curious enough. We must try not to prick their curiosity—hence our southward detour. But for Eshett matters are now more complicated. The drift and the riders have cut her off from her intended path, and further east the defile becomes too steep to descend."

"What can she do?"

Jód made an ambiguous gesture. "There is another path, sound and unmistakable. But it will be five days before we reach it."

Five days. I have five days with her instead of two. His heart leaped: selfish, guilt-ridden, overjoyed.

"Eshett will have walked in a mighty circle by the time she reaches the canebrake at Maskiar," Jód continued. "Let us hope she finds her people waiting as she imagines."

"Are you saying you don't know if there's anyone there?"

"I am," said Jód, "but that is between her and the desert. Now then, tell me about the Well of Riphelundra."

"The pit?" Kandri shook his head. "What can I tell you? We're lucky to be alive."

"That is a truth we must all strive to remember," said Jód, "especially when one travels in your company, assassin."

Kandri bit down on a sigh. "I've told you before," he said. "I'm no assassin, and neither is Mektu. General Tebassa has it all wrong, we're nothing special. We just . . . got in the way."

"How do these lies serve your purpose, when the truth stands naked for all to see? Did you not throw yourselves into the Well?"

"*Throw* ourselves?" said Kandri. "I was attacked with a knife! Why would I throw myself into a pit?"

"Who can say?" asked the Master. "In obedience to a God, perhaps. A lesser God, a God of malice and heartbreak, but still a God. Certainly it was an inspired maneuver."

"Master Ifimar, please speak plainly. Remember I don't know your ways."

"There, that is another lie," said Jód. "You know them quite well. You knew that the Wasp, once disturbed, would leave sentinel insects above ground. Sentinels who would roam the canyon for days. Sentinels who would race back to the pit and bring down the full fury of the swarm on the next creature larger than a rabbit who chanced near."

"Devil's ass!"

"You deny it? You deny that you set a trap for the Prophet's next band of killers?"

"Yes, I deny it! I had no idea!"

"And the deep water, where you plunged to escape the Wasp yourself?"

"We never reached any water," said Kandri. "Dust is all that saved us—dust, filth, sand. We were buried in it."

"Nonsense. You set a trap. As you did on the summit of Alibat S'Ang."

"On the mountain . . . things were strange," said Kandri carefully. He had no intention of discussing yatras with Ifimar Jód. "We were betrayed, we let ourselves get cornered. The Rasanga—"

Jód hissed, cutting Kandri off, and his dark eyes flashed a warning. "Do not speak of them in anyone's hearing!" he whispered. "Why do you mention Rasanga?"

"Because they're out to kill us, of course."

"Are you saying to me that the men on your trail are *Rasanga*? The commandos, the death-priests of your Prophet?"

"I thought you knew."

Jód quickened—very nearly doubled—his pace. Of course the whole train was obliged to match him. Startled voices rippled back along the caravan. Animals brayed and snorted.

"They're not all men, either," said Kandri, shuffling at his side. "Most Rasanga are women, in fact."

Jód spared him a glance. "You think to teach *me* about those killers? Let us test your knowledge, then. How many Rasanga exist, across the Army of Revelation?"

Kandri was taken aback. "We were foot soldiers," he said. "No one told us that kind of—"

"Six hundred," said Jód, "one third of whom are with the Prophet at all times, and another third divided between her legions. And the last third, the last two hundred: those she has seeded across many lands, to kill and to provoke, to steal and kidnap and extort and terrify. Whatever furthers her vision of a continent under the thumb of her children.

"But I have known them since they numbered twelve—all men, when the division was formed. One of those twelve gave me a whetstone, telling me it was a gift from Her Radiance. To this day I sharpen my knife with that stone."

"You came to my country as a boy?"

The Caravan Master snorted. "Why would I set foot in Chiloto lands? What could I have hoped to find there but enslavement in the Prophet's army, and death fighting Važeks, or some other enemy not my own? The Rasanga came to us, Mr. Hinjuman. My father was compelled to teach them the ways of the desert, along with others of our clan. They were excellent pupils, and the training continues to this day, although my family long ago foreswore it."

Jód shook his head. "General Tebassa says that you are prodigies of killing, you and your foolish brother. I do not doubt him, but you have failed this time. No Rasanga will die in your trap. They will recognize the sentinel wasps and avoid the gorge altogether. All you have done is create a howling commotion that echoed the length of the Vasaru. I meant to lose our enemies before we set foot on this plain with its cursed nakedness. If those killers ride out and cut us down before we can hide again, only you will be to blame."

"Your men were desperate to show me that pit," said Kandri.

"My men are superstitious peasants. What is your excuse?"

No answer was likely to satisfy, Kandri decided. He walked on, waiting. The Master was not finished with him yet.

"My father did not teach the Rasanga everything," said Jód at last, "but he did teach me. We crossed the Sumuridath Jal eight times as father and son, serving the great merchant families as my people have done for many hundreds of years. On one of those crossings we were stranded for an entire year in the Blackwind Mountains, our camels dead and us too far from the next water source to depart unaided. Another year we were buried alive when a dune collapsed at Ravashandul's Wall, and all but five of us perished. In another, fever swept our ranks at Famine's Table, in the desert's deepest heart. Spalak, the Submaster of this caravan, buried his closest friend at Famine's Table. He has never been the same."

"Spalak?"

"You will have seen him at the rear of the caravan. He wears an earring of black and yellow beads."

Once again, the grim-faced veteran with the probing stare. "He's your second in command? He never talks."

"Our Submaster is not one for pleasantries," said Jód, "but he is a great fighter, and his knowledge of the desert is vast. There are few men or women in this world whom I would trust with my life. Dothor Spalak is one. He has been with us since I was a youth in my father's service, and Važek rule stretched as far as the Crescent Palmeries. In years of peace we used the common routes over plain and lathban, but in wartime we followed paths known only to the desert scholars. Paths even they had long neglected, paths forbidden to mapmakers, paths like a secret of the blood."

"Your father was a Caravan Master as well?"

"The finest in Urrath," said Jód. "Even in his day he was like one returned from times forgotten, like a saint out of the Basul Scrolls. When he died, travelers across the desert shaved their heads in mourning. I walked with my uncles' caravans for long years afterward. When they died in turn, I looked long into the eyes of the Gods who dwell behind the sun. I declared my wish to become the next Master of the Ways of the Sumuridath, and the Gods saw fit to approve."

He shot Kandri another of those looks. "If we escape your Prophet's killers, it will be by paths that I alone can show you. Is that clear?"

Kandri drew a deep breath. He nodded.

"Good," said the Master. "And note this as well: you must never underestimate my drivers. Superstition is not the same thing as stupidity. They are brilliant, after a fashion—but they are easily led astray. A single lie, a single liar, could bring death to us all."

"But I'm not leading your camel drivers *anywhere*. I've hardly spoken to them."

"I did not mean you, boy. I meant the one who is filling their heads with the Prophet's teachings, her tales of fear and deliverance. That one, that whisperer, is the one we must identify and deal with. For the next attack may not be so clumsy. It may be a knife drawn swift across your sleeping throat. Or your brother's, Hinjuman. Or your uncle's. Tell me, who was it dragged you to the pit?"

Kandri went rigid.

"You have not learned their names, of course," said Jód. "No matter: I know them all. Describe the man."

Kandri said nothing. The dryness in his mouth had nothing to do with the heat.

Whomsoever you name shall be executed.

Yes, but named in answer to Jód's questions, not the Prince's. Nirabha was not offering to kill anyone. He was offering a warning. The one with killing in mind was Jód.

"Many drivers were there," said Kandri.

"Indeed? Women and men alike?"

"No, no women."

75

"Someone must have taken the lead," said Jód.

Kandri fixed his eyes on the distant hills. A certain driver had, in fact, taken the lead. The man with the clouded eye and the kind, coaxing voice. *You have to look, Mr. Kandri. Once only. Mandatory.* The man who, of all the drivers, had been most friendly from the start.

"You think this person's another follower of the Prophet?" he asked.

"Which person, if you please?"

Bastard. You're trying to catch me out.

What if Jód was right, though? What if that kindly voice was coaxing driver after driver to Orthodox Revelation? What if it goaded six or eight men into attacking next time, instead of just one?

What if the man was innocent?

Jód's glance grew impatient. Kandri held a life between his thumb and forefinger. And realizing this, he found that there was only one answer he could give.

"No one took the lead, Master Ifimar. And they never meant for me to fall into the pit. The maniac saw a chance to kill me and took it, that's all. He didn't have any help."

Kandri expected anger at the obvious dodge. But the Master's face was merely thoughtful.

"Lies are a moral failure," he said, "and you, boy, are addicted to lies. I will pray for you."

They marched in silence. Kandri thought: *I'm running from people who kill for no reason. I won't become one of them. Shove that prayer up your ass.*

"Do you understand why I keep the truth of your situation from my drivers?"

"I suppose you don't want to frighten them."

"And what harm is there in frightening them?"

Kandri disliked these schoolmaster questions, but he answered, "Fear makes you careless, doesn't it? Makes you miss things."

"Indeed," said the Master, "but there is one thing above all that they must not miss too dearly: home. We are still in the Outer Basin. They could still abandon us, still turn and flee, or so they tell themselves. Yes, they have sworn oaths. But certain horrors will prompt a man to break his oath and run for his life."

"What clan do they belong to, your camel drivers?"

"You would not have heard of it."

"I wanted to make an effort—"

"To be social with them? To chat pleasantly about the food, the weather, the things all clans hold in common? A noble sentiment to be sure. But then many pleasant topics are deadly serious to those whose lives are governed by them. Others become a matter of life and death when discussed in ignorance. Sounds carry in the desert, and words cannot be recalled. The drivers' clan is not yours, and not mine. If they wish for you to know more than this, they will tell you."

He spoke with sharp finality. Kandri thought again of Eshett's words: *You of all people should understand why someone might want to hide.*

"The driver who attacked me knew I had become the Prophet's enemy," said Kandri. "Someone's sure as hell talking about us."

"Most of the drivers will not listen to that someone, fortunately. And while I know of your deeds, I remind you that you are forbidden to speak of them. If anyone is to broach the subject with the drivers, it shall be me."

"When will you tell them?"

"Possibly never," said Jód, "and certainly not until we have passed the Crescent Palmeries. We shall meet other travelers in the Palmeries; it is the busiest oasis in the desert save the Font of Lupriz."

"So if our drivers are too frightened—"

"They may abandon us there, begging or buying their way onto other teams."

Kandri took a deep breath. Mektu's babble had been even more dangerous than he'd imagined.

"Thank you for explaining," he said. "May I ask you one more question?"

Jód consented with an elaborate sweep of his hand.

"Why can't we smoke? Everyone else does."

To Kandri's astonishment, the Master smiled. Kandri found the look far more disconcerting than Jód's typical, low-boil wrath. The smile was not one of pleasure.

"This concludes our business, Kandri Hinjuman. Go and walk with your sweetheart, the desert's daughter."

Kandri jumped, startling the dogs. "If you mean Eshett—"

"Who else?" said Jód. "Go to her, drink of her wisdom while you may. But I warn you to recall my prohibition: your carnal joys are suspended while you walk with this caravan, save for those your own touch provides."

"My own—Gods below, Master Ifimar, what did I ever—"

"Our chat is over, Hinjuman. Blessings be upon you."

ଔ

Smiles or not, Kandri knew he had deepened Jód's hatred. The Master had grasped in an instant that he was refusing to cooperate in the matter of the drivers. Kandri did not regret his choice to protect his cataract-afflicted friend, but there would be consequences. Jód would watch him as never before. How could he possibly defy the man further? How could he be with Eshett?

They had defied Jód's order the very night it was given. As he made his way to her now, Kandri wondered just how harsh the punishment could be. Beatings, reduced rations, extra work? He would take them. Any worse would be hard to inflict, unless Jód beheaded people for lovemaking.

Eshett's face brightened as he approached.

"Where's Mektu?" he said. "Shouldn't he be fastened to your arm?"

"Your uncle's having a talk with him about that." She bumped his shoulder with her own. "And you and I have five whole days."

"I'm sorry, for your sake."

She narrowed her eyes. "I've been trying to get home for a year. I can wait five days. Or are you that keen to get rid of me?"

He didn't bother to respond. Eshett smiled and glanced away.

"Last night when we were finished," he said, "I dreamed of the Mountain of the Gods."

"Flatterer." She laughed, still looking away. But Kandri was sober, now.

"It's not the first time I've been there," he said. "But this time, I saw the world go mad. I saw Eternity Camp come to life and chase after us. And the

Chilotos followed them. I mean all of them, every last Chiloto in Urrath. And the animals, the soil, the hills—"

"Spare me."

"All right."

A trio of mercenaries lurched past them, insolently close. At their lead was Woeden Surk, the mercenary commander, an enormous fighter with an outthrust jaw and suspicious, heavy-lidded eyes. The left corner of Surk's mouth seemed forever on the point of lifting in a sneer. Now it did so, as his muscular elbow grazed Eshett's breast—no accident, of course. Without a thought Kandri made for Surk, one hand reaching for a machete that had not yet been replaced.

"*No*," whispered Eshett, catching his sleeve.

The mercenaries walked on. Surk looked back over his shoulder at Eshett, studying her up and down.

"Ignore them," said Eshett. "They leer at all the women—the drivers, Utarif's soldiers, even Talupéké. Especially Talupéké, in fact."

Kandri shook his head. "They have *no idea*—"

"What she's capable of? Neither did we, until we saw it. Captain Utarif's warned the brutes to keep their distance."

"He's a good man, Utarif," said Kandri.

"Yes," said Eshett. "Leaders like Surk use their tongue as a whip. Better ones don't have to. Jód doesn't scream at his drivers. Of course—" Her gaze swept back along the caravan. "—you don't have to scream, if you've put a man like Spalak on their heels."

"What kind of man is that?"

"A killer," said Eshett. "Don't be fooled by the gray in Spalak's hair. Look at his earring: yellow bead, black bead, over and over. He's a Parthan, Kandri. Each of those beads is a kill."

So Jód kept an assassin at the rear of the caravan. Kandri was not especially surprised. "What about the Master himself?" he asked. "You told me he was a Parthan, but his ears are bare as a baby's. Does that mean he's never killed?"

"Not at all," said Eshett. "Jód is not just any caravan leader. He's an *Aebris Sredereb*, a Master of the Ways."

"A guide, you mean?"

"A guide!" she laughed. "Kandri, an Aebris is a holy office, a calling. Only the Gods are allowed to alter the body of an Aebris. An earring would be a desecration, and the drivers would refuse to travel with him. *The Master keeps one foot in heaven*, we say. Like a priest. That's why Jód can't boast or swagger like those *uduch*, those mercenaries."

"They are pigs, aren't they?" said Kandri, bristling. "Ang help me, if they keep looking at you like you're some kind of—"

"Whore?"

"Candy. I was going to say candy."

"You watch yourself," she said. "What good will it do me if you kill one of them? And what if they kill you?"

"Not likely."

"Because the Gods love you so much."

"No, because I was trained in battle-dance. The Prophet's a monster, Eshett, but she did teach us to fight."

She took his hand for a daring moment; he had curled it into a fist. Gently she teased his fingers open.

"Just stay clear," said Eshett. "I'll let you know if I need help, *anjastha*."

He smiled, and she smiled to see that he recalled the word she'd taught him: *Anjastha*, lover. For a few more nights.

"What's a glass drift?" he said.

Her smile vanished. She glanced to the north. "Death," she said.

"Meaning what?"

"I don't want to talk about it," she said. "Never go near a glass drift. But if you do, and the wind blows from that direction, run downwind. Run as fast as you can. And speaking of downwind, you need a bath."

"Not going to happen for awhile."

"You'll get a bucket-bath at the Palmeries. There's water enough."

Kandri watched her strong limbs working, the calm alertness of her eyes. Like Jód she trained them on the horizon, leaned toward it like the face of a loved one across a table. He wanted to kiss her eyelids. He wanted her breath rasping against his ear.

"I put it back," he said, lowering his voice. "The knife, I mean. The mattoglin."

She glanced up at her pack, lashed above the saddlebag on the camel beside them. "Why did your brother steal it?" she asked.

"Hell if I know," said Kandri. "He told me some rubbish about it worrying you."

"Of course it worries me," said Eshett. "It's worse than a toothache. I see it in my sleep."

"Bury it," said Kandri. "Somewhere outside your village, under some tree or rock you won't forget. Pry a jewel off the sheath when you need money for something. But keep the knife intact. *Those* jewels, the ones on the blade, they're just—"

"Yes," said Eshett. "The ormalid alone—"

"The what?"

"Ormalid. The great blue jewel. It must be worth twenty times all the goods in this caravan."

"I love the thought of you being rich," said Kandri.

She laughed. "I've never even *known* a rich person. At least . . ."

Doubt creased her face suddenly, as though a suspect thought or memory had abruptly surfaced. "What is it?" asked Kandri.

Eshett shook herself. "Nothing, nothing at all."

"Tell me," he pressed.

But Eshett just looked at him wryly. "You tell *me* something," she said. "What exactly do rich people *do*?"

Now it was his turn to laugh. "Whatever they want—that's the point. They can sit on their asses or go sailing or have orgies or collect rare bugs. Doesn't matter. They'll still have food."

But it was not a good time for laughter, really. "Listen," he said, "you can't talk about the mattoglin. You understand that, don't you? Not for years. Not until the Prophet's forgotten all about it. But when she has—"

"I'll sell it, and have wells dug all over the western desert. And send my nieces to school."

Something in her voice said it would never happen, that she was reciting the plan just to make him stop talking. He noticed that she had tugged the sleeve of her cloak over her left hand, and was holding it there with two fingers.

"Something wrong?" he asked, nodding at her hand.

"The wind makes my burn itch," she said.

"Burned yourself making flatbread, did you?"

She looked at him, frowning. "This is my *old* burn," she said. "You know."

Kandri was bewildered. Gently, he put his hand on her wrist, tugged back the sleeve.

"Jeshar!" A raised red scar bisected her palm. He turned her hand: the scar crept up to her wrist and encircled it like a bracelet.

"Eshett! What the hell happened to you?"

"My sister's wedding feast," said Eshett. "I told you weeks ago. Boiling molasses, a crowd in the cooking tent. Don't stare, it's not the first time you've seen it."

"But I've *never* seen it before," Kandri protested.

She pulled away, annoyed. Kandri was flushed and shaking. He had known her for weeks now, made love to her thrice. How could he have overlooked such a scar? He had kissed that hand. She had touched him with it.

Could she possibly be lying? There had been fires aplenty when they fled over the plain of the Lutaral: fires from heaven, great blazing orbs hurled down from the sky. The *Darsunuk*, people had shouted: the Time of Madness, and the fires the Gods' own tears.

None had landed near him, but Eshett had made the crossing miles away, with his uncle. Still, what reason could she possibly have to lie to him? And if one of those nightmarish embers had struck near her and sprayed her with fire, wouldn't it have burned more than her hand?

He thought of Mektu's strange words from weeks before: *Eshett has a secret. Something she's afraid to tell a soul.* His brother had, once again, noticed more than Kandri himself.

He risked another glance at her hand. No, it was not that complicated: he was just a dumb pig. The scar was obviously old. Eshett caught him looking, shook her head in despair. But her fingers reached for his again and gave a surreptitious squeeze.

"You're as bad as Mektu," she said. "Maybe if I'd burned my tits."

೦೩

Kandri did not know what to make of his feelings for Eshett. There was a litany he returned to, almost hourly now: *I love one woman. Her name is Ariqina and she changed my life. I set out for Kasralys to find her. Eshett knows and doesn't mind because we never meant for this to last. We're lovers, we're not in love.*

All that was the simple truth, wasn't it? Why then did Ifimar Jód's words echo in his mind like cries from a cave?

Her burden is greater than you know.

Of course he was frightened for her. The traitor Stilts, once General Tebassa's right-hand man, had no doubt mentioned Eshett when he betrayed them all to the Prophet. Their enemies knew about this desert woman, this Parthan, who had run with the fugitives all the way from Eternity Camp. Who had helped Kandri hide the body of the Prophet's son.

But it doesn't matter, Kandri told himself. For Stilts was dead, and the Rasanga had never seen Eshett's face. Once she fell back into the fold of her people, she would be just another nomadic Parthan, lost in Urrath's immensities, erased.

No, it wasn't fear for her that tormented him. Nor even the thought that he would never see her again after a night or two, never touch her again.

So what in Jekka's Hell is it?

The sun beat down, the sky ahead quaked with heat. Kandri turned and walked backward, studying the dusty, stinking centipede of the caravan. Who could he talk to? His uncle was furious; his brother was jealous and insane. Talupéké was half insane.

And Jód? Kandri nearly laughed aloud. Jód would be praying about now—praying with silent fervor that the next attacker was more capable than the first.

Speak of the devil. There, behind the brooding Spalak at the rear of the caravan, the ghost of the first maniac suddenly blinked into existence, nodding and chattering to himself, cradling his thumb.

Maybe I'll talk to you.

The ghost looked up at him, as though he had heard the thought Kandri sent his way. In his eyes there was less menace than there had been in life: there was almost, strange to say, an appeal. Then the dead man's toe caught a stone; he stumbled; he was gone.

No one to talk to, no one to ask. Eshett too was a ghost (Kandri's thoughts had run wild). She had come out of the night and would vanish into it again, she'd leave no trace, all the memories would fade to shadows, her secret glances, her frowns of concentration, the smoky taste of her skin.

Lovers, enemies. The living. The dead. Was it all just happenstance, start to finish? Bits of straw blown apart or together by vagaries of wind? And why was that idea, of all the mad and curious notions he had grappled with since deserting the army, the most intolerable?

Second Interlude

Kandri, Kandri, was it ever in doubt? Of course it's happenstance, my host. We are all prey to that blind brute.

Yet think again. What could be more liberating than the glorious symphony of cause and effect? To mourn happenstance is to mourn that a cup falls down and not up when knocked from a table, that hail must break a window rather than mend it, that the universe plays one song and not another. Happenstance is the earth you walk, the blood your body warms, the stars' gyrations, the light by which you see. It is also what unites our two peoples, whether we like it or not.

You love Ariqina. That will-o'-the-wisp named Eshett (not her true name, I think) loves you. Mektu loves both women, not least because you do yourself. And while I have far less access to their minds, I can say with confidence that your uncle and the half-mad Talupéké love you both, and throb with guilt when they catch themselves wishing they had never met you, wishing they could just walk away.

Happenstance, indeed. Why should that thought make you bitter, when the word contains all life's mystery and possibility and promise, along with its fragility, its doom? Could you live with the alternative—with inescapable purpose, a role you had no choice but to perform? Of course not. You'd howl. You'd chafe at that bit until your gums bled, and if you found no way to spit it out, you'd run mad. All the same you lament, rend your hair and clothes, cry out to the Gods in indignation at your wondrous mortal freedom. It is one of the strangest qualities of the human mind, this hunger for a play script, this craving for a Master Plan.

The trouble starts with memory, or rather the lack thereof. If I could but speak to you—if you could hear me without horror and pain—the whole of my message would be a plea:

REMEMBER!

Practice memory. Refine it, nurture it, cherish that embryonic gift! On what other pedestal do your achievements stand? What else but memory keeps them from vanishing into the mire?

Don't interrupt; I know what I'm saying. You, Kandri, watched your grandfather's mind decay: foul, cruel, horrible. Now imagine living long enough to witness the decay of generations. One hundred thirty generations, in my case. In that time I have entered nearly six hundred human minds. I have shared in their glories, their pleasures, their agonies. I have slipped away as death approached, for the wind and void are always waiting for my kind, and a host is the only shelter. But with some hosts I stayed long enough. I watched that merciless loss, memory dripping like soup from a cracked kettle, leaving hunger and a stain.

The same leakage can hobble a careless nation. This too I have witnessed. Poetry, history, moral philosophy, scientific law. That engineering magic of your father's, which Her Radiance longs to pervert into weaponry. Those fabulous machines of the Xavasindran doctors: light without heat, cold without ice, surgery performed while the patient sleeps. The architectural miracles of the Kasraj. Lañatu music. Sutku mathematics. These are little hearth-fires, Kandri. You must feed them, or they die.

Consider your own clan's great invention: the *solaprus*, those epic Chiloto histories in verse. Miracles of memory they were: tales of great deeds and small mercies, proud Chiloto queens and cunning Chiloto villains, exile and discovery, dynasty and war. Tales spanning centuries—and *memorized* for centuries, passed down verbatim from parents to children in the darkness after evening meals. Three decades ago they were still being taught, by a few brave souls. Your Prophet tried to turn those last storytellers into weapons as well—weapons of meaning, stories of heaven's sanction of her rule. Failing, she simply killed the storytellers.

Today, hardly anyone your age has even heard of *solaprus*. To speak of them is forbidden; the word itself is a crime. Absolutely no one can recite those masterpieces. No one save a handful of yatras, these demons you despise.

Memory, then: that's the cure for your fear of happenstance. You're very welcome. No charge.

No charge, either, for your glimpses of the dead. Again, there is nothing to be afraid of. We yatras straddle numerous worlds—distant pasts, potential futures, cul-de-sac realities orphaned alongside your own. We see these mirror-worlds, gazing out through your eyes. We cannot help it. And sometimes, very rarely, our hosts see them too.

The world of death is one of the nearest, first cousin to your world beneath the living sun. And the dead respect you, Kandri. Rare indeed is the ghost that harms a living soul, unless that soul first strikes at them.

No, the dead are the least of your problems. And certainly the least of mine.

Listen, host: when this particular yatra sparked to life (cold, frightened, motherless, a speck of plankton in a roaring sea), there was no desert where you stand. Oh, it was coming. The dunes were spreading this way. Emperor Ravashandul was losing sleep over them, dreaming of his Desert Wall. But here all was still green. Rice flourished, gallery forests lined the rivers, the River God's children ran laughing after midnight through sleeping villages, farmers rose at dawn and wondered at their tiny footprints.

Minds were more comfortable then. Mortality stood hulking in a corner, but the rest of the house was bright and cheerful, the furnishings simple and few. Today, when I take up residence, I shuffle through worries and resentments and suspicions and self-doubts, piled like rubbish to my knees. You do clean house, now and then. You sweep the doubts aside for love, lovemaking, childbirth, war. And children's minds are little changed from the old days. Things of beauty, those young minds, like new-built towers on a summer hill. Windows open. Ample sun.

That of course, is what makes them such alluring targets. And why our law *absolutely forbids* any trespass into the minds of children. No exceptions. No debate.

By the Last Voice, have we arrived at a world where it must be debated?

Children are soft-shelled creatures, wildly growing and changing, far too delicate to touch. There is no pardoning a yatra who invades a child: the crime is as venal as rape. Indeed it is a form of rape.

We live by a code, we yatras. We are far more law-abiding than you. When we inhabit your minds, we touch nothing, change nothing. This too is fundamental law. Oh, we have the power—some of us more than others— but that does not compel us to use it. Do you break windows, crystals, the bones of helpless animals, merely because you can?

We are the finest of guests. We make no sound, leave no footprints. We resist even the urge to dust or part the curtains. Our host is no more aware of us than the portraits in a gallery are aware of the night watchman who patrols the darkened halls.

Do the portraits dream of the watchman? Perhaps, in one of the countless mirror-worlds through which our reflections scatter. But in this world, we yatras are the soul of honor. We are not selfish or grasping. And we are no menace whatsoever to your children, for *we do not touch them.* At the very most, we listen—from a distance, and in awe.

But we too have our criminals.

Sometimes, the watchman begins to speak to the portraits—not in his thoughts, as I am doing now, but aloud. Perhaps he shouts and listen for the echo. Perhaps he taunts them, threatens them with the maid's rag and solvent, or his night stick, or the contents of his surreptitious flask. Sometimes, lonely and depraved, he enjoys how the faces in the portraits recoil in fear.

If I could speak without harming you, Kandri, I would share what I have only just understood. Your brother is not lying. One of us did assault him, terribly, at the tenderest age. He fought back and won, and that is a miracle in itself. But his mind has never fully healed.

I have despised him. I'm ashamed. A being like myself crept inside his mind and bloodied every chamber, every wall. Mektu Hinjuman, without aid or guidance, drove the yatra out. He told us, did he not? The fight for control, the jaws closing on his mind, the headlong rush to the neighbor's farm and the desperate leap into the smokehouse. The sealed door, his oath to suffocate before surrender. His blackout.

I thought it all fantasy and fibs, like the better part of his talk: no one drives a yatra out with threats. But he did. The scars are there, plain to be felt by any of my people with the sense to seek them.

Do you understand, my host? Mektu, a boy of six, bested a creature of thirty centuries or more, a torturer of monstrous depravity and strength.

I make no excuses. I ignored the clues, and there were many. A dog once burned will cringe at the first whiff of smoke; a human once assaulted by a yatra will sense another yatra's presence where no others can. Mektu caught my scent back at Eternity Camp, when I dwelt in Lord Garatajik. Who believed him? Not you, Kandri, and you had plenty of chances.

Almost as many as I had myself.

When Garatajik tracked you to that burial yard, his nearness (my nearness) must have been a horror for Mektu, the purr of a tiger in the brush. How else could he have failed to hear the man declaring himself your ally, thanking you for killing his gore-debauched brother Ojulan, promising to stop his mother's war?

What did my presence do to Mektu, in that instant? Was he reliving the battle in the smokehouse? Did some instinct deeper than thought guide his knife?

A more urgent question plagues me, too. What happened three days ago on Alibat S'Ang? Your brother fell, twitched, gibbered in a credible yatra-voice. He mimicked your Prophet to an uncanny degree. He appalled and distracted your enemies, left them ready for ambush, saved your lives.

None of it was my doing, except for the relief I gave you from crippling pain. The rest—no, I have never attempted such deeds. I am not great among my people. I lack the power of our ancient kings. I could not have reached out and controlled your brother's mind—not without tearing a mortal hole in your own.

He spoke the simple truth to the camel drivers, before your plunge into the pit. He's not possessed. Not by me at any rate. But spawn of hell: can it all have been an act? The writhing, the voices, the agony at unseen blows? Can any human do *that* to himself at will?

And if not—

Well then, if *not*—

No, no, I cannot walk that path. Mektu has suffered enough. Oh, he might yet heal, if he is indeed himself, and finds love enough, and if you are not all murdered or swallowed by the sands. Without question, he deserves to heal; indeed he deserves all the praise and sympathy we might bestow. Unfortunately, he's still an ass.

That night Jód stopped the caravan at moonrise. An hour's rest: the drivers flung themselves down. Kandri was about to follow their example—his whole-body bruises from the pit were just beginning to assert themselves—when he noticed Ifimar Jód walking with his hand on the arm of a young camel driver. The gesture was kindly, even affectionate. It was like seeing another man.

The young driver was tall and lean. He walked with Jód to the rear of the caravan, where Spalak appeared to be expecting them. Kandri watched as Jód addressed them, the tall youth and the grim Submaster. The youth nodded eagerly at first, proud it seemed to be included in this conference with his betters.

But gradually the youth grew still, and Kandri saw that he was frightened. He spilled water from the faska Jód placed in his hand. When Spalak touched his elbow, he flinched.

The youth and Spalak laid their outer cloaks and most of their possessions at the Master's feet. Spalak even discarded his sword, though he kept a long knife on his belt. The two stood there in nothing more than headscarves and breeches. Then Jód stepped forward and handed each of them something flat and tiny as a coin. Spalak at once placed the object in his mouth. The youth stared at the thing on his palm a moment before doing the same. At a last word from Jód, Spalak and the youth dashed away into the night—back, it appeared, along the path by which the caravan had come.

Rear scouts, thought Kandri. Seeking the enemy and running light, the better to stay ahead of them, and to return in time for a warning. Kandri watched Jód bend and tie up their possessions in the cloaks. Then, as though feeling eyes on his back, he stood and faced Kandri. The Master was no more than a silhouette, but Kandri felt his fury like waves of heat.

Exhausted though he was, Kandri lay sleepless for the remainder of the hour. It was almost a relief when they rose and marched on under a still-climbing moon. Jód's pace too fast for talk, too fast for anything save the effort not to fall and be stepped on by the camel behind. Had the scouts returned? Kandri could not find them in the crowd, and it was only gradually, as his gaze slid up and down the caravan, that he realized they had yet to return.

Deep in the night, he saw the drivers frowning and glancing over their shoulders. He looked: there was nothing behind them save the pale, persistent ghost of the maniac, his would-be killer.

"Don't look at him," said Mektu.

Kandri was shocked. None of the camel drivers had thus far shown any awareness of the ghost. Nor had Chindilan: Kandri had spied him looking back when the dead man was shining like a beacon to his eyes, and the smith had been quite unaware. But with Mektu Kandri had avoided the subject: his brother's fear of the supernatural was boundless.

"You can see him, Mek? The maniac? Could you see him from the start?"

"Don't make me," said Mektu. "I'm not the same as you. If I meet his eyes I don't know what will happen."

"Nothing will happen, fool. But we're the only ones, I think. To the others he's just not there."

"Then what are these fuckers looking at?"

An excellent question. Kandri studied the drivers' faces. No, it wasn't the ghost. Their eyes were darting, traveling, searching the night. "Brother," said Mektu, "do you hear something?"

Kandri raised his head. *Did* he hear something? A faint voice crying out, perhaps? Or had Mektu simply put the idea in his head? As he cast his eyes about, he saw that Talupéké was moving away to one side of the caravan.

Away from other noises. She had the right idea.

He hurried after her, and Mektu followed. Still as a hare the girl watched them approach. When they drew near, she said simply, "It's them."

Kandri held his breath. Very faintly, the sound reached his ears:

Oorlulu-Kralulu-Kelulu-Lhor! Oorlulu-Kralulu-Kelulu-Lhor!

It was the kill-song of the Army of Revelation.

ଓଃ

The caravan fled. Kandri did not know if the drivers recognized that mocking, ululating cry—a cry he himself had once flung at the Prophet's enemies—but all of them had grasped its essence, which was death. No further thought of rest or sleep. Hour upon hour, they ran through the dark.

Luck, or the Gods' favor, was surely with them. The sound did not come again, and no Rasanga or other servants of the Prophet appeared in the night. As the dawn broke Ifimar Jód slowed their headlong pace at last. And with the first light, Spalak came running from the north.

He reached them with the last of his strength. Drivers' hands caught his shoulders, propping him up. Jód halted the caravan and rushed to his Subcommander, and Spalak toppled into his arms. He tried to speak, head lolling on Jód's shoulder. When at last he succeeded Jód put back his head and gave a clipped cry of grief or rage. The whispers swept the caravan.

Dead. The boy is dead. The Rasanga have murdered him.

Jód helped Spalak hobble along the caravan, through the drivers' cries and sobs. When they drew near the brothers, the Master looked at them with loathing. His eyes were bright.

"The death-priests you did not see fit to mention," he said, "passed within a mile of our last place of rest. A large force, a deadly force. By the grace of Ang our paths are diverging: my evasions appear to have misled them, for now."

"What happened to the boy?" asked Talupéké.

Spalak dropped his eyes.

Jód looked hard at Talupéké, as though the question were indecent. At last he said, "Spalak and the boy split up, watching the enemy from a distance. But the boy stumbled, and the Rasanga heard him and pounced. He knew his fate then. He swallowed the poison capsule I had provided, and Ang closed his eyes in death."

"His name was Themasar," said Spalak suddenly, and his voice was deep like Jód's, but smoother, and full of sorrow. It was the first time Kandri had heard it.

"He was brave, and swift as a wolf upon his feet," said Jód. "We dare not stop to mourn him as he deserves, for the Rasanga will correct their course soon enough." He turned a scathing look on Kandri. "If you had been more candid, young Themasar might still be among us. How shall you atone, Kandri Hinjuman? How many shall join him before the end?"

6. SIREN'S HARBOR

General Agathar was on the road out of Cauldron Farm before the messenger himself, with no escort but his daughter-in-law and a pack of hunting dogs. A stiff wind from the sea had blown the sunny morning away. He was cold and rode stiffly, sore in his neck and shoulders. A rain so fine it was almost mist filled the air, slithering beneath their ponchos, soaking them through. The road was deserted; the grand estates bordering his own lay bleak and gray. Even the sorrel deer they passed looked miserable.

Statuary House.

Those two words in the King's missive, more than all the coded hints of danger, had compelled this haste. When his eyes fell upon them, he had felt a change in his surroundings, as though some buried titan had moved in his sleep, sending tremors through the land he loved.

He had expected a summons—what else could have put the messenger in such a froth?—but to the capital, perhaps for some wedding to which the King had forgotten, until the last possible moment, to invite him. Or to which the King *had* invited him: earlier this year he had ignored two such invitations, hoping silence would cause less offense than refusal. Weddings bored him; royal weddings bored him almost to tears. After the second invitation he had begun the wheelchair subterfuge.

But no one married at Statuary House. On his first visit, forty-seven years ago it was, certain guests had been called discreetly from table, including the man on Agathar's right. He never forgot that proud old officer, eyes quizzical but unafraid, dabbing the corners of his mouth with a linen napkin as he went.

Moments later the absent guests' plates were cleared and their chairs removed from the hall. No one spoke of what was happening, unless it was the servants, in whispers. But across the table from Agathar, a rather gaunt and hungry-eyed young barrister from the capital met his eye and grinned—Agathar could still see his white teeth shining among the candle flames. At the time, he knew only that the barrister was apprenticed to someone at Statuary House and that he was said to be clever and ambitious. The young man raised his glass and nodded, as though he and Agathar shared some happy secret.

Five decades later, on his most recent visit to Statuary House, Agathar had stepped out onto a dark, storm-swept balcony above the sea and faced the same barrister, standing there in cold wind and colder moonlight. Agathar had become the military hero of his age. The barrister, one Lord Sulmurg, had become Master of Statuary House, and Special Inquisitor of the Kingdom of Shôlupur.

Long wars lay behind them, along with the better part of their lives. Many times across the years Agathar had spoken of the people called away from the table. Sulmurg had never answered with more than a smile and a twinkle in his eye. But that night on the balcony he had finally acknowledged the crime.

"You feed your lizards, Agathar. We feed our sharks."

"My lizards are vegetarians," Agathar had countered, instantly regretting the comment. The Inquisitor had turned to face him, beaming.

"But they rip each other to pieces, do they not?"

"Only if provoked."

"You do them a disservice," said Sulmurg. "You provide food without effort, make them lazy and fat. Worse still, you erode their fear of human beings. Why not harvest them? The Sutku clan in the mountains considers iguanas a delicacy, you know."

Agathar had just walked away. The Sutku were all dead, at least in Shôlupur, but arguing with the Special Inquisitor was like wrestling an eel: no winning, no shoulder to pin to the ground.

Sulmurg would preside over this emergency council as well, since it was convening in his house. Unless he'd caught an arm in one of his own torture devices and been killed.

Agathar had never wished death on any person, though in battle he had killed with lance and bow and sword and strangulation. But how he despised Sulmurg—his laugh, his methods, his influence with the King. And the fortress itself: loathsome, depraved. It was a point against the general's own estate that it was a mere six hours from Statuary House.

ɞ

The rain strengthened, black clouds shouldering in from the coast. When they reached the Morsitka Pass with its stone signal tower the eight soldiers billeted there were standing at attention, terrified and drenched.

He freed them with a salute and a smile. No inspection today. But as always, he stopped his horse for a few breaths at the summit. Long enough to look east into the kingdom's heart.

Somewhere out there beyond his sight stood Nebusul, greatest city on the continent save one alone. Between him and the unglimpsed capital, a sea of rich pastureland spread its bounty, pale gray and brown here at winter's end, but soon to erupt in wildflowers and the emerald greens of new kvinith, the tall wild grass of the hill country. And there too were the deep wet woods that were the Kingdom's glory, and small hamlets beyond counting, and lakes like melted coins. Shôlupur, eternal Shôlupur, defiant of the rain.

Isula pointed to a distant spot on the Coast Road, where a vague red shape blurred the highway. She gave him a questioning look.

Agathar did not need to consult his telescope: not after the life he'd lived. "Infantry," he said. "Half a legion at the minimum. That's the rearguard, closest to us, which means they're making for the capital. Unusual, to see such a large exercise in weather this foul. Of course I approve."

She made a face at him, spurred her horse on.

Below the pass the valley was flooded, and the dogs had to swim. Agathar's toes were numb, but the riding had loosened his back, and the stench of wet horse was as sweet in its way as the perfumed vines in his garden. Provided he filtered the memories that smell evoked, let only the right ones surface in his mind. The oldest. The newest. Never the abyss in between.

When the water rose even higher his daughter-in-law slid from her horse and lifted the smallest dog onto her saddle. Before she could remount, he pointed to another.

"She's hardly any taller, that runt. Give her here."

Isula looked up at him, her black curls wilted by rainwater. She touched her chin with thumb and forefinger: a question. She had not spoken since the death of her husband and daughter three years ago, but Agathar could follow a fair amount of what she said with her hands.

"One for you, one for me," he said. "What, do you think I'll drop the bitch?"

Isula lifted the squirming creature into his hands. She flashed him a smile: a rare sweet sight. They crossed the flooded valley with the dogs upon the horses' withers, set them down as they ascended, and reached the gate of the village of Siren's Harbor by mid-afternoon.

ɔ8

The black brick wall, like the village it guarded, was crumbling. The sentry post was abandoned, the rusty gate stood ajar. They could hear the great northern ocean beyond the cliffs but not see it: the people of Siren's Harbor were denied even that.

Agathar tugged a ring from his finger, held it out to Isula.

"Show this to the brewer. He'll give you a room and a seat at his table. We're old friends."

She slipped the ring onto her finger, lifted an ironic eyebrow. Agathar chuckled.

"Finish your hunting by this time tomorrow, do you hear? I'll be ready. One night in this town will be more than enough."

Isula gestured at the fortress, touched her chin again.

"It's a War Council," said Agathar, "but that's just a fancy name: I'd know if the Scarlet Kingdom were going to war. Still, there must be trouble somewhere. A skirmish with the Kasrajis, maybe, or some crisis with our friends in Važenland. I've told you how these small matters upset His Majesty, ruin his tranquility. But they're small nonetheless. I'm sure this one's no different."

Isula dropped her eyes, frowning.

"Right," he said. "I'm sure of nothing, except that you're impossible to fool. But even if we're facing some true urgency, I'm still retired. I'm not leaving my orchids in your hands."

She grinned, and he pressed his advantage. "The deed to Cauldron Farm is with my solicitor in the city," he said. "The estate details as well. It's all yours, of course."

Isula's dark eyes took the measure of him. "I'm not being morbid," he said. "Just practical; at my age one takes nothing for granted. In any event, the solicitor knows that I place all trust in you."

She cleared her throat. His heart leaped at the sound of her voice. She had studied music; he had heard that voice silence a theater bursting with drunken lords and princes; she had won his son's heart with song.

When will you speak, Isula? When will you tell me how they died?

She glanced at him and recoiled, as though he'd said the words aloud. He reached for her shoulder, but she turned the horse and rode swiftly westward, her hounds like surf about its legs.

"I didn't ask," he murmured.

And yet he had thought the questions, once again. Questions she was afraid to hear, let alone attempt to answer, and that could make no difference anyway, since death was death. He watched her vanish. He passed through the gate alone.

Siren's Harbor: a sad stone fishing village without shrine or temple, wrapped like an old scarf about a headland on the Actumian Sea. Nothing lived or grew on the headland; it was white and smooth as a skull. But crowning that skull was Statuary House. Among his reasons for hating the tall stone fortress was this, how it loomed above the fisherfolk, used them as a garment and a shield and gave nothing in return. The villagers never climbed the hill, averted their eyes from its summit. Like everyone in the Kingdom, save princes and army commanders, they were forbidden to speak of Statuary House.

He rode straight through the village; no point in delay. Gaunt maidservants looked out from lightless windows; young men watched his progress from doorways reeking of wine. He passed a rambling structure that looked for all the world like a collection of sheds and porches hammered together in the space of an afternoon. SOLDIERS' HOME, guffed a crooked sign. On its listing stairs and landings, they gazed at him, men and some women, vacant, frail. Here an eye missing, here a nose, there the stump of an arm waved away flies. His own age, these people, and retired from the same profession.

He stopped long enough to put a purse into the hands of the matron of the Home, but not long enough to chat with the soldiers, not today. Forty-six of these shelters across the Scarlet Kingdom, and a three-year waiting list to claim a bed. He went on. In the alleys, refuse steamed, children gazed hollow-eyed from shelters of scrapwood and tin.

What had all the battles been for?

The sun, thank the Gods, chose that moment to nudge the stormclouds aside. He rode uphill in soggy, spreading brilliance, the village behind, the sea a mad indigo before him, the gulls wheeling, laughing at his gloom. Atop the white headland, Statuary House looked innocent and scrubbed.

଼

But the King's letter had lied. There was no War Council, no officers, no bustle of clerks and secretaries frantic with manifests and decrees. No national crisis. And no assembly of any kind. There was only Lord Sulmurg, black-gloved hands on hips, grinning at him from across the courtyard.

"Welcome, River Dragon," he crowed. A provocation, of course. Sulmurg knew quite well how he disliked the nickname.

Agathar closed the distance between them. "What am I doing here? How long will it take?"

Sulmurg was his junior by five years or more, but the man looked older, pale from his years in archives, laboratories, dungeons. His gray eyes crouched deep in their sockets like furtive crabs. He leaned closer to Agathar and sniffed.

"You reek of dog. Wet dog."

"Answer me," said the general.

"You'll be in the north tower. The finest chambers in the house, incidentally. Would you care to borrow some clothes?"

"No."

"Not my own, I wouldn't sully you with them. But I have whole wardrobes full of outfits, you know. They . . . accumulate."

The general looked him up and down.

"What are you thinking, you old schemer?" said Sulmurg.

"That you won't believe me, and yet I'm free to say it anyway," said the general. "You should retire. This very day. Walk out of here and never return. How many years do you have left, my lord? Perhaps fifteen? Perhaps only five? What God ordained that you should spend them in the depths of this hell-house? In the darkness, inflicting pain? Just this morning the sun was out and the land was green and beautiful. I expect you failed to notice."

The Inquisitor gave him a crafty smile, as though they were sharing a joke. "This is all your doing, isn't it?" he said.

Agathar narrowed his eyes.

"This gathering," said Sulmurg. "This secrecy, this last-minute intrigue. All you, at the end of the puppet-strings. What better way to exhibit what remains of your influence than to upstage me at this most critical hour?"

"I have no idea what you're talking about."

"I should have guessed," said Sulmurg. "Therel Agathar, the military genius. The hero who left the fray when he wished, regardless of the needs of Shôlupur. Who dared his King to try to extract another day of service. But now! You're burning for the last and greatest glory, are you not?"

"What glory? Explain yourself, or stop wasting my time."

"Did you bombard His Majesty with letters, tell him you alone could deliver the prize? Confess, Dragon! I'll find out anyway, you know."

"I was summoned," said Agathar quietly, "to an emergency War Council, very much against my will. And all I see is sham. The house is empty; the emergency nowhere to be found. You may feel we have old scores to settle, Lord Sulmurg. I have no such obsession; in fact I rarely think of you. But if this proves to be malice on your part, you will indeed learn something of my remaining influence."

Sulmurg looked at the general anew, as though reconsidering the very identity of the man before him. "You won't make *me* responsible," he said. "I told them to leave you rotting among your flowers."

"If you didn't arrange my summons, who did?"

"That would be me, General," said a voice on his left.

Agathar jumped, making Sulmurg roar with laughter.

There by the postern door stood Obekri. Kalen Obekri. A tall, bright-eyed man with the weathered look of a sailor or a nomad. Arms crossed. White shirt frayed at the collar. Neat beard gone to gray.

He crossed the courtyard, gazing only at Agathar. His face shone with a complicated light: happiness contending with something dreadful or repellent, or was that just the sun in his eyes?

Agathar was dumbstruck. Obekri was his oldest friend. He was not a soldier but a naturalist, a man who studied rivers, wetlands, lakes, and all the teeming life they contained. The King had sent him to Wostryl to advise the general how the scorched and poisoned battlefields might be made green again. It was a stroke of genius, and left the defeated Wost clan hating Shôlu-pur less than they might have. But—

"What in hell's larder are you doing here?"

"Yes, enlighten us, woodsman," said Sulmurg. "Are you just a present for Agathar? The King might have tidied you up a bit, if that's the case."

Obekri did not even glance at Sulmurg. "You look well, General. Peace-ful, in a word."

Agathar said nothing.

"What has it been? Two years?"

"Closer to three."

"The fault is mine," said Obekri. "I've been but little in the north. I meant to visit you nonetheless, but then—" He made an uncertain gesture. "—my life has not been my own."

"Whose is?" said Sulmurg. "We are subjects, not sovereigns in miniature. We possess many freedoms, and the wealth and time to enjoy them. But in the last analysis, our lives are the King's."

"I think the general will require those clothes now, my lord Sulmurg," said Obekri quietly. Then he took Agathar by the arm. "Come, I'll show you to your chambers."

For the second time in as many minutes, Agathar was stunned. *Obekri just gave Sulmurg an order. In his own house.* The Inquisitor was visibly furious. He took a step toward Obekri, all the muscles in his face gone rigid.

"The King's business—"

"Will suffer if his general develops pneumonia," said Obekri. "Send the clothes, and a samovar. That will do for now."

He turned away, ushering Agathar toward the postern door. Agathar expected Sulmurg to erupt, flaying this common-born rambler with words, since he presumably could not do so with knives and needles. He glanced sidelong at his friend. *Why are you sparring with that deadly creature?* Lord Sulmurg had cultivated power in Shôlupur for half a century. His tendrils had crept into the courts, the religious academies, the homes of leading citizens, the councils of the King. His memory, like Agathar's, was prodigious. And Sulmurg never forgave a slight.

Obekri led him through the doorway and onto a narrow staircase. "Watch your step. They've not lit the torches yet."

He closed the door, plunging them into darkness. "Kalen," said Agathar, "what is happening here?"

Obekri's hand fumbled for his shoulder. Old friend. Old familiar touch. "We'll talk above," he said.

The light grew as they ascended: there were windows on the courtyard and the sea. They passed through the grand room reserved for Agathar, where a maid was arranging flowers on the bedside table. The floor above was an elegant reading room, with dark bookcases, a round cherrywood table, and a great map of the continent of Urrath painted on the curving wall.

"One more," said Obekri. "Do you need to rest a moment?"

"Go to hell."

Smiling now, Obekri resumed the climb. The general followed, breathing hard and trying to hide it, until Obekri shouldered open a trap door.

Blinding sun, thrashing wings: ravens startled into flight. The two men climbed out onto the roof of the tower, mossy and slick from the rains. A stout wind was blowing. Agathar walked to the battlements, steadying himself. He glanced over his shoulder at the opposite turrets, then turned his attention to the village.

"You can see the fishermen's wharf," he said without turning. "Come here, take a look."

"I don't care about the wharf," said Obekri.

"Neither do I," said Agathar, "but Sulmurg keeps a lip-reader among his retainers. You'll want your back to the other tower before you speak."

Chuckling, Obekri stepped up beside Agathar. "Nothing's changed, has it? You enter a room and check the exits, the number of strides you need to reach them. You climb a tower and assess the threats."

"Everything has changed, in fact," said Agathar.

Obekri paused, lowering his eyes. "I sent condolences," he said at last. "Brief, I know; but what can one say? Your son, your granddaughter. A loss like that—"

"I want to speak to you as a friend, Kalen, but not before you disperse this cloud of devil's flatulence and *tell me what is happening*."

Obekri's eyes widened. "You really don't know?"

"Tell me!"

"Kasralys, old friend. Kasralys is happening."

"What are they up to?"

"Who, the Kasrajis?" Obekri shrugged. "They seized two of our ships at the mouth of the Ghel. They entered a Shôl temple, in violation of treaty. Their royals are sclerotic, of course, but they have a shrewd young Chancellor, one Lady Kosuda. They say 'Lady' came with the office; she's really a commoner, like me. Unlike me, she can be bloody-minded. She fed a number of our agents to her wolves."

"Typical frictions. None of that is a threat."

"Of course not," said Obekri. "Indeed, Kasralys *is* no threat, nor has been in decades."

"Then what more have you to say?"

Obekri cleared his throat. "Our King means to lay siege to Kasralys," he said. "Don't laugh, Therel. It isn't funny."

But the general could not help himself. He dropped his chin, pinched the bridge of his nose. The laugh was silent, but his body shook. Idiocy. Farce. He would be home this time tomorrow.

"The King," said Obekri, "is in deadly earnest."

"So he enlists a naturalist, of course," said Agathar, wiping his eyes. "What is your task in this deadly earnest venture? Will you threaten them with soil erosion?"

"You're not really amused, are you?"

"I am, but I won't be much longer. You dragged me here for nothing."

Obekri leaned into the parapet, flexing his leathery hands. It was a strain, this speaking without eye contact, this arguing with the sea.

"You also worried me, and my daughter-in-law," said Agathar. He gestured at the fortress. "I've never heard of a conference in Statuary House except in times of national crisis, or to discuss the darkest secrets of the Crown."

"This *is* a crisis," said Obekri. "I tell you, the King intends to take the Fortress City *within a year*. He is not the man you remember, Therel. And the man he has become—that man you may not like."

"Does it matter?" said Agathar. "I didn't like the original."

"It matters," said Obekri. "For one thing, he cares not a fig for the support of nobles like yourself. He ignores them, scorns them, scorns the very families who once fought in his corner."

"My own family?"

Obekri hesitated. "It has not come to that," he said.

As a child, the young Prince Grapahir had been consumptive, and many feared that the rigors of the disease had left him feeble-minded. When his mother the Queen lay dying, the realm had split between supporters of Grapahir's claim and that of an elder cousin from the provinces—a glamorous braggart, a chaser of adolescent girls. The crisis had culminated in a rowdy meeting of the Grand Assembly in the castle ballroom. There, Agathar's own mother had decided the matter for the whole of the kingdom. Her words were legend in Nebusul:

"My daughter is but six, my lord," she said to the skirt-chaser, "yet she will one day dance within this hall. And never but never shall *yours* be the hand on her waist."

"He owes us his very crown," said the general, "and the whole capital knows it. He may ignore a great many things, but not that."

"Don't be so certain," said Obekri. "He wants war, Therel; he's a man possessed. And he means this siege to be different."

"Of course," said Agathar. "Eleven's the charm."

Obekri closed his eyes. "Debating with an Agathar. Of all the *rankest* fates in this world."

"Most rank, not rankest."

"Stop proving my point."

○შ

Enemies had, in fact, marched on Kasralys on ten previous occasions, if the histories could be believed. Agathar was rather certain that they could; he had written the newest of them. Some of the siege efforts had been doomed affairs; others had been brilliant, or simply unrelenting. But Kasralys had stood like a rock, like the great mountain it was part of, unconquered and insolent in its perfection for three thousand years. The whole continent knew this, and had long ago made peace with the fact. Except for Shôlupur.

"Kalen, Kalen, someone's made you their fool." Agathar shook his head, watching the sun dance on the waves. "Grapahir is throwing fits again, but they will pass as they always do. Lay siege to Kasralys! The idea would not last three minutes in his War Cabinet, if he even takes it that far. To say nothing of the Treasury, or the outrage in the provinces."

"It has gone to the War Cabinet," said Obekri.

Agathar grew still.

"Three minutes were all they needed to roar their approval. And the provincial governors are converging on Nebusul as we speak."

"To debate—what? A general mobilization against the Kasraj? Open war, with the Kasraj?"

"*Elimination* of the Kasraj, Therel. Total defeat, and the walls thrown down. Our flag raised over the Palace of the Imperium, and our ascent to unquestioned supremacy in Urrath."

"Rubbish, sewage, dung," said Agathar. "Talk to Kimburac; he'll snuff out this nonsense like a candle."

"He would try, certainly."

"*Try?* He would take no prisoners. General Kimburac is the conscience of the army, Kalen, and he fears no man alive. You should have started with him. The King knows better than to pick a fight with his own tactical commander."

"General Kimburac has been missing for a fortnight," said Obekri.

For the second time that day, Agathar felt a change in the world around him. This time the air itself seemed to grow heavier, closer, pressing in from all sides.

"Missing?"

"There are rumors of a grave illness," said Obekri. "He was treated in the royal hospital, but moved elsewhere in the dead of night. His own wife does not know his whereabouts."

"Someone must," said Agathar.

"True," said Obekri, "but that little avails us at the moment. Lord Sulmurg claims the King appealed to the Xavasindrans to treat Kimburac's ailment, whatever it is. The foreign doctors will neither confirm nor deny his presence in their clinic. But then, they never do."

"Where's our friend the baron, then? He will *never* consent to this farce."

Obekri grimaced. "Baron Morsu has been dispatched to the March of Thieves."

"To *where?*"

"I promise you, it's the truth. Word reached the court of two brothers afflicted by demons. Possessed, if you will. They slew a son of the Chiloto

Prophet, then moved on to Mab Makkutin and left that city on fire—the city, and half the Lutaral. Real terrors, and it's believed they have help. Perhaps of a supernatural kind."

"What does this have to do with the baron?"

"The Prophet wants them dead at any cost, and her legions are pouring east out of the Cinderwood. They've not approached our frontier—they know better—but our King has charged Morsu with securing the March of Thieves all the same. He does not want the so-called Enlightened One's army to stray into our territories. And he does not want these demon-touched brothers to slip north either—imagine the panic that might ensue. If they appear, his orders are to slay them with all their company, down to the very pack animals, and to pile goods and corpses alike into a bonfire."

"Possession. You believe a word of that?"

"I believe that Morsu was sent away before the War cabinet met. And that Kimburac's illness could not have been more convenient. That I believe."

"War with the Kasraj," said Agathar. He turned and locked eyes with Obekri, lip readers be damned. "Kalen, this is preposterous. Have you seen the Nine-Mile Rift, that great shelf Kasralys is built upon? Have you seen the walls above it, the walls below?"

"No, but you have."

"They stand five layers deep. The outer wall has three tiers and a moat. The inner wall is ninety feet of flawless granite, above a cliff twice that height. The gates are works of genius against which no ram can feasibly be deployed. And behind Kasralys, do you know what you find? The sheer south face of Mount Kasq, a vertical mile of rock. Above that a glacier, sawtooth peaks, perpetual snows. And the city is rich, Kalen. Rich and enormous. They have whole farms and stockyards and inexhaustible springs within those walls. They have years' worth of grain squirreled away in caves. They have the friendship of the mountain clans, and of nations in the east. I could go on."

"Don't," said Obekri. "I read your address on the subject this morning. 'An army could lash like the sea against Kasralys for a decade and not break her.' That was twenty years ago, however."

"Nothing has changed."

Obekri forced his lips into a smile. "You were right the first time. Everything has changed. They lost half their fleet in a typhoon. They can no longer be certain of the support of either Alapnysh or Mostuc at the mouth of the Thask. We, meanwhile, have gone from strength to strength. Our country is larger, richer, and better loved across Urrath."

"Not for long, if this talk continues."

"Our standing army is thrice the size of the Seventh Realm's. They are the husk of an empire; we are just coming into our own. They live in the failing twilight. We live in the dawn."

"Who the hell are you quoting *now?*"

"They are old greatness. We are the ascendant power. We have the better engineers, the better mills, the better armories."

"Speculation, much of that."

"Damn your quibbling!" cried Obekri, slapping the parapet with both hands. "Say it, as you did twenty years ago. 'No power in this world can take Kasralys.' Speak, Therel! I'm dying to hear it from your lips."

"No power in this world . . ."

Agathar's voice trailed off. They had never lied to each other; it was the bedrock of their friendship. He did not want to start now.

"A new siege of Kasralys?" he whispered. "Kalen, it must not be. You understand that, don't you? The lunacy of it. The utter ruin for us all."

"I understand that perfectly," said Obekri. "I have not become a monster, Therel."

"The way you spoke just now. What was I to think?"

"That I've been enduring such talk for months, while you fed lizards and pruned your trees." Obekri's hands were shaking. "You ask why I dragged you here. Can't you guess, River Dragon? You're here because I begged His Majesty on my knees to go no further before speaking with you, despite your oath to end your days on Cauldron Farm. Because you're Therel Agathar the genius. Because nearly everyone I meet with *has* become a monster, very suddenly, and it scares me to my core. Because they can ignore a simple woodsman but not their Magnus General. Because if there's anyone left in the Kingdom who can stop this madness, this avalanche, it's you."

7. TEARS OF THE GODS

The desert," said Eshett, "is more than you people imagine. More than the *lathbans*, the sand seas, one dune after another to the edge of the world."

"That's not true," said Mektu, scratching at his side like a dog with fleas.

"You're telling *her* about the desert?" said Talupéké. "Be quiet and listen to her, fool."

"No, I'll keep talking," said Mektu. "She's been kidding me all day. Making things up just to see if I'll believe her. This is why I don't like Parthan girls."

"Make him stop, someone," murmured Eshett.

Sunset was near, but the heat had not broken. The caravan was tucked into the shadow of rocks that jutted from the earth like titanic vertebrae. Some miles off, a herd of antelope with corkscrew horns drifted over the plain.

Kandri and his companions lay in the dirt like landed fish, blinking at the empty sky. All save Mektu, who scratched his side almost as vigorously as he peppered Eshett with questions.

"Are you telling me it's not sand? The desert isn't *sand*?"

"Of course it's sand, you babe," said Chindilan. "There's sand underfoot, sand that buries villages, sand storm-whipped two miles into the sky. Sand in your food. Your bedding. Your hair, teeth, private parts—"

"Sand in ass," offered a camel driver mournfully.

"It's sand and much more," said Eshett. "It's gravel, slickrock, scale earth, ironpan. It's *koeli*, dust rivers. It's mountains, canyons, sinks. And water— yes, there's water, if you know where to look. Shared water, *meio*. And water secrets, *meikurús*. There are paths to wells marked in code on Parthan maps, or carved into cliffs. There are streams that run free under the sky for just one or two days a year, and sink underground the rest of the time. There are rivers a hundred miles long and six inches deep."

Talupéké laughed. "Do you really know all this, Eshett? Or do you just want us to feel like idiots when we die of thirst?"

"She's a Parthan," said Captain Utarif. "They know all the desert's secrets."

"Everyone be quiet, you're distracting her!" said Mektu. "Go on, Eshett. What's a water secret?"

"The kind of secret that could keep you alive."

"For example?"

Eshett bit her lip. She wanted to smack him, Kandri thought.

"A cistern," she said at last, "under a mountain deep in the Sumuridath. It's eight hundred feet deep and full of water, ancient water from the bones of the earth. No one knows who built it or why; it is older than the memory of my people. My grandparents took my father there for a blessing on his seventh birthday, but they traveled by night, and never showed him how to find it again. They were sworn to guard the secret, even from their children. Now my grandparents are dead, and the secret died with them."

"Eight hundred feet deep—" Talupéké's smile was incredulous. "—and they died without telling *anybody*?"

"It was a water secret," said Eshett simply. "Other families may still know about it, somewhere. The desert has so many kinds of strangeness—so many peoples, animals, plants."

"Not plants you can eat, I'll bet," said Mektu.

"Some you can eat, and some that eat you," said Eshett. "The *islik*, now: we passed a few this morning. Waxy leaves with a bright purple edge."

"I saw them," said Mektu. "Very pretty. I almost picked some for you."

"If you touch those leaves your flesh blisters, then melts and drips from your bones like wax."

"Fuck a shaggy sheep!"

"The plant feeds on flesh," said Eshett, "and there are worse creatures, many. The closer you get to the center, to the Heart Basin, the more dangerous everything becomes. The Heart Basin is not for people. Everyone understood this, once."

"I understand you just fine," said Captain Utarif, "but this spot is comfortable, and for the next half-hour I'm going to pretend I didn't hear a thing."

"Happy ignorance," said Chindilan. "The wisdom that drips from an old man's mouth."

"Not as old as you, you fat-assed ironmonger."

The two men closed their eyes. They had lived through the same wars, albeit in different armies, and had become fast friends.

"What did Jód want with you earlier, by the way?" Chindilan mumbled.

"Asked if I was good with a bow."

"And are you?"

Utarif said nothing: he had fallen asleep between one question and the next. Soon Chindilan too was gently snoring. The brothers and Eshett watched the antelope by the fading light.

"Scratch, scratch, scratch!" said Eshett irritably. "What's bothering you? Why can't you be still?"

"It itches sometimes. My old wound. It's not normal."

Kandri sighed. "Leave it alone, Mek. It's the most beautifully healed wound I've ever seen."

"I wish you'd never dragged me to that clinic. I don't trust Outworlders. They were strange. They were cold."

"And you're shameless," said Eshett. "Kandri saved your life by taking you there."

Kandri wiped his face with his headscarf. He wanted desperately to be alone with Eshett; two of their five days were already gone. If only the others would sleep, he could signal her, meet her behind those rocks . . . but Mektu talked and talked, and the little surgeon crouched ten yards away, lancing a boil on a driver's foot. A little farther, Woeden Surk and his mercenaries sat in a circle, picking at their teeth with twigs. Kandri caught Surk and another mercenary studying Eshett like a prospective purchase. He met their eyes, stared them down. At last, smirking, they turned away.

"You wish for lore of this land?" said Eshett suddenly.

The brothers sat up straight.

"Hear me, then. I will speak of the fall of Omipraj."

Kandri felt a tightness in his neck. The world had gone strange and threatening. "Eshett," he said, "are you playing a joke?"

Her cadence had completely changed. Instead of her usual lilt and rasp, she spoke with a stern and somehow old-fashioned intonation. The change was so drastic that it was almost as if she had become a different person.

"A time there was when the sun was kinder, and the rains came winter and spring. The land yielded grain, and the grain fed cities. Three cities, holy and hidden. Balatuam. Sanulsreya. Omipraj."

Kandri's dread was growing by the second. *That is not Eshett. That is not how she talks.*

"Each city had its palaces, its covered markets, its sacred trees. Olives and cedars about the temples, cinnamon and panyak in the courtyards. Dream trees, holiest of all; the sartaphs would hang a man who injured them. Curtain trees, spread in walls of living lace."

The yatra, thought Kandri. *Has it been in her all along?*

"There were night gardens," said Eshett. "Some just for stargazing, some for watching moths drink nectar under the moon, some for hearing the music of the dead."

"Eshett, stop," whispered Mektu.

"The Sartaph of Omipraj," she said, "ruled from a great tower clad in bronze, a relic of an earlier city around which his own had been built. His soul was gentle, and he played a flute of glass, and those who heard it forgave any who had wronged them, and their hearts were filled with love even for the mountain people upon whom they made war. But one night the Sartaph overheard his son and daughter conspiring together, saying how they would poison him and rule Omipraj themselves. They were not of age, these children of his heart, and it was said later that they were not in earnest, only playing a reckless game as children do. But the Sartaph believed, and so despaired, for they were as the sun and the moon to him, and he stripped them naked and had them driven out into a wasteland to die."

Kandri turned in desperation to his uncle. Wake him? Call the surgeon? Shake Eshett by the arms?

"That night the Sartaph stood in the tower window, hoping against hope to see his children return. But it was the Night Queen of Ramisith who came to him, dark and radiant in the moonlight. 'Play for me, Sartaph,' she commanded, 'for my death too was at the hands of those who should have loved me. Play, play a song from your heart.' And the Sartaph could not refuse, for such is the power of the Night Queen over those who spill innocent blood. He played a tune favored by his children. But as he gazed at the Queen the tune was altered, and became a spell of madness, and every soul who it heard it felt the Sartaph's own agony and remorse. Nightly he played, and on to sunrise, spurning sleep and food and company. Delegations approached the bronze tower to plead for silence, and later mobs to demand it. But the tower withstood them, and the Sartaph played on."

Mektu's eyes were wide; his lips moved in wordless fear. Kandri knew the signs: *yatra panic. Terror of possession.* No one felt it more deeply than his brother.

"The people fell upon one another," said Eshett, "or marched on neighboring lands in mobs, never to return, or simply fled screaming from the spell of music, and so Omipraj was lost."

Do something, thought Kandri. *Break her out of it, call her back—*

Only one idea came to him. He leaned forward and kissed her on the cheek.

Eshett started and looked at him. Mektu looked at him too, shocked for a second time.

"You're quite the poet," said Kandri. He tried to sound casual. He actually sounded as if a dog had closed its jaws on his testicles.

Eshett touched her cheek. "Why the hell did you do that?"

It was her natural, chiding Eshett-voice. Kandri sighed as though released from a nightmare. Eshett looked at each brother in turn.

"Is there a reason," she demanded, "that you're staring at me like twin toads?"

Mektu laughed, overloud, waking Chindilan with a start.

"*Jeshar!* What's the matter with you?"

"Nothing! Ha!" Mektu snatched at Eshett's hand. "She was just—entertaining us."

"Entertaining? Ang's blood, let me sleep."

"Ha *ha*!" Mektu was so nervous he was almost in tears. Kandri rubbed his temples. Nothing about Eshett was out of the ordinary. Had it ever been? Was he losing his mind?

"Hell of a ruckus," grumbled Utarif, opening one eye.

"It's him," said Eshett, pointing at Mektu. "He pesters me night and day about the desert. So I told him. I couldn't stand it anymore."

"At least *you* were quiet about it," said Chindilan.

"I'm quiet!" shouted Mektu. "She's entertaining! Everything's fine! But I do have a question, girl—"

Eshett shot him a withering look.

"Those hidden cities," said Mektu. "Those gardens and things. All the splendor. Is it gone?"

"Mostly."

"But not all gone? Mostly isn't *all*, after all. Isn't that true, brother, I—"

Eshett pressed her hand to his mouth.

"Don't waste water," she said. "Keep your hands off things you're ignorant about. Then you might live to see something beautiful. Out here there's nine hundred kinds of death for every fool who thinks he can make the crossing. You people call these the Ravenous Lands. That's the one thing about them you get right."

୧୫

Of course he began to chatter as soon as Eshett dropped her hand. But at that moment Ulren appeared.

"Silence, idiots!" he hissed. "Captain, why are you sleeping? The time has come!"

Utarif sprang to his feet like a younger man. "Where, man? Speak!"

Ulren gestured at a great rock some fifty yards to the west. It stood apart from the general outcropping, a flat-topped sentinel the size of a mansion.

"He is there, but you are nearly too late! Run, run!"

Utarif snatched up his bow and sprinted for the rock. "What's happening? Who's there?" demanded Mektu. "Do you mean Jód?"

"That's Master Ifimar to you!" snapped Ulren in a whisper. "Now be silent, like everyone else! If we fail he will learn who is to blame!"

The light was nearly gone, now. But there was enough for Kandri to see that it was true: every last driver and soldier was holding perfectly still, as though all received the same warning, the same threat.

Utarif slung his bow over his shoulder and began to scale the rock. When he reached the flat summit they saw the head and shoulders of a second man—yes, that was Jód—rise just long enough to gesture urgently. Utarif crawled to him on hands and knees, and both men's bodies merged invisibly with the rock.

All was still. Mektu looked beseechingly at Kandri. Ulren kept one hand raised, demanding absolute stillness. Minutes passed. Bats jigged overhead. The sky darkened further behind the rock.

Mektu exhaled, an explosive belly-noise. "Too much! I can't bear it, the tension—"

Kandri pounced on him, crushing Mektu's face against his chest. His brother kicked and shoved—and then the bird appeared.

It streaked out of the west, a great black shadow of a bird, astonishingly swift. *Jihalkra's eagle! The pet of the Prophet's son!* Kandri was immediately sure of it. And of much worse.

They know where we are. They've been tracking us all along.

The eagle flew arrow-straight. Its path would bring it directly over the rock where the two men waited. But at the last minute it veered left, cutting wildly away from the rock.

"It's seen them," whispered Chindilan.

Ulren hissed: "The man did not even shoot! Useless bastard! We shall die now, the Prophet—"

A second bird shot up from the rock. Much smaller, it struck the eagle square in the chest. The raptor stalled and fanned its wings; the creatures merged into one rolling, careening shape. Neither cried out. The eagle twisted and tore at the smaller bird, which from below was all but impossible to see.

Pop. A sound like a far-off fiddler plucking a string. The eagle jerked, tearing sighs from the watchers below. Its wings went limp. It dropped, lifeless, near Ulren's feet.

Talupéké, twenty feet away, put her head back and whooped. "*Nobody shoots like the captain!*"

The arrow had pierced the eagle's abdomen and emerged near its spine. The smaller bird, untouched by the shaft, stood up from the corpse and looked at the circle of humans. It was a tiny owl, sand-colored, half the size of a crow.

"Safiru!" said Ulren, delighted. "Fine work, madam! You're the best of your kind!"

The little owl spread its wings, gingerly at first, as though to see what might be broken. Satisfied, it leaped from the ground and was gone.

"So that's a pocket owl," said Kandri.

"Worth her weight in diamonds ten times over," said Ulren. "Safiru has been with Master Ifimar for years, and comes from a line bred by his family. The Master showed Utarif great favor, trusting him not to skewer her by mistake."

Chindilan squatted by the carcass of the eagle. With the tip of his knife he raised one of its legs. A brass ring circled the leg just above the talons.

"This is Jihalkra's steppe eagle, all right," he said. "I forged that ring myself, and marked it with the Prophet's seal." He shook his head. "What a beautiful creature. Such a waste."

Jód and Utarif stepped out of the darkness. "We must bury the eagle swiftly," said the Caravan Master.

"Allow me," offered the surgeon, lifting the bird by its neck. "I'll just have a look at its stomach contents first. Professional curiosity."

"You will do nothing of the kind!" snapped Jód. "Desert hunters cut their eagles twice a year, and train their dogs to know the blood. The Rasanga, moreover, hunt with Shefetsi maulers, the finest tracking dogs in all the world. They are not as wise or steady as our two Ramisith running-hounds, but they can sniff out one drop of blood in thirty miles of wind. Even Safiru here, my little champion, I must now wash with precious water. Do you see now why I forbid you to smoke, Kandri Hinjuman?"

"But the drivers—"

"Smoke one leaf, and one leaf only: that of the fire-weed of Dresheng, which torments and confuses the noses of the maulers. You are welcome to join them, if any will share their supply. But be warned: even the desert-born require years of initiation. Until you acquire the taste, fire-weed is hideous, like smoking the hairs plucked from an old man's ears, held together with his wax."

It was a testament to the Master's authority that no one so much as smiled. Jód looked again at the surgeon. "Handle the eagle as little as possible, and bury it deep. Leave no trace whatsoever upon your person."

The surgeon grunted. "Didn't know what I was volunteering for. Story of my Ang-forsaken life."

He puttered off with his burden, and Jód departed as well. The others began to scatter, preparing for sleep. Kandri found himself alone with his uncle.

"Ear wax," said Kandri.

"Might come to that," said his uncle, and now they did laugh, hard and silent, holding each other up.

But Chindilan was somber again before long. "Wish I could have kept that ring."

"A trophy, Uncle?"

"Hell no," said the smith. "A reminder, I suppose."

"Of what?"

Chindilan turned to face him, scratching his beard. "Jihalkra used to feed his bird these little treats. Thin strips, like parchment. Rolled in date sugar and dried. They were human flesh, Kandri—Važek flesh, from the battle-fields. He forced some poor bastard in the village to make those hideous things. Just *because* they were hideous, you understand? Because they would appall anyone who knew about them. It worked, of course. I felt sick every time he brought that bird to the weapons shop. But later he decided we were used to it."

"Used to it?"

"We weren't reacting with the same shock when he fed the bird. It galled him. So he starting bringing this jar around." Chindilan's jaw was clenched. "Put it up on my workbench beside his eagle. Took off the lid, so the bird could snatch what it wanted. I thought they were olives at first."

"Don't tell me."

"Eyeballs. Važek eyeballs, packed in brine."

Kandri looked away into the darkness.

"My point," said Chindilan, "is that it was never the eagle's fault. Ang made that bird to be clean and fine and free, didn't she now? Not a killer's instrument. Not a slave. And perhaps Ang All-Merciful had the same in mind for the Prophet's children—and all of us Chilotos. Health, love, freedom, flight. But it hasn't worked out that way. You and I and your brother, and Ariqina if she's out there, and your father, wherever he is. We're the lucky ones. We're pissing out the poison, day by day. But there's half a million poisoned in our clan."

"She's not a God, Uncle," said Kandri. "She won't live forever, you'll see."

"She may not have to. The damage is done. Weren't we all fed a diet of horrors, Kandri? Taught to swallow vile things? And if Chilotos march as a people over Urrath, what then? Won't there be somebody waiting with hands on a bow?"

ឃ

Another day crawled by. They rose before dawn, walked past midday, made camp under the sun-shields in the afternoon's murderous heat, walked late into the night. Jód was weaving a roundabout path toward the eastern hills, moving from one place of concealment to the next. The glass drift still shimmered to the north. The riders, whoever they were, made no appearance.

The next morning, breath steaming as they walked, Kandri asked the man with the clouded eye about the glass drift. What was it, exactly? The man offered one of his gentle smiles.

"Death by blood, Mister Kandri. If it comes, you must run."

Kandri walked beside him in silence, hoping he would elaborate. At last the man said, "Many dangerous things in the Sumuridath Jal. And additionally, we are late. Winter is ending."

"Isn't that—" Kandri pointed up at the sun. "—the worst danger of all?"

"*Avru*, the sun?" The cloudy-eyed man laughed. "No, no, not true. Sun climbs and falls and never surprises. Like the mother bear. It will kill you, but not if you avoid." He nodded at Ifimar Jód. "A good Master makes sure you avoid."

"What *is* the worst thing, then?"

"Rain," said a second driver.

There were hisses of agreement. Kandri smiled, thinking they were teasing him. But the drivers' faces were deadly earnest, morbid with recollection. "Yes, true," said his friend. "In the desert, the worst is rain."

ఴ

A rumor wormed its way through the caravan: Jód had spotted someone behind them with his telescope. The Caravan Master admitted nothing, of course, but struck a pace even faster than he had on the day Kandri mentioned the Rasanga, and shortened their water breaks from ten minutes to three.

As the story grew, it reached Kandri's ears that Prince Nirabha had also stolen a look through the Master's telescope. At the next water break, Kandri approached the Prince and asked if the rumor was true.

Nirabha's face was troubled. "I saw something," he admitted. "But for an instant only. A flash of movement, then nothing at all."

But in that flash?

The Prince nodded in Jód's direction. "The Master was irritated that I had used his scope, when he had merely asked me to hold it a moment. He had been examining the tall rocks behind us, where we sheltered the day

118

before yesterday. Naturally I trained the scope there myself. But I saw nothing to account for this . . . panicked retreat. What I saw was a solitary figure, a child, standing still upon the rocks."

Kandri froze. "A child?"

"Is it not strange?"

"Boy or girl, Your Highness?"

"A girl," said Nirabha. "Waiflike, and in rags."

Kandri felt the world closing in.

"Of course I told Jód that we must go to her aid, lost Parthan daughter or whoever she might be," said the Prince. "I regret to say that the remark infuriated the Master. 'There is no one to aid,' he said. 'And you, who have made free with my telescope, must not imagine that you can make free with my leadership as well.' Since then we have not spoken."

"What did she look like, this girl?"

"You must recall that I barely glimpsed her," said the Prince.

"So you remember nothing?"

Nirabha shrugged. "I thought she was exceedingly pale. An albino, were I to venture a guess. My dear Mr. Hinjuman, are you ill?"

He was, in fact. He turned and doubled over and vomited before his shoes. It was only a small, foamy puddle of spit, but the worst part was knowing that he was not truly ill at all. Only afraid. He had vomited to silence a still more embarrassing impulse—to run, blind and heedless, away from the horror behind them.

"Finished?" said Nirabha.

"Yes," groaned Kandri. "I'm sorry, Your Highness."

"We royals vomit too."

Kandri forced a laugh, and the Prince moved away. He should warn Mektu, Kandri thought. But no—that would be a dreadful mistake. His brother had enough to be frightened of.

He watched a shiny black scorpion climb a stone. The Prophet's servants were still hunting them, of course. But *that* servant. How could she possibly be here? She moved too slowly; did not ride or run but merely walked, slow and dreamlike, on a girl's stick-thin legs.

The scorpion waved its foreclaws at him cheerfully.

She can't be following us. The Prince saw a girl, a normal girl. Not—

He vomited again. It was this fear that would kill him. Not heat, not scorpions, not the enemy's blades.

Not the touch of the White Child.

℅

Jód drove them on. Once more Kandri and Eshett found no way to be alone—not for ten minutes, not for two. It was maddening. Nothing but space around them, infinite and empty; and yet someone was always there, always watching. The wordless Spalak. The leering Surk. Above all, Mektu, Eshett's all-day shadow, jealous of her every glance.

Mektu, who had known her in the army brothel.

Mektu, who had purchased her services (that is what men called it, *services*) before Kandri knew she existed. Mektu, who liked to torture Kandri by speaking of what they'd done.

Mektu, who also tried to claim Ariqina. Who told the world they'd been engaged. Who spoke of her body with vulgar familiarity.

Of course (Kandri reflected for the thousandth time) Mektu had *not* slept with her. Ariqina herself had told Kandri that she'd wanted no one else since their first night together. Nor had he: the very thought had made him laugh. Yet Ari had nonetheless insisted that they each promise to tell the other if the feeling changed.

"People talk about lying for love," she whispered, naked in his arms. "That's all wrong, Kandri. It doesn't happen. We only ever lie from fear."

He had never once seen Ariqina fearful. Which meant his brother's talk of sleeping with her was mere spitefulness, born of a strange need to bruise his brother's heart. Only this, Kandri told himself. But what if Mek learned about him and Eshett? What would he tell Ari about them, if they found her waiting in that glorious city? How would he twist the simple facts of the affair?

A wiser part of Kandri knew better than to gnaw that particular bone. Ari would perceive the truth about his time with Eshett no matter what anyone told her. In some ways—terrible thought, but undeniable—Ari was like the Prophet. She was not a normal person. She had an instinct for honesty that caused deceptions to spontaneously combust. He would not need to explain a thing. Ari would simply know, as she would know that Kandri still loved her precisely as he had for every minute of the ten years he had known her and the four since they first made love and the three since she refused to marry him and disappeared. It had never once been otherwise. In her presence he was as naked as the day he was born.

No, his fear was far simpler. On some nights it took the form of a vision: Ariqina standing before him—honest, beautiful, blameless—and explaining that it was over, long over, that the dream he had chased across the width of Urrath must be abandoned, because another had her heart.

It was agony, that vision. But there was a third possibility, one he could not bear to contemplate. That she had never made it to Kasralys. That some day, somewhere, the word would reach him that she had chased her own dream but never attained it, that she had been taken by fever, stumbled from a clifftop, stumbled into the path of war.

To think of losing her love was like contemplating his own annihilation. But that would be better, infinitely better, than to learn that she had left this world before him.

છ

"*Ikkada!* Fire!"

One hundred twenty voices, shouting at once. Fingers pointing at a spot in the distance, many miles to the north.

Kandri, turning an instant too late, saw no fire at all. Only a great plume of dust, and a rolling cloud of grit and sand near the ground.

"God of my Keeping, something fell from the sky!" cried Prince Nirabha.

"It happened in the Lutaral as well," said Chindilan. "People were calling them the Tears of the Gods. *Jeshar*, I thought that was once in a lifetime."

Whatever had just occurred had shaken humans and animals alike. Goats cried like newborns; camels snorted and shook their heads. The hairless dogs tucked their tails.

"They heard it, didn't they?" said Mektu, gesturing at the animals. "Or maybe felt it through the earth. You know what this is about, don't you? The *Darsunuk,* the Time of Madness. Everyone says it's coming."

"Not everyone," said Ulren, "just village bumpkins, simpletons who fall for that sort of—Gods! Again!"

This time Kandri saw them: three fireballs, much closer than the first and dazzling even by daylight, with black specks boiling at their hearts. They crashed to earth in a straight line across the barrens, flinging earth into the sky. The last point of impact was somewhere between the caravan and the eastern hills.

But something even stranger was happening. When the nearest fireball struck, Kandri felt a tug at his belt—sharp, then gone. Just enough to throw off his balance. And up and down the caravan it was the same: men and women stumbled. The camels broke ranks, bashing and shouldering each other.

Two seconds at the most, and the strange tug was gone. No injuries, no damage. The drivers wrestled their beasts back into line, but their composure was shattered.

"Darsunuk," they said, turning to one another. *"Darsunuk elub etri!"*

"Ang save us," murmured Chindilan, "they believe in it too."

"So do I," said Talupéké, who for some reason had drawn her knives.

"Hush, Tal, no theatrics," said Chindilan. "And put those damned things away. You planning to stab a fireball?"

They bickered like father and daughter. Kandri watched the dust clouds rise over the flats. *Darsunuk,* Time of Madness, the great wave of disorder that could drown the world. Before this month he had never heard of the Darsunuk—although some of the Prophet's visions were equally ghastly. But as the brothers had fled east the word had sprung up everywhere. Some claimed the Darsunuk was but a few years off, others that it had already begun. And for a week now the fires had been falling. Usually they were no more than shooting stars, like those that had made Eshett laugh in his embrace. But on the night they crossed the Lutaral, the tears had made it to earth. Lighting brush fires, exploding like suns. And today, in broad daylight—

"Ikkada!"

The blast came from behind him, tearing screams from men and beasts. Kandri whirled. Searing light. A mass of flames tall as a palace, not a hundred yards from the caravan. Earth leaping skyward in a volcanic chaos. The drivers howling, the camels stumbling, falling—and the same weird tug at Kandri's belt, but infinitely stronger than before.

It was his new machete. The iron blade was pulling, straining for the fire. And beside him, Chindilan's axe was skittering across the earth. The smith lurched after it, looking like a man chasing a crab.

Up and down the caravan, metal objects—swords, helmets, hammers, cook pots—were rushing and rolling toward the fireball, even as debris from the impact began to pelt them like rain.

Iron to a lodestone. Kandri had seen it before, in his father's workshop. *But iron to a ball of flame?*

The tugging ceased. The rain of sand and gravel dwindled, then stopped. But the cries went on. On Kandri's left a mercenary appeared to be fighting a camel. Then he saw that a knife had pinned the warrior's hand to the shoulder of the frenzied beast.

Talupéké stood gaping, her left hand empty. "I didn't throw it," she said. "It jumped, it flew from my hand!"

The camel bucked and screamed. The mercenary at last caught the knife's grip in his free hand and wrenched it loose. As a comrade bound his wound, he looked over his shoulder at Talupéké, pure hatred on his face.

03

The tower of flames collapsed into a spitting fire, rising from a crater the size of a courtyard. Warily, the travelers recovered their tools. Chindilan picked up his axe with a frown. An object like a shard of black ice clung to the axe-head.

"Iron," he said, dumbfounded. He touched it, jerked his hand away. "Pit-fire, it's still hot!"

The shard trembled a moment on the axe head, then dropped to the ground. Kandri and his uncle looked at each other, and then at the rest of the caravan. Other such shards were dropping like leaves: from clasps, buckles, padlocks, spear-points, swords.

"Those fucking things might have killed us!" said Mektu.

"They were part of it, part of the fireball," said Kandri. "It shattered when it struck the ground. Did you see the others? They had black hearts, like the coals in your forge, Uncle."

"I saw them," said Chindilan, "But *Jeshar*, burning lodestone from heaven! What sort of world have we stepped into?"

"A world indifferent to your deaths," muttered the surgeon, rushing by with an armful of bandages.

"Very helpful," growled the smith, glowering at his back. "*Harach*, Mektu, you're right, we're lucky men. Ang spared us this time."

But Ang had not spared all her creatures. A second camel was stumbling in agony: the beast had broken its foreleg.

"My archers can dispatch that beast for you," said Utarif to the Master.

Jód did not deign to answer him. Instead he glanced at Spalak, who nodded gravely. He came forward, and Jód held out his own black sword.

Spalak drew the sword, leaving the scabbard in Jód's hands. He circled the flailing camel, studying it like a sculptor might a stone. The camel bellowed, then lashed out suddenly with its hind feet, missing Spalak by inches. There were cries from the drivers. Spalak merely turned sideways to the beast. Then in one fluid motion he whirled in and beheaded the camel on the upswing and leaped clear of the blood.

The camel fell, and Spalak cleaned the sword on its flank. Kandri realized that he had never seen anyone—save the Prophet's own Rasanga—strike as quickly as Spalak.

Eshett was right. He's a stone cold killer, that man.

"Mr. Ulren," said Jód, "empty those saddlebags and see them buried. We must leave no sign of our passing."

"There's . . . one more fallen, Master," said Ulren.

"Another camel?"

"No, Master." Ulren made a reluctant gesture. Thirty feet away, a driver lay motionless on his side. The earth by his shoulder was dark with blood.

Jód cried out, a sound of such pure anguish that Kandri felt a pang in his chest. The Master rushed to the man and knelt. Touching his forehead, he whispered a prayer, then closed the man's eyes and rose to glare at the onlookers.

"This man was our beloved friend. He has four children in Sendu. How did this happen? Speak!"

There were witnesses. One had seen a dark flash; several had heard the *clang* as the splinter of sky-iron struck a heavy samovar, a trade item, right through the saddlebag in which it which was packed.

"That one, Master Ifimar," said Ulren. He pointed eagerly at Fish. Mektu's camel gaped at Jód in its characteristic way. On its saddlebag was a small, fresh stain.

Jód walked up to Fish and touched the stain, revealing a small tear in the saddlebag. Probing with two fingers, he drew out the jagged metal splinter, still moist with the driver's blood. He turned to gaze at the brothers, pain in every line of his face. And also wonder, a strange fascination. He pointed at the flaming crater where the fireball had struck. Then, pensive, he drew a line in the air. His finger passed over Kandri and Mektu and ended on Fish. Without lowering his hand he regarded the brothers again.

"Abominations," he said.

Mektu hid his face in his elbow. Jód stalked away, leaving Kandri scalded by the word, the nearest drivers muttering and aghast. *You vicious bastard*, thought Kandri, watching the Master depart.

Eshett approached him, eyes astonished. "A miracle," she murmured.

Kandri barely heard her. "Abominations," he snarled beneath his breath. "Right out loud, for everyone's benefit. And he was looking straight at us."

"Does he know?" asked Mektu. "That the Prophet calls us that?"

Kandri laughed bitterly. "It wasn't a fucking coincidence."

"He wants us dead, brother," said Mektu. "He'd give one of his lungs to see us bleeding on the ground."

"You almost were," said Eshett.

Kandri started; Eshett's eyes were moist. With a shaking hand, she made a gesture similar to Jód's own, tracing an invisible line. She had seen the flight of the splinter, she said. A foot from Kandri's temple, inches from Mektu's ear. And then, as if to assert itself after sparing them both, it had caressed the driver's jugular, opening it with the precision of a knife.

ↀ

The dead man was wound in cloth and his body lashed atop a camel. The drivers sang their prayers and crouched down, as they had by the pit of the Wasp, to dab their foreheads with dust.

But what to do with the beheaded camel? A grave would take too long, and might be hard to disguise. Simply abandoning it was out of the question: the vultures alone would ensure that any eyes that scanned the country would be drawn to the spot.

"A sling between two camels," suggested Mektu. "Just until nightfall, when we stop and bury the thing."

"And what would that say, to any fool who watches us?" snapped Ulren. "Merely that we are hiding something, that we are so fearful of discovery we must hobble along with a headless camel. Ang save us from Chiloto inspirations."

"Better than no inspiration at all," said Eshett, and for the next hour, Mektu strutted and grinned.

Jód's solution was sensible if unpopular. Ten drivers were dispatched to tip the carcass into the crater itself, and to shovel earth upon it with all possible speed. Ten more were sent to bury the celestial embers. The drivers blessed themselves, gazing up at the heavens with fear and remorse. They managed to bury the camel, and even to snuff the bulk of the flames, with no obvious sign that the Gods had taken offense.

But the smoke billowed on, unstoppable, no matter how feverishly they flung earth into the crater's maw. At last Jód canceled the hopeless task. All that day the black clouds rose behind them, drops of ink falling upward into the glass of the sky.

ↀ

"Eshett?"

Kandri opened his eyes. Beside him, stone-faced, Eshett did the same. His brother lay on the other side of her, propped on one elbow, watching her.

Murderous heat. It was past noon on their fourth day; the hills seemed close enough to touch. They were resting in the shelter of a drywash, an empty riverbed, but the protection it afforded was only horizontal—protection from searching eyes, not from the mallet of the sun. Every last driver, soldier, and mercenary had squeezed beneath the sun-shields. Most were attempting sleep.

"Eshett?" Mektu repeated.

"Yes?"

"The path to your village? The safe one Jód has in mind? It turns off in those hills ahead, right?"

"You know it does," said Eshett.

"We'll be there tomorrow. That's what Mr. Ulren says."

Eshett said nothing.

"Wouldn't you rather stay with us?"

Kandri could have kicked him. He opened his mouth to speak but Eshett stopped him with a look. She sat up slowly, touched Mektu on the cheek. Then she rose and went to cast herself down among the women drivers in their separate shelter.

Woeden Surk, the commander of the mercenaries, watched her movements with lewd absorption. He caught Kandri's accusing look and flashed him a grin. Then he turned to Captain Utarif.

"You ought to send your girlies to that tent as well. Not right for them to curl up beside the men, is it? Folks are likely to get ideas."

Captain Utarif was trimming his nails with a small pair of scissors. "Not folks who like their current number of teeth," he said mildly.

Despite his rage at both Mektu and Surk, Kandri found himself smiling. He was growing fond of this captain.

Woeden Surk rolled onto his back and crossed his bulging arms. "Don't say I didn't warn you," he muttered.

"No need for that sort of talk," said Utarif. "We're in this together."

"I won't be responsible, is all," said Woeden Surk. "You ought to send them away."

"You ought to fight the urge to interfere with my unit."

"That's just what I'm talkin' about," said the mercenary. "Urges."

His men guffawed. Kandri sat up with a premonition of doom. He glanced at his uncle: still asleep, thank the Gods. But Mektu had heard it all.

Four of Utarif's soldiers were women. The oldest, Grandmother Kereqa, had speared a man dead at forty feet just a few days earlier. The youngest, Talupéké, was beaming at the mercenaries, as if she appreciated the joke. But her hands were reaching for her throwing knives.

They were not on her person, fortunately. Both her knives and her sword lay next to her grandmother, on the opposite side of the old woman from Talupéké herself. The girl no longer slept with her weapons. It was an arrangement for everyone's safety.

Kereqa appeared to be asleep, but as Talupéké reached for the knives her eyes snapped opened and her hand caught Talupéké's wrist. Her other hand wagged a finger: *No.*

Talupéké's grin faded into something far more alarming. For a long moment she looked into her grandmother's eyes. Then she dropped her gaze and slowly lay down.

Captain Utarif's eyes were still on his nails, and his expression had not altered in the least. His right hand, however, lay gently on the hilt of his sword.

Belly up, Woeden Surk gave his testicles an ostentatious scratch. Kandri and Mektu exchanged a look, and for an instant there was perfect understanding between them. Neither had the least fear of Surk, ox-strong though he was. Talupéké was another matter entirely.

The third woman soldier had gone rigid in the act of braiding her hair. Kandri did not know her name, but he decided that she must know Talupéké well enough. She was watching the girl as one might look up at a cliff from below, when a tremor shakes the earth.

8. MASKS

"Chiloto. Chiloto. Up."

Where was he? Who was hissing his name? Whose rough hand was on his shoulder?

"Look lively, slowcoach. The Master wants you, now."

Ulren. Kandri blinked and shivered. The stars were still bright, the Pilgrim Moon a red smudge behind the hills. "It's not even morning," he said.

"It will be before you move your arse."

Kandri pulled on his cloak and sandals. He shuffled after Ulren, hugging himself, trying not to step on anyone. So precious, the last fragile minutes of sleep. He resented their loss, and hoped his face said it plainly.

Ifimar Jód was the only member of the caravan who regularly slept in a tent—a small, airless tent, but a tent nonetheless. He was seated now in the threshold, cross-legged. Dowi, brother to Tana-Dog, lay curled beside him like a serpent, watching Kandri with one bright eye. A hooded lamp sputtered before the Master, casting its diffuse glow on a small rug spread upon the earth.

"Ang's peace greet your soul at waking," said Jód. "Sit down."

Kandri lowered himself stiffly to the rug. *No philosophy*, he prayed. *Not at this hour. Let it be something else, anything, reprimands, insults—*

"Do you ponder the afterlife, Hinjuman?"

Storm of shit in a priest's red pajamas.

"Do you imagine it will bring eternal joy?"

"I have no idea in the world." Blabbering bastard. Let me sleep.

"What if it does not resemble this human sphere in the slightest?" asked Jód. "What if it is governed by birds or insects? Or still lesser creatures, the flukes and parasites that breed in stagnant water?"

Kandri rubbed his face. The dog gave a sigh of despair.

"Perhaps we are doomed one day to take our place among such creatures, for all eternity. Soaring high, flitting from plant to malodorous plant, creeping in the soil, wriggling helpless in a dewdrop."

I'm a good person, Kandri thought. Damn good, even as a child. That time I found the coin purse at school? Did I keep it? No, I—

"Or perhaps the afterlife is only one of witness," said Jód. "No form, no voice, no body. And no eye to see with, yet seeing all the same, seeing without end, as the Gods play out their games with this world. Such are the beliefs of the Elaru clan, whose burial caves are to be found in the hills ahead."

"What got you thinking about all this, Master Ifimar?"

"An attempt on my life," said Jód.

"What?"

Glowering at Kandri, Jód reached for something behind him in the tent. He tossed it on the ground beside the lamp.

Kandri was suddenly wide awake. The object was a rolled cloth bound in twine. One end of it was falling open, and burned. Looking closer, Kandri saw blackened paper rolled up with the cloth.

"Parthan spellcraft," said Jód. "My face flannel, stained with a spot of blood from a scratch I took in the Arig Hills. A page written in my own hand, torn from my book of meditations. And finally, a lock of my hair—" He touched the back of his head. "—stolen, as I have just discovered, in my sleep."

He scratched the dog behind the ear. "Dowi is trained to alert us to many things. One is fire. She caught a whiff of smoke an hour ago, and her eyes snapped northward. I rose and saw a tiny flame well out on the flats. I sent her ahead of me but followed as fast as I could run. But I was too late. When I reached the spot there was only a dying fire of twigs and leaves. And Dowi, with this talisman in her teeth."

"Then someone's following us, shadowing us? Someone who hates you in particular?"

Jód shook his head. "There were signs of someone fleeing in haste: Dowi surprised the fire-starter. But she would have bayed if she saw an enemy, or even an unknown face. The person was known to her." He gestured at the rolled cloth again. "Only Parthans—and very few of them—have the skills to unlock the evil of such a talisman. If the one who made it had such skill, and had finished the burning ritual, he or she could have stopped my heart cold."

"But why would any of the drivers target you? Master Ifimar, were they *forced* to make this journey, against their will?"

"No," said Jód, "but neither did they consent to aiding you. I warned you that there might be more devotees of your Prophet among them. And if they know you and your brother to be the Twin Abominations, what shall they make of the one who gives you his special protection? Is it any wonder that he too must be condemned?"

"But why bother with spells and such, whoever they are? Why not just brain us with a rock in our sleep?"

Jód leaned forward and raised the lamp. He opened the hood a fraction of an inch, so that a lone beam struck Kandri's face. "Only when we learn *who* can we hope to learn *why*, Hinjuman. I ask you again: who was it led you to that pit?"

Kandri looked down at his hands. *So this is why I'm here.*

"Resist me no further," said Jód. "Who is it you are protecting? That person deserves no mercy, fool. Even now he may be whetting the knife."

A lone bird's trill. A flaw of light in the east. Once again Kandri recalled the Prince's warning: *Whomsoever you name shall be executed.*

"You think the responsibility too great?" suggested Jód. "That is nonsense. You will not be responsible. You will only hasten what I would learn by other means—and by speaking now, you may spare your brother, your uncle, even yourself from another attack. My justice is not your burden to bear."

Condemn a man to death, thought Kandri, *because this lunatic found some burned cloth and paper.*

"Damn your silence!" hissed Jód. "Speak! For your own sake, for your family's. The hour is later than you know."

The camp was waking; the camels raised the black rosebuds of their heads. Somewhere a woman was singing, artless, for no one but herself. Kandri looked away into the dark.

"I can't help you," he said.

 C3

The heat that day was slightly less than the worst they had experienced. Consequently, Jód led them on straight through the day and into the night, with only momentary breaks for water. Breaks where one might squat or sit but never recline. That was forbidden. Ulren, patrolling the length of the caravan, declared with a certain glee that Jód had ordered him to stomp on any head that touched the ground.

"Evil man," grumbled Kandri.

No, no! cried half a dozen drivers, startling him. Right practice for caravans, Mr. Kandri, necessary practice, never recline, the dead recline, we must not join the dead.

"I simply can't understand these people," said Chindilan. "Anyone would think they delight in being tortured."

"No," said Eshett. "They simply don't want the burden."

"The burden?"

"Of deciding when to be tired. That's a torture in itself—counting the miles, the minutes, wondering if they should go on. They leave all of that to Jód. And they've learned over years that it's better. Their minds are free to go elsewhere, even if their bodies are in pain."

"So he can ask *anything* of us?" said Mektu. "March us until we drop dead by the trail?"

"Of course not," said Eshett. "Everyone has a breaking point. A good Caravan Master knows better than to reach it."

"What happens at the breaking point?"

Eshett looked at Mektu, struggling for patience. "We're a long way from there."

"I'm not."

"Yes you are."

෪

"Uncle," said Kandri, "did the Old Man ever talk about Ifimar Jód?"

He and Chindilan trudged shoulder to shoulder, stupid with fatigue, stumbling against each other and the camels. It was dark and chilly; the yellow moon had set, but the Pilgrim still smoldered low in the sky. The drivers were singing in their secret tongue, low words like water trickling in a cave.

"Your father knew more people than he talked about."

"Answer my question, Uncle."

Chindilan sighed. "For once—just *once*—couldn't you keep your mind on things that matter?"

"This matters," said Kandri. "Jód must have *some* reason for hating us."

"What Jód hates," said Chindilan, "is the notion that protecting you could get him and his drivers killed. Let the past sleep, boy. The present's trouble enough."

"I thought you were done with evasions," said Kandri, "since our little cup of tea."

His uncle flinched. They had drunk that tea a month ago, in General Tebassa's lair in the Arig Hills. It was there that Chindilan had told him of the extraordinary connection between Lantor Hinjuman and the Prophet. Kandri was still reeling.

They had been children together in the Sataapre Valley: his father, the reluctant mascot of a cheap little gang; and the girl, a frightened prisoner. Not in an iron tower or cold marble palace, as the myths would one day assert. Not in a dungeon or a famous jail. No, the Prophet-to-be was locked in an orphanage. A nothing of a place. A crooked little operation at the end of a dusty road. Kandri himself had passed it a thousand times and never suspected. No one suspected. But the evil done within its walls had shaped the world.

"Talk to me," said Kandri. "Secrets are no good for anyone."

"Is that a fact? Then I suppose you'll be in a hurry to tell your brother who you're hoping to find in Kasralys. You *should* tell him, you know."

"Stop changing the subject."

His uncle snickered. Kandri waited, trying to read the silence, his uncle's vast unease.

And all at once, he had it. "Jód," he said. "You knew Jód as well, didn't you?"

"Not really," said Chindilan.

"Not *really*? Pitfire, you knew him. That's why he had an opinion about you the day we reached the caravan. About your fucking *honor*."

"Watch your tongue," snapped Chindilan. "I may be old, I may be thick. Some days I feel I'm a waste of matter. But I'm damned well honorable."

"I'd like to go on believing that," said Kandri.

Another silence. Kandri let it stretch out. The ice was giving way.

"It was a quarter century ago," said Chindilan at last. "And even then we barely spoke. I was in Jód's presence for less than an hour."

"Jód said he'd never set foot in Chiloto lands."

"For all I know, he hasn't," said the smith. "We met at the gates of Mab Makkutin. It was my first year in the army."

"What was my father doing in Mab Makkutin?"

"Settling accounts with Jód after a desert crossing. Heading for home. I wanted to go with him—he was a bit of a wreck—but there was no hope of getting leave."

"Papa went home alone, then?"

Chindilan sighed. *Here it comes*, thought Kandri.

"He went with a friend he'd picked up in the desert. Well, friend is one word."

"What's a better word?"

"Wife," said Chindilan. "He went home with Uthé, boy."

Kandri missed a step, blundered into Alahari, and barely managed not to fall under the feet of the camel behind. "You're lying," he told Chindilan. "Lying, or mad."

"Neither, I hope."

"You said you didn't know where my birth-mother came from. You *always* said that."

"Correction," said Chindilan. "I always said that you should ask the Old Man."

"I'm twenty-four years old," said Kandri, "and I'm learning *now* that my birth-mother was part of Ifimar Jód's fucking caravan?"

"Oh no," said Chindilan. "She was with them only for the last few days. They met her in a village near the desert's edge. She was in desperate trouble. Same as all those kids."

"What kids? You mean *those* kids?"

"Of course."

For the first fourteen years of Kandri's life, his father had come home with children. Always at night, always from the east. Kandri thought of them as turtles: silent, slow-moving, heads shaved against the inevitable lice. They were war orphans. Empty pockets, empty stomachs, empty eyes. His father would be gone the next morning to find them permanent homes. Kandri loved them, these instant brothers or sisters, but they never stayed. A week or two, at the very longest a season. When they left he never saw them again.

Desperate trouble. So the Old Man had brought Kandri's birth-mother to that house by the same road. Perhaps even for the same reason.

"That's why she was so good to them," he said. "She would give them our last spoon of rice. I hated her for that, sometimes. But she had to, didn't she? Uthé was one of them. One of Papa's rescues."

"Yes," said Chindilan, "his first."

"When I was small I couldn't understand why they kept coming. Why they were all he talked about, all that ever seemed to matter. And you, Uncle. You hid this for years."

"Now, Kandri—"

"Twenty-four years."

"It's what he wanted," said Chindilan.

"Well that's just fine then."

"I told you a month ago I was sorry, damn it all! How many apologies do you need?"

"How many more shocks do you plan to give me?"

Chindilan sucked a breath through clenched teeth. "Fair enough," he said.

୧୫

After that cup of tea, the world had suddenly made sense. Lacerating sense. Only then had Kandri seen with any clarity the two figures whose encounter had shaped it. Lantor, his father, a small scared boy guarding the door of the house of torture, the orphanage his gang had turned into a brothel. And the girl, trapped inside, who would grow up to be Her Radiance the Prophet, Mother of All Chilotos, deliverer, demon, at war with all the world.

The boy could have helped her. Could have unlocked the door, let the girl flee into the warmth of that long-ago summer evening, into a different life, a normal life. Could have prevented, maybe, all the horrors that followed. The prophecies, the War of Revelation. Death and murder like a perpetual wind over Urrath, the storm without end.

She had begged him: *Open the door, let me out of here!* But Lantor Hinjuman had refused. He had not wanted any trouble. He was afraid.

Those orphans he brought home were acts of atonement. But they were not, could never be, enough.

"It was some thirty-two years later when he met Uthé," said Chindilan. "He'd been to the East, apprenticed with the Gods know whom. Great engineers, great thinkers—'the pride of Urrath,' that's what he said once, after a lot of drinks. He'd become an inventor, a genius. And surpassed all his teachers, or so I've always suspected.

"And none of it mattered to him one wit, Kandri. He still carried the doom of Urrath on his shoulders. He'd not found a way to stop the bleeding inside."

"Jód halted the caravan in her village, is that it?"

Chindilan nodded. "For some eight days, as I recall. There were kinship ties between the village and Jód's family, and then a storm blew up in the west. Your father had time to listen to Uthé's woes. And to consider what he might do about them."

136

"What kind of trouble was she in?"

"The kind that made him marry her fast."

Kandri snorted. "Should have guessed. How noble of him."

"*Harach.*" Chindilan elbowed him sharply. "Always the simplest answer with you. He knocked her up. Is that all you can imagine?"

"Well, didn't he? You said it was a quarter century ago. I'm twenty-four."

"There's more to your father than a dick!"

Chindilan bit his lips: his voice had carried. The drivers looked away, glad for once to exaggerate the language barrier. Further back, the dark outline that was Spalak faced them squarely. Kandri could almost feel his probing eyes.

"Lantor," hissed Chindilan, "did not sleep with your mother until they were married."

"So he told you."

"Never once in my life have I caught that man in a lie. I dare say neither have you."

"But he was *already married to Sepu.*"

It was all Kandri could do not to scream it. *Sepu* meant *second mother*. It was his nickname for his beloved stepmother, Dyakra Hinjuman, mother of Mektu and his other half-siblings, the woman who had drawn Kandri into her heart and home when Uthé Hinjuman died of snakebite.

"Dyakra," said Chindilan, "was the first one he told."

Kandri had not expected that. But did it matter, really? Weren't the fundamentals the same?

"He was the luckiest bastard in the world to have Sepu. He didn't need two wives."

"You're just being a fool now, Kandri," said Chindilan. "When Uthé turned up, Jód flatly refused to add a runaway girl to their caravan—not one who could bring down the wrath of a whole clan on their heads. 'They will ride up from behind and slaughter us like chickens, Hinjuman!' is what Lantor said he shouted."

"So marrying Uthé—"

"Was the only way he could get Jód to agree. It was also the only way to convince her Parthan family to let her leave a terrible situation."

137

"What situation? You said Papa didn't get her pregnant with me until they were married. What was the emergency?"

"*Jeshar*, you're like a wolf after a bone."

"Then share your Gods-damned precious bone!"

Chindilan rubbed his face. "Listen up, then. Members of another clan of desert guides—rivals of Ifimar Jód—had become smitten with the Prophet. They'd met a few of those young Rasanga, the ones Her Radiance sent to train in the desert. They became believers, these guides—believers, and fanatics. They swore their lives to Orthodox Revelation—forever, unto death—and started bullying the rest of their clan to do the same.

"One of those was Uthé. She had a suitor among those young fanatics. The boy was nagging her daily, maybe hourly, to give her life over to the Prophet, and marry him. She didn't want to do either. She knew she had to get out of there or be swallowed up by the faith."

"That's it? That's why Papa helped her?"

"Why do you doubt me, damn your eyes?"

What a question. Rich as treacle tart. "Go on," he said aloud, "tell me the rest."

"What else is there to tell? I met your birth-mother the same place I met Ifimar Jód, at the gate of Makkutin. Along with a few hundred camel drivers—not these drivers, of course."

"It was a whole different team?"

"Almost entirely. Ulren was there, charming as he is today. I heard some chatter about Spalak, but he never made an appearance. Kandri, there's no more mystery to unearth here. Your birth-mother was overjoyed, felt she'd been delivered from death. She would have run off into the desert without a camel, without food, without a *gham* for her future. And now she was safe. I saw her drop to her knees in front of Jód, and then . . ."

Silence. Kandri's hands were in fists.

"All right, this is a bit strange," said Chindilan slowly. "I hadn't thought of it in years, Ang slay me if I lie. Probably it's nothing, but—"

"Just tell me."

"Your mother meant every word of thanks she said to Jód," said Chindilan. "He didn't have to let her join the caravan, after all. But I don't think she liked being near him. In fact I'm sure of it. She got up and rushed away before the man could say, 'You're welcome.'"

The smith looked up at the star-bright sky. "I remember now. Jód turned to Lantor and asked what would become of her, and Lantor said he'd been sincere about his marriage vows, that he would care for Uthé and do his best to fall in love with her. Jód looked pleased with that. Then he stepped away to fetch your father's camel. And Lantor turned to me quickly. 'If you ever cross that man's path again, tell him nothing of Uthé,' he told me. 'Not a word, you understand? Her future's her own. She's cut the past away with a knife.'"

Kandri started. "So Jód, he—"

"No," said Chindilan. "Lantor swore the man never touched her, never had a chance. And for the few days Uthé traveled with the caravan she never once left your father's side."

"He could have attacked her on some earlier journey," said Kandri.

"Yes, that's possible."

"But you don't think so?"

"I don't," said Chindilan. "Uthé didn't exactly hate Ifimar Jód. It was . . . stranger than that. As if he cast some kind of shadow."

"Shadow, Uncle?"

"As if he reminded her of something she never wanted to see again."

☙

By dawn they were hungry and freezing and footsore. The dry river had ended, disgorging them back onto the plain. There was no more cover, no more hiding places between where they stood and the next line of hills.

They were much taller and steeper than the Vasaru range at their backs. These hills were sharp-sided, with cliffs and boulders and broken summits. Far to the north and south they dwindled gradually back into the plains, giving the range the likeness of some vast reptile breaking the surface of a waveless sea.

Menacing or not, the land at their feet was the most gentle they had seen in days. There were cacti and wiregrass, sun-blasted shrubs, even a few tiny flowers, offering petals small as lemon seeds to the sky.

Kandri was gnawing his last morsel of breakfast—dried apple, tough as a boot—when the word swept through the caravan.

Riders!

All heads turned north: some thirty riders on horseback were thundering toward them over the plain. Where had they come from? He fumbled for his telescope, but there was no point. The riders were already upon them.

Jód halted the caravan. Utarif's soldiers drew their arms and formed a circle around the brothers, Chindilan, and Eshett. The mercenaries gathered to Woeden Surk.

"I count thirty, more or less," said Kandri.

"Jód saw seventy on the Vasaru Plain," said Chindilan, scanning the horizon. "If these are the same riders, where are the rest hiding out?"

"Archers, to the fore!" said Captain Utarif. "Don't fit your arrows yet, though: I'll not start a fight by accident."

The horses were beautiful: dappled white and chestnut, broad of hoof. They outnumbered the riders; clearly some were pack-horses, though all were wild-eyed and strong. The riders, men and women alike, were heavily armed. Swords, rapiers, flint-headed spears. Oddest of all, they appeared to be masked.

"What the living fuck?" said Talupéké.

The masks were moon-yellow, with large openings for the eyes and narrow slits at nose and mouth. They were mottled and rough, as though made from mud-soaked paper or leaves.

"One thing's certain: they're not Revelation Army," said Chindilan. "We're still a step ahead of the Prophet, by the grace of Ang."

The riders formed a line some fifty feet away and studied the caravan, their faces like a row of deviled eggs. At the center of the line, one mask stood out: blood-red among the identical yellows. Its owner was a woman on a splendid red-and-white dappled horse. By the others' looks of cautious deference it was clear that she was their leader.

All grew still; for a moment the only sound was the wind. Ifimar Jód, black sword in hand, glanced over his shoulder at Spalak, and it seemed to Kandri that a look of deep understanding passed between the two men. Then Jód walked out to meet the riders alone.

The woman in the red mask raised her arms above her head. Each hand gripped a broad-bladed sword, and white ribbons trailed from her forearms, creating a suggestion of wings.

"Who the hell *are* they?" said Mektu.

"Clowns, Mr. Mektu," said a driver, miserable with fear.

"That's not funny."

The man retreated behind his camel. "Clowns, not funny, thank you please."

"Oh Gods, learn to talk," said Mektu.

Ifimar Jód bowed to the woman, towering above him on her horse. Both sheathed their weapons, but Kandri still read danger in their bodies, and the woman's eyes.

"Grandmother," said Talupéké, "I think I've seen those bastards before."

"You have," said Kereqa, "in the Arigs, when you were scarcely old enough to walk. They are great fighters, ruthless and quick. Their legends say they were never defeated by the empire of the Kasraj."

"A lot of bush clans will tell you that," said Chindilan.

"But how many refuse to speak Imperial Common?" asked Kereqa. "These people will not utter a word of it: they call it the language of surrender. And yet they embrace the evil name the Kasrajis gave them."

"Which is?" said Mektu.

"*Akrunu Haggath*. Slaughterhouse Clowns."

"On second thought, fit those arrows," said Utarif.

Among the camel drivers, whispers flowed like smoke—*Clowns, masks, death.*

"The *Clowns* bit, that makes sense," said Mektu. "But *Slaughterhouse?*"

"It is oddly . . . specific," said Chindilan.

"Haggath," grumbled a low voice behind them.

It was the Prince's hulking manservant; Kandri had never before heard him speak. "Haggath!" he said again. "That is a place in my city. The meat place."

"Ripheem is quite correct," said Prince Nirabha. "The Haggath is the great butchers' quarter of Kasralys. And yes, there is a clown troop made up of meat packers, and they do paint their faces. But they are a charitable society, raising money for the poor."

I'm losing my mind, thought Kandri.

The Prince gestured at the mounted warriors. "No, these are not the same people at all. Perhaps our legions met on some expedition long ago, and were reminded of the clowns of Kasralys? How very fascinating. I wonder when it occurred."

"Go and ask them, Prince," said Mektu. "I'll be fascinated from here."

"There's nothing charitable about *these* people," said Eshett. "They have a reputation. They're known to be hard."

"What does 'hard' means, in this case?" asked Kandri.

"They burn out the tongues of their enemies. They believe the soul resides in the tongue."

"So it does, in certain cases," said the Prince with a glance at Mektu.

"They're modest, in a strange way," said Eshett. "They consider mouths to be mating organs, and noses obscene. My father says that the prisoners who die from the tongue-burning are the lucky ones. Those who live become servants—mindless, voiceless, barely human anymore. The Clowns use them until they fall dead."

"Adorable," said Captain Utarif, "but not our problem today. If it comes to a fight we can kill these thirty—provided the mercenaries do their job. But I'd feel better if we knew where the rest were lurking."

In fact the mercenaries did help, but not in the way anyone expected. Their leader, Woeden Surk, raised a scarred fist and shouted a few words in a strange tongue.

Strange, but not exactly unknown.

Kandri turned to Mektu. His brother's face was ashen.

"Was that—could that *possibly*—?"

Mektu hid his face in his elbow.

The red-masked woman answered in the same language. A few of the mercenaries laughed.

Chindilan, appalled, sidled close to the brothers. "It's true," he whispered. "They're speaking Važek."

ᙏ

Kandri went cold all over. He recalled with searing clarity the last time he'd heard the language. It had been spoken by a Važek soldier on the end of his spear.

A vision of the man rose before him: defiant eyes, tattered uniform, hands clutching uselessly at the wooden shaft, blood-spittle on his lips as he barked some curse or prayer or sarcasm. Whatever it was you said to the enemy who'd just taken your life.

Another flash, another memory: his first day of training at Eternity Camp, and a mural on a wide stone wall. Marauding Važeks in attack formation, bristling with pikes and glaives and bloodied halberds, eyes fixed and inhuman, mouths open in a war cry. The new conscripts were made to stand before it at attention for a quarter hour, until the drill sergeant shattered the silence with a howl.

"Važeks! Depraved, ruthless, fearless, cruel! For some of you in this yard, these faces will be the last things you ever see. If you're not man enough to fight to the death, these monsters will take your homes, take your mates, take your country. They nearly did it in your grandparents' day. They hate you to the depths of their souls, Chilotos. They always will."

ᙏ

Jód beckoned to Woeden Surk, and the mercenary leader slouched forward and crossed his arms. He began a halting exchange with the woman in the red mask.

Chindilan rubbed his face. "Piss of the devil's dancing girls!" he hissed. "Are *they* some mad sort of Važeks?"

"No," said Kereqa, "they are the Slaughterhouse Clowns. But they are certainly speaking the Važek tongue."

"And so is Woeden Surk," added Captain Utarif. "I don't like this at all. If these Clowns have embraced the Važek tongue they may have embraced Važek hatreds as well. You Chilotos should keep your heads down. Of course—" He glanced at the mercenaries, lowering his voice still further. "—you'll still be traveling with *them*."

"Your general wouldn't have attached us to a caravan full of Važek sympathizers, would he?" asked Chindilan.

"My general," said Utarif, "had no way whatsoever to get you across the desert. No way but this caravan—and it had already set off."

"Because he sent it off," said Kandri, "without us."

Utarif glanced at him sharply. He opened his mouth, then checked himself and shook his head. "General Tebassa does not deal with mercs, Hinjuman. Jód hired them on his own."

Kandri studied the captain's profile. His eyes were troubled. *That's not what you were about to say.*

ങ

The red-masked woman abruptly stopped speaking. Jód gestured at Woeden Surk, demanding a translation. The mercenary shrugged.

"War's come to their homeland," he said. "The bitch Prophet—her words—drove out their allies the Važeks a month ago, then burned everything. But she also says this wasteland here belongs to her people, so we need her blessing before we cross."

"A fabrication," said Jód. "What else?"

"Begging your pardon," said Surk, "but she says if we're going to walk around with our mouths uncovered, why not show the world our arse-mouths too? That exactly what she called 'em, arse-mouths, did you ever—"

"What *else*?" snapped Jód.

"She says the fireballs are a punishment for naked mouths, among other sins," said Surk, "and she has a colt to sell if you're interested. Also a servant."

"Servant?"

"Or maybe a captive. She wasn't clear." Surk muttered in Važek, and the Clown leader turned and barked a command. A horse was led forward out of the company. On its back was a lumpy, canvas-covered shape: a body, Kandri knew, even before it squirmed.

"She says she'll take payment in kind," said Woeden Surk.

A moan escaped the heavy canvas. The body was tied over the saddle like a butchered sheep. At his leader's signal, the nearest Akrunu slid to the ground and tugged at the canvas until it parted.

Kandri felt his throat constrict. A bruised and battered face dangled by the horse's flank, twitching and blinking. Kandri could not tell if it was man or woman, old or young. The hair stiff with filth and blood. The lips pale and swollen. They moved, trying to form words, but the only sound that came was that moan of despair. A noise that might issue from a mouth without a tongue.

The red-masked leader was talking again. When she finished, Surk looked at Jód.

"She says he's a Važek soldier. Hard working and strong."

"She just claimed to be in alliance with the Važeks!" shouted Chindilan. "She's *speaking* Važek, by the Gods."

"This one's a traitor and a runaway," said Surk, grinning widely. "Reminds me of someone. Can't quite put my finger on it."

Jód pointed at the captive. "Even if I were *tirmassil* scum who bought and sold human lives, I would not pay a hair-thin copper for that man."

"Didn't you hear me, *Master*?" Surk was having fun. "She wants payment in kind. She's offering the captive, along with permission to cross her territory."

"And in exchange?" said Jód.

"Those two." Woeden Surk pointed and Kandri and Mektu. "She demands them."

"Then she can come over here and get measured for a new arse-mouth!" shouted Mektu, pointing with his machete. "Tell her, I want to hear you say it, I want—"

Eshett socked him in the arm.

"She picked them out at a glance," Surk went on. "Chiloto faces, Chiloto hair. She says you can keep their possessions. Hand them over naked if you like."

Jód's hands were in fists. "And you laugh at this, you rejoice?" he demanded.

Woeden Surk spread his hands in a gesture of innocence, but his smile widened. "I told her you'd object. That you had a strange fondness for the louts, even though they were forced on you. She's not particularly understanding. She says you're heading in the wrong direction."

"How is that?"

"She's convinced you mean to sell those two," said Woeden Surk, "but the buyer who will pay real money is behind us. Meaning the Prophet, of course."

He laughed, and his men guffawed on cue. Then Surk added, "They mean to fight us if you refuse."

Captain Utarif snapped out a hand signal. His archers—five of the nine soldiers—trained their arrows on the red-masked woman.

"I don't suppose this needs translating," said Utarif.

The riders burst into high howling, strange and distorted from behind their masks. Two began to urge their horses forward, shielding their leader. The woman stopped them with a shouted word. Contemptuous, she faced the arrows pointed at her chest.

Jód, slow and deliberate, drew his sword again. He was seething, but his eyes were not on the leader of the Clowns. They were on Woeden Surk.

"Tell her to be gone, with her insults and atrocities."

The mercenary nodded, still looking amused. He spoke to the red-masked leader. In reply the woman gave a kind of low, trilling snarl. Kandri drew his own machete. Beside him, Talupéké reached over her shoulders, fingers resting on the handles of her knives.

The red-masked woman barked another command. The rider who had dismounted once more covered the captive's face. He stepped to his horse and remounted, and the Akrunu began to turn their steeds away.

"Wait," shouted Kandri.

Thirty masks swiveled to face him. So did all his companions.

"I'll buy the prisoner," he said.

"Silence, silence!" Ulren was livid. "Meddling bastard, this ain't your affair!"

"He's right for once," said Mektu. "Have you gone mad, Kandri? Buy the prisoner? What for?"

"For fifteen gold." Kandri gestured at Surk. "Kasraji true gold. Tell her. I'll get my purse."

"That's *our* fucking purse," said Mektu, "and that's a quarter of the coin Garatajik gave us, we're going to need it, you have no—"

"Stop it, Mek."

In a kind of dream, Kandri made his way to Alahari. As Woeden Surk addressed the Clown leader, he opened the saddlebag and fished out the purse. On his left, Dothor Spalak watched him with fascination. Ifimar Jód had turned to stone.

"She wants twenty," bellowed Surk.

"All right."

"Kandri," said Chindilan, "what the hell are you doing?"

Kandri did not look at him. Hands shaking, he counted out twenty of the heavy gold coins. He rounded his scandalized brother and uncle and walked into the open space between the caravan and the Clowns.

The flat of Jód's sword struck his chest. Kandri looked up and met the Master's burning gaze.

"Why?" said Ifimar Jód.

Kandri's mouth was dry. "I've killed them," he said. "Vaẑeks, on the battlefield. I've killed eighteen or twenty."

"They are dead and gone, Hinjuman."

"My father," said Kandri. "All my life he helped strangers. Even my mother was a stranger, I wouldn't be here if he'd done nothing—but you know that already, don't you?"

"I know your birth-mother too is dead."

"But you don't know why my father helped them all. You don't know how the Prophet—"

Jód lifted his chin with the sword-tip. Kandri held his breath. The Master's rage like a bonfire, burning without light.

"One single day," said Jód.

He lowered his sword, sheathed it, and held out a hand for the gold. Kandri passed him the coins. Weighing them in his right hand, Jód approached the prisoner. With his left hand he once more uncovered the battered face.

The red-masked leader was chattering, pointing: she wanted Jód to show her the coins.

Dothor Spalak coughed.

A stream of drool fell from the prisoner's mouth.

Jód spun on his heel and flung the coins at the Clown leader. They flashed in the sun, striking her and her mount, falling like bright rain to the dust.

"*Bithrel*," said Spalak, "perfection."

Horses nickered. Jód's left hand was scarlet. In the same whirl of motion he had drawn a short knife and slit the prisoner's throat.

"Aw, shit," said Woeden Surk.

His men pressed forward, as did every other fighter in the caravan. The Clowns, struck dumb for an instant, burst into a high howl like a shared delirium. The sound was blood-chilling. Ifimar Jód did not move.

Swords whirled over masked heads. Horses pawed the dust. But the red-masked leader sat with eyes locked on Jód and said nothing. At last the howls died away.

"The man's windpipe almost turned my blade," said Jód. "You tried to sell us a victim of the Throat Rust. Dismount and take your payment, foul spawn of the slaughterhouse. If you dare."

The Clown leader looked at the scattered coins. Base avarice at war with common sense. Thirty of her people against the same number of mercenaries, as well as Utarif's soldiers, the brothers and Chindilan, Spalak and Jód. To say nothing of the camel drivers, some of whom at least would help in the fight.

The red-masked leader shot a last glance at Surk, whose wooden grimace did not change. Then she wheeled her horse around, shouting to her people. Seconds later all thirty were galloping to the north. Common sense had prevailed. No slaughter today for the Slaughterhouse Clowns.

But another forty of her people were out there.

9. A CHILD OF HER RADIANCE

The patient awoke to discover a white baboon crouched upon his thighs. He was rather sure he was in hell.

The creature was unbandaging him, peeling encrusted dressings one by one from a wound on his chest, and eating them. It grunted softly, absorbed in its work.

Darkness, heat. Smoky lamplight splashed on a wall. The bed so high it might have been an altar on which he'd been placed, face up, readied for the knife.

A scream, he thought. That's what the moment calls for. But he knew that the baboon would, at the very least, respond in kind, and the thought of hearing its voice was somehow even more terrible than what it was doing to him. The man's legs ached; the baboon was large and potbellied and its nails were sharp. Was this his private damnation, his fate? To watch this monster open him layer by layer to the end of time?

The creature stank of sweat and dander and spoiled food. But behind the reek he detected a finer smell: the brisk, clean odor of creosote. He sniffed. No, not quite creosote: that was creosote *bush*. In flower. A harbinger of spring.

This was not Hell then but merely Gathen, where the bush grew thick upon the plain. The scent cleared his thoughts a little. Enough to note the weakness of his body, the many stitches in his chest. Enough to recall a carriage ride, three days and nights it must have been, and each rut and stone in the highway jolting him from his drug-induced sleep. Enough to recall, much earlier, the fascinating sight of a dagger sliding between his ribs.

I have been in a coma. I lay in the dirt and my blood pooled around me. Someone was kneeling in it, shouting. How curious that I survived.

Names returned next. First his own, Garatajik, Secondborn son of Her Radiance the Prophet. Then the names of the brothers who had danced and gibbered in his dreams. Kandri Hinjuman. Mektu Hinjuman. His chosen couriers, his heroes. No sooner named than knifing him.

Gods of Death, they were just peasants. Village boys given machetes and marched to the front. You utter fool. What possessed you to place the world in their hands?

The lamp was somewhere behind his head. The baboon's lips moved, as though it were not just picking at his bandages but reading them.

Fool or not, he was more lucid with each breath. He recalled that he must pretend to hate those brothers, to speak of them as accursed, the Twin Abominations, the blight foretold by prophecy. He must say that he had not asked anything of them, not conversed on any subject, only tried to enforce his mother's justice. That he had no idea where they had gone.

He recalled other names as well.

"Sleepyhead."

The baboon fixed its round, babyish eyes on him.

"Get your fat foul body off my legs, if you please. I want to use them."

The baboon placed a paw on his cheek. The touch was inquisitive. They had known each other for twenty-five years.

"What sadist left me alone with you?"

The baboon leaped straight up, screaming, that scream Garatajik hated above all sounds in the world. Time slowed. He had leisure to marvel at his failure to recognize that the beast had been sent there to kill him. He saw its claws spreading, its lips curling back from those obscene fangs, the zenith of its ascent and the way its mouth reached for him even as it fell. He observed his own puny efforts to shield himself, weak arms rising, a quarter turn upon the bed—

He saw a flash of steel. The metal scales of a serpent that struck like lightning, coiled twice about the baboon's chest, twisted, snapped back. He saw the animal jerked sideways with inches to spare, felt its breath on his face, heard the solid *thump* as it hit the floor.

The whip!

He rolled over. The baboon squatted there on its haunches, feigning innocence, licking its paw. The steel whip held it prisoner two yards from the bed. At the weapon's tip hung a disk of razor-sharp steel. The other end trailed away into the shadows.

Garatajik's heart slammed in his chest. *Kisjithek*, viper whip. An insane device of articulating scales small as bees' wings. There was only one such weapon in existence, and one hand capable of wielding it.

The dwarf. Ang in heaven. My mother's dwarf is in the room.

He had to think before he acted, before he moved so much as an inch. None of what had just occurred should have been possible. The white baboon was his mother's pet. Save for brief walks about Eternity Camp, she kept it near her at all times. And the dwarf—

Not yet. One menace at a time. The baboon had just tried to kill him. Old, screaming, sugar-addicted Sleepyhead. His mother believed against all evidence that it was a gentle animal, and so she failed to notice the rage it directed at certain soldiers, merchants, ambassadors, Garatajik himself. The creature had an uncanny ability to sense when someone wished his mother harm.

But others noticed. Others who whispered in the Prophet's ear. As a consequence, those at whom the baboon screamed had a tendency to vanish. Now someone had let the creature into Garatajik's chamber, hoping it would tear out his throat. Someone close enough to his mother to arrange such a thing.

The whip flexed, python-like, forcing the baboon to shuffle across the floor. Latches clicked. Sliding doors parted, and a somewhat brighter lamplight spilled into the room: enough to reveal the creature scampering away. The doors closed again. The whip slithered away into the dark.

Nothing moved. Somewhere a cat yowled, barely audible. It yowled again and ceased abruptly, as though stabbed.

For the first time in several decades Garatajik felt like shouting for his mother's protection. He had been saved from a deranged animal, but what was to come might be worse. Could the dwarf really be there, just yards from him in the gloom?

If it was rare to see Sleepyhead without his mother, it was much rarer to catch any glimpse whatsoever of the dwarf. The rank and file believed that only doomed men saw his face. Of course everyone in his family had seen him on occasion—a silent executioner, a shadow in a darkened hall—so it could not be quite as bad as all that. Unless everyone in his family was doomed from birth.

What if the game was up, his treason discovered? What if his mother had clung to his side since the attack? She might have plied him with drugs. She might have questioned him and learned the truth.

Or perhaps—he forced his eyes to follow the whip again into the blackness—she was still *trying* to learn it?

A loyalty test? For her own son, a Son of Heaven, nearly martyred for the faith?

Was he being watched, even now? To see if he betrayed himself, cried out his secrets, begged for mercy? Or merely cringed in the darkness, as only a guilty man would?

But the dwarf—

Enough! You're a loving son of Her Radiance. You're a soldier in the War of Revelation. You're a believer. Sell it, sell it or die.

"Barigorm?"

The dwarf, a being infinitely more dangerous than Sleepyhead, crept from the shadows, coiling the whip, his bright eyes appearing before the outline of his body. His mother's guardian stood just over three feet tall, but he was barrel-chested and immensely strong. He was mute, but that had never mattered. The whip spoke for him. As a boy, Garatajik had seen him use it to cut the hands—both hands—from a merchant accused of overcharging his mother. The dwarf had other weapons, too, should they ever be required.

"We thank you, Master Barigorm. We were . . . in some distress."

The dwarf stood watching him, a statue in the dark. The last twelve inches of the viper whip dangled from his hand, the disk-blade rocking like a pendulum. He was waiting. Waiting with a certain defiance, if one could read any motive in that face that never saw the sun. Waiting, no doubt whatsoever, as he had been ordered to wait, for Barigorm's life had been one ceaseless essay in obedience to the Prophet.

Garatajik held his gaze, expressionless. They might suspect him, but he would not give himself away. The matter was simple now that he perceived it: lose your nerve and die screaming, devoured by blackworms, buried in rats. Be a thing of ice and live.

In one fluid movement, Barigorm spread his hands and bowed. It was merely his duty, the same as any Chiloto who approached a Son of Heaven, but this time the gesture meant everything to Garatajik. His mother had not denounced him. She had not learned the truth, not peeled back the layers of his mind like that monkey had his bandages. There was still hope.

"You have frightened Sleepyhead, my child."

The voice, thin and warbling, came from the darkness beyond his feet. Garatajik felt a sudden cramping in his stomach. Barigorm backed away into the shadows, bowing in the direction of the voice.

"Try to warm to him, Garatajik. Love is all he requires. He has always loved you."

"Mother," he said, "I've grown a beard." For so he had: a thick, short beard.

"You have been asleep this past month and more," said the Prophet. "We trimmed it, of course—all the world knows your love of good grooming— but with scissors alone; I would not let anyone near you with a razor. You twitched like the very devil, my Secondborn."

He squinted at the darkness. "A month? I have slept away a *month?*"

"As I say, we almost lost you. The Abomination clearly meant to pierce your heart. Lucky for you he could not find it."

Wide-eyed in the darkness, Garatajik touched his chest. How blessed wonderful, to breathe.

"All the same, your lung deflated like a balloon," added the Prophet. "The doctor says you may labor to breathe from now on."

Garatajik traced the edge of his wound, reliving again that horrible attack. Mektu Hinjuman had come out of nowhere, said not a word. Of course he thought he was defending his brother—saving him, even, from the clutches of the Prophet's loyal Secondborn. The knife had been silent too, gliding into his chest. As if it knew its business was obscene.

And there had been something more—something terrible, uncanny. In that instant, as his chest imploded and he fell upon his knees, something had fled from him. A bodiless invader, a second mind. It had felt the wound as keenly as Garatajik himself, this creature. It had left him for dead and departed, slipping out through the window of his fading eyesight.

Yatra. That is the word. I played host to a yatra. But it did not hate, did not wish to destroy me.

"It . . . pitied me."

"What do you mean, *it*?" snapped the Prophet. "The doctors had no pity, or scorn, or love in their heart. No vision either. All of them are the same."

He was barely listening. *The yatra pitied me. It knew what I had to live for. A lover, a cause. And it spoke kindly as it departed. It wished me safe passage through the lands of the dead.*

"But I did not die," he said aloud.

"No indeed," said the Prophet.

"Who attended me, Mother?"

"The finest doctors in Urrath."

Xavasindrans, thought Garatajik. It was the continent's old, self-depre-cating joke: the finest care in Urrath was at the hands of non-Urrathis. And under the Plague Protocols, the only non-Urrathis allowed on the continent were Xavasindran medical missionaries.

I've been possessed by a yatra, and interfered with by Outworlders. Jekka's Hell, I've been under their knives.

Don't react. Don't betray yourself. Speak of the trivial, be quick.

"Well, radiant mother—"

"Fatuous fool," she shot back.

"—what have I missed, besides the start of spring?"

"Your eldest brother's birthday."

Oh Gods. Jihalkra's fiftieth. The rites. The Presentation of the Crown!

It was, in the scheme of Orthodox Revelation, about as far from trivial as one could get. His very return from the east had been impelled by his brother's upcoming Presentation: if he had failed to make the journey he could never have returned at all. But now—

"I am heartbroken," he said, with all the feeling he could simulate. "I trust my brothers were all in attendance?"

"No, they were not. Our beloved Ojulan lies in a casket, dead."

"I meant—"

"Of course you did. And do not wring your hands over your absence from the Presentation. Jihalkra forgives you. We will all of us forgive you, that. You were wrestling with the Shadow of Death, boy. You could not rise and kneel before your brother, even if . . ."

Garatajik pinched the bridge of his nose. *Even if your prophecies declared that I should, when he first glimpsed his crown. I have undermined your teachings, left a blemish on your face. That is something you will never forget.*

"Open the doors," said his mother, in a voice meant for someone else.

The sliding doors parted again, wider this time, and Garatajik recognized the walls of the Traveling House, his mother's elegant but collapsible war cottage, where she dwelt on those rare occasions when she traveled beyond the Chiloto heartland. He was in a room off her bedchamber. The hulking wardrobe he had played in as a child stood beyond her bed. The baboon had climbed into its own bed, a canopied thing of red satin which more than a little resembled a throne. No windows, no daylight leaking in at any door. It could be midday for all he knew.

"Mika will shave you now," said his mother.

"I should like that," said Garatajik. In fact he did not give a damn about his beard—but Gods, how he needed time to think! His mother's voice had unbalanced him. Over the years he had heard it suffused with affection, fury, regret, coldest loathing. But never, until this moment, cynicism. *We will all of us forgive you . . . that.*

"Your eyes have suffered too," said his mother. "No one thought to wash the sand from them, for hours after you fell."

"My eyes feel fine," said Garatajik.

"You will wear darkened glasses outside this room. And no reading. Those are your doctor's orders, not my own. I trust will find it easy to obey a fellow scientist."

Rather than your Prophet. He could almost hear the words. Was she toying with him? Had she captured the boys' uncle, his faithful servant Chindilan, and ripped the truth from him with torture?

Six women approached: Rasanga, tall and beautifully arrayed in gold collars and nose rings and indigo scarves over their breastplates. Also armed to the teeth. To his astonishment, they knelt before him, three to either side of the bed, and hid their faces behind folded hands.

Garatajik was taken aback. Such obeisance from the proud Rasanga was reserved for the Prophet herself—and perhaps for his elder brother Jihalkra, the Firstborn, the High King to Be.

"We are honored, Mother, but—"

"You must give them permission to rise."

This was entirely too much. He waved a hand at the six killers; they rose and wheeled him into the larger chamber. Propped him up with pillows, facing the gauzy curtains of the Prophet's bed. Took up positions around him and their mistress, serene as statues, uncomfortably close.

Within the curtains, his mother lay like an embryo, curled on one side, both hands near her mouth. A small, gaunt woman. A delusional with arthritic hips. The greatest monster on the face of Urrath. If he lunged now . . .

The Rasanga would seize you, throttle you, snap your neck if you were lucky. And if you weren't . . .

Always thus. A seeming ease around her sons, but no chances taken. Guards who never slept, who watched every motion of every hand.

Light footfalls beside him. Garatajik turned and smiled.

"Mika! We are very happy to see you."

She had materialized out of nowhere: Mika, the blind woman who shaved the Sons of Heaven and the limbs of the female Rasanga, and had no other duties in life. It had not always been thus. Mika had served his mother fifty years, from the days when the Prophet was merely an unlucky girl in the clutches of a warlord holed up at Hunger Cliff. Mika had bathed Garatajik and his brothers in their infancy, trimmed their fingernails, combed and oiled their hair. Years of kindnesses. The extracted splinters, the bee stings soothed with cactus pulp ("Don't cry, my little Lord. The cactus remembers. It will sting the bee tomorrow.").

She bowed low, practically kneeling, and her ancient legs shook. He reached down from the bed and touched her shoulder. "We hope you are well, auntie, and that your birds are well provided for."

She smiled, too abashed to speak. Her teeth were crooked but intact. She reached for his hand and felt its contours, front and back. "This is how I see you," she had told him forty years ago, "how I know if you are joyful, or if something troubles your heart."

What was she seeing now?

He had not lain eyes on her in years. No mystery, that: a mere five months had passed—Pitfire, six now—since his return from the east. He had, perforce, resumed his charade as a Son of Heaven. He had also dedicated himself body and mind to the Cure. The theory he was hatching was so extraordinary that he lay awake with it whole nights in the Palace of Radiance. Most days he had resumed work at four. There were studies to review, three thousand pages of field notes to analyze. A planet to deliver from the Plague.

And on top of all that, the rebels. He had learned of their presence in the ranks before his departure for Kasralys, years ago now. But they had been dead by his return—or worse than dead; some matters of state even he could not probe. All save Chindilan, quiet Chindilan, the listener. It had taken Garatajik months to recruit the smith to active treason. Who could blame him for hesitating? Ang knew what had become of the man—exiled along with his nephews, presumably. Or dead. Or worse.

With the smith's help, he'd found a few more he could trust: secret insurgents, terrified of their dreams. They were excellent dreams: of ending the war, of liberating the Chilotos from their adoration of his mother, of making a republic of the Orthodox Dominion, this empire of hallucination and blood.

Fine dreams, and doomed. Some of the rebels wished to strike at once; Garatajik had persuaded them not to try. An attempt on the Prophet's life would almost certainly fail. And if by some miracle it succeeded, what would follow but catastrophe?

Orthodox Revelation had a script to follow, a recipe. The Prophet could only die because of monstrous treason, but if such should occur she would become a spirit, invincible and sleepless, everywhere at once. In the hearts of all believers, she would lead them on, illuminating Heaven's Path more brightly than she ever had in life. And the war: that would only accelerate. Her surviving sons would pursue it with absolute ferocity, right to the end, when all of the clans of Urrath submitted to their fate.

Mika laid out her razors on the foot of his bed: small, tiny, minuscule. She whipped foam in the same bowl of dented tin she had used all his life.

Garatajik knew that if their mother died, the unity of the Sons would shatter. Jihalkra would be named King of Kings, but the rest would burn with envy. They would watch his every move, and would turn on him if the chance came. He was a fearless soldier, Jihalkra, and a most cunning tactician. But he had his weaknesses. He led his people like a golem, like a walking stone. He showed them no warmth, lacked an understanding of what warmth might entail, or why one should bother with it. Above all, he hated speaking. He could pass whole weeks among his troops without addressing them, barely murmuring to the aide at his side.

Such flaws were not lost on his brothers. One day they would take knives to these flaws, pry them open like oysters, pounce on the flesh within.

Mika brushed the foam into his beard. She was over one hundred years old, but her hand was rock-steady as she shaved him. A hand that had never killed. Also, as he recalled with conviction, the first kindly touch in his life. One of the only.

Through the gauze curtains, his mother's eyes were twin slivers of moon. And Garatajik knew suddenly that his reasons for avoiding Mika had nothing to do with time. He loved the old woman. In all the lands west of the desert, he loved no one else. Perhaps he had loved Chindilan. Perhaps the smith's best friend, Lantor Hinjuman. But both men were gone, and that other—the true companion of his heart—was making east for Kasralys, and there was no one else who knew him, not one, save this hobbling Mika with her blade and bowl.

That was why he had never called on her, never sent word. If he fell, he would doom anyone he favored. Even now he was putting her at risk.

You're trembling, man. That has to stop.

He closed his eyes, tried to surrender to the joy of warm lather, sharp clean strokes. He did not succeed. He could feel the others around him— warriors, mother, monkey, dwarf. None of them were blind.

"The Xavasindran doctors who treated me," he said carefully. "I should like to thank them in person."

"Of course," said the Prophet, "but be wary. You know I do not trust these foreign doctors. From the start of our holy war they have been eager to advise us, to influence our choices."

"I will be careful, Mother."

"And the Xavasindrans are not the only Outworlders in our midst. Before your return from the east, my brigadiers conducted a man into my presence who called himself Eyelash."

"What a curious name."

"Eyelash Thruko. He was quite the flatterer. It was he who brought me the gift of the golden mattoglin, which the Brothers Hinjuman took from Ojulan, along with his life. Oh, he was *most* well spoken, this Eyelash. He warned me of the growing power of Shôlupur, the Scarlet Kingdom. He claimed there would be war between the Shôl and the Kasrajis."

"Not again, surely," said Garatajik.

"The man was an Outworlder," said the Prophet. "Not a Xavasindran— his flesh was as dark as yours or mine. But an Outworlder all the same. He was not aware that I knew it, that I had pierced his shadows. Of course Outworlders are blind to the spirit. Eyelash Thruko. He was false, false to the core."

"Did you execute the man?"

The Prophet did not answer. *Ah, you let him go,* thought Garatajik, *and you're still chewing the cud of that mistake. Change the subject. Cool her down.*

"If you think it right," he said, "I will kneel in the sun to honor my elder brother, just as I would have done at the Presentation, had I been able."

"That is a kindly thought, Garatajik," she said. "We will ponder it."

"Be my guide in this, Mother. I do not know how to make amends."

A soft chuckle from the bedclothes. "You will worry yourself sick."

"No doubt," he said. "Tell me, why have we come to Gathen?"

The Prophet bolted upright. The baboon gave a startled hoot. The Rasanga nearest her recoiled, pulling Mika away with them. His mother flung the curtains aside and stood from her bed, eyes blazing, hands closing on his arm.

"Someone spoke."

Garatajik shook his head. His mother leaned close, then closer still. Her necklace of dog's fangs smacked his chest as she raved.

"No one was to visit you without my consent. Not a doctor. Not a nurse. Not a bodyguard. Not the bedpan boy. Not the high legion priest. Not a Gathen whore. Not a stray Gathen fly. Those were my orders, my orders, but someone has disobeyed. Was it Thruko? How could it be Thruko, can he reach into my private chambers, where I dine, where I undress? Who has failed us so profoundly? When did you wake, Garatajik, and who has been whispering in your ear?"

"No one, Mother—"

"WHO IN THE REALM OF ALL THE GODS-EXCRETED DEVILS HAS BEEN WHISPERING IN YOUR EAR?"

"I smelled the creosote—"

"THE WHAT."

"—bush, the creosote bush. It grows nowhere else in such profusion. Nowhere but Gathen."

Silence. The Prophet straightened, then turned and stalked across the chamber. He mopped her spittle from his face. Of course there was a scream worse than the Sleepyhead's, how could he forget?

"Not Thruko, then."

"No, Mother, no."

"It could not be—not in the flesh," she muttered. "It was not yet autumn when he quit Eternity Camp. But what a stain he left. The tattlers, the spies."

"Spies? An Outworlder dares to afflict you with spies?"

She waved the question away. "We are riding to war together. You have never cared for this life of struggle, or how I must live to lead this cause. You think that prophecy blinds me. That I perceive the motions of the spheres, the fate of clans and continents, but miss the smaller matters. The disposition of my servants. The mood of my sons."

"I think no such thing, Radiant Mother, I—"

"Man of science. Student of nature and its laws." She crossed the chamber again and stood over him, hands in fists. "What good has it done you, Secondborn? Have you ever stopped to consider? What good has it done a living soul?"

I found a cure for the World Plague. He dared not say it. Not to her, not to anyone.

"Tell me, scientist," she said, "what do you know of the Suzruk Blight?"

Suzruk. Suzruk. "I'm not—or rather—is it a beetle?" he stammered.

"Grub, a grub. A wormy grub." She spat the words, looking him up and down. "A canker. A pest that withers crops. Broad beans, wax beans, yams, potatoes. More people—more of your own people—have died of it than at the hands of the Važeks, but I do not suppose it factored in your studies. Never mind, I will teach you. *Suzruk*, from Kasraji *sazisrk*, executioner. Oh yes, it leaves death in its wake, but it is very colorful, very fine to behold. Deceitful, like so much of nature. It would be better for Urrath if we snuffed it out."

Terror, instant and absolute. Once again, he had missed the obvious. She wanted to kill him after all.

"It has just one use, suzruk," she went on. "Oh, not for many. Not for one soul in a million. But the great seers of Urrath have always known. Dry the insect in the sun. Grind to powder, inhale through the nostrils, or infuse with tobacco and smoke. Do you know what follows?"

Garatajik bit his lips. Nothing to be gained by speaking. Much to be lost.

"You think I will say that it brings on my visions," she said, derisive. "That is not it at all. Minor sorcerers, mystics, village conjurers: let *them* reach for transcendence with a drug. Let *them* swoon and thrash and stutter. I am no such fool. I have no need of a drug to show me the Mountain of the Gods, son of mine. I live there. I walk with the immortals day and night, instrument of their pleasure, prisoner of their truths. The suzruk powder brings me back to earth for a time. It mutes the roar of Prophecy. It is the weight I tie to my ankles, that I may descend and speak as others do."

She drugs herself into sanity. He stared, forgetting to breathe. *Gods above, can we increase the dose?*

"You never told me," he whispered at last.

"I am telling you now," she said. "And I will tell you a second thing: my eyes do not fail me, when I return to earth."

"I never supposed—"

"You went east to complete your studies, Garatajik. We were proud of you. It was ever as the stars foretold, that you should have learning above us all. But learning can go astray."

His jaw went rigid. He wanted to lie, to plead his innocence. But he knew the logic of her rule. Such pleas were a kind of confession. Those who uttered them were doomed.

"They have all been praying for your recovery," she said. "Your brothers, your generals, your troops. They have given alms to the Collector of Souls, made a circle of bonfires three miles in diameter to ward off ghouls, yatras, cannibal spirits. And all your people, Garatajik. They have come to a standstill, praying that you live. The Chiloto nation has held its breath. Even Mika here has fasted. Resume your work, Mika dear, time is short."

Garatajik had never felt less a Chiloto. He loved the clan neither more nor less than other clans, although he had studied its history and knew what it had survived. It could not claim him, all that suffering, all that death. A change had taken hold and he was powerless against it. He had become a Kasraji, not by blood or citizenship but by the laws of the heart. This birth-family of his was an accident, the Gods' tasteless joke.

The Prophet stood with her back to him, gazing at the flickering lamps. "I will address the army," she said, "and tomorrow Jihalkra will lead them north to meet the host of the Važeks."

"Tomorrow?" Garatajik raised himself on the pillows. "Are you ready for such a battle?"

"I am done with old stalemates," said the Prophet. "Urrath is changing, the river of history is in flood. And my champions, my sons: they must be planted in the soil where their kingdoms will take root."

Garatajik's stomach gave another twist. *They must*, not *you must*.

It was time, of course. Her teaching made it clear. After the Presentation of the Crown the believers of Urrath must begin the Great Partition, the slicing up of Urrath into territories for her sons to rule. One by one in the years to follow they would all be shown their crowns, allowed to hold them, to read the name of the land of their future dominion. Never mind the other clans, whose eagerness to be conquered was presumably slight. Never mind that three of those clans were larger than the Chiloto; and of those three, two were powerful enough to drive the Army of Revelation into the sea. One almost had to admire her vision. Its supreme simplicity. Its indifference to fact.

"Our first duty, however, is to holy blood," she said. "The Abominations must be taken and slain."

"They must die in greatest agony, the monsters," he agreed. *Too eager, watch yourself.*

"Taken, tortured, expunged from memory," she said. "They must be given to the fire, along with any nation that harbors them."

"Yes, oh yes."

Mika drew her razor along his cheek. It occurred to Garatajik that his mother would sacrifice this old woman in the blink of an eye if it served her purposes. She would, if it suited her, have his throat cut and blame the old woman for her clumsiness—for ignoring his "twitch."

"The Hinjumans," he said. "Have you some rumor of their whereabouts? Some sighting?"

His mother hesitated. "You are keen for news of them?"

"I have . . . burned for it, Mother. As you say: they have shed my brother's blood. And you know what I felt for him."

"Yes," said the Prophet, "I believe I do."

Garatajik lowered his gaze. *Stop chattering, idiot! You're crossing an abyss on a bridge of straw.*

"They fled east," said his mother, "over the Yskralem and the Lutaral, and a rain of fire struck that country as they passed. We know for certain that they took up with General Tebassa, that slippery eel."

"You have a spy among Tebassa's soldiers?"

"We may," said the Prophet, "but this was another's spy, as it happens: one we intercepted on the way to his masters, and obliged to speak. From him we learned that Tebassa had given shelter to the Abominations, and the whole of the Seventh Legion marched south on the news. We massacred Tebassa's little army, and have collected a new stronghold in the bargain: the Cavern of the Owls."

Her own eyes became somewhat owlish, riveted upon him, unblinking. "Tebassa himself slipped away into the hills, however. Along with many of his . . . unusual guests."

Garatajik focused all his will on maintaining his composure. *Many?*

"The Twin Abominations eluded us," she added, "once again."

"The whole of the Seventh Legion could not apprehend a pair of deserters, eyestained and notorious?"

"They were gone before the first troops arrived—into the desert, probably, and the Seventh has no camel detachment. Nor are there camels enough in all Urrath to sift the Sumuridath Jal for two assassins who do not wish to be found."

"And yet you do not look worried, Mother."

"How good to know the truth is written in my features," snapped the Prophet. "I do not worry, no. The White Child has their scent now, and distances mean nothing to her. She does not move swiftly, our little girl. But she will find them out, though they hide in the deepest caves under the Nightfire Mountains, or the dry snows of Famine's Table, or indeed at the bottom of the sea."

"Pray, who is she, this White Child? You have mentioned her before."

"She is rage and retribution and hurricane and fear. She can speak to the ancient ones of the desert, the spawn of the Shroud, and they will do her bidding, which is my own. If the Revelation Army cannot find the Brothers Hinjuman, our Child will. But we have chatted quite enough, Garatajik. I wish to know if you can walk."

To the gallows? Garatajik laid a hand on his chest. "I have been asking myself the same question. Rising from this bed may be the hardest part, these stitches—"

"Yes or no."

"Yes, Mother. Briefly, anyway."

"Then finish his face, darling Mika. We want him looking his best. And you: bring his spectacles."

One of the Rasanga approached. The dark glasses looked absurdly delicate in the warrior's hands: smoked glass, copper wire, collets of wool to cut off light from the sides. He slid them on and was plunged into utter darkness, even the lamps reduced to pinpricks.

His thoughts went wild. The glasses were as good as a blindfold, and his mother's prisoners were always blindfolded on their way to the gallows. And noble prisoners were offered a shave. He was suffocating. His mother was toying with him. She had done so from the start.

Then he felt Mika's hand upon his shoulder. Mika, who had lived in this sightless realm twice as long as he had been alive. Mika, who would pass into a still darker land soon enough. She steadied him, drew the razor over a last bit of stubble: finished. He heard the click as she folded the razor, and the warm, wet cloth rubbed his face again, as in the days of his childhood, bathing him clean.

He pressed her hand with his own, felt an answering squeeze, and then the Rasanga hustled her away.

The next minutes were a blur. He was helped to his feet; his muslin was stripped from him; a rather funereal winding-cloth enveloped his torso. A heavier cloak enveloped him. Garlands of lilies and hyacinth descended on his shoulders, and the Prophet herself dabbed his forehead with honey, as one did with newborns. And corpses.

Why not an apple in my mouth?

He shuffled blind across the chamber, a Rasanga to either side. He could hear his mother walking before him with the baboon. Sliding doors, a distant brightening, the murmur of many voices. Someone guiding his feet into sandals. Then the Prophet, irritable: "*Yes*, right now, have we not waited long enough?"

Heavier doors, groaning hinges—and at last, a flood of daylight. Through the lenses it was muted and pale, but still daylight, thank the Gods. All the simple things one neglects to cherish, until the moment of their loss.

After the first dazzle he found that he could see. They had stepped out under the portico of the Traveling House, which had been erected on a bluff. The sun was high, the air hot and still. His elder brother Jihalkra was there already, tall and beautiful and heartless, medals covering his chest.

And below them, tens of thousands strong, stood the Army of Revelation. Silent, motionless, a sea of warriors blanketing the stark Gathenian plain. Three entire legions, possibly more. Assembled to observe an amputation, the Prophet's own flesh turned against her. The death of a blood traitor, her son.

Of course they were here. His punishment had to be witnessed, talked about, spread to every corner of her realm. No one could be left in doubt. Many had heard her famous claim: "I would cut off an arm for my people— cut it myself, with the arm that remained." Disposing of a son would be a simple matter.

"No gallows, Mother?" he heard himself say. "I expected a noose, or a broadsword and a basket. How are we to proceed?"

His voice so thin, a bird's voice, a sissy squeak. She looked him up and down, a bit cross-eyed and vague—perhaps the suzruk was wearing off. He wished for stronger nerves; he wished to curse her in a voice like thunder, a speech this multitude would never forget. *You cannot kill me. I am one of the authors of the Cure. I am the only member of your family the world has reason to love.*

"Kneel, Secondborn Son of Heaven."

Her voice blasted from her chest. As though the whole house behind her had spoken, and the bluff on which it stood. It rolled out over the legions and returned as an echo. Garatajik dropped to his knees. *Magic*, he thought. *How does one fight an enemy possessed of magic? It's not fair.*

Jihalkra drew his sword. Straight, simple, tapered like a blade of grass: a beautiful sword for a beautiful king. He raised the weapon above the throng.

Lowering it, he kissed the blade, reversed his grip, and offered his mother the hilt.

"Ah," said Garatajik, chuckling. "You'll do it yourself. I should have known."

She took the sword. Her eyes were locked on Garatajik, but he was not certain that she could see him, or anything in this world. *I do not ascend the mountain. I live there.*

Why not lunge? No one constrained him. The Rasanga would cut him to pieces, but that was going to happen anyway. Perhaps he would lay hands on his mother, one finger even, in the manner she deserved.

She rested the blade on his right shoulder.

"Garatajik the Merciful, Lord of Urrath, second fruit of my womb, delight of all my days."

Please, he thought. She moved the blade to his left.

"You who in two years' time were to behold your crown of kingship, as your elder brother has lately beheld his own. You who would then receive the name of that land the Gods have selected for your dominion. Hear now what they reveal to me."

I hate you, I spit on your prophecies. Say it, say it aloud!

"The Twin Abominations were sent to take you from us, as they did our beloved Thirdborn, Lord Ojulan the Fair. But you survived them. You have wrestled with the Shadow these thirty-six days and defeated it at last, and the Gods are pleased that you should have your reward. Come forward, children."

Garatajik looked wildly about. Jihalkra glared at him with unmistakable hatred. His mother's glazed eyes drifted over the legions.

At the foot of the bluff, a procession had emerged from the numberless soldiers. First a phalanx of pikemen in dress uniform. Then a dozen from the Orthodox Guard, splendid in their red sashes. And then, by the Gods, his brothers. Etarel. Satim. Geptim. Brapatim. Besul. Nasul. Pithtul. Ared. His eight younger brothers, the surviving Sons, the whole rapacious rat's nest together. They were carrying a wooden litter on their shoulders, upon which rested a small but elegant chest.

Drums played as they ascended to the Traveling House. The Prophet stood aside. A table was placed before Garatajik, and Etarel and Satim, the oldest of the eight, raised the chest from the litter and set it before him. "Open it, brother," whispered Etarel.

Garatajik looked at Jihalkra: the man was seething. He glanced at his mother: she was looking through him, at some world or future only she could perceive. They hated him, and suspected him of treason. And they dared not kill him, yet. He had to go on performing. He opened the chest.

The crown was wrought iron enfolding great teardrops of amber and opaltine, and a twisted vine of solid gold. It was no ancient relic; indeed he guessed it was fresh from the casting. A new crown for a new kingdom, at least in his mother's fevered mind. Which kingdom, exactly? He found the answer engraved in silver on the inner rim:

THE CITY OF KASRALYS AND THE TERRITORIES OF HER REALM

ভ

"You will make a fine guardian of Kasraji art," said his brother Jihalkra, expressionless. It was not, of course, a compliment.

"You will sit where the Emperors sat a thousand years ago," said his youngest brother, Ared, wide-eyed at the thought.

"It was not so long ago as that," said Etarel. "I expect our learned brother could tell you to the year, if not the hour."

Their voices came as if from another world. Garatajik was still on his knees. He felt like laughing, but he hated the thought of the cackle that would come from him. A sound of madness. The family trait.

"The Court of the Emperors still stands," said the Prophet, running a hand through Ared's curls. "And the White Stone of the Kasraj still looks down upon it from the Tower of Eroqas. But your brother Garatajik will not require the Stone. That we will remove to our own country, for Jihalkra the High King to wipe his feet upon, as once the Kasraj wiped its feet on all the clans of Urrath."

"And Garatajik?" said Ared.

"Oh, he will be at home in Kasralys—in what remains of it after the war." She turned him a gaze flat and merciless. "Garatajik, our scholar. How we must all revere him. But first he must help us take the continent."

A silence. Garatajik cleared his throat. "What small powers I have—"

"Put your crown away," snapped the Prophet. "What powers you have will be at Jihalkra's disposal, for as long our struggle endures. You are his first advisor, now, Garatajik. You will observe his progress—you, with your most *educated* eye. And you too will be observed, of course."

"Day and night," said Jihalkra.

"Let us break bread and celebrate," said the Prophet. "It has begun, our great march over Urrath. And where will it end for *you*, Secondborn? Can you tell me?"

Garatajik looked from face to face. *Where it will for all of us. Massacred by a united Urrath, contemptuous of your lunacy, your bloodthirsty dreams.*

"I don't—that is, who can possibly, of the several—"

"With victory," she said. "With the defeat of Kasralys, and your own installation there, and this crown fastened forever to your head. Do you understand, my obedient, my loving child? You are off to battle tonight in the service of your brother, and you will not leave his side until the war is won."

10. PARTING PRAYERS

"Slaughterhouse Clowns."

Mektu laughed, although his face was anything but mirthful. He was marching beside Eshett, chattering nonstop. "And they wanted our scalps, mine and Kandri's. Criminals, they said. I'll bet they've never heard of us, that they just saw two Chilotos and wanted to kill them on principle. Don't you agree?"

"No," she said. "Stop talking."

It was late afternoon; they had marched without a break for seven hours or more. But Jód had achieved his goal: they were climbing into the hills at last, the hills where Eshett would turn aside for her village. A beautiful cactus flourished here, pale green but crowned with waxy orange petals: Eshett called it flame-of-the-hills. The camels labored in single file; the way was very steep. Kandri blinked the sweat from his eyes. His tongue felt as dry as the leather-hard fruit he gnawed each morning.

You have desert blood from your birth-mother. Until now he had flattered himself that some of Uthé's toughness must have passed to him. Nonsense. He took after Sepu, his stepmother, who wilted in the sun. An hour ago he had remarked to the camel drivers that it was hot. They assured him he was mistaken.

"You're right," Mektu was saying, "who cares about the Clowns? It's the Prophet's killers that matter. Everyone knows they're out there."

"Everyone *will*, if you can't keep your voice down," said Eshett.

Mektu blinked at her like a newborn calf. "You should make the crossing with us, Eshett. We'd be safer. You could teach me things."

"I doubt that," she said.

"You teach Kandri," said Mektu. "About the desert and other subjects, Parthan ways of—"

"Kandri knows a few things already," said Eshett. "Like not wasting your breath. Water escapes on your breath."

Mektu shot Kandri a glance. "He's the one wasting water," he said. "Look at him sweat."

Kandri bit back a retort: once he began to light into Mektu he might never stop. *Wouldn't you rather stay with us?* The selfish little shit. What kind of friend would even hint that she should stay?

He gnawed his fury right to the hill's jagged peak. Here a gap opened in the rocks like a missing incisor, and the camels passed through one by one. Beyond, the boulders stood tall and close together, creating numberless paths.

Jód led them deep into this maze, winding and doubling. Kandri lost all sense of direction. The heat pressed down like a boot. But at least they were hidden: in that wilderness of rocks, the Prophet's death squads could have passed within half a mile of the caravan and been none the wiser. When Kandri shared the thought with Chindilan, his uncle made a face.

"I can't argue with that," he admitted. "Jihalkra never had but the one eagle, so we can hope no one's looking down from the skies. But the truth is I'll be glad to be out of here. Stilts betrayed us in a place like this."

After several hours the company passed abruptly into a large open space. It was a kind of natural amphitheater, hollowed out like a dish. Ancient cedar trees grew around its perimeter, stark and bent, a circle of witches in a gale. Kandri watched the drivers bend and touch their roots where they erupted from the dusty earth. As they had done at the Well of Riphelundra, they rubbed a bit of that earth against their foreheads, praying all the while.

Large as it was, the space was soon overflowing with camels, dogs, goats, and people. When at last everyone was accounted for, Ifimar Jód climbed onto a large flat rock near the center of the hollow.

Kandri felt certain an address was coming, but the Master did not speak to them at first. He stood watching the night sky, broad arms crossed on his chest. Then one arm shot up, and something all but invisible alighted near his wrist. It was Safiru, the pocket owl. Jód held the tiny creature close beneath his chin, stroking it and speaking in a whisper. He removed something small and well-chewed from his mouth and fed it to the bird. "Go, now," he said. Soundless, the bird leaped from his arm and vanished back into the night.

Only then did Jód look down at the company. "We have made a swift crossing," he said. "We will rest here until midnight, if the watch reports no danger. After dark we may risk a cookfire. See to the animals and drink a measure of water. Then sleep, and may the peace of heaven fill your hearts. All too soon your trials recommence."

♈

The drivers arranged the camels in a spiral around the humans, a wall of flesh within the walls of stone. There was no room to spread out. Eshett once more withdrew to the company of the woman drivers; Talupéké once more handed her weapons to her grandmother. The mercenaries, all leering smiles, studied them both.

They slept, first in stifling heat and then in shadows. But by the last glimmer of twilight Kandri saw a figure rise from the women's area and slip away among the rocks. He sat up; no one else stirred. He pulled on his boots and followed and Eshett seized his hand and tugged him deeper, headlong, running in the dark. They went a great distance, and for a wild moment he imagined they were eloping, just running off, to hell with the future and the past. Then she turned and her cloak was open and she growled into his shoulder, the words fast and imperative, but she had reverted to her Parthan tongue and he caught none of it, the only certain message was her touch, her limbs, the plea no one could ever fully answer, the need that was an end in itself.

☙

The dry wind moaning. The cackle of some distant bird. He lay on his back with Eshett's cheek pressed to his shoulder and her knees on either side of his hips. The stillness briefly perfect. No gap between their bodies, no room for doubt or fear. They were no longer two beings, no longer even one. They were something mindless and eternal, a desert stone carved by wind into a form suggesting life.

Eshett raised her head and sniffed.

"*Gamapindi.*"

"Gama—?"

She rose from him and moved in a crouch, making for one end of the little niche where they had fallen together. He stood up, alarmed. He'd brought no weapon. He'd not expected to go a hundred yards.

He began to follow her but she was already returning, pulling him back down, drawing her cloak over them both. She was chewing something. A wiry scrap of a plant that trailed from her mouth and tickled his chest.

"What is it, a root?"

She bit off a piece of whatever it was and chewed vigorously. "Open up," she said.

The plant was tasteless at first, but as he chewed his mouth filled with a sharp, cold taste, like a mouthful of snow and juniper. He gasped, and the feeling rushed to his throat, chest, fingertips. His muscles spasmed; his limbs tightened and twitched. Eshett laughed and he laughed, for the sensation was nothing but wonderful, and her kisses were like the touch of a sea-creature, sharp and electric, nearly painful, deliriously sweet.

Eshett, Eshett. Who are you?

The stars changed color. The spaces between them were textured like parchment; the hills themselves had a pulse. He watched from beneath her as she reached for those hills, or some space beyond them, one hand outstretched and groping.

Do you even know? Are you a mystery to yourself?

He sat up. Time had leaped forward; Eshett slept at his side. He shook her gently; they had stayed too long. What if Jód roused the caravan and they were nowhere to be found?

But Eshett slept on, and suddenly Kandri felt an overpowering compulsion to move. He rose and staggered toward the end of the niche where she had found the plant. He felt that his body had grown dense and elemental, that he was joined to these hills by binding energies from unthinkable depths; that his veins were continuous with the veins in the earth.

Leaving the niche he found himself atop a high cliff, looking out across a wide, broken land. Moonlight flooded it, making its pleats and cracks and boulders stand out like details in a woodcut. But something was wrong. He could see with arresting clarity, but he could not judge distances, could not determine where he stood in relation to the scene before him.

He froze. Seven creatures, moonlit, were clambering through the rocks below. They were ape-like, with hair in ropy tendrils and long fangs protruding from their lips. They had a spider-like way of crawling among the stones, using both hands and feet, gripping with splayed fingers and toes. He was immensely glad that they seemed to have passed the niche already and were gliding away.

Then the creatures paused, looking back over their shoulders. A pale light was following after them, and a moment later Kandri saw that it came from a girl.

At the sight of this new being Kandri was almost overpowered by fear. A young girl. Bone white. Bone thin. Long limp hair and a tattered gown that trailed in the dust. He knew the figure. It had the face of the Prophet—the Prophet before her gifts, before bloodshed and misery and magic. Before Revelation changed her utterly, forever.

The White Child. A demon, Mektu had called her. But even that word failed to capture the horror of this being who wore the Prophet's face, answered to the Prophet's will. She caught up with the spider-apes, and the latter chittered and groveled about her knees.

The Child stopped again, standing very still, and the fear in Kandri exploded. She sensed him. She was reaching for him with her mind. He fell back, burying himself in the shadows. The girl began to turn, and as she did so Kandri saw her terrible, beautiful eyes, coal black without iris or pupil, twin tunnels to a realm where death was sovereign, life fugitive and suspect, eyes that were searching for him, eyes that would never let him go.

A jolt, a gasp. He was lying beside Eshett beneath her cloak. She frowned and pinched him and told him to be still.

"A dream," he said aloud. "Oh blood of Ang, it was a dream."

"Was it?" she mumbled.

"Don't tease," he said, annoyed. "You shouldn't have drugged me, damn it. What were you thinking? Why did I—"

"Hush," she said, caressing him. "Hold me. After this it's over for us, fool."

Kandri made himself kiss her eyelids, but his lips were trembling. "We need to go," he said.

Eshett's hand slithered between them. She smiled. "You can't escape that easily," she said.

"Escape?"

Her eyes snapped open: jet black. No irises. Twin pools of death.

This time, he screamed.

This time, Eshett woke in an instant and clapped a hand over his mouth. *Nightmare, Kandri, nightmare, that's all it was.* And when he saw her natural eyes and calmed himself at last she agreed that it was time they returned.

☙

Back among the others he slept like the dead. But after what seemed no more than minutes he felt a toe nudging him awake. Smells of wood smoke and sizzling fat. The fire was some distance away and so hemmed in by bodies that he could barely see it.

"Midnight, Mr. Kandri," said his friend with the clouded eye. "Time to eat, then to journey. Leave our enemies behind."

The man was smiling, kindly as ever. *You*, thought Kandri, *are no killer, no secret fanatic. You're just a man who invited me to pray beside a well.*

What would it take for him to know, and not merely hope, that that was true?

"Go and eat," said the driver, and Kandri did. The meal was sumptuous—three dates apiece, hot broth with mutton fat—and when it was over Jód climbed once more upon his rock.

"Rest a minute longer in Ang's holy darkness," he said, "for there will be no rest for many hours when we resume. This night we will press east through the hills, and greet the dawn at the Spire of Atimaku the Exile."

The drivers stiffened, sharing glances of alarm. Their looks did not escape the Master. "There is nothing to fear in this country," he said, "and less for you than any clan in Urrath. Do you fear to lay eyes on an ancestor's house?"

Jód did not give them long to contemplate the question. "You may pray at the Spire's foot if you like. I shall do so myself. We will not linger there, however, but carry on at once onto the Marastiin Floor."

If mention of the Spire had worried the drivers, now they looked as though they had been ordered to beat their own children. "Many have passed over the Floor and lived," said Jód swiftly. "Dothor Spalak is one. I myself crossed the Marastiin in my fifteenth year."

The drivers could not look at him. Some pressed the ends of their scarves against their faces, ashamed of their terror, the tears starting from their eyes. *What in Ang's name*, thought Kandri, *is the Marastiin Floor?*

"With heaven's help," Jód went on, "we shall make the Crescent Palmeries before the ninth rising of the moon. And in the shelter of that oasis we shall slaughter our last goats and roast them whole."

There were some fragile smiles. Jód turned to face Eshett.

"As for you, desert daughter: the time for choosing has come. The left-hand path from this hollow descends to the great dust river, the Koeli Irga. Following it, you may pass unseen to the canebrake at Maskiar—if that is truly your wish."

"It is," said Eshett.

"Your path is your own," said the Caravan Master, "but I would tell you once more: no word has reached me of a settlement at Maskiar."

"What?" cried Mektu. "No settlement? She can't go then, can she? No settlement!"

He turned to Kandri with a look of panic. Kandri set a hand on his shoulder, although Jód's words alarmed him as well. He tried in vain to catch Eshett's eye.

"I passed that way as a younger man," said the Master. "I saw its emptiness for myself. Nothing lives at Maskiar save cane and bramble—and one grove of stunted trees, a mourning grove left by a vanished people, rising untended from the fen."

"My people are there, Master Ifimar," said Eshett. "We're Nine-Year Parthans: we don't stay longer anywhere, unless we're prisoners. By the time other clans learn where we've built our village, we're already thinking about a new one. And this is the eighth year. I can't wait any longer."

The Master nodded. "As you will, desert born. Will you accept my parting prayer?"

Eshett approached him in silence. Jód stepped down from the rock and laid his broad hand on her forehead.

"May the Shepherd of all true souls attend you. May you sow peace and wisdom, and harvest love. And may heaven bless your people in the hour of your return."

Spalak led Eshett to a nearby camel and unlashed the pack that held her meager possessions—meager, save for the jewel-encrusted mattoglin, the rough shape of which Kandri could just see outlined in canvas. She touched it, met his eye for an instant. Even now, heart bruised and body aching for her, Kandri had to smile. This woman from a clan of nomads was making away with the Prophet's treasure, the most costly and exquisite object Kandri had ever seen. That it had been taken off the corpse of the Prophet's monster of a son, Ojulan, made it that much sweeter.

"Jód's sending her off *alone*," said Mektu. "That's wrong, that's out of the question. We got her into this mess."

"Which is why we can't tramp up to her village with the Rasanga on our heels," said Kandri.

"No," said Mektu, "but we can keep her with us." He snatched at Kandri's elbow. "Eshett needs us, brother. Trust me. I know her better than anyone."

"The hell you do."

Mektu turned with a start. "What does *that* mean?" he demanded.

Kandri closed his eyes; he had very nearly broken his promise.

"Just forget her, Mek," he said. "She's better off without you, without me, without *any of this in her life*. Much better. Don't be selfish."

He regretted the final word even as it left his lips. Mektu's eyes gleamed with a rage such as Kandri had rarely seen. His mouth worked, as though he were about to shout an accusation in Kandri's face. But he could not do it. He bit his lips and walked away.

○ჳ

The drivers were all afoot now; the camels stood ready for the trail. Jód motioned to Ulren, who came forward with something ornate and lovely. It was a faska, very much like the leather water-sacks found everywhere in Urrath. But this faska was sewn with hundreds of turquoise beads, and even, to Kandri's amazement, shells.

"Palm wine for parting," said the Master. "And this batch is exceptional, made from the fruit of the great sentinel palms about the Fountains of Lupriz, which lift their fruit to heaven as an offering." He beckoned to Eshett. "Drink and engrave us in your memory, desert daughter. Who can say if our paths will cross again?"

Ulren brought the wine to Eshett, who took the faska in both hands. Her eyes passed over the crowd, and she whispered a few words in her own tongue; Kandri fancied it was a prayer. Then she drank.

"Eshett, I don't *want* you to go!" bellowed Mektu.

He ran forward and clutched at her waist. Eshett choked, spraying Ulren with wine. Jód whirled on Mektu, hands lifting as though to tear him to pieces, but Mektu only clutched Eshett tighter. "Stay with us, you have to!

178

You can't vanish, you can't toss me away like a bone! Kandri, tell her! She has to *stay!*"

Chindilan and Captain Utarif pulled him off Eshett, trying to muzzle his shouts. When Kandri followed, Mektu lunged at him, struggling in the others' grasp.

"You pig! You don't care if she exists!"

Eshett flashed Kandri an imploring look: *Keep away from him.*

Lamps were snuffed. Camels and drivers began to flow from the hollow. Mektu dropped to the ground and hugged his knees. The surgeon bent over him and shook his head like a disappointed schoolmaster.

"This one's nerves are permanently disordered," he said to no one in particular.

Kandri stepped close to his brother. "See the impression you're making? Get up now. Show them who you are."

His brother looked away with a sneer. Kandri held out his hand.

"There's no choice, brother," said Kandri. "We'll miss her always, but—"

Mektu leaped up and struck him in the face.

It was not a blow meant to break his jaw, but it was close. Kandri felt the shock of it pass within him like an echo along a tunnel. He was dimly aware that he was staggering, that everyone was shouting, that his uncle and Utarif were restraining Mektu by force.

"You damned walking miscarriage!" Chindilan shook Mektu by the shoulders. "You want to end up alone in this world? That man's your nearest kin!"

"He's a pig fucker!"

Flat taste of iron: Kandri's mouth was full of blood. The mercenaries were laughing with such pure joy he almost felt Mek had done a good deed. The drivers stared at him, whispering. *His own brother did that. Malediction, shame.*

"Drink this, it's antiseptic," said the surgeon, handing Kandri the ceremonial wine.

"Away now, to the road!" Ulren barked at the drivers. "Stop gawking. Chilotos will be Chilotos, after all."

"Do not fall behind," Spalak warned Kandri as he left. "In the dark the path is easily missed."

Mektu's face was creased with rage and despair. Kandri moved away and drank. The wind increased; sand and grit whirled in little cyclones, and the palm wine tasted of cat piss on his tongue. But when drivers, mercenaries, camels, goats, and dogs had all filed onto the trail, Eshett pulled Kandri aside once more.

He leaned into her, undone. Her cheek was wet against his own.

"Eshett," he whispered, "that scar. Tell me the truth."

She pressed two fingers to his lips. What if he behaved like Mektu? What if he begged her, forget your family, abandon them, walk with me into this furnace, this silent death?

"Be good to Ariqina," she said, and it was the first time she had ever said the name of his lover, his only other lover, the woman they both knew he belonged to body and soul. Then she drew him down for a last bruising kiss and was gone.

11. DARK HOMECOMING

"And Ariqina Nawhal: she wants a meeting too."

Lady Kosuda stopped in her tracks. "The doctor?" she asked, although she knew perfectly well who her aide was speaking of.

"Yes, milady," said Lisrand. "The Chiloto with the brilliant smile. The one who says 'Plague' and makes it sound somehow appealing. You've met her before, I think?"

"We've . . . crossed paths," said Kosuda.

She glanced back along the alley, which was narrow as a servant's passage and smelled of coal and incense and rotting fruit. Silence, peace: even the street dogs had called it a night. It was here, after missions beyond the city, that she typically parted ways with her company. At one end of the alley, under the dim flame of the street lamp, stood the carriage that had met them at the Flying Bridge—and which now, conveniently enough, hid the alley from view. At the opposite end was a plain locked door through which Kosuda often found it prudent to disappear. The door let into the kitchen of an abandoned household. From the kitchen, one descended to a wine cellar, thence an empty storeroom, and beyond more locks and keys, a second staircase deeper into the earth. The latter ended in a network of tunnels known to only a few dozen of the city's teeming souls. Kosuda could not eliminate her rivals' gossip about her comings and goings, but she could make it harder for them.

Take twice the care you imagine necessary, old Colonel Nefiru had advised. *You can step out from the shadows whenever you like. You can never step back in.*

Nefiru would be eager for details about their sting operation—although by the code of secrecy she herself had written, she should not tell a soul. Not even him, her beloved mentor in both statecraft and spycraft, the man who had groomed her for the post. She would tell him anyway, of course. Her successes brought him such obvious, if always understated, joy.

And it had been a success: her people safe, Ramu's treachery exposed, Shôl agents captured, the alliance with the wolves renewed. A triumph; but as with love or battle, the climax was followed fast by exhaustion, and the road back to Kasralys had never felt so long. When at last they walked under the Sky Gate they were all swaying with fatigue.

And there he'd been at midnight: Lisrand's office boy, the merciless runt. Laden with scripts, letters, notices, edicts, commands, the unprocessed discharge of three days of Kasralys business. The city cared not a whit for their fatigue.

"Can't this Dr. Nawhal speak to someone else?"

"She asks for you by name," said Lisrand. "It's underlined."

Kosuda found herself repressing a smile. *She wants to see you, that vision of a girl.* A foolish thought, a faithless thought. Kosuda already had a lover, and that was challenge enough. And what did such a request mean, anyway—or for that matter, eyes with a dancing light behind them, eyes in a gorgeous face? From what Kosuda had observed, this Ariqina was all business, had no friends or idle hours, could speak of nothing but sick wards and stomach acid.

Gods, but that reminds me of me.

"You have some unclaimed minutes in three days' time," said Lisrand, glancing over his ledger. "Fifteen, to be precise. And of course, there's tomorrow." He held up an empty page. "No appointments. But also, no leave for any of us. What's afoot, milady? Another mission?"

"You'll find out tomorrow. What does she want, this Dr. Nawhal?"

The First Marshal squinted at the doctor's missive. "Doesn't say. But she calls it *a matter of utmost urgency for Kasralys*—as do another nine I've seen already, I might add. But you'll want to answer the earnest young thing. You can't resist—"

"I beg your pardon?"

Lisrand looked up at her. He raised a small square of parchment. "A reply card, milady, with the stamp affixed. I've never seen you toss one away."

"Ah. No." *Blood of the saints, stop acting the fool.*

A muffled coughing reached her ears. It came from the carriage at the end of the street. Kosuda glanced at its dark shape and sighed.

"Give me three minutes," she said.

✲

The carriage driver lowered the footstool as she approached. Kosuda opened the door and climbed into the darkness and sat on the crude wooden bench. The man across from her shifted in his chains. Just the two of them, as it had been by the river. But that was where the similarities ended.

"What did you mean, 'There's a first time for everything'?"

The prisoner coughed again. Kosuda reached for the window and tugged the curtain aside, and lamplight fell on the rugged face of Ursad Ramu. He was cold, bruised, filthy, frightened. None of her people had touched him, of course; the damage had been done by rocks and ice, or by the Shôl agents trying to free him from the raft.

"They'll give you a draught of something when you arrive."

Ramu's mouth worked. His voice when it came was a barely audible hiss. "Truth serum?"

Kosuda shook her head. "Just a tonic for your throat. And to help you sleep."

"Your consideration is humbling. But what I should actually like is to see Palachim."

Kosuda grew still.

"Palachim," Ramu repeated. "My sister's boy."

"I know who he is," said Kosuda.

"May I see him, then?" asked Ramu. "We're quite close; he's more like a son than a nephew, and his mother's religious lunacy changes nothing."

Kosuda hesitated. *Would it change something if you knew Palachim was my agent? That we'd never have caught you without his help?*

"I will arrange a meeting, if you're cooperative," she said. "And you can start by answering my question. 'A first time for everything.'"

"I should have thought that was plain enough. Our city will be taken from us, Chancellor. Her luck has run out."

Our city! thought Kosuda. *The one you called a malignancy twelve hours ago!* But her face and tone betrayed nothing of her rage. It was a tool she relied on, this mask of indifference.

"Only a fool," she said, "would deny the role of luck across the centuries. But work and wisdom count for more."

"Very true," said the Ursad, "and our enemies are short of neither wisdom nor brute strength."

"Kasralys has gifted servants."

Ramu shook his head. "She has you. The plural overstates the case."

"This city," said Kosuda, "is a fortress like no other in history, anywhere in the world."

"It will be taken all the same."

"By the Shôl?"

"No, by the giant anteaters of Kinutuk. Of course by the Shôl. Who else?"

He had snapped out his answer with unusual haste. *Ah, who else indeed?* thought Kosuda. *Is that a question you're keen to avoid?*

"And how will the Shôl accomplish this miracle?" she asked.

"Either through a campaign of merciless starvation, or by a blow so swift that we are felled before we know we've been struck."

Kosuda shook her head. "An assault will simply founder against our defenses, which are impregnable. The fighting force does not exist that could drive us back within the confines of the city. But even if it did, we would exact such a terrible price in our retreat that the invaders would wish they had never heard of the Seventh Realm. And the waiting to follow? All to our advantage. While they camp broken and bleeding on a plain stripped bare, we will be here above them, untouchable, dining on beef and mutton and good Kasraji grains from our stores. And if they persist beyond a single season, our allies from the east will march to our aid, as they have done for centuries."

"Not out of love," said Ramu.

"Out of love, sometimes," said Kosuda, "but always with the knowledge that Shôlupur unchecked would be a menace to all Urrath, and that Kasralys is their sole defense against that day."

"Shôlupur also claims the mantle of protector of Urrath."

"Says the man who insists he has never set foot in the Scarlet Kingdom."

"If you ignore my warning, Chancellor," said Ramu, "it will be to your everlasting shame."

Kosuda closed her eyes. She didn't care for him to know it yet, but she was not about to ignore his warning. On the long ride home her thoughts had turned a corner. It could happen. Shôlupur could be that tragically stupid: to throw away its wealth, its standing in Urrath, the lives of its soldiers. And while of course they would never take the Invincible City—*that* idea remained a fantasy, a farce—they could wound her, leave her scarred and impoverished for a generation. Such horrors as that *could* come to pass. Indeed they had, many times before.

Say for a moment that it was true. The Scarlet Kingdom was mobilizing, preparing for a siege, transforming their country, once again, into an engine of war. A doomed choice, and therefore indefensible. But it begged one overarching question: *Why?*

Yes, the Shôl were their greatest rivals—and, as they never let the world forget, the first realm to break free of the old Empire of the Kasraj. But they were also a practical people. They did not worship the sword, like the Važeks, or hang on the words of deranged clerics, like the Chiloto. They were capable of examining the might of Kasralys and drawing the sensible conclusion. The only conclusion. The city could not fall.

What, then, could drive them to such madness?

"Let us speak again of the Prophet," she said.

Ramu's gaze sharpened. His lips quivered, forming words he seemed too startled to speak. *I've got your full attention, suddenly*, she thought.

"The Prophet?" he said at last. "That isn't possible. The Chilotos are too far away."

"What isn't possible?" she asked.

Ramu's breathing appeared troubled. He stammered: "You don't truly— you can't have reason to think that *she*—"

"I am not the one being interviewed," said Kosuda. "Tell me what you know, Ursad. Before sunrise, preferably."

"An assassination," said Ramu. "When I was tied to that raft, you told me there had been an *assassination*. In her family, the Prophet's family. Oh my dear Gods."

He clutched her arm. She did not resist him; he was chained after all. His flesh was trembling and cold.

"You people," he whispered. "You schemers and spies. Was it you? Did you send killers across the continent, to kill one of her own?"

"Of course not."

"For the love of Ang, woman, tell the truth!"

"The Kasraj dispatched no one to strike the Prophet, nor ever has," said Kosuda. "Why in the Nine Pits would we provoke that madwoman, or her enormous clan?"

"Why would you? That's right, why would you?" Ramu sat back, but his eyes darted ceaselessly: window, ceiling, floor. He was struggling to calm himself, with limited success.

"Ursad," she said, "someone got to you before us, didn't they?"

"Like hell they did. Apart from your abuse, I've been just fine, thank you very—"

"Tell me about Eyelash Thruko."

Ramu grew absolutely still.

"I know you lied about him on the raft," said Kosuda. "I know he's more to you than just a rumor."

Their eyes met. Slowly, Ramu shook his head.

"He went west for a time," she said, "perhaps to the Chilotos, and the court of their Prophet. But we know he has returned to Kasralys. Is he the one who turned you traitor? Did he coerce you, threaten your family?"

Another shake. Ramu flexed his shackled hands.

She hesitated, then made a swift decision and plunged on. "We have drawn a net about Thruko. It will not be long before we close it. We will have the man, as a prisoner or a corpse. He will have no further power over you or your loved ones. But I have never seen his face or learned his purpose. Is he an agent of the Shôl like yourself? Or does he serve some other master? Tell me, Ursad. Tell me who he is."

Ramu's eyes shifted away.

"What I can't work out," said Kosuda, fighting rage again, "is what you think to gain by resisting me *now*. At the river's edge you hoped for rescue. But now? What hope is left? A prisoner exchange? Never. You will die of old age first. Those men we fought by the river?" She shook her head. "Gone, erased. They never saw you. Indeed, they never reached the river at all. The whole party died somewhere between the frontiers of Shôlupur and the Martyrs' Plateau."

"But that is false," he said.

"It is the truth as your King Grapahir will hear it."

He lunged at her, chains snapping taut. "Never," he hissed, "call Grapahir my King."

Kosuda regarded him carefully. "Grapahir rules the Scarlet Kingdom outright," she said. "When you betray our secrets to the Shôl, it is him you serve."

"What in the devil's red bowels do you know?"

"Less than I need to," she admitted. "Less than I will, when this masked dance of ours is over, and you say something true."

"The insults you ply me with," he snarled. "Perhaps your kind can't even feel them."

"My kind? My kind?"

"Not women who love women," said Ramu, with an impatient sneer. "I mean Mapuris, Chancellor. Your foundling clan. Exiles, castaways—foreign features, foreign skin. You were tossed on Urrath's shores in untidy batches, like waifs to the almshouse."

"I think your mind is wandering," she said.

"You do not fit here," he said. "You will *never* fit, no matter how much of your life's blood you pour on the altar of this city. Don't you see that—you, of the famous intellect? You're not one of us, and behind the smiles we despise you for it."

"Who despises me?" said Kosuda. "Not you. I'd have noticed."

"Oh, but I do. I'm a true son of the Realm. Tell me this: where is the name 'Kosuda' in the Annals of the Imperium? Where are the records of your family's deeds, or the deeds of any of your clan? Is there a foundation beneath your feet, Mapuri? No, there is nothing. There are beggars of older lineage, more beloved by us all."

"Ramu," she said, "what is happening here?"

"There are public lavatories that have served the realm longer than your clan."

Kosuda sat back. Nothing in her face or voice betrayed her feelings. And yet she was in desperate shock. Ramu was a proven traitor, but never in ten years had he revealed a whiff of such loathing. How had he kept it from her, and from all her agents? How had it never surfaced in the hundreds of hours they had watched him?

"Come clean to me," she said quietly. "I swear by Almighty Ang, it's the best path that remains."

"You swear," he mocked.

"And whatever my post and honor allow me to do for you, I shall."

Ramu looked out the window. A little three-note chime was ringing faintly in the distance: a moss wagon, alerting the cloistered Aburi Brethren that their meditation drink was on the doorstep.

Skies of fire, it's almost dawn.

"You like to say that it's your job to keep the city safe," said Ramu. "I have a word of advice, Chancellor. In the spirit of *coming clean*."

He beckoned. They leaned closer together. Ramu brought his lips to her ear.

"Find another job."

He turned back to the window and would answer no more questions, not even with grunts. Shaken, Kosuda stepped out of the carriage and closed the door. Ramu was afraid, that was certain. But not of any punishment she might inflict.

Lisrand was still waiting with his cursed scripts. "Give Ariqina Nawhal her appointment," she said, marching up to him. "And have Palachim in my chambers by eleven. I want to prepare him to face his uncle."

"Best make it noon, milady. Your breakfast with the Grand Illim—"

"Oh Gods, breakfast. Can you get me out of it?"

Lisrand stopped, and Kosuda felt a twitch of guilt. They were both road-filthy and stank of sweat and horses. They'd eaten nothing since dusk. Here in Calspath District the taverns were shuttered and the windows black, and it was a long walk to Stone Gate or Lurusk with their all-night kitchens for the sunless shifts. Lisrand would go to bed hungry, or else gnaw something dry and cold in his garret above the counting house. If she ever let him finish.

"Breakfast it is," she said. "Go on, what else?"

Lisrand rifled through the remaining forms. "Brawlers at the lakefront: someone's barge has been sunk. A child gone missing, last seen at Wulfair Court."

"Get someone on that. Goncu, maybe. She lives nearby."

"I'll see to it, milady. Let me see . . . an historian at St. Aburik's wants to meet you *instantly*. Seems he's discovered a manuscript that will 'shake the world.' Quite an old fellow; I've seen him about. Palachim studies with him, in fact."

"Have Palachim find out what he wants."

"As you will," said Lisrand. "Here's a winner, now: Lord Isar accused of dalliance with the Lady Orm, lately engaged to Isar's cousin. She entreats you to prevent a duel."

Kosuda leaned against the sooty wall. *Four days*, she thought. *I've been gone just four blessed days.*

Lisrand went on, relentless: "A lewd play, hairy chests and such . . . tax collectors chased out of Coppersmith's. The devil spotted on the Imperial Heath."

"Shall we bring him in for questioning?"

"No editorials, milady, we're almost through. Your godson's naming rites tomorrow evening at Yafnar Tower. Dog fights in Calspath. A priest murdered by his choir master. A suicide—"

Lisrand stopped again. Kosuda looked at him, alarmed. This time his silence was utterly different. He stared at the card, then lifted his eyes to his mistress, lost.

"It's Palachim," he said. "Palachim has hanged himself, in the stables."

છ

An hour later, daylight rising and the horses stamping and nickering for food, the body was still there among the rafters, sixteen feet above the floor.

The stables stood at the center of the Imperial Riding School, where young Palachim had trimmed hooves and carted manure since childhood. Where his father kept both war and racing steeds, and made equestrians of Kasraji youth. Where neither Kosuda nor Lisrand had jurisdiction—at least not public jurisdiction, the sort they could own up to, the sort needed before their agent could be lowered to the ground.

Heartsick, Kosuda and Lisrand sat outside the tack room, sipping coffee provided by the grooms, glancing at the stables across the hay-strewn yard. A lone constable stood there, dispatched to the crime scene by the Gods knew whom. Above and behind him dangled Palachim, riding pants streaked with shit and his head bent at a sickening angle against a beam.

The constable looked as restless as they were. The Master of Deeds had still not arrived, and it was he who would have to sign the death certificate, checking the appropriate boxes:

☒ UNWITNESSED
☒ SOLITARY
☒ SUICIDE

Kosuda knew the form all too well. Every unnatural death in the city generated such a form, and every form passed through her own hands as well, before entering the sad files of the Rigat.

"It must have been quick," said Lisrand.

"Yes," said Kosuda. "That's one mercy."

For Palachim had not hanged to death, not exactly. The noose was tied to a rope-and-pulley device used for lifting hay into the loft. The rope's other end had been hitched to a Lañatu war horse. And there, beneath the boy's swaying feet: a bullwhip.

Kosuda could see it all, plain as a diagram. The lash of the whip, the charging animal. Palachim wrenched skyward, probably dead of a snapped neck before he reached the beam. Certainly dead when his skull struck oak.

The horse had broken free, but the body had not fallen. The pulley wheel turned in one direction only. A safety mechanism. Kosuda pinched her eyes shut.

"He had a lover, didn't he? That dance instructor?"

"Yes," said Lisrand, "although he claimed it was nothing serious. The woman's married but her husband's long since made it clear he prefers the company of men. We had eyes on them, of course."

Kosuda tossed her coffee in the dirt. What a ghastly tangle. Ramu, a spy for Shôlupur. His nephew Palachim, dead in the stables behind the school where he worked as a cover for his own spying life—the life to which Kosuda herself had recruited him. And the boy's parents: colorful, divorced. The father a Sartaph and a commander in the Iron Legion. The mother a religious mystic. Both born to wealth so assured, so guaranteed to continue, that they hardly seemed aware they possessed it.

Where the hell was the Master of Deeds? The delay was galling, unworthy of the boy's dedication. To say nothing of his beauty: a lean, strong youth of nineteen, black hair woven into braids like mooring lines. A face one smiled to remember, the face of a teacher who would also, always, be a student, in love with the next thing to learn. A face that, whenever it turned to you, brightened with interest and sympathy.

A face like Ariqina Nawhal's.

That he was also an agent of the Chancellor's Inspectorate was something they could never tell a soul. The Inspectorate was tiny compared to the Imperial Clandestine Service, the realm's famed and ancient guild of spies. It got by on a fraction of the latter's funds and could not petition the Rigat for more. But the Inspectorate had a singular advantage: scarcely anyone knew it existed. The Grand Illim's father had authorized its creation just twenty years earlier, in part to keep an eye on the Clandestine Service itself. The old monarch had well understood that a house of spies will go its own way if not watched—and that the watchers must be few if he was to control them.

Few, and utterly anonymous. Even in death Kosuda's agents could not be thanked.

At least she could be honest with the man beside her. "When I cut him from the Martyrs' Plateau operation," she said, "it was not just because of his uncle."

"Had you lost faith in Palachim?"

"No," she said. "I had lost faith in my decision to recruit him. Something is off about that whole family, Lisrand. I can't put my finger on it, but it's there." She sighed. "I was going to ask for his resignation. Give him back a normal life. It was not too late for him."

Except, of course, that it was. They both looked at the body. Still as an icicle. Mobbed by flies.

"Was Palachim faithful to his dance instructor? Was he sleeping with anyone else?"

Lisrand shifted uncomfortably. "After the Winter Ball—"

"Besides her," said Kosuda. "I know about her."

Palachim had left the Winter Ball with the young woman who had played Kosuda's double on the Martyrs' Plateau, the woman who had just managed to control her coal-black horse. Both had reported the liaison promptly. Kosuda was happy for her agents to bed one another—post-coital confidences were best kept in-house—but she imposed one absolute condition: they must tell her. In her mind she could still hear Colonel Nefiru's warning her from his sickbed:

Nothing in their souls, nothing cherished like a secret flame, must be hidden from you. Not if you are to protect them, and make of them true servants of the Realm. Have no doubt, Kosuda: someone else will learn of that cherished thing and use it to destroy them.

Kosuda trusted Nefiru, in this as in all matters. Even an invitation, even a wink between two agents had to be reported. She did, however, allow them to choose between reporting to her and Lisrand. Nearly everyone, for some reason, chose Lisrand.

"They broke it off after a fortnight," said her aide. "There's been no one else but the dancer, unless he's been sly as a weasel about it."

"Who else did Palachim spend his time with, in recent months?"

Lisrand scratched his beard. "His crazy mother, whenever she summoned him. Our own combat instructors. He'd made great strides as a swordsman. And that professor I mentioned—the historian with the world-shaking manuscript. Palachim was keen to develop his mind."

"Talk to that professor," said Kosuda. "If anything whatsoever feels odd, bring him to me."

Her aide nodded. "There's Palachim's father as well," he said. "The Sartaph. A prize pig if I may say so."

"You may not," said Kosuda. "Not to anyone but me. That prize pig wants to be Secretary of War, if not First Counsel to His Serenity."

"He was vile to his son," said Lisrand.

"So he was. The Sartaph never forgave Palachim for *settling*—his word—for the post of schoolmaster."

"Is that what stood between them?" Lisrand puckered his lips. "The old heel might have whistled another tune if he'd known his boy was an agent of the Inspectorate, fighting day and night for the Kasraj. Just how bitter a feud are we speaking of, milady?"

"Quite," said Kosuda. "They weren't on speaking terms. But Palachim wasn't about to kill himself over it."

"He killed himself for *something*, though," said Lisrand. "That means of death took preparation, brooding over."

She nodded. A cavernous yawn overtook her. "You should go home, milady," said Lisrand.

"One of us must stay here, no matter how it looks."

"You've not slept in days."

She smiled bleakly. "Have you?"

"Yes, on the journey out," he said. "I have that gift, you know. Sleeping afoot, sleeping on horseback."

"And cats can dance. I doubt you ever closed your eyes."

"You look a fright, milady. Hair is like a raven's nest."

"Flatterer," said Kosuda. "But we shouldn't both linger here, true enough. No way to explain such . . . interest."

"I'm glad to hear you say it."

"Which is why you're to go home."

"Milady, no! It's the Chancellor's presence that will raise eyebrows, not her aide's."

"Are you giving orders now, Lisrand? Were you promoted without my knowledge?"

"I was not," he said, "and thus His Serenity is not expecting *me* for breakfast within the hour."

Oh, pissing witches!

"You'll need most of that time just to reach the palace, and beforehand—"

She gestured for silence. He was right again: beforehand she would have to dress for court. The death of a teacher, a stable hand—someone she could not even admit to knowing—was no excuse for filth in the presence of the Grand Illim.

They stood up. Lisrand took no pleasure in his logical victories, and that was something she admired: pettiness was alien to the man even in jest.

"This shit is liquid rust," he said, scowling into his cup. "Gods, for three minutes at Cathqimar House."

"Coffee with a chaser of brandy," said Kosuda.

"Best idea in days."

"This dancer," she said, "had she spurned him recently?"

Lisrand shook his head. "We left them happily in bed four days ago."

"I want you here when they cut him down," said Kosuda. "I want you to study him. Find some excuse."

"Certainly, but where's this going, milady? What do you suspect?"

Kosuda just looked at him, and Lisrand's eyes slowly widened. "You don't think it was suicide," he said at last.

"I think there's a great fucking hole where his motive ought to be. And there's . . . the other matter."

Lisrand mouthed the name: *Eyelash Thruko?*

Kosuda nodded. She too avoided speaking the name. "We're close, Lisrand."

"We've been close before."

"This is different. This time I can smell the bastard."

"The bastard still lacks a face and a domicile," he said, "not to mention a cause we're sure he's fighting for."

She snatched his mug, threw back his coffee like a shot of rum. "This time," she repeated, and started away.

"One thing, milady."

She froze; her aide's voice had changed. Lisrand toed at the grass between the cobblestones.

"Palachim's mother . . . well. She was seen outside the Orfuin Club."

"She *what?*"

"It was four years ago. We hadn't recruited Palachim yet. We hadn't even made contact."

"Outside? Tell me what in hell that means."

"We believe she'd just exited the club."

Damnation of all the Gods. The Orfuin Club. A marble monstrosity in the oldest district of Kasralys. Secretive, cloistered, its members rich beyond imagining. The lair of Sky Lords, sartaphs, vindictive generals, dagger-eyed dowager queens. And utterly opaque: Kosuda had yet to find a single informant willing to speak of what occurred within those walls. It was a black hole in the city. And her dead agent's mother had been inside.

"Lisrand," she said, "that woman is Ramu's sister."

"I know it."

"She is also a religious lunatic, a cultist. She chatters on about the Rain King and the Chiloto Prophet. She goes to court functions and speaks of the Opening of the Pits."

"She may not be a club member," said Lisrand. "She could have arrived as someone's guest, and left alone. It happens. We thought little of it at the time."

"Obviously not, since I'm learning of it now."

Lisrand straightened his back. "Milady, the old Kasraji families are always vying for invitations to that club. It's not all shadows and fear. They have fetes for children. Weddings as well."

"The old Kasraji families," whispered Kosuda, seething, "have produced three traitors in as many years—four, counting Ramu. And those are just the ones we've apprehended. What if she is a member? People enter that club and vanish. We don't see them again for thirty days, and when they surface it's on the far side of Kasralys. Or out on the Sacred Plain. It's a pipe, a rat tunnel. They can bypass our checkpoints, come and go from the city as they please."

"Yes, milady. But Ramu's sister's about as active as a barnacle. She lets Palachim run her errands, she won't even walk to the—"

"Stop fucking explaining why it doesn't matter. You're telling me now because it *might*."

"I'm telling you," said Lisrand, "because I've just remembered."

Kosuda looked up sharply. She knew at once what the admission had cost him. Lisrand had forgotten a matter touching on the security of the Realm. And Lisrand never forgot a thing. It was his greatest asset, his memory: "that inexhaustible glutton" he called it. She had never known it to fail.

"First Marshal," she said, "you're on holiday."

"If you want my resignation, you've only—"

"Am I speaking in code, Lisrand?"

"No, milady."

"Did I mention resignation?"

"No."

"Am I an idiot, to cut off my right hand? Save your breath: it's no again. I've worked you like a pack animal, and you've let me because you're a prince at heart. I'm the one who's failed."

She took a deep breath. In the silence, she heard the toll of the distant, thunder-deep bell in the Tower of Eroqas.

Breakfast. The Illim. Kosuda swore again. The Grand Illim was no emperor, but he was as impatient as any tyrant of old, and would break her to pieces if she displeased him.

"Wait here for the Master of Deeds," she told Lisrand. "Inspect the body. Learn the name of whomever they send to inform his kin, and who among the latter bothers to visit the morgue. And make a note of anyone who shows their face here before they take Palachim away."

"Of course, milady."

"You're right, you know. It's likely that visit to the Club means nothing."

"*Likely* is a fool's comfort," said her aide, miserable.

"At six bells we hold a council with all our people," said Kosuda. "I'll bring wine. You'll bring a written description of how, where, and in what manner of bliss you plan to spend your fortnight's leave. But Lisrand—" She leaned in, lowering her voice. "Start your holiday in two days' time. Tomorrow I must have you at my side."

He looked up, eyes gleaming. There was the fire she counted on.

"Tomorrow, milady?"

"Tomorrow we take him at last."

She left him holding the coffee cups, marched across the barnyard in the direction of the dead man, her true believer, servant of the city that would never cheer his name.

The constable watched her with a guilty expression, as though guarding the dead were somehow shameful. What accounted for such emotions? Failing the living: *that* was shameful. Failing those who trusted you to lead.

"Lady Chancellor!"

A woman's voice. It was another of her operatives, rushing in through the gate. She ran to Kosuda. Wordlessly, she passed her mistress a city form.

Kosuda scanned the report—CERTIFICATE OF ACCIDENTAL DEATH— and nearly handed it back to her agent, irritated. A mishap. This could damn well wait. Then she saw the name, and felt the hammer of impossible coincidence strike her full in the chest.

Palachim's lover, the dance instructor.

By suffocation. A chimney fire. Her rooms filled suddenly with smoke.

Kosuda looked back across the yard. Lisrand was watching her, reading her stillness. *You can't shield him from this. And you can't delay another minute.*

She thrust the missive back into her agent's hand. "Lisrand," she said. "Give it to him, and then clear out. Too many of us here."

She crossed the rest of the yard. No time now for the meditation that sustained her; no time to pray for the city's dead. Or for the Shôl agents, true believers themselves no doubt, whose lives had bled away into snow. Why did she do so, anyway, for every soul that left this world? The Gods were not waiting for her whispers. They would do as they pleased.

Palachim and his lover in a single night. It's you, Eyelash, isn't it?

Two years trying to corner Eyelash Thruko. Two years, and she still did not know his face. Or his voice. Or the master he served.

But she knew where he would strike next.

You bloodworm, she thought as her eyes grew moist. *Your games in my city end tomorrow.*

The constable stood to attention as she passed the stable door.

"Lady Chancellor."

"As you were."

But would any of them be as they were, ever again? In the gloom behind the constable, Palachim hung with lips pressed together and head to one side, as though considering the question.

12. FRACTURE

After Eshett's departure, Jód led the caravan east over a high plateau. The night was cold, the land wind-scoured and broken. The drivers marched in silence. No singing, as on other nights; the specter of the Marastiin Floor hung over them.

Often they crept in single file beside deep clefts and fissures, trying not to look down. In these places Chindilan began to stumble. After the first such mishap Kandri stuck to him like glue, ready to seize his arm. After the third, his uncle confessed that his eyes were troubling him.

"Why in Hell's privy didn't you *say* anything?" Kandri demanded.

"Because it's nonsense, that's why," said Chindilan.

"Nonsense? I can see your squint by moonlight."

Chindilan stopped squinting. "Nonsense," he repeated. "My eyes are dry, that's all. Stop hovering, boy. I'm on this lark to keep *you* alive, not the other way around."

"How long has 'nonsense' been making you fall on your face?"

"Since the salt-blindness in the Yskralem."

"Is it getting worse?"

His uncle made an ambiguous grunt, and Kandri winced. That was a yes.

As for Mektu, he had withdrawn from everyone but his camel, Fish, at whom he launched a quiet stream of invectives. Kandri kept his distance. His thoughts were still too tangled, and his jaw too sore.

As dawn broke the path began to descend. They found themselves in a country of undulating hills, metallic-gray and astonishingly uniform, like drops of quicksilver on steel. There was just one flaw in the pattern: barely two miles ahead, a great splinter of rock pointed skyward. It was a tower, straight and needle-thin. Even as Kandri perceived it, a large carrion bird lifted from its peak and flapped off to the north. The tower's shadow, like a dark blade, reached back for them over the lifeless hills.

Kandri turned to the nearest drivers. "Is that the place Master Ifimar mentioned? The Spire of Something?"

The drivers answered with clear discomfort. *Of Atimaku. Yes, Mr. Kandri, very famous, very old. Here before the Kasraj. Here before the Parthan Fracture.* But they did not like the Spire, and hid their faces from it as though from something terrible or obscene.

The trail led to the foot of the hill on which the Spire stood, and the agitation of the drivers increased. Strangely, Kandri noticed some of them lifting small stones from the earth and placing them with care in their pockets. *Lunatics. Next they'll be putting rocks in their shoes.*

As they drew nearer, Kandri could see that the only windows were a row of small round openings at the very peak, like a row of portholes. He could see no door of any kind.

"What use is a tower without a door?" asked Prince Nirabha, more to himself than those around him. "Strange, is it not? Yes, very strange and perplexing."

"Oh *rather*," said Mektu, in a pitch-perfect imitation of the Prince's voice. The mercenaries barked with laughter; even some of Utarif's men had to fight down smiles. Nirabha blinked at Mektu, confused.

Ripheem, his enormous servant, rolled up to Mektu like a boulder. "You will not mock my lord the Hraliz," he said.

"Isn't that what I just did?"

"Mek," sighed Kandri.

"I won't do it again." Mektu made sheep's eyes at Ripheem. "Not right now, I mean, not immediately."

"*Mektu!* For the love of Ang, can't you just be—"

Kandri broke off. Two camel drivers—his friend with the clouded eye and the woman with the amber nose-stud—were rushing toward them with anxious gestures.

"Please and thank you!" hissed the woman, glaring.

"You must not be noisy or frivolous," said the man. "Not here, not at Atimaku."

"I'll keep him quiet, and I'm sorry," said Kandri. "Tell me though: what frightens you? Is there a curse on the Spire?"

The two drivers exchanged the briefest glance, then hurried off without answering his question. The Prince and Ripheem drew apart from them as well, and Mektu worked his face into a caricature of the servant's long, doleful countenance. Once again there were sniggers.

Then Spalak appeared out of nowhere with eyes full of wrath. Mektu quit his act with a jolt and scurried ahead of them.

"Where's my Fish? I need a toothpick, damn it, a comb . . ."

The Submaster turned his gaze on Kandri, but said not a word. They marched around the dreadful Spire and carried on through the hills.

Some minutes later a voice, high and distant, hailed Kandri from behind. He turned—and almost cried out. A face, a face in one of the Spire windows! He pointed, and then dropped his hand even more swiftly. There was no one; the round windows stood empty, black.

But who had called to him? Kandri was near the back of the caravan; only a handful of drivers were behind him. "What is it, friend?" asked the Prince, glancing where Kandri had pointed.

"I thought—" Kandri stopped himself, frowning. "Did you call me, Prince? Did you say my name?"

"Heavens, no."

"I thought I heard a woman," said Kandri, "but it could have been you."

The young royal's voice was, in fact, more high-pitched than most men in the caravan. He looked at Kandri, thoughtful and perhaps disappointed. "Mr. Hinjuman," he said, "are you, like your brother, in need of someone to ridicule?"

ᚳ

The day crept by. Jód permitted them an hour under the sun-shields: barely enough to recover their strength. With the late sun hot on their backs they set out again, pursuing their own shadows east.

Spalak appeared again at Kandri's side. "Why did your brother strike you, before the Parthan woman left?" he asked.

Kandri was taken aback. He could not imagine why the distant Submaster would take an interest in his fight with Mektu, let alone seek him out to discuss it.

"Perhaps you wonder," the man continued, "if I am asking as Dothor Spalak, free man of the Sumuridath, or as the spy and servant of Ifimar Jód."

Kandri gave him a noncommittal look. *Hadn't gotten there yet.*

"I am mindful of my place," said Spalak, "but you need not fear that what you tell me will go any further. I noticed your conflict with Mektu long before you came to blows. And also your concern for him. There are few bonds more powerful than that between brothers, whose souls were forged in the same mother's womb. For good or ill, that bond will define you."

"Do you have a brother, Mr. Spalak?"

"We are not speaking of me. This Parthan woman, now. Or some prior lover. Or your mother's affection, your father's esteem. Or skill with arms or dance or music. All these rivalries are but phantoms, cobwebs to be cleared with one stroke of Truth's sword. Truth is a thing of iron, not of mist."

"You talk like the priest in my village." *Who I tried to strangle.*

"It was a priestess who opened my eyes to the world. Are you a man of prayer, Kandri Hinjuman? Do you have faith in the hosts of heaven?"

"I've been known to pray."

"To the Gods directly? Or through the intercession of she whom they call the Enlightened One?"

Kandri decided he was in no hurry to answer. Where was this interrogation going?

"Come, I am merely curious," said Spalak. "You strike me as a man of deep reflection. Does no part of you still revere your Prophet?"

Kandri's heart had begun to quicken. "She is *not* my Prophet. Not anymore."

"But you still recognize her power, I think. A power far beyond human."

"I recognize her desire to kill me, Mr. Spalak. And my brother, and our family, and our friends. To kill anyone who doesn't toe her bloody line."

Spalak's face darkened. Kandri thought he had given offense; perhaps a Submaster too expected the members of a caravan to bow and scrape?

Spalak bent and lifted a smooth stone from the earth. He placed it with care into a pocket of his cloak. Kandri decided to try again.

"What are the stones for, Mr. Spalak? I saw the drivers collecting them as well."

Spalak was not surprised by the question; indeed Kandri had a feeling the man had hoped to be asked. "Walk apart with me," he said, "and I will tell you."

Kandri obeyed with reluctance. He was confused by this new eagerness to talk. "Master Ifimar might prefer silence on the matter," said Spalak, "but he has not forbidden the sharing of stories. Not yet."

Another veiled swipe at Jód. Kandri looked at the hills.

"You must not question the drivers about Atimaku," said Spalak. "Their history is bound up with this tale, and it is a tragic history, and a burden. Do I have your word?"

Kandri shrugged. "All right," he said at last.

"Know then that we are passing through the ancient country of Ramis-ith, that once was prosperous and green," said Spalak. "Atimaku, a minor prince of this land, descended from the hills in his youth to the ruling city, and there became the lover of the Queen of Ramisith. This was no misdeed, for she had taken other lovers, and cared deeply for all her people. And the people loved their Queen in turn, and began to say that she perceived things to come that were fair and beautiful before others could do so, and so they called her *Sanulbithor*, Queen of the Dawn.

"As for her husband the King, he welcomed Atimaku. He was very old, and great of heart and understanding. He loved them both well, and did not begrudge the pleasure they took in each other, and they returned his love and were his champions. It was a rare time of peace in this country."

Kandri sighed. "Why do I have the feeling—"

"Because happier tales are soon forgotten, that is why," said Spalak. "One day a former lover of the Queen, whom she had passed over for Atimaku, took terrible revenge. He knew the Queen's deeper secret, and when the opportunity came he shouted it from a high window, and many heard before he was silenced. The Queen had a man's genitals, not a woman's. In some lands this fact could not have been turned into a weapon against her, but the folk of Ramisith worshipped an ancient God of bleak severity, whose laws were etched in stone. This God held his people like indifferent coin, without promise or covenant, and to defy him was to court disaster on a scale beyond imagining."

"Defy?" said Kandri. "Wasn't she born that way?"

"Such a birth amounts to disobedience. It is much the same."

"But the Queen—" Kandri frowned; this was hard to work out. "—must have had the same equipment during that 'rare time of peace.' I guess the God never looked under her clothes."

Spalak shot him a warning glance. "Do not make light of this tale. The priests of this dark God pointed their finger at the palace and declared the Queen an Abomination."

"Abomination!"

Spalak looked at him sharply. "Just so. The word has power, does it not?"

Now Kandri was scowling. Had Jód told Spalak everything about them? "Go on, then," he said.

"Abomination," Spalak repeated, "and thus unfit to rule. And the people were terrified. At the high priest's orders, they lay siege to the palace, and when the Queen tried to escape in the night they stopped her carriage and burned her to death within it. And her spirit, which had only ever been one of kindness and humility, rose in smoke above the carriage and declared that the gardens and vineyards of Ramisith would become as you see them—dust and sand—and that she herself would haunt the desert as its only sovereign. The Night Queen she would become—"

"The Night Queen?" Kandri had heard the name before. Eshett had spoken it, during her tale of the Sartaph who murdered his children. The evening of her strange, sudden trance.

"That is the title she claimed," said Spalak. "The Night Queen, sovereign of the desert, dead but undying from that night on, until the sins of Ramisith were all atoned, and a new age of plenty could begin. 'This is not my wish, but my doom, just as yours,' she told them, 'for I must witness all that is to come.' And then the old King himself came to the place where the carriage yet burned, and shouted in his heartbreak that the only abominations were the God of wickedness who condemned her, and his priests. And for this blasphemy his own guards turned on him and forced a scorpion into his mouth, and he died."

"Splendid, glorious, great," said Kandri. "And that's quite enough, Mr.—"

"At daybreak," Spalak went on mercilessly, "the people grew frightened of their own deeds, and the dead Queen's words, and turned to young Prince Atimaku to lead them. But Atimaku too had changed. He gathered the people in the city center, renounced the faith, and crushed a likeness of their savage God beneath his heel. Then he reminded them of a kindred clan, simpler and more loving than what Ramisith had become. No one had seen hide or hair of this cousin-clan for many years, but Atimaku said he would find them, and called on any who would seek a better life to follow.

"And no one dared. They were afraid to leave the comforts of Ramisith. The Prince told them he would wait for three days beside a rock north of the city, for any who found their courage. Alas, his fate was already sealed. On the first night he saw dim shapes atop a hill and thought his people had come to join him, but out of the gloom came a pack of famished wild dogs. The ire of the God he had renounced shone in their eyes, and they devoured Atimaku flesh and bone.

"On the third day some in the city had a change of heart, and went to join the Prince on his quest. They found the earth defiled with his blood, and though they wept they were not deterred. They raised the great Spire and prayed that Atimaku's soul might alight there and know peace. Then they went on into the north, seeking their cousin-clan. But whether or not they succeeded none can say, for the followers of Atimaku were never seen again."

Kandri sighed. Of course they weren't.

"Some say the Night Queen herself visits the Spire when visitors approach. As for her lover, Atimaku: if he lingers here, it is in agony—"

"Oh Gods."

"—for the dark God's fury burned so bright that even his soul was torn to pieces, and could not reassemble for the last journey into the arms of Eternity."

"Oh *Gods!*" Kandri could contain himself no longer. "What a nasty old fable. Why the hell did you think I should hear it?"

Spalak's gaze was severe. "It is more than a fable, Hinjuman. The Parthans say that the desert itself grows outward like a cancer from the place where the Queen was slain. I do not know. What is certain is that clans from one end of the desert to another pray to the Night Queen. In the east she has a mighty Pillar, more holy and enchanted than this Spire; indeed it is a wonder of Urrath. The stones some of us have collected will be placed at its foot: a stone from the Queen's native land, to ease her suffering in exile. You might wish to carry one yourself."

"Carry a stone across the whole of the desert?"

"Exactly so. Our camel drivers, now—"

"Hold on, let me guess," said Kandri. "They believe they're descended from this Night Queen, or her lover Atimaku. Or from the ones who built that ugly Spire."

"No," said Spalak. "Ramisith perished, and Atimaku's followers disappeared."

"Then who—"

"These men and women," said Spalak, gesturing at the drivers, "are the cousin-clan Atimaku's people went looking for. Do you see now why they are afraid? The ghosts of their brethren, who gave up everything to seek them and failed, weigh on their souls. And they fear that the wrath of the God who killed Atimaku is not yet spent."

"Joy to all the world." Kandri rubbed his temples.

"Divine wrath lingers about the Spire like a whiff of smoke, Kandri Hinjuman. Smoke from a burning carriage, a murdered Queen. Master Ifimar was daring—some might use another word—to lead these people here."

СЗ

By sunrise the gray hills were smaller and farther apart. The Spire of Ati-maku had vanished behind them, but the mood of desolation lingered. No one was immune. Prince Nirabha and Ripheem walked shoulder to shoulder, as though troubled by the same dark memories. The little surgeon muttered to himself, studying the camels as if expecting some calamity to befall them.

Spalak's morbid tale lingered in Kandri's mind. He was intensely annoyed with Spalak, and even more so with himself for being so easily rattled. All the same he had lifted a small stone from the trailside and tucked it away inside the calfskin pouch.

Just ahead rose the last sizable hill. As the caravan moved around its base the lead drivers began to moan. Before them stretched an ash-white basin of astonishing extent, beginning at their feet and stretching beyond the horizon. A harsh wind raked over it, flinging dust and grit into their faces.

Talupéké stepped up beside Kandri, shielding her eyes. "Why the fuck are we here, again?" she asked.

It was like the surface of some brutal, alien world. The plain was blanketed in tall, elongated rocks. They stood in lines straight as sunbeams, one behind another to the edge of sight. Most rose about ten feet tall, but a few soared to a hundred or more. No two were alike, and yet they shared an eerie, overall shape, which was of cloth flung over jagged pillars and whipped sidelong by the wind. Nothing moved, yet every stone evoked motion. Violent motion, irresistible force.

"The Marastiin Floor, Mr. Kandri," said the cloudy-eyed driver. "Now the hard times begin."

"Begin?" said Mektu.

He shot a glance at Kandri, wry but nervous. He had yet to say a word to his brother since his violent fit in the hills, but he had begun to walk near him again, and to eavesdrop.

Kandri glanced at the driver. "The rocks all face east," he said.

"Into the wind. Like us, Mr. Kandri. Grovel before your Gods."

"That's the spirit," said Talupéké.

Murmurs along the caravan: Jód was calling for their attention. When all eyes were upon him he bellowed over the wind:

"We embark now, and there must be no confusion. I set the pace. You will not lag. You will not fall down. You have one task before you, and that is to walk the Floor. Succeed and you will feel the favor of heaven, where no deed of courage is overlooked. But I warn you now: keep your chins raised and eyes forward. It will not go well for any caught staring at their feet."

He said no more, but marched straight into the forest of stones. The drivers hissed and whistled at the camels, and the whole company filed after the Master.

Kandri's first sensation was relief. The tall stones' shadows blocked the wind a little, and provided relief from the morning sun.

"I'm missing something," said Chindilan. "The Floor is huge, but there must be something more to all this bellyaching than that."

"Old man's right for once," said Talupéké. "You'd think we'd stepped into hell. What would these drivers have made of the Stolen Sea?"

"We've seen worse," Kandri admitted.

"'Chin up or else!'" Talupéké smirked. "Was that supposed to be a threat? March with General Tebassa for an hour and you'll know what a threat sounds like."

"I don't doubt it," said Kandri. But he thought it a typical, odd remark from Talupéké. She never missed a chance to brag about her general, whom she loved like a difficult father. Of course Tebassa was strong and fanatically determined, and the devotion of his troops was a legend. He was also paralyzed below the waist—never likely to march with anyone again. When he had ordered Talupéké to join the desert expedition, he had looked, she'd confessed, as though he were saying goodbye.

☙

The shadows were short-lived. The wind soon rose as well, making them blink against the flying dust and grit. The next problem to emerge was the footing. The wind had cut the very stone on which they walked into endless grooves, irregular in shape and height. Each step was awkward and hazardous, and as the dust collected on their sandals they began to slip. The camels bellowed, struggling for balance. The humans cursed and stumbled.

The first ten minutes in this washboard land were uncomfortable. The first hour reduced Kandri's ankles to throbbing misery. By nightfall, the caravan resembled a train of arthritic elders, hobbling to a silent melody of pain.

Eight days, went a sudden whisper through the caravan. *We will be eight days on the Marastiin Floor.*

☙

The Master allowed for little rest. By night they crept over the grooves by moonlight; by day they moved from shadow to shadow. Only at midday, when the stones provided no shade at all, could Jód be counted upon to order a rest.

Mirages danced between the stones: washes of blue and silver that could only be water, cool and life-restoring, fanciful and false. The wind moaned in ten thousand voices, each clawed from the air by cruel stone fingers. The voices never tired of their subject: nothing more than agonized defeat.

On the third morning the skeletons began to appear. Most were mere jumbles of bones, dragged here and there by wind and scavengers. But some were immaculate, seated with their backs to the stones. One held a shattered cup, another the bird-thin bones of an infant. Two lay embracing, skulls close together at the foot of a stone, fleeing the wind a final time.

It was a wind that had blown forever, Kandri thought, aware that he was flirting with delirium. A wind that carved rock like so much soap, etching the softer minerals away, leaving this fleet of tall, narrow stones to sail forever into the face of the enemy.

Like us, Mr. Kandri.

The midday rest seemed to end seconds after it began; Kandri had not yet managed even to unclench his jaw. He rose and pulled on his sandals in mute stupefaction, wetted his lips with water, rose and walked. *Your task is to walk.*

Away to their left, nine camel skeletons loomed out of the vaporous heat, nose to tail. The surgeon muttered something about "useful compounds" and made his way to them, clutching a hammer and chisel.

"Little fucker's brain is poached," said Talupéké.

"Bit of respect if you please, sister," said Captain Utarif.

Kandri agreed with Talupéké: the surgeon did look deranged, fussing there among the bones. Sun-maddened. Of course the girl herself did not look much saner, her face twisting now into a smile, now a frown, now a bitten-off, ferocious word that never quite left her lips. How close were all of them to the edge?

He watched the surgeon jam a long bone upright in a crevasse and begin to scrape it with his chisel. *Not that close, anyway.*

But in the night, Kandri stepped over the legs of a human skeleton and saw it lift its dark sockets in his direction. The move was barely visible, a finger's width, and the skeleton dropped its gaze just as suddenly, as though hoping Kandri hadn't noticed.

"Pitfire!"

Hands flew to swords, bows, machetes: his cry alarmed everyone near him.

"What is it, Hinjuman?" demanded Captain Utarif.

Kandri pointed wordlessly at the skeleton—just as Alahari's wide foot came down on its leg. No protest was forthcoming.

"Snake, was it?" said the captain.

"Snake?" Kandri was breathless and abashed. "Yes it was, a snake. A rattler."

"Walk clear of those bones!" said Utarif, waving, and the latter half of the caravan shifted a few yards to the right. He looked at Kandri over his shoulder. "Most discreet rattler I've ever come across. Nothing's rattling."

"But one damn fool's rattled," said Woeden Surk.

After that Kandri caught skeleton after skeleton glancing at him—him alone, no matter how far he kept from them, no matter how close the others passed. Sneaky, he thought. They were so utterly still, and then *click*. Tiny, deliberate movements that made his flesh crawl. He dared not cry out again, but he knew the others could see him jump.

Their gaze became a torture. He thought, *Why me, you grinning bastards? Leave me alone, I'm in a hurry. I have a letter for Dr. Fessjamu. Well of course you've never heard of her: she's a brilliant Kasraji doctor and you're just old bones. And when she reads this Cure she's going to make you scarce, do you hear, she's going to save the lives of millions of fine, fleshy men and women who keep their bones on the inside and don't leer without good cause. No, I won't be staying. Dr. Fessjamu is waiting and so is Dr. Nawhal, my Ariqina, and once I'm through those city gates I'll throw my blades away and be her assistant, her nurse, her cook, I'll wear a motherfucking apron and I'll never kill, never draw blood again, don't you wink at me you shits, I don't know you, I'm no friend of the dead.*

Then he looked over his shoulder and saw the ghost of the maniac, nodding and speaking to the skeletons, bending to touch their foreheads like a consoling priest.

○ঙ

On the fourth day a man broke his ankle. Jód had him tossed over a camel like a sack of grain. But first he stripped the man to his waist and delivered sixteen lashes. The driver wailed and shivered upon his knees, his torn back gleaming in the sun. Pointing at him, Jód turned to face the other drivers.

"His weight will slow the camel who must bear him now. This cannot be. If we tarry in this land none of us will survive it." He turned in a circle, raking each of them with his eyes. "The next to fall, man or woman, young or old, will be punished by our Submaster. Take note: Mr. Spalak's whip is laced with salt."

No one else fell in that crossing. They hurled themselves on, a careening battalion of the battered and lost. Chindilan swayed and heaved; the brothers had taken up position at both his elbows without a word. Mektu stared at the horizon, head wobbling, a crazed smile on his face. Kandri had passed beyond pain into numb surrender: from the thighs down he was another being, an animal whose limbs jerked and plodded with no instruction from his mind.

But on the eighth day they saw hills rising in the east. The drivers cried out, then squatted down to bring dust to their foreheads as they had done beside the pit. Jód paused, saying not a word, but when he looked back over the caravan his face shone with quiet pride.

℘

They reached the hills at sunset. The drivers were weeping freely, and some broke out singing in their secret tongue. Soon Jód halted the caravan and let them sleep through the night: a long, blissful sleep. "The Master is pleased, he commends your valor," Ulren shouted at them, making even this announcement sound like a scolding.

As he drifted off, Kandri mused that Jód's merciless pace had not been entirely senseless. They had flown east, made up for lost time. *And if we'd ever stopped like this, ever let ourselves collapse—no, not even salted whips would have gotten us moving again.*

The next day they walked more slowly. The hills were mild underfoot, and pale aromatic shrubs grew in the folds between them. Kandri's legs became his own again. He was very thirsty, for the water ration had been reduced. But he took his cue from the drivers, none of whom seemed concerned about water. As night fell the reason appeared.

"*Sharasúm!* Oasis, oasis!"

The happy cries came from the front of the caravan, which had ascended a high, round hill. "We must have reached the Crescent Palmeries," said Old Kereqa. "It is fifty years since I beheld them. I never thought to again in this life."

When Kandri reached the summit he felt a surge of animal joy. It was too dark to see the oasis in detail, but he could make out the feathery crests of palm trees, thousands strong, and the pinpoint lights of torches and lamps. There were scores of these lights already, and more appeared by the minute, as though night spirits were waking into darkness, opening their glowing eyes.

Other people! Kandri laughed at his own foolish excitement. He wanted to race down the hill and run between them, shouting, although he had no idea what he would say.

Chindilan looked at the brothers. "Your father used to talk about this place," he said. "It's an obligatory watering hole, no matter which way you're headed—although those from the west go *around* the Floor, unless they're stark raving like us."

"It's beautiful," said Mektu. "There must be girls."

"Doesn't matter," said Chindilan.

"Why not?"

Chindilan clapped Mektu on the shoulder. "Because, nephew, you look like a rat with scurvy walking around on hind legs."

"Chilotos! There you are!"

It was Ulren, caustic as ever. "Why are you always the hardest to find? Come along, Master Ifimar has something important to tell you."

"If it's important," said Kandri, "he should have sent Tana-Dog."

Ulren's face grew so tight Kandri thought it would rip at the cheekbones. He spun on his heel and led them forward, hands flexing at his sides.

They found Jód in a crowd of drivers and fighting men; Spalak attended him, holding a lamp. Woeden Surk and the other mercenaries stood in a cluster, looking belligerent as usual, now and then eyeing the women in Captain Utarif's unit.

Jód beckoned the new arrivals closer. "Chilotos," he said, "we shall part company here."

The brothers and their uncle froze.

"When we descend to the oasis," said the Master, "you will travel north along the spine of these hills, and thence to Abisthu's Land, as we call that country. You will go well provisioned, with camels and water aplenty. I will honor General Tebassa's wishes and send his nine soldiers to guard you. The mercenaries, of course, will remain with the caravan."

Kandri felt chilled to the bone. *What in Ang's name is he doing? Abandoning us, casting us out?*

Chindilan caught his eye, made a small, subtle gesture: *Tread carefully.*

No one, in fact, seemed pleased with Jód's pronouncement. Utarif looked astonished: clearly this was the first he had heard of Jód's orders. Spalak's thick eyebrows knitted in a frown. Even the surgeon was gaping, as if at some gross injustice. The camel drivers—those near enough to catch the Master's words—looked afraid.

"That is all," said Jód. "I will take my leave of you."

No parting prayer, no wine. Jód motioned to his deputy. "Mr. Ulren, you will supervise the division of goods. Prepare yourselves, Chilotos. In ten minutes we shall be underway."

"Master Ifimar," said Kandri, "why is this happening?"

Jód turned to him with narrowed eyes. "Because I command it," he said.

"We took an oath to obey you, sir, but—"

"Hear him! Hear the Chiloto!" snapped Ulren. "*'But.'* That did not take long."

"Now hold on," said Chindilan. "My nephew's just curious about your order, Master Ifimar. He isn't questioning your right to make it."

"That is precisely what he has done," said Jód.

"No one here wants to offend you, Master—"

Mektu started to lift his arm; the look on his face said *I do!* Eyes bulging, Chindilan slapped his arm down. The mercenaries leaned on each other, shaking with silent laughter.

"We don't know your ways," Chindilan went on. "All we've got is our own good sense. And we'd have died a long time ago if we stopped thinking for ourselves."

Jód looked long into his eyes. "You swore to their father that you would curtail their recklessness," he said at last.

"I did," said Chindilan, "and also to keep them alive until we found him."

"Lantor Hinjuman has a noble heart," said Jód, "and for his sake I will disregard tonight's impertinence. But hear me, boy—" He turned his sharp gaze on Kandri. "—I am not answerable to you, nor to any of your kin or comrades."

"I humbly beg your pardon, Master," said Kandri. Finding none, he swept his gaze over the rest of the crowd. "My burden is this caravan," he said, addressing them all. "Its welfare, its survival, the safe delivery of its wares. If I send for water, you bring water, not idle questions. That must be perfectly clear."

"It is clear," said Utarif, "and so is our promise to you. Obedience in all respects—save one."

Jód whirled to face the captain. The set of his jaw did not change, nor the line of his mouth. But the camel drivers around him began to back away.

"You are too eager to invoke the exception," he said.

Captain Utarif stood a head shorter than Jód, but his training as a warrior was written in his limbs, his whiplash glances, the very plant of his feet.

"I'm not eager at all," he said, "but I'm even less eager to die of thirst in these Ang-forsaken hills. That's bound to happen if we lose our way."

Jód took the lamp from Spalak. "I will speak with you apart, Captain Utarif. You—" He pointed at Kandri. "—come along as well."

He set off through the crowd of humans and animals. When Kandri started to follow, Mektu grabbed his arm.

"Stay here," he whispered. "Wait him out."

"The hell I will," said Kandri. "You want Utarif to speak for us?"

"Utarif's orders are to keep us alive," said Mektu. "If we stay with the caravan, he has to do so as well. Besides, all this is a trick."

"Why do you say that?" said Kandri.

"Because it's obvious, fool, just look at Jód's face. That man wants us dead."

It was not the moment of reconciliation with Mektu Kandri had hoped for. "Let go," he said, "and stop worrying yourself into fits. If Jód wanted us dead he'd kill us here and now."

"You can't be that dense," said Mektu. "Of course he wants to be able to *deny* that he killed us, so that he can stay right with General Tebassa. He's sending away *everyone* who might tell the General what became of us. And think of this: the Prophet has drugs that make you talk—talk yourself silly. Talk until you drop on the ground."

"Who gave them to you?"

"And other drugs to stop you from lying," Mektu went on, oblivious. "So what happens if Jód's captured, eh? He needs to be able to say he doesn't know where we are. If he kills us, he can't say that, because he'd know where we died, where he disposed of the bodies. No, he needs us to walk off and perish alone. And we will; we'll die of thirst out there, or be eaten by—"

"Let *go*." Kandri jerked his arm free. "Ang's fanny, Mek, your shit talk could fill a hundred barns. You don't know *any* of that."

Mektu glared at him, hurt. "I'll tell you what I know," he said at last. "If we leave the caravan, nothing will ever be right again. We'll regret it. You'll regret it. You'll see."

CB

Jód and Utarif waited with the lamp at their feet. As Kandri approached the Master's eyes were blazing. "Father of asses," he hissed. "You wish to know why I am dividing the caravan? Your Prophet's lunacy infected one of my drivers, enough so that he threw his life away in an effort to kill you."

"I noticed that," said Kandri.

"How many others are hiding in my ranks, awaiting their moment to strike you dead? Can you tell me? No, you cannot. And how by the flame-wraiths of Osheym are we to learn?"

Utarif crossed his burly arms, a smile twitching at the corner of his lips. "By drawing them out, eh? Making them think this is their last chance to strike."

"And failing that, to mislead them," said Jód.

"Mislead them?" said Kandri. "I don't understand."

"Be still and listen, dung lizard. You will *not* be going north as I announced. The minute we are out of sight, you are to turn and walk *south*, into the greater hills that edge the lathban, and thence to the hidden oasis at Weeping Rock. A mile beyond Weeping Rock is a crossroads, hard by Rav-ashandul's Wall. At that crossroads we will await you."

"Weeping Rock?" Utarif looked doubtful.

"A secret place," said Jód, "and thus likely to be deserted. Not so the oasis at hand." He pointed down the hill. "In the Crescent Palmeries there are bazaars and brothel-tents, games of dice, cock fights, traders in women and children. Also, traders in words: certain men do nothing there from one day to the next but spy on travelers, so that they may peddle their gossip to anyone who pays. Do you wish them to peddle news of *you*, Hinjuman? No, you wish to live. Despite evidence to the contrary."

Kandri's face was hot. He wanted to put Jód in his place, to speak of all the terror and treachery they had suffered in the last month alone. But he could not afford to provoke the man again.

"Prince Nirabha and his servant will go with you," added Jód. "They have nothing to do with your crimes, but the servant is a giant, and the Prince is—a prince. They are too strange, both of them. We cannot parade them about the Palmeries."

"So now they're my problem," grumbled Utarif. "Two more helpless bastards to keep alive."

"When a fool insults a stranger, it rebounds on himself."

Utarif snorted. "Maybe so. But those Imperials are still nothing to me."

"Imperials?" asked Kandri.

"Don't you know who he is, then?" Utarif gave a mocking salute. "Nirabha Ibru Ilasfar, Lord of the Citadel, penniless Prince of the Seventh Realm." At Kandri's blank look, he added, "That's Kasralys, lad."

"Kasralys! He's a Kasraji?"

"Your powers of deduction do you credit," said Jód. "But the captain is right: this Prince is not a man of great influence. The old royal families still exist in the Fortress City, but their power and wealth are gone. Prince Nirabha may be descended from emperors, but his only grand possession is his name." A look of slight contempt crossed Jód's face. "The man could not even afford his passage with us. He had to borrow the funds, and leave his escort—all but the one servant—behind with the general to work off the debt."

"And Tebassa won't make that easy," said Utarif. "But Master Ifimar, we're none of us desert born. How do you expect us to find this Weeping Rock on our own?"

"Do you think me a murderer?" said Jód. "I will send guides with you, of course."

"Meaning Spalak."

"Spalak?" Jód was abruptly furious again. "Why Spalak, by the blood of the saints? Why do you imagine I would send away our Submaster?"

Utarif raised an eyebrow. "I didn't imagine," he said. "The man just told me he'd volunteered."

"And I declined his offer. You will leave such considerations to me, Captain Utarif! As indeed Spalak himself should have done."

Utarif shrugged. "My mistake."

"I have chosen two guides already," said Jód. "Drivers who could walk blindfolded through the Khasabilari Hills. And your elder, Kereqa—she too has been to Weeping Rock."

"Decades ago," said Utarif. "She told me."

"You will reach the Rock in two days," said Jód, "and the crossroads the following morning. We will arrive before you, for although we shall rest awhile at the Palmeries, the path beyond is arrow-straight, while your own is quite the opposite. We will await you at the crossroads—through the day's heat, if necessary. But our lives are in peril too. At sunset on the third day, we go on."

"Why didn't you tell us any of this before?" Kandri demanded.

Jód's look was incredulous. "Tell Mektu Hinjuman, and expect him to be silent?"

"You might have informed *me*," said Utarif. "I can't protect these two if you won't take me into your confidence."

"And I could not have protected them if I had," said Jód.

"Why not let me worry about that?"

"Why? Why? Is there to be no end to this badgering? There is a traitor among us, Utarif! Perhaps more than one. And their target is about to vanish in the night."

With a rush of shame, Kandri understood how prudent Jód had been. From their first day with the caravan the Master had been obsessed with betrayal. Now at last they had a chance to flush their enemies out in the open.

"Only minutes ago," Jód continued, "Mr. Ulren reported that our trade wares have been rifled, searched—and not for the first time. Whoever is plotting against us is also a thief."

Utarif frowned. "That's damned peculiar. If something of value goes missing, you'd only have to search us one by one to expose the traitor."

"Unless the thief plants it on someone else," said Kandri.

"Quite possible," said Jód, "if their aim is to destroy our unity, and slow us to a crawl as we bicker and fight. The golden mattoglin you sent away with Eshett would be ideal for such a purpose. However did you acquire such a thing?"

Kandri took a deep breath. "We took it off the body of Ojulan, the Prophet's Thirdborn."

"I thought as much," said Jód. "One more reason for the Prophet to hunt you high and low. But of course that blade is a minor prize. The real treasures the Enlightened One craves are the heads of the Twin Abominations."

"And someone in this caravan's ready to die to help her do it," said Utarif. "How did the Prophet ever get her hooks in these people, I'd like to know."

"The reach of her vile words is strange indeed," said Jód. "Was it not your general's own man, sworn and seasoned, who nearly handed the brothers over to their Queen?"

Utarif looked away, brow furrowing. Jód was speaking of Stilts, and the reminder clearly hurt. Kandri too felt stricken. *You trusted him, didn't you, Captain? Revered him, like we did. Loved him, maybe.*

But could they be making the same mistake again? Kandri had been preoccupied with the thought that another worshipper of the Prophet might spring from among the camel drivers. What if the blow came from some other quarter? What if a traitor lurked among the very soldiers Tebassa had sent to guard their lives?

"Do not punish yourself unduly for your blindness, Captain," said Jód. "Mr. Stilts was a Naduman. They are a very learned people, and for some that learning extends to conjury and illusion."

"Stilts was no magician," said Utarif, "just a circus performer."

"It was to his advantage to appear so, in any event."

219

"The traitor still among us is the one that concerns me," said Utarif. "You've never asked my opinion, Master Ifimar, but we all know the obvious candidate."

"I did *not* ask, that is true," said Jód, suddenly bristling with fury, "and you of all people should know better than to judge a man for the sin of a dark demeanor."

"It's more than demeanor, isn't it?"

"Dothor Spalak and I have walked in the same caravans for forty years," snapped Jód. "We came of age together. He could no more betray me than I could betray myself."

Utarif was taken aback. "Who said anything about Spalak?" he asked. "I meant that animal, Woeden Surk."

"Surk?" Jód spat out the name. "Put him out of your mind. He is a creature of perfect greed. If he turns on us, it will be not be at the orders of the Prophet. His God is a purse; he has no room in his heart for the seductions of faith. No, if Her Radiance has inserted someone false into our ranks, he will be far less obvious than Woeden Surk."

Who, then? Talupéké and Kereqa had killed the Prophet's warriors before his eyes. But that still left six soldiers.

Or seven, Ang forgive me. Kandri glanced sidelong at Utarif. Such a good man. So capable and decent to everyone, so fair.

So much like Stilts.

"Watch your words among the others," said Jód. "Tell no one that you will double back to the south. And *never* mention Weeping Rock."

"And you'll be waiting for us, three mornings from now?" said Kandri.

"Why must I repeat it? Do you doubt my word?"

Kandri bit his lips. *Of course I do, you tricky bastard.*

So, clearly, did Utarif. The captain was holding very still, fixing Jód with his gaze.

"We'll take the Sparavith camels, if you've no objection," he said at last.

Jód started. For the first time in the journey, something had caught him completely off guard. At last he shrugged.

"The Sparaviths were a gift from your general, for friendship's sake. If you would reclaim what was freely given—"

"They're bred to match the speed of a barrens horse," said the captain. "If Kandri and Mektu have to make a run for it, they'll need the fastest steeds we've got. And of course I'm not reclaiming them for long, am I? Since we're only talking about three days?"

Jód spoke through clenched teeth. "Use them. It is of no moment to me. And now we must be off—your nattering questions have delayed us too long already. I charge you, Captain, with explaining matters to the Prince."

☙

Jód dove in among the drivers, shouting for Spalak as he went. The Subcommander trailed after Jód with obvious reluctance. Before he disappeared, he gave Kandri a sharp look over his shoulder.

You volunteered to guide us, thought Kandri. *Why? And why did that offer fill Jód with such rage?*

He looked around for his brother, but found himself walking instead into a confrontation between Talupéké and Woeden Surk. The mercenary leader towered over the girl, speaking from the side of his mouth and jabbing at her chest with a grubby index finger. Twelve or thirteen of his men stood around them; like Surk himself they seemed darkly amused. Talupéké's smile was indifferent.

Surk noticed Kandri, turned him a sneering grin. "My nephew's *just curious,*" he said in a crude imitation of Chindilan. "Is that how it's done in the army of your holy bitch? 'General sir, I'm *just curious* about your order to charge the enemy. Care to sit down and discuss it?'"

The mercenaries laughed, deep in their cavernous chests. Kandri walked up to Surk and looked at him until the laughs died away.

"No," he said, "that's not how it's done."

"These people have been on the run for a month, Surk," said Captain Utarif from beyond the ring of mercenaries. "In constant danger, sleeping rough. Have some sympathy."

"A month of sleeping rough." Surk made a sucking sound through his teeth. "Ang's blood, that's hard. A cause for tears and lamentation."

Kandri studied the mercenary—broad flat face, muscles heaped on his shoulders like lumps of coal. *What are you after?* he thought. *Bloodshed? What the hell do you stand to gain?*

"Commander Surk has it right," put in Ulren. "The only danger to these fools is themselves."

"Not the point, is it?" said Woeden Surk. "They're too fresh, that's the point. Runts like them shouldn't be talkin' back."

Talupéké kicked the ground in her awkward way. *Gods, no,* thought Kandri, struggling to catch her eye. Where the hell was his uncle?

"Three years in the Prophet's army," said Woeden Surk, gazing at Kandri. "Little ass-rag. I've been at war for *sixteen and counting*. I've fought clans you've never heard of. I got tied down on a nest of fire beetles in the Far Fehinj. I killed bears in the arena in the Scarlet Kingdom, with a dull knife and no shield. I've got three inches of Ghalsúnay spear broke off in my chest."

"How did you beat the infection?" asked Kandri.

"Infection?"

"Three inches of filthy wood, and no infection?"

Woeden Surk made a phlegmy growl. "I'm a man, if that means somethin' to you," he said. "What's more, I'm an officer. You don't talk back to me."

"They can say what they like," mumbled Talupéké. "They're not fucking soldiers." After a brief pause, she added, "Difference is, they know it."

Any remaining mirth drained from the mercenaries' faces. Woeden Surk looked Talupéké up and down.

"What about you, girlie? You fucking soldiers?"

Kandri leaped between them. It was his first impulse, and he knew as he did so that he had just saved a life. Not Talupéké's, of course. The girl's smile was back: the same mad, damaged grin she had worn under the sun-shield on the dry riverbed, the last time Surk had opened his mouth. But tonight she was armed.

"Tal," said Kandri, "don't."

Her cheek twitched. Her face just horrible, the laughter in her eyes a scream. She crossed her arms over her chest, hands gripping her shoulders. The gesture looked defensive, but it was quite the opposite. She was reaching for her knives.

Kandri knew his own worth as a fighter. He would stand a fair chance against a man like Woeden Surk. He also knew that in a certain state of mind this girl could go through him like a sword through paper. Still—

"You can't fight all thirty of them."

Her eyes flicked left and right. Unconvinced.

"Don't do this, Tal. We won't make it without you. And . . . you'll break my uncle's heart."

His last words were the only ones that reached her. Talupéké looked around for Chindilan. She started to curse, but the oath died on her lips. After a moment, she raised a corner of her mouth in a smirk—so suddenly childlike—and walked away.

Shaken, Kandri turned back to Woeden Surk and found Kereqa staring him down, their faces inches apart. The old woman's eyes were sharp as ice. Surk was chuckling, pleased with himself.

Idiot, thought Kandri. *You're as good as dead.*

☙

But minutes later the mercenaries, along with nearly everyone in the caravan, were filing away toward the lights of the Palmeries. Some of the drivers sang as they went; others laughed like children. Those left behind—the brothers, Chindilan, the Prince and his hulking servant, Utarif and his team—set off northward. They would maintain Jód's ruse until the caravan was well out of sight.

The guides Jód had chosen, two young men, wept in the arms of their closest friends. At the last moment, each removed a necklace of painted beads, or seeds perhaps, and pressed them into waiting hands. The friends clasped these artifacts to their hearts with words of encouragement, *We will see you again, brothers, we will guard these for your return.*

But Kandri thought of prisoners in Eternity Camp, and there were many, pressing talismans or trinkets on their wives or sons or daughters, before their hands were bound and the blindfolds affixed and they were marched up the gallows stair.

II. THE WALL

"You must not love the creatures of the desert," said the Night Queen to the pilgrim, "for they will vanish at your approach. They are shadows thrown by firelight on the walls of a cliff. Draw too near and you will block the light."

"But my Queen," begged the pilgrim, "I have been a year on this journey that I might meet your children."

"You must see them in the words I speak or not at all," she answered sadly. "This very night a mother points you out to her daughter: you are the shadow, cast by an unknown flame against a cliff you cannot see. In her loneliness the desert child reaches for you, eclipses you, you are gone.

"Such is the law of all worlds. Long ago some dared to break it, but they fell through the shadow-portal and have not returned."

RAMISITHAN PROVERB

FROM *PARTHAN TESTIMONY AND DEMEANOR* BY THEREL AGATHAR

13. SHADOW AND STORM

The guides were indignant. Jód had told them that the assignment was an honor, but Kandri imagined it felt more like exile. The fireballs, the Clowns, Jód's breakneck pace: all this and more had conspired to change the drivers' opinion of the brothers. Rather than good luck, they were now revealed an overflowing spring of exactly the opposite. But Jód had spoken and his word was law.

In keeping with the planned deception, they made north for several hundred paces, then stopped and listened. When they were certain that the caravan was out of earshot, they reversed course, moving south along the ridge.

Kandri saw the looks the young guides exchanged. Quiet vexation, *No one tells us a thing.* Jód must have explained how to enact the deception without a word about his reasons. What had they said to the other drivers, in the secret language of their clan?

Old Kereqa marched just behind the guides, leaning on her spear like a walking-staff. The moon was a low crescent, bathing one side of the hills in a submarine light, leaving the other in darkness. The wind blew cold against their backs. They walked without speaking, each intent on the trail, which was treacherous in the shadows, and on the tricks and pitfalls of their private thoughts.

Kandri's face was swollen on one side. He looked at his brother, loping along in his crooked fashion: part soldier, part ape. No hint of an apology. Kandri thought of his parting from Eshett. *Be good to Ariqina.* He recalled her exact words but not the tone she had taken—a whisper, a command? And her kiss: neither the taste nor the sensation of her lips would come back to him, no matter how he groped for the memory. It was almost as if the kiss had not occurred.

He doesn't care if she exists. What the hell had his brother meant? And what had he expected Kandri to say? How could those who cared about Eshett want her to do *anything* but leave them, return to her people and a life without fear?

"Stop, fool."

It was Talupéké, her voice a furious whisper. He was so deep in himself that he had walked right into the girl. Everyone had stopped: the guides had frozen like deer. The silence held for ten long seconds, until Kereqa looked back at the others.

"Did you hear nothing?" she hissed. "Come, your ears are younger than mine!"

"I heard," said Captain Utarif. "A patter, like tumbling stones. From the path ahead."

"Stones," said Kereqa, "or perhaps running feet."

The soldiers drew their blades as one. Kandri rested a hand on his machete, cursing his wandering mind. He had not heard a thing.

"Small feet, if feet they were," said Chindilan. "A jackal, maybe?"

"*Sirchasp,*" whispered the younger of the two guides, obviously shaken. Then, in his broken Common: "Is cat. Little cat. Black also."

"Yes," said the older guide. "Sirchasp. Black and little cat."

"Sirchasps?" Kereqa looked at the guides. "Have you met such creatures before?"

"Is black and little—"

"*Little black cat,*" grumbled Mektu. "That's what you're trying to say. Ang's blood, learn to talk."

"Yes," said the older guide. "Little cats come from talking."

"Always pretty words," said the younger guide. "Make you love, then steal child. Keep child forever."

"Or the manhood time," said the other.

"*Until* manhood, you mean?" said Chindilan.

The older guide nodded again. "Yes please. Or the woman time."

"Shut your mouths, I can't stand it!" cried Mektu. "Captain Utarif, why are we listening to these mules? Who knows what they're saying? Little cats who steal children!"

"We must all calm our fancies," said Kereqa. "Any number of desert creatures could have made that noise."

"Then who cares?" said Mektu.

"You'll care, if we walk into an ambush," growled Utarif. "I don't know this country, but I've fought your Prophet for nine long years, and I know this much: she uses anyone she can. Spies, gossips, slavers, mercenaries. If she hasn't seduced them into worshipping her she buys their services."

"But the Rasanga are far behind us, Captain," said a young private whose breaking voice was like the croak of a frog. "Aren't we sure of that much? We've run due east and seen no sign of the Prophet. She can't have jumped ahead of us, so she can't have laid any traps."

"Can she not?"

Everyone turned. The voice belonged to Prince Nirabha. The young royal stood flanked by his hulking manservant.

"Her Radiance is said to have once decimated a great Važek battalion by learning *before the battalion itself* that no reinforcements had been dispatched from Važenland. She was four hundred miles to the south at the time."

"You believe in her powers?" asked the croaking private.

"I do not know, my good fellow, but—"

"Of course she has powers," said Mektu. "She made the White Child, didn't she? And she can do things to men, that's a fact. She can look at you and shrink your balls up inside. So far you'll never find them again."

"That's enough," said Chindilan.

"Prince Nirabha is correct," said Utarif. "We take nothing for granted where the Prophet's concerned. Keep your eyes open. Archers, I want bows in hand. And private—" He turned to the same croaking youth. "—put your gloves on."

His last words jolted all the soldiers. The croaking private glanced at his comrades.

"Do it!" snapped Utarif.

The youth obeyed, wriggling his hands into a pair of thin leather gloves. Kandri and Chindilan exchanged a baffled look: Utarif was not prone to shout at his troops. The archer drew an arrow from his quiver, reluctance in his every move. As they set out again, he saw the other soldiers draw slightly away from the youth.

They're frightened, thought Kandri, watching them. *What in Jekka's Hell is so special about those gloves?*

Third Interlude

"They're frightened."

I like that. *They're* frightened, your soldier boys and girls, of a pair of gloves they can cast aside whenever they like? Perfect nonsense. The sort of thought that gives your species a bad name.

Listen to me, Kandri Hinjuman: *I* am frightened. I, your yatra passenger.

For something has changed. Some power among us I have not wished to see, to recognize, has stirred. It woke to wrath when Ifimar Jód announced the splitting of the caravan. It raged then, even as your brother raged at you over Eshett. And I hid from that wrath, deep within you, horrified, not daring to move or speak or think. It sensed some great loss to itself in Jód's decision. It toyed with killing him. And I, bunkered deep in your distracted mind, saw that it had the power to kill him, and whispered a prayer.

Do not ask me to name the intruder! Yatra, virghast, incubus, foundling of the Pits. I do not know. I dare not guess. But of this much I am certain: like me, it travels with you, invisible but aware. Like me, it is ancient.

Unlike me, it is vile. Unlike me, it wishes you nothing but misery, murder, pain.

Unlike me, it occasionally slumbers, and even when it stirs there is a screen or mist between it and the world. I am grateful for that mist. For what if it senses me? I know the answer already: it will try to subdue me, to purchase my subservience with threats. Failing, it will attack me in all its power, seek to drive me from my host, or destroy me outright.

I do not wish to fight such an enemy. I do not think I would survive. And you, my host, would stand even less of a chance.

As for Mektu, I must walk the path I shunned before. Of course he deserves credit for that miracle on the mountain. He has gifts, certainly. He can mimic, feign emotions, fool the credulous, stun those who think they've seen it all. Yes, he is often savage, childish, crude. But sometimes he is inspired, and the source of that inspiration is part of the great and beautiful mystery that draws me to human beings. Your Ariqina would call it *the spark*. All Urrath knows it as the Sacrament, the cup filled at the Well of Fire, the drink that should mean death but instead means vision, transcendence, change. All these glories may be found in noxious Mektu. Nor should they ever be denied.

But his performance on Alibat S'Ang? That was not skill alone. Mektu was singled out by this other creature—and briefly injected with its power. That creature, evil though it is, did not wish the Prophet's servants to kill you. It needed you alive, or at least some of you. The ones it did not consider essential it helped you kill, or simply pushed over the cliff.

Who does it consider essential now?

Watch your brother, Kandri. Watch him as you might a spy or a cornered animal. He fooled the Prophet's killers, and perhaps he was even himself when he hatched the idea. But in its execution he was—I am certain of it now—possessed.

The night wore on, and the sound did not come again. The wind died away; the silence was broken only by the camels' grunts and flatulence and a jackal's far-off wails. The moon descended; the hills cast devilish shadow-fingers over the barrens to the east. The hills were shorter here but even more jagged, and the trail meandered among them like a wayward moth. Kandri's stomach growled: he had eaten nothing but a bite of seed cake and two brown apple slices since the previous morning. Remembered dishes cut a depraved caper through his mind. Red rice with chilies and sausage. Carrots blended with cream.

"Well, Mektu," said Chindilan suddenly, "there's your sand."

Everyone stopped. The smith was pointing east through a gap in the hills. Kandri caught his breath. Vast dunes rose in the moonlight, one behind another, in immaculate curves like drifted snow. The nearest broke against the hills where they stood, groping with sand-tentacles at the folds and crevasses of the rocks. The furthest rose like mountains in the distance, blotting out the lower stars.

"Fah," said Mektu.

Kereqa's old eyes swept the dunes. "That is *Lathban Nidu*, the Little Sand Sea," she told them. "The Parthans say it was born of human folly, when the Death Wind from the heart of the desert found its way blocked by Ravashandul's Wall. Perhaps that is only a story. I have never seen the Wall. But the Nidu I glimpsed from this very trail thirty years ago, chasing smugglers who had tried to cheat General Tebassa. We killed them not far from here and gave their flesh to our dogs."

"Who cares?" said Mektu. "I don't fucking care."

The Prince looked at Kandri. "Is your brother always so charming?" he asked.

Talupéké broke into a grin. Mektu turned to Nirabha, opened his mouth to speak. But something, perhaps the other's very mildness, made him falter. He looked away again, murmuring disjointed words. Prince. Sand. Shit.

Kandri turned to Kereqa. "Little, you called it? I can't see where it ends."

"Nor can I tell you," said Kereqa. "This is as far east as I have ever roamed."

"There are much greater lathbans," said the Prince. "But the Nidu is unusual: it has arms like a starfish. And here where the Nidu contends with the hills—oh, this is an infamous place."

"Are you saying you've been here?" demanded Utarif.

The Prince shook his head. "Only in books, Captain. The Desert Collection in the library of Saint Aburik's College. In Kasralys, of course. As I prepared for this journey it became my second home."

"Why do you call this land infamous?"

"All watering-spots in a desert are infamous—for the story-teller, that is," said the Prince. "One is said to be guarded by traps, another by ghouls aslumber. One has been deliberately poisoned; the next is the lair of some desert beast. Fact and fancy commingled, of course—and more the latter than the former. But the books agree on a few points. This region was inhabited as recently as the last century. One may still meet with herding folk in the spring, and parties of warriors from the more bellicose clans, on their way to raid the green Lutaral. But no settlements, not any more. Only the ghosts of the departed, and other spirits."

"Spirits," said Mektu, overloud. "That's not true, is it, Uncle? He's just saying that to get a rise out of me."

"But of course it's not true," said the Prince. "I never thought you would take it as such."

"You're not so smart," said Mektu.

The Prince looked at him, bewildered. His huge manservant cleared his throat, a sound like chains dragging stones. Mektu was biting his lips.

Say something, thought Kandri, desperate. *Change the subject.* "What about animals, Your Highness?" he blurted, thinking of the giant Ornaqs in the Stolen Sea.

"Animals?" said the Prince. "There are many. And they're to be welcomed, even the deadly ones, for they mean that water is not too distant. Around this lathban are owls, foxes, antelope, spitting lizards, snakes. An especially handsome sidewinder rattler calls it home."

Mektu's eyes had never left the Prince. "Handsome," he said. "*Especially* handsome. Are you fond of snakes, Your Highness?"

Nirabha gave him a cautious smile. "I suppose I am, truth be told. There is nothing superfluous about a snake. I admire their perfection of form."

"They don't crawl into your kitchen, then?"

"My kitchen, sir?"

"A snake crawled into Kandri's mother's kitchen when he was fourteen," said Mektu. "Kandri's my closest blood and I can't live without him, you see. But in fact we're only half-brothers. His birth-mother Uthé died when that *handsome* snake bit her foot."

"But that is horrible." The Prince turned to Kandri with a look of grief. "My good man—"

"It was ten years ago," said Kandri. "Stop it, Mektu."

Captain Utarif made an irritable gesture. "If you're all quite ready—"

"And worms?" Mektu demanded. "You admire them too?"

"Worms are excellent detritivores," said the Prince.

"Because right now, I think my own mother, and our little brothers and sisters, might just be hanging over a blackworm pit, gnawed from the legs up, tortured by the Prophet's—"

"Shut your mouth!" snapped Chindilan. "You know that's not true. Lord Garatajik—"

"Promised to hide them, to keep them safe," said Mektu. "Nice words, those."

The Prince's voice grew colder. "If Lord Garatajik gave you his promise, you have nothing to fear. His word is good."

"Oh," said Mektu. "Oh my. Thank the Gods. Did you hear him, brother? We have nothing to fear." He looked hard at the Prince. "Where's your mother, then? Busy with her embroidery?"

"Silence! Vomitous babbler!"

It was the manservant. He surged toward Mektu, his whole form radiating violence. Mektu gave a simian sideways leap, one hand on his machete. Utarif and his soldiers crushed forward, blocking the servant's advance.

"Let him go, I'll fight him," snarled Mektu. "Who's vomitous, you pock-marked toad?"

"Enough out of you!" hissed Utarif. "Your Highness, I'm shocked. I'll tolerate no brawling in this company. Am I clear?"

In fact the Prince had already stayed the man, with the lightest touch on his arm. He nodded to Utarif.

"Ripheem is no brawler, Captain; he is merely protective. I will speak to him apart."

"You'll do more than that, Prince: you'll answer for his deeds. And *you*—" Utarif turned to Kandri. "—keep this fool brother of yours quiet, or I'll do it with a gag."

Kandri raised his eyebrows; the idea was immensely appealing. Still, he was shaken by Nirabha's words. *The Prince is a friend of Garatajik, the author of the Cure.*

Nirabha was bowing to Mektu with great dignity. "Mr. Hinjuman," he said, "I beg forgiveness. I had no malice in me when I spoke of ghosts and spirits. Had I an inkling that such things worried you—"

"They don't," snapped Mektu. "Why should I be worried? It's left me alone since Alibat S'Ang."

"What has, my friend?"

"Stop pretending," said Mektu. "I know you've heard the talk." He nodded sharply at Kandri and Chindilan. "I'll bet you asked them if I was worth bringing along. Kandri's the one everyone wants, everyone looks up to, the one carrying—"

He broke off. The Prince looked at each brother in turn.

"Carrying . . . ?"

Mektu stood silent, guilt twisting the line of his mouth. Kandri willed himself to unclench his fists. Utarif and his soldiers knew about the Letter of Cure, but clearly the Prince did not. General Tebassa had kept it from him. *And Tebassa does everything for a reason.*

Nirabha glanced over the company. "I am the only one in the dark, it seems. Come, Kandri Hinjuman: what are you carrying? Does not the danger I face in traveling with you give me some rights?"

Kandri froze. Tebassa always had reasons, but he was not infallible—he had, after all, nearly tossed the Letter on a bonfire. And in Kandri's heart he still felt as he had when he argued with Chindilan: secrets were a poison among friends.

Nirabha was waiting. Kandri touched the Letter through his shirt and looked him in the eye. "This," he said, "is a cure for the World Plague. Garatajik wrote it out. He discovered it with help from doctors in your city, Prince. And one doctor from our country, Ariqina—"

"Who loves me, who's engaged to me," said Mektu.

"—set off for Kasralys to help with that work."

"What?" cried Mektu. "You don't know that. Did Ari tell you that?"

Kandri gestured for silence, fighting a searing urge to kick his brother in the gut. Nirabha was staring at him as though he had changed into some sort of mythical beast, horns and wings and tail.

"You personally," said Nirabha, "bear a letter from Garu—from Lord Garatajik?"

"That's right."

"Give it to me."

He stepped forward, hand outstretched, but Captain Utarif cut him off. "I'm sorry, Your Highness," he said, "but Garatajik entrusted the brothers with that letter, not you."

"He had no letter to entrust when last I saw him!" said the Prince. "He had found no cure. It was driving him mad."

"All the Prophet's sons are mad."

"Not him," said Nirabha. "He is a genius. And my closest friend."

He started forward again, and now the huge Ripheem came up beside him. But Utarif's soldiers knew their duty. They surrounded the brothers, hands on the hilts of their swords. Once more Nirabha paused.

"Have you even bothered to *read* this Cure?" he demanded.

"We can't," said Kandri. "He wrote it in a language none of us speak."

"I speak nine," said the Prince. "Show me. I insist."

"No, *I* insist," said Utarif. "Even if Kandri chooses to show you, it will have to wait for a less preposterous moment than this."

Nirabha struggled visibly to control himself. "The most vital, the most *transformative* discovery in a thousand years," he said, "and he puts it in the hands of two . . . *imbeciles*, two hayseeds who could not tell a salve from a purgative, who—"

He broke off: his gaze had shifted to Chindilan. The smith was turning in a circle, a look of horror on his face.

"Utarif," he said, "where are the guides?"

&

The party scattered up and down the trail. The two men had vanished without a trace. Kandri stared into the gorges on either side of the path. Nothing moved under the moonlight on the western slope, and the darkness on the eastern side was impenetrable. They called out, but not too loudly. No one imagined that the guides wished to be found. The soldiers snarled under their breath, cursing the name of Ifimar Jód.

At last they regrouped. The camels stamped and snorted, distressed by the commotion. "How in Jekka's Hell did they slip away unnoticed?" said Utarif. "Where were your *eyes*, people?"

On Mektu, thought Kandri. *On the clown. He made this possible.*

"They were here when we paused to look at the dunes," said Chindilan. "I saw them; they were checking the camels' girth-straps."

"They were scared," said the croaking private, gloved hands twisting on his bow. "And what if they were right to be, Captain? What if they know something we—"

"Enough, boy," said Kereqa.

A sudden chill came over Kandri. He looked at his uncle. "Checking the straps, you say?"

The others grasped his meaning at once. They whirled to face the camels. What Kandri saw carried a plain, sharp message: *That's our death.*

Water was licking down the legs of two camels. Fresh water. From cuts in the saddlebags where the faskas were stored.

Prince Nirabha shrieked: "Get them, grab them! Save what's left!"

Kandri and Talupéké pounced, tearing open the saddlebags. Water gushed and spilled: the bags were flooded; the faskas within were slashed at the seams. A debacle. Some tried to catch the water in their own faskas, but most of it had already gone. Others mopped at the puddles with their headscarves, or bent down to suck with their lips.

It was over. They stood in a circle, speechless. The guides had also taken water for themselves: ten full faskas, along with some of the food.

"Water inventory," said Utarif at last. "Bring out every last bag."

The loss was worse than they feared. The only surviving reserves were the six faskas in the lead camel's bags, which had not been touched. Everyone in the party also carried one faska on their person, but these had not been refilled since their separation from the caravan. None was more than half full.

"About twelve faskas, once we refill from those six," said Utarif. "And we're fourteen. Do I need to explain how bad this is? Wring every drop from those scarves. Drink from them, right now before it's lost."

Mektu shouted: "Those fuckers, they were trying to kill us!"

"They may have succeeded," said Nirabha.

"That's not clever, Prince," said Mektu. "But I'll tell you who is: Ifimar Jód. He didn't dare get rid of us in person, because his drivers have grown fond of us. But he found two sons of whores prepared to strand us here to die."

"No one needs to die if we keep our heads," said Utarif. He turned to Kereqa. "You've been to this oasis, sister. How close are we?"

"Quite close," said Kereqa. But Kandri caught the hesitation in her voice. She turned to face the broken hills. "Weeping Rock is well hidden. If you do not know what to look for, you will pass it by altogether. The Parthans who took me there did so for love of General Tebassa. But they were not glad to be doing so. They certainly never intended me to return."

She flicked a hand at the southbound trail. "Somewhere ahead lies a cleft in the hills in the shape of a keyhole. That is the doorway to Weeping Rock, which lies below the door like a sunken garden. A beautiful place, small but unspoiled. The cleft faces east, a long stone's throw from the trail." She paused, frowning. "Better if we seek it by daylight."

"Master Ifimar told us you knew the way," said Nirabha.

"What he told you I cannot account for," said Kereqa. "I claimed only that I would know the Keyhole cleft if I saw it, and that I could keep this trail to the first glimpse of the sands. But the sands move. They advance, or retreat, or drift sideways with the years."

"She doesn't know," said Mektu.

"I know when a search by night is wasted effort," said Kereqa. "An east-facing cleft will be in shadow at this hour. We will never see it."

Mektu sighed loudly; Talupéké turned him a dangerous look. But even her fellow soldiers struggled to hide their unease. Kandri looked at the maze of hills spreading endlessly to the south. *Twelve faskas for fourteen people.* The sun would rise in a matter of hours. Before it set again their water would be gone.

They would last the night, perhaps even through the day that followed. But no longer. *We find that oasis, or we die.*

Even then, of course, they would not be long out of danger. How were they to locate the crossroads without the help of the guides? Ifimar Jód had sworn to go on without them at sunset on the third day. In that sole respect, Kandri trusted the man completely.

They set out again, the silence between them deeper than before. Kandri realized that it was even later than he had imagined, for in no time the moon began to set behind the western hills. The darkness slowed them still further. Even the sure-footed Sparaviths began to miss their steps.

When the moon vanished altogether, Utarif gave the order to pitch camp.

"No fire," he said, "and no idle talk; that's a waste of your strength. Make the swiftest meal you can. There's dry goat flesh, but don't eat more than a scrap tonight: it's salted. And then sleep. The Gods know we won't sleep long. Brother Ebeja, first watch goes to you."

The goat flesh was like wood: delicious, salted wood. Kandri gnawed his portion like a muskrat, lying prone in the fine wool blanket General Tebassa had provided. The blanket he had wrapped around himself and Eshett two nights before. Was she home, in the arms of her people? Had they danced and shouted at the sight of her? Had they wept?

Pray that she's happy, Kandri. So immersed in love that she gives no thought to you or your brother. And you: forget her as well, or try at least. You have other things to think about. Other people.

Kandri smiled to himself. The voice in his head—so utterly real, for just a fancy—was Ariqina's.

03

"No, sir!"

Talupéké. Shouting. Kandri bolted upright.

"I was wide awake! I never closed my Gods-damned eyes!"

Pale orange light: the very first hint of dawn. Kandri struggled to his feet. Most of the others were up already, hugging themselves against the cold.

Talupéké stood facing Captain Utarif, hands in fists, so charged with fury she seemed almost to be lifting from the ground.

"It could have taken less than a minute," said Utarif. "A dash in, a dash out—"

"*I didn't fucking fall asleep!*"

Utarif poked her hard in the chest. "You curse at me again, girl, and I'll give you a reason to lose some sleep. Tebassa may be far away, but his law is right here, right now."

"Yes, sir."

"I'll not stand for insubordination."

"No, sir. I'm sorry, sir."

Bunched in Utarif's hand was a red shawl. Even in the dim light Kandri could see that it was finely made, with bright sequins, and gold embroidery along the hem. The captain held it up before her eyes.

"I know what you've faced, sister," he said. "I know damn well what you're struggling with. But if I find out you're lying—"

"It's no lie!" cried Talupéké, beginning to shake. "I don't f— I don't wear that sort of thing, Captain! It's . . . lacy."

"Lacy." Utarif turned to face the rest of the party, raising the shawl in his fist. "I found this between Talupéké's bedroll and my own. It was not there when we lay down. Whose is it? Speak up, and don't you dare waste our time."

No one answered him. Utarif turned in a circle. In quick succession he spoke to every member of the party, soldier and civilian, and every last man and woman told him the same. They had never seen the shawl before.

The light was growing swiftly. "You're asking me to believe," said Utarif, "that we've had a fucking visitor in our sleep?" He looked again at Talupéké.

Mektu sniffed. "It's perfumed, isn't it?" He reached out, lifted the trailing end of the shawl to his nose. "Fresh flowers," he said. "*Harach*, that's nice."

The shawl went from hand to hand. When Kandri held it a shiver passed along his limbs. The scent was faint, but extraordinary; his mind filled with visions of flowering trees and vines in the jungles of the south.

Talupéké sniffed the shawl and made a face. "You think I'd f— I mean—"

"Conceded," said Utarif. "You'd not be caught dead wearing scent. All right: break camp. But there's one task before we move."

He held up a tiny copper funnel. "Bring out your faskas: we're dividing the reserve water now. Do the honors, Talupéké."

Talupéké started. "Captain, ask someone else. I don't want . . . to be responsible."

"Responsible? For Ang's sake, girl, that's an order. You've got the steadiest hands."

One by one, Talupéké brought out the five untouched faskas. With infinite care, she broke each seal and topped off everyone's water bag. When the last reserve faska was empty they exchanged dismal looks. What they had just divided was less than they had drunk since the sabotage and theft.

Kandri found himself gazing at the dusty earth at the their feet. Most of the area had been stomped and scored by their feet, and those of the unhappy camels. But between these were markings of another kind.

He bent down. They were the tracks of a small animal. Not a bird or a hoofed beast, or the scatter-tracks of a lizard. This was a neat and graceful creature. "A cat," he said aloud. "I've found the prints of a cat."

His words caused a commotion. They discovered identical tracks all about the camp site, weaving among the spots where they had slept. Dust prints crossed their packs and bedrolls, and even the cloaks in which they'd slept.

"There are prints on your shirt, Uncle," said Mektu, poking his belly. "Look there. It was standing on you."

Chindilan jumped and brushed his shirt. "A cat!" he said. "The guides spoke of some sort of cat, didn't they?"

"Black and little," said Mektu.

"A *sirchasp*, yes," said Kereqa. "A clever animal, impossible to catch. They are said to be wise to human ways. They cause mischief, and steal food. But I did not think such creatures were to be found in this part of Urrath."

"They're found in bedtime stories, if you ask me," said another soldier.

"Whatever you believe or doubt, something was here." She turned abruptly to Talupéké. "Granddaughter, what is it? Are you unwell?"

Talupéké had not moved during the search of the camp. She was holding her own faska, unsealed, as though about to drink. But she did not drink.

"You look strange, girl," said Mektu. "Drink a little. You need it."

"Fool!" snapped the Prince's valet. "Why make her drink, if she is not thirsty? Who knows what is to come?"

Talupéké looked at her grandmother—and then, strangely enough, at Kandri. Her cheek gave a violent twitch.

"Sister—" Utarif began.

"*Surthang atha ilebente!*" she said. "Lord of Death, pass us by!"

She dashed her water to the ground.

⍰

The second uproar was worse than the first. Once again headscarves sopped at the mud. The other soldiers cast hateful looks at Talupéké as she carried on with her invocation of Surthang, Supreme God of Death. Her grandmother tried to take her arm, but Talupéké shook her off and stalked away.

Utarif barked at her: "Stop where you are, sister! I'm not done with you."

Talupéké ignored his command, quickened her pace. Chindilan plunged after her. Nirabha whispered to his servant. Mektu hid his face in the crook of his arm.

Gazing at them, Kandri felt sick with foreboding. *It's us who are coming apart at the seams.*

He turned to follow Chindilan. But a hand on his elbow stopped him. It was Kereqa.

"Your uncle will calm her, if anyone can."

"We don't have time, the sun—"

"She has given the smith her trust. Let him try to use it."

"We can't just fucking *stand* here!"

But they did, and Kereqa was right. Minutes later Talupéké came stalking back, explosive in her silence, hands in fists. She glanced at Utarif, waiting for her punishment. The morning light caught the tears on her cheeks.

The captain looked her up and down. What was there to say? The girl had thrown away her water, and perhaps her life. They would try to share with her, but Kandri doubted she would accept a sip from anyone.

How long had she had a pact with death? From their first days together she had claimed that a God was whispering in her ear, hinting at her fate. But Surthang? The Bringer of Silence, the Sower of Despair?

You're a child, Talupéké. He blinked a tear out of his own eye, annoyed with himself. Because of course that wasn't true. She was sixteen. She'd started fighting and killing at thirteen, an age when he had still been making forts out of rocks and scrapwood on Candle Mountain. She'd not been a child for a very long time. But she might well be the first of them to die.

Utarif stood watching her with a severity that forbade any approach. But at last he turned to the other soldiers, jolting them to life.

"See to the camels," he said. "We're heading out. Let's find that oasis before the sun cooks us alive."

⌘

But the oasis did not want to be found.

They had come into a wilderness of sharp-sided hills, broader and more severe than any before. Red earth, red cliffs, scorched black here and there like the walls of a furnace. Dry gullies teasing them with thoughts of flowing streams. Low, cruel cacti. Needle-encrusted vines.

All that morning they followed Kereqa's lead, pausing when she paused, scanning the cliffs for any remotely keyhole-shaped cleft. The path descended lower and lower, to the very roots of the hills. For a time the shadows kept them cool enough. But as the hours passed the sun climbed higher. It grazed the tufted ears of the camels first, and the wise beasts lowered their heads. Minutes later they had to lower them further.

No cleft appeared. Or rather, hundreds did—some as small as cupboards, others huge as temple façades—but did any resemble a keyhole? No, no more than they did any number of other shapes: a wedge of cheese, a rolling pin, a vase.

Along one high, narrow bend in the trail they looked down into a ravine and saw corpses. Two human corpses, with brass bangles and earrings and long bright teeth. The flesh dried to gray enamel, cracked and flaking from the bones.

By noon Kandri had drained half his remaining water. *No more until sunset*, he promised himself. But the heat had scarcely begun.

Around one rocky turn, the path suddenly divided.

The soldiers groaned aloud. Kereqa looked down each path in turn.

"I have no memory of this place," she said. "One of these could be a new path; thirty years have passed. And we traveled by night, that other time, so perhaps I missed this fork altogether."

"Doesn't matter how it happened," said Mektu. "Lost is lost."

They chose the eastern path, since their goal was an east-facing cleft. Less than an hour later the trail divided again, and again they bore east. But now they all knew they were fighting despair.

Kandri's mouth grew dry. He saw Mektu anxiously squeezing his faska. Talupéké walked beside her grandmother, who was speaking in low tones: "All wrong . . . that last ridge . . . the sand was never . . ."

The sand reached for them from the east, groping among the rocks in huge tentacles that obliterated the path. These were the arms of the lathban, the great sand sea they had glimpsed from the hilltop. Kandri had thought them beautiful; now they were sobering obstacles. The sand was fine and loose. He felt it suck and cling to his every step as they ascended the first dune, the bite of it against his cheeks as the wind sheered it from the summit.

When they reached the crest he looked back, appalled. His first dune, his first half-hour, and his legs were aching as though he'd climbed a mountain. How did anyone stand it for weeks on end? How could he dream of lasting months?

The next dune was taller still. As he dragged himself to his summit, the answer to his question came. The familiar answer, the army answer: *You'll manage because you must.*

In the remote distance, sand rose in a whirlwind, danced fitfully along the spine of the dune, collapsed.

"No shade for hours yet," murmured Utarif, close beside him. "And Kereqa's lost at sea."

Kandri glanced at him. Utarif had spoken for his ears alone. Was he asking for advice? If so, he'd come to the wrong man. For hours Kandri had thought feverishly about their plight and gotten nowhere. Ariqina called such efforts "chewing on a stone," and that was just about right. A dry stone with sharp edges. A stone that cut the tongue.

"We're blind down there among the rocks," he whispered, "and that's exactly where we can't afford to be blind. We could miss the entrance. Hell, we may have *already* missed it. And if that's the case—"

"Then we're corpses, sure as that pair in the ravine." Utarif smiled, but his sunken eyes were more ghoulish than amused.

"Captain," said Kandri, "tell me about your archer's gloves."

Utarif drew a hand across his face. "It's not the gloves. It's the arrows he handles them with. Spore arrows. General Tebassa received them as a gift from the Xavasindrans. He's done those Outworlder clans a few favors, you see."

"Black Hat likes to do favors," said Kandri.

"And to call them in," said Utarif. "But these arrows, Hinjuman: they're obscene. When one strikes its target, a capsule bursts on the shaft and fills the air with a fungal poison. No need to draw blood—you just aim for the center of a crowd. I've seen one arrow strike a tree and kill ten fighters standing beneath it." He sighed. "I've also seen one dropped by accident—in a barracks. That day we lost five of our own."

"Five dead? Because someone *dropped an arrow?*"

Utarif nodded. "And a sixth saw her fingers rot after she handled the arrows with sweaty palms. The spores aren't in the capsule alone: they permeate the wood itself. Horrible, horrible tools. But they just might kill Rasanga at a distance. The general had nine of those arrows, but he's down to four, now. Two are in the hands of his bodyguards. The other two—" He gestured at the croaking private. "—are with that lad."

The others were ahead of them now, slide-stepping down the dune, and still the captain did not move. Kandri watched him, mystified. *Say what you want to say.*

"The Prophet tried to cozy up to the Xavasindrans too," said Kandri at last, "but I never saw any Outworlder tools in the army. What the hell did Tebassa do for them?"

Utarif gave him a warning look. "There are questions I've learned not to ask the general," he said. "'What deal did you strike?' was among the first. But there's one question I damned well should have asked, as soon as I got my orders."

"And that is?"

"Who really owns this caravan."

Kandri almost lost his footing. "Don't stare at me, boy," said Utarif, glancing quickly at the others. "Don't repeat a word of this, either. My soldiers have enough to worry about."

And you don't know if you can trust them all, thought Kandri. *Not after Stilts.*

"Do you mean that Jód isn't really in charge?"

"Oh, he's absolutely in charge—his word is life and death here in the desert. But he's also lying. He's not working for that Dimas fellow, the supposed owner of the camels and the goods. That man was a prop, a decoy. Someone was pulling his strings."

"Who, Captain?"

"If I knew, would we be talking?" said Utarif. "I don't have a clue. Or rather, yes, I have clues—three clues, in fact, but I'll be damned if they're enough. The first is that this mystery-owner was known to my general, and counted on his aid. No one but Tebassa could have equipped a caravan so well, so quickly."

"Maybe Black Hat needed to move some goods himself."

Utarif shook his head. "General Tebassa is a soldier, not a merchant. He leaves trade to his customers. But here's my second clue: whoever was pulling the strings wanted that caravan *gone*. I mean instantly. Out of the West, out of danger, as fast as humanly possible."

A vulture with scarlet wattles drifted over the facing dune. "What was the hurry?" asked Kandri. "Captain, was it about us?"

Utarif shook his head. "Impossible. All this got started before we'd ever heard of you or Mektu, or the death squads nipping at your heels."

"You'd heard of my father, though."

Utarif smiled. "The great engineer. Or the mad inventor, depending on who you ask. Yes, we'd heard of Lantor Hinjuman. The man whose skills were not for sale—not to anyone, at any price. That impressed my general, and enraged him too. But your father was long gone—two years gone from the Lutaral. No, this didn't involve Lantor either."

"What's your last clue, then?"

"Deep pockets," said Utarif. "This mystery owner was spending money like a king drunk on love. He bought everything the general put before him. He bought all the best camels and provisions in Mab Makkutin *in a single night*. And that, of course, is insane. Jód will tell you—any veteran of the desert will tell you: *Start in haste, die in haste*. When you rush, you overlook things. A cough among your drivers. Straps that chafe until your camels have open sores. Mold in the silage. Bad seals on your faskas."

"Bad mercenaries," said Kandri.

Utarif inhaled through gritted teeth. "Woeden Surk is a human pustule. We'll see how he conducts himself in a fight, though. His men are strong enough. But our mystery owner never wanted mercs to guard his caravan. He wanted us, as a matter of fact."

"I gather Tebassa wasn't interested."

"He's not for sale either," said Utarif, "as that fool Dimas learned to his shame. I watched him try to bribe the general with a little chest of gold. 'You can part with a few dozen soldiers, Black Hat,' he wheedled. 'Always more where they came from.'

"You can imagine how that went over. 'Not for all the gold in the Horde of Balishan would I feed my children to the desert, you dog,' said the general. Dimas must have had very specific orders from our mystery person, however, because he didn't give up. He pulled out a pouch of emeralds and set it beside the gold.

"That put an end to the dance. Tebassa had Dimas carried outside and tossed in the cesspool behind the latrines. The love and loyalty of his troops: that's the general's wealth, and he knows it. Come on then, we're lagging behind."

He and Kandri started down the slipface of the dune: step, slide, sway, slide. "But he did send you, finally, when we came along," said Kandri.

"And don't you forget it, Hinjuman," said Utarif. "What he did for you, for the sake of that Cure you're carrying: I've never seen him do anything of the kind."

Kandri said nothing. Guilt and pain had driven that decision, he knew. The general had lost his own family to the plague. And he had come close to burning the Letter of Cure before he learned what it contained.

"This mystery owner," said Kandri. "Did Tebassa help him in any other way?"

"Certainly," said Utarif. "He introduced him to the best Caravan Master in Urrath."

"Jód."

"Jód. He's the only one of us who's met the owner, the only one who knows his name. Tebassa never breathed a word to us soldiers. But he did tell us one thing: the owner offered to pay Ifimar Jód *four times* his usual fee for a desert crossing."

"And the catch?" asked Kandri.

"Haven't you been listening?" said Utarif. "Leave now, that was the catch. Leave instantly. You thought my general ordered the caravan to start without you, from spite? That's precisely backward. He *delayed* its departure for as long as he could."

"Not for us he didn't," said Kandri bitterly. The memory of Tebassa's abuse had not lost its sting.

Utarif smiled. "No, not for you. He delayed it because he and Jód are old partners—even friends, to the extent that Jód's capable of friendship. And the general feared his friend was walking into a trap. He wanted to inspect every pack on every camel, to find out what he was getting Jód into. I led that inspection, as it happens. We tore those packs apart."

"Did you find something?" asked Kandri.

"Of course. Sataapre wool. Sendu leather. Indigo and shells from Kiprifa, resins from the Obik Fens. Potency creams made from fox testicles. Brass candlesticks. Straight razors. Shirts."

"Fox testicles?"

"Scandalous, isn't it?"

"But who in Jekka's Hell cares so much about fox testicles?"

"Quiet!" said Utarif—they had nearly caught up with the others. "No one, of course. We've overlooked something—something that made the owner push like a madman to get that caravan underway. Jód himself is burning, boiling to know what it is. And so is the traitor."

"So you still believe there's a traitor in the caravan?"

"I know there is," said Utarif, "and so do you. Stilts didn't betray us alone. Jód said it himself, someone's been rifling through the trade goods. Searching them, one camel at a time."

"It's the Letter he's looking for," said Kandri. "We know that much."

"Do we? Are we sure the traitor even knows a Cure exists? And what if the traitor was after that golden mattoglin you sent away with Eshett? Trouble is—" He gave an exasperated sigh. "—it might not be either one. You brought both those treasures with you, but that rummaging in the saddlebags started before we arrived. Jód himself admitted that much. Said he didn't want me suspicious of my own."

"So the traitor was part of the original caravan—"

"Assuming there's only one."

"—and is looking for something it was already carrying. What the hell could it be, Captain?"

Utarif shook his head. "I've run through the inventory fifty times. *But it must be there*, in some saddlebag or basket or bundle. And to our traitor that something matters the way you matter to the Prophet. Beyond reason. Beyond anything in the world."

଼

Down among the rocks the heat was worse, throbbing from every surface. One of the soldiers choked on a sip of water, spraying it from his mouth.

"I can't swallow," he croaked. "Throat's too dry. Ang's mercy, I want a proper cup of—"

"What you want is to look for that Keyhole," said Utarif. "Focus on that, do you hear me? Nothing else matters."

Around the next turn, the path divided once more. The party stopped with a collective shudder. Two trails, two identical gorges. No way to choose among them.

Kandri's lips felt like tissue paper, crackling. *What if Jód did want to be rid of us? What if those guides were just following his orders?*

"Hold a moment. Look up there."

Utarif was pointing up at a spot high on the cliffs overhead. Kandri shielded his eyes and saw a flat, narrow ledge.

"Right at the juncture of the gorges," he said. "From there we could look down into both, and maybe a few others besides."

"If we were birds we could do even better," said Mektu. "So what?"

"I'm going up there. Catch your breath for a few minutes, everyone."

"Forgive me, Captain," said the Prince, "but that is suicide."

"Nonsense." The captain dropped his pack, cracked his knuckles. Kandri studied the cliff: bald, sheer, undercut. Utarif could not be serious.

"This is wrong," said Old Kereqa. The others murmured in solemn agreement, but Utarif cut them off.

"I didn't convene a fucking plenary! And we can't go on guessing, can we? Relax, all of you. I'm a fine climber."

"No you're not," said Talupéké, "but I am."

She kicked off her sandals. She tugged off Chindilan's ring and placed it in his hand.

"Stop right there," said Utarif. "You're weaker than any of us, thanks to your little libation to the God of Death. *Harach*, as if he needed an appetizer."

Talupéké bent double, rubbed her hands in the dust.

"Forget it, circus girl, you're in no shape to—"

Talupéké scaled the wall like a lizard. In mere minutes she was crouched atop the ledge, peering away across the twin gorges, shielding her eyes.

"I'm sharing my water with that circus girl," said Chindilan, glancing sternly at the others. "I hope I'm not alone."

Awestruck, they watched her return. She made it look like descending a ladder. She dropped the last six feet and stood among them, and Kandri saw that she was barely sweating.

"To the west—" she began.

251

Then her knees buckled. Chindilan caught her, eased her down. And Kandri thought with horror: *Of course she's not sweating. She's dry as a gourd.*

He reached for his faska, but Chindilan was quicker, pressing his own into her hands. Talupéké gave him a frightened look.

"You saved me before," she rasped. "But this time you can't. The God said—"

"Shut up and drink," said Chindilan. "Tell me about your God some other time."

Still watching Chindilan, she took two sips small as teaspoons. As if to drink more would be to bind herself to some impossible debt.

"Let's have that report," said Utarif.

"To the west there's a dead shrub, maybe," said Talupéké. "A mile or two down the trail."

"What else?" said Utarif.

"Nothing else. There's no other difference between the paths. Just rocks, gullies, dirt, sand flows. Nothing green or alive. And no fucking Keyhole— sorry, sir."

Kandri winced: her words were like a blow to the chest. He saw the same despair in all their faces—all but the Prince's, that is.

"Plants," said Nirabha, "do not occur in the absence of water. It is far better than nothing."

"No it's not," said Mektu. "A dead shrub, *maybe*? That's nothing at all. But we know one thing: our trail leads east, if we ever escape these hills."

Utarif looked at Kereqa. The old woman shook her head. "Even a dead plant is some evidence of life. I would not ignore it, if the choice were mine."

"We're sweating, losing water," said Chindilan.

"That occurred to me, smith," said Utarif sharply. Then he sighed. "You're right, we've got to make every drop count. And every step. That's why we're going to set up the sun-shield, here and now."

"What, stop?" cried Mektu.

"For an hour—by then we'll be in shadow again, with any luck. Then we'll start down the western path. If we find nothing and have to double back, at least we'll be in better shape to attempt it."

"But we can't be late for the rendezvous!" said Mektu.

"Is shouting out the obvious a tradition in your family?" asked Utarif.

"No, we're soft-spoken," said Mektu. "But we can't be late. Jód will leave us behind, you'll see. Give him one little excuse."

"You gave him that already, back at the pit," said Chindilan.

"And he left us, Uncle. So we'd better not be late."

"Babbler," spat the manservant, Ripheem.

They spiked the sun-shield between the cliffs. The camels, who could not possibly fit into its shade, ducked their heads under the canvas and moaned in indignation. The croaking private volunteered to stand watch out in the sun, with only a tented headscarf for shelter. *That's what a good captain inspires*, Kandri thought.

He and Chindilan both tried to share their faskas with Talupéké, but it took a direct order from Utarif to get her to drink.

"No food," said Kereqa. "We must be still and calm."

Even beneath the sun-shield the heat was miserable. They lay like the already dead; time crawled like the flies on their faces. Kandri glanced at Kereqa, seated cross-legged against the cliff. Bone-thin face, bright eyes peering out from thickets of wrinkles. *Thirty years.* What if her memory was faulty? What if she had forgotten a whole day of travel, some fundamental turn?

We could be miles from the oasis. We could be just about anywhere.

"Captain Utarif?" said Mektu softly.

No answer. The captain's eyes were closed.

"Captain Utarif?"

Ripheem growled in his throat. This is how death will come for me, Kandri thought. I'll be listening to my brother's drivel as I die of thirst.

"Captain Utarif?"

"What the *hell is it*, boy?"

"Even if we find the oasis, we're still in trouble. That man will leave us to die, I tell you."

Utarif heaved a sigh. "Jód's as cold as they come, but he's not a monster. Back at the pit, he slowed the caravan the very minute he was sure we'd escaped the Wasp. He hoped you'd make it, somehow. He wanted you to catch up."

"That was before Kandri mentioned the Rasanga," said Mektu. "Now he knows how much the Prophet hates us. I'm not saying it's Kandri's fault—although it is his fault—but the *point* is we'd better not be late—"

"Say that once more," barked Ripheem, jolting everyone awake.

"We'd better not—"

"He means, sir," interrupted the Prince smoothly, "that he hopes you will *not* feel compelled to say it again."

"Then he's an imbecile, he said just the opposite." Mektu sat up, indignant. "And who's this slab of lard to order me around? If he wants to fight I'll shame him, Your Royalness, I'll—"

"Don't move! Don't move or you're dead!"

It was the croaking private, on watch. The others leaped up, groped for weapons, poured out from beneath the sun-shield. Kandri ducked around a camel, machete in hand. Then, like everyone else, he skidded to a halt.

The youth had an arrow trained on a stone about twenty feet up the path. Behind it, stealing glances at them, was a woman a few years younger than Kandri himself. She wore a white cloak with the hood raised over her head, and bright rings on the hand that touched the boulder. Her face was breathtaking: eyes large and gleaming, lips full, skin a midnight black.

"Private, lower that bow!" cried Utarif. "You there! Who in Jekka's Hell are you?"

The woman did not move.

"We won't hurt you," called the captain. "You startled us, that's all. Where have you come from, girl? You can't possibly be alone."

She shook her head. "Family," she said.

"You're here with your family?"

By way of answer, the woman rose and stepped away from the protection of the stone. Slender, barefoot, eyes delicately lowered. Her black hair cropped short like that of the soldiers. In one hand she clutched a twisted branch to which a handful of dry leaves clung.

"What's that for?" said Mektu, retreating a pace. "A spell branch, a witching branch? Are you some kind of witch?"

She looked up at him sharply, and her eyes drew gasps. They were not just bright: they were silver: a metallic glimmer where the whites should have been, surrounding irises of deepest black. If they were human eyes, they were unlike any Kandri had ever seen or imagined.

The woman lifted the branch. "For tea," she said. "What is *witch*?"

She stepped closer. Those strange eyes showed no fear and perhaps even—did they imagine it?—a touch of amusement. Kandri stood rigid with wonder. There was something both uncanny and immediately familiar about this woman, the fluid grace of her movements, her flame-thin form.

Utarif shook himself. He went to his camel and unbuckled a saddle pouch and withdrew something neatly folded and bright. It was the mysterious red shawl.

"Did you—" He waved a flummoxed hand. "—misplace this?"

The woman broke into a radiant smile. "I leave in the night. Is mine, yes, and thank you."

She went to Utarif and took the shawl from his hand. Then, soundless, she made for the path through the eastern gorge.

"Is your family that way?" asked Kereqa.

"Yes," said the woman.

"Close, are they?"

"No."

She began to glide down the path, not looking back. The party stood as though turned to stone.

"Pitfire, girl!" shouted Chindilan at last. "What brings you to this miserable place? What's your family doing, while you're gathering twigs?"

The woman turned her head, just enough for them to see the mirth in her expression.

"Swimming," she said.

ଓଃ

If this was a trap—some ridiculous, overelaborate trap—no one in the party cared. They seized their belongings and the camels' leads and stumbled after her. *Swimming.* The word had grabbed them by the throat.

She led them down into the gorge. Kandri caught his brother's eye, gave in to a smile. Even if this woman was deceiving them, she was clearly not dying of thirst. For the first time all day they had reason to hope.

But the heat did not relent. It had taken on physical form: moving forward was like pressing through walls of blunt needles that did not quite break the skin but came nearer to it with every step. The path serpentined; the throbbing cliffs drew close enough to touch. Now and then a gap opened to the east, where the dunes towered high above their heads.

All at once the woman turned off the path and began to scramble down a slope of naked rock. After a confused moment, bunched up and cursing on the trail, they followed. The way was hazardous: a globe of slick rock, over the curve of which they had to creep like ants. The camels snorted and flattened their ears, and who could blame them? One false step and they would fall, in a chaos of bags and broken limbs. But the Sparaviths kept their balance, and at last the ground leveled out.

They had entered a second canyon. The cliffs were orange and almost translucent, like walls of wax. Gossamer sand underfoot. From a hairline crack in one wall, a pale green vine reached for the sky.

The woman quickened her pace; they followed stumbling and blinking. Sometimes she vanished around corners, but when they trudged on they always found her waiting.

Talupéké began to cough. Each time the sound came, Kandri winced. The girl's voice was so dry it was like the rasping of wood against wood. His hand went to his faska; he could spare her a sip—but no, his water had been gone for an hour or more. And the others: did they have any left? They were weaving, now, feeble with thirst. Sunset was still far away.

"Where in Jekka's Hell has she gone?" said Mektu suddenly.

For the woman had disappeared. They rounded the next bend, and the next: she was nowhere to be seen. They called out, and their voices rolled back to them along the canyon. There was no other reply.

"She's tricked us, hasn't she?" said Mektu.

"We don't know that," said Kandri.

"I think we do. I think she meant this to happen from the start. We're so deep in the canyon now we'll never be able to climb back out. Not in the shape we're in. We've followed her to our deaths."

"No more of that," said Utarif. "No more talk at all, until we're out of this scrape."

Mektu leaned back against Fish. He seemed about to slide to the ground. "Girls," he said. "Bug-eyed lying girls, and meat-killer clowns. This entire desert is full of assholes."

Fish turned and bit his arm.

While Mektu was screaming and smacking the creature, Old Kereqa padded ahead, barely lifting her feet from the ground. As she neared the next curve in the canyon her face began to change. She raised her arm and pointed.

"There it is! There!"

The others staggered forward. Around the bend, the left-hand cliff hung over them like a storm cloud. At its foot was a six-foot-gap shaped more or less like a keyhole.

Weeping Rock. Kandri had begun to doubt that it was real.

"I missed the path altogether," said Kereqa darkly. "Were it not for that girl, we should have perished, and on my soul the blame."

"It's *not* your fault, grandmother," whispered Talupéké.

"Ang in heaven, I hear it," said Chindilan.

Kandri shivered, for he heard it too: the loveliest sound ever to reach his ears, that faint sweet susurrus, water falling from a height.

14. WEEPING ROCK

The oasis was like a temple, roofless and glowing in the last light of day. A sunken temple, echoing not just with water but also voices and even—were they imagining it?—the sound of a flute. Beyond the Keyhole, the ground dropped away in giant steps, one ledge beneath another, with the high cliffs soaring over all. Straight down through the ledges ran a staircase of weathered stone. At its foot opened a broad, flat space of earth and sand.

And there was the water: a whisper-thin falls, dropping sheer as a curtain. Part of it struck the rocks below, but most fell straight into a round pool already in shadow. The pool was narrow but looked quite deep. A few yards from its rim was a boggy patch thick with greenery. A few stunted palms shaded this wallow, and among them stood one ancient, barren, sun-tortured fig tree, which reached out a long, lone branch for the falls, and perhaps felt their kiss, for that twisted branch alone was in leaf.

The flute fell silent. Men and women turned to face them. Some were swimming; others sat beneath the water-curtain, bathing in the spray. All naked, save for the young woman they had followed here. Four men, four women. Raising his eyes, Kandri saw a second group looking down from one of the ledges above.

The staircase was no easy matter for the camels. They descended slowly, teased by the song of the water. Small scarlet birds flitted by like notions, plucking insects from the air.

The swimmers left the pool without haste, pulling on their clothes. Kandri only realized he was staring when he felt the dig of his brother's elbow. The people were beautiful: slender torsos, long graceful limbs. All with eyes of that same astonishing silver. All moving with the same fluidity and poise.

I've seen it before, Kandri thought with certainty. *But where, where?*

The strangers on the ledge above were clearly elders: some might have had a few years on Kereqa. They sat very still, watching the newcomers with unreadable faces. But the bathers were young, not one above his own age, Kandri thought. The men were tall, slightly fragile-looking: no warriors these. The women's hands were delicate, plucking cloaks and sarongs from the rocks. Their glances full of laughter, though not one made a sound.

At last they reached the oasis floor. Mektu gripped Kandri's arm. "Gods, brother, are they real? Do you see them?"

"I'm not blind," said Kandri.

They moved toward the pool, and the whole company moved with them, like a herd of goats to a trough. But the young woman blocked their way.

"*Siro*. Wait."

No force in Urrath would have kept them long from that water. And yet they stopped. The woman gestured to Kereqa: *Your faska.*

Kereqa handed it over. The young woman knelt and submerged the bag in the pool, filling it swiftly. She rose and gave it back to Kereqa, then moved on to Talupéké with the same gesture.

"We're too dirty," croaked Talupéké. "That's the problem, Captain. They don't want our filth in that pool."

"*Siro*, yes, very dirty," said the woman.

Three men, dressed now in billowing trousers, came to help her at the task. Soon everyone in Kandri's party was drinking, gulping, gasping with relief. The water had an acrid smell and an aftertaste of slime, but as he drank Kandri could not imagine a deeper joy. It was like being reborn.

One of the men stepped forward, smiling broadly. His black hair hung to his elbows in a riot of knots and braids. He placed a hand on his chest.

"*Iu marugon brata*. Love of stars for this meeting."

Utarif glanced at the others, perplexed. "Well. Thank you. Some of us were near death."

"No more," said the man.

"You're here alone?"

"Stay tonight, maybe tomorrow," said the young woman. "Then away."

"We're Chilotos," tried Kandri, "and Lo'acs, and a few other clans. What about you?"

A long pause. The strangers looked at each other, grinning, as if the question had stumped them. At last the young woman touched her chest and said, "Nachasps?"

It sounded like a question. "Nachasps?" echoed Utarif. "Is that the name of your people?"

"Nachasps, not people," said the man with the long tresses. He made a scrubbing gesture. "Clean. Then you, *hmmm*, rest or—*ecthur*, Fiasul?"

"Swim," said the woman. "You swim after clean. Or not swim, rest, drink tea."

She pointed to the boggy spot near the palms, and Kandri saw that there was water there, a low channel fed by overflow from the pool. "For animals," she said. "Also washing clothes."

"Your name's Fiasul, darling?" said Mektu.

"Fiasul," she said, and laughed. "Not *darlink*, what is that?"

Under the gaze of the motionless elders, they led the camels to the boggy patch, where the beasts fell to slurping with a singular will. The younger strangers, meanwhile, fetched buckets of water from the pool. They passed these and several scraps of cloth to Fiasul and the man with long braids. Smiling, the pair looked at Kandri and his companions. Their silver eyes did not blink.

"Are we simply to disrobe in front of her?" said Ripheem.

"I will," said Mektu, and did.

Others matched his example, if not his eagerness. As Kandri peeled off his own grimy tunic, he was treated to the sight of Mektu, stark naked, being scrubbed like an infant by this strange, silent woman. She was methodical and absorbed, a cat cleaning its young, and she left no crease or crevice of his body unwashed.

The young man approached Chindilan, who was undressing with dignity. *Jeshar*, thought Kandri, *two hours ago we were dying, and now—*

Doubt shook him, a spasm of the nerves.

He looked up at the ledges, the stairs to the Keyhole, across the glowing pool. Bracing himself for some betrayal, some attack.

Nothing had changed. The strangers carried buckets back and forth from the water, silent as mimes. Kandri felt ashamed of his panic. He feared these people because they were different, because their eyes were beautiful and strange. As if strangeness meant menace. As if his own clan were not baying for his blood.

Then he caught Utarif's eye. The man's smile a mask. "Captain," Kandri stammered, "I don't think—I mean, perhaps we shouldn't all—"

"Disarm at once?" murmured Utarif. "Wouldn't dream of it. Fact of the matter—"

He beckoned to three of his soldiers, and led them to a spot where they could watch the whole of the oasis, and the stairs.

Relief washed over Kandri. How could he ever trust again, after Stilts' betrayal at Alibat S'Ang? *To hell with trust. If you're safe enough to give it, you don't need it anyway.*

But his bitter thoughts vanished like a dream when Fiasul set to work on his skin. He nearly moaned. The frigid water, the soft linen traveling his body, the unspeakable pleasure. To die now. Ang's mercy. And how sick in the head had he become, to think ill of these strangers? Why would enemies bother with *this?*

"You're simply good people, aren't you?" he said.

"Good," she said. "Not people."

"Nachasps," he said. "Is that—do you have to do with Sirchasps, somehow?"

"Sirchasp is cat, black and little. I am Nachasp."

"All right," he said, defeated.

She was tireless. Now and then she gave her companion a mirthful look.

"Fiasul," he said, "people—warriors—are hunting us. Terrible warriors. Maniacs."

She lifted his scrotum; he jumped away. She *tssk*'d and told him to be still.

"You don't understand, girl," he sputtered. "Those bastards, they'll kill us all."

"Stop talking," she said.

"We should fill our bottles and go," he said. "You people, you're gentle, but to them you'll just be someone who helped the abominations. *Harach*, abominations, that's a word that means—"

She pressed a hand to his mouth. Her silver eyes locked on his own.

"No one will find you here," she said.

ଔ

The sun fled to the highest cliffs; the birds began a chattery evensong. Utarif rotated his troops, allowing all to partake in the washing ritual. Soon everyone had been bathed, and waved forward to the pool.

Everyone, that is, but the manservant Ripheem. Still fully dressed, he backed away when Fiasul turned in his direction.

"Oh come, there's no cause for modesty," said Nirabha. "Pretend you're at the mineral baths in Serrekín District, at home."

"That is different, Hraliz," he said. "Those baths are . . . particular."

"Well she is not," said the Prince, "but if you prefer to wait for the shaggy fellow—"

"I prefer neither. I am not a child."

"Then show us, my good man, and be quick," said the Prince. But his servant recoiled: *Show us* was perhaps the wrong thing to say.

"You stink," offered Mektu. "Like a butcher's undershirt. Like a toad fried in grease."

Ripheem gazed at him with loathing. He walked to a far corner of the oasis and stood with his back to a boulder, crossing his great arms. At last it was the Prince himself who carried buckets to his servant, and bid him scrub beneath his clothes.

Kereqa and Chindilan, meanwhile, had been escorted up the stairs to the ledge where the elders sat. Kandri saw them seated near the edge, overlooking the pool. Both his uncle and the elders were laughing. Even Kereqa's cautious eyes looked more at peace.

A splash. Talupéké had thrown herself into the pool. Mektu, the croaking private, and two other soldiers were already swimming, along with several of the strangers. Talupéké surfaced with a roaring laugh.

"It's cold as all hell!"

For a moment—only a moment—she might have been any girl of sixteen. But her comrades did not laugh with her, did not approach. Kandri winced. Something about her warned others to keep their distance. Not just now, but always.

"Krandee!"

Fiasul's voice. She sat beside another woman near the falls. Fiasul was still dressed; the other wore only a necklace of silver, bright against her skin. They were holding hands like sisters, or sweethearts perhaps. Fiasul beckoned him nearer. He approached, feeling the spray against his cheeks like a brushing of wings.

"Swim, swim," cried the women over the noise of the falls.

"Later," said Kandri.

"Cold later. Swim now."

He just smiled. He would not swim. It had nothing to do with modesty and everything to do with fear. He could swim well enough—Mektu had taught him years ago—but water would never be his element. Not since his eighteenth birthday, when the stream that gave life to his village had almost taken his own.

The women studied him, and their teasing smiles faded into something kinder. He bent and splashed water on his face. When he raised his eyes Fiasul stood beside him, extending her hand.

"We go up," she said. "See the Wall."

"The Wall?"

She led him up the stairs to where the elders sat. They numbered eight, and they smiled at Kandri but did not rise. Chindilan and Kereqa, he saw now, had climbed to a higher shelf set back from the first. It appeared to be a lookout spot: the towering cliffs parted there, leaving a window on the east. The two stood as if hypnotized by what they saw.

"Young friend."

Kandri looked down: a very old man, probably the oldest of all the Nachasps, had reached up and taken his hand. He pressed it tightly between his own trembling palms. Then he looked at Fiasul and grinned.

"*Idiparath sel sebu.*"

Fiasul shook her head, and the two exchanged a few more words. The old man patted his hand, the floating touch of a grandfather. At last he sat back with a shrug.

"What was that about?" asked Kandri.

Fiasul dropped her gaze. "He speak lie."

"What lie?"

"He said you are easy. *Sunuth*, I don't know how to say it. Trick?"

"To trick? He thinks I'm easy to trick? How could he know one way or the other?"

"You fight for the Prophet, but not believing the Prophet. Not loving her."

Kandri frowned. It did not shock him that these people knew of the Prophet—was any name better known in Urrath?—but he had not expected to be identified as one of her troops.

"These?"

He pointed to his own eyes, and Fiasul nodded. She had seen the cactus-oil eyestain, that slight hint of violet that marked every Soldier of Revelation for life. He had underestimated these people. He had been so distracted by their extraordinary eyes that he had forgotten his own.

Obscurely angry, he said, "I did believe in the Prophet, once. She did some good in the world."

"Maybe believe but not love," said Fiasul.

"How would you know?" he said.

"*Abek*, Fiasul," said the old man. The others made sounds of earnest agreement.

"*Keder, keder, abek.*" Fiasul sighed, glanced at Kandri. "Come now, see Wall. Old man wanting tea."

264

He stood between his uncle and Kereqa, gazing east. He could not speak. He could not make room in his mind for what he saw.

"The tales were true," said Kereqa. "I never believed them. I never thought such a thing could be built."

The desert sprawled before them, red in the sunset, terrifying in size. Endless barrens of gravel and stone. Naked hills. Phantom suggestion of mountains in the distance. Above all, sand. An ocean of dunes, boundless, sinuous, marching away to the horizon.

And against that ocean stood a wall.

It was a titanic ruin. Taller than the spire on the Prophet's Palace of Radiance, Kandri thought, and wide enough for twenty to walk abreast upon the battlements. It began with a vast tower—swamped by sand to some fifty feet—and ran on forever, beyond forever, vanishing to a pale red speck where earth merged with sky. Crenellations, cracked horse-tooth defenses, stood along the near side, and every ten or twelve miles another tower raised its head, blind and broken, guarding nothing.

"That," said Chindilan, "is the Empire of the Kasraj. What it was capable of, at its height."

"Ravashandul's Wall," said Kereqa. "An emperor's challenge to the desert. Or as some say, to the Gods themselves."

The Wall split the earth in two. On the north side, the land was a flatter version of what they had seen in the hills—earth, rock, gravel—and in the rare fold or crevasse, a hint of thornbrush or cacti. But on the Wall's southern flank the dunes pressed like a besieging army. Great as the stone monstrosity was, the dunes were greater. They crested and broke against the Wall in wind-smoothed mountains, and the very tallest spilled over the ramparts to drift on the wind into the lands beyond. In other places the dunes had broken through the Wall outright, swallowing fragments the size of castles, flooding northwest through the gaps. Conquering new lands.

"The Gods are winning," said Chindilan.

"They are," said Kereqa, "but not our beloved Ang and her children: Surthang the Death-Sower is victorious here."

Kandri turned to Fiasul. "How far . . . does it go?"

"Far," she said. "To Sanulsreya, then more miles. Desert Wall is very long."

"Sanulsreya?" In what dream had he heard the name?

"Old city," said Fiasul. "From Wall you cannot see it. Lost to sand."

That was it: Sanulsreya was one of the cities Eshett had spoken of, in her trance-like speech.

"Why doesn't everyone follow the Wall across the desert?" he asked.

Fiasul laughed aloud. "You are like baby, Krandee. Wall is long, so long. Even very long. But desert is long like thing of Gods. Also dangerous. Also leading from nowhere to nowhere."

"Dangerous how?" asked Kereqa.

Fiasul gestured with her chin. "You staying north side tomorrow, not south. Is better that way, until winter ending. Stay out of sand."

Chindilan cocked an eye at her. "That's up to our Caravan Master, darling. But is there something we should know?"

The Nachasp woman laughed again. "*Darlink* again, what is that, I am Fiasul."

She left them there, with a last mischievous glance. Chindilan's mouth twitched above his beard. "Baby Krandee," he said.

"They don't even try to say *your* name."

Kereqa smiled gently. "Here is something to be glad of, both of you." She pointed at the tower where the wall began. "Just before the sand begins," she said. "There is a trail running north to south. It is difficult to see, only a line of dust upon the stone."

Kandri shielded his eyes. "I see it. Barely."

"Follow it south," said Kereqa.

Squinting, Kandri traced the path with his eyes. Half a mile south of the Wall, it passed through a curious space: a circle of tall, rough-hewn stones. And there at the center of the circle it was bisected by a second, even fainter trail. This second trail ran back to the hills, entering them five or six miles north of where they stood. East it vanished into sand.

"The standing stones are the crossroads," said Kandri, "where Jód promised to meet us."

"Yes," said Chindilan, "and it's barely four miles from where we're standing."

"Then where the hell is the caravan?"

"That is odd," agreed his uncle, "but not so odd. We're early, if you can believe it. Jód's not expecting us until tomorrow."

For a moment Kandri was stunned. But it was true: all the thirst and fear and strangeness since their departure from the caravan had occurred in just two days.

"We should get down there *now*," he said.

"Should we, though?" said Kereqa. "The crossroads are exposed: we would be visible from all directions. Jód himself will likely stop the caravan at some hidden vantage."

"Kereqa's right," said Chindilan. "Down there we'll stand out like flies in the cream. And if we're attacked, that's no place to make a stand. Better to sleep here under cover, and head for the crossroads with the sunrise. Even if they reach the crossroads in the night, Jód's promised to wait until the following sunset. That gives us all day to walk four miles."

The smith turned Kandri a grin. "Let your brother say, 'We can't be late' a few more times. We'll spring the good news just before Ripheem stomps on his head."

Kandri's smile was faint. "We shouldn't sleep here," he insisted. At their startled looks, he added, "The Nachasps. They're wonderful, of course. But they're also—"

"Freaks," said Kereqa. "That is the word you're looking for. But I tell you there are odder clans in Urrath. The Eralu have the clawed feet of bears."

"That's a myth, sister," said Chindilan. "My cousin married an Eralu. His toenails were ugly but perfectly human." He looked down at the silver-eyed strangers. "Nothing ugly about them, is there? Sleek as minks, and generous as well. They snared six rabbits today. I believe we're to be offered a taste."

"But how did they get here?" pressed Kandri. "They have no camels. How far could they have come?"

"The hairy fellow spoke of that. 'We know water places—big, small, very small.' He meant wells, I suppose. They must drift from one to another."

"Jód didn't mention any other wells," said Kandri.

"Jód mentions as little as he can get away with," said Chindilan. He clapped Kandri's shoulder. "Tell Utarif your worries; he's also spooked. But what worries me are those butter-slippery stairs. Let's join the others. It's damned near dark."

க

"Strange, top to bottom," said Captain Utarif. "You don't have to convince me of that. But strange how? I don't see these people selling us out to the enemy like a pack of stinking *Tirmassil*, do you?"

Kandri found that he did agree. But then, as if from a darkened room, the vision pounced: Stilts, beloved Stilts, pushing an innocent man from the cliff at Alibat S'Ang.

"I don't trust them," he said, "but then I don't trust anyone fully these days. I seem to have lost the knack."

Utarif gave him a long look, and his face changed, tightening as with the memory of a blow.

"General Tebassa," he said, "is my savage grandfather: by inclination, not by blood. It's the role he plays with most of his soldiers. But Stilts—he was even closer. My birth-father died in a jail in Mab Makkutin; I barely knew him. By the time I met Stilts I was seventeen and not looking for a father, or so I told myself. But I thought of him like a father. I loved him like one. And you know how that ended."

Kandri nodded, averting his eyes.

"You're on an extraordinary path," Utarif continued. "You and your brother and that old smith you call your uncle. There's something about the three of you that I can't put my finger on. But I'll say this much: if your instincts tell you we should be wary of this place, I'll not be the fool who ignores you. We'll sleep elsewhere: down the path a few miles, somewhere we can't get cornered."

"Thank you, Captain," said Kandri. Then a thought came to him, and he asked, "Which way does Ifimar Jód intend to take us from here?"

"That's a dullard's question," said Utarif. "East, unless you want to rush into the Prophet's arms."

"I meant along which side of the Wall," said Kandri. "Fiasul told us to stick to the north side. She said the dunes weren't safe in winter."

"Fiasul is a strange bird, Hinjuman. And Ifimar Jód has crossed this desert fifty times. Leave the navigating to him. And listen." Utarif raised a warning finger. "Not a word to the others about shifting camp, do you hear me? Let them have a couple hours to relax. I've set a watch at the top of the stair by the Keyhole, and another on the opposite trail down to the crossroads. When I give the order, we'll see how our Nachasp friends react. If they try to stop us, we'll know they were never friends at all."

Kandri nodded. "That's a good plan, sir."

"Glad you approve. Now get your ass up to the Keyhole and relieve the corporal. I believe she wants a swim."

Kandri did as he was told. He would not have minded seeing the corporal take to the water; she was lovely, and her large eyes reminded him distantly of Ariqina. But by the time he had replaced her at the Keyhole the night was pitch black: so black that he could only make out the cliffs above them by the absence of stars. He paced. Warmth would be the next to go. Looking down on the oasis he saw a small fire at the center, and an even smaller one on the elders' ledge.

Night birds called. He pumped his arms, keeping warm. Now and then he heard soft laughter from below, or a splash.

Then a flickering light appeared on the stairs. It jerked and bobbed and nearly went out. But at last it resolved itself into Mektu. He was cradling the candle in both hands, cursing the trembling flame.

When he reached the cleft he told Kandri he was relieved.

"Utarif sent you?"

Mektu looked at him askance. "I volunteered," he said.

"Ah, well."

"Try their tea—it's bitter, but it grows on you. And take the candle. Those stairs would be the death of a billy goat."

Kandri fumbled for the candle. But Mektu did not let it go.

"I'm sorry I hit you, Kandri. I haven't slept since."

"Jekka's Hell, you've suffered more than I have," said Kandri.

"Something's all wrong inside me."

"The only thing wrong with you is all the shit you believe."

"I've never healed."

"The arrow wound?" asked Kandri, suddenly alarmed. "It hasn't grown worse, has it? Gods, you should have *told* me."

"Not that," said Mektu. "I never think of that any more. The Outworlders saved me. They're magicians."

"Then what are you saying?"

"I'm saying that I've never healed since the smokehouse."

Kandri closed his eyes.

"I always believed I'd won a victory," said Mektu. "That I'd driven the yatra out of me for certain. Others thought so too. Even Ma said so."

"Ma? You talked about the yatra with Ma?"

"Of course, and she believed me," said Mektu. "The Old Man believed me too. He just said I was lying because he was afraid for me. I hated him for that, for denying what had happened. But maybe he had good reason, Kandri. The priests might have put me to death, if they thought a yatra was inside me."

"What did Ma say?"

"That I'd done a great deed, probably. Scared a yatra into letting me go. 'Forced its mouth open' is how she put it."

Kandri was stunned. Mektu's mother, his own beloved Sepu, absolutely never lied. Not for comfort, not for convenience, not out of pity or anger or fear. But . . . *probably*?

As if reading his thoughts, Mektu leaned closer above the candle. "The night after it attacked me, I couldn't sleep at all. I climbed out on the porch roof and heard them talking, Ma and the Old Man. She told him some yatras would rather die than let go of a soul once they'd claimed it. She said that we're like wild horses for them—they have to break us, it's a point of pride. If you can't stay on the horse, other riders laugh at you.

"Then she got very quiet and I had to hold my breath to hear. She said I might have just chased it deeper inside me. Way inside, like a bear into its cave."

"You think it could have lurked there, all this time? For *eighteen years?*"

"Why not?" said Mektu. "Those things live forever."

"Mektu, listen to me. We had three years in the army. We've marched with officers, with generals, with the Sons of Heaven themselves. At Eternity Camp there were *thirty thousand other people* it could have jumped to. Why would it stay curled up inside you?"

"For the same reason it chose me to begin with. Because I'm different."

"*Harach*, you sure as hell are. You fought it like a Gods-damned tiger. Even if it did hide within you for awhile, it would jump ship at the first good chance. And by now it's had thousands of chances. Things that live forever aren't stupid."

Mektu looked into his eyes, and a fragile smile appeared on his lips.

"I miss her, brother. I miss home."

Kandri just nodded.

"We can't ever go back. Our own people would stone us to death, and turn Ma and the kids over to the Prophet if they tried to help us."

"We can't go back," Kandri agreed. "Uncle's all we'll ever have."

He might have added, *besides each other*. He might even have said, *and Ari, if we find her waiting*. But he said neither. Mektu reached out and touched his chin.

"I'll never forgive myself for that."

"Oh shut up," said Kandri. "I've thought of smacking you a few times, Ang knows. Forget it."

"You mean that?"

"I tend to mean what I say."

"Yes, you do. That's the best thing about you, brother." He laughed, that old snicker-whinny that Kandri despised. "We've shared everything—really *everything*, isn't that so? Do you remember when I took you to Sed Hemon to see the girls?"

"Can't say that I do."

"The girls *bathing*, the Nawhal sisters—with no clothes on. Ari was there too."

"You sure I was?"

"The Nawhals—those gorgeous—Kandri, you lying *pig!*"

Kandri doubled over laughing. And the candle went out.

∞

No matches, of course. Weak with laughter, Kandri hugged Mektu in the dark. His mirth departed quickly. There was one more thing he had to learn.

"That day on Alibat S'Ang—"

"I don't know," said Mektu. "All right? I don't know if I managed all that myself, or if a yatra used me like a Gods-damned puppet. And it scares me, it fucking scares me to death. You satisfied?"

"I wasn't thinking about that," said Kandri.

"You weren't?"

"I was thinking of Stilts. How he pushed Mansari over that cliff. His friend, his fellow soldier. And then he turned and told us to jump. Three times, Mek. Why did he keep insisting that we jump?"

"He knew what the Prophet had in mind for us. The torture. The worms."

"Would he care, if he's a believer? We killed the Prophet's son."

Mektu shook his head. "You should have asked him, before *he* jumped. Or . . . rolled. That was strange too, of course. Seemed like he had some kind of attack."

"I looked down from the cliff when it was over," said Kandri. "Just for an instant, before the mist closed in. There were pine trees, far below. And something else."

"What something?"

"Canvas, maybe," said Kandri.

"What do you mean, canvas? Canvas tied to the trees?"

"Or a net."

A very long silence. Kandri felt guilty for his poor recollection. The fighting had been so savage, death so near.

"You're dreaming," Mektu said at last.

"That's what I think," Kandri agreed.

"Because if there *was* a net, something to catch us—"

"There was no other way down, except through those Rasanga."

"If there was a net," Mektu said again, "then going over the cliff would have made all kinds of sense. And maybe Stilts—"

He shook himself. "Horse shit, Kandri. You heard them. The Rasanga spoke to Stilts like one of their own."

"But they didn't entirely trust him."

"No one entirely trusts a traitor." Mektu tapped him gently on the temple. "I think the sun cooked your head today. Or maybe I knocked something loose."

☙

Kandri felt his way down the steps. He was touched by Mektu's apology, but doubted the peace would last. *We've shared everything.* That was perfectly true. Deployments, desertion, secret lessons with their father, the Prophet's irrevocable curse. And Eshett: she had been in Mektu's arms before his own, if only in a brothel. And—

No, not Ariqina.

In the darkness, he felt the copper ring from the fever-syrup bottle, still around his thumb where she'd slipped it four years ago. *She never touched him. Mektu's lying through his teeth.*

As he neared the oasis floor, the smell of meat woke a hunger he had pushed aside for days. Other candles guttered in the night breeze, illuminating faces, bodies huddled close. Kandri walked to the fireside: there were the rabbits, skewered, sizzling. He knelt between two strangers, warmed his hands. The pensive corporal was here, her face wet and gleaming. Across the flames he saw the woman with the silver necklace, dressed now and listening to Prince Nirabha.

"In my city we light fires on rooftops," said the Prince, "and on hills, towers, mountain citadels. Any high place, where we may send a little light back to heaven, by way of thanks. Once a year we even climb to the glacier that hangs above our city—the glacier that will be our doom, they say, should the Gods decide to let it fall. Youths who would serve the nation must launch a fire balloon from that ice. The colors they choose declare the calling to which they aspire: red, blue, green, orange—warrior, teacher, healer, scribe.

You must see it to believe it, my dear: the firelight reflected in the ice crystals tall as trees, the glowing faces, that flotilla of balloons."

"We have these here," said the young woman. "*Grasthu*, terrible. Long strings hanging."

The Prince shook his head. "No strings. In my land we simply let them go."

"In your land," she asked, "eating many people?"

The Prince sat up straight, then laughed. "We are not speaking of living creatures, my dear. Only balloons."

"*Bloons*." They laughed together. Her small hand was on his knee.

A ceramic jug made its way around the circle, steam wafting from its mouth. "*Abek*," said Fiasul's companion, catching Kandri's eye.

"Tea, Hinjuman," said the pensive corporal.

"I know."

She did not hear him. Her eyes were locked on the man with silver braids, gliding by in the half-light.

Kandri wet his lips with the tea, then changed his mind and passed it on. When he looked back at the circle, the pensive corporal had risen to follow the man.

The rabbits were delicious. There must have been more than six, for everyone was given a good portion. Kandri did not refuse, but he ate his portion quickly and rose. Where was Utarif? Surely it was time to set out.

Following voices, he groped his way to the pool's edge. Two men laughing, moaning a little. The croaking private and one of the strangers. He heard them splashing, fumbling together. He could not see a thing.

The private was a *lulee*, then. Kandri shook his head. Did it matter? Should he care?

Every Chiloto man knew his duty to hate them, of course. What they did was diabolical, said the priests and schoolmasters. It made you feeble. It spread disease. Kandri had played his part, chanting *Lulee* at the old men who lived together at the edge of the village, grinning at the insults scrawled in chalk upon their door.

But that was another life. A life of stupid certainties, a life of faith. Schoolmasters, priests: why trust the bastards? *And while you're at it, why trust yourself? What do you know of love?*

He'd killed for it, to be sure. For love of the Prophet, his people's savior, that murderer and fiend. And when real love—shattering, soul-changing love—had come for him, he'd blinked. For Kandri had never told Ariqina he loved her. Except for a thousand times in silence, idiotic silence, in the months before she disappeared.

Fuck them all. Fuck the gifts of loathing they'd bequeathed him, this fever swamp of a mind. Twenty years of lies about the soul, and here he was: replete with solitude, in a desert alone.

"Krandee?"

Fiasul's voice. Turning, he saw a candle gliding toward him. She was no longer smiling, and for some reason he liked her better for it. She reached out and touched his face; he jerked his head like a startled horse.

"I'm not good company at the moment," he said.

Fiasul laced her arm through his own. The gesture was so easy and familiar it was as if they had walked like this for years, in sight of everyone, joined for life.

"Did you hear me? I—"

"So much trouble," she said. "Bring you here, wash you, make good *abek*. You think I am making poison in *abek*?"

"Not poison, no."

"Even the big stupid one drinking *abek*. Not Krandee. So much work."

She led him into the darkness, up the spray-slippery rocks, around the curtain of water to a hollow place against the cliff. She eased him down by her side.

"I have to find Captain Utarif," he said. "Do you know where he is?"

"Yes." She slid a hand under his shirt. The concave wall pressed them together.

"You are careful, Krandee. That is good. Stay longer alive."

His breath came short. Her hand played with the hairs on his chest, then moved to the calfskin pouch.

"This is what?"

"Nothing important." The biggest lie of his life. Somehow he did not like her touching the Letter of Cure. Even when she bathed him he had

275

worn it, shifting the belt to keep the pouch away from her sopping rag. The rawhide stitches were tight as sinews, and the letter inside protected with wax. But one could never be too careful.

Gently as he could, he removed her hand. The woman's fingers intertwined with his own, dancing, exploring. She found the copper ring on his thumb and grew still, as if at some momentous discovery.

"This, I think—"

"Yes, that's important."

Ariqina's only gift. He could hear her laughter, that night in the clinic as she slipped it onto his thumb. *I have you now, Kandri Hinjuman. I'm the master of your soul.*

He should get away from this stranger, from her kindness and her questions, the purr of her body, the tease of her voice.

"I am sorry," said Fiasul.

"Sorry?" he said. "What the hell for?"

"Sorry that you bear a wound."

"They've healed," he said. "I'm lucky, no infections, wound spirits are a miracle—"

"Not true," she said. "Some wounds close without healing. That wound I gave you when I left the Valley, for instance."

"I searched, Ariqina. For weeks, until they locked me up. Why did you go?"

"I didn't take another lover," said the voice in his ear. "If you thought that of me, you're unkind. Yours wasn't the only heart I broke."

"I never thought that, Ari."

"Yes you did."

He brushed her cheek with his lips. It was the most natural thing in the world to know that she was Ariqina—of course she was, who else—but how could she accuse him of such coldness?

"I would have gone with you," he said. "If you'd asked me, given me a chance."

"I couldn't," said the voice. "Not after that evening, that priest—"

"Father Marz?" The mention of the cleric touched a rage in him that nearly burned away the mist. "I knew it, I knew from the start. He forced himself on you."

"No," said Ariqina. "He tried. It made him furious that he was weaker than a girl. But he raped me all the same with his words. There's your answer, Kandri. That's why you never saw me again."

"What do you mean, with his words? What did he tell you?"

She grew still. Kandri knew the secret was crouched there, trembling, a bird in her mouth. And since it would not take flight he tried to free it with kisses. The sweetness broke him, he had sought her in Eshett, missed her to the edge of madness; the bird leapt floundering from mouth to mouth, and then she turned away to breathe and it escaped, vanished into the night.

She clung to him, weeping on his shoulder.

"Ari," he whispered, "is Mektu . . . part of what happened to you?"

She whispered a *Yes*, and then a fiercer *No!* She burrowed into his embrace, sobbing, shaking in his arms. Kandri raised his eyes. The oasis was a dark, distant valley, a land glimpsed through the wrong end of a telescope. The candles snuffed, the moon nowhere to be seen. Only a last throbbing of orange coals where the fire had danced.

"I won't leave you, Ari," he whispered. "Never again. I swear on my life."

In his arms the woman lay still.

⦃

"Fiasul?"

"Shh. Too much fearing. Too much mind."

"Don't do that, don't touch—"

"We are Nachasps, Krandee. We pay for what we take."

"I think I drifted off."

"Not yet, darlink-boy."

"I had the strangest dream."

"Dream nothing. Only rest, I protect you. And maybe you protect me."

⦃

A weight on his ankles. Kandri woke to broad daylight—mouth dry, cheek sand-crusted. Talupéké was sprawled across his shins.

"Tal?"

She was naked. Someone's cloak thrown over her, no more. She stirred, blinked, gaped at him. Her body slow, as though rising from the depths of a lake. And he was no different. He sat up; she rolled off his legs. They were in the center of the clearing, twenty yards or more from where he'd lain with Fiasul. He was dressed, but his sandals were missing. Some yards away three men lay motionless: Mektu, Nirabha, and the croaking private.

"The fuck," slurred Talupéké.

She was all right, then.

Kandri crawled to the others. The Prince was fully dressed but Mektu and the private were naked as babes. He shook them; they groaned. Kandri rose unsteadily to his feet.

The rest of the party was scattered about the oasis, some stirring, most dead asleep. The pensive corporal and Captain Utarif lay tangled like lovers at the foot of the stairs. The camels knelt under the palm trees, heads resting on one another's backs.

"Wake up," Kandri rasped, swaying where he stood. Then, filling his lungs and shouting: "*Dumb bastards, snap out of it, wake up.*"

The remaining sleepers twitched awake. Some with nervous laughter, all with embarrassment, Utarif and the pensive corporal mortified. None harmed, as far as Kandri could see.

But of the strangers there was no sign at all.

ശ

They sprang to action. Where were their weapons, their faskas, their shoes? For a few terrible moments they feared that the deception carried out by the guides had been visited upon them again. But no: their faskas were undisturbed. Their foodstuffs were not only intact but supplemented with bread and dates. Their missing clothes were found in the camel bags, neatly folded. Salve had been applied to their blistered feet.

"Someone's trimmed my nails," said Mektu, raising both hands. "Look at me, Uncle. I'm like a schoolgirl."

But Chindilan was looking past him, bewildered. "My axe," he said, "is in that Gods-damned tree."

So it was, nestled high in the fronds of one of the palms. Other items—bows, blades, headscarves—also festooned the treetops. The brothers' telescope dangled from a sling made from Kandri's headscarf. Mektu snatched it down, laughing. "They haven't robbed us. They're just tricksters. They played us a joke before they stole away."

"You speak too soon," said Kereqa. "Our sandals are still missing, and who knows what else?"

"My arrows, that's what else," said the croaking private. He looked hard at the captain. "*All* of them, sir."

"Idiots," said the captain, seething. "It will serve them right if they poison themselves. Right, inventory! What else have they taken?"

"My book of memories," said Kereqa, "although I place it beneath my head when I sleep."

"My good knife," said Chindilan, "and devil's spit, my tinder box! Anybody seen it?"

"My ring!" cried the Prince, gaping at his naked hand. "Damn them, the pilfering dogs!"

"Hard luck, Prince," said Mektu. "An heirloom, was it?"

"To hell with heirlooms," snapped the Prince. "That ring is encrusted with Nfepan sapphires. I intended to sell it."

Mektu grinned—and then looked suddenly mortified, and made a dash for the camels. Kandri could not begin to think what he was worried about losing. He touched his own ring—that worthless band of copper, more precious to him than a crate of sapphires. *Praise Ang almighty, if she'd stolen—*

He clapped a hand to his chest. The knowledge cut him like a blade of ice. "Oh no, *no—*"

The calfskin pouch, and with it the Cure for the World Plague, were gone.

15. CROSSROADS

No one shouted at him. No one said a word. But their faces—his uncle's long look, his brother's disbelief—were worse than any rage. The torture lasted only a moment, however, for with a clarity of mind quite absent the night before, they sprang to the task of catching the thieves.

The pensive corporal, with Captain Utarif's telescope in hand, raced up to the high ledge overlooking the desert and the Wall. For a few interminable seconds they watched her gaze sweep the desert; then she turned and made a throat-cutting gesture: *No one.*

Of course this narrowed the hunt only slightly. The Nachasps could have fled back up the trail beyond the Keyhole, or in either direction on the opposite trail: up into the maze of hills, or down toward the crossroads and the Wall.

"They could be *beyond* the crossroads by now," said Chindilan, "if they walked through the night. Hell, they could be—"

"It hasn't been that long," said Kandri. "I'm sure of it, I—woke up, for a moment. But we have to search those trails *now.*"

"Look who's thinking sharp all of a sudden," said Utarif. Nonetheless he divided them swiftly into teams. "If you catch sight of them, close. Don't give them a chance to scatter. Knives against throats, people, and no discussion. Get the letter. Then they can go to hell."

"Those pigs," said Talupéké. "I thought they *liked* us."

"Thoughts like that can wait," said Mektu.

"Right for once," said the captain. "Get moving, and run as fast as you can. But not too far: a mile at the outside. Then get back here, no matter what."

"A mile?" cried Kandri. "What if we don't catch them in a mile?"

"How many forks did we pass, Hinjuman?" said Utarif. "How many more will we find on the crossroads trail? And what if those slippery rats take to the hills where there's no path at all? We're shooting arrows in the dark here, and it's all we can do."

"Captain, *we have to get that letter*. We're talking about the Plague, about the whole Gods-forsaken world."

"If only you'd kept that in mind," said Prince Nirabha, "before you snuggled up to a snake."

"Leave him alone!" snapped Mektu, rounding on him. "I saw you, Your Specialness. That girl was practically in your lap, and you were robbed too, and besides, *you're fond of snakes*."

On his last words he poked Nirabha hard in the chest. It was a grave error. The servant Ripheem leaped for Mektu with a roar. Knocking Kandri and Chindilan from his path, he clamped one hand on Mektu's wrist and cuffed him open-palmed across the face with the other. The force of the blow was staggering: Mektu's head rolled to one side, and for a moment he went limp.

Kandri saw disaster about to happen: his brother was already recovering, and his free hand was groping for his machete. Kandri seized his arm even as Ripheem grasped Mektu's shirt and lifted him from the ground.

One-handed. Gods of Death.

"No one who walks this earth," he snarled, "lays a hand on the Hraliz."

And then, just as suddenly as he had erupted, Ripheem grew still. Once more the Prince had intervened, whispering to his servant, a hand on one massive shoulder. Ripheem's face worked. His right arm was drawn back in a fist.

"That is enough, brave one," murmured the Prince. "This man is no danger to my person. Merely a buffoon."

Mektu's legs flailed. "Toad—kill him—squash—"

"Shut the hell *up*, Mek," snapped Kandri. "Prince, if this attack dog of yours can't tell the difference between—"

"You fools!" came Kereqa's voice from a distance. "Pull your heads from your anuses! I have seen them!"

They whirled. The old woman had labored up to the trailhead opposite the Keyhole. "They are out upon the sand already, making for the Wall and the desert beyond. What are you waiting for, heaven's commandment? Ride after them, ride!"

ಐ

It was the only thing to be done. But they had just four camels, and the first mile of the trail was too steep for even the Sparaviths to navigate with riders. It was not until the hills grew tamer that they mounted, and smacked the animals into a run.

Kandri, Mektu, Talupéké, Utarif. Inferior riders on extraordinary mounts. The others, led by Kereqa, they left to follow afoot.

The crossroads, Utarif had shouted back at them over his shoulder. *Wait for Jód. We'll rejoin you by nightfall, come what may.*

His words dreadful. His reasoning flawless. They would either catch the thieves quickly or not at all; that was certain. They had taken only what they could seize in an instant: headscarves, faskas, blades, telescopes.

Kandri's eyes ached. *All your fault. The fault of your loneliness, your lust.* He had thought he would be remembered as the killer of the Prophet's firstborn. And perhaps he would be—by the Chiloto masses who cursed his name. But the scholars, the Ariqinas of the world: they would remember him as the one who let the Cure slip through his fingers. The one who condemned millions to an endless future of Plague.

If anyone remembered him. If memory itself survived the world's rising frenzy.

Garatajik! he thought. *What the hell were you thinking? Just one copy, in a language no one speaks? Why not a thousand copies in forty languages? Why not scatter them like seeds?*

The old mystery tortured him as never before. Garatajik must have had a reason. He was the secret enemy of his mother the Prophet. His mere survival was proof of his brilliance. Besides, Uncle Chindilan revered him like a saint, and Chindilan was the best judge of character Kandri had ever known.

And your brother stabbed him, stabbed the author of the Cure. The Prophet's right, we're abominations. Everything we touch, we destroy.

Another source of misery was his ass. He was slipping in the saddle, chafing, unable to still himself no matter how he tightened his legs. He was clumsy, he was top-heavy. His inner cheeks, he thought with terror, were going to bleed.

The army had trained him for exactly twenty minutes as a camel rider before declaring him not worth the trouble: he was a mountain youth, they reasoned, and would expire in the heat if deployed to the desert. Kandri, inclined to agree with them, never mentioned his birth-mother. He was given boots and a machete. He would fight the War of Revelation afoot.

"Too rigid," called Utarif, glancing his way. "Watch Talupéké, she's a natural. Or watch me." He gripped the forward ring on the saddle. "That's your anchor. Keep it close. And sway *with* the camel, don't fight the motion. Loosen your back, and your ass will stay where it should."

Kandri tried to loosen his back and nearly pitched over the camel's shoulder. But the captain's advice was sound, if difficult. With a few minutes of effort Kandri did manage to stop the chafing. Blessed deliverance! He looked at Utarif with wordless gratitude, and the captain smiled.

"Get in the habit of talking to your beast. They understand everything. Not the words, but the feeling. Tell them they're safe, that they're good and clever, that they matter to you. Tell them it's their job to walk, walk forever, and you'll take care of the rest."

In spite of everything, Kandri smiled too. "Is that what you tell your soldiers?"

"Don't push it, wise ass. Not today."

 C8

The hills grew smaller yet. Dry earth gave way to grit and sand. Then they rounded a last bulge and the world opened, the gravel plain and the sand ocean beyond, and just two miles ahead, the circle of stones marking the crossroads. Beyond it, the Wall rose like a continent, battered and half-buried on the near side, the toothlike crenellations huge and cracked and crumbled. The white scar of the trail they were following slinked out toward the ruin, sand crossing it in streamers on the rising wind.

Talupéké had taken the soldiers' telescope from her grandmother; now she swept it across the land. "Nothing," she said. "They must be behind another dune."

"Or behind the Wall," said Utarif. "We could scale that first great dune and step right onto it, I expect."

"What good would that do?" said Kandri. "Even if we saw them on the far side, we'd be three hundred feet over their heads. We could wave, I suppose."

Only after he finished did he realize he was shouting, and not merely over the wind.

"We could also," said Utarif, "look down among the other dunes. On *this* side."

"Oh. Yes." Kandri's face was burning. "I'm sorry, Captain, I'm not—"

"We'll make for the crossroads," said Utarif, "and hope they show themselves."

He charged off without another word, and the others followed. And here in the open Kandri saw at once the greatness of the Sparaviths. His camel exploded into its run. Soon its legs were a blur, swift and graceful as any horse's, but longer.

Kandri was not graceful. He took the ring on the saddle in a death grip, cursing the camel's lack of a mane. He bounced, and the bounce was like an endlessly repeated kick in the balls. He could only pray that Utarif knew how to keep them going in the right direction. And how to stop.

In minutes flat they were nearing the stone circle at the crossroads. Up close, the stones were jagged rectangles: some broken or toppled, but most standing high as the camels' ears. The wind combed through them, a lament. The blown sand lay against them in drifts.

Utarif cried, "Whoa!" and reined his camel in. The beast skidded obedi-
ently to a stop and the others followed its example, raising a dust cloud that
was quickly shorn away on the wind. Talupéké sprang from her mount to the
top of a stone and wrenched open the telescope.

"Nothing," she said as before. "They could be atop the Wall, hiding
among those teeth." She pointed up at the great stone merlons.

"Behind the archery placements?" said Mektu. "Not likely. But they
could be inside the tower."

"They could be *anywhere*," growled Utarif. "And the wind's growing by
the minute. I wish your Parthan was here, or Jód, or someone who could tell
us if we're looking at a storm." He sighed. "Right, sister, we're climbing that
dune. You Hinjumans get into the shade, drink some water—and be ready to
ride, you hear? Don't shout for any reason. We've each got a telescope. If the
Nachasps are there, I'll give you a clear signal, north or south."

"What if they're up where you're going, on the Wall?" asked Kandri.

"Then you'll see us kicking their asses." He glanced sharply at Kandri.
"Stop blaming yourself, Hinjuman. They bewitched you like they bewitched
us all. You suspected it before anyone."

"And then ignored it, did nothing," said Kandri.

Mektu nodded in vigorous agreement. Utarif gazed at them a moment
longer.

"The both of you need to calm down," he said at last. "Listen to your
conscience, not your guilt. And have some faith in yourselves, and each other.
It's not misplaced. All right, Tal."

The two soldiers thundered off toward the dune. "Faith," said Mektu,
watching them, "is the last thing in the world you want a Chiloto to have
more of. Faith is what fucked us over to begin with."

"There's more than one kind of faith," Kandri said.

Nothing now but to wait. They nudged their camels into the shade. The
sigh of the wind like old women in mourning. Kandri looked at the deep
drifts forming against the circle of stones. He thought of the ancient burial
stones near his birthplace in the Coastal Range: frost cracked, tumbled, artifacts of some clan vanished from the earth.

Nothing but stones to prove those people ever existed. His father had said that. He supposed one day it would be the same for his people, the people of the Sataapre Valley and the village of Blind Stream. And for the thousandth time he wondered, with a pain like nails to the skull, what had become of their family.

They sipped water, passed the telescope back and forth. It was terrible how slowly the two soldiers climbed: not even Sparaviths could run up a sheer dune-face. The Wall had deformed the nearest dunes: rather than the lovely hawksbill curves of dunes further out in the lathban, these were ramps and wedges, leaning against the offending stone. The great tower at the Wall's end stood half-submerged, a lighthouse swamped by a monster wave.

"Must be hell up there—the wind I mean," said Mektu. "We could shout all we liked and they'd never hear."

"Someone downwind might," said Kandri. He twisted in his saddle, aimed the telescope back at the hills. Chindilan, Nirabha and his servant, and the remaining soldiers were descending onto the flats—on foot, of course. They would be a long time in arriving.

And still there was no sign of the caravan. The more Kandri thought about it, the more troubling its absence became. How could it possibly have needed longer to reach the crossroads than Kandri and his companions? Jód had been clear that the caravan's path was a straight line, while their own, Ang knew, had meandered like a stream.

Utarif and Talupéké were halfway up the dune. Kandri turned his brother a glance. "The Prince was right, you know. I did this to us. You all trusted me to carry that letter, and I—"

"What happened to you," Mektu interrupted, "could have happened to anyone. Let's just get the damned thing back."

Kandri had to look away. This was the Mektu he could not do without, the one who had carried him unconscious from a battlefield. The one for whom love was greater than vanity, greater than spite.

"Mek," he said carefully, "were they . . . kind to you? Not just friendly, more than that—"

Mektu raised an eyebrow at him. "You'll have to be more specific. Fiasul, now. Tell me how she was *not just friendly.*"

"Oh fuck off."

"Give me the long version. I don't mind."

Kandri smiled, although he knew Mektu hoped for a laugh. There was no laughter in him, nor ever would be again, unless they somehow recovered the Cure.

He blinked; the memories were returning. "She knew things, somehow. Names of people and places. Things I never talk about. She knew about me and—our lives back then."

And Ariqina. He had almost said it aloud.

But Mektu was not paying attention. "Fiasul," he said. "I would like to grapple with her. To grapple and have sex."

"Aren't you a bundle of surprises."

"I'll bet you two did everything," said Mektu. "The way girls like you, it just isn't fair. I wish you'd grow a wart on your nose."

Kandri looked away. What *had* they done together? What was even possible between Nachasps and humans?

"Last night was worse than my eighteenth birthday," said Mektu. "I can't remember anything after I jumped in that pool. But someone must have dragged me by the armpits: there were marks on the ground, and my heels were rubbed raw. And you, speaking of heels, wake up with Talupéké—"

"I did not *touch* Talupéké!"

"I know that—for one thing, you don't have a death wish. But you must have been out like a six-day drunk not to notice when she—Kandri, what is *that*?"

He pointed to one of the standing stones, about thirty feet away. As with all the stones, sand lay drifted deep against its southern face. But something small and dark, about the width of a hand, was protruding from that drift.

Kandri passed his camel's reins to Mektu and slid to the ground. Sand whipped about his ankles. The thing by the stone was tufted like moss. He crossed the circle, leaning into the wind.

His stomach lurched. The tufts were human hair.

He knelt and groped in the sand and found an ear, a jaw, a forehead. He scooped sand away in armfuls. He cupped his hand around a buried shoulder. He braced himself and pulled.

A man's head and torso burst from the drift. A dead man, eyes ruined, cheeks bloodied, mouth forced open by a gag. Kandri tore at it but there was no soul here to save: behind the twisted cloth, his mouth had filled with sand.

That face.

Mektu was shouting something, a bleat downwind. Kandri whipped out his knife and cut the gag. Then he gasped so deeply that sand entered his own throat. Choking, he leaped to his feet and backed away.

The dead man was a camel driver from their own caravan.

"Kandri, come back!"

He was the elder, the one who had tried to explain the prayer to Mektu by the edge of the pit. How in Ang's name had he come here—bound, murdered, alone?

Unless . . . he was not alone. Unless he was placed here quite intentionally, to draw someone in—

Kandri whirled. But all he could see was Mektu across the circle, gesturing with the telescope, screaming. With a blade in each hand Kandri raced back to him.

"What the hell were you doing, Kandri? They're at the summit, mount your camel, get ready to ride!"

"The dead man—"

"I see him—terrible, tragic, Ang rest his soul. Now tie your fucking headscarf and—"

"He's one of ours. A driver from the caravan."

A look of dread crept over Mektu's face. He sat and gaped at the corpse. With trembling hands Kandri reached up and pulled the telescope from his grip.

Chindilan and the others still looked far away. Utarif and Talupéké stood on the dune's crest, scanning the desert with their own scope, peering down between the dunes. He saw Utarif shake his head and pass his camel's reins to Talupéké. Then the captain made for the Wall.

"Jód would never do that to one of his own," said Kandri. "He has codes he follows, rules. If he killed a man he'd behead him straight away and call it justice. He wouldn't stoop to torture."

Utarif stepped onto the Wall as simply as one might step from grass onto paving stones. He made at once for the further edge, crouching lower as he went, and was soon gone from sight.

"He'll be looking down on the north side," said Kandri. "Looking for the Nachasps. Say a prayer, Mek."

But the captain returned in no time at all, and gestured to Talupéké: a sharp slash of the hand. Nothing there. Kandri closed his eyes, trembling. *Breathe. Now breathe again.*

When he opened his eyes Utarif was jogging along the Wall toward the tower, appearing and vanishing behind the broken crenellations. A few yards from its arched doorway, he stopped, gazing into the shadows, holding very still.

"He's seen something now, hasn't he?" said Mektu.

"Or heard something," said Kandri.

Utarif glanced over his shoulder at Talupéké. Kandri swung the telescope: the girl was gesturing frantically: *No!* But when he returned the scope to Utarif the captain was stepping through the arch.

"He's gone inside," said Kandri. "Damn the bastard! I hope he has one hell of a good reason."

"Brother," said Mektu, "if the caravan reached here before us, where has it gone?"

They glanced at each other. The horror of the question flowed between them on the keening wind.

Kandri's gaze moved to the other standing stones. A sand drift against each one of them, smooth and deep. And although he felt a strong urge to turn away—to ride off somewhere, anywhere, to cease thinking, to forget— Kandri found himself approaching another stone and plunging in his hands.

The second corpse was also familiar: one of the women drivers, beaten savagely about the head. When he cut away her gag it was encrusted not only with blood and sand but with shards of her teeth.

Mektu shouted questions, his voice torn away in the wind. Kandri tried to shut it all out. The next two drifts contained nothing but sand, but the one after that—

"Shit of the Gods!"

Something flinched at his touch. Whoever lay buried there was alive.

He probed deeper, found a chin, a neck. The figure squirmed. Kandri locked his hands around an upper arm and wrenched.

It was Ulren, Jód's bulb-headed second in command. He lay on his side, wrists and ankles tied behind his back, eyes pinched shut. The rope binding his limbs was also wound tight about the stone, forcing him to lie against it in a torturous position. He had managed to spit out his gag, and so had been able to close his mouth against the sand. *And that's why you're alive*, Kandri thought.

He cut Ulren free, brushed his face, scraped sand from his ears and nostrils. Then he opened his faska and dribbled water on Ulren's lips. The man began to cough; Kandri held him against his knees. He was too weak to sit up.

"Can you hear me?"

Ulren nodded.

"How many victims here?"

The man twitched, as though remembering were an agony. He held up three shaking fingers.

"Counting you?" Kandri shook him gently, then raised his voice to a shout: "Three counting *you*, man?"

Ulren nodded again. Kandri felt a momentary relief: at least there were no more bodies to discover.

The deputy beckoned; he wanted to speak. Kandri bent his ear close to Ulren's mouth. The man's voice when it came was a halting rasp.

"I thought you were a spider, a spider, come to suck my blood—"

Delirious. That was no great surprise.

"Who did this to you?" Kandri asked.

Ulren turned him a caustic smile. He pawed at the faska, and Kandri let him drink. The man was in a pitiful state but did not appear mortally wounded. When he finished drinking he looked at Kandri with loathing.

"You want to know who did this? You did, you vipers. All your fault. Your Prophet's army was waiting to pounce on us, an hour after you went your merry way."

"*What?*"

"They were camped in the oasis, in the Crescent Palmeries," said Ulren. "If the Master had only kept you with us, as you begged him to, we might have handed you over and been done with this nightmare."

"How many, Ulren? How many soldiers?"

"Some three hundred—horse cavalry, they were. And twelve Rasanga—"

"Twelve!" cried Mektu. "Twelve Rasanga? Are you sure?"

Ulren squinted at him. "Eight women, four men, riding those hellish sandcats, led by a bitch who looks like she eats scorpions for breakfast. And he asks me if I'm sure."

Kandri steadied himself against the stone. Twelve Rasanga—more than he'd ever seen assembled, except as bodyguards to the Prophet herself. And all on sandcats, the deadly saber-toothed *sivkrin*, larger than lions, mastered by no one in the world but the Prophet's commandos. And three hundred cavalry.

And three hundred Tekkel cavalry. All of them, looking for us.

"They beat Master Ifimar straight away, just to get our attention," said Ulren. "Beat him until he could barely crawl. Then they asked if we'd seen a pair of brothers traveling with their uncle and a whore."

Wincing with pain, he sat up against the stone. "We said no, every one of us. We lied for you snakes. But they didn't believe us, and—" He flinched again. "—they had a way with fear. Never even had to threaten us. They just waited, staring us down, stroking those demonic cats. And suddenly two of the drivers fell on their knees and begged for mercy. They swore they loved the Prophet and always had. They would have ratted on you then and there, but the Master beat them to the punch."

"*He* ratted us out? Jód himself?"

Ulren nodded. "Told them he'd sent you north along the ridgeline. And somehow the Rasanga knew he spoke the truth. They took off hot on your trail."

Kandri closed his eyes. Jód had not spoken the truth, of course. He'd sent the Rasanga in the wrong direction.

"They punished us for lying, before they went," said Ulren. "Killed four of us—one for each of the four they wanted. They meant to start with that quack surgeon, but he whined and whispered and talked his way out of it somehow, the clever bastard. They moved on to the mercenaries, cut two of

291

them down, and then two camel drivers. One was Master Ifimar's cousin, a boy from Harul Makkut. He lost family for you, snakes. What have you done for him? For any of us?"

"That's the last you saw of the Prophet's forces?" Kandri demanded. "Riding north?"

Ulren looked from brother to brother.

"What's wrong, why don't you answer?" demanded Mektu. "Did you see them again or not?"

"There's something else, isn't there?" said Kandri.

Ulren's voice was tight with loathing. "The mercs," he said, "abandoned us ten minutes later."

"*Jeshar!*" shouted Kandri. "What, all of them?"

"Every last pig-faced, Važek-loving one. Took camels, and water of course, and went off into the bazaar to find a desert guide to take 'em all back east. Left us to bury their so-called comrades. And Jód couldn't do a thing to stop them; he'd only just staggered to his feet. Spit of the Gods, why did he ever let you travel with us?"

Kandri looked at Ulren's bruised and wrathful face. He was still withholding something.

"The Rasanga killed four of you," he said. "Woeden Surk and his thugs deserted. But how in Ang's name did you end up *here*, buried in the sand? And where's the rest of the caravan?"

"Brother, something's wrong," said Mektu, his eyes on the dune. "The captain's still inside the tower, and Talupéké's shouting in the doorway." He glanced at Ulren. "You need to pull yourself together."

"My brother's right," said Kandri. "We're getting out of here. Can you walk?"

Ulren gave him a peculiar look, as though the question were a trick. "I'm not sure," he said at last.

"Well, start by standing up," said Kandri. "My uncle and the others are on their way; you can wait for them if you like. But if we get the signal from Captain Utarif, Mek and I have to ride like hell."

"No!" shouted Ulren.

His cry startled both brothers. "What do you mean, no?" said Mektu. "Why shouldn't we?"

"Because—" Ulren waved his hands, urgent but vague. "You don't know the rest."

"Then tell us, but talk fast," said Kandri. "What else happened at the Palmeries? Where's the caravan?"

Ulren grimaced, as though at some fresh pain. He slid a hand beneath his tattered coat.

"Ulren!" cried Kandri. "Jód didn't turn back?"

"Oh, no," said Ulren. "He wouldn't dream of turning back. Although the Gods know I'd have done so, long since. Before the flats, before Vasaru and your little trick with the Wasp. But no one listens to Ulren." Blinking, he looked up at Kandri. "What's your charm? Will you tell me?"

"Our charm?"

"You slip through death's buttery fingers, every blessed time. The pit, the Wasp, the Rasanga. You're like a pair of Gods-damned sidewinder rattlers, that's what you are. You should have died when the heavens flung fire down on us. That shard of sky metal had your name on it, but it killed poor Sabin-jur instead. Why?"

"No idea," said Kandri, extending his hand. "Now will you please make an effort, or do you intend to lie there until the wind buries you again?"

"I'll make an effort," said Ulren, and jerked Kandri's arm.

The move caught Kandri utterly by surprise. He toppled against Ulren, and in the same moment felt the bite of steel at his throat. Somewhere in his rags Ulren had concealed a knife.

"Don't move!" he hissed. "Don't so much as breathe, either of you. Just throw it there at my feet."

Kandri lay rigid. The blade was pressed so hard that the merest twitch from Ulren might slash his jugular. Mektu, seated on the camel above him, was admirably composed.

"Throw what, exactly?" he asked.

"You know bloody well," said Ulren. "The knife, the golden mattoglin. I know it's on your person. Get it out now."

For a moment, even with the blade at his throat, Kandri could think of nothing but the sheer wonder of Ulren's greed. The man had been buried, hog-tied, left for dead. Whether or not his legs still functioned was unclear. And yet he was attempting to rob his rescuers—of a treasure neither of them possessed.

"We gave it away," he said, trying not to swallow. "We don't have a thing you could want."

He could feel Ulren's teeth against his ear. "True enough," he said. "I don't want the mattoglin. I want to live, is all. I want to survive this crossing, feel the touch of a loving whore at the Font of Lupriz." He looked at Mektu again. "Throw it to the ground, pig, or by Hell's black altar, your brother dies."

"I'm sorry," said Mektu.

"Ulren," said Kandri, "we gave the mattoglin back to Eshett—"

" 'Course you did, I watched you."

"—and she took it with her, to her village. That's the truth. I swear on my life."

Ulren sneered; his eyes had not left Mektu's face. "How about you, pig? Care to swear on the same? On your brother's life?"

"I'm sorry," Mektu repeated. He lifted an elbow, fighting the impulse to hide his face.

"Mek? Mek?"

"I had a feeling about this one," said Ulren, glowering at Mektu. "He was stuck on that Parthan whore. But not just on her body, mind you. She had something he wanted. He kept sidling up to her pack—it was lashed on the camel behind my own—and pawing at it, squirming."

Kandri stared at his brother, dumbfounded. Mektu seemed physically unable to look at him, as though his neck had developed a kink.

"And before we parted ways with the girlie," said Ulren, "your dear brother snuck over to her pack and pulled out that golden beauty and stuffed his own dagger in its place. He was quick, but not quick enough. I saw that great blue bird's egg, the ormalid, plain as I see your ugly nose. The mattoglin he shoved in a hurry under his shirt. And it's there right now, ain't it?"

"No," said Mektu, "it's gone for good."

He stood in the stirrups, lifted his shirt. Nothing there, save his machete and the scars of old wounds. "The Nachasps stole it," he said, "like they did the Letter of Cure. I woke up and it was gone."

Fury washed over Kandri—fury at Mektu alone. "You did it again," he said. "You stole the fucking knife *again*."

"I had to, brother."

"You're a shit dog with yellow mange."

"Dog, pig, viper," said Mektu. "I'm a whole fucking zoo."

Ulren demanded to see the contents of the saddlebags. Mektu slid to the ground and began to open them, one by one, turning the camels to face the pair slouched by the stone. Kandri tried to look at the dune-top, but Alahari-Rana was in the way, and he dared not move more than his eyes. When at last his camel shifted, Kandri's heart sank even lower. The dune-top stood empty. Like her captain, Talupéké had vanished from sight.

When Mektu had turned out the last saddlebag, Kandri joined Ulren in cursing him. Mektu stood quaking in the onslaught, but soon began to shout back: he was forced to take it, something compelled him, the yatra compelled him, the yatra was behind everything that went wrong—until the Nachasps "with their tea-and-rabbit trick" put him to sleep.

"Nachasps?" said Ulren. "The ones with the eyes?"

"Silver eyes, that's right," said Mektu.

"They don't exist."

"Tell that to Prince Happy-Lap. Tell that to Kandri, for that matter. Oh, they exist. Silver eyes, and nice round bottoms, round like your head, and they're not just friendly, either—"

"Shut up, shut up both of you."

"He's telling the truth," said Kandri. "They stole all kinds of—"

Ulren twitched, and a sharp, thin pain erupted in Kandri's throat: the knife had tasted flesh.

The man seemed barely in control of himself. "No mattoglin. So rot in hell. Stinking Chilotos! You can march down to Jekka's darkness with your great bitch in the lead. I should have waited. I should have let them hear this shit for themselves."

"Let who?" said Kandri.

"Shut up!" screamed Ulren. "You jackass bunglers, you should be dead, I hope the spiders get you, first you give it to the Parthan whore, then you steal it back, then you let some moon-eyed pixies take it off you in your sleep!"

"Yes!" bellowed Mektu. "Why don't you believe me?"

"*Who cares if I believe or not, you demented fuckwit?* They *never will!* Ah, Gods—"

With a violent motion he shoved Kandri aside. Mektu leaped to his brother's aid. Ulren, not lame in the least, sprang to his feet and ran.

Kandri touched his throat: no vein slashed, his life wasn't ebbing away. He stood up, stanched the blood with his sleeve. Mektu whipped off his headscarf and wound it about his neck.

What was happening? He looked around, groping for some explanation. Chindilan and the other travelers were within a mile now, pounding doggedly closer, and for a moment Kandri thought Ulren was waving to them. But no, he was running at an altogether different angle—southward, toward an infinite bleak nothing.

"That man is barking mad," said Mektu.

"I'm not sure," said Kandri.

As they watched, Ulren stripped off his tattered shirt. A moment later, his pants. Naked to his sandals, now, he blundered on, waving his garments above his head.

Mektu glanced at Kandri. "You were saying?"

When Kandri made no reply, Mektu turned away and began coaxing Fish to kneel. Ulren ran on, shaking out his clothes like empty sacks.

"Barking, raving, drooling," said Mektu.

"Brother—"

His voice turned Mektu like the lash of a whip. From around the base of the tower, riders were appearing by ones and twos. Riders on horses, not camels. They were four, and then six, and then nine, and still more after that. All heavily armed and galloping straight for the crossroads.

"It's the Meat-Clown fuckers!" cried Mektu.

Twelve. Fourteen. Kandri could see their moon-yellow masks, huge eyes, black mouth-slits. "We've been set up," he said.

Sixteen in all. From behind them, Ulren was screaming: *Don't have it, never touched it, not my fault!*

The Slaughterhouse Clowns drew their swords as one.

ɞ

In a rare miracle of understanding, the brothers set their backs to the same tall stone. There was no hope in flight: even if they outpaced all their enemies, where would they go, what would they drink? And how could they leave the others—most of them on foot—to face the riders alone?

Akrunu Haggath. Kandri tried not to think of Eshett's stories about their treatment of captives. Atop the dune, Utarif and Talupéké were still nowhere to be seen. What was happening in that tower? Had the soldiers been ambushed? Were the Clowns there as well?

Kandri looked to the west: Chindilan and the others were sprinting toward them across the plain. They had started off closer than the Akrunu, but they were afoot. For several minutes, the brothers would have to fight alone.

Several minutes: an eternity.

They were going to die.

No. Think. The problem wasn't those whirling swords—not yet anyway. The problem was spears: half a dozen of the Clowns carried spears. He and Mektu could slide behind the rock if the Akrunu charged, but what if they were smarter? What if they closed in from all sides?

Kandri's decision came in a flash. He leaped for his frightened camel, unhitched the saddlebags and pulled them down. They were thick leather, sun-hardened and stiff. He heaved the bags to Mektu.

"On your left arm," he shouted, already reaching for the second camel.

The bags were awkward, hard to grip. They might not turn a straight-on thrust. But as makeshift shields they were much better than nothing. They freed the camels, smacked their haunches to make them run: they would only get maimed. But the Sparaviths would not flee: they only retreated into the circle of stones and stood their ground, stamping and braying.

The Slaughterhouse Clowns did not charge at first, but galloped in a wide ring about the stones, taunting the brothers with shrill cries. Kandri searched for their leader, the red-masked woman with ribbons trailing from her arms. He could not see her among them.

"The Clowns set all this up," he said. "Ulren knew they were watching, getting ready to ambush us."

"I don't want to be a slave," said Mektu. "If we're losing, you cut my throat."

Kandri shot him a warning look. The riders were hooting, howling, tightening the circle. A spear flew, fast as thought, and shattered against a stone inches from Kandri's head.

"The mattoglin!"

He could not tell which of the Clowns had shouted, but the other fifteen cried out in approval, shaking their weapons above their heads. *So that's all it comes down to.* Greed, plunder. The Clowns' hatred of Chilotos was just an excuse.

"When they ride through the sand drifts we can get them," said Mektu. "The horses will stumble. The Clowns don't know about the bodies."

"Of course they know, you ass," said Kandri. "They put the poor bastards there."

Mektu looked at him, blinking. "Where the hell is Tal when we need her?"

Kandri glanced again at the crest of the dune—no sign of the girl or the captain. And now the circle tightened even more.

"I hate them," said Mektu. "Those masks—"

"Brother," said Kandri, "they've spooked you. Don't let them."

"Worry about yourself! They haven't cut my dick off yet. Or my tongue. That's what they do, right? Burn out your tongue?"

"Tongues, masks, slaughter," said Kandri. "It's all about fear, don't you see?"

"The mattoglin!" shouted the same rider. "Throw it down and live!"

"We don't have it, idiots!" shouted Kandri. But he was thinking, *When did they learn Imperial Common?*

"We will tie you down and dissect you with a razor!" bellowed the rider. "Give up the mattoglin! We will not ask again."

"See that?" said Kandri. "They want it without a fight. They're cheap."

Mektu looked into his eyes, and Kandri saw his fear melt away into certainty. Kandri grinned at him. The grin of the deranged. *Army tactics, brother. Achieve insanity. Then you can't be stopped.*

"Cheap mother fuckers," whispered Mektu. Kandri pulled his brother close and kissed his forehead and then the madness took over, and Mektu roared, an impossible sound, overpowering the wind—

"CHEAP! MOTHER! FUCKERS!"

—and they whirled into battle dance, that ancient thing Chilotos had built instead of cities or monuments or schools, instead of clinics, that blade the Prophet had sharpened and handed back to the Army of Revelation, and the Clowns broke form at the spinning onslaught. Kandri leaped straight into the arc of the sword descending for him—into the arc, through the arc—and he seized the man and fell backward, toppling horse and rider and the edge of his machete slashed the man's throat to the bone against the earth. As the horse kicked to its feet he rolled with the man above him and a spear passed through the corpse and nicked his ear. He slid on the ground, the horse stomped his thigh, he did not feel it, he was under the horse and out beyond the circle of riders and back in again for blood.

No thought. The black gift of his training. He caught the sword of the next rider with the flat of his blade and let his arm give way until both hilts were near his face and then seized the other's wrist in his teeth and bit down grinding through veins until he choked on blood and there was another dead man, another soul to taste and swallow and forget.

Their allies came. He saw his uncle bury his axe in a rider's chest. He saw Kereqa bring down another with her spear, calmly, from a distance. He caught a wild glimpse of Mektu riding off toward the tower, riding behind a corpse, a man he'd killed but not yet unseated, groping around it for the horse's blood-slicked mane. He saw the Prince's servant break a man over his knee.

For two or three hideous minutes they were invincible, touched by something potent and malign. Then all at once the Slaughterhouse Clowns appeared to remember their own name and nature, and the battle became a nightmare. The Clowns leaped from their horses with demonic screams and landed running and slashing. They drove a wedge through the defenders, scattering them. Kereqa fell, and the croaking private cried out and flew to her aid and was felled in turn by a mace. Kandri leaped at the Akrunu before he could strike the youth again, and the Clown fled before him, laughing, actually laughing.

"Run, run, you sow's-ass ugly—"

His uncle's eyes, flashing a warning. Too late. Explosion of pain at the back of his skull, and darkness like a flood.

❦

Sand in in his eyes, blood and grit in his mouth. He raised his head. The world pitching and sliding. How long was his blackout? Seconds, a minute? He felt no pain, knew no sensation but the joy of living faces, one after another, Kereqa bloodied but standing, the croaking private crawling but alive.

He gained his knees. Howling wind, riderless horses. And eight surviving Clowns, fleeing on foot around the base of the dune, back toward the tower from which they'd come.

Mindless bloodsuckers. All that for nothing. We don't even have the fucking knife.

"Mektu! Mektu!"

Prince Nirabha was shouting his brother's name, his uncle was shouting it, everyone was. Kandri rose and saw Mektu at a great distance across the flats, standing over a dead Akrunu, machete limp in his hand. To his left, a horse was trotting away.

Oh Ang's blood, no.

300

The eight Akrunu who had fled the larger melee were almost upon him, and Mektu had no idea. His back was turned. He was staggering.

No chance whatsoever of reaching him before the Clowns. And the hateful wind blasted full in their faces: Mektu could not hear. They screamed nonetheless. Their voices were straws in a gale.

Tears washed the sand from Kandri's eyes. He ran, but the Clowns were five hundred yards ahead if they were five. The cry torn from his throat like a death in itself. This was despair. He ran like a mindless thing. Like a body without a soul.

And the eight Clowns died before his eyes.

A single arrow had struck the earth at their feet. No one was hit, but the first to run past it fell writhing, tearing away her mask, clawing at her mouth and eyes. Those behind dropped like wheat cut down by a sickle. They rolled and gasped and twisted, and in seconds they were still.

Mektu stood unharmed. It was as if the Gods had intervened. Kandri whirled in a circle, still choking on tears.

Far above on the wind-whipped shoulder of the dune stood Utarif and Talupéké. The captain held a bow in one hand. A bow he had not possessed when he scaled the dune.

The brothers' eyes met over the mounded dead. *The spore arrows.* Utarif had recovered at least one of the terrible weapons, and a bow to launch it with. The shot had been extraordinary: banked into the wind, it must have been, and placed far enough to spare Mektu but near enough to catch eight Clowns in its puff of death.

Chindilan's hand clapped his shoulder. "All right, Kandri?"

Kandri looked at him, trying to find his voice.

"Three of the Clowns were mercenaries in disguise," said his uncle. "*Our* mercenaries, in Akrunu masks. They spoke Imperial Common, if you noticed."

"They're working together," said Kandri.

The smith nodded, scowling. "Woeden Surk must have done some fast talking that day on the plain. As for our Nachasps friends, I suppose they abandoned those arrows somewhere in the upper part of the tower. The arrows and the bow. We're damned lucky the Clowns didn't find them before Utarif did."

Kandri gazed up at the soldiers again. Talupéké had tied something flowing and red about her neck. Releasing the captain, she made for the camels, abandoned some yards higher up the dune.

Utarif, sand blowing like surf about his calves, looked down on him sternly. Indeed so sternly that Kandri felt it and grew still.

The arrows and the bow, he thought. *And what else? Is it possible . . . ?*

Utarif broke into a smile. With deliberate slowness, he held up the calf-skin pouch.

"Great Gods, he's recovered the Letter of Cure!" shouted Chindilan. "Ang bless and keep that man!"

Kandri nodded in a daze. "Ang bless and keep—"

The next instant returned in nightmares to his dying day. A sand-colored shape exploded over the dune and pounced on the captain. It was a gargantuan spider, bloated and spiny as a sea creature, with egg-cluster eyes and legs like jointed masts.

Utarif never saw it coming. It took his body in its mandibles and his head in its mouth and then the head was gone and the body lifeless, and a fan of blood flashed and vanished in the wind.

Kandri was screaming, everyone was screaming. Talupéké was flying back toward the captain, but even as she drew her knife the dune seemed to swallow her, as though she had fallen into a pit. Or a burrow. Seconds later she was clawing free, still making for the monster. But to what possible end? The spider turned away with Utarif's corpse in its mouth. It drew its long legs in close to its body. It jumped.

The leap took it out of sight beyond the shoulder of the dune. Talupéké, frenzied and stumbling, gave chase. For one instant a trick of the wind brought her scream to their ears—a girl's scream, and a soldier's—and then she too was gone.

16. IDEALISTS

Magnus General Therel Agathar met the eyes of the hunting dog. *That's right*, he told it silently, *I am a bloody fool.*

Late afternoon. A sea breeze swept cold over the soggy hilltop, highest point in the district of the capital. The hill was crowned with a war memorial, first and most important in all the Kingdom of Shôlupur. Agathar was on hands and knees. He could see the shadow of a long outstretched arm, but it would never do to look up at the statue until the rites were observed. He bent lower, crawling under the first of three spun-silver wires that formed a triple cordon around the memorial. His back and elbows ached, but that was the way of it. No approaching the sacred without the greatest humility, not even for generals or kings.

But a dog? It would have dashed forward to sniff, and perhaps lift its leg, if Agathar's daughter-in-law had not restrained it. Now it cocked its head and studied the general, as though reconsidering his place in nature's hierarchy.

How little upheld it. They both had dicks. The dog's, moreover, was still in demand: Isula made a fair income, lending her males out to stud. And this hound could run like the wind, leap and snatch a flushed quail from the air, smell a fox around the shoulder of a mountain, stop a leopard with a snarl.

"So why don't I serve you?"

"Beg your pardon, General?" The lieutenant flailed behind him, squelching. Agathar waved him off.

"Nothing, nothing. Get up, don't stain your trousers."

"You'll have to bend slightly more, sir, the third wire—"

"Is the lowest. I'm aware."

He dropped to his elbows and scuttled forward. The wires enforced a ritual obeisance before the first hero of the Kingdom. Agathar endorsed the custom, believed in its necessity, for what good was an ideal before which one never bowed? Yet each year it grew more difficult. Six or eight more and it would be beyond him. Then he would take his place among the ancients, pardoned and pitied, renewing their vows from the window of a coach.

Or else it will not matter— The thought pounced like a cutthroat. *—because we will have been ruined by a fool's war of aggression, and Nebusul sacked in the reprisal, and all of us in pyres or in chains.*

How easily it could happen. The historian in him knew.

How deep the sedimentary ruins, cities beneath cities, graves beneath graves, civilizations ground down to meal.

How hard to believe in the danger on any given morning in spring, with new green on the hilltops and seabirds drifting like kites and the valleys quilted in fresh-planted fields. This morning. One more blind turn in history when there was still time to act.

He squirmed under the last wire. He sat back on his heels and rubbed his neck. The statue towered above him on its wordless plinth: a young woman with the posture of a goddess, the ravaged gaze and tattered clothes of a war refugee. Left hand cradling the wren that had alighted there on the Morning of Liberation. Right arm stretched up to heaven, beseeching.

"Mother of Rains," shouted Agathar, loud enough to carry to the onlookers, "I come again, your grateful child."

The old words, so effortless, so unmatched at stilling a crowd. Thank the Gods he was spared that today. Barely a score had gathered on the hilltop, counting the dogs.

"You who fought our case in heaven's tribunal, who sang to the clouds until they wept deliverance, drowning the fires of the enemy. By your song was

Nebusul saved from burning. By your prayer did the Kingdom survive its day of birth. By your love are we instructed. By your compassion are we taught compassion, mother to child, century on century, peace begetting peace unto Urrath's hour of perfection. We follow behind you, savior of our city and our souls."

We follow behind, intoned the onlookers.

He sat silent a moment. Words mattered only if you felt them.

He rose to his feet. Outside the wires, Isula stood holding the dog's lead, beautiful and desolate. She was not glad of this visit to the capital. Like Agathar she had been born here. But Isula had renounced Nebusul—along with speech—after the city took the lives of her husband and daughter. *I hope never to set foot in that cesspool again.* She had scrawled that on an envelope and thrust it at him, the one time he'd tried to make her explain. But here she was, and no mystery about her purpose. She was protecting him.

And so was Obekri. There he was beside her, hands in pockets, favoring him with a smile. The general had given him the first good news in a fortnight, he said, by hiring a carriage right there in Siren's Harbor and making for Nebusul at once, to talk some sense into the King.

An assault on Kasralys. Gods below, I've been asleep. Agathar had written books on war: not just its conduct but its origins, its blundering preludes. This one he should have foreseen. In the rumors of press gangs and debtor's lists. In the shifting language of royal edicts: GUESTS IN OUR KINGDOM SHALL SUBMIT TO WEEKLY INSPECTION OF THEIR LODGINGS. FOREIGN FAITHS SHALL RESPECT THE PRIMACY OF SHÔL TRADITIONS OR BE BANNED. In the promotion of men like Lord Sulmurg, the show trials of accused Kasraji spies. In the extraordinary taxes collected twice this year—or was it thrice, by damn?—for "the valor and readiness of the armed forces of Shôlupur." In those canceled visits from the King.

"The old buzzard didn't want to alert you," Obekri had told him on the ride from Siren's Harbor. "He didn't want you shredding his war plan like the paper doll it is. The younger generals, the rank and file—what would they have done, if Agathar himself had denounced the notion of a siege? No, he needed them all to think you indifferent. Retired to gardening, writing, eccentricities. Too happy to give a damn."

Or too old and daft to form an opinion.

Agathar climbed the stone steps of the plinth, eased around the twelve-foot Mother of Rains. He stroked the bronze wren for luck as he had done since childhood. Then he raised his eyes and studied the place of his birth.

The coast, first of all: sheer and savage. Dark bird-crowded rocks, turquoise shallows of the continental shelf, and the far, frigid blue of the Actumian Sea. Monstrosity of nature. Twenty days to nearest landfall. Effectively boundless, given the Quarantine.

"Volcurinath," he whispered. It was the nearest port of the Outer World, a land he would never see. Today children were not taught even such basics: the other continents, the great Outworlder cities, their largest clans. Over the centuries the fog of forgetting had crept in at every window. Dampened libraries, rotted archives. Blackened mosaics with mold.

Sometimes the foreign doctors broke the silence: *Our elephants are snow creatures. They are covered in wool from head to foot.* Chance words, offhand stories. Good enough for Urrath, those crumbs.

He lowered his gaze from sea to city. Nebusul, City of Joy! Bright innocent colors, azure and oxblood, verandas of blinding white. Fourteen hills, some still draped in native jungle, others so dense with dwellings they resembled nests of bees. Ten colleges and twenty-three public gardens and a punting lake and a zoo. The multi-hued castle at the center, a fever dream of spires and onion domes and bridges and keeps. And about the whole of Nebusul slithered the great red wall: a mighty defense, built by Shôl hands, and yet less loved than the city's other features. That wall had been the project of the occupying Kasrajis, and the hands that had built it had been enslaved.

It was not the greatest city of Urrath—everyone knew who held that prize—but it was the undisputed second. Some described it as more beautiful than its arch-rival. Others contended, rather more persuasively, that at the very least its army stood supreme.

Fool, fool, fool! he accused himself again. *Of course the King wants to put that notion to the test!*

So, apparently, did the bulk of the army. For every spot he examined in the city below—every place a fighting force might train or march or muster—was in use. In the ancient field called Shepherd's Common, mounted

306

strike teams were racing, leaping trenches, weaving among posts. At the Royal Fairgrounds, footmen in their thousands stood in ranks, spears vertical, looking like a bed of nails. Even in the garden of the Academy of Music some battalion had mustered, engaged in mock hand-to-hand.

Agathar had a good idea who was leading those drills. The officers he trusted most—General Kimburac, the Baron Morsu—might have been sidelined, but Agathar had signed off on every promotion above the rank of major for thirty years, and most of those he'd approved were surely still in uniform. A decade in retirement was not so long.

When I'm finished with you, he told those officers silently, *you'll be shamed before this city, before your children, before your Gods. You'll wish you'd retired yourselves, rather than let this madness sweep you up.*

But no, no (he breathed deep; the eyes of the statue were upon him): you didn't stop a war with invective. You stopped it with love. He would not set out to destroy their pride or make them beg forgiveness. He would address them as he always did, as equals under heaven's gaze. Quiet chats, private chats. Starting with the King but extending to all of them. Hell, he'd be at it all night, making his case to the enlisted men over cups of pulqo, nailing the coffin shut. He would appeal to their dignity, speak to their souls. And he would enlist them, one after another, to demolish this plan in public, to tell the truth in every district of the city and every province of the realm, that such a war would bring only loss and poverty and despair.

That was his way, not vengeance, not spite. That would inoculate his country for a generation, and let him die in peace.

ଓଃ

As he stepped over the wires—no obeisance required as one left—he saw that his entourage was distracted. Some new commotion in the city. Even Isula and Obekri were gazing to the north.

The lieutenant hurried to his side. "General," he said, "allow me to note that I followed your orders precisely. Your carriage entered the city by the Pike Bridge over the Tidal Basin."

"I wasn't asleep," said Agathar. "I saw how we approached."

"And no scouts went before us, sir. No heralds. You wished to arrive unseen, and I bent all my thought to that end."

"What the devil's the matter?"

"Perhaps you should take another look, Magnus General."

The lieutenant gestured at the others, clustered at the hill's shoulder, gazing north. Agathar crossed the soggy green and stood beside Isula and Obekri. All eyes were on the castle. Obekri, looking grimly amused, passed him a pair of field glasses.

"So much for quiet diplomacy," he said.

Agathar swallowed an oath. Citizens of Nebusul were swarming toward the castle along a dozen streets. By the thousand. Old and young, running, walking, hobbling. It was like watching great flocks of sparrows converge on a field.

"They're making for the Coronation Green," said Obekri.

"And so must we," said the general.

The Coronation Green projected like a marble tongue from the castle, leaping high over gates and gardens and reflecting pools, to end in a round dais overlooking a central avenue of the city.

And out along that tongue King Grapahir himself was walking, stiff and slow, within his constant retinue of guards and courtiers and kin. He was already two-thirds of the way to the dais. Agathar could see his wrinkles and his thick gray curls, like an untidy barrister's wig, sprouting from beneath the Cedar Crown. Twenty men and women in scarlet livery marched ahead of him, goose-stepping, with black wooden cases the size of doctors' bags in their hands.

"Do you know what this is about, Therel?" whispered Obekri.

"Working on it."

"Our King was in silent retreat all morning, sir," said the lieutenant.

"I was informed."

"And this cannot be a review of troops. Our King never inspects his armed forces save on horseback."

I know, I know. Stop telling me things I know.

The big dog nuzzled his hand. Agathar scratched its ear by reflex. And suddenly, he saw the whole charade.

"Get back," he shouted, waving at the small crowd about him. "Back from the overlook, out of his sight. Damnation. Hurry!"

Everyone rushed to obey, though not one saw the need. Backing away himself, Agathar glanced once more through the field glasses. *Spawn of the Pits. Too late.*

King Grapahir was looking up at Agathar, and before the general could fully retreat he raised both arms in greeting. The swelling crowd let out a roar.

"He's got his own spotters," said Obekri.

So he did: one of the courtiers had a telescope trained on the hilltop even now. So organized, so beautifully choreographed. Agathar had made a lifelong practice of visiting the Mother of Rains at every homecoming, before all other tasks—before visiting his own mother, in fact.

No choice. Agathar mimicked the King's gesture. The second roar was louder than the first. The city was greeting him, welcoming the hero's return.

The general dropped his arms, which felt suddenly leaden, constrained. He was caught in a net, and it would be much harder than he had supposed to cut his way free.

King Grapahir reached the Green. The twenty blank-faced civil servants had spread around its perimeter. With practiced swiftness they set down their boxes, unlatched them, and withdrew twenty gleaming trumpets. Rising, they faced Agathar and blasted out a long, strident musical phrase. Isula's hunting pack, along with half the dogs in the city, responded with howls.

"They're playing 'Fearless, We March,'" said Obekri. "Very subtle, that."

"Kalen," said Agathar, "you know the location of the Xavasindran Medical Mission?"

"Across from the Oyster Pier," said Obekri. "I know it."

"My daughter-in-law has my signet ring. Take it from her, and present it at the Mission Gate. Tell them it is my wish that you pay a visit to General Kimburac at his bedside—if he is truly a patient there."

"You believe they will admit me?"

"With my ring, they will. Take Isula's horse. Ride at once. And if he is not there—"

"I will find him," said Obekri.

Agathar nodded. "We need him with us, Kalen. We have been used."

"Used by whom?"

"Sulmurg, of course," said Agathar, gesturing at the Green. "He may not have reached the capital yet, but his creatures were lying in wait."

"Sulmurg." Obekri gave a mirthless laugh. "Come, that hardly follows. Sulmurg detests you."

Agathar turned to face him, narrowing his eyes. "You still cannot see it?"

"I confess I can't," said Obekri. "This is a hero's welcome, the very last thing that serpent would arrange."

"You think?"

"I'm sure of it, Therel. You must forget about Sulmurg, and keep your mind on—"

Agathar seized his arm. "I do not believe you are with him," he said, "but if I find that you are, I will have no choice but to crush you both together. You know that."

Obekri's gaze was horrified. "You are accusing *me*—"

"No, not accusing, just—"Agathar closed his eyes. "I'm sorry. You did not deserve that tone."

"But the substance? That I deserved?" Obekri was trembling with rage. "Therel. My closest confidant, my—no, it's too hideous. That you imagined for one fleeting instant that I might serve that torturer, that beast."

"What we can't imagine is what kills us, Kalen. I must be perfect now, don't you see?"

"*I see you tossing away forty years*—" Obekri checked himself. The others, save for Isula, looked tactfully away. "Forty years," he went on softly, "in which I always, always took your side, fought in your corner. Though my influence was slight, of course. A civilian, a woodsman, his defense of the great man laughable—for those who noticed it at all."

"I noticed," said Agathar, bereft. "Forgive me, I'm nervous, I don't know myself."

"Nor do I, it seems." Obekri was fighting tears, and would not win the fight much longer. "I shall take the footpath," he said, "and you had best find someone more trustworthy to visit the Outworlders' clinic. Good luck, River Dragon."

He turned on his heel and slid through the little crowd, pausing only to place a stern kiss on Isula's cheek. General Agathar, helpless, watched his oldest friend walk away.

C&#x8;

The chanting began as soon as the carriages left the hilltop. Ardent chants, full of ferocity and hope:

River Dragon! River Dragon!

Agathar sat back in his seat, the curtain half-drawn. Citizens were flocking to both sides of the road, more by the minute, roaring his tiresome nickname. He be damned if he'd wave. That too was part of the trap Sulmurg had laid for him: to be so enmeshed in public adoration that he would have no choice but to succumb to the war-fever, join the idiot crusade.

Isula rode beside the carriage on the red gelding; her dogs bayed as though starting a hunt. *I must send her home. Or to Mother's at the very least—she will be safe from these vipers there.* But did he believe that, was he sure? *They will try to use her, as they used poor Obekri. I should have left both of them out of this.*

For it was clear to him now that the reception was an ambush, and that Obekri had become Sulmurg's tool. Almost certainly an unwitting tool, but no less useful for that. Who else could have ensured that he, Agathar, would race to the capital without delay? Who else would he have trusted? Obekri's pleas for him to stop the war-madness had only served to hasten his involvement.

Agathar rubbed his eyes. What a splendid double-blow the Special Inquisitor had landed, to lure him from hiding, and to leave him no better than *almost* certain about his beloved friend.

Of course Sulmurg was not acting alone. There were circles of warmongers, clubs of warmongers, temples where the faithful prayed for blood. *Break the wall, slay the Kasraji wolf, melt the old Imperial throne! Death to the enemies of Shôlupur!*

Death to prosperity and the dreams of our children. Death to peace.

And then there were halls of embittered soldiers. Not the finest, by and large. Certainly not those who had lost the most. No, the truly bloodthirsty were less the survivors of wars than the survivors of indifferent careers, deskbound, dust-coated, the ones no one had ever cheered for, the ones for whom no lovers had eagerly undressed.

Any of them, all of them, might now be Sulmurg's tools.

But they will not prevail. They think me a creature like Sulmurg himself, driven and defined by vanity. What a surprise I have in store for them.

ෆ

"Agathar! We are so very glad to see you! Come, rise, my friend! Enough kneeling for one day." Grapahir touched his forehead, and for the second time that morning, Agathar rose from his knees.

The King was slightly younger than Agathar, but a lifetime of dissipation had left him sallow and squint-eyed. A childhood blow (rumor held it was his grandfather's fist) had knocked an incisor out of true; when he smiled, he kept his lips firmly sealed.

"They tell me your farm is reverting to jungle," said the King.

"An exaggeration, sire, it merely—"

"'You don't know him as I do,' I countered. 'The forest primeval is Agathar's inspiration. He'll have planned it that way.'"

Grapahir spoke as though they were alone, sipping brandies in some corner of the castle. In truth they were the focus of some fifty thousand eyes. The Coronation Green stood like a rock above a sea of faces, young and old, women and men, wealthy and threadbare. On the Green itself stood a mix of royals, ministers, and military leaders. The gray-haired Crown Princess, Grapahir's daughter and confidant. Her six children by five men, all since disgraced. A clutch of minor sartaphs, thrilled to be part of the pageantry. Two generals rather more decorated than when Agathar had seen them last.

Beside the Crown Princess stood Sulmurg's much-younger nephew, the improbably handsome Sartaph of Larisalt. Bright eyes, chiseled jawline, flawless skin. More like a sculpture of a sartaph than a living person. There was nothing about him to recall his crooked, hollow-cheeked uncle. Nothing but the dead smile he aimed at Agathar.

"You arrived here before my inquisitor," said the King, following Agathar's glance. "Larisalt is here in his stead. A fine young lord—clever, quick-handed. Fast becoming a celebrity of sorts. But see how I gossip already. I have missed you, my dragon."

The crowd on the Green stood at rigid attention as Grapahir led Agathar to the balcony. The city held its breath. The trumpeters, bowing deeply, backed away from the pair.

"Your Majesty," whispered Agathar. "This welcome—I have no words to express my—"

"Nonsense, old friend. The people demand no less. You and I are both helpless in the grip of their love."

"If you could but grant me the favor of a private word, sire, our beloved country will be the better for it, I swear to you."

"We shall have a number of private words," said Grapahir, "and without delay, you may be certain. But smile first, and hold your tongue a moment. This must be done, Agathar. You know it already, in your heart."

"What must be done?"

"Smile, I say."

Agathar smiled, and Grapahir smiled back. Then, with his own palsied hands, the King began to unbutton the general's coat.

It was a fine new traveling coat, brass buttons polished to gold, donned in haste in his carriage. The King pushed it from his shoulders and let it fall to the ground. Agathar stood now before the multitude in only his sweat-damp-ened shirt and trousers—the same trousers he had muddied in the crawl beneath the wires. Grapahir, beaming, turned to one of his grandchildren, who stepped forward and handed the King a second garment.

Dress uniform. Of course. Sulmurg's nephew caught his eye. The man's smile had broadened.

They believe this flattery will make it harder to refuse, thought Agathar. *How little they understand me, after all those campaigns.*

"For the honor and glory of Shôlupur," cried the King, in his shockingly loud public voice, "we welcome our beloved subject—"

He wrapped the coat around Agathar's shoulders.

"—our first warrior, our kingdom's delight—"

A new hat followed. Scarlet wool, golden braid.

"—our irreplaceable Magnus General, back into our service—"

The mob went mad. The King kissed him on both cheeks. He went on talking, but not even Agathar could hear what he said.

〆

Twenty minutes later, the old King granted him that private word. Grapahir disliked public appearances as much as Agathar himself; it was their one point of flawless accord.

They retreated to a lonely chamber in the east wing of the castle: a gray room of hulking furniture, landscape paintings, blank-eyed busts of ancestors forgotten. The fire snickering in the hearth did little to dispel the cold. For some reason, all the curtains were drawn.

Servants whirled ahead of the King, lighting candles, moving obstacles from his path. Two enormous chairs were placed by the fire, between them a table with a tea service and a platter of nectar-sticky cakes.

The King thrust a book into his hands. "My fireside reading," he said. "History from another perspective—a Chiloto perspective, if you can believe it. That is the first Shôl translation."

Fine calfskin, a handsome volume—but when Agathar read the spine he nearly flung the book to the ground. *The Five Atrocities*. A notorious screed, composed at the behest of the Chiloto Prophet. A retelling of the worst abuses of the old Empire, with Chilotos in the role of heroic victims, tireless freedom fighters, and one-day leaders of an Urrath reborn. It was the sort of book Agathar despised above all others: deeply false, but marbled like a cut of fatty meat with enough truth to fool the credulous.

"You look positively alarmed, General," said the King. "Fear not, I do not believe everything in that book."

So you believe some of it?

Not trusting himself to speak, he forced his lips into a smile and set the book down beside the cakes. Grapahir waved out the servants—and then, to Agathar's surprise, his bodyguards. Doors slammed, the candles flickered. He sat and nodded for Agathar to do the same.

"The Persuasion Room," said the King. "Don't ask me how it comes to be called that. Perhaps my father came up with the nickname—he locked us in here, sometimes, if we misbehaved—or perhaps the term dates back a thousand years."

"Your Majesty's castle is but half that old," said Agathar, "and this wing, if memory serves, is younger still."

"Trust you to know," said Grapahir with a smile. He sat back in his chair and studied the general through the smoky gloom. "You are everything they claim, Agathar. Learned, judicious, fearless, endlessly active in the mind. And let us not forget: adored. Yes, adored and trusted across the kingdom. If I were a man given to envy, I would lavish the emotion on you."

"My King is far too kind."

"Not so, Agathar. Were it not for your tactical brilliance, we might all be speaking Važek today. Eat some cake."

"Thank you, Excellency. I fear the journey has left my stomach rather unsettled."

The King made a face of concern. "Retirement takes a toll on the constitution, they say."

Agathar dropped his eyes. He had not missed these audiences; it was a comfort to know that today's would be the last. Grapahir drank off a whole cup of tea, watching Agathar over the rim. He patted his lips dry with a napkin, set down the cup.

"Well," he said, "you may proceed to the urgent matter you invoked on the Green."

"Thank you, sire. Indeed, nothing could be more urgent. Your Majesty knows full well that I have no love for the rulers of the Kasraj. They are vain, corrupt, acquisitive—"

"General."

"—and if ever harm befell your kingdom, they would shed no—"

"General."

The King's smile was brittle. Agathar bit his lips.

"You may proceed, I was about to say, *after* you assist me with this minor task. Look there, in the corner." He gestured. "I could summon the guard, but an old King must make a point of doing things for himself now and then."

Something in his tone made Agathar's hands clench in his lap. He twisted, peering over the back of his chair. The corner was empty save for an oversized oil painting of Mount Inuvtuk, snow-crowned and savage, and a lesser painting of a figure in repose.

"Sire?"

Grapahir rose and crooked a finger. "Easier to show you than explain. Bring that candlestick if you would."

Agathar followed him across the silent room. The hot wax that dripped on his knuckles shouted *Lies, danger, death!* Reaching the corner, the King pointed at the smaller of the paintings. "Beautiful, is she not? Do you recognize her?"

The painting depicted a naked woman upon a divan or day bed. "To judge by the lilacs in her hair," said Agathar, "that is Countess Eland."

"Yes," said the King. "Eland the Idealist, at her most bitter end."

The divan stood in a dark forest glade. The Countess rested on one elbow, eyes heavy as though she had just woken from sleep. Her gentle smile made it plain that she was not yet aware of the animals—tiger, hyena, strange feral dogs—slinking from the shadows around her.

"You're the historian," said Grapahir. "Did she truly meet her end that way?"

"Improbable, sire," said Agathar. "It is true that Eland was found in a wilderness, her body partly devoured. But she had feuded publicly with her father the Grand Sartaph over his wholesale cutting of the royal forests. Scholars generally concur that he ordered her throat cut before abandoning the body."

"To her woodland friends," said the King. "Always better to leave nothing to chance, as my grandmother liked to say."

"Ang's boundless love for our Queen," said the general automatically.

A shard of memory blazed to life: the old woman, bent already but twice his height, thumping toward him over hand-trimmed grass, the center of a storm of jewel-heavy fabrics and perfumed smoke and courtiers and flies. *Look at him!* The shriek of an albatross. *Look at the little patriot! Shôlupur will devour this one when he comes of age!*

"She had an enduring wish," said the King, "to leave her country stronger than she found it."

"Then her death was surely peaceful, sire," said Agathar.

"Quite the opposite," said the King. "Shôlupur was diminished. I know you won't agree. You would tell me the *facts*, as you call them. Wealth and petty victories. Better harvests, wider roads. But my grandmother *lived* the years you only write about, my dear historian. She knew how Urrath saw us. 'The shine has left the armor,' was how she put it. We were no longer respected, Agathar. We were no longer feared. A terrible thing at the close of a life, wouldn't you say?"

Agathar lowered his eyes. What he would say is that the old Queen had died senile, had confused the decline of her own body with that of her realm. And now her son was nearing the same age. Woe to all Urrath that its monarchs never retired.

"Now help me with this one," said the King.

He reached for the larger painting of the mountain. Agathar, still mystified, gripped the frame's opposite side. The painting must have weighed sixty pounds, but together they wrestled it to the floor. "Well done," huffed the King. "You see? We are stronger than we appear."

In the wall where the painting had hung was an iron door, bolted, three feet square. Agathar looked at Grapahir: the King's eyes were melancholy. He stepped forward and struggled with the bolt. Hinges moaned as the door opened. A chilly draft swept the room.

With that draft came certain odors, faint but unmistakable. Sweat. Urine. Shit. The King retrieved the candle and beckoned. "Look in," he said. "Look down."

Beyond the door, a narrow stone shaft descended into the earth. The candle's light did not reach far, but Agathar heard the sound of moving water below.

The King dropped the candle down the shaft. There came a faint cry and a shuffling sound. The candle guttered and went out, but by its brief light Agathar knew what he had seen: a man, some thirty feet below. Gagged. Wrists bound behind him. Naked, save for a pair of thick socks. The man stood awkwardly in these socks upon thin strips of metal which ran from left to right across the shaft.

"General Kimburac too is an idealist. He would not—"

Agathar seized the King's throat, slammed him up against the wall. Grapahir wheezed; his bejeweled circlet clattered to the ground.

"Let him go," Agathar whispered. "Do it, give the order. Or by the Gods, you monster, I'll finish you here."

He was not strangling Grapahir—not yet—but his hands shook with a rage he had not felt in years. In the time since his son's death, and his grand-daughter's. The King's eyes went wide: he had assessed the strength of that hand upon his throat, the desperation on the face of his old General. But he made no move to speak.

"Sulmurg put you up to this," snarled Agathar. "You must know he's peddling poison. Devil's bile, Grapahir! You'll never meet a more true and honorable man than Kimburac! He's incapable of treason."

"Refusing your sovereign's will is treason," said the King, his old mouth crushed against the wall.

"Not if the sovereign has gone mad."

"We are not mad," said Grapahir, "but what word would you apply to yourself, Magnus General? Do you think for one moment that you have taken me by surprise?"

Agathar tightened his grip. The King gave a hiss of pain. "Razors!" he spat.

"What do you mean, razors?" Agathar forced himself to loosen his fingers.

"Kimburac is standing on razors. For the moment the socks protect him, but he cannot sit down or even kneel."

"A new sort of torture. Did you grow bored of the pool and candles?" He leaned close to the shaft. "Don't shout, General Kimburac," he called softly. "This is Agathar. We're getting you out of there."

From the darkness, a moan. Tortured, beseeching.

"Killing us will not save him," said the King. "Nor will it stop our kingdom from marching on the Seventh Realm."

Agathar felt a pounding behind his ears. "What the hell," he demanded, "do you want from *me*?"

"You know already," said Grapahir. "We want your service, your mind."

"I will *not* lead this kingdom into war with the Kasraj!"

"Quite true, you shall not. Larisalt will lead the campaign."

Shock followed on shock. "That one?" cried Agathar. "Sulmurg's nephew? That dandy, that veteran of precisely nothing?"

"The theatrics may be awkward at first," the King admitted. "Larisalt is adored—his looks alone guarantee it—but no one imagines he has half your skill in war. The people demand you, Agathar. It is because you are here that they are chanting 'Victory' with such faith. You will be the face of the campaign, therefore, until the Great Host departs from Shôlupur."

"And then?"

"You may cede much of the public glory to Larisalt. But never fear: he will follow your orders in the conduct of the war to the letter. I have Sulmurg's word on that."

Sulmurg's word! The pounding behind his ears grew so powerful he thought his skull would crack. "But you are old," the King was saying. "When this campaign is over you will be spent, exhausted, burned down to a stub—and yet our kingdom will still require a war hero. Someone young and vigorous and pleasant to the eye. It's the part Larisalt was born to play."

"Theatrics," said Agathar. "You truly have gone mad."

"And you, Agathar, will do what you do best. You will plan the attack, be its architect and overseer. You will shepherd Larisalt, wind him up each morning like a mechanical bear. And you will *not* fail. Shôlupur will not fail. The Scarlet Kingdom will take Kasralys, realm and city both. Our flag will be raised over the Tower of Eroqas, and the world's order changed. That is what is going to happen."

"You don't need this war," said Agathar. "The Kingdom's safe already. No power in Urrath can threaten her."

"There is a world beyond Urrath, General. While you played the hermit out there on Cauldron Farm, we have learned much of its intentions, and its strength."

"You've been speaking to the Xavasindrans?"

"And why not? *You must be ready to speak to anyone with knowledge, my King, without favor or prejudice.* That was what you prescribed, in the days when you served us gladly. We look forward to the return of *that* Therel Agathar. In the meantime, we will introduce you to our new Xavasindran liaison, a humble sort of man named Eyelash Thruko. He is just come from Kasralys."

"And wasted no time in warping your vision."

"Our vision is our own," hissed the King. "You will hear him out, Agathar. Only then may you try to convince us that Kasralys is no threat. Now let me go."

Agathar's mind was racing. Grapahir had not even spelled out the cost of refusal. He did not need to. Sulmurg had coached him well.

"Not another word," he said, "until Kimburac's free. Or I *will* kill you, here and now. For Shôlupur if nothing else."

The King hesitated only a moment. Then his hand groped for the portrait of Countess Eland and knocked it from the wall. Behind the portrait was a small iron lever. "Raise it," said the King. "I cannot do it with your hands on my throat."

Agathar stood still.

"Blood of Ang," hissed the King. "Do you think it's *him* I care about? Raise the lever and your man is free."

Agathar moved his right hand to the King's throat, fumbled for the lever with his left. It was heavy. Indeed it took all his strength. But he managed, and as soon as he did he felt movement in the castle wall. A balance tipped, counterweights descending, gears driving chains.

The King squirmed. Agathar released him and leaned into the shaft. In the darkness, Kimburac made a low sound, hope or horror—and then the King jerked Agathar back roughly by the arm.

An enormous block of stone fell down the shaft, missing his head by inches. Precisely fitted to the space, it dropped like a maul upon Kimburac. The seal it made against the walls of the shaft obliterated any sound.

"He is free," said the King, rubbing his neck. "Those razors are matched to deep grooves in the fallen stone. His flesh has been pressed like so much garlic, down into the river beneath our castle, and with the next storm that river will rise and wash the last traces of him from the blades. Your decorated head would be down there too, if I hadn't moved to save it. Remember that, you ingrate."

Agathar steadied himself against the wall. "I'll denounce you," he said.

"Certainly," said Grapahir, "if you wish your daughter-in-law to go the way of Kimburac."

Agathar slowly raised his eyes. The King met them and took a hasty step back. He laughed, but his voice was shaky. "There, there's the dragon," he said. "There's the man I need."

"You'll be dethroned," said Agathar. "Kimburac and I are loved. You're hated, feared—"

"Wrong, General, the people love me already in their way. And they shall do so all the more as I lead them to supremacy in Urrath, a rightful destiny that has eluded them for centuries." Grapahir shook his head. "You will not gamble with Isula's life, I think. But Lord Sulmurg cautions me not to presume. He thinks you just cold-blooded enough to let her die. And after all these years, I must concede that he knows you best. So: to your silent daughter-in-law, add your mother. She may be ancient, but she can still feel pain. And there are others you love. Three at least we have foreseen. Will you give them all into his hands?"

Agathar's mind was bleeding. The King shook his head. "No, you will amend your behavior and apply yourself to our cause. The first legions will depart by mid-spring. You and Larisalt will ride at the vanguard, and you will not return until the deed is done."

"A sinful deed. A blasphemous deed."

"Leave morality to the priests, man," said Grapahir. "You will dine this evening with the War cabinet. In the morning you will begin your review of the Scarlet Guard. As for your King—" He gestured, contemptuous. "—spare him your presence henceforth. Send letters. Send a lieutenant or a page. I will receive you again within the shattered wall of Kasralys, when I place garlands of victory about your neck."

"Never, never, you animal—"

"It shall be garlands, Agathar, or something far less comfortable. Now get out of my sight."

17. GONE AWAY

Everyone who could run began to climb toward the spot where Utarif had fallen and Talupéké disappeared. No one could reach it quickly. The dune's western face, wind-sculpted against the tower, was too steep to climb; the only way to ascend was by the same path the two soldiers had taken, up the south-facing slope. The croaking private and the pensive corporal ran in the lead, but Kandri was close behind.

Motion in the corner of his eye: several dunes to the east, the gargantuan spider was departing with astonishing speed, gliding over the surface of the dunes like an insect upon a lake. They could not see its mouth and Kandri was glad of that. A moment later the spider vanished around the shoulder of the dune.

By the time they reached the spot in question, the wind had erased all evidence of the soldiers' deaths. Nothing remained but a few smooth depressions already filling with sand. On their knees, they dug in those cavities, fearing what they might find but needing to find it all the same. They were not successful. If Talupéké too had been killed, the creature had borne her body far away. Nor was there sign of the captain: not the bow he had recovered, not the arrows, not one sand-coagulated drop of blood.

Not the calfskin pouch with the world's future sewn up inside it, a miracle that would never be realized, a seed fumbled into the sand.

The dune yielded one thing only, and it was Chindilan who found it and tugged it free: a red shawl with sequins and gold embroidery, identical to the one that had appeared next to Utarif in the mountains.

The shawl Fiasul had accepted from his hand. *Mine, yes, and thank you.*

CB

The four Sparavith camels allowed themselves to be captured. It was somewhat more work to apprehend the gibbering Mr. Ulren, but Ripheem caught up with him at last, and even persuaded him to put on his clothes. Like a constable with an anxious drunk, he hauled Jód's second in command by the arm across the flats and up the dune. Ulren spat and cursed and struggled, evidently horrified that the spider—or spiders—might return.

"You sack of mule shit," said Mektu. "We saved you, dug you out of the sand. Why didn't you warn us?"

"Why didn't you keep an eye on your things?" snapped Ulren. "If you hadn't let yourself be robbed by pixies there'd have been no trouble to begin with, and I'd have never been tied to that stone! The Slaughterhouse Clowns would have taken that blade and left us in peace."

"That is a lie," growled Ripheem. "The Akrunu Haggath wanted the brothers, hated them."

"You're a clod," said Ulren. "They hate Chilotos, like anyone with sense. But mostly the Clowns want plunder from this world and nothing more. And it's the same with the shit-dog mercs, which is why they took up together. Plunder and greed. Sell a golden knife. Sell two deserters back to the Prophet. It's all the same."

Kereqa stepped toward him. Her eyes were bright, her voice lethally restrained.

"Where is the caravan, Ulren?"

"Away, gone away."

"Dog!" shouted Nirabha, startling everyone. "Two are dead, one devoured before our eyes, and your hands are far from clean in this matter. Answer the question without evasion or sniveling. Gone away *where?*"

"East, Prince," said Ulren, looking chastened. "Deeper into the Sumuri-dath. Along the barren side of the Wall, as the Master always intended. He would have waited, but the Clowns didn't want him interfering when you lot arrived. Leave or be slaughtered, they said. And Master Ifimar couldn't argue, with no mercenaries, no men at arms. Some of our drivers are handy enough in a scrap, but those—" He gestured toward the heap of Akrunu bodies below. "—would have cut them to ribbons. And if they'd turned back—well, the Rasanga won't be happy to learn that Jód had sent them on a goose chase. You can't blame Master Ifimar. He had no choice."

"How is it you knew about the spiders? Did they attack the caravan?"

"No," said Ulren, "but we've faced them before. The Master knows when they're about, somehow. He's a God, a God of the desert. He can see things invisible to the likes of us."

"The bastards we just fought aren't all the Clowns," said Chindilan. "Barely half, I'd say. Where are the rest?"

"I wasn't privy to their schemes, was I?" said Ulren. "But I know one thing: they left a watchman, somewhere. Back in the hills, maybe, or in them ruins to the north. I heard that woman who leads them—what a devil she is!—talk it over with Woeden Surk. They wanted someone to observe all this from afar, in case the ambush failed. As it did."

"Despite your best efforts," said Mektu.

Ulren turned to him, sneering. "I did warn you, matter of fact."

"You said you hoped the spiders would get us," snapped Mektu. "That's not a warning, that's a crazy man's jabber."

"Call *me* crazy!" said Ulren. "Ha ha, ain't it priceless, coming from this gooney bird? At least I don't speak in tongues or throw myself into pits of hornets. And last I checked, no yatra had burrowed like a maggot into *my* soul, thank you very—"

Kandri struck him in the mouth, and once more for good measure in the stomach.

❧

They climbed in the footsteps of their fallen comrades. All of them undone. The pensive corporal was stone-faced; she had woken just that morning in the Captain's arms. The croaking private wore a look of shamed denial, as though someone had told him a blasphemous lie and ordered him to believe it.

Kereqa, who in the span of nine days had lost her senior officer, her granddaughter, and her younger brother Stilts, was now in command of the remaining half-dozen troops. Her face was closed, her eyes narrowed to slits against the wind-driven sand. Kandri thought she had never looked so old.

Kandri himself felt nothing. That was how it worked. His birth-mother had died of snakebite. Ari had vanished; his father had vanished; his comrades in the Army of Revelation had died around him like blighted crops. The army had taught him to fight, to hack and stab, to murder, but it had also taught him not to feel until he could afford to. He had grown a shell that closed by reflex, granite-strong, airtight. He would walk and eat and fight and scheme and feel nothing. Even when he drove his fist into Ulren's chin he felt nothing. The pain would come later: fangs, claws, crucifixion. In a moment of safety, it would pounce.

Fiasul had warned them, after a fashion. *You staying north side, not south. Is better that way.* But none of them had heeded her words.

C3

At the summit the wind was roaring, scalping the dune, flinging sand in their faces. Kandri squinted, gazing east along the Wall's impossible length. The enormity of the structure. Like a highway in the sky. On its right, sand seas, battering. On its left, a three-hundred-foot drop onto barren land.

They stepped out upon the Wall. Underfoot the colossal bricks were smooth and polished, rounded at the corners like bars of soap: untold centuries of blasting sand. To their left the tower loomed like a castle, its entry arch so tall a camel rider could enter without ducking his head.

What else had Utarif found there?

Prince Nirabha, crouching low against the wind, crept close to the sheer drop on the Wall's north side. He shielded his eyes and looked east. Returning, his face was grim.

"I cannot see the caravan, ahead or behind," he shouted. "Consult the telescope. But I fear Master Ulren has lied to us again."

Kandri's telescope revealed no caravan either: only endless miles of flatland, the narrowing line of the Wall slashing into the distance, the towers at even intervals, the rare breaches where the dunes had punched through into the north.

"What the hell are we to do?" said Chindilan. "Trust that bastard, and light out ourselves? If we can't locate Jód we'll perish out here. We'll never find the next well without a guide."

Ulren swore up and down that he had told the truth. He suggested that the Master might have led the caravan through one of the breaks in the Wall. "To wait out the day's heat," he said, "and give you a chance to catch up, if you survived. That first gap's no more than five miles off."

"You expect us to believe he led them *into the sand*, where those fucking spiders are?" said Mektu.

"I told you, the Master can read the desert," said Ulren. "Besides, he'd not be taking them far. Even a hundred yards would get them out of sight."

"We agreed to meet *there*," said the croaking private, pointing down at the crossroads. "If Jód is a man of his word, he'll return for us."

"Jód promised first and foremost to take care of his people," said Kandri. "We're an afterthought."

They debated several minutes longer, huddled behind the camels, but in the end it was clear that the majority favored pressing on. Kereqa gazed out once more across the tops of the dunes, and now the tears flowed freely on her wrinkled cheeks.

"My granddaughter is no more," she said, "and we will not find her body in that waste. It was a risk to climb to this spot, but now we must take that same risk again. For if we travel atop the Wall the danger will be infinitely worse."

"You speak the truth," said Nirabha. "The spiders could burst from the sand and be upon us in seconds. We must descend and round the tower, and walk beneath the Wall upon the flats."

There were nods of agreement. Mektu saw the emerging consensus and flapped his hands. "The tower, what about the tower? Captain Utarif found some of our gear inside, but I'll bet there's more."

"Nothing that will save us if we do not catch up with Jód," said Kereqa. "I should love to have my book of memories restored to me, but there will be no more memories if we die of thirst, or allow the Rasanga to find us."

"What about that ring of yours, Prince?"

"They will not have cast a ring of Nfepan sapphires away like an apple core," said Nirabha. "And if by any madness they *have* done, we would need three days with bright torches to find it in that monstrosity of a tower. Let us go."

Mektu shook his head. "I can't believe you people. Anything could be in there. The mattoglin could be in there."

Ulren laughed, a small, spiteful noise. "Even now, the greedy—"

He broke off, catching Kandri's eye, and quickly shuffled away. His instincts were sound: Kandri was at that very moment picturing himself beating Ulren senseless, stabbing him, tossing him from the Wall. And why not? He could do as he liked and damn the consequences. It no longer mattered. He had lost the Cure.

They turned once more to face the dunes. But before they could lead the camels back into the sand, Chindilan boomed at the top of his lungs: "Stop, stop, you miscreant shit!"

Mektu was running for the tower door.

Groans and curses from the soldiers. *Useless idiot. Let him go. Let him die.*

Kandri cursed as well. But his brother had come within a whisker of death just an hour before, and Kandri had been helpless to prevent it. He was not helpless now.

"Someone—my camel—"

He dropped the reins and dashed after his brother. He heard Chindilan pounding behind him, spitting obscenities.

Mektu reached the archway and vanished into the dark. Kandri reached the spot twenty seconds later. Unlike his brother, he paused: the interior was huge and impressively black. Arrow-slit windows admitted blades of light, but they only seemed to amplify the darkness. Amorphous shapes loomed like objects in a dream.

Halfway across the floor, something jerked and stooped and darted. Yes, that was Mektu, searching, scurrying like a rat. Nothing else in the tower moved.

"You great ass!" he hissed, not daring to shout. "Get out here *now*!"

"Go to hell," said Mektu.

Kandri plunged within. The interior was cool and full of echoes and moans: the wind scraping, probing, dragging at the ancient structure. Fallen stones. Heaps of masonry. Dust rising in slow, twisted columns, like dancers on the floor of the sea.

Mektu was far away across the chamber, bending over a deeper blackness in the floor. Kandri stalked toward him, hands in fists. As he drew near he saw that the darkness before his brother was a large opening in the floor. It was quite wide, and built right against the wall of the tower. Mektu stood as if fascinated, staring down through the gap.

"Don't you dare!"

Mektu stepped down into darkness and was lost to sight.

Kandri, out of his mind with fear and rage, drew his machete and raced across the floor. *They're going to leave us, the soldiers will leave us, this time they won't put up with your Gods-damned—*

His toe caught something soft but heavy. He tried to recover but it was too late: he came down hard, and the thing beneath him made a bubbling, wheezing noise.

A body. A Nachasp body, lifeless. Its throat slit ear to ear.

Kandri rolled away in horror. The face leered at him. It was the same old man from Weeping Rock, the elder who had been impatient for his tea. The silver eyes half-lidded but still gleaming in the darkness. Mouth forced open. Blood dried thick on lips and throat.

Someone had cut out his tongue. Kandri stood and turned in a circle. Those other shapes, all around him: bodies from wall to wall.

He shuffled on. The eyes of the dead winked at him in flashes of silver. Then just to his left he saw a corpse that did not wink. A corpse in a yellow mask.

Fiasul's people had walked right into the ambush meant for the brothers and their companions. How many had perished? Was Fiasul herself somewhere below, stabbed or beaten to death, her tongue burned to slag in her mouth? In the silence, her voice came back to him, strange words between the kisses he had not quite fended off. *I protect you. And maybe you protect me.*

A distant screaming. Ah, but that was just his mind.

He reached the spot where Mektu had vanished. The gap in the floor was a stone ramp leading down into the tower. Beneath each window lay a scallop of wind-smoothed sand. At the floor below the ramp leveled out into a wide landing before descending further.

Chindilan, wheezing and furious, appeared at Kandri's side. They looked at each other in the gloom, shaking their heads. What was there to say?

"I can't *really* leave him, Uncle. Much as he deserves it."

"I know," said the smith, "but hurry. The others are waiting, for the moment. But we can't push our luck."

They started down, hissing his brother's name. The corpse of another Akrunu lay sprawled on the landing.

"That's only the second Clown I've seen," said Kandri. "Most of these dead are Nachasps. They were massacred."

"Well, they put up some sort of fight," said his uncle. "They're not as helpless as they seemed at Weeping Rock. I'll be damned if I can guess how they go about their killing. There's no blood on these Clowns."

Kandri squinted into the darkness, then descended again. Halfway down to the next level, a small black shape lay crumpled on the stone.

"Devil's spit, Kandri," said his uncle. "That's a cat."

It was a cat. No larger than the barn cats of the Sataapre, but so different in build—sleeker, skinnier, with hair so sparse that its skin showed through, stretched and pleated like the skin of a bat. The cat's neck was broken: its head looked back between its narrow shoulders.

The little creature appalled Kandri somehow. It was wrong that it should be here, wrong that it had died here, wrong that someone had inflicted such cruelty. On an impulse, he squatted down and touched one silken foot.

The body was still warm.

Chindilan had continued down the ramp, and Kandri rose and hurried after him. *Sirchasp*, he thought. *Black and little cat*. But even as he drew level with his uncle, he froze, and put a hand on his uncle's arm.

"Do you hear something?"

"I hear the wind, and I hate it," said Chindilan. "Outside of that, no, I don't believe—hello, what's this?"

Collapsed against the wall was the corpse of a Slaughterhouse Clown. The smith bent down before it and pulled something from its belt.

"Is that . . . your knife?" Kandri asked.

"Damned right it is!" said Chindilan, eyes bright with satisfaction. "I made this beauty on my grandfather's anvil—first time I ever met his standards with a blade. One of the Nachasps took it off me in my sleep. *Jeshar*, why did they rob us? They've paid a big fucking price."

"Mektu's not here," said Kandri, glancing around the empty floor. "When I find him, I—oh Gods, Uncle—"

"I hear it."

"That's not the wind."

The noises came from deeper in the tower. Men's voices, shouting and cursing. Far below they seemed at first, but in a matter of seconds they grew louder and nearer. With them came an altogether different sound. A clattering echo. It too was growing loud.

Chindilan widened his stance, axe held high. Kandri drew his machete, braced his heel against the wall.

"Kandri! Uncle!"

It was closer to a stage-whisper than a shout. Mektu appeared, a wraith from the gloom, sprinting and waving his hands. *I could drop him like a tree*, thought Kandri, helpless with rage. *My leg, his shins. . . .*

"Damn you to hell, Mek!"

"Look out! Look out!"

Mektu all but tackled them, driving them back against the wall. The clattering noise grew suddenly louder, and even as Kandri's mind placed the sound three men on horseback thundered up the ramp.

Woeden Surk.

And two of his mercenaries. The warriors were riding Akrunu horses, and looked as amazed to see members of their former caravan as Kandri was to see them.

"Leeches!" bellowed Chindilan. "Backstabbers! Piss-swilling hogs!"

They did not stop. They were not riding to the attack but carrying on up the ramp to the tower's upper floor. Yet Woeden Surk, eyes red with hate, swung a long, bright blade in a backhand arc as he passed the smith.

Kandri's hand shot out, jerked his uncle back by the hair: the blade missed his throat by an inch. All three riders pounded up the ramp and were gone.

Kandri looked at his brother, who hid his face in his elbow. The blade in Surk's hand was the golden mattoglin.

Always the mattoglin! He realized suddenly that it was this, the precious knife, that had lured his brother into the tower. "What is *wrong* with you?" he hissed. "Why can't you let the damned thing go?"

"I'm sorry," said Mektu.

"Why are they fleeing?" Kandri demanded.

"You mean *who* are they fleeing."

"All right, bastard, *who*?"

"No idea."

"Shut up! Get after them!" Chindilan was already charging up the ramp. The brothers came to their senses and bolted after him. In seconds they had left the smith behind, flying across the upper floor of the tower and out into the blazing sun.

Surk and his men had ridden straight through the soldiers, straight past Ulren and the Prince and his servant, all of whom were now watching their departure, stunned. The three mercenaries were galloping away atop the Wall.

"Where do they think they're going?" said Mektu. "Deeper into the desert? That makes no sense at all."

"What did you see on the lower level, Mek?" asked Kandri.

"Dead bodies," said Mektu. "Clowns, Nachasps, mercenaries. At least, I thought they were dead, but then a few of them began to crawl around. There were horses, too—more horses than people, and most of them were standing. Then some of the humans stood up, groaning and swaying. It was strange. They looked like they'd been drugged."

"Like us, this morning," said Kereqa.

"Then some of them noticed me, and I ran," said Mektu. "I wanted to warn you, Kandri, but I didn't dare shout."

"They must have thought we'd execute them," said the pensive corporal.

"Can't say it's a disagreeable notion," snarled Chindilan. "Who knows how things might have gone if they'd been true to their word?"

"I can," said Prince Nirabha. "The Slaughterhouse Clowns might never have planned our ambush. Our party might have reassembled peacefully at the crossroads. And Captain Utarif and Talupéké might not be dead. But I will note—" He glanced coldly at Mektu. "—that all this death might just as well have been avoided if you had not stolen the mattoglin."

Mektu glared at him, flustered. Ulren gave a throaty laugh. "I told 'em, Gooney Bird, while you were prancing around in that tower. They've a right to know that they're traveling with a thief."

"In this one matter," said the Prince, "I concur with Mr. Ulren."

Ripheem crossed his arms, looking deeply satisfied. Mektu squinted sidelong at the Prince and began to rummage in his pockets. "Say you're sorry," he demanded.

"What's that, my bumptious fellow?"

"Sorry," repeated Mektu, "for calling me a thief."

"Pig feathers, I will not," said Nirabha. "For you *are* a thief, Mektu Hinjuman."

"Don't you push me," said Mektu.

"If you stood nearer the Wall's edge I should be tempted," said Nirabha. "But merely tempted, have no fear. My actions result from *choice*, not mindless impulse. We are different in that way."

"I'm not a thief."

"Then you have authored a dictionary all your own."

Ulren cackled with delight. Mektu's jaw worked as though he had a mouthful of grain.

"A thief," said Ripheem, "and a pesky fly."

"*Pesky?*" Mektu glanced at the Prince, who shrugged in nonchalant agreement.

It was, apparently, the last straw. Mektu pulled his hand from his pocket. There on his palm lay Nirabha's extraordinary ring, its clusters of sapphires blazing in the band of heavy silver.

"Gods of Perdition!" shouted the Prince. "You found it, how in the name of—"

Mektu whirled and flung the ring with all his might.

Nirabha gave an inarticulate cry, reaching out with both hands. But the deed was done. Mektu had perhaps been aiming for the doorway of the tower, but a squall of wind caught the ring as it left his hand and bent its arc northward. It winked at them, a blue spark in the sunlight, and vanished over the Wall.

For a moment, everyone was speechless. Nirabha's arms slowly lowered to his sides. Ripheem's mouth hung open. Even Mektu looked stunned.

"My my, he's a special prick," said Ulren.

Slowly the Prince turned to face Mektu. "Nineteen centuries," he said. "Mother to daughter, father to son. You miserable, you *shameless*—"

Ripheem charged with a roar, his great hands grasping for Mektu's throat. But this time Mektu was ready. He slipped sidelong through the giant's arms, and sank three blows to his ribs before Ripheem could turn to face him. Ripheem staggered sideways with a groan, but he looked more embarrassed than injured.

Kandri, Chindilan, and the soldiers surged between them. Kereqa was seething. "Idiots!" she snapped. "Have we braved death to watch you squabble like brats in a nursery? We have true enemies, if you care to remember."

"Look there!" said Ulren. "They've stopped running, for some reason."

It was true: the three mercenaries had ridden about half a mile, to a point where a dune crested over the Wall like the sea over a breakwater. And there they had stopped. The horses, whipped to a gallop minutes before, twitched and pranced in confusion.

"What's gotten into them?" said the croaking private. "Afraid of the sand drift? It hardly looks dangerous."

The drift could not have been more than a foot deep—far too shallow to hide a spider. Then something protruding from the sand caught Kandri's eye: it was a dark, low mound. All three mercenaries were studying it. Woeden Surk nudged his horse forward.

"Your telescope, Hinjuman!" shouted Kereqa.

Kandri raced to his camel and pulled the scope from the saddlebag. By the time he trained it on Surk, the mercenary leader had dismounted and was standing over the mound. He prodded it with his toe, cried to his men over his shoulder. Then he bent down and lifted something from the sand.

It was the pouch with the Letter of Cure, which Utarif had raised in triumph a moment before he died. Surk had plucked it from a limp, sand-buried hand. And suddenly Kandri knew what lay at Surk's feet.

"Talupéké!" shouted Kandri. "Ang's sweet tears, he's found her! Mount up, mount up!"

He shoved the telescope into his bag. He said nothing about the Letter of Cure, even though he had watched Surk pass the strap of the pouch over his head. He did not need to. Talupéké was reason enough for them to charge.

But they had only four camels—and none of them were kneeling. Kandri knew it was just possible, by brute force and swearing, to climb a standing camel. You jammed a foot into the pit of its foreleg. Hoisted your body by a stirrup. Hooked a knee over the gooselike neck. And prayed that the creature would not buck or bite you or kneel after all, in sympathy or spite.

Such offenses were beneath the dignity of the Princess of the Golden Heart. Alahari watched his efforts with serene indifference. Mektu was likewise trying to scale Fish, while the others coaxed the last two camels to their knees.

Kandri gained Alahari's withers. By now Woeden Surk had freed the girl's body from the sand. He dealt her a savage blow to the face, then began to drag her by the armpits toward the edge of the Wall.

Why beat a corpse?

The answer burst in him like one of the fireballs on the plain. There was no reason at all to beat a corpse. Talupéké was alive.

He clawed his way into the saddle. Alive, and barely conscious. Alive, and beyond their help. Surk was just yards from the precipice. He was going to toss her from the Wall.

Kandri bellowed with all his might: "Don't you do it! We will *kill* you!" But Surk could not hear him, and would not have cared.

Sudden howls at his back. Floundering, Kandri looked over his shoulder: a second posse of riders had surged from the tower and were storming past his companions.

Slaughterhouse Clowns. Eight of them, swords and spears raised high. At the lead rode their red-masked commander, white arm-ribbons snapping in the wind. They cried out in unison, a falsetto war-cry that managed to be both bloodthirsty and sarcastic.

Woeden Surk took one look at the Clowns and dropped Talupéké like a sack. Waving at his men, he sprinted for his horse and remounted. The other mercenaries were already riding for their lives.

The Clowns thundered past those nearest the tower without a glance. But the croaking private, obeying some impulse, drew his sword and feinted at the commander's horse. Kereqa screamed a warning, but the youth had committed to his effort, whatever its aim. Perhaps he hoped the horse would shy and throw its rider upon the Wall.

It did not shy, however. As she passed the youth, the leader of the Clowns brought her broad-bladed sword down like an executioner's axe and cleaved the private's head in two. The body stood a moment in the fountain of its desecration, then crumpled sidelong, sword clattering on the stone.

Paralyzed, Kandri watched the eight Clowns pass him as though he did not exist.

ඥ

Nor did Talupéké merit their attention. Nothing existed for the Clowns but the mercenaries, it appeared. Did they know that Woeden Surk had the mattoglin? Had the mercenaries assaulted one of the women? Whatever it was had smashed their alliance to pieces. The Clowns were out for blood.

Kereqa was the first to reach Talupéké. Kandri and Mektu, in their saddles at last, arrived to find the girl retching and spitting blood, her head in her grandmother's lap.

"Surk broke two of her teeth," Kereqa yelled over the wind, "and when we have avenged our comrade I will break that man's arms and legs."

"You won't get the chance," said Mektu. "The meat freaks are going to dice him."

"She says the Nachasps fell into a trap. Their dead lie all about the tower."

"We know," said Kandri.

Chindilan appeared, eyes fixed on Talupéké. Even before his camel stopped he swung a leg over its withers.

"Do not dismount!" shouted Kereqa. Talupéké nodded, making a tortured sound in her throat. She pointed after the fleeing mercenaries.

"But the Clowns—" said Mektu.

"To hell with the Clowns!" cried Kereqa. "That great hog Surk has the Letter of Cure! Ride, ride him down! Now of all moments you must not lose faith."

Talupéké made the sound again, mouth working, tears in her eyes.

"The mercenaries will not escape," said Kereqa. "Sooner or later, they must turn and fight the Clowns. At that moment you must help them win— and *then* deal with Surk. That is your best hope, Hinjumans! Do not squander it."

"But Tal—" began Chindilan.

Talupéké's hand found a stone. She flung it. The smith's leg jerked; he cried out in pain.

Talupéké spit out a mouthful of blood. "What are you waiting for, you shit monkeys?" she screamed. "Ride!"

337

18. VANISHING POINT

Every word of praise about the Sparaviths was true: they held their own against the barrens horses, even though the surface beneath their feet was mostly stone and not sand, the terrain of their natural advantage. But while the extraordinary camels could match a horse's pace, they could not exceed it. The Clowns were barely half a mile ahead, but the gap persisted, no matter how the brothers and Chindilan urged their mounts on.

The Clowns in turn were about the same distance behind Surk and his men. They too seemed unable to close on their quarry. All three parties were galloping flat-out for their lives, or toward the end of their lives, toward the Wall's vanishing point in the murderous desert, and no one, for the moment, had the upper hand.

Kandri knew in minutes that the chase ahead would be a nightmare. The Wall was smooth but had weathered unevenly. Some of the great bricks had heaved or sunk, creating sudden ledges, and the seams were obscured by the wind-driven sand. There were great cracks and fissures, heaps of stone where the crenellations had collapsed. And the wind itself was now an outright threat, violent and capricious, roaring like floodwaters over the levee of the Wall, howling through its stone teeth, slamming into the camels from one side only to change its mind and blast from the other. Alahari needed little urging to avoid the sheer drop on their left, but the defects and debris often forced them nearer than Kandri liked. Nor was the Wall's right-hand edge a place of safety. Drops of sixty or eighty feet separated the dunes, and where the latter stood high the wind launched sand at them in sheets and streamers.

Five miles, then six. They passed a human skeleton, immaculate, a rust-gnawed chain still fastened to its neck. They galloped straight through the next watchtower, and bats flowed about them like a storm of ashes. Kandri could feel the effort Alahari was making to keep her balance, weaving among obstacles, punched left and right by the wind. Mektu was faring no better with Fish, but their uncle, astonishingly, rode like a champion. He was soon in the lead, broad buttocks high on the animal's back, shoulders level with his hips.

Kandri watched him, amused and irritated at once. *You've ridden camels before, you sly old bear. You might have told us.*

The smith turned his head, astonished at something he'd seen. Kandri followed his glance.

What in Jekka's boiling Hell!

It was gone so quickly that he could almost have dreamed it. Hallucinated. Seen nothing all. But when he looked back over his shoulder it was still there, seated in the wind-shelter of the parapet, watching them with lively interest.

A black cat.

ॐ

The first mercenary died minutes later, when his horse lost its footing and cast him from the saddle. The horse itself recovered but would not be caught. The man fled on foot as the Clowns swept nearer. At the last minute he flung himself at a dune and began to climb, scrabbling like a squirrel. The Akrunu speared him with casual accuracy, never breaking their stride. Pierced in four places, the man slid face-down and came to rest with his feet against the Wall.

All this Kandri watched like a silent performance. But as he galloped past the spot he saw another black cat standing on the dead mercenary's buttocks, sniffing at his wounds.

Nine miles or more. The wind tore foam from the camels' mouths. By luck or strength or force of terror, Woeden Surk had pulled somewhat farther ahead of the Clowns. He was, Kandri had to admit, a fine horseman, outpacing his pursuers on their own steed.

But the other mercenary was in peril. His horse was laboring, missing steps, as though troubled in one of its hooves. The Clowns behind him had narrowed the gap to a hundred yards.

Eight of them on his heels. No hope for that one. But how much hope did he, Mek, and Chindilan have? Could they kill eight Akrunu, after the mercenaries fell?

Turn and fight, his mind begged Surk and his underling. *We'll help you, even now we'll help you. Five against eight are the best odds you'll get.*

The best odds any of them would get.

Surk galloped on. Kandri began to wonder if he had any plan at all. Just a mile ahead now loomed the first point where the Wall had collapsed, where all this racing and flailing had to end. There were still a few escape points before then, a few spots where the dunes climbed all the way to the ramparts they were galloping along. But at the breach itself there was no way down—none but leaping to one's death. The dunes, with nothing to lean against, had fanned out flat through the gaping hole.

Chindilan's gaze snapped left.

"Oh, lovely, lovely, fuck my favorite dog!"

On the plain below, a swarm of riders was sweeping toward them from the north. Horse riders, hundreds of them, a battalion's worth. And a vanguard riding something else, broader and stronger. They were miles off but closing swiftly, flying over the russet land.

Mektu gave a wordless yowl and tried to drive his camel faster.

Kandri too felt the spike of fear, like a malign injection. Nothing at all like the fear the Clowns had provoked when they attacked at the crossroads. This was an intimate, familiar fear. Ulren's words came back to him with scalding clarity: *three hundred on horseback, twelve Rasanga on those hellish Sandcats.*

The Army of Revelation had caught up with them at last.

Turn, you bastard.

Surk would not turn. He had no intention of fighting the Clowns. And he had a new incentive for speed: the Prophet's forces were making for the breach, where they could pass through the Wall and ascend the dunes.

And if they gained the breach first, and held it?

Well, then they were all fucked together. Mercenaries, Clowns, the three idiots in pursuit. Either they would take to the open sands or reverse direction, flee back along the Wall—and lead the army straight to Talupéké and Kereqa and the others.

That could not happen. But even if Surk and his underling managed to scramble down one of these dune-faces, race across the breach and climb again, who would be bringing up the rear but the idiots, the object of the Prophet's wrath and the army's fascination, the threesome that had dragged them all into the desert?

Run, Alahari-Rana, run your heart out. Please.

The mercenary on the stumbling horse had taken to glancing over his shoulder. Each glance threw off his balance; each glance showed the Akrunu closer by a horse's length. The nearest had lifted spears to shoulders. They were almost in range.

Surk flung something down upon the Wall. It was not the pouch with the Letter of Cure, but a long, flat bundle, too heavy to be lifted by the wind.

The leader of the Slaughterhouse Clowns reined in her horse beside the bundle. Her riders broke stride as well, but a gesture and a scream from the woman sent them galloping on. She speared and lifted the bundle. It was a canvas saddlebag, and in seconds she had torn it open and rifled the contents. A twitch of fury. She flung the bag down—no mattoglin, clearly—and raced after her fellow Akrunu.

The ruse had bought the mercenaries only seconds. Far from enough. The breach was within half a mile.

Kandri's hatred of Surk had grown into a physical pain. He wailed, he moaned with it inside. *You're galloping toward a cliff. Turn and fight, you dumb, greedy, suicidal—*

Surk rode his horse off the Wall.

It was a drop of eight or nine feet to the dune-top, the last thinkable point of exit. The horse, magnificently, landed on its feet, and Woeden Surk stayed in the saddle. But when his underling attempted the same maneuver his horse shied, planting its feet and flinging the mercenary headfirst from the Wall.

The man rolled and slid downslope a good twenty yards. Woeden Surk did not even look back. The Clowns, meanwhile, accomplished the leap one after another, flawlessly. By the time the mercenary stopped sliding they were upon him, taking aim with their spears. Kandri shuddered. The man never gained his feet.

"Right here, boys, here or nothing—"

Chindilan turned his camel sharply. It was a far gentler exit: merely a large step down for the Sparaviths. Chindilan was right—they dared not attempt a nine-foot leap—but it meant extra time on loose sand, which even for a camel was a slower terrain than stone. Their quarry pulled ahead.

At the fissure, the dunes fell away to nothing. The descent was steep, and their long-legged camels fared worse than the horses. By the time they passed the blood-soaked body of the mercenary, the Clowns were already racing across the level sand before the mouth of the breach, and Woeden Surk was halfway up the dune beyond.

When at last he reached level ground himself, Kandri was rewarded by a clear view of the plain beyond—and the advancing battalion. So close. Just minutes. The white-robed Rasanga well ahead of the rest, their sandcats stretched out and sprinting, paws hardly seeming to touch the ground.

Ang's love, how close we came to being trapped!

On they pushed the Sparaviths, straight up the opposite dune. For a few paces they were sheltered from the wind, and the silence was so abrupt and strange it was like a noise in itself. Kandri suddenly became aware that he was in pain. Blows, cuts, bruises, blisters. He ached all over. Worse than any of these, however, was the abuse his ass was taking in the saddle.

"The cats," said Chindilan, mopping his brow. "Not the sandcat monsters, the little ones—"

"I saw them," said Kandri. "They're what the guides were talking about in the hills, aren't they? *Little cat, black and little cat*—"

"We're all going mad," said Mektu.

"In the same way, at the same time?" said Chindilan. "Explain that one to me."

Mektu looked glum. "The yatra," he said at last. "It's toying with us. We've failed it, and now it's taking revenge."

"Failed it how?"

"We lost something it cares about."

Kandri and his uncle studiously avoided his eye. They could no longer dismiss Mektu's fears about the yatra. But trusting his pronouncements about it was another matter.

"Drink some water, both of you," said Chindilan. "You're burning."

Kandri took a long pull from his faska. Just as fear had distracted him from the pain, the mad wind had made it easy to ignore the sun. No shadows to speak of: it was high noon already. They had water enough for today, perhaps even tomorrow. But what of their camels? How long could they keep running?

He put the question to Chindilan, who scowled and shook his head. "Longer than the horses, you can be sure of that," he said. "They drank gallon after gallon at Weeping Rock. Horses can't do that, can't pack it away."

"How long will the horses last?"

"Do I look like a bleeding veterinarian? A good while. They're barrens horses. But when the thirst hits those poor brutes they'll not be good for anything, save a buzzard's banquet. *Harach*, they're doomed already."

"And we're not much better off, are we?" said Mektu. "It's simple. We find the caravan when this is over, and Jód finds us a well to drink from. Or we don't, or he doesn't, and we're through."

No one answered. The wind swallowed them again. They watched Surk regain the Wall and start to gallop, and then the Clowns, one after another. As they neared the summit themselves the first sandcat-mounted Rasanga burst through the fissure and began to climb.

"It's *not* that simple," Chindilan growled above the wind. "There's fifty other ways we could die."

CB

But over the next hours—excruciating hours of sun and scorching wind—
no one died, no one faltered, no one managed to close the stubborn gaps.
Woeden Surk rode on like a distant lure, a mirage floating ahead of them, his
form bent by the glare. The eight Slaughterhouse Clowns were spread out
over half a mile. And barely two miles behind Kandri and his companions,
the Rasanga. Twelve Rasanga, with the cavalry at their heels.

Kandri felt his ass was being beaten into a textureless mass, beaten like the
army used to beat the mutton, with mallets, working it into something that could
be chewed. That process took minutes; this one was never going to end. Although
perhaps it had reached the chewing stage; perhaps his ass was being gnawed off
right now by the abrasion of Alahari's hump. He would know when his thighs
separated from his torso. When pieces of him fell senseless on the stone.

The mangling of his ass was nothing, however, compared to the torture
of his thoughts. *Your doing, your doing*, went the singsong refrain. *All you had
to do was stay awake, keep your mind on that letter, keep your hands off that girl.
So what if she had Ari's voice?*

He gazed into the blinding distance. The figures ahead were capricious
flames. Was that Woeden Surk or the Akrunu leader, insane with greed for
the golden mattoglin, riding to her own death as much as anyone's?

He realized suddenly that the figures in the lead were approaching another
breach in the Wall. Not a total collapse, this time: the sand had punched
through the upper third of the structure, about a hundred feet of stone. The
top of the dune lay across this V-shaped gap like a thick and muscular arm.

There was nothing preventing a rider from stepping into that sand. But
the wind in the gap was cyclonic. One moment it was shearing away great
curtains of sand into the north; the next it flung that sand skyward or let it
drop like gravel on the Wall.

Deathtrap, thought Kandri. *Absolutely no one could*—

Woeden Surk drove his horse into the maelstrom. It balked, slowed to a
jerking, twitching walk. But he drove it on, bent low in the saddle, kicking
with his heels.

The Clowns reined in their horses at the edge of the breach. One launched a spear at Woeden Surk only to see it whisked away like a straw. None of them seemed anxious to step into the sand.

The brothers and their uncle slowed. Eight Slaughterhouse Clowns backed into a corner: that was no fight Kandri wanted. Another stab of misery gripped his throat. The idiocy of the chase. The futility.

"Gods, that pig can ride," said Mektu.

Surk's horse dragged itself through the last yard of sand. It climbed with a shudder back onto the stone, and the mercenary at once began to whip it for speed.

"Why are they waiting?" said Kandri. "Devil's ass, they're letting him get away!"

"They'd better find their courage," said Chindilan.

Kandri looking over his shoulder. The Rasanga were closing fast. Behind the commandos, riders twenty ranks deep thundered along the Wall.

The men cursed and the camels paced. Woeden Surk was already far off, and still the Clowns did not advance.

"Mother fuckers!" said Mektu. "We're going to have to attack them!"

They nudged their camels closer. The Akrunu were aware of them, and certainly aware of the Prophet's forces close behind. But all eight were looking forward—into the blowing sand, or beyond it.

"Mektu," said Kandri, "get the telescope out."

Mektu brought Fish alongside Alahari and dug the instrument from Kandri's saddlebag. Rather than hand it over, he raised it to his own eye and focused.

"I don't believe it."

"What, what?" Kandri and Chindilan shouted together.

"I mean I do not fucking believe it."

"What in Jekka's Hell do you see?" cried the smith.

"A cat. Just—a cat. Those stupid, gutless—"

Kandri leaned out and snatched the scope from his brother. It was true, by the Gods: a small black cat was seated just beyond the collapsed area, watching the Akrunu, wind-whipped but motionless, tail tucked around its feet.

"Mek's right," he said. "It doesn't look dangerous."

"It's a barn cat!" said Mektu.

Chindilan pulled at his beard. "Some kind of superstition. A bad omen, a sign."

"You don't understand," said Mektu. "This is a cat, a little kitty, *Meow, meow—*"

"It didn't do a thing to Woeden Surk," said Kandri.

"Do?" Mektu was apoplectic. "What the hell could it do? Spit on him? Scratch his horse?"

The Clowns appeared to be having a similar argument. They were shouting, gesturing, shoving one another. They drove their horses to the edge of the sand and back again, circling.

By now the Rasanga were barely a mile off. "Kandri, Uncle?" shouted Mektu. "We're out of time. We have to charge."

"Wait," said Kandri.

Mektu faced the Clowns and bellowed: "Afraid of cats, are you? Look at the ones *behind us*, bastards! Ride on!"

"I doubt they can hear you," said Chindilan, "but you can be sure they've seen the Rasanga and their sandcats."

"Then they're crazy and we have to fight them," said Mektu.

"Not yet," said Kandri.

"Fuck your 'not yet'!" Turning again to the gap, Mektu cupped his hands about his mouth and screamed to wake the dead: "IT'S A KITTY! AND YOU DUMBFUCK CLOWNS ARE ABOUT TO LEARN WHAT SLAUGHTER IS! RIDE YOUR HORSES, CHICKEN SHITS!"

Chindilan told Mektu to save his breath—for what, Kandri wondered?— but even as he spoke, the eight Clowns gave a howl of defiance and plunged into the whirling sand.

Oh, thank the Gods.

The brothers and Chindilan drove their camels toward the gap. The Clowns were bent double against the wind. Their horses plowed forward shoulder-to-shoulder, high-stepping as though walking in surf.

On the Wall, the little cat flicked its tail.

The Clowns picked up speed as Kandri and his companions reached the edge of the gap. "We don't have to wait," said Mektu. "They don't care about us; all they want is the mattoglin. Hell, they probably think we're still in league with the Prophet."

Now the Clowns were halfway across. The little cat raised its hackles. Kandri looked at his uncle but could read nothing in his face. Behind them, the Rasanga were closing with hideous speed.

Mektu nudged Fish into the sand. Kandri whispered a prayer and followed.

"*Stop!*" howled Chindilan.

Both brothers obeyed. And in that instant the spiders pounced.

They erupted from the dune just below the Clowns, eight or nine of the creatures, terrible in their swiftness, a wave breaking in wrath and blood. The eye could not follow. Spiny bodies, mandibles, long flexing legs. The carnage was instant. Torn necks, limbs, torsos, brief spasms, blood frothing away on the wind. Horses bolting with madness in their eyes. One wounded animal leaped from the Wall with half a mercenary dangling by a stirrup.

The camels reeled and fled. Kandri, Mektu, and Chindilan fought to master them, but it was no use: even Sparaviths had limits. Clinging to Alahari, Kandri glanced back and saw that it was over. Blood smeared the jaws of the spiders. They crouched in the blowing sand and gorged.

The fact that they were charging straight at three hundred enemies was, at first, beyond the camels' comprehension—but the dagger-toothed sand-cats proved impossible to ignore. At last they heeded their riders' screams and imprecations and turned a second time. Once more they charged for the gap.

Kandri thought he was dreaming. The spiders were gliding away down the dune, one after another, like docile sheep. One only remained, larger than the rest, towering above the carnage. And beside it stood a woman. She was perfectly unafraid, even steadying herself against one of its massive legs. Then she turned and looked squarely at the men, and her silver eyes flashed in the sun.

Fiasul.

She was wrapped in the same white cloak she had worn in the hills, but about her neck she had tied a slash of scarlet cloth. Even as they watched, the great spider bent its head to the sand, and Fiasul sprang upon its back.

She raised a hand to them: *Hello, goodbye.* Then the spider followed the rest of its brood, gliding with that same eerie, water-bug motion down the side of the dune. Fiasul rode on her knees, gripping its thorny carapace, white cloak whipping like a flag.

Of the little cat there was no sign.

ᘓ

Scraps of Clown—boots, bones, ornaments—peeked blurrily through the sand. Despite his loathing of the Akrunu, Kandri was sickened. Eight lives gone in an instant. For nothing. For greed.

They crossed the gap, staggered and slow, but once back atop the Wall the camels ran with a will, grasping as clearly as their riders that only death lay behind. Close and ever closer: nothing in the gap hindered the Rasanga; they crossed almost without slowing down.

Memories ran like minnows in Kandri's head: Fiasul's gaze as she washed his body, the eyes of the dead Nachasp in the tower, the red shawl at Talupéké's waist, Fiasul's words in the dark. *And maybe I protect you.* Had she called the spiders? Was that massacre a kindness to Kandri, or simply revenge?

Woeden Surk had put miles between them; in the late-day glare he had become a distant speck. Kandri felt rage at the man like a physical affliction, an abscess in his mouth. *Keep the knife, bastard, but give us back the letter, give us the Cure. You don't even know what you've stolen.*

"We'll outlast him," shouted Chindilan, as though reading his thoughts. "He's on a horse, remember. When that poor beast drops dead, we'll close and take him, along with the Cure."

"If he doesn't toss himself over the Wall just to spite us," said Mektu.

"I still don't understand," said Kandri. "Why did the Nachasps take the letter, of all damned things? Why not my telescope? Why not our blades?"

"They took the mattoglin," said Mektu.

"*You* took the mattoglin," shouted Kandri. "You stole it from Eshett. Again."

"I didn't lose the most important thing in Urrath, though, did I?"

"No more!" snapped Chindilan. "Shut your damned mouths and ride. What would your beloved Ariqina think if she heard you? 'A pair of clods, bickering and useless! What did I ever see in them?'"

೮

Behind his back, they glared at each other. Helpless in their idiocy, a whole battalion at their heels.

What *would* Ariqina think? For Kandri it was a scalding question. She would forgive their blunders; she always had. But meanness, smallness of mind? No, not that. Such things touched Ari to the core. She had no defense against meanness because she could not understand it. Ari, doctor to indigents. Ari, schoolgirl, his mad crush and Mektu's, who had left her only dress folded on the doorstep of a mother whose daughter had drowned. On impulse, so that the destitute woman might have something decent in which to bury her child.

He had first lain eyes on her just three days before, when Mektu took him to spy on her older cousins, bathing. The hidden spot near the bath chamber was Mektu's greatest discovery, treasure, and life accomplishment. Her two cousins had disrobed and washed by sputtering lamplight, and the vision of their bodies had gone through Kandri like a spear. Then Ari had stepped into the chamber and extinguished the lamp to save the life of a moth. The cousins departed. And Ariqina sat alone in the chamber and wept.

It lasted just three or four minutes, a brief, quiet hurricane of tears. But those few minutes changed the course of Kandri's life. Ariqina Nawhal. A voice, a shadow, a girl who thought herself alone, consumed with grief for who knew what, sparrow-bone shoulders trembling against the wooden plank that was all that stood between her and Kandri, a sensation in his fingertips, an explosion in his mind, a fresh arrival in the Valley just as he was,

349

a name, a question, a hope. And a frustration to his brother, who had set out to see this new girl naked, and complained all the way home.

Happenstance, he thought. What if the night had been rainy? What if Mektu had not shared? What if no moth had arrived, as if summoned, to smack and hurl its body against that terrible strange fire, helpless in the grip of a fascination woven into its soul?

ᛗ

Kandri never went back to the hiding place. He did not want to deceive this girl, to be ashamed before her, to have something he could not say. As for her beautiful cousins, they no longer existed. Ariqina had banished all other girls from his dreams. Along with all other ambitions, priorities, plans. He was adrift in the awareness of her perfection. He was not yet fifteen.

She passed their house on her way to school and back. Disheveled, wearing the cousins' cast-off clothes, indifferent to his glances, anyone's glances, reading a book as she walked. Or chasing after street dogs, hugging them, cleaning their eyes, pulling ticks. Or laughing at the gangly storks raiding the fish ponds. Or retying a cousin's braid.

He could never speak to her in this lifetime, obviously. She was too rare and ethereal, too good to hear his voice, a sleek brown bird that his farmyard bray would bring down like a stone. He should be satisfied with knowing that she existed, that Urrath held such wonders. To expect more was vain and selfish. Give thanks, he commanded himself, but don't lose your mind.

Then one of his sisters mentioned Ariqina's gift to the grieving mother, and something inside him collapsed. He walked out the door and down the road to her township and spotted her and followed her home. She saw him; he didn't lurk in corners. When she waved from the garden he found his hands were welded into his pockets. He nodded, strolling on, busy with his nonexistent errand.

She was watching him; it was unbearable; this was punishment for his night of spying and lust. His mind and body skinned by her gaze. He chuckled horribly. He had forgotten how to walk. This was love, it seemed, and love was a rout, a mental mass defection of everything one counted on to get through the day: hands, voice, reason, stomach muscles—

"Are you too dignified to climb a tree?"

She had crossed the road and appeared at his elbow. He panicked. Why was she looking at him? Should he look back?

No, no, answer her question! Answer right and she will smile and you will never know unhappiness again. Answer wrong and you'll shrink before her eyes into something vile and dead. A carcass. A toad crushed by a cart wheel, flayed dry by the sun.

"Yes of course. I'm not."

She waited, puzzled.

"I mean I climb. I mean I'm absolutely in love with climbing. If I could I would devote my whole life—"

Her smile: a flood of gold, and his first taste ever of what Her Radiance the Prophet called the Fire Sacrament, the cup drawn from the world's molten heart that sets the soul upon its path. What a strange boy I am, he thought with wonder and fear.

"You can hold me at the waist," said Ariqina, "and boost me up to the first branch. Then I'll lean down and help you up. Worth a try?"

"Tree," he burbled. "Which, what, me?"

"The sunburst oak," she said, "in the field behind the house. It's in flower, but only near the crown. Have you ever smelled the flowers of an oak?"

He looked at the house to keep from gaping at her. The older cousins, fully clothed and predatory, were watching from an upper window.

"They're sweet, but they're afraid of dirt," said Ariqina, taking his hand. "This way, Kandri. I'm so lucky you . . . chanced along."

Ari, who he followed up a tree. Ari, who in days to come he followed into the Valley's hills and roads and distant townships, into books, into the beautiful mad dream of the clinic for the poor, into the meadows where they taught each other love.

Ari, who had vanished without a trace. Ari, the echo he was chasing across a continent. The oasis in the distance that might just be a mirage.

ൠ

Night fell, and the wind died away. No galloping now: the chase had become a war of endurance, and the Wall was black, the hazards numerous as ever. Some of the cavalry lit torches, but the Rasanga had become invisible, and it was anyone's guess how close to the three men they had drawn.

Woeden Surk too had vanished from sight. Each time a dune crested the Wall Kandri strained his eyes by starlight, fearing to see the mercenary already far away down its side. That such a move would be hopeless went almost without saying. Surk's horse would die of thirst and exhaustion. The mercenary's death would follow fast.

But a point came when the dunes disappeared: to the right now as well as the left there was only a sheer and deadly drop. What had become of the sand? Was there a ridge, a second wall, some parallel structure out there blocking its advance?

In the darkness it was impossible to say. But mile upon mile there was no longer a means of egress from the Wall. If Surk had not left it yet, he was trapped.

So, of course, were Kandri and his companions.

An icy cold descended. For a time the Wall itself warmed them, giving back the heat it had drunk through the day, but hour by hour the cold advanced. The glow of the still-hidden moon swelled behind the mountains he had glimpsed from Weeping Rock, sketching in their shape. Animal eyes blazed from crevasses, mounds of stone.

The fireballs came at moonrise. Six blinding orbs, trailing plumes of flame that lingered in the sky. They fell in a straight line across the desert, the first so distant it was like a tiny scratch on a chalkboard, the next perhaps twenty miles closer, then twenty again, and again.

By the light of these momentary flares they saw where the dunes ceased— some five or six miles to the south of the Wall—but not what held them back. Hulking, angular shapes rose and mingled with the dunes, but the light was too brief to reveal very much, and whether the shapes were built or natural they could not perceive.

Most of the fireballs winked out on impact, or lit faint fires behind some distant fold in the land. But one struck close, near a dune's summit, with a flash that turned night into day. Half the dune was gone in an instant. Brittle particles began to strike their bodies like a sidelong rain. In what remained of the dune, a molten object lay throbbing, burrowing, melting its way into the sand, a heart torn from a demon and flung to earth.

In the windless night they heard the suck and roar of flames across the landscape. It was somehow obscene, that red sinking shape. Like the Prophet's vengeance—on the two of them, on the Važeks and the Kasraji empire, on the present and the past. A diseased inspiration. A need that could never be met.

"Boys," said Chindilan, "my camel's gone lame."

Kandri felt as though he'd swallowed glass.

"That's not true, Uncle," said Mektu. "She's keeping up, don't say that, she's fine."

"She's lame," said the smith. "Right front foot, or ankle maybe. I don't think she'll run again."

"She's got something in her pad, is all," said Kandri. "We'll find it and pull it, dig it out."

Chindilan sighed through his teeth. "Camels aren't horses, and their pads aren't hooves. We can try, but don't get your hopes up. And don't stop yet! We need to do this perfectly—and that means *fast*. Dismount, foot check, remount, ride. Sandcats can see in the dark. For that matter, so can Rasanga, or so Lord Garatajik claimed. They're not like us. They're not normal people."

"If they can see in the dark, they don't have to move slowly," said Mektu.

"Not for safety, anyway," said Chindilan. "Fortunately, sandcats tire like any mounts. We're all getting careless: we should have looked back when that fireball lit up the world. Because you're right, Mektu. They could be closing. For all we know they're three minutes behind."

No one spoke. The dark had wrapped them in an illusion of safety, but now death was back, palpable and very near. Kandri tried to imagine how the procedure could possibly be done. Kneeling the camel was out of the question. So was climbing in that jackass manner he and Mektu had barely managed by daylight.

"A rope," he said at last. "One end tied around my chest, under my arms. The other tied to Fish's neck."

"Pig pastries," said Chindilan.

"It can work," insisted Kandri. "I drop to the ground, fix your camel's foot. We fling the rope over the saddle on Alahari. Mek gives Fish a good smack—"

"Fish bolts forward," interrupted Chindilan, "and crushes your chest against your own beast, or hauls you right over her. Or Alahari bolts after Fish and you're dragged bobbing and smacking along on the ground."

"Then cut your camel loose. Slide onto Alahari behind me."

"What, on her hips? Clinging to that hump for dear life, like a cub to a tree trunk? No, Kandri. What happens at dawn, when we need to run again? I wouldn't last ten minutes. And even if I could hold on, I'd slow you down."

"You have a better idea?"

"'Course I do," said Chindilan. "First, I'm the one who ties a rope around his chest, and I check my own damn camel's foot. If I'm able to help her, the two of you pull me up, hand over hand. Might take a few seconds longer, but at least I'll end up in the saddle."

"What if you can't help her?"

A long silence.

Kandri repeated his question.

"Listen to me now," said Chindilan softly. "There's precious few ways this ends that leave *any* of us—"

"Shut up, Uncle."

"I know you mean well, Kandri. But I'm ex-army too, see? I'm done taking orders. There's only one man in Urrath I'm beholden to now, and I promised him to keep you chaff-heads alive. Besides, I've had my fun. Good years, lucky years—"

"Shut your fat foolish mouth," said Kandri. "You're *not* getting off that camel. There's no need, we're just walking. And Mektu's right, she's keeping pace with us just fine."

"She's not lame, she's not," Mektu insisted.

"Stop it, both of you! She's lamer with every step. And I'll ask you again, what happens at dawn?"

Kandri was shaking with rage and fear. He had no answer, but he had to spit out something, anything, before his uncle—

"Another!" cried Mektu.

The fireball flared and vanished and flared up again, over and over, like a stone skipped across a lake. At last it achieved a constant burn and fell earthward in a shower of purple sparks.

"What do you suppose they signify?" said Chindilan. "A change in the state of heaven, a God's passing, a God's coming of age? Is that what the *Darsunuk* is all about, boys? A temporary madness when one regime's over, and the next hasn't begun?"

Fear like cold wires scratched and gouged in Kandri's brain. His uncle did not philosophize.

Once again orange light bathed their faces. Once again it flickered and died.

"Tears from heaven," said the smith, "and the Pilgrim on its way as well. Our wandering moon, Jekka's bloodshot eye." He scratched his beard. "Do you know what they call those six hours when it's nearest this world? When everything grows lighter and pulls toward heaven? You boys were what, three, last time around? Too young to remember."

"I remember," said Kandri. "We couldn't walk normally. We bounced."

"It was a great day," said Mektu. "The Old Man threw a chicken off the porch roof, and that fucker could fly."

"They call those hours the Pilgrim's Kiss," said Chindilan. "Kandri, I want you to do me a favor, somewhere in those six hours. I want you to take Ariqina somewhere gorgeous and make love."

"*Him?*" said Mektu.

"I never had the chance with a woman," said Chindilan, "but my old mates say there's nothing like love during those hours. The way her body answers your touch, how happy you can make her, how you both feel every care in the world's been shorn away." He looked at them. "Your own father said so, among others. I wonder which of your mothers he was with."

"You're confused, Uncle," said Mektu. "Ari's *my* girl, wherever she's gone. But if I find her I'll be glad to—"

"Kandri and Ariqina were lovers," said Chindilan. "There was talk of marriage. We all knew it, the whole family, and you'd have known it too if you hadn't walled yourself up in a fortress of dreams. Don't live in that fortress, nephew. Life is very short."

Kandri felt as if the world had been ripped open. *Uncle said it. He said it right to Mektu's face.* The plain truth, which Kandri had promised Ariqina he would never reveal.

He wanted to take his uncle in a bear hug. *All that lying. It's over at last.*

Mektu did not look at either of them. He gave a kind of tortured chuckle, and the sound went straight to Kandri's heart. Ariqina, so wise about so much, had been dead wrong to demand his silence. It had protected no one; it had cost them all such pain.

Another fireball lit the sky, and Mektu turned with feigned astonishment. "That's seven," he said.

Chindilan had pulled the coiled rope from his saddlebag. "I need you both to be strong now," he said, slinging it over his shoulder. "Here, take this; you'll be needing it soon."

He held out a bulging faska: the very last of his water.

"No way in hell," said Kandri.

Chindilan shrugged. "Be a fool, then. Not much left anyway. Right, I'll be as quick as—"

"If you get down from your camel," said Kandri, "I'm getting down from mine."

"You little bastard," said the smith. "Is it blackmail, now? Think again, because I'll shame you. I'll kick you in circles around this Wall."

"Eight," said Mektu, his eyes lit by fire.

"I'm going to win this argument, Uncle," said Kandri.

"What you're going to do," said Chindilan, "is ride down Woeden Surk and take the Letter of Cure back from him and deliver it, like Garatajik wanted."

"Yes," said Kandri, "with your help."

"You're going to reach Kasralys City. You're going to find Ariqina in some ward or laboratory and get down on both knees and ask for her hand, *that's* what you're going to do—"

"Why are you stopping your camel, Uncle? Don't stop her. Don't fucking get down."

"Nine," said Mektu. "Gods. They're huge."

The flash was bright. His uncle's face glowed for an instant, a match in the dark. Rage-twisted, soaked with tears. And tired, so unspeakably tired. The smith turned in the saddle, raised a leg to dismount.

Kandri lunged for his arm.

"Let go, damn you!"

"Wait, wait, talk to me—"

"Number ten is coming," said Mektu. "Oh shit, any second—"

"Don't make me cut you, Kandri!"

"Cut me, you old hog! You're *not* killing yourself—"

"You owe me obedience, boy, you owe me, I'm your Gods-damned—"

"DEVIL'S PRICK!" screamed Mektu, and the world went mad.

ભ

A searing redness, a demonic wail. A detonation so close and enormous that the stones of the Wall groaned and shuddered. Alahari whirled and bucked and screamed from her chest; Fish bolted; Chindilan's animal collapsed onto her knees, flinging the smith upon the stone.

Mektu was shouting: "Uncle! Uncle!"

From above, a growing scream.

Another!

Roar of wind, blast of heat as an eleventh fireball shrieked low over their heads.

Somehow in that bedlam Kandri thought to look back. There they were, lit by the plume of fire: all twelve Rasanga, terribly close and riding like furies. Two of the twelve were out ahead, and nearest of all was the one who must have been their leader. The one Ulren had recalled with such fear. A huge woman, war-axe in hand, hair streaming behind her in ragged, rust-colored braids. Crouched low atop the sandcat, aware that her moment had come.

Alahari bucked Kandri from the saddle.

He landed on his back under a rain of cinders. He could not draw breath. He rolled over into blood, his own blood, some gash near his shoulder. He raised his head.

The Rasanga leader was within two hundred yards. *A woman who eats scorpions for breakfast.* She raised a black gauntlet as if in greeting, but even as she did so it burst into flames.

Get up, Kandri.

Who was speaking? No one was speaking. He could not get up.

She is going to use that gauntlet to rip out your heart. Get up. Get up now.

He fought to his knees. Blood pumping like a spigot from his arm. She was closing. He raised an unsteady hand.

"Stop."

Not enough. Get to your feet! I will try to help, but you must do your part—

By the Wall's edge, his uncle lay motionless as a corpse.

Kandri stood up. Hand still raised, fingers spread wide.

"Stop."

And the sandcat stopped.

A stricken look came over the Rasanga. She bent and whispered to her mount, the look of triumph changed to wild uncertainty. In Kandri's mind something was tearing, scraping. What did it matter? She had to stop.

Forgive me, human. I cannot do this. I tried.

His hand fell; the scraping ceased. The Rasanga's face hardened as she spurred her sandcat on. For some reason the night sky began to brighten in the south.

All for naught. You must go to the Wall now, and leap.

Brighter and brighter still. His south-facing cheek began to warm.

Leap! said the voice. *Leap from the precipice! Don't let them take you. The tortures your Prophet has devised—*

"Stop."

The fireball, last and greatest of the Tears of the Gods, struck the Wall like the Hammer of Jekka in the depths of his Hell.

಑

The noise was ludicrous, beyond bearing. Then gone, utterly vanished, and Kandri understood that he was deaf. He also understood that the Wall was buckling, and that his hair was on fire. He ripped away his headscarf, rolled in a ball, enveloped his head in arms and legs. *No air.* Smoke scalding his lungs. Flame lifting in a monstrous geyser on his left. Granite bricks large as carriages striking around him, blasting him with shards and slivers. *No air. No air.* He was drowning on the driest of land.

It was the tower of flame itself that saved him, for its ravenous updraft brought a rush of cold, clean air from somewhere below the Wall, and he drank it with tears of gratitude, and rose on blistered hands to crawl away. He found he was crawling uphill: the Wall was listing toward the fire. The huge bricks had cracked and separated, making him stop, turn, double back, a mouse in a maze.

Uncle. Mektu.

He looked wildly about. The fireball's point of impact had been somewhere behind the two lead Rasanga. He could not see their leader, but her sandcat lay ten yards from him, half-buried in smoking debris. The great animal's skull had been crushed and the fur along its back scalded away. Somewhat farther, the second Rasanga lay facedown upon the Wall. Motionless save for one hand, pulsing open and shut like a jellyfish.

The flames collapsed swiftly, as with the lodestone-fireball upon the plain. Kandri stood, light-headed. His upper arm was throbbing. His shirt was soggy with blood. A wide gash below the shoulder, blood spilling like beer from a tap. He turned and looked back once more.

Ang's sweet mercy.

Ninety feet of Wall had ceased to exist. Huge stones had been flung like marbles across the plain. The destruction reached all the way to ground level, three hundred feet below. The drop to either side was nearly vertical.

And just beyond the rupture stood the Prophet's battalion. Ten Rasanga, three hundred cavalry. They clustered rank upon rank, as near as they dared to the monstrous cavity. They were watching him, shouting, cursing. Their silent mouths opened and closed, children playing a game.

Most of the Rasanga were looking down from the Wall's torn edge. *Climb down*, thought Kandri. *You can manage three hundred feet. You can do anything, you holy butchers. Climb down, please.*

The Rasanga looked across the gap at him. At the ample rocks he could throw, the larger rocks he could roll over the edge. They did not climb down. Instead, they ran back to their mounts, gesturing and shouting. In a matter of seconds all ten Rasanga and a third of the cavalry had reversed course, racing back to the southeast.

How far back had it been, that point where the dunes fell away? Seven miles, eight? Far enough to put hours between them. Two hours, maybe, or perhaps even three. But what were three hours to the Rasanga? They would never stop. They had found the Abominations at last.

cg

A flicker in the dark. Kandri spun: there was Mektu, bloody-faced but whole, dragging his uncle by the armpits. Kandri rushed to him, hopscotching through the debris.

"Oh Gods, no—"

Chindilan was ash-covered and still. Mektu was jabbering, shouting through his tears.

"I can't hear you, brother. Is he—"

Alive. He saw the words on Mektu's lips, felt his own eyes grow moist. But his brother was gesturing wildly, and shouting another word.

Arrows.

They were falling like hailstones. Of course: they were still within range, even of the short bows issued to the cavalry.

"Jackknife, Mek," shouted Kandri.

His brother nodded: the jackknife lift. They rolled the big man face-down, lifted him at the buttocks, slipped their shoulders beneath his hips.

They rose together, sharing his weight, and stagger-ran through the devastation. Weaving, pitching. An arrow passed so close to his head that he felt the tickle of its feathers above his ear. He should have been terrified, but that part of him was broken, gagged.

But those feathers, that tickle. Ah, yes. In his mind's eye Ariqina turned to him beaming; he was sixteen; she tucked a pencil behind his ear.

Don't listen to your father. You're smart and you're going to study. We're going places, you and I.

σβ

Then suddenly it was over; they were safe behind a mountain of exploded rubble that could have sheltered fifty, a wall across the Wall. They lowered Chindilan like a great sack of beans, Kandri still enjoying his moment with Ariqina, flirting with her, laughing inside. The smith's eyes fluttered open; he took in Kandri's smile with disapproval. His groggy hand rose and pointed.

Mektu's soundless mouth was screaming *Shit, shit, shit!*

Kandri's arm was sodden with blood. He had draped his uncle across his wounded shoulder and felt no pain at all. *You should have said something, Ari, you imp.*

I'm not there, fool! Snap out of it!

Kandri dropped beside his uncle, pressed his hand tight over his wound. Delirious, blood-deprived, head full of space and sky. Mektu knelt before him, desperate, mouth moving nonstop.

Chindilan pulled Mektu near and kissed his forehead, then squeezed Kandri's free hand between his own bloodied fingers. Kandri laughed with joy. His uncle lived. Their foes could not reach them. All in all it was miraculous luck.

But his laughter had another source. The arrow: he had *heard* it as it passed his head. And that faint, carping, honking, petulant, nasal sound: yes, that was Mektu's voice. He had never before realized that it was beautiful.

"I'm not deaf!" he bellowed.

But now Chindilan was struggling. What was that look on his face, that word he was too weak to shout?

"You!"

Staggering toward them out of the night was Woeden Surk.

The mercenary was gasping, ragged to the point of collapse. But he was not maimed, not dying, and in his hand was the mattoglin, its gold-filigreed blade gleaming in the moonlight.

Surk was marching as fast as his spent frame would allow, as though driven by fear. Certainly something out there had made him reverse course. But as he drew near them he saw the ruination of the Wall, the arrows heaped like straw to either side of the rubble mound. He stopped dead.

A rage flooded Kandri such as he had never known. This was the man who had plotted their ambush at the crossroads, who had watched the Akrunu murder the very people he had sworn to defend, who had tried to hurl Talupéké to her death. Kandri put a hand on his machete and struggled to rise.

His vision blurred. Mektu pressed him back down, roughly.

"Stay put. Can you fucking hear *that*?" Then Mektu rose and drew his machete and walked toward Surk.

The mercenary laughed, smacked the mattoglin against his chest. "You want it, you Chiloto corpse-worm? Here it is. Come and take it from me!"

Then his face twitched and he glanced over his shoulder. What was it he feared?

The answer, when it emerged from the darkness, gave Kandri a shock to rival any on that that endless night. Ten warriors on camels, moving abreast in a dragnet from one edge of the Wall to another. Men and women both. Not one of them from the caravan—and yet all strangely, distantly familiar. He knew them. How the hell did he—

"Oh. Blood of Ang."

It came, the slap of certainty. *Tebassa. All ten were in the caves with General Tebassa.*

Beyond all hope, it was true. A second unit of Tebassa's soldiers had found them, come to their aid. And walking before them were two men.

The first was Ifimar Jód. Lethally enraged. Black sword twirling in his hand with casual mastery, eyes locked on Woeden Surk.

The second man—

"No," said Kandri. "*Harach*, it can't—"

"Ghost," sputtered Chindilan. "That man is a *ghost*."

It was Kandri's thought as well. But this ghost wore spectacles and was smoking a cheroot. An older man, lean and hard and angular about the face. His exhaled smoke into the wind and trained his bright gray eyes on Kandri. The eyes of a traitor. Stilts.

೧

Once more Kandri tried to stand. Chindilan clung to his belt, wheezing and scolding. Mektu had turned to stone. At that moment Woeden Surk might have killed him with ease.

Stilts. Talupéké's great-uncle, Kereqa's younger brother. Stilts, the spy in General Tebassa's ranks. Stilts, the double agent who had led the Prophet's army to Tebassa's door, and Kandri's own party into the ambush on Alibat S'Ang. Stilts, who had pushed his own comrade from that very clifftop, only to fall from it himself minutes later.

You're not here. I saw you fall to your death.

But he was real. Somehow he had saved himself, and found the caravan in their absence. Now Jód, old comrade of the general himself, was being taken in by the man.

"Be still, Kandri, you great idiot!" shouted Chindilan. "Press that wound! Do you want to bleed out and die?"

The newly arrived soldiers were dismounting and drawing blades, eyes fixed on Woeden Surk. "We have to warn them about Stilts, Uncle!" said Kandri. "I should have told Jód before. But why should I have? He was dead. Why in Hell's sewers isn't he *dead*?"

"You're shouting in my ear," said Chindilan.

Others were shouting too: Mektu had come to life and was bickering with Jód. Woeden Surk turned at bay between them. From his stance—disdainful of Mektu, flinching at Jód's every movement—it was clear which opponent he would prefer.

The warriors surrounded Surk. Jód shouted at him, pointing to the stone at his feet. *Drop that blade.* Woeden Surk answered with a gesture involving his crotch.

Stilts shook his head. He walked a few paces away, deeply attentive to his smoke.

Ifimar Jód raised his hand as though to issue an order. No doubt in the world what that order would be. The only mystery, Kandri thought, was that Surk had betrayed so many—the general, the caravan, the Clowns—and survived so long.

Then again, look at Stilts.

But Jód's signal did not come. Something had caught the Master's eye, something to the left of the rubble. He was staring in disbelief.

Around the northern edge of the protective mound, the male Rasanga was dragging himself by his arms. He was blood-bathed from head to foot, and burned horribly, everywhere, as though the blood were boiled pitch. Both legs crushed, and three arrows—his fellow soldiers' arrows—protruding from his back.

He bore no weapon. His white teeth shone through ruined lips. He was sliding like some primitive lizard toward Kandri and Chindilan. Rage in his hugely muscled arms, holy purpose in his eyes. The Abominations were in reach.

A warrior took three steps and kicked the Rasanga in the gut. It was a blow that would have crippled a healthy man, but the Rasanga merely spat and kept crawling.

Then Jód approached, black sword in hand. He set his foot on a bloody shoulder and the Rasanga stopped. He pushed; the Rasanga rolled onto his back and lay blinking at him.

Jód squatted down; murmuring what might have been a prayer.

Chindilan and Kandri both sat up, screaming.

"Back off, back off!"

"It's a trick—"

"He'll have a knife, a razor—"

"*Jeshar*, they can kill with teeth alone, those bastards—"

Jód drew his sword over the Rasanga's neck in a lazy sawing motion. When he reached bone he leaned his weight up the blade.

Never mind.

Jód rose, gripping the man's head by its hair, and in a smooth whirl flung it from the Wall. The wind carried droplets of blood as far as Kandri's knees.

His brother was still jabbering; perhaps he had never stopped. Demand, complaint, plea? Kandri simply could not tell. But whatever it was had its effect on the Caravan Master. He turned away from the Wall's edge and looked at Mektu. He gave a flourish with his hand: *Be my guest*.

And Mektu advanced on Woeden Surk.

03

A look of relief came over the mercenary's face. He kept his eyes on Jód, as if Mektu were not a foe worthy of his attention. Then he sprang like a jackal.

He was about the same height as Mektu but much wider and stronger, and he had clearly used a mattoglin before. The weapon broadened along the blade, adding weight to its swing, and it flared near its tip into three cruel barbs. For all its beauty, it was a fast and hideous tool of murder.

Surk was fast as well. He lunged, and struck at Mektu's throat in a blinding arc, and the power in his arm was shocking. Kandri's whole body seized. But Mektu was gone, whirling away on the balls of his feet, circling behind the mercenary. His face relaxed, his gaze clean and focused.

Battle dance. The old Chiloto art, rescued from oblivion by the Prophet, drilled into every recruit. The discipline was almost useless in the mass butchery of a war front. Not so against a single opponent, however. At Eternity Camp there had been tournaments and prizes. Kandri had once earned a roast chicken. Mektu had been eliminated in an earlier round.

Surk lunged again. This time Mektu climbed onto a stone. As Surk chopped at his legs Mektu retreated, making the man reach farther with each swing.

A technicality, Kandri recalled. *A rules violation. He never actually lost.*

At Surk's fourth stroke Mektu leaped over his head, turning as he did so, and landed facing his opponent, whom he still had not tried to attack.

Gods, he was angry. He wanted that chicken.

Surk whirled and lunged again. Mektu retreated, put a pile of rubble between them. Surk bellowed, and the word came faint to Kandri's ears.

"Coward!"

Mektu's gaze was as quiet as a painter's studying a canvas.

"Stop running, worm! Fight like a fucking man!"

Mektu leaped nimbly around the rubble, not allowing Surk to close. The mercenary paused, his great chest heaving. Mektu crouched down on his haunches, looking rather like a dark, filthy frog.

Woeden Surk's gaze swept over the onlookers with hatred. "You know," he shouted, "that I'm doing you a favor."

Jód crossed his arms. "A favor, backstabber?"

"When I kill this one, you're a third of the way to freedom. Cut down his brother and their uncle, and the world might let you live."

Jód turned his back on the mercenary.

"Cut them down!" bellowed Surk. "Cut them down or be cut down with them—if not by the bitch's army then by Clowns, if not Clowns then bounty men, flesh traders, some other thieving mob. The word is out. The bitch will pay their weight in *diamonds*. You'll never be safe until they're dead."

"We are out of time," said Jód. "Finish this, Mektu Hinjuman."

Mektu was still in his frog-squat. His face calm as ever, he locked eyes with the mercenary.

"Coward," sneered Surk again.

Mektu tossed his machete aside.

"No! Mek! No!" screamed Kandri and Chindilan. The watching soldiers shook their heads; even Stilts looked thunderstruck. And Woeden Surk charged with a roar.

Mektu rose to face him with a stone in each fist. He feinted left, sprang right. Surk mirrored him clumsily and ended up with legs spread wide.

Mektu let fly a stone. It struck its target, Surk's kneecap, with devastating force. The mercenary threw his head back and howled.

The second stone caught him in the temple. Surk fell; his injured knee would not support him. Mad with pain, he rose on his good leg, drew his arm back to swing.

Mektu leaped, drawing in his limbs as he rose. As he descended he lashed out with a blinding kick that caught Surk's fighting arm at the elbow. The arm jerked horribly. The mattoglin sprang from his grip and Mektu plucked it from the air and brought it down as he landed through the base of Surk's neck. The blow sank deep. Blood gushed like a bucket overturned.

Mektu snatched at something as the man fell back. He jerked it away from the body, its leather strap cut by the same killing blow. He cleaned the mattoglin on Surk's trousers even as the mercenary twitched his last. He crossed the stones to Kandri, dropped the calfskin pouch at his feet.

"You owe me," he said.

Kandri pulled the pouch near. The Letter of Cure was safe, its seal unbroken. There was hope yet for the world, and for himself.

And yet even in that moment a new fear was being born. Mektu was gazing enraptured at the mattoglin, stroking the fat blue jewel on its handle, turning its blade to catch the light of the moon. His face shone like that of a child handed a marvelous plaything.

And all at once Kandri knew that Mektu's joy was unnatural. And he cursed himself for not having seen it before.

The mattoglin. Its menace had been there from the start. On that evening Kandri first glimpsed the priceless weapon in his uncle's workshop—and wrestled with the urge to touch it himself. On the night the Prophet's son attacked him with it in the dark. Each time Mektu had stolen it from Eshett.

It had overpowered the Nachasps, the mercenaries, the Slaughterhouse Clowns. And what had spurred them to this ride of madness and death? What but lust for the mattoglin?

Day by day, mile after mile it had goaded them, fooled them, brought them ruin. Until here at last Mektu had claimed it, killed for it, and the mattoglin had leaped from Surk's hand to his own like a living thing choosing sides.

The yatra. It's not in any of us. It's in that blade.

Fourth Interlude

You see it now, Kandri. And thanks to you, so do I.

Of course you are only half right, for nowhere in your wildest dreams have you considered that there might be *two of us* in your unfortunate company. It took you long enough, my dear host, to accept that there might be one.

But the second of us—the criminal yatra, the monster—dwells there in the blade. More specifically, in that luscious blue ormalid at the hilt. A changeless jewel, harder than diamond. Nothing softer would have served the purpose.

And what a purpose. For the ormalid is a prison, a cage for the monster. Some human—praise the long-dead soul!—had the skill and wisdom to trap the beast within the jewel. Wiser still would have been to encase the jewel in lead and drop it in the sea. But we must not ask for everything. The beast was trapped—and oh, the centuries of pain prevented by that deed! Within the jewel-cage the beast's powers are greatly muted, though not altogether erased. It can still whisper. It can lure and fascinate. And it can peer out and identify a weakness.

For a while you imagined that it had crawled into your brother's mind. Reasonable enough: just look at his antics. Look at his past, and the tale his mother whispered, that his near-death in the smokehouse might have driven it deeper within. She was wrong, of course. Mektu triumphed in the smoke-house. Whatever being invaded his six-year-old mind fled that day, never to return, leaving gifts of fear and scars.

But today's Mektu has been used all the same—by the yatra that dwells in the mattoglin. And that yatra is a beast, I tell you. A beast that has found something useful in Mektu's scars, one jackal sniffing at the mouth of a bur-row abandoned by another.

A beast that sings to him, croons his name.

A beast that lent him power once, for purposes of its own. A beast that concluded it was better to risk killing him, leaving him mutilated within, than to fall back into the Prophet's hands. A beast who broke our sacred law, made tools of human bodies, human minds.

And my existence? No, you did not suspect a thing. Why should you, when I was hiding from that monster myself, scarcely breathing, hoping it would not catch my scent? Why should you, when I have kept the yatra law?

But you haven't kept it!

. . . ?

And you're not hidden anymore. I hear you.

You . . . cannot.

I hear you, I hear you! I, Kandri Hinjuman, have a yatra in my soul!

ॐ

Boy. You must be silent.

Don't you give me orders!

Boy. Kandri. Do not address me. The beast will hear you and come for me, come and dig me with its red claws from my cave.

MY CAVE. MY SOUL. MINE.

Yes, yours—always, forever yours. I am no thief.

You spoke when I faced the Rasanga. Get up, you said. Leap from the Wall, you said. You wanted me to hear you!

Kandri, Kandri, I was talking to myself. From you I wanted only obedience—and that only to save you, as a last resort. And I failed. I would not risk destroying you to make you obey. I am not like that beast.

Who else were you talking to but me? When I faced the Rasanga, when I held out my hand?

Hush, boy. Do not address me. For my sake and your own.

Why are you inside me? What do you want?

I could make you forget, you know. I could simply—

I'll shout, I'll tell everyone! They'll kill me, Jód will cut off my head like he did the Rasanga, but I'll beat you. Yatra. Yatra! YATRA!

Silence! I surrender! Yes, I have whispered in your ear, now and then, when death was ready to pounce. I've tried to help. I know it harms you, shakes your sense of the order of things, pricks a hole where the germ of madness might slip in. Yes, I tried to stop the Rasanga tonight, when all seemed lost. I did that. I was desperate. You were so close to recovering the Letter of Cure.

But I am not like that beast in the mattoglin. What I do, I do out of compassion, not avarice or hate. My sin is to have cared for the plight of your species—yes, even to the point of breaking our supreme law, to tamper with human minds.

With my mind!

It was only the least touch, the least whisper.

You're a monster, a criminal—

I am a criminal. My restraint will count for nothing when my people learn of my deeds, as they learn of all transgressions in time. But the law! I revere it. My cause for breaking it is sound, reasonable. I may have damaged you, Kandri, but we are allies all the same. I am a good yatra, a considerate guest.

Now for the love of all that lives, will you calm down?

Calm down it says!

Please.

Calm down? I'm possessed. It was never Mektu, never Eshett. It was me!

You're not possessed, Kandri. Merely visited.

All along it was me!

I will rest here in silence. You'll learn that there's nothing to fear. Listen, Kandri, listen to the silence. That's better. Your mind's your own and always will be.

I thought—

Yes you did, but it's just your own thoughts in your head, no one else's, fear itself was the enemy, you can see that for yourself. Good, very good. Breathe in and know you're safe. Breathe out—

And FORGET.

ↂ

"Kandri, wake up!"

Chindilan slapped his face. Everyone was watching him. Mektu's hand still gripped the golden knife. The wind had once more begun to blow.

"What's wrong?" said Kandri.

"What's wrong?" said Chindilan. "You were delirious, that's what wrong. Talking a mile a minute. 'It was me, it was me!' We couldn't shut you up."

Mektu approached him, cautious as a hunter stalking game. "Who the hell," he said, "were you talking to?"

Kandri blinked. He had no answer. There was a void in his mind where the answer should have been. "Myself?" he said at last.

His hand was still pressed to the wound on his shoulder. "We need to see to that," said Chindilan. "Ang's mercy, but you've lost some blood."

"Too much to know what he's saying," said Stilts.

Kandri whirled on him. Or tried to: his body answered only slowly to the commands of his mind.

"Don't talk about blood," he said. "You're soaked in it. Soaked in all our blood."

"Sounds to me like my nephew knows exactly what he's saying," said Chindilan.

Stilts shook his head. "I'm no traitor. I'm your friend and always have been. We had nets strung to catch you, below the cliff at Alibat S'Ang. General's orders, and the general's plan."

"Hogwash," said Chindilan. "Nets under a cliff."

"My family ran a circus, you old fool," said Stilts. "We knew exactly what we were doing."

"But why do it? Of all senseless ideas!"

"Not senseless," said Stilts. "Desperate. You said it yourselves: the Prophet would chase you to the ends of the earth. You'd never be safe, nor anyone who helped you. Only if you were dead, only if the Prophet's own commandos *saw* you die, would they call off the hunt."

Jód pointed at Stilts. "Twenty-seven years have I known this man," he said. "Like his general, he lives by his word."

Kandri's head felt hollow; it took an immense effort just to speak. "Master Ifimar," he said, "the Prophet's commandos *knew* him. They spoke to him like a comrade."

"Of course they did," said Stilts. "They'd paid me a small fortune to be their traitor. My general was amused to be receiving so much gold from one of his fiercest enemies. And even more amused by the lies I was feeding the Prophet."

Kandri froze.

"The Naduman was a double agent, boy," said Jód.

"Triple agent," said Stilts. "Your Prophet tried to turn me against my one true master, General Tebassa. I let her think she succeeded, but the only one I betrayed was that monster herself."

"Then why lie to *us* about it?" demanded Mektu.

Stilts' eyes flashed with sudden anger. "Because," he said, "there was a *real* traitor in the general's ranks. Someone tipping off the Prophet about our movements, about our bunker in the Cavern of the Owls. About the general's decision to help the two of you escape.

"That fall from the cliff would have been your liberation, boys. Her own servants would have reported your deaths. But again—the spy. Whoever it was also had to be convinced—which mean that *everyone* had to be. Don't you understand? If the least whisper of doubt about your deaths reached the Prophet, her hunt for you would go on."

"As it does now," said Ifimar Jód. "While we talk, the enemy is riding. And a storm comes too, a great beast out of the Heart Basin—the worst in years, perhaps. Is the boy too weak to travel?"

"I'm not," said Kandri. "I can ride. I just need—"

"Blood," said Stilts, "about two faskas' worth. No, Master Jód, he can't walk a tenth of the distance. Or even keep himself upright in a saddle."

"Yes I can. You don't know."

"You're swaying as you stand there," said Mektu. "As a matter of fact— catch him, catch him!"

They pounced. Their voices clashed in Kandri's ears.

"Damnation, worse than he looked—"

"Cut his shirt away—"

"Get a bandage, a proper bandage—"

"*Jeshar*, he's out. Ease him down."

Fifth Interlude

That, dear host of mine, was far too close.

I have done what I can. I have patched you up, erased your knowledge of me. I can only pray the patch holds—and that you never again need my aid. I do not think you would survive that aid. Yatra-terror in humans is like certain allergic reactions: worse with each incident. If you were to detect me again, the fear might send you raving, running like your brother, to whatever stand-in for a smokehouse you can find.

Now all my sins are doubled. I have brushed away a piece of your memory, that sacred core of human existence, stone and mortar of your soul. I killed it. Yes, I *killed a small part of my host.*

No more than what perishes on a hard night's drinking, I console myself. But is that the truth? I plied my brush in a panic. What if I damaged other memories? How can I know?

You've been reckless with memory yourself, of course. You suffered a cracked skull that almost killed you in the army. You've been spectacularly drunk. But again, I grope for justification. You did not drink *me.* I never asked your permission. I broke into your house, and now I have done the unforgiveable: stolen that which I can never return.

I have watched the moon pass from full to bitten crust and back again thirty-two thousand four hundred sixteen times. Reveled in three thousand summers. Watched seeds burst open and grow into titan oaks and drop their limbs and perish, returning peacefully to earth. Never, never have I sunk so low.

The Eye of Creation knows my deeds. Why lie to myself, then? I dwelt in Garatajik when he sought the Cure. I whispered, goading him: *Don't stop, don't rest, you will redeem this world!* You could say that I inspired him. Or you could say that I abused him, drove him to work until his mind screamed for rest and his eyes no longer focused, blind to the perils that gathered around him, the shadow-presence of Eyelash Thruko, the closing net of his mother's spies.

Vanity on my part? A desire to push you ephemeral beings out of the way of the careening boulder of your fate? To give you fighting odds of building something enduring—truly enduring, on the scale we yatras know?

And you, Kandri. What if I had killed you tonight? What if my brush-work had failed, and you remained aware of me, a worm between your temples, and that awareness proved so ghastly that you jumped?

It's worse yet. Look at yourself—gulping air, sweating ice, heart pounding like a regimental drum. As I distracted Garatajik from his danger, I distracted you from your wound—from the fact that your life-blood was gushing from your shoulder. What if I *have* killed you? Whom do I fly to next?

I differ in degree, not in kind, from that beast in the mattoglin. I am a parasite. I gaze into the mirror and loathe what I see.

19. A PAIR OF DRUNKS

A knife, slashing what remained of his shirt. Worried hands stripping him to the waist. The burn of wound spirits. A bandage passed over his shoulder and around his chest. His own hands weak and cold but locked on the calfskin pouch. He would not part with it again.

Frightened voices, faces crowding out the stars. *Are you mad? Sling him over a camel? Did you see that gash?*

Shouts and insults: his uncle and Mektu confronting Stilts, and the Naduman's look of sorrow. Behind him, also sorrowful, the ghost of the maniac from the pit, still cradling his thumb, his regret clear enough but ambiguous in origin.

He's a wounded man, not a saddlebag! That was Chindilan. *He'll be shaken apart on the trail. He needs rest and stillness.*

Neither is possible here. Ifimar Jód. *Not for any of us. We must make haste.*

And then Stilts: *There is another way.*

The Naduman continues in a low voice, but is abruptly drowned out by cries of disbelief, and from Mektu, expletives.

I understand your fear, says Stilts, *but can you not grasp their own? Beings like us slaughtered scores of them in that tower. Listen: none of us can stay here a moment longer. What I propose—*

I saw Captain Utarif! Mektu's voice rises to a howl. *Dead before his knees could buckle. And now you want—*

What I propose is his best chance, Mektu Hinjuman.

As if—Uncle Chindilan, seething—*we'd be foolish enough to trust anything you say.*

Stilts points a finger at the dark lands to the south.

Say yes to something, or stand here bickering and watch him die. She is out there, good as her word, and my man is with her and her people. Even now they are working to reunite us all. But they will vanish with the storm, and there will be no help from any quarter once they're gone. The decision falls to you two, as his family. Now clear your heads and make it.

∝

His eyes are full of starlight: he is face up to the void. Lashed upon a makeshift stretcher, which hangs suspended like a painter's platform against the side of a camel. Flies tickle his forehead. Dunes tower above him, a monstrous sea.

He cannot brush away the flies: his arms are lashed against his torso. The calfskin pouch is once more secured upon his chest. His wounded shoulder burns.

Where are the others? What has become of the Wall?

A figure rides hunched on the camel above him. Kandri cannot see a face. But every two or three minutes, a red firefly blooms in the darkness, chased by a faint, wind-swallowed whiff of smoke.

∝

Time passes; the stars disappear. Chips of dawn light blaze on the summits of the dunes. The camel has stopped; he is being lowered to the ground. In the still-black shadows crouch a dozen figures, watching him with eyes of silver. Behind them, two shapes like great round tents, surrounded by curious struts or beams.

Then one of the tents moves, or rather sidles. Kandri gasps, struggles to sit up. A hand presses down on his forehead.

Stop thrashing, says Stilts. *You'll tear open that wound.*

Get me away from them!

He is shouting—but no, he isn't; the cry is only in his mind. Then a new voice reaches his ears.

Song of Imlu! Is that who I think it is?

Yes, says Stilts, *that's Kandri Hinjuman.*

I thought I'd seen the last of this Chiloto hmm, *specimen.*

That purr, thinks Kandri. Ang's love, I know that voice.

His brother and uncle are back there with Jód, says Stilts. *It's a miracle they've come this far.*

Your word, not mine, says the new voice. *That sniveler Ulren called them sidewinders, after the rattlesnakes. I do not think it was a term of* hmm, *endearment.*

I like that, says Stilts. *Fast, slippery, impossible to catch.*

Flat heads. Forked tongues.

Stilts chuckles. *You admire them, Mansari. Admit it.*

Cʘ

Bright sun, parched lips. He is floating above the sand. No longer on the stretcher but a woolly hide, a sheep's hide, through which a great many knobs or stones jab his body. *What prick*, he thinks, *decided to lash me over stones?*

Oddly enough they are not painful. Nothing jolts or bruises; his glide is as smooth as a boat downstream, an insect on the surface of a lake.

Memory returns. And the urge to scream.

I am on the back of a spider.

Even worse, he is pinned. Cords wind about his arms, legs, torso. Only his wounded shoulder and his neck are spared.

He lifts his head. A black porthole swivels to face him, dilates. A clammy horror envelopes his skin. The porthole is one in a cluster of eyes, each large as a dinner plate, in a globular haystack of a head. The same eyes that fixed on Utarif. The same mouth, the same mandibles, drawn back like crossbows ready to fire.

Ang All-Merciful, help your son.

⅋

The eye released him at last. Kandri turned his head and saw Fiasul kneeling at his side, her white cloak snapping in the wind: the spider ran with astonishing speed. Fiasul gripped the thorny knobs on its back, leaning with its movements. She did not seem to be directing its course.

She touched his shoulder. No smile, no spark of laughter. The touch was a gesture of assessment, not comfort.

"You stronger now," she said. "But move slow, Krandee, or you bleed."

She tugged at a knot on the binding cords until she worked it loose, and Kandri found his arms and torso free.

With great care he rose to a sitting position. Dunes sprawled around them, endless scallops and serpentines. Ahead in the distance rose a line of brown hills: very tall, but hazy and indistinct.

Another spider was running beside them with two figures crouched on its back. One was a Nachasp man. The other, to Kandri's amazement, was Mansari. Like Stilts, he was an officer in General Tebassa's private army. His body and bearing had confused Kandri from the start. He seemed curvaceous, like a woman, and his movements recalled the sly gray tom that hunted rodents in the courtyard back home. Kandri saw that he rode the spider with the same ease as the Nachasps, fearless and effortlessly balanced. Then he remembered. *Kereqa's circus. Of course.* Mansari had been the tightrope walker.

The spiders ran with bodies held high, like bundles of cargo suspended from the cranes of their legs. But it was their feet that astonished him. Everywhere else the spiders were encased in that crab-shell armor, but the feet were broad, dense masses of hair and claws. A froth of spittle or webbing formed a spongy pad beneath each foot. The sand did not stick to this froth but stiffened on contact, like water frozen suddenly to ice.

378

The stiff sand gave them purchase. The spiders were not running across the dunes. They were skating.

He twisted about. Many miles behind them, a thread of smoke curled away into the wind.

"That is Wall," said Fiasul. "Still burning. Long time burning."

"Where are we?"

"Close to city. Your friends follow with camels. They take care like us, stay low on dunes, out of sight from Wall. But camels are slower, reaching city in dark."

"A city? Out here?"

"Human city. Very beautiful and dead."

Ruins, then: perhaps the ruins of Sanulsreya that both Fiasul and Eshett had spoken of. Kandri squinted: he could see nothing ahead but the strange billowing hills. He turned and gave her a long look.

"Your people, Fiasul," he said.

"Many die. The mask men."

"I know. I'm sorry."

"They kill us like animals. No reason. We don't understand."

"I don't either," he said.

"We give them all to the spiders, ugly mask men of shit. But it is too late for my family. Why do they kill, Krandee? They want brother's golden knife?"

"It's *not* my brother's!"

His ferocity startled her; in fact he had startled himself. *The yatra in that blade! It's why her people died. Why Surk wouldn't surrender, why the Clowns chased him to their own deaths. It's why Mektu kept stealing the mattoglin.*

And now the knife was back in his brother's hands, and Eshett, who alone might have talked sense into Mektu, was gone.

Fiasul was still watching him, a new thought troubling her silver eyes. *You sense it, don't you?* Kandri thought. *The damned knife is working on me too.*

"Did you give Utarif to the spiders?"

The edge in his voice was not lost on her. "No," she said. "Spiders love Nachasps, but humans they will never love. If Nachasp is not there, they make food from humans."

"Why didn't they *make food* out of Talupéké?"

"She is wearing scarf. Spider learns language, like human dog. Scarf is Nachasp word for *friend, good thing.* You understand?"

"More or less."

"I am sorry for the captain."

"*About* the captain," said Kandri. "Me too."

"Very good man. Loving much the other humans."

Kandri nodded. In his mind he saw a network of forking paths: all the other ways things might have gone, might have ended, since they parted ways with the caravan. His party dead of thirst within a mile of Weeping Rock. A poisoned arrow missing its target, and his brother cut to ribbons by the Clowns. The Gods' fiery tears incinerating Mektu or Uncle or Kandri himself. The Prophet's forces just a little closer, a little faster, and so taking them all, leading them back to Eternity Camp, to the blackworm pits, to unendurable pain.

And you. He kept his eyes on Fiasul's hands, those hands that had caressed him in the dark. *If you hadn't robbed us like a posse of second-rate bandits, none of this—*

"Nachasp is thief," said Fiasul, as though reading his mind. "Yes, true, we are always thiefing. But we pay for what we take. Always, every time."

"This time?"

"Yes," she said. "One kind of payment is this: we take troubles away. When your people come to Weeping Rock, we know there is worst kind of trouble. There is curse. We talk together, decide you are good people with love inside. We decide to free you of this curse-thing you carry. What is it? We talk long in the night. Something treasured but bad, wicked. We try to learn what is it."

"It was the knife, Fiasul."

"I know now. But then we do not know. The curse hides its face from us, hides from our touch. And we cannot leave you cursed."

"So you took many things."

"And the knife—" She was weeping, silver tears from silver eyes. "—calls to mask-men, and they kill so many Nachasps. We are strong, Krandee, strong and wise. But curse is stronger. We take it. We pay."

ભ

It was not a line of hills; it was the storm, the "great beast" Jód had spoken of. Now that his mind grasped what he was seeing, the enormity of the phenomenon was overpowering. The storm was farther away than he had imagined but six or eight times as tall, churning dust and sand a mile or more into the sky. In the time since his waking it had visibly grown.

Atop the other spider, the Nachasp man signaled to Fiasul: a raised finger, a shake of the head.

"He saying storm is near," said Fiasul. "We will not rest today. We run on, since you do not die." Her look was gentler now. "I am glad you do not die."

She gripped his hand, and Kandri's anger and suspicion vanished. Shame and gratitude flooded him, clashing energies, and behind them both was sheer wonder at her presence, her existence.

"You're not . . . entirely of this world," he said, feeling entirely an idiot. "Part of you is in another place."

"You and I go to that place together," she said, "at Weeping Rock." She blinked at him, as though trying to recall a dream. "Say her name again. One time. Your lover's name."

"Eshett."

Fiasul frowned and shook her head. Kandri shuddered. There was no hiding from her.

"Ariqina," he said.

"Ah—!" She flinched as though he'd jabbed her with a needle. "That is it, the one who shaped you, wounded you, *that* is where you still bleed. Krandee, is that human love?"

"Yes."

"Horrible thing!"

"Let's stop talking, all right?" *What if Ari is nowhere. What if she died years ago.*

"Like bad food, sweet and rotten, hurt you, make you die."

"Sometimes."

"The love thing! I don't want it, Krandee! I don't know what it is!"

381

"Love is a crazy fucking monkey chewing the back of your head."

"No one said it before," said Fiasul, dropping wretchedly beside him. They swayed another half-mile in silence. Leaning together like a pair of drunks.

"Will you tell me something, Fiasul?" he said.

"What something?"

"Can you change into cats?"

"*Tss*, stupid question. If I am cat, I am cat. Otherwise I am Nachasp."

"But that doesn't explain *anything*."

"First you want something. Now you want anything. You rest, or else bleeding again. No more crazy talk."

ଔ

The dunes grew smaller. They raced on toward the boiling storm front, but to what shelter, he wondered? Could any ruin break the force of *that*?

He had no say in the matter, of course. He could not fight this mistress of spiders. But what of the rest of their party? What of Talupéké and Kereqa and the others, left so far behind? If they carried on along the Wall, they could shelter in one of the ruined towers. But the Rasanga and the Prophet's cavalry were also riding that stone highway, and their paths were bound to cross.

And his brother and Chindilan, Stilts, and Ifimar Jód? "They won't make it, will they?" he asked. "On foot, on camels? How could they?"

"Rasanga never find them," she said. "Staying low like us. Wind hiding tracks."

"It will hide a lot more than their tracks, Fiasul. It will bury them alive."

"You are fearing *storm*?" Fiasul shook her head. "Storm kills foolish, Krandee, not wise. They have Caravan Master. And we have spiders. If storm comes we sleep in spit."

"I beg your—*what*?"

"Spiders dig into ground, make bed of spit, and we sleep there, under their bodies."

"Devil's red ass I will!"

"Foolish," she chided. "Is safe and comfortable, whole storm sleep like baby. Like baby in stomach of the mother."

"Please stop."

Fiasul looked at him with pity. "I could never stand to be human people. You miss the best parts of life."

ଔ

He felt like laughing, or screaming. The storm had grown unthinkably huge, an oncoming wave high as heaven. The light was all wrong, as though he were seeing the world from the bottom of a glass of tea. Every instinct told Kandri he would be obliterated, scrubbed away like a stain. On they flew toward the beast.

Strangely, the wind in their faces had weakened. It was as if all the violence in nature were being sucked into that colossus before them.

The dunes became broader and lower. Knuckles of granite broke through them like the peaks of buried mountains. Then all at once they were among ruins again: shards of old walls, towers, paving stones strewn like discarded toys.

They rounded a great ocean-swell of dune—and Kandri's eyes went wide. Before them, a staircase rose out of the sand. It was enormous, sweeping away from them to left and right in great serpentines until it vanished among the dunes. To Kandri it seemed as though the earth itself had welled up here in solid stone, and some clan of astonishing industry had simply carved it into stairs.

At the summit, hundreds of steps above them, ran a wall. It hardly compared to Ravashandul's Wall, but it curved away among the stones like the staircase until it was likewise lost to sight. And where another wall might have had turrets, this one had statues—the remains of statues—facing outward in postures of defiance. They were utter ruins, features melted by centuries of wind until they resembled soap carvings left out in the rain. But Kandri could see that they had never depicted humans. One had a woman's body with the head of a lion, or perhaps a bull. Another was like a rearing horse with a lizard's tail, its outstretched wings whittled to stubs. And a dog-tiger.

A stork-boy. A goatish man brandishing a spear and an enormous eroded cock. A fish-headed woman with gigantic, broken breasts.

"Sanulsreya," said Kandri.

"Yes," said Fiasul, "but Nachasps call city *Kusmirenon*, Gift of the Moon."

"That's beautiful."

The spiders turned and glided swiftly along the foot of the half-buried stair. In her broken Common Fiasul told him that the statues were little Gods, befriended by the Night Queen and persuaded to stand guard over her city. Kandri found it hard to focus on her words. He watched the sky and thought it ready to crush them, grind them invisibly, a boot of glass. *What's happening?* he thought. *Why can't I hear the storm?*

Fiasul ceased her tale and gave a sudden whistle. She pointed: above them, the wall was breached. Mansari whistled in response, and with a disconcerting weightlessness the two spiders began to spring up the stairs.

"We are late," said Fiasul. "Storm very close."

"Hadn't noticed," said Kandri.

When they reached the top, the spiders slid through the breach without slowing. Beyond the wall stretched a level expanse of stone, three hundred feet wide or more, empty save for drifting sand. They crossed at a run. Kandri saw that the far edge of this level area dropped away, sheer as a cliff.

And at the bottom of that cliff lay Sanulsreya, still and eerie and submarine. The city lay in a great sunken circle, lower than the lowest saddles in the dunes outside. If Ravashandul had resisted the desert with brute strength, Sanulsreya had burrowed beneath it, sealing herself within a dike.

The cliff receded cone-like as it descended, making the floor of Sanulsreya wider than the aperture above. Darker, too, especially in the failing light. As they skirted the cliff, Kandri saw structures of great size and weird, geometric shape. They were less ruined than the guardian statues but no less strange.

They came to an inner staircase and descended—carefully, for the stair was almost too narrow for the spiders. Down at street level there were sanddrifts high as houses, and other areas with almost no sand at all. They passed among gaunt shapes that might have once been mansions, temples, schools.

Glimpses of long, straight boulevards, dust devils racing here and there like fairy messengers, building to building, door to time-stolen door.

"Nachasps living here before human people," said Fiasul, "with wind cousins, lovers from stars. All gone now. You take moon's gift, long ago. Humans are thiefing much more than Nachasps. We only take small things from pouches, pockets, belts. You take world, and keep it, and never pay."

She watched him, as if for sign of an argument. Kandri was thinking of his own Sataapre Valley, green and bountiful and ignorant of Urrath. Simpleminded, blessed.

And as if his thought of home had summoned them, Sanulsreya was suddenly peopled with ghosts.

He cried an obscenity, startling Fiasul. *So many of them!* And yet so dim—ever so much fainter than the dead that trailed behind the caravan. Like schools of fish, they glided along the lifeless streets, waving to one another, pushing handcarts, pausing to gossip without a sound. A man led a donkey to a sand-filled basin and the animal began to drink. A woman polished empty air until Kandri saw her reflection in the ghost-glass. Three children flew from a doorway, mute mouths open in laughter, vanishing as they neared the spiders and reappearing beyond.

"Gods save me," said Kandri, "they're all still here."

"Who?" said Fiasul.

He turned to answer—and like an image that vanishes when one bumps the mirror, the ghosts were gone. "The people," he said. And then, before she could correct him: "The . . . human people. They're everywhere."

She met his eye. "You see them?"

"I did see them."

"Maybe you are favorite of the Night Queen, Lady of True Sight. Mine at least."

"Your what?"

"Favorite."

The spiders stopped. Their saucer-eyes swiveled back to face the riders. Their bodies settled to the ground.

Before them loomed a great hulk of a building, larger than any they had passed. It too was conical in shape, rising like a geometrically perfect stone hill to a wide, flat roof like a dais. Kandri saw no doors or windows. But a few yards from where they stood, a wide gap opened in the side of the building. In the darkness of that opening he saw a staircase descending, half swamped with sand.

"Human temple," said Fiasul, "making around the well. There is sweet water like Weeping Rock. Enough for caravan. Not enough to swim."

The other riders had already dismounted. A deep quiet had settled over them; the air felt unnaturally still. The Nachasp man vanished around the curve of the building. Mansari ran to Fiasul's spider, and she leaped down to embrace him.

"Stolen child," she said, and Mansari smiled as though it were his name.

"The storm comes from there," he said, gesturing beyond the temple. "In minutes it will strike like the very fist of death. We must secure the precious *hmm*, cargo, sister. Untie him. Let us see if his legs are any use."

"I can walk," said Kandri, tugging at the cords.

Between Fiasul and Mansari (who was gentle, despite his mocking tone), Kandri was eased to the ground. He staggered, light-headed. "The doctor will do what he can for you," said Mansari.

"Doctor?"

"Your stout little surgeon. The caravan is here already, Hinjuman. Camels, drivers, dogs. They were halfway here already before your *hmm*, adventures on Ravashandul's Wall."

"But we left so many back there—"

"Other Nachasps have gone on spider-back for Talupéké and Kereqa's party, with Stilts along to vouch for the transport. As for Jód and the rest, they are all mounted on camels, and have been riding hard. The Master knows a place in the outer ruins where they can ride out the storm. No *hmm*, mansion such as this, but it will serve. When the storm passes all will rendezvous here. Get below, Hinjuman."

He gestured to the stair.

"What about the two of you?"

"What about us? My sister here is a Nachasp. I am a *hmm, hmm*—just get below."

"You go ahead. I'll be right behind you."

"You'll be grist and blood!" Mansari seized his arm and tugged. "Do not argue with me, buffoon! All this effort has been to keep you alive!"

Fiasul touched Mansari's shoulder. She spoke a quiet word in the Nachasp tongue. Mansari looked at her in exasperation. When Fiasul repeated the word he threw up his hands in surrender, and ran—not for the safety of the temple, but back toward his motionless spider.

"Where is he going? Isn't he staying with us?"

She touched his chin, turned him gently to face her. "Krandee," she said, "I am not seeing you again."

"You might, though," he said. "I might come looking for you."

Nonsense words, he thought as soon as he had spoken. But Fiasul was grave. "Maybe you look and not find," she said. "Or maybe you look and find Nachasps second time. Then you stay forever, like Stolen Child. Once is allowed. Twice is forever. Be careful, Krandee. Be sure."

Her eyes held a sober warning. Was this what had so terrified the faithless guides? Were those silver eyes a snare?

"Maybe tomorrow you forgetting me," she said. "Maybe soon, human people seeing Nachasps no more. Run, now, hide under temple. Also—"

"I have one more question," he interrupted.

"Always one more!"

"By the falls, when we . . ." He made a helpless gesture. "You spoke in her voice. In Ariqina's voice."

"No," said Fiasul, "I speak in my own. *She* speak in hers."

Kandri closed his eyes. Hopeless, impossible. She was right here before him, severe, breathtaking, brushing his fingers with her own. But her soul was under other stars.

"What I need to know is this," he tried one last time. "Was it real? I heard her voice, and the words she spoke through you."

"Not through me."

"All right! That's not—well, damn it, is she alive? Does all this mean she's alive?"

"How are you so *stupid*?" Fiasul shouted. "Yes, obvious! How talking if not alive?"

Kandri pressed a fist against his mouth. *Let it be true. Let it not be some Nachasp dream.*

"Where?" he croaked. "Can you tell me where?"

"Very far, stupid boy. Very extremely. That is all."

"All right," he said. "Thank you, Fiasul."

"You are *crying*?" She stamped her foot. "Why is that, and also me? Go away now! That is the monkey, fucking monkey, human love."

"I hear something," he said.

"Hide, hurry, or else you join the ghosts. Also, that night at Weeping Rock, you and she make child."

He turned to her, gaping.

The storm blasted around the temple with the force of an exploding dam.

III. THE BRIDGE

If the crack is fine enough, no one will notice,
and the boy who drops the chalice sighs with relief.
A century on it may shatter like an oath
as his granddaughter brings the wine to her lips.
FROM *IN THE KASRAJI TWILIGHT* BY EYELASH THRUKO

20. A SERVANT OF THE SEVENTH REALM

"What? What?"

"Your pardon, professor. You are summoned to court."

The professor sprang to his feet. Blinking, befuddled. Had he truly nodded off? How mortifying, on this of all possible occasions! And this young man with folded arms was waiting to escort him to the palace.

"My things—just a moment—I've been six hours on this bench."

Six hours in General Petitions! His escort, resplendent gray and purple of an Inner Palace functionary, did not acknowledge the remark. He merely watched, impassive, as the professor retied a shoelace, smoothed his thinning hair.

The great hall throbbed around them, the echo of a thousand voices dashing itself to pieces, waves among rocks. Petitioners occupied all the benches and spilled onto the floor, whole families chattering, carping, dozing, drooling, and still more queued in the anterooms. Vendors and beggars sidled up to them, hawking their charms, flowers, wounds. Yes, he'd nodded off—over a book, like a caricature of scholarship, like the old man he'd become.

"I found these at your feet, sir."

His spectacles. On the escort's spotless glove, the frames of dark, discolored antler sat like a reproach. Worn out. Nearly ready for the bin. The professor took them sheepishly.

"Very good of you, I'm blind without—"

"Of course, sir. This is yours as well?"

His valise. The professor snatched it, startling the youth. He gave an apologetic laugh.

"All nerves!" he said. "I've thought of nothing but this visit for days. When the secret comes out—Ang's grace, lad, when it comes out! All Urrath will be speaking of it. That may sound grandiose, but I assure you it is an understatement."

"How splendid, sir." His escort had the eyes of a mule.

"In point of fact," the professor continued, "it will leap *beyond* Urrath. It will compel a change in all the world. Yes, the entire world. But I dare say that change will be difficult. It must be managed, prepared for. And that is why I have come here first. Before daybreak, you know."

"I take it you're alone, professor?"

The boy had not listened to a word. Never mind, others would.

"Quite alone, lad. I am a private citizen."

"Have you suffered a rash, cough, hives, chills, fever, or flux of the bowels in the previous fortnight?"

In other words, are you a danger to the royals? "None of the above," he said. "I'm the picture of health."

"And for the record, is this your written hand?"

The young man held up a sheet of linen paper. The professor frowned: it was the very petition he had submitted that morning. Or rather, the top half of the petition. The bottom half, with a full statement of his *extraordinary* discovery, had been torn away.

"That is mine," he said, "but why is it mangled? I addressed the envelope to Mathir Calaribas, Minister for Peace and Security. I was promised—"

"Your petition arrived intact, sir, have no fear. Our superiors tear these sheets deliberately, so that the two halves may be compared before the appointment, ensuring we've brought the right person to court. It's a common practice."

My petition, however (the professor was rigid with indignation) *is as far from common as could ever be imagined.* But it was not his fault, this errand boy. The professor took a breath and smiled again.

"We're old schoolmates, you know, the minister and I. We roomed together in our final year. Granted, we've not met since his appointment to the Rigat. But we are close all the same. When his son was born—"

"If you're ready, sir. Long walk to Blackwood Hall. And mind the flag-stones; they're a bit rough by winter's end."

"Lead on."

The garden-style door by which they left Petitions gave an unhappy groan, startled to be in service. The path beyond, sandwiched between buildings, was edged by rubbish bins, garden tools, sweepings from the grounds. A shortcut: the professor felt a certain glee. How many visitors were plucked from the mob in General Petitions and escorted to Blackwood Hall, at the heart of the Inner Palace, where for sixteen centuries the deepest matters of Kasraji security had been decided?

From the alley they stepped out into the faded splendor of the Northwest Gardens, a great serpentine of rose beds, perfume trees, neglected monuments, fish circling in ornate tanks like jewels pondering their sentience. Further back, gazing wistful at the path, stood the rain-softened statues of the Founders of the Realm. Eyikoru, Cymbarim, Yafnar, Eroqas. Out of those minds, an empire, most terrible and splendid of human accomplishments. One faith, one law, one language for the continent. The dream of order. Melted away like those stone faces, never to return.

"And so much better for everyone."

"Sir?"

"Nothing, I was just—" *Talking to myself, like an old buffoon.*

They passed the cypress grove with its holy tombs and reliquary, the Keldic bear at the door of the War College, the Thirivu Fountains where the sea nymphs made a ghostly keening, none knew how, for the drowned children clutched in their black marble arms. So beautiful, even in winter! He would not gawk, he was not a farmhand. But neither would he repress the joy he felt singing in his blood. Why should he? Thirty years since he'd walked this path. And even then it was the rarest of honors, a distinction for which his colleagues had either roared approval (the loving few) or sneered (the jealous many). To offer testimony in the Imperial Rigat! To address the Chamber of Forty! To speak, on one precious occasion, to three members of the Sky Dynasties, direct lineal descendants of the Emperors.

All that really happened. It was not a dream. And didn't the women love him suddenly, forgive him his hollow chest, his inkstained fingers? Hadn't the girl he married flashed her first smile at him after just such a visit? *It's you they're all talking about, isn't it? The clever one called up to the palace.*

Yes, he'd rated once. There was a portrait somewhere in this sprawling complex—one of thousands, of course—of the Young Lions of Kasraji Letters, Imperial Year 3613. He'd been just nineteen when he posed with that group of gangly, eager scholars. Nineteen, and basking in the city's embrace of his first book. *Liberated By Defeat: The Moral Rebirth of Kasralys in the Twilight of Empire.* Radical, many had called it. A torch to the cobwebbed notions of agonizing decline. Today, half a century later, its ideas were so broadly accepted that no one bothered to cite—let us be honest, to remember—from whose pen they had sprung.

Obliterated by Success. That could have been the title of his biography, if one had ever been written.

They'd been predicted, biographies. Plural. There had been some discussion. And then none, silence, a silence of decades. His life had been the inverse of the city's own.

"Would you care to take the lift, Professor?"

"The what?"

"The lift, sir, the service lift." They were suddenly at the foot of a great granite stair, leading up to a high, huge courtyard looming over the gardens. His escort pointed to a mechanism just beyond the staircase, a stately thing of cables and counterweights, and an iron enclosure like a monkey cage. "I can shake up a pair of hands to turn the wheel. Otherwise it's sixty steps up to Blackwood Terrace."

"My dear boy," said the Professor, "I climb St. Aburik's Hill every day to my office."

"Very good, sir."

And very much a lie. He was retired and neglected his office, for days or weeks at a time. If he wanted a book he sent his errand-boy. He had become a man who paid the young to act in his stead.

Well, he was acting now. *Calaribas! What a prize I have for you today!*

He huffed and grimaced; the young man visibly struggled not to leave him behind. How was it possible that he'd forgotten this staircase? *Because you never felt it then. Because you raced up to the Terrace bearing your books as a rescuer bears a child from a fire, as a soldier his comrade from the field. And you did not slow down until you reached the Hall.*

He would not slow down today, either. He pressed on over the crowded yard, startling his escort, not deigning to look back at the sweep of Kasralys, greatest city the world had ever known. That could wait. Perhaps he and the minister would step out on the Terrace with brandies. Something of the kind would surely be called for.

In the Grand Salon of Blackwood Hall, nothing had changed. The ink with which he signed the visitor's book was the same cobalt blue; the guards by their columns of porphyry were still as young; the flames in the great hearth chewed the same nine-foot lengths of oak. It was toward that fire that his escort steered him now.

"If you'll have a seat, sir, the minister will be with you shortly."

The professor walked with dignity to a leather couch near the hearth. He nodded his thanks to the escort, tried a last friendly smile. The young man imitated his expression like someone given the choice between smiling and scrubbing latrines. Then he handed over the torn upper half of the professor's letter, turned on his heel, and marched away.

CB

Oh heaven's womb, these couches—after six hours on that Ang-forsaken bench. And Calaribas, coming out to collect him personally! The professor had not expected such a gesture.

And as his body relaxed and his limbs warmed, he understood suddenly that he did not care about a brandy on the Terrace, the praise he might receive, his name on the lips of lords and princes. He'd had all that. He didn't want it to return. As a matter of fact he could think of nothing he wanted less.

It had been a kind of horror, that fame. The corrosive vanity, the smile that was not his smile, given to people who were more useful than loveable. The exclusion from genuine friendships. The suspicion that no man or woman ever approached him but for hidden ends. The speech writing, the interminable sessions of the Chamber of Forty, the mind-numbing diplomatic councils, the famished demands of the Realm.

I am retired, he thought with giddy delight. *My fire sacraments are behind me. By the Gods, I don't have to impress a soul.*

A servant appeared with a glass of water, and a steaming towel to freshen his face. This one smiled without effort. The professor shook the fellow's hand.

Why had it taken him so long to see the obvious? He might have gone with his discovery to the papers. He might have proclaimed it at the Congress of Imperial Historians in the spring. But he wanted nothing of the kind! He had sought this difficult appointment with Calaribas precisely so that his old friend could protect him from very fame he had craved in his youth. The public outcry, the public *explosion* that would follow the revelation of his secret: Calaribas and his staff were welcome to that. The professor's life was rich and full. He had two children, five grandchildren, and their love was enough.

Somehow his heart had filled with quiet joy. *I am here for them*, he realized. *Not for myself; that chapter is complete. This is an act of service—and is that not why I chose this life? Is that not how I began?*

A muffled sound from behind him. The professor twisted about, smiling already. The sound was a gasp of surprise, of recognition. It was the voice of his old friend.

But no, it was not after all: merely two strangers hustling through a doorway, snapping it shut behind them. But that voice! It was so perfectly like Calaribas. How could he be mistaken?

Old fool. Don't make a scene. Not today of all days.

He sat back on the couch, removed his spectacles, gave them a guilty wipe against his sleeve. It was only when he replaced them that he realized that everyone else in the salon had risen to their feet.

A prince of the realm stood watching him, arrayed in gold and indigo, servants to either side. Heart in his throat, the professor jumped up and bowed. He recognized the man: Prince Limajur, not merely a Kasraji prince but one of the thirty-six Sky Lords of Urrath, of whom it was said that no door on the continent, from rude shack to royal bedroom, could be closed.

Limajur was one of the youngest of the Sky Lords. He stood in the doorway opposite the one through which the two strangers had vanished. Silent, uneasy. He surveyed the room as though it might contain some threat. At last, making up his mind, he beckoned. The professor hurried forward, holding his valise in a death grip. As he bowed again the Prince reached out and touched his shoulder.

"We are, eh, honored, yes," blurted Limajur. "You're the scholar. Very good. Why don't you come along, then? Some refreshments. A better place to talk."

He turned and stalked out, and the room exhaled. Gaping, the professor charged after him. They marched down a candlelit hall, the young Prince silent, the professor struggling furiously for composure.

Limajur was not an active voice in Kasraji affairs. Indeed he was barely educated, if the rumors were true. But a Sky Lord, all the same! One of the keepers of the Pact of Blood, by which the Gods placed this world in human hands.

Calaribas is moving faster than I dared hope. He has not even seen the proof of my claim.

Of course the proof was right here in his valise. But to persuade a Sky Lord to attend the moment of its unveiling! Even from an old friend, it was an astonishing act of trust.

He tripped—over a wrinkle in the carpet, or perhaps his own feet.

In a flash, the servants became soldiers, catching him in hands of iron, forming a wall between professor and Prince.

"Is he all right?" asked Limajur.

"I am, yes, never better," babbled the professor. "So clumsy—I beg your pardon, my lord."

The Prince's mouth worked as though chewing a lemon. "You," he said, "beg *mine?*"

397

The remark baffled the professor, but it was not for Sky Lords to explain themselves. They proceeded up an ebony stair. Through doors the Prince's bodyguards unlocked one after another. Up a second stair, and a third. The professor was dizzy and winded. Flare of a match. Hands turning him by the shoulders, smells of spirits and roasted meat.

"Do sit down," said the Prince.

They had entered a tiny drawing room, lamplit and cozy. A tower chamber. Windows at knee level gazed down on the hexagonal perfection of Blackwood Terrace. On the table before him was a plate of steaming delicacies—roast beef, tubers, persimmons, figs, a dark flagon of wine.

"Go on, no reason to wait," said Limajur.

"My lord?"

"Eat, man. Drink some wine. I would, in your place."

"My lord, I am so deeply honored, but . . . did Minister Calaribas speak to you?"

"Calaribas . . . ?" Limajur glanced at his servants, who discreetly shook their heads. The Prince's eyes drifted to the door.

"Do you . . . know the nature of my discovery, my lord?"

The Prince, as if he could no longer restrain himself, snatched a cut of bloody meat from the platter and wolfed it whole. "Absolutely not," he said, licking his fingers.

And with that he was gone.

✇

Alone, the professor steadied himself on the chair. He had not, of course, sat down: to do so while a Sky Lord remained standing would have been unthinkable. How very odd it all was. Limajur had no interest whatsoever in his discovery—perhaps in anyone's discoveries, in the whole march of human intellect? Why then had he become involved at all?

Could he be acting on another's behalf—opening doors, as it were? The professor knew quite well that the upper floors of Blackwood Hall were off limits to anyone of his own, simple stature. It was the domain of generals, sartaphs, spies: those few who answered directly to the Grand Illim of Kasralys. Those whose every breath was devoted to the safety of the Realm. Surely that was why his old friend had arranged for him to be escorted here?

"Professor Barunin."

He whirled. A man in a dark gray coat was standing just behind him, straight and still. He was slender, almost elfin, with bright eyes and a kindly smile. His arms hung straight at his sides; his hands were neat and quiet. A small white scar, roughly wing-shaped, marred his left cheekbone and moved when he spoke.

"You know my name," said the professor. *Someone. Finally.* "I am Barunin, yes."

The stranger extended his hand. "Please forgive me for startling you, professor! I am so happy to make your acquaintance."

They laced their fingers together: the most formal of Kasraji greetings. Where had the man come from? Had he slipped in as the Sky Lord departed? But that was impossible: the professor had not looked away for an instant.

And the chamber had no other door.

Which could only mean that the man had been here all along. In the shadows, against the wall—behind that bookshelf, perhaps. And again the professor thought of Prince Limajur's eagerness to depart.

"Did the minister send you?" he demanded. "My missive was directed to him."

"I regret to say that Minister Calaribas is quite unable to join us," said the stranger. "I will attend you to the best of my abilities, poor substitute though I am. My name is Thruko, but I hope you will call me Eyelash—" He touched the scar on his cheek. "—the nickname I take with friends."

The professor was speechless. Still smiling, Thruko put a hand in his coat pocket and withdrew a folded sheet. He winked at the professor. "Do you suppose we match?"

It was the bottom half of the petition: the substantial half. "Good!" said Thruko, when the professor held up his own portion. "Now we can both speak freely. I would like to toast you, sir. Indeed, I *will* toast you, with your permission."

He crossed to the table and filled two small cups from the flagon. The wine was thick and all but black: true Imperial wine, ancient and priceless. Thruko held out both cups, beaming. The professor took the cup from his right hand.

"You, Professor Barunin," crowed Thruko, "have made the greatest historical discovery in at least three hundred years. To your intellect, and your dedication."

He drank. The professor drank. The wine was acrid and sweet at once, not pleasant but madly evocative. Wild bees, ruined temples. Lost vineyards in the pocket valleys of the Nightfire Range, guarded by gryphons. Old lords in decaying strongholds, poring over pages of the *Apocryfeni Kasraj*, reading late into the night.

"You understand what I have found, then?" asked the professor.

"Understand it!" said Thruko. "My dear sir, I expect that no one understands it as well as you. But for my part I am transfixed. I've thought of nothing else since I was shown your petition this morning—indeed I have delayed my departure from this city by a day, at some danger to myself."

"Danger?"

"Tell me only this," said Thruko. "Have you attempted to explain your astonishing discovery to anyone, in any manner, outside of what you wrote in this petition?"

The professor hesitated, obscurely frightened by the question. Thruko's eyes held him like the gaze of a hawk. At last his training as a scholar came to his rescue.

Attempted to explain. When in doubt, give a literal answer.

"No, sir. I felt it was vital that I inform the Palace without delay. I have worked to great advantage all my life with the Kasraji authorities."

"As indeed have I," said Thruko, beaming, "although with a different branch altogether. But not another word until you eat! You have missed luncheon by hours. I shall keep you company if that will induce you."

They ate. The professor gripped his valise between his ankles. He could tell that his last statement—his discretion, that is—had made Thruko immensely happy. Unless it was merely the food—extraordinary, fit for an emperor—which the professor had almost failed to notice in his agitation.

When they finished Thruko's eyes were merry. He dabbed the corners of his mouth with a napkin.

"If they were to march us to the gallows after such a meal, would you complain? I should not."

"Master Thruko—"

"Eyelash."

"I am quite lost, sir," said the professor. "You affirm that my discovery is historic, but add that you don't understand it—"

"As well as you," corrected Thruko, raising a finger. "I did, of course, read your petition with care. Shall we test my comprehension?"

The professor made a twitchy gesture of assent.

"You claim," said Thruko, "to have found the testimony of four survivors of a terrible fire, one of the greatest catastrophes in the annals of Urrath."

"Yes indeed. The Bandritramal Fire."

"Bandritramal. The port garrison. A town where Outer World ships made landfall once, under the strictest medical supervision."

"Yes," said the professor, "in accordance with the terms of the Quarantine, and the Plague Protocols."

"A town struck by a fire so horrendous that it consumed every structure within its granite defenses. And every living soul."

"Yes, every last. Or so we have always believed."

"But now," said Thruko, "we have the voices of these four, who did *not* perish. Who crawled to freedom by means of a storm drain running beneath the wall. Who fled in terror, and dared not speak of what they knew for decades."

"Yes," said the professor, leaning closer. "And by the Gods, what they *knew*—"

"Came from the loose lips of an Outworlder who perished in the fire along with the rest. A guest in Urrath, who had become too fond of Urrathis—their customs, their women, their beer."

"A Xavasindran doctor," said the professor, "like so many before him and after. But this one was a true friend—to Urrath, I mean, to us. Not to those who dispatched him thither. He is quite forgotten today, but his name will be taught to schoolchildren, sir, when the histories are revised. As they *must* be revised. For this doctor—"

"Claimed that those who imposed the Quarantine never, but never, intended to lift it, medical advances be damned."

"You have it, sir! Horrible, unspeakably horrible—demonic, I should say. But *absolutely incontrovertible!*"

Forgetting himself, the professor shoved his chair back from the table and lifted his valise. "This folio," he declared, "is evidence of a crime so vast it beggars belief."

"Go on," said Thruko.

"It is not ancient. It is but a hundred years old, whereas the Quarantine itself has endured three times as long. But fully a century ago this crime was already underway. For the doctor's confession was clear: that Urrath was closed behind the walls of Quarantine *for the continued profit of the Xavasindrans.*'"

"The Xavasindrans?" Thruko's eyes widened. "My dear professor, you know as well as I do that those doctors comprise a *charitable* mission. They may have failed to cure the Plague thus far, but they have treated the lesser wounds and maladies of *thousands* of Urrathis and never taken a penny. When has there ever been a question of profit?"

"You will see for yourself," said the professor, "when this folio has been translated, and shared with all the world. For the good doctor had more to say. Twice before his time, in those first three centuries of Quarantine, *the Plague was almost cured.*"

"Oh, come now."

"The proof is in my hands, sir. The mystery was all but untangled, a formula nearly in reach. But the doctors who were reaching for it?" Professor Barunin shook his head. "They vanished overnight. Recalled from Urrath by their masters—or else killed here in Urrath, and their bodies spirited away."

"But professor! Whatever for?"

"Profit, sir. The doctor is eloquent upon the subject, and I committed to memory the choicest passages. To wit: 'My superiors have long since abandoned all desire to cure the Plague. There is far too much wealth to be extracted from the world by managing it. By selling half-cures and temporary salves, for treating the symptoms. They are the wealthiest persons ever to walk the face of this earth. They own fleets, islands, armies, banks. They want for nothing, and fear nothing, save one thing only: a true cure for the Plague.' Quite a lot of detail follows, but that is the heart of it."

He sat back, closed the valise over the folio, and met the stranger's eye.

"I do not know if Urrathis are truly carriers of this Plague, which cuts down Outworlders as the reaper cuts his grain. But this much is certain: the Xavasindrans are not here to cure the malady. We are hosting a predatory force, Master Eyelash. We are living a lie."

In the silence, the professor heard the cry of a falcon somewhere over the city, the trembling of the window casement in the breeze, the faint tick of a clock.

"Yes, you are," said Eyelash Thruko.

⚃

The professor shot to his feet. Thruko drank off his wine and rose slowly, a broad smile on his face. He reached for the professor's arm, but the other recoiled, pulling the valise against his chest.

"I know this is strange for you, friend," said Eyelash Thruko, "but it is equally strange for me. We are living in a time more wondrous than our minds are made to comprehend. And you and I, professor, are among the few who will ever grasp the whole of it. What your long-dead doctor says is perfectly true. The Xavasindrans are not here to cure the World Plague. They are here to ensure that it is *never* cured."

"But that is madness, lunacy—"

"No, that is commerce. Few die of the Plague here in Urrath, but in the Outer World its victims are legion. We Outworlders have no natural immunity. The people beyond these shores—all those millions—live in terror of an early, agonizing death. And they pay dearly for anything they believe makes them safe."

The professor was fighting an almost overwhelming urge to bolt from the chamber. Could he make the door, was it possible? And what would happen then?

"Pay whom?" he whispered.

"My employers," said Thruko. "Suppliers of preventative drugs, palliatives, cures as false as harlots' smiles. These, and a battery of substances to reduce the suffering that always comes in the end."

"A crime syndicate, Master Eyelash?"

"A syndicate of clever persons. And yes, the richest men and women this world has ever known. Think of it: their customers are infinite, and captive literally *for life*, and there is nothing they will not part with in exchange for a little hope. A little, mind you. Never too much, if the flow of gold is to be sustained."

"But what part does Urrath play in this, this hideous—"

"Urrath, my dear Barunin, is the secret laboratory. The disease was born here. It traveled abroad in the lungs of Urrathi merchants, sailors, slaves. And yet you *are* immune, for the most part. Where better to study the Plague? And since it is forbidden territory, where better to tell the world that you are working to conquer it once and for all?"

"An evil, an *unforgiveable* fraud—"

"That judgment I leave to heaven," said Thruko, "but a clever fraud to be sure. Alas, not quite clever enough, though. For a cure *has* been found."

"A t-true cure? For the Plague?"

"An absolute cure, a final cure. And the proud doctors of your city, with no help whatsoever from the Xavasindrans, played a crucial role in its discovery, along with a rather brilliant son of the Chiloto Prophet.

"But the description of the Cure, the formula—that has gone with two foolish boys into the heart of the desert. And there it shall either vanish, like most everything that enters the Sumuridath Jal, or be taken off their corpses and burned." Thruko turned him an apologetic smile. "Either way, the world will never hear of it."

Run. Run if your legs are still capable. Run to save your life.

Thruko crossed to the window and knelt, gazing down on Blackwood Terrace. "That woman by the fountain," he said. "Do you see her?"

RUN! The command was now a scream in the professor's head. Somehow he could not do it, could not accept what was happening. He rounded the table, his body weightless. He squatted down by Eyelash Thruko.

"Is that the Chancellor?"

"Lady Kosuda, yes," said Thruko. "I have the greatest respect for her—and for you, Barunin. You and she are both detectives, after a fashion. And you are among the very best at what you do. That folio of yours—what a damning testament, what a singular find! As for Kosuda, she has been shadowing me for half a year, aware of my influence, circling ever nearer. For a week now she has been close to succeeding, and I knew that I must flee Kasralys while I still could. Today—well, as you can see, there she is, about to enter this hall in force."

"You're one of them," said the professor, ashen. "Gods of Death, you're a Xavasindran."

Thruko shook his head. "I merely oversee their work," he said. "If I were a Xav you'd have noticed my amber-yellow skin, would you not? But there are many clans in the Outer World, and some of us can pass for Urrathis. You cannot spot us by the shape of our eyes, professor. Nor by the color of our skin.

"That has not, however, thwarted Lady Kosuda. Her foresight has been—" He shook his head. "—exceptional. Nearly equal to my own. Kosuda is like a fastidious rat catcher, who before she begins her efforts, takes care to seal the doors, one by one."

Again he smiled at the professor. "I am not a rat, though. Much more of a rattlesnake. Very hard to catch indeed."

The professor's lips were trembling; sweat had soaked his shirt through. *I shall act. I shall break this window and scream for her aid.*

He squatted motionless at Thruko's side, thinking of his mother and father, his friends.

On the Terrace, Kosuda began to march. Precisely on cue, men and women scattered about the yard rose from benches, ceased pretending to admire the roses. Eight in total fell in behind her. All were converging on Blackwood Hall.

"To spend one's life among persons of sincerity," said Thruko. "Not literal sincerity—that has never been an option for some of us—but sincerity of vocation, of commitment, of work for a chosen end: that I count a blessing above all others. I hope in some measure you feel the same?"

"I feel frightened," said the professor. "Some vocations are simply wrong."

Smiling, Thruko turned his face to the sky.

"I thank Usthe my protector for this day, Professor Barunin. This short time in your presence, your fine qualities, your clarity of mind."

"Please—"

Thruko made a shushing sound. He put his arm around the professor, who was blinking through tears. His other hand, quite gently, closed on the handle of the valise.

"You must preserve that clarity now," he said. "You are a true son of this city, a servant of all Urrath, a man of principle and faith. Rejoice, professor. Who could look upon your life and not be moved?"

☙

Four minutes later, when Lady Kosuda burst into the chamber, she found a number of curious things. An open window. The remains of a fine meal. The body of an aged man with a bone caught in his throat. A fire rapaciously consuming the last of a manuscript that blazed and sizzled with lamp oil, and not a drop of wine or water left to snuff it out.

21. A REUNION

SANULSREYA, MIDDLE BASIN, GREAT DESERT OF URRATH

15TH DAY OF SPRING, 3662

"And people think *I'm* the reckless one."

Mektu's voice, cutting through fog.

"You're awake, Kan, I know it. I saw you move."

A black chamber. A bedroll on stone. Tattered cloak rolled into a pillow beneath his head. Far away, through multiple arches, a sunbeam like a pillar of fire.

"Malingering, that's what this is," said Mektu. "Open your eyes."

He opened his eyes. His brother squatted by his elbow—a shaggy, scabrous apparition.

"I dreamed of the Mountain again," said Kandri. "The Mountain of the Gods."

"Who cares? Dreams are boring. Happy new year, by the way."

"It's . . . spring?"

Mektu laughed. "It's been spring for two weeks; we just didn't stop to notice. The new year started while we were crossing the Marastiin Floor. Back home the lambs must be dropping. And the girls will be sewing dresses for the Thaw Dance in Ashfield."

Kandri shook his head. "Outlawed. Years ago, by the priests."

Mektu frowned at him. "No Thaw Dance?"

"You're forgetful."

"Maybe so. But you're a chicken-headed halfwit. You almost got yourself killed."

Kandri blinked at the distant sunbeam. "How long have I—"

"Four days," said Mektu. "That storm trampled you like a bull. You even reopened that shoulder wound. It was a class act, brother."

Kandri raised a hand to probe his forehead. Every part of him ached. "Fiasul—"

"Yes," said Mektu. "She dragged you in, screaming for help. But she wouldn't go beyond the bottom of the stairs. It was the oddest thing. The storm was *torturing* the world outside, but did that scare her? Not a bit. What scared her was a roof over her head. 'Nachasps needing sky,' she told us. The minute we had you in hand she turned and ran, and the storm closed around her like she'd jumped into the sea."

"The others, back at the tower—"

"The Nachasps brought them," said Mektu. "They did everything Mansari asked of them and more. And it's no wonder they love him so much—they raised him."

"Raised him!"

"His first fifteen years. 'They plucked me one night from a caravan,' he told us. 'I was a babe of thirteen months. After that I never saw another human; in fact I doubted they were real. It was a childhood of *hmm*, distinction.'"

"Stolen child," said Kandri.

Mektu nodded. "The guides talked about children like him, remember? *Raised until the woman time, or the manhood.*"

"Ang's blood," said Kandri. "No wonder he reminds me of a cat."

"He's half the reason they helped us," said Mektu. "The other half was—well, you and Pixie."

"Don't call her that."

Mektu looked at him oddly. "He went back with them, Mansari did. After twenty years with Kereqa's circus, and the general's family. That was their price, brother. And somehow I don't think it's temporary."

Kandri lay back, stunned. Fiasul's words rose in him: *Be careful, Krandee. Be sure.*

"Why are you smiling?" he asked.

For Mektu was smiling: a troubled smile, but a real one. "Because we're free men," he said. "It's happened, at last. We've shaken the Rasanga, the army, the Clowns. Even Jód says so: 'Nothing that walks this earth can track those who flee into a lathban under storm.' Can you believe it, Kan? No one has any Gods-damned idea where we are."

Kandri closed his eyes. *Could* he believe it? In his mind's eye he saw the figure of a bone-white girl in a tattered gown. Perhaps he had only dreamed her, that night with Eshett among the rocks. But the Prince and Ifimar Jód had seen her in the plain light of day.

"Drink some water," said Mektu.

Kandri kept his eyes closed. By sheer will he drove the vision of the White Child from his mind. But the very effort flooded him with a new vision, vast beyond thought, and once more he was seeing Urrath from the Mountain of the Gods. Urrath in blackest night. Urrath burning and smoldering under the Gods' burning tears. Urrath crawling with armies, with laboring millions, with siege engines and great shackled beasts. Urrath waking into war.

"Free men," he murmured.

"Free to make straight for Kasralys," said Mektu. "At least as straight as the desert allows."

Kandri opened his eyes. He held out a groggy hand and Mektu clasped it. His brother was desperate to comfort him, to give him reasons to heal. But Kandri knew that he would only ever be free on the day he learned the truth of Fiasul's words. If only she meant them simply. Not as a puzzle, a ghostly enigma, a cat but not a cat. If only he could draw one breath in the certain knowledge that Ariqina was alive.

છ

"It's a wonder, this temple. The heat never quite finds its way inside."

Mektu's nervous chatter had gone on for ten minutes or more, and he was not through yet. "Some of the chambers have murals—wars, weddings, monsters, forests—*forests*, in this sandbox! Underneath the main chamber there's a room with hundreds of round holes in the walls, and each hole has a stopper of clay. Stilts says they're tombs. He even showed me where the ghouls had tried to claw them open."

"Ghouls!"

"Don't worry, we've checked every last room. No ghouls left in here, but they could be elsewhere in the ruins. That's one reason Jód's in a hurry to set off again. It's almost a shame. The well here is a gift from heaven—sweet, clean, cold."

"And we're all back together?" said Kandri, still struggling to believe.

"The whole caravan," said Mektu, "and nine more soldiers. And Stilts. It's a miracle, all those people—but I won't talk about that."

"About what?"

"Forget it," said Mektu. "The doctor said not to disturb you."

Kandri laughed: more pain. "You came in here to disturb me, jackass. Doesn't matter; I'm glad you did. But if we're all here, what's there to be disturbed about?"

"The Clowns cut down that private like a dog, Kandri," said Mektu. "And Captain Utarif. I keep seeing what that thing—"

"Try not to," said Kandri. "Think of better moments. Think of him laughing with Uncle."

Mektu nodded and looked away. Kandri studied him, uneasy. "There's something else, isn't there?" he asked.

Mektu stood—or rather bounded up like a Jack-in-the-box. He made an anxious gesture with both hands, then squatted just as abruptly, his smile slightly crazed.

"Nothing whatsoever," he said.

Kandri sat up (tiny spears to the ribcage) and gripped his shoulder. "Tell me the truth," he hissed. "Someone's hurt, aren't they? Mek, is it Uncle?"

"Oh, no. You're the worst by far."

"Then what's the matter?"

"Nothing, nothing! Besides, I promised."

"Shit on a griddle, Mektu! You've as good as told me *now*."

"That's not true. I never even mentioned her."

"Mentioned who?"

Mektu hid his face in the crook of his arm.

Kandri crawled away from him, sweating with pain. At the wall he braced himself and stood. Vertigo, weakness. Mektu, still hiding his eyes, prattled on about how well he'd kept his promise.

Kandri staggered toward the beam of sun. The first archway let into a room stacked with harnesses and saddlebags. In the second, a dozen camel drivers squatted around a tower of clothes, hands busy with needle and thread. The men saw him and leaped to their feet.

"Mr. Kandri! Mr. Kandri!"

They crowded around him, beaming, patting his cheeks. He smiled for them, his face dry as a corpse, and staggered on into the chamber of the sunbeam.

"Not my fault!" Mektu was shouting. "I told him to rest! I never said a word about—*that*."

The chamber was round and enormous, with a great domed ceiling, and the beam fell straight down like chiseled gold from a square hole in the crown of the dome. Passages led away into blackness on all sides, and looping the chamber above was a ruined balcony, its dark arcades suggesting further rooms or hallways.

Great as it was, the room was crowded. Most of the camel drivers were here, along with scores of camels. The little doctor was examining Kereqa's teeth. Jód, Stilts, and Prince Nirabha were huddled about a stone table; they had yet to notice Kandri. But Chindilan and Talupéké had, and were rushing toward him with stricken looks. A dog yipped. Ulren pointed at Kandri. The doctor turned and threw his cap to the floor in a rage.

"I *told* you to keep that bent screw of a brother away from my patient!"

"Kandri, you shouldn't have risen!" Chindilan seized his elbow. "We need you healed boy, and soon. The journey from here will be pure hell."

"The old man's right for once," said Talupéké, taking his other arm. "Go on, get out of here."

"First tell me what's happened," said Kandri.

"Don't fuck around," said Talupéké. "Your muscles feel like dishrags, you've lost so much blood."

He could hear the fear in her voice—*in Talupéké's voice*—and did not for a moment believe it was about his health.

"I'm going to kill someone," he wheezed, "if you keep treating me like I'm six."

"Kandri Hinjuman!"

Jód himself materialized before him—and Pitfire, even *he* was afraid. The Master leaned close and whispered in his ear.

"Afterbirth of a dog! Once again you endanger us all, who risked so much to bring you here alive. Return to your chamber, and do not stir from it again until—"

A woman screamed, in agony or madness or both. The cry rent the chamber, and the faces around him twitched.

"I didn't tell, I didn't!" cried Mektu.

The scream came again—furious, bereft. And Kandri realized to his horror that he knew the voice.

"Oh Gods, no—"

With a violent motion he shook off the hands that held him. He lurched through the crowd, passing camels, cook stations, mounds of gear. The screaming came from the far side of the chamber. The others trailed in his wake, cursing, snatching at his limbs.

"Don't get too close," said Chindilan, "and don't despair, Kandri. The doctor says it could be temporary. She could get better, do you hear?"

Kandri rounded the last of the camel drivers. And stopped dead, swaying in place.

Eshett, ragged, emaciated, stood near the wall. Her bare arms strained toward him, clawing at the air. Nails bloody. Hair plastered with grease and filth. In her eyes, no recognition. In her mouth, no human words.

Around her neck was an iron collar, fastened to a chain. The chain in turn was padlocked to a ring set in the chamber wall.

"She returned to the caravan the day after we left it," said Chindilan. "Jód says that she was perfectly normal when she arrived—but only for the first few minutes, as she looked everyone over. Jód asked if she had found her village. 'No,' she told him, 'there was nothing, only a marsh, you were right.' Then she asked where you and Mektu were. Jód admitted that he'd sent us away. And something snapped inside her. She started cursing, wailing, swinging at people."

"They told her we'd be back, but she didn't believe it," said Talupéké. "They had to gag her. She could have brought the Rasanga with her screams."

Feeling half mad himself, Kandri started toward her. This time Chindilan and Talupéké seized him with force. "Not another step!" said Chindilan. "She doesn't know you, or any of us. She won't let anyone but Tal and Kereqa near her. She's an animal, Kandri. An animal in pain."

Eshett lunged. The chain snapped taut. The iron ring bit into her throat, cutting off her scream. In Kandri's chest something was breaking. Was it his fault, somehow? Had he wounded her? Eshett had sworn from the start that their lovemaking was a thing of the moment, a sweet end to a union that was always temporary, a carnal goodbye. If anything, he had regretted their parting more.

"She's choking herself," he said.

"She'll quit when we back off," said Talupéké. "Or when she passes out. Either way."

Once more Eshett lunged, her bare feet scraping and slipping. Her reach was the reach of a drowning woman for a rope.

But she was not reaching for him. Her gaze was fixed at something over his shoulder. Kandri turned. His brother stood as if pinned to the spot, looking back at her, and his gaze was almost as odd as Eshett's own. There was pity for her, certainly, and fear and remorse. But there was also a wary defiance, a ferocity.

His hand rested on the hilt of the mattoglin.

Kandri turned and marched toward him. Where his strength came from he could not fathom, unless it was simply rage, rage like a furnace, fed and stoked until it glowed. His brother retreated a step.

"You did this," said Kandri. "You took it from her."

"Because she hated it," said Mektu, baring his teeth. "I took it to protect her—at first, at first. That's the holy truth, Kandri. But now things have changed."

"Changed? You've killed her, Mek. Killed her mind."

"I did?" said Mektu. "Who gave her the knife in the first place?"

Kandri swung at him. A clumsy gesture; Mektu dodged with ease, and his follow-through landed Kandri on the floor.

A bare foot, Chindilan's foot, came down hard upon his neck.

"Lie still!" snapped his uncle. "Tear those stitches again and you're as good as dead."

Kandri twisted. Chindilan put more of his substantial weight into the foot. Then Stilts appeared at his uncle's side. Behind the black spectacles, his old eyes creased with concern.

"The smith is not exaggerating," he said. "You've managed to rise and shamble around and act the fool, but so what? Tomorrow night we set out again. How long do you think you'll last? Half a mile? Three quarters?"

Kandri's chest was heaving. He knew that Stilts' words should horrify him. And perhaps they did, in some part of himself he could not reach. From the edge of the chamber, Eshett's howling went on.

"Fortunately," said Chindilan, "Jód's given permission for us to set you in a sling once again, for as long as a week."

"As he plans to do with Eshett," added Stilts, "except that you won't be gagged."

Kandri shut his eyes. *Why Eshett? Why did it have to be her?*

"But a week is nothing," said Chindilan. "Your shoulder needs to rest for three at least. And longer if you don't behave."

Kandri stopped fighting; there was no one to fight. His uncle stepped back and helped him gingerly to his feet.

"You don't need to worry about *him*," said Mektu. "Kandri always behaves. He's the good one, remember?"

The bitterness in his voice spoke volumes: they had been fighting while he slept. Chindilan, and no doubt others, knew that Mektu had stolen the mattoglin back from Eshett. And they knew that somehow that theft had played a part in her madness.

But no one save Kandri had guessed the truth. His uncle still doubted the very existence of yatras. Kandri himself had doubted their existence, until . . .

When? He had carried the mattoglin for a while and suspected nothing. But at some point doubt had been replaced by certainty, and he had known, absolutely *known*, that a yatra was among them. He thought he should able to pinpoint the moment, but where the memory should have been there was a troubling blankness.

Eshett shrieked again. Mektu looked up suddenly into Kandri's eyes. "She's still in there," he said. "She's not gone. I'm sure of it."

Her scream rose and fell. A moan, a sob, a cackle.

His brother was trembling. Kandri found he could not apologize for trying to strike him. He thought of Eshett walking through the night after leaving the caravan. Alone in her dust river, desert insects screeching from the banks. Feeling troubled for no clear reason. Stopping at last to take the mattoglin from her bulky pack. Finding Mektu's dagger there instead. Cursing him but carrying on, *To hell with all of them. It's finished now, I'm free.*

But she was not free. The yatra had sunk a hook in her mind. A hook that tugged and tore at her the further she pulled away from the mattoglin. Until the pain drowned all other feelings, blotted out all other thoughts. Stopped her in her tracks, in agony. Turned her at last to chase after the caravan, hour upon hour, only to discover when she reached it that the brothers and the mattoglin were gone.

No, he could not forgive Mektu yet. Far worse, he could not warn him. Could not say what was obvious now: that the yatra they had feared for so long, since the rash of signs and rumors at Eternity Camp—was right there on his belt, using him, riding him for a purpose it alone understood.

ᘓ

"You're the world's worst patient, damn your eyes," said Chindilan. "But you're not quite a lost cause. We'll take care of you if you let us."

Kandri let Chindilan help him back to his darkened room. He lay down. His uncle lowered himself stiffly to his knees beside Kandri's bedroll.

"Maybe the Old Man did hate you," said Kandri.

"Because he saddled me with protecting you two?" Chindilan shook his head. "I was furious when I said that, Kandri. Those wasps might have killed us all."

He looked away, frowned, scratched the back of his neck. Then, reaching some decision, he held up several folded sheets of paper. They were fine linen, although dusty and creased.

"That's from Stilts," said Kandri.

"The paper, yes. The letter's from me. And you're not to read it until I'm dead."

Kandri just looked at him.

"Dead or lost to you," said Chindilan, "and don't give me that eyeball. Took me days to write that thing."

"Why can't I read it now? Why can't you just *tell* me?"

"You'll understand when the time comes. For today just keep it safe. As a matter of fact, why not put it in that pouch of yours, next to the Letter of Cure?"

Kandri hesitated. "You mean it, don't you?" he said at last. "I can't read it unless you're—"

"You think I'm joking?"

"No," said Kandri. "I only wish you were."

He opened the pouch without removing it. Chindilan peered inside. "Ang's blood, the Letter of Cure looks as good as the day we received it," he said. "Garatajik positively embalmed it in wax."

"General Tebassa added another coat."

"Least the bastard could do," said Chindilan, "after nearly burning the thing."

He slid his own letter into the pouch beside the Letter of Cure. To Kandri it seemed that a weight had lifted from his uncle's shoulders.

"Enough of this," said Chindilan. He reached out, and Kandri felt his hand, leather-hard from decades at the forge, gently brush his eyes closed.

"Empty your mind, lad. Sleep as much as you can."

"Eshett could have left us in Mab Makkutin, or even sooner," said Kandri. "She wasn't bound to us. Why didn't she tell us to go to hell?"

"Because love's a magic potion of stupidity," said Chindilan.

"I've seen the Mountain of the Gods," said Kandri. "I've sat there in the starlight, looking down on the world."

"Stop talking, lad. I prefer you sane."

"It's the world that was insane. Crawling, murderous. The land itself. You can't look away when you see something like that."

"You can forget it later, like a normal person."

"I want to help her, Uncle. But look at her. How in the Nine Pits can I help?"

His uncle sighed, an old soldier near the limits of his strength. "Not dying," he said, "would be a good place to start."

22. FAMINE'S TABLE

Sleep took him with predatory swiftness, and for many days that followed Kandri never quite escaped its jaws.

But even in dreams—the tortured miasma of them, the quaking landscapes, the leering eyes—certain facts rose to the surface. He was feverish. They had fled Sanulsreya. The drivers had slung him on the painter's platform once more, tied a black cloth over his eyes. He had swallowed a narcotic; the doctor poured it into his mouth and tipped back his chin. *That should help him to be sensible. Although in one with so little sense to begin with, I make no promises.*

The days swirled together, leaves clogging a drain. Heat and cold, needles of sunlight through the bandage, the drivers' walking-songs by night. His fingers resting on the calfskin pouch. The two dogs riding atop a camel ("Nothing stops them but the open sand," says Ulren). Alahari-Rana's dry nose snuffling at his ear. Eshett's muffled screams.

Daybreak. Talupéké walking beside his platform, stealing glances at him, swearing under her breath. *Brain fever. What the fuck. That's a symptom, not a disease.* Her glance angry and fearful. Her dry fingers press a date into the pouch of his cheek.

Midday. Stifling air beneath a sun-shield, stinking bodies, biting flies.

More gruel, more water. A cloth wiping his forehead. His uncle's voice. *Lie still, don't toss and worry so. There's no one chasing us, boy.*

Eshett's screams. Or the memory of her screams. Or anticipation of the next.

Dusk, coolness, clean copper light. Sudden chills traveling his body with fingers of bone. The surgeon, muttering under his breath as he changes Kandri's bandage. *I will never forgive those who condemned me to this journey. Heal them? Of course, what a question, that's my job is it not? But forgive them—no, not in this lifetime or a thousand to come.*

Whiff of a cookfire. Eshett wailing like a soul in hell.

What are you thinking, Prince? Talupéké again, and from a further distance, Nirabha's answer: *That if the old sources are correct, this Lathban Othurge'ul is so enormous it could hide the whole of my country within its sands.*

Midnight. Deep cold. A gulp of sweet resinous tea. Stilts, tucking a stone, fire-warmed, into Kandri's shirt.

Daybreak. Spalak's face brooding over him. *Your body is healing,* he says (or has said, or Kandri expects him to say), *but what of the corruption in your soul?*

Night again. His brother marching at his shoulder, one hand on the mattoglin, dried tears on his cheeks.

ᛒ

He was walking. They had brought him down from the painter's platform and set him on his feet. But when had it happened? There was no notch in Kandri's memory, no hatchmark. And with a sensation like free-fall he wondered how much else had been erased.

Not just forgotten: erased. That was the horror of it. In his illness—or was it earlier?—he had suffered some gross violation. A claw, a whisper, a parasite gnawing his brain . . .

He shook himself. Delirium, nothing more. Fight it, fight for clarity or die. Your task now is the same as on the Marastiin Floor: to go on walking forever. To be that thing that never stops.

But walking was a torture beyond dreams. Kandri had never been so frail. His arms dangled like rags. Sand chewed at his feet, rasping in his sandals until the soft skin of his ankles bled. His legs were two drowning children he rescued endlessly from the sea. Lift the first leaden body above the water. Stand it hopelessly on its feet. Heave up the second. Return to the first before it sinks again. Return to the second. Return to the first.

Eighteen days, or was it nineteen? Was it perhaps twenty-four? He could never sustain this, despite the nearness of friends, the stark promise from Ulren that *You'll leave this land afoot or in the stomachs of vultures, Chiloto.* He stumbled often into the soft rump of Alahari-Rana, grateful for the guiding star of her anus when his mind began to drift.

ങ

By night he was beset by strangling doubts. He saw his life as a charcoal drawing on a cave wall slick with soot. Kandri Hinjuman, earnest boy from Blind Stream. Raised by two mothers and the man they shared. Poorly schooled, ignorant of everything. Vain and petty as only small-town boys with many younger siblings can be. A dreamer, a chaser of girls. Until the new girl arrived and speared him with her honesty and laughter and brilliance and naked pain.

Finally, miraculously, with her love.

But the cave-artist had had a change of heart. Scratch the girl. Leave the spear. See what becomes of the boy.

He slapped his own cheek, hard, and tried to see the world around him. Lathban Othurge'ul. Infinite dunes, glass-splinter stars. Red reptile eye of the Pilgrim rising in the east. Was he to believe that the village boy had found his way *here*? Was that likely in the least?

Of course not. The spell would break. This night of chill wind and murmured songs in a secret tongue would drop like a gauze curtain, and he would be back in his old bed on Candle Mountain, nine years old. Or in the room he shared with Mektu a few years later. Or in a meadow, tangled with Ariqina in love's aftermath, on a warm Sataapre night.

He hungered, he craved that moment of waking. It never came.

This, then, was the truth: the noiseless caravan, like a serpent skeleton on the move. Even his friends made strange by moonlight. And behind them all, the accumulating dead, incandescent, the rattle on the serpent's tail. There was the maniac, still cradling his thumb. Woeden Surk and his mercenaries, fearful, diminished by defeat. The tall youth who had run with Spalak and swallowed poison. The croaking private with a hand on his scalp. Captain Utarif, resolute as ever, eyes on his surviving troops.

Several times Kandri mustered his courage and faced them, daring them to approach, seeking their eyes. The act made them flicker and vanish, like fish into the depths of a pond.

One day they will speak to me. One day I will know why they're here.

But even as the thought came to him, he saw a new figure among the dead. It was fainter than the rest, and disappeared altogether before he could look at it squarely. Kandri was not sure if it was man or woman, old or young. Yet he felt he knew the face: knew it intimately, as though he had run his hands over its contours in the dark.

The new figure had another kind of distinction. The other ghosts comprised both friends and enemies, but in all of them, even the maniac, anger had leached away to nothing. As though they were separated from the living by centuries, not days or weeks. They glanced at Kandri, if at all, with weary remorse.

Not so the newcomer. Its form was obscure, but its purpose blazed like the fires on Ravashandul's Wall. Alone of all the ghosts, this one hated Kandri and wished him death.

ભ

The wretchedness of those days was offset by a blessing Kandri had not dared to hope for: Eshett had begun to improve. Her screams dwindled to moans, then to whimpers that held less terror than sheer bewilderment. Finally they dropped to nothing, blank silence, and her face looked tortured no longer. When they gave her food she ate like a human rather than a wolf. She would not suffer anyone but Talupéké and Kereqa to approach her, however, and her eyes still searched for Mektu day and night. When they found him, her body trembled and a low keening began in her throat. Even Mektu seemed finally to grasp that he could not come near.

The change in Eshett swept away much of Kandri's own misery. Still more vanished when he realized that his own strength was returning. He was not yet fully himself, but he was far from the invalid who feared that every step would be his last. His muscles had learned to stop fighting the sand; with no conscious thought he had begun to mimic the drivers' rocking, floating stride.

Spalak was right: his body was healing. The awareness brought such a burst of pleasure that he nearly laughed aloud. He thought with defiance of the ghost who hated him. *You can forget it, bastard. I'm going to live.*

◌

The next dawn, Ifimar Jód led them straight up the windward slope of the tallest dune since Ravashandul's Wall. In his new good spirits, Kandri could not have cared less, but a part of him wondered why they were climbing at all. None of them could afford to waste energy. Why not simply go around?

The answer came at the summit, like a blow to the gut: mountains, dead ahead. Vast and menacing, oxblood-red, the highest peaks dusted with snow. They were the same mountains he had glimpsed from Weeping Rock, and later from the Wall. They had come and gone like fever dreams, but now they were far too close to ignore.

Jód motioned for everyone to gather. A stiff wind tore at his cloak and beard, and his face was more grim than usual. He spread his arms wide.

"In the cool of the night we crossed a line together," he shouted. "The middle regions of the Sumuridath Jal are behind us. We have entered the Heart Basin."

Looks of shock, cries of anguish. Jód waited for the silence to resume.

"The mountains before us," he declared, "form the outer wall of the highlands we call Famine's Table. It is a place never meant for human kind.

Few have ever beheld it so close. Far fewer, a handful in history, are those who have entered that realm and emerged alive.

"We are fortunate to have three of that handful: myself, Submaster Spalak, and Mr. Ulren. They have explored the lesser mountains: I alone have climbed to the Inner Table, that country in the clouds. But even the lesser mountains are terrible. The malign power of the Highlands spills down upon them like steam over the lip of a cauldron. In another season, I might lead you around the hills, but that is not among our options. Summer is near; the Killing Heat is near, and the shortest road out of the desert is through Famine's Table. Follow me, and have courage. In three weeks' time, if Ang allows, we shall rest in the marble baths at the Font of Lupriz. And ten days beyond that oasis, Kasralys City awaits."

Marble baths! Kandri's very skin responded to the words. He knew almost nothing of the Font of Lupriz, but now the idea of it brightened in his mind like a star in the east.

"But you must not lie to yourselves," said Jód. "The worst is here before us. Death is here, for any who stray from my guidance." He swept a pointing finger across the crowd. "The wise shall live, if Ang wills it. But the foolish, the disobedient—these the land shall claim in its bottomless hunger, and none shall save them, neither I nor any God of heaven's host."

As he spoke these last words, he stared at something beyond Kandri's shoulder. Kandri turned: there was Spalak, meeting the Master's gaze unblinking, a burning intensity in his eyes.

ಐ

Another two days passed before they reached the foothills. With every mile the red wall of the mountains loomed taller. Scraps of cloud—the first clouds Kandri had seen since the Lutaral—gathered over them at daybreak, and by night lightning flickered in the peaks.

The first hills were widely scattered and sharp, like dry elbows thrusting from the sand. The caravan snaked in among them, east by northeast. Within a few miles, however, the sand gave way to a brittle, crusty soil, and then to a parched loam that compressed underfoot with a sound like crusty snow.

Astonishingly, there was life. The first manifestations were trees: dark, leafless thorn trees, widely scattered and forbidding. Soon these were joined by cacti and a second sort of tree, low and rock-hard and thick with stubby leaves like peeling scabs. Then all number of strange underbrush: climbing cacti, wiry grasses, ground-hugging plants that resembled streamers of leather. A few small birds flashed by, soundless and barely seen.

"Horrible, he tells us," said Mektu, "but this isn't half as bad as being out on the sand."

"Just remember what Eshett told you," said Kandri.

"About not touching myself?"

"What? No. About all the dumb ways to die in the Sumuridath."

"You mean the plant that melts your flesh? That sort of thing?"

"Yes," said Kandri, "that sort of thing. Touch yourself all you want. Don't fucking touch anything else."

Mile by mile the brush grew thicker, and the signs of life more pronounced. Nests like woven sacks hung from the thorn trees. Long-tailed mice burst from cover, and miniature deer fled at their approach. There were signs of menace, too: grass growing in clumps like bouquets of black needles, bird skeletons impaled on the thorn trees.

Late morning a trio of predators sidled by in the undergrowth. "Hyortus, hyortus!" shouted the drivers. The sight of them turned Kandri's stomach: unholy fusions of wolf and wildcat they seemed. They stood no higher than his knees, but their chests were deep, and their teeth were jagged saw blades. The drivers screamed at the animals and threw enough stones to drive off an elephant. The hyortus vanished, but the drivers remained deeply shaken.

Ulren relayed new orders from Jód: both humans and camels were to walk in tighter formation, and no one was to step into the brush for any reason, not even to urinate. During their midday rest under the sun-shields the drivers whispered and huddled together despite the scorching temperatures, and had to be cajoled into attempting sleep.

Kandri had almost managed to nod off himself when he felt a tap on his forehead. Mektu again. Before Kandri could complain, his brother raised a finger to his lips, glancing meaningfully to the north.

Kandri rolled over and looked. Fifty or sixty yards from the sun-shields, two figures stood in the meager shade of one of the thorn trees. They were very close together: one stock-still, the other gesturing urgently. It took Kandri a moment to realize he was looking at Spalak and Ifimar Jód himself. The Master stood motionless; Spalak's hands were working before his face.

"Are they fighting?" Kandri whispered.

"I don't—"

Jód's hand flew up and caught Spalak's wrist. Spalak twisted and grappled, and the two men became a tangled blur.

"—believe there's any doubt," said Mektu.

In was over in seconds: lightning-fast though Spalak was, Jód was even faster. He overpowered the younger man and pinned him bodily against the thorn-tree, both arms twisted behind his back. They stood there a moment, faces inches apart. Then Kandri saw Spalak give a reluctant nod, and the Master released him. After several deep breaths he faced Jód and bowed with slow dignity. Jód raised him by the shoulders, then embraced him. Spalak's arms were rigid at his sides.

ଔ

Three days passed. Famine's Table loomed over the caravan in a dark red wall. Jód was leading them around the great central peaks, but still deep into the mountain complex. From the first peak they scaled, Kandri turned and looked back. Open desert spread endlessly in the distance. These highlands, greater by far than his home country of the Sataapre, were still no more than a rock jutting lonely from an ocean of sand.

That night they camped in a hollow against a cliff, and Jód gave his blessing for a bonfire of thorn-tree branches. The fire was welcomed by all, for with the darkness a deep chill had descended. The Pilgrim Moon rose scarlet above the cliff.

"She's a little closer and brighter each night," said Chindilan. "Before we know it, we'll all feel like we have wings."

"The Weightless Day is distant yet," said Prince Nirabha. "There will be months of tremors beforehand, and the winds gone mad, and finally the moaning of the earth. Such at least I have read—for I was still in the womb when the Pilgrim last visited this world."

"I can remember two previous visits by the Fever Moon, as we call it," said Kereqa. "The winds were terrible indeed, and the tremors caused great damage along the rim of the Yskralem."

"A rockslide cut off our village for ninety days, last time around," said Chindilan. "Even the war came to a halt. But I don't recall any moaning earth."

"Perhaps our Nightfire Range is more talkative than your own," said the Prince. "And these mountains, these hermits of the desert? I wonder what they would say?"

"'Get lost,'" said Mektu. "'Leave us in peace.'"

Kandri thought of the great mass of the highlands looming over them, and had the disconcerting sense that his brother was correct.

છ

After a sparse evening meal, one of the drivers began a song in their secret language. Soon she was joined by an old man with a bamboo flute, warm and clear as the willow flutes Kandri recalled from childhood, before they were banned by the priests. The song had many verses, and while Kandri could not decipher a word he felt he had never heard such longing in any tongue. He saw his brother's face, spellbound and serene. Old Kereqa wiped a tear from her eye.

"Gods above," said Chindilan, when the last verse was sung. "That's the most lovely thing I've heard since my youth."

Kandri felt much the same. He turned to his friend with the clouded eye and asked the subject of the song. His friend looked uncomfortable. An anxious whisper swept the caravan, and soon Jód came striding up to the fire.

Kandri rose, expecting fury—there were ten million ways to misstep with the Master—but to his surprise Jód looked at him with approval.

"Your question cannot be answered," he said, "for that song is an old secret of our drivers' clan. Still, they are pleased that you ask. Your love for their music gladdens their hearts."

"I've never heard anything like it," said Kandri.

"You have, in fact," said Jód.

Kandri started. "I don't understand, Master Ifimar."

"You have heard such music in your cradle, in your birth-mother's voice. And also in the blood-song that is your birthright, the chorus of ancestors whose souls bequeathed you your own."

Don't sigh, Kandri told himself. He was beginning to regret his curiosity.

"The art of memory is taught nowhere so well as in the desert," the Master continued. "Prince Nirabha has his libraries; we Parthans have our voices, and our minds. These men and women carry volumes within them. Songs, poems, proverbs, tales. From elders to children they pass, around small fires, over centuries of sleepless nights."

He faced Kandri again. "Such knowledge is a priceless gift. And it dwells within you, Kandri Hinjuman."

Load of rubbish. Kandri kept his face blank.

But Mektu was indignant. "Only him?" he said. "Is that what you're saying? What about me?"

It wouldn't do, thought Kandri, *to collapse into giggles*. But his face must have revealed more than he intended, for the Master's eyes grew stern.

"You know so little," he said, "and yet you doubt so much."

"I tried believing," said Kandri, "like a good Chiloto. Look where that got me."

"Your birth-mother was a child of the sand."

Kandri shrugged. "That didn't change anything for me. She never even spoke of the desert. I had the feeling she hated it."

"You see, Master Ifimar?" said Spalak. "It is just as I told you. He is indifferent to his blood."

Kandri turned: the Submaster stood just behind Tebassa's soldiers. His body was rigid and his face hard with judgment. Kandri found himself enraged. *Why do you care, you pious prick?*

"Enough, Spalak," said Jód. "You have amply conveyed your feelings in this matter."

"To you alone, Master—" Spalak made the slightest bow. "—and glad I am to hear you say so, for I confess I thought you had not heard me."

"You will hold your tongue, Submaster," said Jód.

Spalak's gaze swept over the caravan. "I tell you, this boy has hacked away his roots—roots that run deep in faith and virtue. He is without father, family, or God."

A swell of dismay flowed among the drivers, as those who spoke better Common translated for those who did not. Then Uncle Chindilan rose to his feet. He took his time about it, but as he faced Spalak his body seemed to glow with rage.

"Without a family?" he said quietly. "I'd like to know what in all the blood-slicked halls of hell you mean by that."

"I mean what I say," Spalak answered.

"Fah," said Kereqa. "This bickering is beneath us. Why let it continue, Master Ifimar?"

But Jód remained silent. He appeared more deeply shocked than at any moment of their journey. He gazed at Spalak as he might a perfect stranger.

"I'll thank you to restrict your comments to your own offspring," said Chindilan. "As for me, I swore to guard these two in their father's absence, and to the best of my poor powers, I've done so. Whether the Gods have smiled or cursed us I'll leave to them."

"Do you expect the Gods to applaud your forbearance, ironmonger?" asked Spalak.

"Now now, gentlemen!" said Stilts, tossing the stub of his cheroot into the fire. "Let's not forget that we've all just filled our faskas from the same well, reeking though it is. And we've not done badly as a team in the Sumuridath—reeking though we are."

Loud laughs of relief. Even Chindilan managed a smile, although Spalak and Jód still glowered in silence. *Bless you, Stilts,* thought Kandri.

From the outer ring of onlookers, the surgeon called out testily: "What's it to you, Naduman? What's your point?"

Stilts raised his eyebrows. "Merely that songs are better than arguments," he said, "especially for companions of the road."

"Companions!" groused the surgeon. "A better word might be 'millstones.'"

"What is there to argue?" said Spalak. "The boy's soul is adrift, and I alone am willing to say so. He hangs above the Pit of Damnation, with no help from any of you—least of all his brother."

He spoke the last word with naked scorn. Mektu exploded to his feet. "I *am* his brother, you camel-fucked old cunt, and I'll slice you open like a Gods-damned jacket potato if you insult him again. Kandri's soul's worth a thousand of yours, *hara bachim*, you don't know the first fucking thing."

Kandri, dread swamping his mind, threw his arms around Mektu and hauled him back. Everyone had risen. The beads on Spalak's earring gleamed in the firelight. This was a gifted killer, not a lumbering mercenary. Against him, Mektu would stand little chance.

Spalak was jeering: "*I* do not know? Listen, fool: all the fiends in Jekka's Hell are laughing at you, roaring at the infernal jest! I am not the one raised in ignorance here! Tell me, Mektu Hinjuman, how long have you believed that he is—"

"Spalak," said Jód, "kneel and bare your neck."

If the silence a moment before had been unsettling, now it was terrible. Spalak gazed at the Master in disbelief. The soldiers gripped their sword hilts, watching for Kereqa's signal. The drivers backed away from the fire.

Jód's eyes were burning. "You are not deaf, I think."

"My words were vulgar, Master Ifimar," said Spalak, "but no less true for all that. The boy must be reconsecrated, he is a beacon for all the ills that spawn beneath Urrath, there is nothing for it but to—"

"Am I the Master of the Ways?" said Jód.

Spalak checked himself. "You are the Master of the Ways," he said at last.

"Kneel," repeated Jód, "and bare your neck."

Spalak looked a long time at Ifimar Jód. At last, with stiff dignity, he dropped to his knees.

He unwound his headscarf first, then spread wide his traveling cloak. His neck was bare now, save for a thin cord of leather that vanished beneath his shirt. He closed his eyes and stretched his arms out straight to either side. Whether the gesture meant acceptance or defiance Kandri could not tell.

Jód reached over his shoulder and drew his black sword.

"Master, don't!" cried Ulren shrilly. "*Aebris Sredereb*, you'll curse us all, spilling family blood—"

Jód pointed the blade at Spalak's neck. He gave a sharp thrust, and a wail escaped the drivers. But Spalak himself did not so much as wince. The Master had not harmed him—not physically. His sword had merely lifted the leather thong about Spalak's neck and cut it like a blade of grass.

Jód put his hand inside Spalak's shirt and lifted something away. It was an amulet, simple but striking: a circle of blood-red stone. Inlaid in silver upon it was a single word in flowing script.

Jód raised the amulet above his head. "The *Athzimazl Joridur*," he cried for all to hear, "second highest of all honors in my line of Parthans. Thirty years ago, Spalak, my father placed this about your neck himself. And on me he laid the solemn duty to observe your adherence to its code. To tender further honors as you earned them, as I have done many times. Or to strip you of the Athzimazl, if you strayed.

"So you have done tonight. Within the confines of the desert, you are sworn to obey me without exception. You have bent or resisted my orders several times on this journey, but for these I chose not to punish you, thinking your own conscience would be punishment enough. I was wrong. You have scorned my authority before the whole of the train, with no excuse but passion. Do you recall my father's words, Spalak, from so long ago? Speak them, if ever they held weight for you."

Spalak remained kneeling, eyes tightly shut. After a moment, he said, "'Passion excuses nothing—unless we would allow it to excuse everything. In the desert, mastery of self divides the living from the dead.'"

"You remember," said Jód, "but you are an oath-breaker all the same. By the oldest laws of our people, your blood is mine to harvest, your flesh mine to bury or to burn."

Kandri's nails bit into his palms. The drivers stood frozen in terror. Jód raised his sword high behind his head.

And secured it across his back.

"A lifetime of honor may be lost in a night," he said, "but not my honor. I love thee yet, Spalak. I hold your life in escrow—your life and your Athzimazl. For what remains of this journey you are stripped of rank and privilege. What is lost may be earned anew, in time. But you must not stray again."

He tied a knot in the leather thong and slipped it over his own head. "Brother," he said, "do you wish to speak?"

Brothers! thought Kandri. *Of course they are!* How had he not seen it? Jód was the elder by ten years at least—but the likeness was there in the eyebrows, the cheekbones, even the words they spoke. Above all, in the two men's comprehension of each other, a knowledge deeper than love or hate.

Spalak's eyes gleamed in the firelight. "I have been a fool," he said. "Your warning shames me. It is more than I have earned. Tonight you have stripped me of a terrible burden."

"Then there is no more to be said," Jód declared. "Rise and help Ulren review the camp perimeter. And let all to whom rest is permitted seek it now."

◌§

"Kandri?"

"..."

"Kandri? Brother?"

"..."

"You awake?"

"Gods, Mek, how could there be a stupider fucking question, you poke me, you lie there whispering my name—"

"I can't sleep either, Kandri. I can't stop thinking about that bastard Spalak. What came over him? Why was he talking about your soul?"

"*Harach.* He's a zealot. He was schooled by some sort of priest. I don't know what God he follows, or why he latched onto me. But I know I'm exhausted."

"He's the one, he's the Prophet's spy. I told you from the start that I suspected him."

"No, Mek. No way in Hell. Spalak's mad as a moon calf, but if he were a follower of the Prophet he'd just kill me. He'd never for one minute think my soul could be saved."

"Do you think he's in love with you?"

"I think you're flinging ideas around like chicken feed. Stop talking. Uncle will kick you if you wake him up."

"I'm not always wrong, Kandri."

"I know that. Just almost always."

"Eshett is a little better each day."

"I know."

"So you see? I didn't kill her when I took the mattoglin. She's going to heal, become herself again. And then she'll know why I had to take it. And we'll be all right, the three of us. And Uncle."

"I hope so, Mek."

"But no more jokes about being her lover."

". . ."

"Kandri?"

"You sleep with it, don't you? You sleep with that mattoglin against your chest. You're fondling it right now, as we speak."

"Don't you ever touch it, Kandri. It's too late for that. Too late for anyone to help me—you, Eshett, anyone. In the end I'll lay it down by myself."

"What do you mean, in the end?"

"When the time comes, I'll know."

CR

That night a driver strayed from the camp. Perhaps he was sleepwalking; perhaps he had a bone to pick with one of the drivers on watch. No one afterward could say. He had walked barely twenty feet from the encampment when the hyortus rose like silent demons from the brush and flung themselves on him from three sides. His screams tore the night wide open. Kandri

432

heard the frenzied snapping and tearing of the animals' work as he and scores of others charged into the brush.

The hyortus fled before the onslaught, but not without torn mouthfuls of the man, who lay mauled and thrashing, his face only recognizable as such by its position above his throat. How to help him, how even to begin? They did not have long to wonder; in seconds the man lay still.

It was the start of an avalanche of misfortunes. A second driver stepped on an emerald-green scorpion at first light while searching for a place to bury the first. The surgeon's drugs proved ineffective; he died moaning and shaking and was buried beside the man without a face. They left the accursed spot as soon as the ceremony was over; the drivers sang a long prayer of mourning as they walked.

By dusk they were much higher in the mountains, but still the vegetation grew thick. It was then that one of the soldiers who had come with Stilts noticed a pair of woolly leaves stuck to his trousers, and bent to brush them off.

"Ouch!" he cried, jerking back his hand. "Those aren't leaves, they're bloody—"

He fainted dead away.

"Sleepworm, sleepworm!" cried a driver, pointing.

"Blood of Ang, wake the blighter up!" shouted Ulren. "Hurry! Now!"

Already the victim's hand had begun to swell. His fellow soldiers shook him and slapped his cheeks, but he slept on.

"*Glah*, you blunderers!" Ulren shoved his way forward and stomped on the victim's crotch. The fallen man gasped and curled into a ball. The nearest soldiers lifted Ulren from the ground.

"Swill hog! Lay him down! Give him a taste of what he just dished out!"

Then the crowd parted: Ifimar Jód had arrived, followed closely by the surgeon. "*Zamgur*," said the Master. "I have never seen the swelling advance so quickly—release Ulren; he has saved the man, if that is still possible. Surgeon, quickly—"

"I *am* moving quickly." The surgeon rummaged in his medical bag. "Ah, damnation, there he goes."

For once more the victim was asleep. Kneeling, the surgeon drew a needle from his bag and jabbed the soft flesh beneath the victim's eye. This time the soldier woke with a scream. When his eyes managed to focus he found his comrades pinning him to the earth, the surgeon fastening a tourniquet, and his entire forearm bloated like a grotesque yam. Above him, Ifimar Jód raised his sword.

"*No, NO—*"

The sword fell. The cut was clean. "No other way," shouted Jód over his howls. "The zamgur's poison was racing swift in your blood, and already your eyes were closing again. From that sleep there would have been no waking."

"Another worm in the brush here," said Talupéké, crouching and pointing with her knife. "And Jekka's Hell, a third—watch your step, Uncle."

"Don't I always?" said Stilts.

Talupéké squinted at the brush. Suddenly her eyes went wide and she leaped to her feet.

"Get back! Get back! The ground's boiling with the fuckers!"

ఴ

The worms covered an area the size of a lake, but by good fortune they had not walked far into the lake. Only one other driver was bitten, and she had the presence of mind to amputate her own finger within three seconds of the bite. More blood, more agony; but in the end she lost only the finger. "*Amri taraji*, the Gods are merciful," she declared, smiling as the surgeon bandaged her hand.

He snorted. "Is that what you'd call the bastards who made a place like this?"

All day the trail rose steeply. They marched now in fear of every leaf and stick and bramble, but the day passed without further incident, and the worst that befell them that night was sleeplessness, as they lay listening to the cries of animals and imagining horrors in the underbrush. Lightning danced among the high peaks above them, and once or twice the bolts struck nearby, and Kandri tasted metal on the wind. The man who had lost his arm lay in a tortured swoon. Talupéké sat up beside him, brushing flies from his stump.

Every hour or so he would wake with a cry, reaching with his good arm for a hand that was no longer there.

The next morning a curtain of smoke cloaked a portion of the sky: somewhere below the hills were on fire. The bone-dry winds spread the fire swiftly: soon a broad crescent behind them was alight. Jód turned them abruptly into the wind, plunging down into an unburned valley and slogging up the far slope.

When at last they reached the new summit, Mektu looked back in disgust. "A five-hour zigzag," he said. "Why the hell are we in these mountains at all? Why didn't we just go around?"

"You heard Jód," said Kandri. "The summer's coming. We're out of time."

"This can't be saving time! Up, down, through cracks and canyons, attacked by animals, poisoned by worms."

"Every time we've second-guessed him we've been wrong," said Chindilan.

"Forget about us," said Mektu. "Look at the drivers: they're miserable. *They* don't think we should be here."

"Who would you rather see in charge?" asked Prince Nirabha. "Spalak, perhaps? Or Ulren?"

It was the rare question to which Mektu could find no retort.

Up and farther up Jód led them, along the sides of red chasms and under cliffs black with iron, red with rust. Through briars they had to attack with machetes. Through stands of trees cracked and stunted but stubbornly alive. The wind surged and gusted: now scorching from the south, now bitterly cold off the towering peaks of the Inner Table.

For ten bewildering minutes they found themselves blinded by a storm of wind-whipped ashes. Something about them was not right, however: Kandri felt cool pinpricks where they touched his skin. He studied his palm. Not ashes, but a dry crystalline snow.

"Now I've seen everything," said Kandri, as the flakes collected like crushed glass on rocks, camels, cacti. But Spalak, who had taken to walking close to him, responded with a thoughtful shake of his head.

23. LAMPS IN THE DARKNESS

T hen all at once salvation beckoned. They rounded the blunt horn of a mountain and saw the land beyond it falling away in vast pleats and folds of rock—down, down, all the way to open sand. The descent looked longer but somewhat gentler than the climb had been. Jód had led them over the spine of Famine's Table.

Talupéké clapped a hand on Mektu's shoulder. She nodded to the east, where the mountains marched on nearly to the edge of sight. "That's why we didn't go around, genius. Devil's piss, it's lucky no one listens to you."

"You're right, girly!" shouted Ulren, voice shrill in the wind. His eyes were merry with relief. "Master Ifimar's done it again! And the news is better than you know. He's got a bearing on the path to the Font of Lupriz."

"A bearing?" said Talupéké. "What does that mean? What sort of bearing?"

"Secret, secret!" chortled Ulren. "The Master tells who he likes. What matters is this: it's a mere twelve days from the edge of Famine's Table to the oasis, and the path's as straight as a king's highway, with no rocks or ridges or chasms to go around."

"One mile at a time," said Stilts. "We still have these mountains to escape."

Ulren was not listening. "Twelve days to civilization! Twelve days to those marble baths, and meaty joints on the fire, and them big-arsed

Luprizana girls to scrub away your sorrows, so to speak." He elbowed Mektu in the ribs. "What do you say, Gooney Bird? Scrub-scrub, eh? Scrub scrub scrub."

"You turn my stomach, sir," said the Prince.

"How big, exactly?" Mektu asked.

C8

By late afternoon they had descended nearly halfway. Below them now the ridge divided like fingers on a hand, creating three winding canyons that dropped away steeply toward the sand. There was no obvious difference between them, at least from this height, but Jód stood contemplating the land a long time in the lowering sun. To Kandri it seemed that some stark choice was troubling him: he could not recall such an obvious display of uncertainty in the Master at any time in their journey. Slowly, as though fighting himself, Jód turned and looked over his shoulder.

"Bring Spalak," he said.

The disgraced Spalak was at his side moments later. The brothers spoke in low voices, as Jód pointed to each canyon in turn. Then, just as Kandri had seen him do once before, Spalak laid aside his belongings, weapons included, although this time he kept a cloak against the cold. And this time Jód provided no companion, nor a poison capsule to carry in his mouth. They regarded each other warily. Jód lifted his hands as though to grasp Spalak by the shoulders. Spalak made a hasty bow, and Jód's hands faltered and dropped. Spalak turned and ran swiftly down the ridge.

The caravan descended another hour, to the point where a choice between the canyons was inevitable. It was by now pitch dark, and Jód ordered a beacon fire kindled on a shelf overlooking the canyons to aid in Spalak's return. While drivers and soldiers took what rest they could, Jód paced beside the fire, gazing down into the deep-cut gorges that opened beneath them.

"He can't see anything," said the pensive corporal. "Not until the moons rise, anyway. He's just wasting his strength."

"You want to tell him that?" asked Talupéké.

That night Kandri slept deep and dreamless. He woke but once, and raised his head to see Jód still standing by the beacon fire, telescope in hand, the twin dogs curled at his feet.

You shamed him, thought Kandri, *and now you've sent him off to prove himself, and you're afraid you've sent him to his death. Why does it always go wrong? Why the hell can't brothers be friends?*

Jód was still there at dawn, and now his great telescope stood upon a tripod. As the day brightened he let the fire die, but gave no orders and spoke to no one save Ulren. Hours passed. It was a windless day and the heat grew swiftly, until it felt almost as fierce as the worst days in the open desert. For the first time in the mountains they retreated under the sun-shields. Jód remained by his telescope, barely seeming to breathe.

Late in the afternoon Kandri woke to find Stilts nudging him in the ribs. "Shake off those cobwebs, lad. The Master wants us, and he's none too patient."

Kandri crawled blinking into sun, and he and Stilts made their way through the camels to Jód's shelf. Kereqa, Chindilan, Ulren, and Prince Nirabha were already there. Jód's eyes were red, his face haggard with sleeplessness. When he saw Kandri and Stilts he beckoned them near.

"Some crisis has befallen Spalak," he said. "I feel it, sure as I feel the skin of my palms. I ordered him to assess the safety of the canyons, and to return by dawn at the latest. I sent my owl with a message: she knows Spalak, and would go to him. She has not returned. I go now to seek my brother, but I do not know in which of the three canyons he may be found—and whether the evil that he has encountered may strike us down as well."

"Let's go together, then," said Chindilan.

"Yes," said Kereqa. "We are one company, and should face the danger together."

"Enough," said Jód. "I have spoken."

Stilts cleared his throat. "If it should come to battle, our unit is—"

"*Silence, all of you!*"

Only then did Kandri realize how consumed with dread the Master was. Jód's mouth worked, and it was several moments before he trusted himself to speak again.

"I have known you three these many years. I am aware of your wisdom—and revere you as an elder, Kereqa. But not even you may question my orders. You will stay and watch for our return with the telescope—and you will not linger beyond another sunrise.

"Each day the heat increases, and there is no well between us and the Font of Lupriz. You carry twelve days' water loaded on the camels—twelve, and perhaps a little more. But without my guidance or Spalak's, you may stray from the path, and twelve days may become fourteen, or twenty. With or without us, you must go on."

"Go on *how?*" asked Kandri. "None of us have been here before. It's damn near certain we'll stray from the path."

"Not if you heed me, and pool your wisdom," said Jód. "Bend down and look through the telescope—but do not touch it. I have aimed it with care."

Kandri looked first, crouching before the long scope. He blinked, frowning. Jód had pointed the device at a tall white rock, quite invisible to the naked eye. At such a distance it was blurry and pale, but Kandri thought its form very strange: like a barren, twisted tree capped by a wide saucer.

"That is the Olukru Tsamid, the Pillar of the Night Queen," said Jód.

"Is it indeed!" cried the Prince, delighted. "Let me look, please! All my life I have dreamed of climbing the Olukru Tsamid! In Kasralys we call it the Tower of True Sight."

"That is another of its names," said Jód. "From the summit you may see many things, if you are favored by Her Highness, and the God with whom she intercedes."

"You can't mean that a flesh-and-blood Queen lives on that rock," said Mektu.

"No, not flesh and blood," said Jód, "but neither is she gone. When you step out upon the dais you will understand. For the moment, what matters is this: the Olukru Tsamid stands exactly halfway to Lupriz from this spot, and it is very tall. Whether or not the Queen bestows her gifts, you will from its summit be able to observe the Curtain Rift that marks the northeast shoulder of the Heart Basin—and with a fine scope such as this, the wall of the oasis itself."

"Lupriz is walled, Master?" asked Kereqa.

"You did not know?" said Jód. "Lupriz was once the innermost ward of a mighty city, with ninety fountains for the delight of its people, and herds of goats and cattle and antelope, and irrigated fields. Greater Lupriz is lifeless now, and its outer settlements are dust. But two thousand souls still dwell within the High Court Wall, and the grandest fountains still flow.

"You must make straight for the Olukru Tsamid. Keep it always in sight. And when you reach it, wait there for Siraath the Morning Star, in the hour before dawn. Keep your right shoulder to Siraath until she fades from sight. Walk only so long as you are sure of your course. If doubt assails you, wait for her return. Then you will find the Siramath Stair which climbs the Rift, and the scourge of heat will ease a little. Carry on each day in the same manner, and you cannot help but strike Lupriz—or at worst, the ancient north road out of her, toward Naduma and the Dry Reaches of Shôlupur. That road is marked with cairns and mile-posts for two days' march to either side of the oasis."

Mektu was unimpressed. "I see a rock," he said, "bigger than those around it, and with a weird shape. But still just a rock."

"It must be the Olukru Tsamid and no other that guides you," said Jód. "Study it now, each of you, and commit its shape to memory."

One by one they did as Jód commanded. "I don't like this at all," said Chindilan, after taking his turn. "These gorges are immense, for starters. We'll be days inside them before we can ever glimpse that rock again."

"Three days, approximately," said Jód.

"And they're still part of this wretched Famine's Table, are they not? If you don't return, how are we to choose among them?"

"If I do not return, Mr. Ulren will guide you."

The others groaned aloud. Ulren himself made a sound like a frightened animal. "Master, no!" he said.

"Even you doubt my choice?" said Jód, shaking his head. "Mr. Ulren, this is the hour when you must take yourself in hand. Let Stilts manage his soldiers: heed his guidance if enemies should appear. But the final authority shall be yours."

"I can't!" insisted Ulren. "They're right, Master: Ulren's no good without you. I'd be lost. I'm just a fancy porter, is all."

"No," said Jód, "you are a student of the Sumuridath like myself. Ten crossings have we made together, and you have grown with each. I have been mean with my praise, for your tongue is vulgar, and your fears still work against you. But do not doubt your wisdom, Mr. Ulren. It has been hard earned."

For the first time since meeting the man, Kandri saw Ulren's eyes lose their squint. He stood straighter, his face suffused with wonder. "Master," he said, and then glanced away, too affected to say more. But after a moment he looked shyly at Jód again.

"I know nothing of the canyons, all the same. How would I choose among them?"

"I don't believe you'll have to," said Stilts.

Kandri turned just in time to see a small, swift bird—Jód's pocket owl—flash up out of the canyon. Its tiny wings fanned wide to break its speed. Jód raised his arm, and the bird alighted there without a sound.

The Master stood perfectly still. The owl rolled its head to one side, hopped closer to Jód's elbow, and yawned like a dog after a race.

Jód closed his eyes, and a look of pure serenity stole over his face. "My brother lives," he said. "Safiru has found him alive."

"He's not just alive, Master," said Ulren, pointing. "He's back."

It was true: Spalak was climbing toward them out of the rightmost canyon. After a moment, as though feeling their eyes upon him, he paused and beckoned: *This way.*

CR

"Predators roam the left-hand gorge," Spalak was saying. "Hyortus, and wildcats: I heard their cries from afar. I saw no great threat in the central gorge, but the rockslides there would slow us to a crawl. This one drops severely, but once we descend the way is clear and flat. The walls are high: there will be shade, and perhaps even water. The earth is soft and cool."

They were descending steeply; the camels struggled with the loose scree and shifting cargo. Kandri and Mektu stayed close to their uncle, ready to seize his burly arms if he fell. Just ahead, Spalak went on talking to Jód, describing the differences between the canyons: terrain, footing, vegetation.

Jód cut him off. Why, he demanded, had Spalak not returned as ordered, by dawn?

Spalak looked abashed. He lowered his voice, and Kandri caught only the word "shortcut." Ifimar Jód glanced at his brother, and his eyes said, *You?* But on his face was that rarest of expressions for the Master: a smile.

It was not returned.

CB

Well past midnight they reached level ground. The mountains towered above them, but the canyon's floor was just as Spalak had described it: cool, shaded, flat. All the same it was not a comforting place: the cliffs to either side were sheer and black. The sand underfoot was soft as powder but strangely unstable, as though spread over brittle earth or pockets of air. There were clumps of cacti and small denuded trees. The cries of owls echoed down the canyon.

"I hate owls," said Ripheem.

Mektu glanced at Kandri and winked. "It can talk," he said.

Ripheem started in alarm. He looked at Mektu and growled: "Not so. You lie."

"I meant you, you rhinoceros," said Mektu. "What's wrong with owls? You don't think they're evil, I hope? Did it start with Kasrajis, that foolish old myth?" But Ripheem had taken offense and would say no more.

For the next two days they marched through this shadowy landscape, a blue-black canyon where toads screeched by night and a gossamer mist hovered inches above the earth at dawn. The drivers were frightened of the toads, which rarely let themselves be glimpsed but sang by the tens of thousands.

"Voices of the dead," said Kandri's friend with the clouded eye, speaking low. "They cry to us, they envy us, because we live and they do not. And in addition, they invite us to join them."

"Join them?"

"In the earth. In the song."

"Well I decline," said Kandri. "If there's an afterlife, I don't want to spend it shrieking and squatting on my warty ass."

The driver frowned, perhaps believing he'd been mocked. "Something," he said, "must fill all the hours of death."

လ

Mortal or otherwise, the presence of the toads meant water, and some hours later they found it: a rude well, ancient, corroded, dug by the Gods knew whom. It stank of sulfur but poisoned no one, and though the water smelled of rotten eggs it still revived their spirits. They camped that night beside the well, lighting a small fire of branches gathered from the skeletal trees. The canyon lay silent; even the owls had ceased to call, but Jód posted watches ahead and behind. Kandri drifted off to the sound of gentle laughter from the drivers, and the camels slurping endlessly, ecstatically from their collapsible troughs.

It was perhaps an hour later when he sensed a figure standing by his knees.

He opened his eyes without moving. Eshett. She was shivering; her legs were bare. Someone had given her a sheepskin which she hugged about her torso. The end of her scarf trailed on the ground.

Mektu, six feet away, was snoring like a bull. Kandri's heart leaped. He could have moved his leg and touched her. Eshett was not looking at him, or anyone in particular. Kandri turned his gaze just an inch and saw that Talupéké was wide awake and watching. Eshett looked left and right, bewildered, lost. Then, clumsily, she lay down beside Mektu and burrowed under his cloak.

Kandri lay very still, mind awash in conflicting emotions. His brother still slept with the mattoglin against his chest. Mektu's snoring ceased; he shifted slightly. Eshett whimpered against his back. Mektu, his voice still that of a sleeper, muttered a single word. It sounded like "Mine."

◌

That night Kandri dreamed of a lamp.

It was an immense lamp of ethereal blue, and it bobbed and floated near the ground some thirty feet from where he lay, like a bubble on a gently rocking sea. Its shape was curious: a knobby dome like a tortoise shell, but flexible and large as a haystack.

As he watched, bemused, a second lamp winked to life about ten yards above the first. It descended in a slow, jerky manner that made him want to laugh. A third lamp, barely visible, glowed at a greater height.

A strong breeze was blowing in his dream. The two higher lamps appeared to be struggling against the breeze as they tried to join the first upon the ground. He thought of children reeling in kites. But these kites reeled themselves.

The dream was shattered by cold—a sudden, freakish stab of cold in his left hand. He gasped, wide awake; his muscles spasmed; he tried to jerk the hand away. He could not. The cold had vanished, but so had all sensation in the hand, the wrist, the entire arm.

The camel drivers began to scream.

Kandri leaped up—and barely saved himself from falling. His left arm was dead. He could not move it, and when he clawed at it with his right hand he could not feel his own touch.

"Mek!" he cried out. "Uncle!"

People were running, camels bucking and bellowing. The screams of the drivers increased.

"*Grasthu! Grasthu!*"

The things he had taken for lamps were all around them. More than tortoise shells, he saw now that they resembled jellyfish—monstrous jellyfish, twelve or fifteen of them at least, and still more starting to glow even as he watched. Some had reached the ground; others were still descending. From each creature dangled hundreds of tentacles: long, glassy, translucent tentacles, so clear that they were difficult to see.

The nearest creature bobbed ten feet over Kandri's head. Its tentacles were glued to his lifeless arm.

"Pitfire!"

He leaped away, jerking the creature like a great balloon. Instantly the tentacles contracted, tightening: now the thing was just five feet above him. Kandri's own motion had brought it down toward his head.

"Do not touch it!"

The voice was Jód's. The Caravan Master raged out of the night, brandishing a spark-spitting torch. He lowered the flame until it all but scorched Kandri's wrist—Kandri still felt nothing—and the tentacles glowed like heated wire, and finally snapped.

Jód swept the torch in an arc before him. A wide curtain of tentacles lit up, crackling and burning.

"What are these fucking things?"

"Grasthu, sky nomads," said Jód. "Take the torch."

"Eshett, where is—"

"Take the torch, Hinjuman!"

Kandri seized the torch with his good hand. There were four or five more torches blazing and waving in the dark, and Jód still held one unlit. In his face Kandri saw rage contending with fear—more naked fear than he had ever beheld in the Caravan Master.

Jód reached into his cloak and drew out the owl. "Fly, Safiru, far from these horrors! *Imnath grasti Lupriz.*" He kissed the tiny creature and flung it skyward, where it vanished in an instant. Then he lit the last torch from the one Kandri held.

"Stand with us, boy, we—"

A cry cut him off—a howl, at the last pitch of agony. Thirty feet away, a driver flailed and twisted on the ground as one of the creatures fell upon him. Only his torso still moved; his lifeless arms and legs were tangled in threads like a ruined marionette.

"No!" cried Jód, as Kandri started forward. "*Elumas Ang.* You cannot save him."

The man's scream was like a knife—but the silence an instant later was worse. The grasthu sealed its body around him like a poncho with drawstrings. Kandri could still see the man through its translucent flesh.

Ifimar Jód seized Kandri by the jaw.

"Stand with us! Do not run when I tell the rest to flee. Hold the line. Can I trust you that far, Hinjuman? Tell me, tell me at once."

"You can trust me," said Kandri.

"Burn the threads," said Jód. "Save all the drivers you can. When they are safely away we torchbearers will follow. And never—a thousand times never—lower your torch. One thread upon your torso can stop your breathing, or your heart. Do you hear me?"

But Kandri was looking back along the canyon. The air between the high cliff walls was filled with the creatures. Not scores but hundreds, with more winking to life every second, as if an army of lamplighters were at work. The wind was bearing the whole flood in one direction: right down the gorge and over the caravan.

Jód howled like a captain in a gale: "Upwind! Upwind and out of the canyon! Flee now or perish here!"

The next quarter-hour was like a battlefield rout. The camels stampeded. The drivers bolted after them, snatching up some goods and tripping over others. Those who were unharmed carried their paralyzed comrades or hauled and whipped at limping camels. Kandri saw Mektu and the Prince leading a wild-eyed Eshett away, Ripheem with a driver beneath each arm, Ulren staggering under the weight of a stone-stiff dog. Where was his uncle, or Kereqa, or Stilts?

"Fucking trap," snarled Talupéké, wielding a torch on Kandri's left. "We walked right into this."

Drivers fell, screaming and abruptly silent. Across the canyon, pools of blue light throbbed upon the ground.

In the rearguard, the seven torchbearers fought the grasthu in a ragged line: Kandri, Talupéké, four other soldiers, and Jód. The Master seemed to be everywhere at once, torching grasthu, lifting the fallen to their feet.

"Spalak!" he shouted once, pausing for an instant near Kandri. "Have you seen him? He was walking the perimeter. He volunteered."

No one had seen Spalak, but Kandri saw that the Master himself had suffered some harm or wound. It was not like the paralysis that had seized his own arm, and killed so many. Jód's limbs still functioned, but they were shaking, and he seemed to be fighting to control them.

The torchbearers were ceding ground: they could no more stop the mass of creatures than they could the wind itself. Kandri ran from driver to driver—burning them free, kicking them, shouting at them to run. His eyes stung and his throat felt scorched and raw. His left arm slapped like a dead thing at his side.

And now the screams were coming from behind them as well. In near despair, Kandri realized that the first wave of grasthu must have passed over the camp before any had begun to glow, for they were now descending right in the path of those fleeing for their lives.

"*Tomvé, Mistajavs! Tomvé!*" Jód howled. "Run wide of them!"

Some heard him and were saved. Others ran too close to the landed creatures and stumbled into coiled masses of tentacles. For these poor souls there was nothing to be done: they fell and they died. Kandri saw a driver carried by his own momentum up against the body of one of the grasthu: his legs were paralyzed, but while his upper body yet lived he plunged arms and head into the gelatinous substance, burrowing like a mole, trying to rip the beast apart. When death found him at last he was embedded to the waist.

The fight seemed endless—until suddenly Kandri saw that everyone left alive had fled. Then Jód called to the torchbearers: "Back, fall back! But guard yourselves now most of all!"

They turned and ran, through a ghastly fairyland of the dead. The grasthu that had reached the ground lit their way, and at the heart of each bulbous monster lay a body like a shriveled wick. But none of the torchbearers fell, and after some three miles the canyon walls began to dwindle. Lower and lower they fell, though still sheer-sided. They ran on. Somewhere camels were braying.

Sudden voices: *Master! Here, hurry, climb!*

Atop the north wall some fifty yards ahead, camel drivers waved in a frenzy. *Here, climb here!* Beneath them was a narrow, eroded patch of the cliff wall. It was the gentlest slope yet—gentle enough that it might, just barely, be possible to scale.

Jód turned and shouted: "Do as they say! Drop your torches, you will need both hands! Climb like the devil is after you!"

The torchbearers flung themselves at the wall. The eroded patch was still very steep, and the brittle earth crumbled at a touch. But up they went, the nimbler helping the slow. Kandri saw Talupéké and the pensive corporal hauling Kereqa by her shirt.

The Master himself stood his ground, gazing back along the canyon. Kandri ran to him and was appalled. The shaking in his limbs had worsened. Even his teeth were chattering.

"That's not the grasthu's venom, is it?" shouted Kandri. "No one else has those shakes. What's wrong with you?"

"Mysteries can w-wait," said Jód. "C-climb, boy. You're the last. Do not fall now."

"I'm *not* the last," Kandri shot back.

"Spalak was on the p-perimeter," said Jód, facing the canyon again. "He must have been the f-first to die, or he would have warned us, he—"

Jód's legs buckled. Kandri leaped forward to catch him, but one arm was not enough. They ended up on the ground together. The Master's face was scarred and his beard burned away, but that was not the worst of it. He was shaking uncontrollably.

"My brother—"

"I haven't seen him, I'm sorry. But dying here won't help Spalak."

"R-run. They will b-bury you."

"Shut up and use your legs." Kandri hoisted Jód into a sitting position. "Stand up. You can do this."

Jód bared his teeth. His legs twitched but would not obey him. Kandri rose and gripped the sword-belt across Jód's shoulder. He began to drag the Master toward the wall.

"Leave me, Kandradisurth."

The word shocked Kandri to his core. It was his full name, but no one save his birth-mother had ever used it. Ten years had passed since he had heard it aloud.

Jód smiled, as though pleased by his guess. "P-Parthan name," he said.

Flash of movement: Chindilan was suddenly beside them. "What the living fuck are you doing? Get him up!"

"He's ill."

"Ill? He's about to be a jellyfish snack! We've dropped a rope for him—take his other arm, boy, hurry! The soldiers will haul him up."

Kandri bent low to the ground and twisted his shoulder under Jód's, then reached around with his good arm and managed to catch Jód's trembling hand.

"Kandradisurth," said the Master, "my brother's son."

A kind of void opened under Kandri's knees. He was falling without motion, into a black space without anchor or reason. Beside him, Uncle Chindilan gaped.

"Your m-mother," said Jód, "came to us with a child already in her womb."

Kandri shook his head no.

"Spalak's child," said the Master. "He fathered you, though he was barely a man."

"You're fucked in the head."

Jód did not seem to hear him. "To the Rasanga, he was a plaything. A bit of clay to shape and fill with their madness. An experiment."

They raised him, staggering. The grasthu were within a hundred feet.

"Spalak g-gave himself to the Prophet," said Jód, "and Uthé wanted no part of that faith. Not for herself or her child. This—" He passed his eyes over the devastation around them. "—is what she was f-fleeing. What she and Lantor hoped to spare you, when I married them in the s-sight of all."

"No."

"I speak only the truth, n-nephew."

"Shut your lying mouth!"

They ran. Jód's quaking feet dragged between them. Kandri's chest felt all wrong and his hearing distorted. *You are not my uncle. The man on your other arm is my uncle.*

"It was fated," said Jód. "I knew it the m-morning you caught up with the caravan. Just as Spalak knew you, Kandradisurth. Knew you at f-first glance for his son."

A rope dangled at the foot of the canyon wall. Chindilan whipped it fast around Jód's torso and tied a tiller's hitch. The Master put a hand on Kandri's cheek.

"My brother was c-cured of his madness," he said. "Years ago. He s-swore it to our mother and father. He swore it to *me*."

"Why the hell do you think I care?"

The wave towered above them, ready to break. "Raise him!" bellowed Chindilan. The drivers responded instantly, and Jód began to rise. Kandri and Chindilan followed, fighting their way up the slope, under the shower of earth dislodged by the Master.

"He was cured!" Jód shouted above them. "By the b-blood of the desert saints, he was f-free!"

I don't hear you. Kandri clawed at the dirt with his one good arm. *I never want to hear you again. Lantor is my father, and Chindilan my uncle, and Mektu, Mektu is—*

The shouting of the drivers spiked to horrified screams. What was happening? The rain of dirt made it impossible to lift his eyes. But the dirt abruptly ceased.

A spear, Kereqa's spear, was embedded in the Master's chest. His shaking hands closed on it weakly. His eyes lowered to the canyon floor, and for a moment Kandri was certain that they saw him. And then they closed.

"Free?" said a voice behind him. "Yes, brother, I am. Set free by the Prophet's truth, though I struggled long years to see it."

Spalak.

"I told you by the fire, did I not? You took away my greatest burden, when you shamed me before them all. You let me abandon you, abandon the lying ways that have kept me chained to you, under you, from birth."

Kandri looked down at the man: tall, deranged, not a wound on his body. Spalak turned from his brother and met Kandri's eye. He was smiling.

"Come to me, Kandradisurth," he said. "We will start your life anew. I see it now: you are innocent; this is all a vast mistake. You never killed our Prophet's son. That is unthinkable. You are the child of my seed!"

The screams above them reached a fever pitch. "Climb," hissed Chindilan.

"It was the other boy," said Spalak. "The slovenly ape, the yatra-tortured, the fool with the heart of a jackal. It was him, is that not so? Him, or that fat old sinner at your side? But not you. Not my own flesh and blood."

Spalak's eyes, chin, cheekbones. Time-scarred, desert-burned, madness-twisted. And in spite of all of that, his own.

Climb! Climb! shrieked the drivers.

"I killed Ojulan," said Kandri, eyes swimming with tears. "Mektu wasn't even there."

Spalak's face twitched. "Defend the ape no longer. Come to your true family, your true home, and the home of all pure souls. Come home to the Prophet, and to me."

"You just killed your own brother," said Kandri. "Come to you? Only with a Gods-damned blade."

A voice cried out suddenly from above them. "Kill him, kill Dothor Spalak! Shoot down that deceitful prick!"

It was, of all people, the surgeon. As if in answer, rocks began to fly, and an arrow missed Spalak by an inch. With a last sharp look at Kandri, Spalak turned and ran into the dark.

"*Aida!*" screamed the drivers. "*Now, climb, now!*"

As though slapped awake, Kandri and Chindilan turned and clawed up the last fifteen feet. Hands reached down and hauled them to safety just as the unthinkable bright mass of creatures flooded the gorge.

03

They passed in their silent thousands, balloon-bodies level with the travelers, poisoned threads below. Kandri watched them, reeling. Further east, the diminished gorge fell away to nothing, and the grasthu dispersed like an infinity of marbles upon the plain. He had never dreamed of such horror. Or such beauty. It felt wrong, indecent, that they were one and the same.

Jód was dead and they were leaderless. The drivers held one another and wept. Spalak had corrupted six others, they said: all had escaped on the far

451

side of the canyon, taking a number of camels as well as water and food. But where Spalak would lead them none could say.

The furthest creatures began to wink out, snuffing their inner lamps. No reason to signal each other now. No more feast to announce. Kandri stood rooted to the spot, gazing in the direction Spalak had fled. *Come to me. Come home to the Prophet. We will start your life anew.*

Ten feet away, Ulren squatted on his heels by the canyon's edge, hugging himself and staring at the spot where Jód had died. Only yesterday Jód's compliments had seemed to increase his stature; now he had shrunk into a ball one might have slipped under one's arm without noticing the weight.

Kandri felt a hand on his shoulder.

"He would only have killed you, lad."

It was Stilts. The Naduman had a red welt on his forehead like a spare eyebrow.

"A mere follower of the Prophet can't gainsay her judgments, and she'd declared you and Mektu abominations before all the world. As a matter of fact, it was probably a toss-up whether to aim that spear at you or the Master."

"Why didn't he choose me?"

Stilts looked down on the dispersing creatures. "I don't know, Hinjuman. Maybe because underneath all the talk of holiness and heaven's will, this was personal. Because Jód had hurt him and you had not."

Kandri shook his head. "There was more to it than that. Much more. He has these mad ideas about me."

"As fathers will about their sons," said Stilts.

"So you heard him."

Stilts shook his head. "No one above could hear him, through all the cries and bellows. Your uncle confided in me just now, and then wished he had not. I think he will tell no one else."

"Mektu—"

"Has no idea," said Stilts, "and if you take my advice you'll not breathe a word for the moment. Don't rush, or speak to him in panic. The moment will come."

Kandri kneaded the muscles in his left arm, which was slowly coming back to life. Behind them the prayers had started. The death-rites, in the

Mistajavs' tongue. They had been sung so often Kandri felt he knew them by heart, though every word remained a mystery.

"The drivers are swapping tales," said Stilts. "Jód talked about these grasthu creatures with them, late at night on other journeys. Their eggs fall from the sky like pollen. Like a fine, dry rain. The young hatch and grow beneath the sand, until they join together in a thick mat of bodies, ten inches buried, miles in extent. And then one night the weight of prey walking above them stimulates the final stage. Their bodies produce a gas that lifts them skyward, where they hunt as a pack."

"We . . . walked over them?"

"As Spalak knew we would, when he chose this canyon. This was no accident, Kandri. He meant for everyone to die—everyone but his converts—and he might have succeeded, if whatever poison he slipped Jód had worked as intended."

"Those shakes," said Kandri. "Jód *was* poisoned. I thought so."

"A strange and terrible poison, whatever it was. He was nearly in seizure, there at the end. But he fought through it long enough to save the caravan."

"How many dead?" asked Kandri.

"Eighteen," said Stilts, "counting the Master himself."

"But what in Jekka's Hell had these people ever done to Spalak?"

"Helped you escape, that's what," said Talupéké, coming up on Kandri's left. "You and your brother. Which meant we'd sinned against the Prophet too."

Kandri knew she was right, and the knowledge was like a blade in his ribs. *Eighteen dead for the Brothers Hinjuman. Eighteen more.*

"He never liked us soldiers," said Talupéké. "He must have thought we were lost from the start. But not the drivers. Right, great-uncle?"

"Not the drivers," Stilts agreed. "They were Parthans; they knew the desert and its mysteries. They were a spiritual people. In his madness I suppose he decided that they were ready for the message of the Prophet. Some were. Most were not. The majority, I expect, could not have cared less."

"And that made him madder than a kettle of hornets," said Talupéké.

"He almost told you, Kandri, that night by the fire," Stilts went on. "Jód stepped in at the last minute, stripping him of his rank. Perhaps that was his breaking point. Spalak had become nothing in the order of the caravan, so the caravan became nothing to him. Just a moving clot of sinfulness, a great angry—"

"Boil," said Kandri.

"Exactly," said Stilts, "a boil to be lanced."

Talupéké leaned her forehead against her great-uncle's chest. It was the most vulnerable gesture Kandri had ever witnessed in the girl, and to his surprise he found he envied her. *I've lost my family*, he wanted to tell them. Knowing that was mostly nonsense. Knowing it was partly, mercilessly, true.

Mektu. Chindilan. They would rethink their memories, change their hearts. Shift him sideways a little. Not on purpose, not because they thought they should. It would just happen. They would shift him away from themselves and toward these spiritual monsters, these Spalaks and Jóds.

Help me, thought Kandri. But he had no idea to whom in Urrath he could address the plea.

"Look," said Talupéké, "it's morning at last."

A blazing citrus-slice of sun edged over the horizon, and the first clear beams lit their faces—bruised, burned, filthy, glad to be alive.

Ulren still crouched at the canyon's edge, gazing down into darkness. Kandri had yet to see him move. But here was Mektu, of all people, walking up to Jód's deputy and extending his hand.

Ulren turned his head. Derision, then bald hatred, broke out upon his face. His expression was so utterly savage that Mektu began to back away.

"Never mind then," he said.

But Ulren was not finished. Unfolding his limbs, he rose and started after Mektu. His teeth were bared and his breathing ragged. He drew a knife, and Kandri thought of the sheer power the Prophet had tapped with her curse, how there was no knowing where the fire of such hatred started, or what rain might ever extinguish it, or how much of the world it would consume before the end.

Ulren's pursuit of Mektu brought him at length into the sunlight. Then in a soundless, sand-colored blur a creature alighted on his forearm.

It was Safiru, Jód's pocket owl. It looked Ulren up and down and folded its wings primly and closed its eyes against the glittering dawn.

Ulren gaped at the tiny creature. Mektu, with slow and careful step, closed the gap between them and plucked the knife from Ulren's fingers. Casting it aside, he placed his hand on Ulren's shoulder. Ulren snarled and tried to shrug off the touch, and failing, broke down into long, loud sobs that rang across the land.

೫

There were no bodies to collect, only skeletons, and these collapsed to loose bones when moved: cartilage, like flesh, had melted away. Even the bones they dared not touch: the grasthu had left them steeped in their acidic bile. Gingerly they raked the bones onto cloaks and canvas and dragged them to a place near the mouth of the canyon. When all seventeen drivers were tumbled together on a mound of brush, they placed Jód's bones among them.

"Rest here in your mother desert, Master of the Ways," said Ulren, toneless and faltering, translating the Parthan prayer. "Rest with your brothers and sisters, and be comforted. Sleep in the peace of a land eternal. Forever will the stars watch over you. Forever will the wind cry your name."

Mektu handed him a torch, and Ulren thrust it into the mound. Like the tentacles, the bile of the creatures burned hotter than pitch, but the smoke was caustic and drove them back from the pyre.

"Remember that smell, all of you," said Ulren, raising his voice. "It's the smell of Spalak's treachery. Master Ifimar always knew he was rotten inside. But the Master himself was chained to the man, chained by an accident of blood. Doomed, because that villain was his brother."

Stilts came forward, holding Jód's black sword in a swaddling cloth. He made to throw the weapon on the fire, mouthing a prayer of his own it appeared. But the drivers cried for him to stop.

"Next of kin, Mr. Stilts! We will clean the sword. We will bear it to Jód-kul-Rumir, home of the Master's people in the Far Fehinj. Do not give it to the flames!"

"Next of kin?" said Stilts, raising an eyebrow. Kandri, choked on clashing feelings, quickly turned his back.

"Right, hide it away then," said Stilts. "We'll give it a proper cleansing at the Font of Lupriz."

Nine camels had died too, and they burned these where they lay. They had also lost Tana-Dog, but never found her remains: she appeared to have vanished without a trace. Loud and long they called her, whistling and clapping. Her litter-mate Dowi whimpered and paced.

When at last the flames had no more to feed upon, a keening cry rang out across the wastes. It was Safiru, perched on the shoulder of a camel. Since daybreak the little bird had stayed close to Ulren. Kandri had never before heard its voice, and now that he did he thought it full of heartbreak, as though the owl knew quite well what it had lost. When it finished, Safiru leaped from the camel into the air and sped away to the east.

Ulren, looking aged and careworn, watched the owl disappear. "She'll not be back," he said. "She came to me out of courtesy, but I'm not of the Master's line. She will become a wild creature again."

"Jód's blood may not be yours," said Kereqa, "but his burden and his honor have passed to you all the same. We are in your hands now, Caravan Master."

All eyes turned to Ulren. For a moment he flinched, like a man waiting to be pelted with fruit. Then he drew a deep breath and raised his chin.

"Stow the faskas, and check the seals twice over. No wells between here and Lupriz. Bring me the telescope. And ready yourselves for walking. In five minutes we quit this corner of hell."

24. AGATHAR'S BARGAIN

One day before the Great Host of Shôlupur marched on Kasralys, Therel Agathar bent his nose to a bucket of turquoise-blue squid.

"That is yesterday's catch," he declared.

The fishmonger's eyes widened. "It is not, begging your pardon, Magnus General. Unloaded it my own self this morning, with my sons."

"Hmm."

"*Hmm*, sir? You wound me, I declare. The boys fried some of this catch up for breakfast and swore it was the best of the season. You can ask them."

"No doubt I could," said Agathar, and both men laughed.

Morning in the Port of Nebusul: lowered sails, sullen prostitutes, dogs fighting over fish heads. As a child, he would meet Obekri here at sunrise to watch the fishermen bring in their magic hauls: barnacled, brine-reeking nets overflowing with agate fish, halo fish, ribbon fish tangled like noodles, scarlet rays, salimanju crabs with their blue-flame eyestalks, deadly twelve-foot spinefish, alive and thrashing as they struck the pier.

It was still his favorite place in Nebusul, despite the sadness that came with any thought of Obekri, and the miasma of fish guts fermenting in the heat. And Sulmurg's people, of course: both the common goons who dogged

Agathar's heels and the well-trained spies he never saw but whose presence he felt like an ache in his bones.

Simple enough to guess their orders. *Stop and question anyone he speaks to. Leap on anyone to whom he tries to pass a note. If he deposits a letter, returns a tea cup, drops a scrap of paper, retrieve it. Never, never let him be alone.*

Agathar grimaced. The mere thought of Sulmurg's voice put his teeth on edge.

For forty years the Inquisitor had suspected that Agathar was a traitor. Now, for the first time in all those years, that vile suspicion had become a truth. Agathar, the traitor. Is that how history would remember him? Agathar the turn-coat, who betrayed his people's love. Agathar the deceiver, who smuggled out a letter of warning to the enemy before the great siege could begin.

Esteemed Foe,

It would be vain to hope that you remember me. Thirty years ago this autumn, your operatives slipped unseen across the Line of Blood in Otheym and slew the whole of our forward command, leaving the battalion decapitated. In later years I had occasion to collect accounts of that day. What emerged was a picture of a sortie astonishing for both audacity and execution, and one that very nearly changed the course of the war. That the Scarlet Kingdom at last fought you to a draw we may attribute to our superior numbers, and perhaps a lucky purchase of baryc halberds from Wostryl, but not to our intelligence. Ten years later we met at the Peace of the Pilgrimage. Alas, my oath prevented me from raising matters of the battlefield, past or present. We were tasked with concluding a treaty, your team and mine. We failed and parted in acrimony, and never again have I set foot in Kasralys. But I longed then and ever afterward to offer my compliments, warrior to warrior. Your tactical gifts are manifest, but more important, I am sure, was the training you gave your young operatives, who passed among us like wolves among so many short-legged, fat-arsed kennel dogs. Their quickness and clarity of purpose taught me more in an instant than I had learned from years in military academies. I pray now that you will grasp my own purpose, and my sincerity. Only then may I hope that you will believe what I must say.

Of course it would mean his death if that letter was intercepted. He didn't care. His position in Shôlupur gave him a chance—vanishingly small, but real—to prevent the worst of the horrors to come. How would he be remembered if he failed to try?

The Scarlet Kingdom is marching on Kasralys, sir. It has marshaled a force beyond description, a force against which you have never been tested. It has emptied its coffers. It has united the Shôl under the toxic banners of grievance and revenge. And Colonel: it has resolved to prevail whatever the cost, even if that should require a campaign of starvation lasting a decade. My study of history is a serious one. I swear to you now upon all that is most holy: this siege will be unprecedented. Your walls and your mountain will long protect you. Cebiru and Fehinj may answer your call and march to your aid. The brilliance of your best minds will position you to win certain battles, whatever the odds. The courage of your people will give them strength. All will fail you in the end. And when the Scarlet Guard at last enters fair Kasralys, it will rampage, and three thousand years of learning and beauty will be lost in a day.

"Magnus General," said one of his minders, sidling close, "the Lord Larisalt is waiting."

"Does he spoil if left out in the sun?" said Agathar.

He did not know why the King's chosen Siege Commander required his presence—at the naval port, of all places. What could be the agenda? A last speech, a last chance to weld them together in the public mind? Never, never. He would give no speeches with Larisalt. Let the man blather alone. But to refuse to appear at all would invite confrontation, and traitors could not afford such risks.

I write of your defeat not with pride but with measureless sorrow. A piece of my heart has dwelt in Kasralys since childhood, when I sat down by a small fountain in Runa District and heard the song of the mountain thrush. That boy saw in an instant through the veil of lies he had been told about your people. And the old man he has become—he has no choice but to see through the veil of seductive hopes. Your doom approaches: that is the plain and shameful truth. But another truth is that I retain a certain influence with King Grapahir. I have struck a bargain with the blood-crazed man: if I give him his wretched victory within a year of our departure for the field, he will forbid the sacking of Kasralys. Your lives shall be guaranteed, your homes sacrosanct, your constables left to manage the daily life of the city without interference. Disarmament and disbanding of your army will be swift, but only enough of our own troops will enter the city to oversee the process. You will become a territory of the Scarlet Kingdom, but the great life of the city will go on. I do not pretend that this is justice. I have done all within my power to prevent this war altogether. Nothing will prevent it, sir. To us who love peace there remains only to limit the carnage.

"Give me three squid, then," he told the fishmonger, gesturing at the bucket, "but from a few inches down; none of that fly-strewn mess on top. And a pair of crabs. The Gods alone know when I'll next dine from the sea."

"Their justice is our ruin, sir."

"Even so," agreed the general, smiling. A fishmonger who quoted the Third Epistle of Shôlmnur. Perhaps when this madness was over he could come to love the capital again. *Their justice is our ruin.* Agathar's glance flickered skyward. *What form of justice will you impose on us this time? Defeat and carnage? Victory and carnage? Or some fate too strange to foresee?*

The Gods, as usual, were pleased to answer but not to translate; they spoke in the wail of the seabirds, the sharp wind off the Actumian, those blinding, backlit clouds.

What use is this letter, you may justly ask? Why do I alert you now, rather than launch this ultimatum from the battlefield? My answer is simple. I wish to be believed. My King would call this letter high treason; I hope you will call it honesty. I wish you to know that it was I who extracted this concession from Grapahir, and I who will stay and see that it is honored. If you doubt me—if you wish to destroy me—you have only to send it back with a messenger to any member of the Scarlet Court. I am forevermore in your hands.

When the call for surrender comes, think of this letter. Think of me, and summon all your courage, and persuade your Grand Illim to save his city. A Kasralys under the flag of the Shôl may yet prosper, but a Kasralys without living Kasrajis is nothing: a memory, a tomb.

The fishmonger handed over his purchase, tied up in rubber leaves. He waved off Agathar's coins.

"Don't insult me, pray! I'll not take a bent penny, not from our King's favorite on the eve of war." They bickered amiably, but the fishmonger prevailed: he would brag all week that his goods were fit for Therel Agathar.

Deep brass notes on the harbor breeze. "That's eight bells, Magnus General," said Sulmurg's man.

"Keep nagging and I'll go back for flounder," said Agathar.

The man sputtered; Agathar forged through the crowd. Vendors, sailors, stevedores bowed and grinned at him, and whispered prayers for victory. When they saw (or smelled) his purchase they tried to bury him in further fish. "Skies, no!" he said. "You'll finish me off before the war begins!" They laughed, they loved him. They pushed each other from his path.

Of course it was all a ruse, this old-man-in-the-market act. He'd not come here for fish but to confirm that his treason had been accomplished, his letter dispatched.

The common folk have it right, sir: the Darsunuk, the Time of Madness, is upon us. But in the oldest tales the Darsunuk is not simply an unfortunate moment. It is the prelude to the Darthrod-Dnn, the Sunless Time, when order and reason perish outright, and the light of learning dims, and all the glories of Urrath end in the stomachs of jackals and ghouls.

"Commit to a plan," you once advised your city, "or suffer the chaos that must engulf you in the absence of a plan."

I grope now toward a plan of survival—for Kasralys, for the Shôl, for all the people of Urrath. Will you help me, Colonel? Will you take the hand of this old enemy, who lives now for a future he will never see?

In Desperate Faith,
Therel Agathar

It was a good letter, and a well-chosen recipient: one Colonel Nefiru, "the Barrister" as he was known. A legend in Kasralys—but old now, so very old. Ten years Agathar's senior, and twenty retired from service to the Seventh Realm. A man renowned for both his wartime brilliance and his ethical commitments. A man Agathar hoped would grasp the strangling paradox he faced himself: that sometimes the only way to love one's country was to betray it.

He had considered reaching out to Colonel Nefiru before. Caution had always stayed his hand. He thought of the old warrior like a sack of rice—good lowland rice, set aside in a tin-lined pantry, unspoiled, out of the reach of rats. *Commit, commit to a plan.* He would have but one chance with this old enemy, and the time had come.

Yes, it has come at last. For you, Nefiru, and for my couriers.

Agathar scanned the crowd. His old heart was thumping like a sparrow's, but his smile remained serene. Lord Sulmurg had not managed to purge all his allies. General Kimburac was dead, and Baron Morsu hustled off to the March of Thieves, but there were others. Persons of less influence but equal courage. Persons Agathar had trained for just such an emergency.

There she was. That young woman, first of his miracle-workers. Small, plump, pockmarked. Loading her wagon, watched by her stolid mule.

Look away, look away at once. Don't give a crumb to Sulmurg's beasts. The least hint of recognition could condemn her to torture and death.

The young woman, his courier, was a widow at twenty-one. She took shellfish to buyers in South Nebusul, then climbed into the hills beyond the city, her wagon heaped with chirimoya and serpent apple and other lowland fruits. On her return the wagon would be loaded with wool, hams, honeycomb in season. A tradeswoman. One of the invisible thousands who scratched out a living on the roads.

But among her customers was a certain farmer who lived alone on a spur road beyond a network of weedy ponds. A veteran, lame and nervous. And a keeper of messenger cranes.

It was an all-but-lost art, crane-keeping. Also a dangerous one. The wild cranes had nine-foot wingspans and beaks that could spear a human chest as easily as a fish. But the juveniles were strangely pliant. Captured and treated kindly, they would allow their keepers to rewrite the fly-routes inscribed in their memories. Of course the effort depended on a second crane-keeper in a distant land noticing the leg-tag, recapturing the bird, and working with equal skill and patience to convince it that *Here, here is the destination you sought, here alone is the haven you have always known you needed.* It took years. It often failed. But the birds who bonded with their keepers would spend a lifetime flying between their households, eagerly, asking only for food and rest and love enough before they set off again.

A wonder of Urrath, said schoolteachers to children.

An extravagant hobby, said the few living practitioners, if ever they were found and questioned.

The fastest way a message has ever, in human history, crossed a continent, said Agathar to himself, years ago, when he first held a letter brought by messenger-crane.

In the years that followed, research and good luck and a fanatic's thirst for knowledge yielded the second piece of the puzzle: how to make the message invisible. A leg-band was all very well for hobbyists, but far too risky in time of war. What then? Stuff a letter down the animal's throat? No, there was a better way. The ancient Inuvtri had perfected the method; Agathar found it in a decayed folio in the city archives, and copied it chapter and verse. The letters were etched on jasmine paper, in almost microscopic print. Dried and slicked with hornets' wax, folded into capsules smaller than lemon seeds. Then the crane-keeper, who needed a jeweler's steady hand, would drill the smallest of holes in the shaft of a wing-tip feather. Into this tiny hollow went the letter, with tweezers, and then the hole was sealed with a drop of hot resin.

It was beautiful. The letter became a phantom. Not even the bird could feel its weight.

∞

Agathar neared the tradeswoman. He would have liked to thank her for her service to the cause of peace. But of course he would not speak to her, had never spoken to her and likely never would. For everyone's safety there were always go-betweens.

The letter itself, the warning to Colonel Nefiru, he had composed a week ago. By now it would have passed from hand to trusted hand, and should have reached the woman only yesterday morning. *Six days to outwit Sulmurg. Six days to smuggle a letter eight city blocks.* The crane would need but half as long for its entire flight to Kasralys.

Yesterday afternoon this woman would have passed his letter to the crane-keeper; Agathar was only here to confirm. Blue stones in her earrings meant *Message delivered.* Once he saw them—and suffered through this nonsense of Larisalt's—he would be free to go home a final time.

All the forces of Shôlupur waiting to march where I will, he told her silently, *yet I cannot send one simple letter unassisted. Thank you, Madam. You may have saved our world.*

The mule stamped; the woman turned to face him. She knew better than to make eye contact for even an instant. The eyes betrayed; the eyes could strip her naked to the scrutiny of Sulmurg's men. Instead she bowed and grinned like any other admirer, murmuring *Victory, victory!* as the great man passed.

But the stones in her earrings were white.

He walked on in stark terror, his public smile frozen on his face. *White stones. White stones.* In a flash the code came back to him: *Letter destroyed.*

Not by her. Someone earlier along the chain. Someone who had no choice but to destroy it. Someone who had nearly been caught.

This woman had carried nothing but fruit into the hills. The crane-keeper had nothing to send.

In some thirty hours, Agathar would ride to war. No letter would fly ahead of him to Colonel Nefiru. There would be no warning, no secret alliance between peace-lovers, no plan of survival for both sides. His act of treason had failed.

છ

"Ah, *there's* our River Dragon! Such a relief! We were starting to fear someone had tossed you in the bay."

Lord Larisalt, Siege Commander, smiled at his own wit. The young man was tall and beautiful but his eyes were the flat black of a shark's. He stood framed by the high marble gates of the Epicentral Armored Dockyards of Shôlupur, hands on hips, sizing Agathar up. Twenty soldiers and courtiers arrayed behind him. At his elbow, two young women stood holding his sword and helmet, as though Larisalt might at any moment be required to fight a duel.

Agathar favored him with the smallest bow. "I am sorry to have kept you waiting, my lord. As it happened I—"

"What's that you're carrying? It moved."

"My mother's dinner," said Agathar. "She fares poorly in a crowded market these days."

"Your mother who fears the angels."

Agathar nodded. "She does. That's true."

"Is the old girl afraid of servants too?"

Some of Larisalt's courtiers actually gasped. Indrishela Agathar was ancient now, but in her prime she had been among the most powerful figures in the Kingdom. She remained among the most revered.

"We cook for ourselves the night before a campaign," said Agathar. "Family tradition."

Behind Larisalt, the Dockyards seethed like a nest of ants. Sailors, midshipmen, drill sergeants, porters, canvas tailors, carpenters, mechanics—all were rushing about on a thousand tasks. In the dim light of the vast covered piers, furnaces belched smoke, sparks flew from grinding stones, hammers rang against steel.

Agathar frowned. "What is this frenzy, my lord? The first vessels do not sail for a month."

"A month." The Siege Commander laughed aloud. His entourage smiled with clear unease. Turning on his heel, Larisalt set off at a quick pace, beckoning over his shoulder. "Come along, General. You'll be excited to see this; it has a bearing on our tactics. And my uncle too is waiting."

Agathar followed with the courtiers. *Come along, General!* So that was how things stood.

But what could explain such a whirlwind of effort? The navy had exactly two tasks in this war: to occupy the small port town of Mostuc at the mouth of the Thask, and to launch sorties upriver as far as the Barrier Falls. Nothing more, and they had been ready to do both for a fortnight.

Sailors, officers snapped to attention as they passed. Agathar's confusion was becoming rage. *Damn this boy and his uncle and his King! They have cooked up some new foolishness at sea, and it will end in disaster. How could they imagine otherwise?*

Shôlupur and Kasralys had not fought a sea war in over three centuries. No warship could round the shoulder of Urrath without heading out beyond the Panzcanthyr Reef. To do so would be suicide—not principally because the waters were so hazardous (they were) but because such a vessel would be in violation of the terms of Quarantine.

The Plague burned through Outworlders like a fire through drought-stricken pines. So grave was their fear of it that for the first century of the disease they had attacked and sunk any Urrathi vessel remotely capable of crossing an ocean. In recent decades they had been more tolerant, letting Urrathis build what boats they liked. Only the great clans bothered with warships, however. For one iron rule remained: sail beyond sight of land, and the Outworlders would burn your every ship, port, and coastal settlement. To the waterline, or the ground.

Forty years ago, the Sartaph of Važenland had seen fit to test this rule, routing a fleet well offshore in a surprise raid on Nandipatar. The raid was a great success; the only Chiloto city in existence was looted, and the Prophet's nascent army handed a rare defeat.

The Outworlders' response, however, settled the question of their resolve for at least another century. The Važeks were still a great power, but to this day their coasts lay in ruins, and their navy had ceased to exist.

A detachment of marines, hundreds of them, thundered past in tight formation. "This is lunacy," said Agathar. "These people should be at other tasks."

"Ha!" said Larisalt. "I thought so too, and said as much to my uncle. Oh, what a surprise he had for me. But here we are already."

They had reached the first of the massive covered piers: a tongue of wood stretching three-quarters of a mile out into Nebusul Bay under a great roof of canvas and steel. Moored there bow-to-stern were seven great ships of the Scarlet Navy—all with sailors aloft and gangways busy with stevedores and cranes swinging still more cargo aboard.

Larisalt noticed the general's shocked expression and burst out laughing again. Agathar pushed past him and marched out alone onto the pier. The first ship was the *Evensong*, a good deep-bellied troop carrier he had sailed on himself. All work stopped as he approached. Men and women dropped their burdens and snapped out salutes.

"You," said Agathar to the nearest officer. "Captain Sayebrin, isn't it?"

"Yes, sir!" she belted, clearly amazed.

"What are your orders, Sayebrin?"

"Training exercises in the Gulf of Nebusul, sir!"

"But we concluded those weeks ago."

"A second round, Magnus General. Four hours to launch."

"And who in the Gods' cold heaven ordered a second round?"

"That would be me, Agathar."

The voice came from overhead. It was Lord Sulmurg, leaning from the *Evensong*'s rail. Beneath him, Larisalt was already climbing the forward gangway. His entourage, oddly enough, had stayed behind on the pier.

"You've broken our accord already, damn you," Agathar called to Sulmurg. "Theater-scale operations do not go forward without my involvement. Not in any branch. Not for any reason. You signed your name to that promise in the presence of our King."

"Our King shouted with delight when he learned what this ship is carrying," said Sulmurg, "as you would too, if your love of country were intact. Oh come along, Dragon! The show's about to begin."

03

They seated him to one side of Larisalt, with Sulmurg opposite, murmuring like a lugubrious stream into his nephew's ear. Both deck and rigging had been swiftly evacuated; not even Captain Sayebrin had been allowed back on her ship.

At the Inquisitor's feet lay a small and curious box. Lead body, bronze trim, heavy padlock: a cross between a lunch pail and a safe. Sulmurg gripped it with his heels, but Larisalt kept his own legs averted. He chuckled at Sulmurg's remarks, but his body was coiled like a spring.

The chairs were drawn up to the brink of the *Evensong*'s cargo shaft, fifty feet above the floor of the hold. The shaft had been widened by the removal of deck planks, leaving the belly of the ship splayed open like an autopsy.

The hold, or as much as Agathar could see of it, lay utterly empty. One deck below the men, Sulmurg's people were securing a net of heavy chain over the shaft. Larisalt made a gesture of annoyance. "Is that thing truly necessary? It impedes the view."

"Caution is always necessary, my dear one," said Sulmurg.

"This is a weapons demonstration," said Agathar with sudden certainty. "You've developed something for the war."

"Developed?" said Sulmurg. "You give me too much credit, Dragon. Let us say I acquired it."

Agathar snarled: "Why in the devil's dreams wasn't I *told*?"

"Consider this my manner of telling," said Sulmurg. "Not one, I think, that you will soon forget."

And you didn't trust me to know about it until the eve of our departure. Well, top marks for Sulmurg: a traitor can reveal no more than he knows. And sometimes not even that. *Letter destroyed. Gods, what am I to do?*

Deep in the ship: thumping, swearing, a barked command. Rasp of hinges. Slam of a gate.

"Pay close attention, nephew," said Sulmurg.

Four persons stepped out into the center of the hold. They looked up, blinking: even the dim light seemed to dazzle them. Two men, two women. Early twenties, he guessed. Muscled limbs, cat-crouches. Forming a circle by instinct, backs to the core. Real fighters, whether trained in the arena or the battlefield. And held so long in Sulmurg's dungeon they could barely stand the light.

"Who are they?" he demanded.

"Absolutely no one," said the Inquisitor.

Their shirts were rags, their trousers belted with frayed lengths of rope. One of the men had a pitchfork, the other a common laborer's hammer. The men held them at the ready but seemed aware that they were being mocked: those hands were used to halberds, pole axes, swords. The women carried nothing at all.

Both of the men had shaved heads and beards clearly hacked off by knives. One woman was tall and willowy, the other broad of face and torso with eyes like a bull's. Those eyes had already found Sulmurg. Her mouth twisted in hatred as she pointed at him.

"*Mratashul!*" she shouted. "Beast! Finish this long obscenity at last!"

"You can't blame *me*," Sulmurg answered, leaning forward. "I've been ready for hours. This is the man who kept us waiting." He glanced meaningfully at Agathar.

"Quite right," said Larisalt. "His mother wanted crabs."

"Play out your game, Sulmurg," shouted the tall woman, "or go and be fucked by whatever dog in the back streets of Nebusul will have you."

Larisalt shook his head. "The flower of Kasraji youth," he muttered.

Sulmurg shot his nephew a warning glance. But it was too late; Agathar had heard. *Kasraji youth!*

"Damn you to the Deathless Fire," he said, glaring at Sulmurg. "Whatever you're plotting, call it off, we are not beasts, I will not sit here and—"

"You will, though," said Larisalt. "After all, what choice do you have? Didn't your interview with the King make things plain enough? Or do we need to press your daughter-in-law through that shredder like old Kimburac?"

Sulmurg bent and lifted the box onto his lap. "No call for threats, nephew," he said.

"I am not threatening," said Larisalt, "merely jogging this old fool's memory."

"Ang knows," added Sulmurg, "it could only improve her looks."

"I *am* threatening, you bloodworms," Agathar heard himself say. "Touch Isula and—"

"Touch her?" Larisalt looked taken aback. "Do you think I would stop at touching? Do you know the ease with which my men spirit whomever I like into my chambers?"

"*My* men, technically," said Sulmurg, taking a key from his coat pocket.

The prisoners below were still shouting abuse. "Touch her," Larisalt repeated. "If I haven't already, it's only because, you understand—"

He put his finger down his throat and made a sound of retching. The Inquisitor *tssk*'d in mock reprimand. Agathar was terrified and lost. *Sulmurg is so much better at this than I am. Even this mindless fop is better. I've spent my life steering around the poisoned cesspools at court. They swim in them.*

Sulmurg turned the key in the padlock. Larisalt's mirth changed instantly to alarm. He sat up straight in his chair, eyes fixed on his uncle's hands.

"Take it as threat or courtesy notice, or my oath on the Pilgrim Moon," said Agathar. "Should any harm befall Isula, bastards, I will cut your throats with my own hand, try me at your peril, I have not lived this long by—"

"Do shut up," said Sulmurg. "We both know you're not as mad as all that. You have too many loves, Magnus General. Isula, Obekri, your old scarecrow of a mother. Here, catch."

He tossed something; Agathar caught it by reflex.

Larisalt exploded to his feet. "Saints' eyes! Don't squeeze it, Agathar! Don't break the skin!"

The thing in Agathar's hand weighed about as much as a goose egg, but it was spherical, and its green skin felt thin and brittle. It had a faint, sickly-sweet smell about it that put him in mind of rotten apples.

"What have you done, Uncle?" said Larisalt, backing away. He seemed at the point of shouting for his guards.

"Jogged his memory, same as you," said Sulmurg. "Come, Agathar, you know how things stand. You'll have endless chances to kill us on this glorious campaign. But you dare not kill or even displease us, unless you also find and kill everyone who serves me, including our King. Root us all out before you strike—or condemn your loved ones to the worst agonies your rare mind can imagine. Now be a good sport and toss that thing in the hold."

"What is it?"

Sulmurg's grin broadened. "Just a bit of fun."

Agathar stood frozen. *I've failed my country, my conscience, the world. I've become what this monster always wanted me to be: an instrument in his hand.*

He held out the object to Sulmurg. "I am leaving," he said.

The Inquisitor took back the object only to toss it casually into the shaft. Larisalt gasped. The object fell through the chain net and struck the floor of the hold near the prisoners with an audible *crack*.

One of the male prisoners toed it with his boot. "You missed, cretins," he said, and then madness engulfed the hold.

Both men began to howl—literally howl, a noise so high and alien it seemed to belong to another sort of creature—and to flail, striking out at nothing with hands and weapons alike.

The women leaped back in horror. The taller staggered, bleeding: the man to her left had caught her in the jaw with the hammer, breaking teeth. The shorter woman bellowed: "Stop, it's a poison, it's a drug you breathed in!"

The men did not stop. Looks of revulsion, of blood loathing, twisted their faces. "Devils!" spat the man with the pitchfork, and the one with the hammer screamed, "We won't let you! Stay back!"

"The misery tree, they call it," said Sulmurg. "An iron-hearted tree, with fruits the size of war helmets."

Misery tree? Agathar knew many of the trees of Urrath. This one rang no bell. *I'm old, but not so old that I'd forget a name like that.*

"The fruit itself is sweet and nourishing," said Sulmurg. "But the seed pod? No, that is to be avoided at all costs."

The taller woman moaned something—a name, possibly—through the blood spilling from her lips. "Get away!" cried the pitchfork-man, although the women were not advancing.

"The pod is what I threw to them," said Sulmurg.

The women went on shouting and pleading. But their voices only seemed to fill the men with fear—the crazed fear of cornered animals—and before Agathar could think of anything he might use against Sulmurg, they attacked.

The taller woman died first, on the tines of the pitchfork. The man who wielded it seemed unaware that his victim had fallen. Again and again he stabbed the corpse, shrieking as though still locked in battle. The shorter woman fared better, grappling with the hammer-wielding man and forcing him back until he tripped over the legs of her dead comrade—the only part of the woman still intact. Flailing, he struck the pitchfork-man in the calf with his hammer, and the other yowled and tried to stab him in turn.

Larisalt and Sulmurg were like two men at a boxing match: *Not fair, was it? Girl never recovered from the hammer blow. But look what the other's done: driven that fork through her and jammed it under a floorboard! He'll pay for that—ouch! Gods, he's paying now.*

The hammer-man had sprung to his feet and was quickly braining the pitchfork-man to death. When the deed was done he dropped his own weapon and worked the pitchfork loose from floor and corpse. The short woman snatched up the hammer, but it was no match for the pitchfork, and both knew it. The man chased her about the hold, screaming that his soul would never be the food of devils. Twice he nearly had her. Then he passed close to a stanchion and started in fear. He faced the wooden pillar, raised the pitchfork high, and stabbed.

"Bleed to death! Bleed to death! Bleed to—"

The woman's hammer struck him full in the temple; he collapsed like a slaughtered bull. Larisalt clapped. "Well done, well done, I don't mind saying!" The woman looked around at the carnage, then bent in sudden heaves. Nothing came; she had not been fed.

"The onset was faster this time," said Sulmurg. "More pressure in the seed capsule, better dispersal."

"*This* time?" said Agathar, gaping. "How often have you done this?"

Sulmurg ignored the question. "The seeds float in a nectar within the pod," he said. "As the fruit ripens, the nectar ferments. It's highly volatile when exposed to air. Breathe it in, and you suffer the most ghastly, the most *terrifying* hallucinations. I know this. I took some myself—" A spasm passed over his face. "—strapped down, luckily. I might have torn out my eyeballs. I certainly would have attacked my doctor, for he had grown fangs and scales, and was drooling over my legs. Between us, Agathar, I feel a bit ashamed. No poison I ever brewed is as potent as that of the misery tree."

He closed the box with a sigh. "With enough of these, we might bombard the city into surrender within a fortnight. Alas, we will never procure enough for that."

"Procure from whom?"

Sulmurg wagged a finger. "Never you mind."

"How in Ang's name am I to conduct this siege for you," said Agathar, "if I am not even privy to the supply lines?"

"He has a point, Uncle," said Larisalt.

Sulmurg raised his eyebrows. "Do you think so, my dear? Well, perhaps he may earn the knowledge on the road, if he behaves. For now I will just say that we have new friends—friends in distant places."

Outworlders, thought Agathar. *This Eyelash Thruko.* A nugget of cold formed in his stomach.

Sulmurg's men returned, one deck beneath them. Three carried bows.

All this frenzied work, thought Agathar. *These new exercises offshore. Has Sulmurg come to some understanding with the Outworlders? Are they to turn a blind eye to our vessels when they approach the Reef? Does Thruko have the power to suspend the Quarantine?*

No, no, he was dreaming. Thruko was some rogue smuggler, selling arms to both sides probably. The Outworlders would not take sides. What would they gain by the fall of Kasralys?

"A splendid drug, to be sure," said Larisalt, "and yet there she stands, alive and well." He gestured at the survivor, who was leaning on the pitchfork in a daze.

"Not for long," said Sulmurg, as his men began to remove the chain netting. "It's true, of course: women are quite unaffected. For some reason this disturbs the men severely: in almost every case, they attack the women before one another."

The woman toed something in a pool of blood. It was the cracked seed-pod.

Sulmurg glanced at Agathar. "I was annoyed by the limitation at first. The pods are obscenely expensive. Then I recalled your famous maxim."

Agathar rose from his chair. "Don't quote me, you aborted pig."

"*'The field commander must be many things, but always an alchemist, transmuting limits into gains.'* A worthy insight, Dragon. So I asked myself: how will it seem to poor Kasralys when these pods rain down from heaven, and men fall on women like feral dogs? Some will die, but those who live will carry the tale deep into the city, and won't that be more crippling? The rumors, the sleeplessness, the fear at every hour of the night?"

Agathar staggered away from them. Shame, shame for his country; he would wear it forever like a cloak of lead. *The letter. I must write it again tonight. And somehow, if it kills me, I must send it on its way.*

"How I should love to be a bird," mused Larisalt, his voice dreamy. "To glide past them when the catapults let fly, to see their faces, their helplessness, oh, what I wouldn't—"

A scream of pain cut him off. A man's voice: Agathar whirled and saw both men gazing down into the hold. He rushed back. On the deck below, one of Sulmurg's men lay quivering on his side with the pitchfork buried in his stomach. The woman below was roaring with hate and defiance. She had flung the tool like a javelin. An extraordinary deed, but this time no one clapped.

Bows sang, and she fell dead. Sulmurg's men clustered about their wounded comrade. Grimacing, one tugged the pitchfork from his entrails and held it up.

"Gods of Death!" shrieked Larisalt. He shoved past Agathar and fled for the gangway, screaming for his servants.

The woman had speared the seed-pod with the pitchfork before she threw. It still dangled there. Sulmurg's man dropped the weapon beside his feet.

"Another of my maxims concerns unforeseen consequences," said Agathar.

And then the howling began.

25. THE PILLAR OF THE NIGHT QUEEN

LATHBAN OTHURGE'UL, HEART BASIN, GREAT DESERT OF URRATH

48TH DAY OF SPRING, 3662

Diminished and sick at heart, the caravan set out. The heat came swift and ferocious. Famine's Table had released them into the great surrounding lathban, and for all Kandri had learned of walking on sand, there was no denying what it meant: exhaustion, agony, muscles screaming for solid ground.

The trick is not to think about it.

The trick is not to think.

Ulren had set their course by the Pillar of the Night Queen: six days distant, if the Master's words proved true. But it was not easy to keep the path. The great Pillar could still only be seen with the aid of the telescope, and only from the highest vantages. They had no choice but to thread their way from dune-top to dune-top, pausing at each summit to erect the tripod and adjust their course. There were no landmarks save the highlands at their back. The dunes themselves, scallop-shaped and arranged in endless arcs and folds and files, conspired to lead them astray.

Of Spalak and his company they saw no sign. Kandri wondered what he had told the drivers who had succumbed to his spell. Everlasting glory when they delivered the Twin Abominations up to the Prophet? Or merely the joy of killing her enemies, and thus hastening the day when she united Urrath under the rule of her sons? Had he whispered to them one by one, reciting the lines of scripture that Kandri himself had learned in school? The March of Angels, the path to heaven revealed, the song of creation revealed at last to waking minds, the rain of bliss like a shower of silver on the day foretold?

And of course, the punishment. The annihilation of the faithless. The insidious traps. *If you wait for proof you have scorned the gift of prophecy. If you wait for proof it will come too late. Then you must fall with the rest into blackness, into nothing, a prison without doors or windows, a prison outside of time. In that darkness, regret alone shall be your punishment. But what is regret sustained for all eternity? It is torture, it is madness, it is an ever-hotter flame passing slow over the flesh. It is the greatest agony a soul can suffer, and it will be yours to suffer forever, friendless, alone.*

The fear those words had unleashed in him. The gleaming lure of salvation, if only he surrendered and believed. Kandri could almost hear Spalak's low, implacable voice unspooling the story to driver after carefully chosen driver, waiting for them to swim up and swallow the hook.

But he failed. We survived, most of us. What will he tell them? What new purpose for them will he find?

It was all but impossible to imagine Spalak and his six corrupted drivers assaulting the caravan directly: even after the massacre, they numbered eighty-three. The soldiers were on highest alert, the drivers grim and vigilant. They would not be ambushed again.

But where could Spalak lead his six, except on to Lupriz? The oasis was walled, Jód had said. Would they linger on the periphery, thirsting and exhausted, until the caravan moved on? Would they try to sneak inside at night?

Kandri had dreamed many times of Lupriz, its shelter and comforts. Now when he thought of it all he saw was blood.

ɔ

That first day he stayed close to Mektu and Chindilan. His brother—*Always, he will always be my brother*—had been occupied with Eshett throughout the massacre. Kandri had no reason to think that he had overheard Spalak or Jód in those final moments. Few had, praise all the Gods.

Of course, he could hide the truth only so long. One day he would have to stand before Mektu and speak it. What would his brother do then? What would become of that closeness, that connection that chafed and provoked him but could never be replaced?

As they walked, Eshett turned Kandri a small, uncertain smile. He thought a song would burst from his chest. It was her first look of recognition since the night they parted in the hills. The night they had last made love.

"She spoke this morning," said Chindilan.

Kandri looked at him with hope.

"She said, 'Goose.'"

"Goose? Just—goose?"

"Nothing more, nothing less. I told her we didn't have one."

Kandri did not know whether to laugh or cry. A word, anyway: Eshett's first. Her progress was undeniable. Screams and moans had given way to silence, and a watchfulness that was not that of a madwoman. It was the watchfulness of a stranger, or a friend so long away that neither she nor anyone else recalled how they had spoken to one another: the words they shared, the memories. If they gave her food, she wolfed it gladly. If they rose to walk, she fell in step, and never lagged or complained, no matter what horrors transpired. If they gave her a task—brush this camel, braid this woman's hair—she complied with skill and dispatch. At night she slept like the dead.

But if they spoke her name she only looked at them blankly. If they managed to catch her attention. If she realized they were addressing her at all.

"A lad in my unit caught brain fever in the Obik Fens," said Chindilan. "He nearly died, and when he recovered he'd forgotten everything but his name. We had to teach him the facts of his own life—where he came from, the names of parents, how long he'd been in the Army of Revelation. He took to it all like a schoolboy, and perhaps his mind healed as well. But it was never clear to me afterward what he truly remembered, and what he memorized."

"That won't happen to Eshett," said Mektu. "Her memories are all coming back."

Kandri and Chindilan waited for him to elaborate, but Mektu walked on in silence. At last Kandri clapped Mektu on the shoulder.

"Thank you for getting her to safety," he said. "I couldn't help; I had to keep burning those creatures. But I'll never forget it."

"She put her hand in my pants," said Mektu.

Chindilan turned away with a sigh.

"I thought she was just after this—" Mektu patted the mattoglin on his belt. "—but no, she wanted to touch my manhood, she *did* touch it, she took a good solid—"

"Not now, Mek."

"It was before the grasthu appeared. Everyone else was asleep. And I don't mind telling you that I was shocked. But the strangest part was this: Eshett was surprised that *I* was surprised. She looked at me as if to say, 'What's wrong? You liked this before.'"

Kandri forced himself to breathe.

"But there *wasn't* any before," said Mektu. "I mean, she wanted me, of course. Anyone could see that. But Jód had forbidden us to lie together, and she didn't want to disobey him. You look strange, Kandri, are you sick?"

"Not at all," Kandri said.

"So there was nothing for her to remember," said Mektu. "I mean, except the night I paid for it. You know what I'm saying. Back when Eshett was—"

"Right," said Kandri. "That's enough."

Eshett was not recalling the brothel, he knew. She was recalling nights in his own arms. Her memories were returning, but scrambled. She had lain down with Mektu because something, the ghost of a touch, had told her that here she had found safety, pleasure, peace. But her aim had been off by a few yards.

"I love her," said Mektu, "and the beautiful thing is, she loves me too. You're all right with that, I hope?"

He could not speak, could not tell Mektu the truth: Eshett herself had made him promise. And what good could it possibly do? Even she might not believe him now.

"Just keep her away from the mattoglin," he said.

Mektu clutched at it again. "Why?" he asked, voice suddenly cold.

For the same reason we have to take it from you, Kandri thought. *Because it's home to a yatra and it will kill you. Can I tell you that? Will you hear me? Can I just say it to your face?*

Kandri said it.

Mektu laughed. Too loud and too quickly. When Kandri did not join in he sidled farther away. "It's mine," he said.

Gritted teeth. Tensed limbs. Mektu was ready to explode. He would fight Kandri, fight anyone, before he'd give up the blade.

But it was too late to stop now. "The yatra's in the knife, Mek," Kandri insisted. "Think back to Eternity Camp. All those signs, all that fear and madness. It started right after the Prophet gave that thing to Ojulan."

"You didn't believe in yatras," said Mektu.

"But you did," said Kandri. "Somehow you knew from the start. I should have listened. I'm sorry."

"Sorry, he says. After laughing at me, telling everyone I was a fool."

Kandri bit his lips. It would do no good to say that he'd done nothing of the kind. "On Alibat S'Ang," he said. "you weren't just acting. The yatra helped you, let you speak with the Prophet's voice."

"Why would a yatra help me? The yatra when I was six nearly *killed* me."

"This one doesn't care about possessing you," said Kandri. "Or maybe it can't, as long as it's trapped in that blade. All I know for certain is that it doesn't want to end up back with the Prophet. And it didn't want to end up buried in a hole near Eshett's village, either. Don't you see? Each time I gave it to her, the yatra made you steal it back."

Mektu moved still further away. He looked at Kandri with open hostility.

"I'm not trying to take the mattoglin from you," said Kandri.

"Smart boy."

"*Shit of the devil.*" Kandri tried not to raise his voice. "Keep it away from Eshett, that's all. Whatever's wrong with her began with that knife. She came all the way back from that Maskiar place because of it."

"You don't know that."

"Mek, she was foaming at the mouth. She wants that knife like a drug."

"Not anymore," said Mektu.

"What do you mean, not anymore? Are you saying she's cured?"

"I'm saying she knows better," said Mektu. "I thought you did too, but I was wrong. You're so jealous you can't see what's in front of your nose."

"And what is that?"

"Eshett's made her choice, Kandri, and it isn't you. Some things aren't yours for the taking."

"Things," said Kandri.

"I'm done talking," said Mektu. "The knife belongs to me."

Kandri watched him move away, hand fluttering in an involuntary fashion to the mattoglin. *No*, he thought, *you're starting to belong to it.*

 os

On the second day the heat surpassed all previous extremes. By midmorning some of the older drivers were collapsing, and barely managing to rise again. When a woman came within inches of being trampled by the camels, Ulren stopped the caravan. For six hours they lay gasping and lifeless beneath the sun-shields, too hot to feel hunger, too hot to speak or even think with much coherence. Blue visions of death danced in Kandri's eyes. Ifimar Jód—his Parthan uncle—pinned like a moth to the canyon wall. The drivers inside the luminous grasthu, their bodies softening. The slaughtered mercenaries, the croaking private. Captain Utarif's head torn from his shoulders.

We could all die here, vanish here. A third of us have died already.

No one had recovered when Ulren called them back to the trail. Kandri felt broken, clubbed. Rising to his feet was like lifting stone with his shoulders. The stone lid of a casket, his casket, from within.

That day and the next they crept over the sand, barely speaking. At rest under the shields, the world spun and throbbed. Someone coughed; a hand slapped a fly. All at once it was time to march again.

Late into the night they walked on and on. Cracked lips, clenched teeth, unstoppable, like one of Lantor Hinjuman's amazing toys. The Pilgrim Moon looked down on them, a bloodshot eye that never blinked.

By the fourth day they could make out the Pillar with the naked eye. Through Kandri's telescope its shape was weird and lovely: a pale arm of stone, twisted into a toffee-spiral, reaching for heaven but leaning precariously as it rose. At its summit was a broad court, flat and unwalled, like a serving platter open to the sky.

Prince Nirabha grew more excited with each glance through Kandri's telescope. "It is a relic of the ancient world," he said. "In my childhood, there was a study in oil paints of the Olukru Tsamid that hung in our breakfast room. How I gazed with wonder on its shape!"

"What's a breakfast room?" said Talupéké.

"Only a little chamber off the garden," said the Prince with a smile. "Cold in winter, but that was sometimes an advantage. If I sat there with a book no one disturbed me."

Mektu clasped his hands together and sighed. "I like to think of our outhouse," he said. "The things I discovered there. The things I learned about myself."

"Another chance for mockery," said Nirabha, "from one who cannot tolerate a heartfelt word."

"Another useless rock you're excited about," said Mektu.

"We shall see," said the Prince.

"If nothing else," said Kereqa, "that rock will offer shade, and I will rejoice. This heat will be the death of us."

Kandri looked at her, startled. Never before had the old woman voiced such a complaint—or any complaint. But now he saw that she was changed: her breathing was labored, and her fierce eyes were haunted with the slightest touch of doubt. For her too the massacre had marked a threshold.

Talupéké, who lately never strayed from her grandmother's side, caught Kandri's look. She raised a hand, and he tensed: the girl was about to maul him with words. Then her face twitched and her hand began to tremble.

"Tal—" he began.

She hissed through her teeth and looked away.

☙

But Kereqa, like everyone else, somehow persevered. Before dawn on the sixth morning they were climbing out of the lathban up a steep gravel slope. Beyond it the plain leveled out for a mile, then rose sharply again. The summit of this second ridge was marked by a low wall, miles long, curving away from them to north and south. The ancient bricks were badly eroded; many had tumbled down the slope.

A wash of orange in the eastern sky declared the sun's return. They groped about the wall until they found a gap, then led the camels through it a few at a time. Beyond lay a wide country of toothlike boulders and low windswept dunes. It was forbidding but beautiful, glowing a hundred shades of red and orange in the early light.

At its very center rose the Pillar of the Night Queen.

It was far larger than Kandri had imagined: taller than the great dunes west of Famine's Table, taller than Ravashandul's Wall. It was also the strangest object he had ever beheld. The pillar groped skyward but leaned at a precipitous angle, like the snag of some ancient, wind-tortured tree. Pale white but bathed in fire on the sunward side, it spread in gnarled buttresses at the foot, narrowing and twisting as it rose. But at the very summit the pillar widened into a vast round courtyard, perfectly level and many times the diameter of the trunk that supported it.

"Like a plate held up to heaven," said Chindilan.

"Like a toadstool," said Mektu.

They filed through the gap and began the descent. Now Kandri saw that the basin ahead was studded with other weird formations, twisted and tortured like the pillar but a tiny fraction of its height.

"Do you see the deep groove, spiraling from foot to summit?" said Nirabha, pointing. "That is the staircase, carved into the stone. Who will climb it with me?"

"No one shall!" said Ulren sharply. "Not you either, Prince, unless you've brought the offering: a stone from the Queen's birthplace of Ramisith. That was always Master Ifimar's law, and we will honor it today as we honor him."

The Prince smiled at Ulren. "I thought we might," he said, and took a small gray stone from his pocket. He looked around, suddenly dismayed. "Do *none* of you—"

"I do," said Kandri, to general amazement. He touched the calfskin pouch beneath his shirt. "Right here. I'd forgotten all about it, to be honest. Ang knows if I hadn't, I might have tossed it long ago."

The Prince beamed at him. "Well then, Mr. Hinjuman."

"There are windows along the stair," said Kereqa. "Is it a keep of some sort?"

"I can give no simple answer," said the Prince. "There are chambers within, but the legends of the Night Queen say little of them. The wonders with which she is credited took place upon that open roof."

That roof, or courtyard as Kandri still thought of it, had no wall about its rim. It was smooth and featureless, in fact, save for three narrow standing stones at the center, and a fourth, smaller and darker, alone near the furthest edge.

"What wonders, exactly?" he asked.

"If you join me," said the Prince, "I will tell you as we ascend. Come, the view will be spectacular! Indeed, that may be too mild a word, if the tales are true."

Ripheem moaned low in his chest. The Prince turned to him and laughed. "Stay below, old friend! No harm will befall me."

"I will *not* stay behind, Hraliz," said the servant miserably. "And I too have a stone."

"Not much time for this lark of yours, Prince," said Ulren. "Another hour and the sun will heat this clay up like a skillet."

"In an hour we shall be long gone," said the Prince. "Kandri, join me! You are not indifferent to beauty, like that brother of yours."

"I'm thirsty like my brother," said Kandri, "but yes, I'll climb."

"Then make yourself useful, Chiloto, if you're so determined," said Ulren. "Take your telescope, and try for a glimpse of the Font of Lupriz. Can you manage that?"

"I can manage that, Master," said Kandri.

Ulren turned him a savage look. Then, wonder of wonders, he saw that Kandri had not spoken in derision. He gave an awkward nod. "You'll, ah, be doing us a service," he said. "Very good, very good."

"No one else?" asked the Prince, turning in a circle.

Many of the drivers had stones, but none had any intention of climbing the Pillar. They looked at Kandri and the Prince with a mix of admiration and confusion.

"Is not requirement to honor the Queen," said the woman with the amber nose-stud. "Leave stone by foot of the tower, that is pleasing too."

A few yards away, the little surgeon cleared his throat. "I will make the climb," he said, displaying a rough little stone.

Kandri looked at him, astonished. The short-legged man had struggled in recent days; he looked little better than Kereqa. But he appeared in earnest.

"A morning of surprises," said the Prince. "Let us go."

They jogged ahead. In truth Kandri had not even considered passing the Pillar by: with every mile he had grown more intrigued. Now, as they reached its foot, he could scarcely believe his eyes. The substance of the Pillar was porous, like the dead corals Kandri had glimpsed on the floor of the Stolen Sea.

"It's not stone at all, is it?" he asked.

"Perhaps not," said the Prince. "Some of the chroniclers declare it bone matter. Others, the hardened husk of a plant."

"Nothing could have *grown* that tall," said the surgeon.

"Nothing known to us," said the Prince, "but the world is vast, my good man. There are beasts in the wild places—the Nfepan jungles, the inner vales of the Nightfire Range—that have vanished from other lands. And the past is a sea whose depths we can never plumb. Once all this land may have been covered with such forms as this."

The staircase was carved deep in the porous substance of the pillar, leaving a thick, smooth bannister-wall on the outer edge. The stairs were very steep, and so eroded and smooth it was difficult to say just where their corners had been. Kandri thought of his mountain childhood, waterfalls frozen in the dead of winter. How strange to be reminded of ice.

The climb was even harder than they had imagined: there was no level spot to plant a foot, and nothing whatsoever to grip. All this was made worse by the Pillar's precarious tilt. Kandri tried to brace himself between the Pillar and the bannister-wall, but it was hard work, like climbing up a corkscrew. The surgeon had pulled on worn leather gloves; he looked miserable and enraged. But no one fared as poorly as Ripheem. The huge man slipped and stumbled, crashing down onto his knees again and again. Kandri began to wonder if they had made a mistake.

"See there!" cried the Prince. "O glory!"

An undulating blackness was flowing toward them through the morning air. It was a swarm of bats, hundreds of times larger than the one they had disturbed on Ravashandul's Wall. Huge and soundless it approached, filling a quarter of the sky. Just before it reached the pillar, the swarm abruptly narrowed, as though passing through a funnel. The bats were entering one of the Pillar's upper windows. Seconds later they were gone.

"You are trembling, Ripheem," said the Prince. "Are you quite well?"

"How could I be anything but well, Hraliz?" said Ripheem, a bit too quickly. "I thank the Gods of Good Fortune they made me your servant. How else should I have gone beyond the estate? How else should I have seen, seen—"

He swept his arm over the landscape—and instantly fell again. This time his head struck the wall and his huge legs shot out behind him. One clipped the surgeon, sending the little man tumbling backward down the staircase with a scream.

Kandri lunged and caught his shirt, just managing to arrest his fall. The surgeon seized him in a panic, clinging to his arm, his neck.

"I've got you! Easy there!" Kandri set him on his feet.

"Damnation, Prince!" bellowed the surgeon. "That great bloody oaf nearly killed me!"

You're welcome, Kandri thought.

Nirabha looked at his servant. "Ripheem," he said, "this climb is not for you. Make your way down, please—slowly, and with care. We can afford no broken bones."

"Hraliz—"

"I must insist, old friend."

They left the servant shamefaced behind them. "He took an oath never to leave my side," said Nirabha, "but I should not have let him honor it here. The man is deathly afraid of heights."

Near the top of the pillar the weathering grew even worse, and they were reduced to crawling. Kandri felt light-headed, and once more he doubted the decision to climb. Both he and the Prince had to assist the surgeon in the worst places, clasping his gloved hand and hauling him like a squirming tuna into a boat.

At last they came right under the gigantic saucer-shaped roof. There the staircase became a tunnel, angled sharply upward. They scrambled up the passage, breathless, relieved.

And stepped out into wonder. The surface of the roof dazzled the eye. It was perfectly smooth and featureless, but the sun had reached it, and like mother-of-pearl it danced with rainbows, infinite rainbows, so bright they seemed to lift from the floor like the spray of a waterfall dashed upon rocks. Kandri squinted, shielding his eyes. The Prince, his body bathed in reds, golds, greens, purples, turned laughing in a circle. The surgeon was a small, blazing clot of blue.

Nirabha ran closer to the roof's sheer edge. "The Tower of True Sight!" he shouted. "The stories are true, but they do it no justice!"

"*Harach*, be careful!" Kandri shouted at the Prince. How had he recovered so quickly? Kandri himself was still half-blinded, and almost too dizzy to walk.

"We must leave our offerings at last," said Nirabha, returning to his side. He took a stone from his pocket and set it reverently upon the roof. Kandri reached beneath his shirt, opened one buckle on the calfskin pouch and fished out the tiny stone from Ramisith. He set it down beside Nirabha's own.

"A pleasant custom, is it not?" said the Prince. "To bring a bit of home to a lonely spirit."

"A mindless custom," said the surgeon.

They looked at him, startled. "I brought no foolish stone from Ramisith," he told them, pleased with himself. "I snatched up that little shard while you were talking, Prince." He fished it from his pocket, tossed it casually aside.

"I am shocked," said Nirabha.

486

"Got me here, didn't it?" said the surgeon. "Old Ulren was none the wiser."

Nirabha quite deliberately turned his back on the man. Taking Kandri's arm, he drew him happily away. They were swaying, and laughing slightly; Kandri felt as though he were drunk on sweet wine. The colors raced and pooled and shimmered. The Prince looked out beyond the roof.

"Do you see it, Hinjuman? The blessed land that is Urrath? Do you *see*?"

He made a sweeping gesture. And as he did so, a vision exploded in Kandri's mind.

It was not just miles of country he could perceive. It was thousands, in impossible detail. They were facing north. His gaze took in a red cliff that wound like an endless snake across the desert, as long as Ravashandul's Wall or longer. Directly north, a gargantuan stair was carved into the cliff, broad as a fairgrounds, a staircase for the Gods. Beyond the cliff sprawled flats that glittered like gold, then a forest of cacti, and finally an ashen plain etched with sad gray ruins, the remains of some great city long since abandoned to the desert winds.

"Great Gods, look at the crater," said Nirabha.

At the edge of the ruins gaped a monstrous hole. It was perfectly round, like the craters punched in the earth by the Tears of the Gods. But this crater could swallow a mountain, Kandri thought, and even with this strange new vision he could not see its floor.

"Jekka's Grave," said the Prince.

"Another painting in your breakfast room?" asked the surgeon.

Nirabha smiled but did not laugh. "Not in this case," he said. "That crater is a place of ill omen. Some great loss befell the Empire there, and to this day we do not speak of it gladly. But there, there to the east—"

"Lupriz," said Kandri. "I see it."

Perhaps twenty miles from the crater, a high wall rose among the ruins. It was in the shape of a pentagon, and it looked formidable enough: no desert raiders would easily scale it or sweep it aside. Still, it showed its age: patched in some places, bulging in others. But within the wall Lupriz was magnificent:

stately halls and towers and temples, groves of oranges and lemons and spiny red alamsad, blue reflecting pools, fountains laughing in the sun.

"I have the strangest feeling," said the Prince, "that I could walk blindfolded to the Font of Lupriz."

"And beyond," said Kandri. "So do I."

"You are both hysterical," said the surgeon. "I cannot see the Font of Lupriz, and I happen to know my vision is excellent. I'll rely on Ulren's memory, if it's all the same to you."

But Kandri was not exaggerating: landmarks or no landmarks, he would never now lose the path. And his eyes were drawn still farther. There beyond the oasis was a thing glimpsed only in dreams, a miraculous thing, a proof that prayers were worth the trouble. It was the desert's edge.

And it was nothing but mountains.

His heart fell through his sandals. The mountains beyond Lupriz seemed to go on forever, range upon range, each more forbidding than the last. Then his enchanted gaze seemed to soar, as though he were an eagle gliding at many times the Pillar's height. Now he perceived a low country, serpentine in shape, between two arms of the mountains. The land was green and exquisite, lavished with farms, orchards, villages. There were also dense woodlands, blue lakes rafted in mist, waterfalls tumbling from the sheer walls of the mountains like skeins of lace.

And marching down the length of this country were nine astonishing towers. They were slender but immensely tall, towers of granite and marble, quartz and iron and glass of fifty hues.

"The Towers of Serenity," said Nirabha when he asked. "It was in one of those that I was born. You can see it there, the Tower of Tsakynnasis, leftmost within the confines of the city."

"The city?" said Kandri. And then: "Oh Gods. The city."

For there it was at last: Kasralys, jewel of Urrath, heart of Empire, focus of Ariqina's dreams. The Fortress City, vast beyond description, a wilderness of roofs, domes, gardens, palaces, pools. Backed up to the mountains. Above a great black lake. Behind a wall not even the Gods could threaten. Atop a sheer plateau.

The Prince glanced at him, beaming. "Do you think you could find your way there, now, Mr. Hinjuman?"

Kandri just laughed: the city was close enough to touch. *Ariqina*, he thought. *You have to be there. And when I find you I'll do just as uncle told me, promise you everything, get down on my knees—*

He turned back to the surgeon, and gasped.

A woman stood watching him, her face just inches from his own. She was taller than Kandri, neither young nor old, wearing a black sarong hemmed in silver. A thin gold circlet ran about her forehead, and about her neck hung a string of small oval shells, very white against her jet-black skin. Her eyes held a sadness that stole his breath. They pierced him, sunlight through water. Her lips moved as though she were speaking, but Kandri could not hear a thing.

"Who—"

She was gone, swallowed by the colors that danced on the roof.

"—are you?"

Another ghost?

Stupid question. What else could she be? But all at once Kandri had a terrifying sensation of reversal. He was a trick of the light, present for less than an eyeblink on this ancient pillar, while this woman had stood here from the beginning of time and would remain until time's end.

He was ill. The heat was cooking his brain. He wiped his face with his headscarf and tried to take himself in hand. They were alone, the three of them. The Prince was still looking at his city, overjoyed. The surgeon, oddly enough, was looking at the Prince, studying him, as though waiting for something to happen.

But I saw her. She was real.

Kandri blinked the sweat from his eyes. Saw what, saw whom? A fairy-tale woman? The Night Queen, in blinding daylight?

His mind ached: something was very wrong indeed. He sat down on the rooftop, put his head between his knees. *Ang help me*, he thought, *I'm insane.*

 os

He was flat on his back in the merciless sunlight. The heat of the roof scorched his skin. The dancing colors had vanished. The cloudless sky rocked and swayed.

His body was shaking uncontrollably. Teeth chattering. Hands trembling like leaves in a storm.

This happened to Jód, he thought with horror. *Whatever afflicted him, I've got it too.*

He struggled to a sitting position. Forty feet away, the surgeon was kneeling beside Nirabha, hand pressed to the Prince's forehead, asking questions in a sharp, commanding tone. Nirabha was shaking more violently than Kandri; he seemed to have lost all control of his limbs.

With some effort Kandri rose to his feet. The surgeon turned and watched his approach. Kandri nearly hailed him: *What is it, what's wrong with him, what's wrong with me?* But some wiser part of him knew that the surgeon's reply, if he gave any, would tell him nothing he wanted to hear.

He stopped five feet from the men. The surgeon's small, bright eyes were pitiless. In his left hand he held what looked for all the world like a fishhook. A yellowish substance coated the tip.

"No more lies," said Kandri.

"Right you are," said the surgeon. "No lies. There's no time for them now."

"You've p-poisoned us. And J-Jód. You poisoned Ifimar Jód."

The surgeon shrugged.

"Why?"

"If slugs threaten your garden, you poison them, Hinjuman. Or better still, you force someone to do it for you. Someone like me."

Kandri drew and raised his machete, but his arm was shaking so badly it almost flew from his hand.

"Put that down," said the surgeon, "before you cut off your own foolish head."

"N-not the one I had in m-mind."

"Curious that you're on your feet, though," said the surgeon. "I can think of two explanations. One, my gloves delivered less toxin than I imagined, in which case you'll shudder and ache for a time and then recover naturally. Or two, I delivered the full dose, but the drug is taking longer to reach your brain than I anticipated—in which case you'll collapse rather soon, and die without my antidote. That is what is happening to the Prince."

It dawned on Kandri that he was at last face to face with the traitor everyone had feared. Spalak's ally, perhaps even Spalak's master. The infiltrator in Tebassa's ranks, who had led the Prophet to his door.

"You walking piece of s-shit."

"Will you waste your last breath on such banalities? Your father would be disappointed." He turned Kandri a rascally smile. "Either father. Both men had standards, after all."

Kandri raised the machete above his head. The surgeon turned back to Nirabha, unconcerned.

"Don't imagine for an instant that you're free to harm me," he said. "You want me to save this young man's life, do you not? Even if you convince yourself that you no longer care for your own?"

"K-k-kill him!"

It was Prince Nirabha. He gazed imploringly at Kandri, limbs flailing, body jerking as though plucked by strings.

"Better not," said the surgeon. "There's more at stake than the two of you."

"B-bastard," said Kandri. "You have an ant-ant—"

"Antidote, yes." The surgeon raised the fishhook. "It will suffice for you as well. But I'll toss it from the roof if you don't lay that weapon down."

Prince Nirabha's head was now smacking the rooftop, *thump thump thump*.

Kandri dropped the machete. He could not have swung it; even a thrust was likely more than he could manage. He looked beyond the roof, wildly hoping that the others might glance up and see what was occurring. But of course they were underneath the pillar now. In the shade. Out of sight.

"W-what do you w-wa—"

"You know perfectly well," said the surgeon. "I want you to tell me, without pausing to compose a lie, what in all the red halls of hell the caravan is smuggling into Kasralys."

Kandri stared at him.

"This young royal here came to General Tebassa with a decent fortune," said the surgeon, "and spent it all—every last copper keldrin—outfitting the caravan and whipping it fast out the door. We know this for a fact. We also know who begged him to do it, and put up the rest of the gold: his lover, of course. The Prophet's rebel son, who Mektu stabbed in the chest."

Garatajik? Kandri's mind reeled. Could it possibly be true? The Prince had called Garatajik his closest friend—but lovers, and the owners of the caravan?

"What did they need to move, Hinjuman?" demanded the surgeon. He pointed with the fishhook. "And don't you dare claim it's that decoy around your neck. I'll be taking that too, of course, in the interest of thoroughness. But the real treasure was with us before you joined the team, or else why the secrecy, the mad scramble, the even madder expense? What are they smuggling? The Prince here wouldn't tell me. You bloody will, or we'll watch him die together."

Lunacy, utter lunacy. Captain Utarif and his men had gone over the trade goods fifty times and found nothing but brass works and fox testicles. And Garatajik himself had chosen Kandri to carry the Letter of Cure. *But why hide that from the Prince?* The question had plagued him since Weeping Rock. Now it made less sense than ever.

Unless . . . the letter *was* a decoy, an elaborate diversion from what truly mattered. A load of gibberish, in a language no one spoke. A deception, and Kandri himself the first deceived.

Could it all be a lie? Could Garatajik be just another enemy—using us, using the Prince? Could there be no cure at all?

"Tell me, Hinjuman."

"I d-don't, don't—"

Sighing, the little surgeon dragged his glove across the Prince's forehead. Nirabha gasped with pain. His spasms grew still more violent.

"Another dose and his heart will burst. Don't make me do that. I have nothing against this Prince."

"I'm a Chiloto!" Kandri spat out. "Trust me. The f-faith is nothing but shit. The P-Prophet is m-m-mad!"

"Come now," said the surgeon. "You don't really think I subscribe to your cult? That I'm another Spalak? Our purposes aligned well enough, it's true. But we barely tolerated each other. Spalak's a mystic. I'm a scientist. He serves a holy madwoman bent on conquering Urrath. I serve the ones who already have."

"Wh-who—?"

"Witless peasant," said the surgeon. "You truly believe this continent's destiny is in its own hands? That its wars just happen, nation against nation, king against king? You thought yourself so much better than those mercenaries, but at least they knew what they fought for—money, plunder, whores. And I know as well: I fight because I'm a slave."

"S-s—"

"A slave," repeated the surgeon, his voice sharp with loathing, "to the true masters of this world. I mean the Xavasindrans, and their agent here in Urrath, one Eyelash Thruko. Your natural father could learn from that man. Spalak was clever about the jellyfish, I grant you. But compared to Thruko we are infants, all of us. The Prophet included. Tell me: how would Spalak feel if he knew an Outworlder was pulling her strings?"

He held up a hand, telling Kandri not to speak. "No," he said, "I'm nothing like your father. He wants you dead, the pious bloodsucker—and he'd be just as glad if I died with you, as he proved back at that canyon.

"I don't want you dead, boy. I just need your mission to fail. Whatever it is we're carrying, *it will never reach Kasralys*, do you understand? That is *my* mission, to acquire that hidden cargo, or see the whole caravan reduced to ashes if I cannot. Handing all of you over to your Prophet's bloody fanatics was the only way I could realize the second option. Though it scared me to death each time I or Spalak scattered breadcrumbs in our wake. I've never been sure that devil would speak up for me, if the Rasanga found we were harboring you two, their great Abominations. They might just kill us all in a blood frenzy—even Spalak, the true believer, though he would drink their piss and call it wine."

"The O-Outworlders—"

"Would very much prefer to take that secret cargo and be done with it. But as I say, they will settle for ashes. And I must give them ashes, unless you cooperate. If I allow that cargo to reach the city, my own punishment would be . . . no, no, we won't speak of that."

He twitched, and recovered with an unpleasant grin. "Between us, the Xavs are a bit afraid of Kasralys. Their Medical Missions have never been allowed to set up shop there. They have never cracked the city, nor made puppets of her leaders. Not enough of them, anyway. What to do? As with this caravan, they've prepared a second option. Ashes, again. You're heading to a city marked for death."

He gestured at the Prince. "Some Kasrajis cause more trouble than others, of course. This Prince, now: Eyelash Thruko has been watching him and his secret heartthrob for over a year. They knew Kasralys was in danger. Whatever they've hidden in this caravan will surely play some vital role in the city's defense. Is it one of your father's inventions? I mean your stepfather, naturally. Lantor Hinjuman."

Kandri stood there, shaking. He wondered now if the surgeon had any inkling of the Letter's contents, any notion of a Cure. He thought Garatajik was sending Kasralys a weapon, something to kill with, not to heal.

"Speak, damn you, before you lose the ability," said the surgeon. "What in Jekka's Hell is hidden in that caravan?"

Kandri's doubts abruptly disappeared. The simplest answer was the right one. Captain Utarif was right: the caravan hid nothing. Garatajik had never intended Kandri to join it. The caravan itself was the decoy; his Letter was the prize.

But could Garatajik really have used ninety people, his lover among them, as a lure to draw off his enemies?

Stay lucid. This monster had not killed him yet because he thought Kandri had a secret to share. *He must, at all costs, go on thinking that.*

So what he needed was a lie. A beautiful lie, a perfect lie. A lie to make his brother proud.

Flaming gauntlets! Invisible armor! Magic fox balls!

I'm going to die.

Kandri sank to his knees—not because of the poison; if anything its effects had diminished slightly. But it was too awful to do nothing, say nothing. The surgeon narrowed his eyes.

"Starting to hurt now, eh?"

With those words, hope sprang in Kandri's mind: the surgeon thought he was declining, that the drug was only now kicking in. Could he use that? Was there a way out, even if he was blind to it still?

He dropped, twitching harder, trying to mimic the Prince.

"Don't quit on me now," said the surgeon. "I really do have the antidote—it's quite remarkable, one scratch from this little hook and you'll be your old, irritating self, after a bit of peaceful sleep. So come, help me. My masters will settle for ashes, I say, but they would much rather have the secret. Help me give it to them, and you can go where you like. Into Kasralys. Into the arms of Dr. Ariqina Nawhal."

Kandri's chattering teeth had bloodied his tongue. The man knew everything. His greatest hope, his greatest weakness. He had left nothing to chance.

"If that's not incentive enough," said the surgeon, "consider this, boy: what you and the Prince are suffering now? Nothing, absolutely nothing, compared to what's in store for Mektu. Ah, Mektu—" He shook his head. "—a symphony of pain, and a filthy death to follow. Not my doing, I assure you. It will just happen. That dog's already slipped its chain, Hinjuman. And I'm the only one who can call it back. So talk. Name the goods. And then we'll rejoin the others, all smiles, and be on our way."

Kandri lay quaking, slapping the roof, moaning low in his chest. The surgeon frowned. Was that skepticism? Was he overdoing it? The man knew the symptoms well.

"F-f-fire."

"What's that? Fire?"

"F-fi-fire d-dust!"

Fire dust. What the fuck. No one in their right mind would believe—

The surgeon stood up and approached him.

"Fire dust? An incendiary substance? A weapon of some kind?"

Kandri nodded.

"Where the hell is it, then? I've searched every last Gods-damned saddlebag!"

"Fa-fa-faskas."

"Packed in faskas? You're telling me there are water skins full of this material?"

Another nod. The surgeon's eyes gleamed and his mouth twisted into a smile. "I'd kiss you, boy, if I dared get close enough. And I suppose that letter strapped to your chest is the formula?"

"N-n-no." *Wrong answer, wrong answer.*

"Well, I'll judge for myself," said the surgeon, gesturing. "Take it off."

Movement behind the surgeon. Kandri's heart leaped: *Ripheem.*

The manservant was crawling on hands and knees out of the tunnel. Already he had seen his master, and the surgeon's cold indifference to his suffering.

"Fire powder," mused the surgeon. "Eyelash Thruko will be pleased. You've saved us both a lot of trouble, Hinjuman."

Ripheem crawled nearer, eyes fixed on the surgeon. Every inch of him murderous, a shapeless lion stalking its prey.

Don't give him away!

Kandri focused on the surgeon, who was even now reaching for the Letter of Cure. From the corner of his eye Kandri saw Ripheem rise to his feet.

And stumble.

The surgeon whirled about. With two lurching steps he was back at Nirabha's side.

"Stop right there, toad, or he dies in agony!" He knelt, one gloved hand poised above the Prince's face, the other brandishing the fishhook.

"*Hraliz!*" The servant skidded to a halt, eyes blazing, huge hands in fists. "What have you done, you monster, you worm? I will kill you! I will tear you into pieces!"

"You will do as I say and nothing more," said the surgeon. "Your Prince's life depends on it."

Kandri stopped his shaking: the surgeon's back was turned. As soon as he lay still he knew that the drug's effects had weakened further. *He was right the first time. I didn't get the full dose.*

"Fix him," snarled Ripheem. "Undo this, or with my bare hands I will kill you! I swear it!"

Slowly, silently, Kandri got to his feet.

"And what do you swear by?" jeered the surgeon.

Ripheem straightened. "By my soul, and—my mother's."

The surgeon laughed. "Well chosen! You cannot swear on a wife, of course. And what about children? Ah, but you lack the tools, don't you? They took your manhood when they chose you for a life at court. And yet you worship him. Blood of Ang, these old dynasties! My masters will have done this continent a favor if they manage to kill them all."

Kandri slipped off his headscarf, began to twist it in both hands. He took a careful step toward the surgeon.

Ripheem saw him. *Look away!* begged Kandri silently. *Look anywhere else!*

The surgeon, however, took no notice: his eyes were still fixed on Ripheem's deadly hands. As Kandri crept closer, he went on jeering: "Eunuch! Who was it gelded you? Never mind: what matters is that you're still capable of love. A twisted love, the love of a dog for the master who beats him, but it will suffice. Back off, back off, or he—"

Kandri slipped the scarf around his neck and jerked with all his strength, lifting the surgeon off his knees. A short gasp escaped the man before his breath was cut off. He clawed at the headscarf. Kandri twisted it tighter.

"Use the antidote," he said. "On the Prince. Right now."

Ripheem charged forward. The surgeon groped for Kandri's hand.

"Touch me and I'll break your neck," said Kandri. "We both know your poison's not fast enough to stop me."

"The Prince!" bellowed Ripheem. "Cure him! Fix him!"

The surgeon's arms were flailing. Would he fling the fishhook away, out of spite or terror? Kandri lowered him just enough to reach Nirabha.

"Use it," he repeated, "or I'll kill you and do it myself."

The surgeon's eyes were glazed. "Fix him! Fix him!" howled Ripheem, and in a last lucid act, the surgeon stabbed the hook into the Prince's cheek.

The Prince fell instantly still, a spot of blood gleaming between cheekbone and chin. He lay there in the hot sun, eyes closed, peaceful. Kandri loosed the scarf just enough for the surgeon to gasp.

Ripheem stared down at his master. His mouth worked. He was trembling so badly that for a moment Kandri wondered if the surgeon had somehow poisoned him as well.

Kandri gestured at the Prince. "He's not—"

Ripheem struck him backhanded, screaming in despair. Kandri dropped, the mad colors returning, swallowing his sight. He felt his head strike the roof but the pain seemed to come from a great distance: he was very nearly unconscious.

Fight it. Fight it. Kandri rolled onto his stomach. Wind knocked out, the world spinning mad. He raised his head and there was Ripheem, dragging the surgeon by his headscarf toward the edge of the roof. The surgeon was clawing at the twisted fabric, heels kicking, helpless as though tied to a draft horse.

Kandri reached out a hand: "Not dead," he wheezed. "Your Prince. He's not dead."

No air in his lungs, no voice. The surgeon pawed at Ripheem's hand, smearing poison if any remained.

At the roof's very edge, Ripheem gave the scarf a final twist. Gripped it tight in both hands and spun in a circle. Again and again. Lifted the small man off his feet.

And let go.

The surgeon flew fifteen feet beyond the roof. He flailed, momentarily weightless, Kandri's scarf still choking him. When the screams came, they were not his own but those of the caravan members, beneath the Pillar in the shade.

Kandri lowered his forehead to the rooftop. That was that. Beside him the Prince gave a barely audible moan. In the chaos of Kandri's mind he thought another sound echoed, like a woman's sob from far away. *Get up*, it seemed to say. *Get up. Call out.*

Then a second scream of horror erupted from the caravan. Nirabha's eyes snapped open. Kandri's head snapped up.

"Oh shit. Oh you stupid fucker. Oh no."

The roof was empty. Ripheem had jumped.

26. A VERY OLD WOMAN

Therel Agathar's mother saw angels in her declining years. Most came at midday, sailing down from the fragrant hills, on ambiguous missions to Paval Churi or the ascetics' colony at Scyrna. The angels terrified her. Some had translucent skin through which mysterious organs were visible; others had the flat yellow eyes of snakes. Often they paused to speak to her, recalling the moral lapses of her ancestors and reminding the old woman that her position in the next world was subject to daily, and even posthumous, review.

Agathar had watched his mother age with both admiration and grief. Her bent fishhook of a spine, her vulture's skin. A wheelchair on each floor of her great listing mansion, although he dreaded the thought of her clawing her way up a staircase, even on a servant's arm. In the black prune of her skull was a mind he knew to be superior to his own, no matter how many called him "genius." But over the years that mind had fogged over like a window on a chilly night. It did not help that her angels spoke so often of death.

"You will face them as well, Therel," she declared as he filled her cup with starfish tea. "When I am gone, their attention will turn to my son."

"I count on you to predispose them to clemency," said the general. "Begin with my kindness to lizards. That should count for something, given your description of the blessed host."

"Never grin, Therel. It offends the natural majesty of an Agathar face."

"I am not grinning, Mother dear."

She looked up at him, owl-eyed. Despite spectacles so thick they resembled opera glasses she was nearly blind. "No, you're not," she said. "Have you been rowing again with—anyone?"

With your father, she had almost said, though it was sixteen years since his passing. At least tonight she had caught herself. The lapses shamed her terribly.

She squirmed in the big armchair. He filled his own cup, gulped the tea, swallowing the little live starfish that would bring good luck in the months ahead. He did not wish to speak to her of Obekri. Some rows were too mortifying to explain.

"There was an incident at the Dockyards," he admitted.

"I knew it. You're dreadful company tonight. It's been like dining with a sloth."

"I'm sorry, Mother."

"You've not visited His Holiness the Patriarch in over a year. Why is that, when he prays nightly for your soul? Have you nothing to confess?"

"On the contrary," said Agathar, "I wouldn't know where to begin."

She made a sour circle of her lips. His mother's visions were monstrous, but her beliefs were perfectly conventional. Heaven was a place of punishment and coercion, of indisputable law. *Their justice is our ruin.* Human souls by contrast came from the depths of the earth, that blessed place of fire and darkness, that land of peace. It was there that love dwelt, there that the wise elementals labored tirelessly to coax living souls from minerals and magma. At the moment of conception those souls slipped their anchors, swam upward through miles of solid rock to blossom in their mothers' wombs. Human life began as the ecstatic dance of the underworld, and progressed by stages toward the cold and perfect dignity of the Gods.

The general knew what his mother thought of his progress. He was apostate. He shunned the temples. He was certain that the Gods were real but no longer believed that anyone, anywhere grasped their methods or their plans.

As a rule they stuck to subjects other than faith. "It was not pleasant at the Dockyards this morning," he said at last. "His Majesty's Inquisitor arranged for a spectacle. A house of horrors, really."

"Sulmurg." There was a faint echo in her voice of that old fire, that scalding moral clarity that had frightened kings.

"This is his war, Mother. The rest are finger puppets. The King, the War Cabinet, Lord Larisalt—"

"You?"

He looked up sharply. Her eyes were fierce, whether they could perceive him or not.

"Lord Sulmurg," she said, "has been a blight upon Shôlupur since he wormed his way into the old Queen's court. He will never be your equal in honor or intellect, Therel. He knows this, and hates you for it. But I fear you will never be his equal in the matter of resolve."

"Resolve without reflection is no virtue," said Agathar.

"But still a deadly tool."

He sighed, looking at the mound of crab legs and cracked shells between them. "I've taken steps, precautions," he said. "I composed—"

"No more!" she said. "What sort of fool have you become, to hazard telling me?"

"I wasn't about to go into detail."

"You were, I think, in your heartbreak."

She could barely see, and yet she saw right through him. So many empty chairs around the table. Isula had left before dinner was served, telling them with gestures that she was exhausted. But there were places set as well for his son, and granddaughter, and for Obekri. All of them should have been here tonight.

"If I am heartbroken, it is for what our Kingdom has become," he said.

"Enough!" His mother smacked the table. "Swallow that heartbreak, child. Your stomach can take it, if you wash it down with deeds. Bring my appointment book. We'll get the old gang together for a little war council of our own. Lady Orset, Cousin Elsk and his soothsayer, the Baron Morsu. And General Kimburac of course."

"I ride for war tomorrow," he said softly.

"Tomorrow! Tomorrow? Yes, damnation . . ." Her voice trailed off; she chased a morsel of squid around her plate with a fork. He could feel her shame like the heat of a bonfire. It was the third time she had forgotten that evening.

"So," she mumbled, deflated, "another assault on the Fortress City."

"The eleventh," he said.

"Will it succeed, this time?"

He sat in silence, ashamed in turn, recalling his laughter atop the tower of Statuary House. "It might," he said.

"And you cannot stop it? Not even you, the Magnus General, the hero?"

"Not even I."

"That is the wrong answer, Therel Agathar," she said, her voice rising again. "Or at the very least, the wrong emotion. Deeds! What are you going to do about this lunacy? Choose a course of action and follow it. Call on the Patriarch. Go to your adoring mobs and tell them the truth!"

And watch them torture you and Isula, he thought.

"I did not raise you to despair," she went on. "That is what this ponderous evening is about, am I right? Your despair? Or merely your self-loathing, as you imagine yourself riding in Larisalt's shadow, prosecuting his uncle's imbecilic siege?"

"That is not what tonight is about," he said.

"What then, Therel? We have never had such a morbid wake on the eve of a campaign. What is it you want? I cannot stand this misdirection!"

"I want," he said, "to know how Kimburac came and went from this house without my father's knowledge."

It had been a long time indeed since he had seen shock in her face, and he regretted it. He meant the elder Kimburac, the architect, father of the general he had seen murdered in King Grapahir's trap. He hated to ask about him; he wished no further blows to her dignity. But it could not be helped.

"Or the servants' knowledge, for that matter," he went on. "If any of them had been aware of those liaisons, all of them would have been. And thus again, my father. Several loved him, despite the drink."

His mother pushed her plate away. "I shall retire," she said. "Be so good as to wheel in my chair."

"I've known since my teens," he said.

"Astonishing," she snapped, "since you were twenty before we began."

He was blindsided: she had not even tried to deny the affair. In a jarring way it made him proud of her: past ninety and still ready to duel.

"My chair," she repeated. "I am most savagely disappointed in you, Therel. Dredging up such matters tonight."

"You fail to grasp my purpose," said Agathar.

"I think not, you wretched boy. Don't say it—I'm well aware that you're seventy, but in my presence you're quite capable of devolving to those teens you speak of. Those spiteful years. That is the emotion I could not place my finger on. Spite. You've harbored the wish all these years to confront me—"

"Yes."

"—to humble the pious believer. Who perhaps did not have enough love to go around. Who saved a bit of it for her faith, when you believed it was yours by birthright, all of it, every laugh and teardrop. Just as your father did. My love was his bag of gold, to hoard or squander but never reciprocate—"

"Mother, Mother, I only wished to confront you—"

"—a thing to dust off before balls, weddings, nights at the theater, audiences with the King."

"—with my approval. My understanding of why you loved him, Kimburac that is. Only I feared to offend."

Again, shocked silence. He had to use that shock, that clarity; the hour was so desperately late.

He stood from the table, pointed at her with a crab leg. "You have *not* understood, Mother. I am watched day and night: eighteen men surround your home as we speak. I cannot step into the garden and piss on the roses without word of it reaching Sulmurg."

"Are you being literal? Those flowers were a gift from—"

"I can send no letter, summon no courier, exchange no casual whisper in the street without him pouncing like an alley cat. But there is one letter that *must be delivered*. Tonight. Without his knowledge. This war, this continent—*Jeshar*, perhaps the world itself hangs in the balance. Listen again: I did not ask why you slept with him, or how long it lasted, or whether you thought of divorce, or if you truly believe that these—" He gestured upward.

"—loveless Gods punish those who seek escape from loveless marriages. I asked *how Kimburac came and went.*"

"Just how?"

"Yes, woman, how! The means, not the morals! And before midnight, pray, or I'll—"

"—become a turnip again."

"Yes. What?"

Their eyes met. Then he guffawed, and she took off her terrible glasses and rubbed her eyes. It was a Wostrylic folk tale. She used to read it to him to make him sleep.

"Bring my chair," she said once more. Beaming at him, blind.

⋘

He rolled her to the grand salon. Then she climbed with him—resting often, creaking and sighing like an old elm—up two long flights of stairs to the spare sitting room. The cozy but long-abandoned room, where once she had liked to embroider and look out at the sea.

And to make love to Kimburac. Agathar had heard them, now and again, from his room below. To think that it had once filled him with rage.

She collapsed into the room's only chair. "That thing," she said, pointing at a tall chest of drawers. "Roll it aside, if its wheels have not fused."

They had fused, but he moved it nonetheless, already guessing what it hid. The little door behind it was not even latched. Beyond, a tight spiral stair dropped back down through the mansion.

"An escape shaft," he said, wondering.

"All the big houses of the day had one," said his mother. "You never knew when your fortunes might change, when your sovereign—or his Inquisitor—might decide you had to die." She nodded at the staircase. "It's walled off from the other floors, and even the basement."

"Father must have known of this."

"Your father lacked both curiosity and imagination," she said. "It never occurred to him that my needs were real, or that I would take risks for them."

She looked wistfully at the doorway. "At the bottom you'll find a tunnel. It passes under the gardens and joins up with a second tunnel, from Fulcyd House." She laughed. "Lady Fulcyd's lover was almost as eager as Kimburac. Sometimes they crossed paths."

"Don't tell me I have to sneak through the Fulcyd estate."

"Not at all. The tunnel ends on the grounds of the Temple of Iszmi. There's a gap in the fence."

Iszmi, God of love and fertility. One day he would tell this tale in full. If anyone was left alive to wonder, or to laugh.

But in the morning he would have to tell her of the death of her lover's son. He could not chance the news reaching her from unkind lips. *Iszmi, if you're listening, let her forget it as soon as I speak. For once, let her fog be a kindness.*

"It was always damp this time of year," she said.

"Mother!" he said. "You used the tunnel yourself? You went to *him?*"

She looked at him sidelong, greatly amused. "You thought we shared nothing but this room, did you? Really, Therel, was I ever so easily satisfied? He took me sailing. He let me furnish his house on Canner's Row."

ᝌ

One hour later, the tradeswoman with the mule heard a tapping at her window. A very specific tapping, a pattern that meant *Letter of maximal urgency, guard with your life.* She parted the curtains and found a face ten inches from her own. She gasped, for it was the face of one to whom she had dedicated her life.

The figure was dressed like an old woman: hooded cloak, floral scarf, straw basket over her arm. Greatly afraid, the tradeswoman parted the windows an inch, and the envelope slid into her hand. For the first and last time in her life, her secret employer gazed into her eyes with boundless gratitude.

"To the crane-keeper. Tomorrow without fail."

"I will, sir, I will."

"Your name may never be inscribed where it should be, on the walls of the Citadel of the Fearless," he said, "but there is a final ledger beyond the reach of us all, and there it shall be set down forever."

"I do only what I think right," she said simply.

"That is enough," he said, "and beyond the abilities of many a prince. Farewell, I must go."

"But sir—" She reached out in sudden distress, and just stopped herself from touching him. "—tell me: what is *really* happening? This new war with the Kasraj, this attack? What's it all about?"

He had begun to turn away already, but was arrested by the vital simplicity of her question. In his mind he saw the Kasrajis in the hold of the *Evensong*, howling, killing, dying—and minutes later, the Shôl guards doing the same. Two great enemies, felled by the same Outworlder weapon, the same poisoned gift.

"It is about weakness," he said. "Our weakness, all Urrath's I mean. It is about making sure we go on hating, brawling, breaking our tools over one another's heads."

"All Urrath?" She hunched her shoulders, horrified. "Why should anyone wish such evil on us?"

"I don't know, sister. But I swear on your good service that I shall learn. And when I do—"

Agathar gripped her hand fiercely a moment. Then he pulled the hood tighter about his face and hurried away.

൫

The monks in the Temple of Iszmi had extinguished their lamps; it was well past midnight. In the street, far below the lone window of the third-floor sitting room, the cheroots smoked by Sulmurg's agents dimmed and flared, dimmed and flared. The Pilgrim smoldered low over the wall of Nebusul.

Scarlet moon for a scarlet land.
Pray for your children, war is at hand.

He felt his age, remembering that song. He had heard it on a woman's voice in a tavern doorway, three days before he marched to Važenland on his

507

third deployment. That had been a Pilgrim year too. He had been too shy to speak to the woman that night, but she was still singing in the tavern a year later when he staggered home, and they had married and raised four children, and bickered and loved and bored each other and laughed a great deal until the Plague carried her away in a fortnight.

Agathar turned from the window and crept down the stairs. No light from beneath his mother's door, thank the Gods. But Agathar knew that his own sleep would evade him for another hour at least. No point in fighting it. He felt his way to the library and lit three candles on his desk.

Moments later he heard footsteps outside the library. His eyes snapped to the door. The steps were too quick to be his mother's.

Agathar's hand closed on a brass letter-opener: a pathetic dagger, but it was all he had. Then the door opened and Obekri stepped into the room.

"I still have a key," he said.

"Kalen!" Agathar gaped at him, mystified.

Obekri closed the door behind him. "Pour me a brandy," he said.

"But why did Sulmurg's men let you pass?"

"That I might seduce you, presumably."

Obekri collapsed in the chair nearest the door. Agathar collapsed into the chair behind the desk. The room was very dark beyond the circle of candles. His friend might have been a ghost.

"You were right," said Obekri. "I am a spy for the Special Inquisitor. Your only mistake was one of timing. When you accused me I was innocent. The man came to me yesterday and explained how things stood."

Agathar folded his hands beneath his chin. "How do things stand?" he asked.

"Sulmurg does not—did not—have a spy within your inner circle. Lacking this, he would be arranging for your death as soon as possible, for he feared you meant to conspire with the enemy."

"The fool won't kill me. He can't take Kasralys on his own."

"I comforted myself with just that thought," said Obekri, "for a night and a day. A few hours ago, however, I reflected that the closest friend I've ever known was riding to war on the morrow, and that I might be signing his death warrant if I stayed behind."

"You mean to—Obekri, Kalen, you can't intend—"

"I will ride as your aide, as your interpreter of winds and rain and rivers—as your concubine, some gossips will assume. I don't give a rat's fleabitten ass. I *will*, however, demand one thing of you, Magnus General, and on that score I will accept no evasions."

"Name it," said Agathar.

Obekri looked up sharply. His eyes were fierce, but his mouth struggled into a smile.

"Lies," he said, "convincing and numerous, to feed that snake."

27. THE WATERS OF LUPRIZ

Mektu declared that he would never depart the Font of Lupriz. He would grow old there, he said. He would shun and even attempt to forget the world beyond its five-sided wall.

Birdsong, butterflies, deep sunset shadows. The day's heat lifting like a veil. It was their third day in the comforts of the oasis, and the peace was tangible and delicious.

Except, of course, right here. Mektu paced before them all, waving like a preacher, talking nonstop. "They served us apricots—apricots blended with palm wine, that is. Apricots you *drink*."

"Brothels the world over serve good drinks," said Stilts.

"The place I visited is not a *brothel*, Mr. Stilts," said Mektu, "but I mean it: Lupriz is the best place in Urrath. Why should we ever leave?"

It was clear who he meant by "we," but to drive the point home he planted a kiss on Eshett's forehead. Eshett, smiling vacantly, waved him off like a fly.

No one took Mektu seriously, of course, but Kandri understood his sentiments. Just sitting here in the courtyard of their boarding house, among palms and ginger flowers and walls of creeping angel's breath, was a kind of ecstasy. Out on the sands, he had felt time stop—dead still, with all of them frozen in postures of futility and pain. Now he wished with all his heart that he could stop time again. Or pause it at least, to let him savor these comforts.

Time was having none of it. Ulren had told them to expect a summons any minute from the ruling Sartaph of Lupriz.

"Best behavior, Chilotos," he'd warned. "Let the Prince talk for you; she'll like his pretty speech. No squawking from Gooney Bird."

They waited, but the summons did not come. Kandri, feet propped on an inverted washtub, was sipping his fifth coffee of the day—an oily black brew with date sugar; he could drink it by the gallon and never tire. Stilts was writing in his journal. Talupéké and Chindilan were playing Babaturri, flipping the hourglass, throwing the stone die with its twelve cryptic symbols, slapping down small wooden bricks on the table between them. Eshett, happy and silent, watched the butterflies.

"Where the devil is that summons?" said Chindilan, studying the little bricks. "I'd like to get this court visit behind us. I hate talking to royalty: you dare not look too anxious to please them, and you dare not fail."

His eyes gleamed suddenly, and he shot a grin at Talupéké. "Warned you, didn't I? Babaturri's my game, and I take no prisoners."

Smack, smack, smack, went his bricks onto the table. "Fifty-three!" he said, rubbing his hands together. "What do you say to *that*?"

"That you've never played General Tebassa," said Talupéké, not looking up. *Smack, smack, smack, smack, smack.* "One hundred sixty-five."

"I never liked you, girl," said Chindilan. "Not one little bit."

ᘓ

Lupriz had brought a kind of rebirth. The orgies conjured by Mr. Ulren had yet to occur, as far as Kandri knew. Walls, beds, ample water, decent food: these were the pleasures they had dreamed of most ardently. To be out of the wind, the sand, the withering sun. To see new faces. To glimpse a lemon tree in bloom. An old man kneeling to buckle a granddaughter's sandal. A pack of boys staring astonished at his wild-man-of-the-desert hair, afraid to return his smile, helpless with laughter as he left.

Life, in short: abundant but normal. Kandri would never take it for granted again.

Mektu, of course, wanted more. Within hours of their arrival, he had talked his way into a mansion with a dark red door and steamy windows called *Aclistin Duru* ("Lasting Joy"), and Eshett had followed with a dreamy smile. They had returned hand in hand, beaming, satiated, clean as newborns. Lasting Joy, Mektu explained, was a charity founded by the Sartaph of Lupriz herself.

"A charity brothel?" said Stilts, looking up from his book. "That's a nice story anyway."

"It's not a brothel," Mektu repeated. "It's run by women, just women, and they feed you sweets and undress you and wash your hair and work the splinters out of your heels, and you soak in hot water until you're soft as jelly, and then comes a bucket of cold water to wake you up, and a cup of hot sweet wine, and then the women go with you into the steam room—all right, it's a brothel, but it's heaven too, and every gham we spend there goes to the poor."

"I hope you think of them each time you climax," said Stilts.

Kandri's only concern was how Mektu had paid for his pleasure—and Eshett's, for it was clear that whatever she had done in the mansion had made her happy indeed. The gold and rubies from Lord Garatajik were all in Kandri's keeping, and he counted them the night of their arrival. How had Mektu paid?

On the second day his brother had rushed back to the brothel. Eshett had trailed after him again, but this time she had glanced back at Kandri, an unspoken question in her eyes.

Now, as they waited for the Sartaph, Kandri blew a smoke ring at his brother. "What did you do with your beloved mattoglin, while you were busy in the steam?"

"Kept it with me, of course."

"What, while you were *naked*?" said Talupéké.

Mektu looked at her sheepishly. "It's priceless," he said. "What would you do, if it was yours?"

Kandri shuddered. *Talupéké with that cursed thing. Talupéké in a yatra's grip.* Best not to think about it.

But the girl just laughed at Mektu. It was a welcome sound, for she had little enough to laugh about in recent days. Her grandmother had fallen ill on the trail and had still not recovered.

"You're lying," she said. "They'd never let a crazy-eyed bastard like you walk around in a brothel with a fucking beheading knife in his hand."

Eventually the truth came out. "They have a little chest," Mektu admitted. "They lock the mattoglin up while I'm there."

"So you *do* hand over your toy!"

"I don't," said Mektu. "They keep the key, but I keep the chest. I carry it from room to room."

Talupéké blinked at him. "You carry a padlocked—"

"Yes."

"While you—while these women—"

"Yes."

Eshett giggled. Talupéké stared in disbelief. "You," she said, "are madder than a chicken with its head on backward. And I've seen one of those."

C3

It was almost as if the caravan had ceased to exist. Across the whole of the Sumuridath, Kandri had lived immersed in those hundred-odd lives. He had watched them wake, rise, flinch from the sun, glance hopeless at the infinite landscape. He had watched them swat flies and swallow beetles, come to blows over dice, sing like angels, fondle the camels' scrota. He had watched them give their last mouthful of water to a friend, only to steal another friend's flatbread and swear innocence before the God of Hosts. He had smelled their blended body-reek like a malt of dubious worth. He had watched them weep and sing and fight and copulate and die.

And now they had vanished into the arms of Lupriz—three dormitories for the camel drivers, a fourth for Tebassa's soldiers, and one more for Kandri and his companions. Though out of sight, the dismantled caravan was in fact close at hand—and so was the mystery of its secret cargo.

Did it truly exist? Captain Utarif had thought so. The treacherous surgeon had been ordered to find that cargo or kill them all to prevent it reaching Kasralys. Now both men were dead, and Kandri was still no closer to solving the puzzle.

Moments after Ripheem's suicide, Kandri had understood that he could not let the Prince descend from the Pillar without raising the subject. It was a repellent task. The young man was sobbing on his knees. Kandri crouched beside him, a hand on his shoulder, wondering if Nirabha and Ripheem had ever once been parted.

When the tears ended, however, his questions were blunt. "Are you smuggling something into Kasralys?"

The Prince dried his eyes on his sleeve. "Not at all. That vicious little man was mistaken."

"But you and Lord Garatajik financed the caravan? That's where your fortune went?"

"To the caravan, yes. And to General Tebassa. He was hardly shy about his cut."

"And you still maintain," pressed Kandri, "that you had no idea I was carrying the Cure?"

"I repeat, Hinjuman," said Nirabha, "that I had no idea a Cure *existed*. Garu never told me he'd been successful."

"Then what did you want with a caravan at all? And why such crazy haste?"

The Prince looked close to tears again. "It was Garu's doing. He had learned something horrible—that much he made clear. Something that left him frightened as I had never seen him before. But as with so much else in our lives, secrecy was vital. 'What you do not know cannot be taken from you by torture,' was all he would say. That was in Mab Makkutin. He kept a house there. I only saw it once."

The Prince rose from his knees and looked at Kandri defiantly. "I grasped his purpose much later, in the Khasabilari Hills. The cargo was me. He took my own gold and used it to send me home. The man blamed himself, you understand, for whatever danger I was in. His search for a Cure brought him west, uncomfortably close to the lands he never wished to see again—the lands the Prophet controlled."

"And you went with him," said Kandri.

"For love's sake," said the Prince. "Garatajik was always opposed. He feared his mother would somehow learn of us, and take revenge on me. Perhaps she did learn. Perhaps that very surgeon, damn him forever, sent word that her precious Secondborn loved a man." He smiled bleakly. "You and Mektu are not the only Abominations. Corrupting a Son of Heaven is only marginally less sinful than killing one."

Kandri felt shattered. Amazing himself no less than the Prince, he stepped forward and drew Nirabha into an embrace. "We should form a club," he said.

The Prince laughed, but there were sobs inside his laughter. "That day in Mab Makkutin was the last time I saw him alive. Ten weeks later your brother stabbed him in the chest."

Kandri winced. "So you know about that."

"I know about that."

"Mektu had no idea Garatajik was a rebel."

"Mektu did not pause to find out," said the Prince into his shoulder. "He attacked, like the savage he is."

Having no rebuttal, Kandri had simply led the way back to the long spiral staircase. But one question remained to be asked.

"The Outworlders," he said. "They're not behind all this, then?"

"What a very provincial idea," said the Prince.

"The surgeon claimed to be their servant. He said they were plotting to destroy Kasralys."

"The surgeon was a delusional fool," said the Prince. "Of course Xavasindrans are self-interested. They are here in Urrath to help themselves, first and foremost—and I suspect they enjoy their monopoly on contact with Urrath far more than they let on."

"Is it true that they're barred from Kasralys?"

"Absolutely true. We shut them out for a number of reasons—some sound, others fanciful. But destroy us? What perfect hogwash. There are barely a hundred Outworlders scattered across *the whole of the continent*, my good man. How could a hundred souls threaten the Fortress City?"

☙

Large as it was, the oasis felt crowded. The caravansaries were occupied not by camel trains like their own but by refugees, fleeing some sort of violence to the northwest. Many had come from Naduma, the land of Stilts' birth, along the ancient road Jód had spoken of at Famine's Table. Stilts had gone to these refugees directly. When he returned his face was careworn, but he did not speak of what he had learned.

The survivors of Jód's caravan, however, had fared rather well on the road to Lupriz. There had been thirst and illness—Kereqa was not alone in her suffering—and long nights of fear lest Spalak and his defectors assault them anew. There had been lasting sadness for all the deaths since Famine's Table. But no attack had come, and no one else had died since the Pillar of the Night Queen.

They had even arrived a day early, for the vision that Kandri and the Prince had received atop the Pillar had left them both with an astonishing certainty about the path. Ulren had scoffed at first, revealing a shadow of his old suspicious nature. But their claims matched even when he questioned them separately, and every twist and turn bore them out. If the caravan strayed by a quarter mile, they felt it. At last Ulren resigned himself to navigating by a gift he had not wanted them to acquire.

They had buried the surgeon half a mile from the Pillar of the Night Queen; the prayers at his graveside were cursory. Ripheem was another matter. His death appeared to have broken the Prince, who walked stone-faced behind the camel bearing the canvas-wrapped corpse. He wished to bury Ripheem far from the lathban, lest its sands shift and cover his grave, but in the ferocious heat they could not bear the body far. In the end they carried him as far as the Siramath Stair, that great edifice that scaled the cliff they had spotted from the Pillar.

Nirabha dug the grave himself, gently refusing assistance, and knelt beside the body in silent tears before they lowered it. Two camels dragged a smooth rock from the foot of the cliff, and Chindilan, who had some skill with stone as well as iron, carved the simple epitaph:

RIPHEEM
of the Line of the Tower of Tsakynnasis
Faithful and Beloved Friend

Nirabha's agony was plain to see. But in his mind Kandri still heard the taunts of the surgeon, and wondered if they held any truth. Ripheem had been ashamed to undress at Weeping Rock. Had someone truly cut him, mutilated him? Someone in the Prince's line?

The answer was yes, Nirabha had confided as they neared Lupriz, although Kandri would not have dreamed of asking. "Ripheem was gelded at the order of my elder cousin the Princess Dowager. The mutilation was not especially visible, but Ripheem had faced mockery before, and the pain of it never left him."

"I thought Kasralys was civilized," said Kandri.

"Civilized?" said the Prince. "A two-edged word if ever there was. You must judge for yourself if we are civilized, when you reach my home at last. But make no mistake: what my cousin did to Ripheem is illegal and abominable. It was also common practice before the Empire's fall. To certain Kasraji royals, any practice from the days of Imperial glory is to be clung to, no matter how shameful or depraved. 'Men without seed make slaves without need,' went the hideous adage. No temptations, that was the idea. Not of the flesh, and not of wealth or fame or power—for a eunuch, it was thought, could never truly enjoy these things."

"If it's illegal today, how did she get away with it?" asked Kandri.

The Prince just looked at him. "Spend an hour with my family," he said, "and such questions will never occur to you again. The most we could ever do for Ripheem was to wrest him from the grip of the Princess Dowager. My mother accomplished this when I was nine. Ripheem became my manservant, and that was for his own protection. The Princess had intended to keep him locked inside her mansion all his life, cut off from the world, lest her evil deed become known. Once we sprang him from her clutches, she wanted him dead."

"But she didn't dare touch your servant."

"Let us say that she concluded that the cost would be too great," said Nirabha. "By the standards of the city's elite, we Nirabhas are neither very rich nor very powerful. But like any ancient family, we have some cards under the table, and old debts we may call in."

ༀ

Much to his annoyance, the Prince had proved unable to read the Letter of Cure, when Kandri showed it to him at last. "This language is not one of my nine," he had conceded. "It looks like a kind of proto-Otheymic, and Garatajik did spend a great deal of time among scholars from Otheym."

Kandri had been incredulous. "Enough to learn their language? To *write* in their language?"

"If the fancy took him, yes," the Prince said firmly. "He could learn anything he set his mind to, Hinjuman. My Garu was a genius."

Says the man who speaks nine tongues. Kandri had felt abruptly desolate at the thought of his own stupidity.

"Garu was right," the Prince went on. "We should not have left Kasralys; within her walls we were little scorned. As you say, we are civilized: only a few lulees are murdered there in any given year. But our real dream was to leave all this backwardness behind us, and cross the sea."

Kandri suddenly feared he was talking to a madman. "The sea? You'd be sunk, you'd be executed. The Quarantine—"

"Only exists to protect other lands from the World Plague," said Nirabha. "No Plague, no Quarantine. It's as simple as that."

"Let's hope so."

"But of course it is," said Nirabha. "How do you think the idea to seek a cure first came to us?"

After that they had walked in silence for a good two miles. Kandri was humbled by the sudden understanding that love—just love, nothing more—had inspired the Prince and the Prophet's son to an endeavor that might yet transform the world.

ೞ

"You're done," said Talupéké. "I've crushed you."

Chindilan looked at the bricks on the tabletop with disgust. "My head wasn't in this game," he said. "Next time we'll play for gold."

"Don't do it," said Kandri to Chindilan. "She'll take the shirt off your back."

Talupéké smirked. "I'll take my winnings in labor. This old man can wait on me for a year." She stood abruptly, looking at Stilts. "It's been hours, Uncle, and Grandmother's alone."

"Go to her," said Stilts. "We'll make your excuses to the Sartaph."

Talupéké set off for the hospital where Kereqa lay. Stilts closed his journal with a sigh.

"I'm glad you distracted her, smith," he said. "She hides it, but she is panicked inside. Kereqa has not improved. General Tebassa erred when he let her join this expedition."

"Did he?" said Chindilan. "Kereqa saved our wretched lives more than once."

"At the cost of her own, nearly," said Stilts. "My sister is strong, by the Gods—strong as the Lion of Runar. In the circus, she used to walk the tightrope with a barrel of flaming oil balanced on her head. But even lions grow old. Kereqa should not have attempted the Sumuridath on foot. I think she will recover here, with rest and nursing and decent food. But it will not happen quickly—and that is the tooth that may bite us, gentlemen. Summer is but thirty days away. Even sooner comes the Killing Heat, when escape from the desert is all but impossible.

"We are not trapped yet, of course. A week's march to the east will bring us to the great pass called Twelve Hearts Valley. There we leave the

Sumuridath behind, all Gods be thanked, and once through the valley the Sacred Plain of the Kasraj will be spread before our feet. That leaves us little time to spare. I would not like to linger here more than one more week."

Mektu snorted. "Eshett and I aren't going—"

Kandri raised a warning finger. Mektu hid his face in his elbow.

"Will Kereqa recover in a week?" asked Chindilan.

Stilts heaved a sigh. "Two would be more to my liking—but for the caravan as a whole two is out of the question. There are other dangers than the heat, don't you think?"

He studied them; the silence grew uncomfortable. "I'm not sure what dangers you mean," Kandri said at last.

"No?" said Stilts. "Well, here's one to consider. I spent this morning among the refugees—I mean those poor souls huddled in the caravansaries, driven into exile. Most are from my homeland of Naduma, which lies some ten days up the northwest road."

"I had an idea that *you* were an exile," said Kandri.

"I have been," Stilts conceded, "and what's more, it was my own people who drove me out, not invaders. Still I love that land and wanted to learn what threatened her.

"The fighting's bloody, I'm afraid. A host of warriors from the north has taken over the Eubled, the heart of Naduma where our sparse waters are born. They are digging in—building forts and furnaces, and underground barracks in the style of my people, who are accustomed to life at the desert's edge."

Chindilan nodded. "Digging in against the heat. Waiting it out."

"I think so," said Stilts. "The invaders have driven the Nadumans' little brigades into the hills but haven't bothered to pursue them, the refugees told me. They rob and enslave us, and kill those who resist. But their minds are elsewhere. They are preparing for some future campaign.'"

"Any uniforms on these invaders?" said Mektu.

"None," said Stilts, "but they speak Shôl, and carry arms made in Shôlupur. And more arrive every day."

"The war's spreading east," said Kandri.

"Yes," said Stilts, "but which war, exactly? Your Prophet's war of conquest? We have left that one far behind. She has not managed to conquer the Važeks, yet—and as Prince Nirabha first informed us back in the Lutaral, the Važeks have formed an accord of some kind with the Shôl. If your Army of Revelation should ever break through to the east, their next encounter would be with Shôlupur—and there is no army in Urrath as great as the Scarlet Guard."

"You don't know the Prophet," said Mektu.

Stilts looked at him coolly. "I was fighting her at the General's side while you were still in baby teeth."

"Then how can you assume—"

"That she's no threat to the Shôl? I make no such assumption. I know full well what a hurricane is gathering behind her. But it has not broken yet. If the Prophet should one day triumph over the Važeks, it will have taken her half a century. And the Važeks at their mightiest were never half the power that is the Scarlet Kingdom. No, boys, the Shôl have not marched into Naduma to prepare for the coming of your Chiloto Queen. Some other purpose drives them. Some other plan."

He sat back, gaze sliding to the rooftops. Kandri knew he had not finished. Then he saw that his uncle wore a similar distant expression. Mektu noticed as well. He looked from one to the other. "You've thought of something nasty, haven't you?" he asked.

"Nasty is one word for it," said Chindilan. "Another might be insane." He scratched his beard, looking sidelong at Stilts as if begging the Naduman to tell him he was mistaken.

"Kasralys?" he said. "A siege?"

Mektu gave a little laugh; he thought his uncle was joking. In the silence that followed his look of mirth drained away.

"Well that's just rubbish," he said, still trying to sound cheerful. "Right, Mr. Stilts? Because the one thing everyone says about that city is that it can't be taken. Never has been taken. Never will be."

"That is exactly," Stilts agreed, "what everyone says."

"And exactly where the danger lies, if I'm catching your drift," said Chindilan.

"You've caught it," said Stilts, "but of course it's only a theory—the wildest of theories, but the most horrible if true. For even if it failed, that siege would be a declaration of total war between the Scarlet Kingdom and the Kasraj."

"And you think the Shôl want to use Naduma as a staging-ground."

"Or simply an experiment," said Stilts, "to test the mettle of the Kasraj."

"But why is *any* of this happening?" said Kandri. "I thought both kingdoms were strong and rich and safe. Why go to war?"

"Why now I cannot say," said Stilts, "though the Prince might, if we can persuade him to be candid with us. But remember that Shôlupur was the largest and greatest territory the Kasrajis held in the days of empire. They are bitter rivals, and have clashed many times since the Empire's fall. Each such clash has brought waste and hunger to Urrath as a whole.

"And for us, very simply, it could mean that enemies beyond counting—brigades, divisions, legions—may soon stand between us and the Fortress City. It could mean that our hopes of reaching Kasralys will be dashed on her doorstep, after all we have endured."

ឥ

Once again, the silence. And once again Stilts gave them a probing look. "Now you know my second motive for a quick departure. But there's another you've chosen not to share with me. I can see it in your faces."

"No, no you can't," said Mektu. His voice rang high with sudden nerves. Kandri and his uncle glanced at each other.

"Do us a favor, Mektu," said Chindilan. "Go and roust the Prince out of bed. Tell him that napping at sunset is the worst sort of luck."

"He's had that sort already," said Mektu, "but I'll roust him."

He left the room. Stilts looked at Kandri and Chindilan. "Out with it," he said.

Kandri played with the stub of his cheroot. "It's the Prophet, of course. Her servants—"

"What of them?" said Stilts. "The force we left behind on Ravashandul's Wall had no camels, lad. That Wall was their last hope of stopping us. They could not mount an expedition over the sand. Besides, they had no Gods-damned idea which way we'd gone."

"Those aren't the servants we're talking about," said Chindilan.

"Who, then?" asked Stilts. "Some larger brigade, rounding the desert from the north? Hoping to catch you as you leave the Sumuridath, wherever that occurs? She may go that far, I grant you. But such a force would still be months from this oasis, even if it passed unchallenged through the Gap of Sutku and the March of Thieves."

"Not them, either," said Chindilan.

"We should have told you," said Kandri. "Everything happened so quickly in your general's caves. The Prophet has . . . another kind of servant."

He forced himself to speak of the White Child: the being they had first glimpsed in Mab Makkutin, by appearances a girl of ten or twelve, but deathly white, the white of snow or a shark's underbelly, and her coal-black eyes the only contrast.

"That creature!" whispered Stilts. "Rumors came to us in our stronghold, but I found them hard to believe. They claimed this Child killed the Ursad's elephant."

"With a touch," said Kandri. "It was one of the worst things I've ever seen. And then she . . . felt us, somehow. Mektu and I were peeping out of a window, and suddenly she knew we were there. Just knew, and started after us. And her *face*, Mr. Stilts—"

"Is the face of the Prophet at a tender age," said Chindilan. "The White Child is her creature, maybe even her creation."

"She's using it to track us—track Mektu and me," said Kandri. "And somehow she's mixed me up with Papa—"

He checked himself. Eshett, sensing his distress but blind to its source, reached out and clasped his hand.

"He means Lantor," said Chindilan. "His stepfather, if you prefer."

"I will never prefer it," Kandri hissed, looking at Chindilan with alarm. "*Jeshar*, I won't ever call him stepfather, any more than I'll stop calling you Uncle."

Chindilan's eyes were bright. "You'd better not," he said.

"You have a clear-thinking mind, Hinjuman," said Stilts. He reached out with one ink-stained knuckle and rapped Kandri's chest. "*That's* what decides who your family is. Not blood. Not names. Not custom. Not paperwork. Just the heart, lad. All the rest is noise and pretense."

Mektu's shouts reached them faintly from the interior: *Up, up! You can't nap at sunset! Don't you know anything?*

"Back to this White Child," said Stilts. "What have we to fear, unless she has her own caravan? She can't cross the Sumuridath on foot. She'd be a dried-up corpse before she descended the Vasaru Hills."

"You don't understand," said Kandri. "She isn't natural. I don't think storms and heat affect her at all. She walks, yes, not even very quickly. But when you look again she's suddenly closer."

"And how do you know this, if I'm permitted to ask?"

"Ifimar Jód spotted her behind us, with his telescope," said Chindilan. "The Prince saw her as well."

"And I see her in dreams," said Kandri, "but they aren't normal dreams. They feel like . . . reports."

"Reports."

"Like warnings that she's still on our trail."

"Ah."

Kandri thought of his last night with Eshett, and the horrible insect-apes he had seen walking with the Child. Eshett pulled his hand to her chest.

Stilts crossed his arms and waited, and Kandri found himself exasperated with his composure. "She's real," he said, "and she's coming, and she may not be alone. She'd have caught up with us before if we'd stayed in one place."

"We stayed five days in Sanulsreya."

"Then I don't know!" said Kandri. "Maybe she was within a hundred yards when we finally set out. It's not as if I've read a book about her."

"How long since you dreamed of the Child?"

Kandri swallowed. "A long time," he said. "Not since Sanulsreya, in fact."

"That's good news at least," said Chindilan.

"And here is a bit more," said Stilts. "Lupriz has not been successfully raided in a century. This old five-sided wall has seen better days—I've spotted cracks here and there—but it still stands thirty feet tall, and the Sartaph's guards are well trained. We were made to wait for dawn ourselves, remember, before they opened the gates. For the White Child they will not be opened at all."

"Glad to hear it," said Kandri.

But in his heart he was not reassured. True, he had not dreamed of the White Child for weeks. But had she lost their trail, or merely found a better way to hide, even from his dreaming self?

True, she had only managed to enter the city of Mab Makkutin because she was tiny enough to squeeze through the bars of the city gate—and the gates of Lupriz were oak, with no gaps at all. But would any sort of barrier stop her for long?

Stilts rose, and the other two followed his lead. "We need a curse-breaker," said Stilts flatly, "someone to cut free your kite."

"My—"

"That's what we used to call such curses: kites, invisible kites. You have one tied to you, lad. You drag it with you everywhere, although it's high above your head. So high the Child can spot it from a thousand miles."

"Just me? What about Mektu?"

Stilts smiled. He beckoned them nearer and lowered his voice.

"We've a strong play to make here, if we're careful. For there's one more of us in need of curse-breaking."

He glanced meaningfully at Eshett. "Such a magician could help this one recover her mind and memory. And a curse-breaker is exactly what Mektu needs, to free himself from the golden mattoglin."

"Mr. Stilts," said Kandri, "there is a yatra in the mattoglin."

Stilts nodded. "I've thought so too, since Alibat S'Ang. That day a force overpowered me, just as Mektu started babbling like a man possessed. It tried to kill me, this force. It might have succeeded if I hadn't rolled off the cliff into the nets below. If we're right, the curse-breaker will need to be a good one, no village soothsayer."

"Mektu will never agree," said Kandri. "He'll know at once that we're trying to get the knife away from him. He won't go near any curse-breaker."

"He *will* go," said Stilts, "if he believes the treatment is for you and Eshett. He will go to protect you, as you protected him at the Xavasindran Clinic."

Or tried to, Kandri thought bitterly. The Outworlders had taken Mektu away to treat the infected arrow-wound, locking Kandri in a room by himself. He had heard what he was sure were Mektu's screams, though later his brother had no memory of screaming. They had both been helpless in the hands of those doctors with their cold, miraculous machines.

The thought brought to mind another doctor. He said, "The caravan's surgeon knew about the yatra, somehow. He claimed it was going to torture Mektu. 'A symphony of pain' is how he put it, 'followed by a filthy death.' And he told me that he alone could prevent that from happening."

"Did he now?" said Stilts, eyes widening. "That last bit surprises me. False as a pimp's promise, that surgeon was, but his contempt for magic was plain enough. Not much of a yatra-fighter, I'd have said."

"Forget him, Kandri," said Chindilan. "That murderous little piglet was trying to scare secrets out of you, although you didn't have the one he wanted."

"In any event we must start with a curse-breaker," sad Stilts. "I have taken Ulren into our confidence."

"Ulren!" cried Kandri. "Why the hell would you tell him?"

"Because he's the only one who knows this place—or the Sartaph who rules it. If we're lucky, he'll find a curse-breaker right here in the oasis, and we can be on our way."

"If Kereqa's on her feet," said Chindilan.

Stilts drew a deep breath. "And if she is not, you all will go, and I will remain here with her through summer's end—or longer, if the way to Kasralys is closed. My soldiers will go with you, of course—all of them, Talupéké included."

"She won't like that," said Chindilan.

"Like it!" said Kandri, almost laughing. "She'll tell you to go to hell."

"You're wrong," said Stilts. "My niece is a soldier, and I'm her commanding officer. She will do as I say. Or barring that—"

"What Grandmother says," said Chindilan with a smirk.

Stilts nodded, conceding the point. "Either way," he said, "I'll be the one who stays behind."

"You're staying!" cried Mektu, appearing suddenly in the courtyard with a groggy Prince Nirabha. "I knew you were smart, Mr. Stilts. And we'll be here to keep you company. Won't we, Eshett?"

Eshett looked at him vaguely. "Goose," she said.

❣

Sudden commotion. A plump man in a dark silk jacket burst in from the street. He beamed at them, as though the travelers were the answer to his prayers.

"There you are, brothers and sister! Come with me, come! The day is half spent already!"

"We're quite aware of that," said Stilts. "Are you the Sartaph's minister, then?"

"Oh no!" The newcomer bowed. "I am Omzal, and only her minor suzein. Won't you come now, please? Would it be possible to hurry?"

Gracious but implacable, he bustled them out. They walked swiftly between the whitewashed row houses, running a gauntlet of curious eyes: beggars, children, men on a rooftop placing ceramic tiles, young girls whispering behind their hands.

"You are a fascination for us, strangers," said Omzal. "We welcome thirty or more caravans a year to Lupriz, but it is decades since any came from the Heart Basin. None travel that way, save those in search of death. But you did—and some would have us believe that you climbed to Famine's Table and survived to speak of it! Famine's Table! Of course that is gossip, idle talk."

"Some of us did not survive," said Nirabha. The suzein winced, begging their pardon for his chatter, then chattered further to make up for it. He pointed out the prison of Lupriz, next door to the flower market. He recommended a cobbler. He showed them a door marked with the symbol of the World Plague—a tube or passage blocked halfway along its length—and told them it was a sanctuary for the dying.

"It is a common myth that all Urrathis are immune to the Plague," he informed them. "We have three souls at the moment in torment, Ang give them peace. And there ahead: that is the oldest temple in the oasis."

A windowless temple. Squat bell tower. Red rock dome. Omzal touched his forehead. "Holy to Ebirid, Crier of Midnight, Painter of Dreams. You may have heard the bell—struck at midnight only. The priests have not missed a night in five centuries, it is said."

Despite the heat, Kandri shuddered. The God Ebirid was a favorite of the Prophet; he sent her visions of the world to come. Hideous visions: devils flaying children for laziness; adulterers strapped in their beds and burned; pits opening under cities, vomiting rivers of blackworms and centipedes and snakes.

Transcriptions of the Prophet's visions from Ebirid made their way to all her arch-priests. Father Marz had recited them with relish from the pulpit. Like children across the Valley, Kandri had woken screaming on countless nights thanks to the Painter of Dreams.

Omzal led them on. They cut through alleys so narrow that Kandri could have lifted the glass teacup cooling in a left-hand window while knocking with the brass knocker on a right-hand door. They walked grand streets colonnaded in palms. Around one dusty corner they came suddenly upon a small iron gate, with cool green shadows beyond.

"Another shortcut," said Omzal, producing a key. "The main gates of the Faluvari stand open to all, of course, but this one will save us going around."

"The Faluvari?" said Kandri.

Omzal looked scandalized. "The Gardens, brother! The Gardens of the Faluvari, and the Fountains that are our greatest joy? Have you not seen them yet? Enter, enter, and not another word."

He waved them in through a curtain of fern-trees and flowering ginger. A cool mist touched Kandri's skin—unspeakable pleasure, gone since Weeping Rock—and then he parted the ferns and stepped into the Gardens.

All of them fell speechless. Before them was an extravagance beyond dreams: marble fountains, rising in steps and tiers and terraces, one above another. There were great scallop-shell basins and mosaic pools, water flung skyward in bouquets and follies, water falling in curtains and tumbling down staircase cascades, water leaping in arcs over winding paths.

Hundreds of people filled the Gardens, here in the cool of the evening, and yet it was built on such a scale that it did not feel crowded. "This is the heart of the ancient city," said Omzal. "It beats still, though the years have bruised it, and the city itself is swept away."

"Those people," said Stilts, looking at the crowds ahead, "they're speaking Naduman."

"War exiles," said the suzein, looking uncomfortable. "Refugees. There have never been so many—not in my lifetime, nor in the tales of my family. I pray for them nightly. But come, we are late."

He marched them swift through the wonders of the Faluvari, over ornate bridges, past tanks and fish ponds and fountains carved in the likeness of elephants and eels, dolphins and sea-snakes, nymphs blurred and blinded with age. In places the tanks had ruptured so that the water gushed over the walkways. Kandri felt he was dreaming. *Fresh clean water. I'm wading in it. And the desert surrounds me still.*

There were a few prosperous-looking visitors, but they were far outnumbered by the war exiles: men and women filling faskas and cook pots, or scrubbing their children's faces, or just standing drenched and silent as though the spray might heal them, restore the lives they had lost. Kandri saw a man solemnly divide a single date among three children. And he saw Stilts trying to give comfort to all he could: gripping one man's shoulder, whispering in another's ear, pressing a small purse of coins into an old woman's hands.

But many more hands reached for him—and some for Kandri and the others, these strangers at their countryman's side. Gently, they clung, sleeve and shirttail, eyes pleading for understanding. We would not do this. We were never these people, we stood straight and never begged. Please, brother, do not judge us. Please stay a moment, look at my infant, hear our tale.

They had to pull away, smiling, sorrowful. Kandri felt the hands long after they were gone.

🙂

The Sartaph received them in a sitting room in the north wing of the palace: an elegant chamber of marble and colored glass, doors thrown open to receive the evening air. Moths fretted circles around the oil lamps. Tailless cats lounged about the floor.

The Sartaph herself, a bright-eyed woman in late middle years, looked less relaxed. She was seated on a low dais at the far end of the room, flanked by fully a dozen spearmen. Dark silk robe, high collar, silver buttons up to the neck. More silver on her ears and fingers, a band across her forehead studded with jade.

Mr. Ulren had arrived before them, and stood near the dais, rigid as a choir boy. He and the Sartaph watched as their guide led them forward. When the man stopped, they did the same and bowed low to the Sartaph.

"Travelers," she said, "rise and be welcome." Her voice low and resonant. Kandri straightened.

"We regret this delay in receiving you," the Sartaph continued. "We took ill even as you entered Lupriz, but we are quite recovered. Now tell me: is it the custom west of the sands—or in Kasralys herself, I must ask, honored Prince—to bear arms into the chambers of one's host?"

Damn the fool! Kandri repressed the urge to look over his shoulder. Moments ago, they had surrendered the few arms they carried to the guards in the palace vestibule—all save Mektu, who had argued for an exception, hugging the mattoglin like a lover. He had been roughly expelled.

"It is neither customary nor fitting, Your Grace," said Stilts. "Our friend has a nervous disorder."

"Is he a danger to the peace? Will he use that splendid blade on one of my subjects?"

"Never, Your Grace," said the Prince, surprising Kandri greatly. "He is a thorough fool, and outlandish in his speech, but he means no harm. And he will cause none, unless attacked."

"But from the mattoglin he will not be parted."

The Prince nodded gravely. "His fixation on the weapon is an aspect of his sickness, Your Grace. We should have preferred to leave him in the boarding house—"

"But I summoned your whole company," she said, "for I wished to see the faces of all those Ifimar Jód was conducting across the desert when he fell. Master Ifimar was a Marshal of Lupriz, our patron and sometime emissary. He was our friend—"

She broke off, glancing sternly away, and Kandri saw at once that this woman had taken the news of Jód's death very hard indeed.

"Mr. Ulren—*Master* Ulren now, forgive me—was about to tell me the tale. But have others remained behind in that boarding house? Where is Dothor Spalak, brother to Ifimar? He too is beloved of this house."

The travelers looked at one another. Ulren looked almost ill.

Prince Nirabha bowed again. "Honored Sartaph, friend of my Tower and my city," he began, "it is the cruelest of ill fortunes that compels me to—"

"He murdered his brother," said Kandri, to his own amazement and chagrin. "In cold blood. And he very nearly killed us all."

The guards stirred, gaping. Cries and whispers burst from the adjoining rooms: they had an unseen audience, it appeared. But when the Sartaph rose from her chair the silence was instantaneous. Wordless, she descended from the dais and walked up to Kandri.

"Who are you, boy, to burst out with such an accusation?"

Raven-fierce, she held his eye. The air in the room seemed to thicken. A moth caught fire within a lamp.

Kandri lowered his eyes. The question had pounced on him, seized him in cruel canine jaws. Who was he?

I'm his son. Spalak's son, the fanatic who killed his brother for the Prophet.

I'm his son. Lantor Hinjuman's son, eaten alive by his guilt over the Prophet.

I'm her son, as every Chiloto is the son of Her Radiance the Prophet.

I'm the abomination she's sworn to kill.

"Is he deaf?" snapped the Sartaph, turning to the others. "Who is this ragged man who tells me Dothor Spalak killed his own flesh and blood?"

"A witness," said Chindilan at last. "And I'm another, Your Grace. It's the truth."

"Spalak has turned to Orthodox Revelation," said Stilts. "We understand that he was first exposed to the cult in his youth. It appears he never ceased to believe."

"And you did not kill him?"

"He fled with six of our drivers," said Stilts, "after leading us into a nest of grasthu that took eighteen lives. Spalak meant for us all to die there, Your Grace. And so we should have, but for the swiftness of Ifimar Jód in responding to the trap."

"Where did they go, Spalak and his six?"

"We have seen nothing of them since the carnage," said Stilts. "But surely they will follow us here—unless there is a watered path out of this corner of the desert that does not run through Lupriz?"

"There are several, Naduman," said Ulren, "and Spalak knows them as well as anyone in Urrath, save the late Master himself."

The Sartaph walked halfway back to the dais. She spoke without turning, eyes on her darkening gardens.

"Jód is slain by Spalak's hand, and Spalak himself has been seduced by Revelation, and he led you into a nest of sky jellies ready to hatch."

It was not a question, and yet it was far from a statement of accepted fact. The travelers held their tongues.

"Do you know, any of you, how long we have enjoyed the commerce and company of Ifimar Jód?"

After another silence, Ulren cleared his throat. "I know, Your Grace."

"Do you know, any of you, of our unloved neighbor to the west, that hellshaft we call Jekka's Grave?"

Murmurs again from the unseen listeners. Kandri felt a prickling of the skin on his arms. She could only be speaking of the gargantuan crater he and Nirabha had glimpsed from the Pillar of the Night Queen.

Once more Ulren answered, his voice little more than a whisper: "I do."

"As companions of Master Ifimar," said the Sartaph, "we gladly extend you the freedom of Lupriz, and will provide you all help and courtesy within our power."

Stilts bowed again, and the others quickly followed suit.

"Our rule, moreover, is famous for its lightness of touch," said the Sartaph. "We tolerate no violence within these walls, but outside of that stricture we interfere as little as possible in the affairs of our people, or our guests. Bending others to our will is not our preference, nor our custom. That said—"

She turned slowly to face them.

"—you stand within the ancient and inviolate *Sartaphate* of the Font of Lupriz, and I am her sovereign. And should I learn that any part of this monstrous tale of yours be false, I shall invite His Highness the Prince Nirabha to quit my province for his own—"

Nirabha looked up in shock. "Your Grace—"

"—but the rest of you, protected by no treaty, I shall deal with as deceivers were in my ancestors' time, and you shall go in chains to Jekka's Grave and be lowered into that darkness, and I myself will beat the iron drum that summons the ghouls at the bottom to their feast. Am I clear?"

Dead silence. Kandri's heart slammed in his chest. *No,* he thought, *I wish you'd just speak your mind.*

"Very good," she said. "May you find balm and healing in our settlement. Our baths, they say, have no equal in the world. Oh, stand up straight, will you. All this infernal bending."

They stood up straight. The Sartaph looked at them, no longer threatening. Kandri saw that her eyes were moist.

Were you Jód's lover? The thought exploded in his mind. *Did news of his death break your heart? Is that why you were 'taken ill'?*

It was an effort not to stare. This woman was powerful and regal and blazingly smart. Also shaken to the core.

Jód's lover . . . or Spalak's? Had that madman—the father who would never be his father—shared this Sartaph's bed?

"Go and rest," she commanded them. "Our chamberlain will show you out."

Ulren, gathering his courage, murmured something low.

"Ah yes, the curse-breaker," said the Sartaph. "As it happens, you're in luck: we can provide far better than a mere solver of charms. Go to Belac Bajamthal the exorcist. You at least have heard of him, Prince."

"I am speechless, Your Grace," said Nirabha. "Belac Bajamthal, here?"

"You did not know?" said the Sartaph. "He is a Naduman like you, Commander Stilts, and well-traveled like most of your clan. For long years he has been a guest of Kasralys, true, but Lupriz was always his home. And we are proud of him: Belac the Exorcist has no rival anywhere in Urrath. Demons fear him as rabbits the wolf. He will cleanse you all of curses, if you truly suffer them. Although I shouldn't wonder. Any of us, if we dared—"

She never finished the statement. She dabbed a silk sleeve against her eye.

"Compliment his sculpture; he likes that. And tell him to send the bill to me."

☙

"Belac Bajamthal!" said Nirabha as they made their way back through the darkened streets. "I had no idea the man had left Kasralys."

"Who is he?" asked Kandri.

"My good man, he is the exorcist of our age," said the Prince. "He drove a wrathful spirit from the Palace of the Grand Illim himself, when fear of the thing had paralyzed the Rigat, and thus the city as a whole. For that deed Bajamthal was given the highest honor the city can bestow: the title of Brother-Defender of the Realm, and a dwelling in one of the Towers of Serenity for the whole of his life. The Sartaph is bestowing a great favor: Bajamthal's services do not come cheap. Go at once, before she changes her mind."

"We'll make inquiries tonight, and visit the man as soon as he's willing," said Stilts.

"Why did he leave Kasralys, if they honored him so well?" asked Kandri.

Nirabha shrugged. "He is old now, I imagine," said Nirabha. "Perhaps the bustle of Kasralys is no longer to his liking."

"Then he's come to the right place," said Ulren. "This is a little speck of paradise, with its fountains and girlies and good food. But it's still a speck, and we'd best remember that. Long days in the desert still, before the green plains of the Kasraj."

"Well we know it, Master Ulren," said Kandri.

"Hmm," Ulren sniffed. "None better than you and the Prince, I suppose."

It was the truth, of course. But that morning Kandri had realized something strange about the vision he had received. The path ahead to Kasralys remained etched in fire, so that he felt he could walk it in his sleep. But the one behind—all those long miles between the Night Queen's Pillar and Lupriz—had faded like chalk wiped from a blackboard. Only the palest ghost-image remained.

For Nirabha it was the same: "All gone, or nearly gone," he'd confessed to Kandri. "I doubt now that I could find my way back even to poor Ripheem at the foot of the Siramath Stair."

Was the gift of the Night Queen only a loan, then? Or had the surgeon's drug caused some lasting damage to their minds that only now was taking effect? Would other memories trickle away? Would they become like Eshett?

Fertile ground for anxiety, but before Kandri could plow any further someone shouted his name. A man was running toward them from the street ahead, waving urgently. As he drew near Kandri saw that it was the driver with the clouded eye.

"Mister Kandri, where have you been?" he demanded, gasping for breath. "Come with me. Very quickly. Your brother, he is attacked."

28. A VISIT TO THE EXORCIST

It was not the sort of emergency he feared, but Kandri soon realized it was the one he should have expected. They found Mektu in the yard of the camel stables, bleeding from nose and scalp. He looked demonic painted with so much blood, and his behavior heightened the impression, although neither wound proved serious. He was wild-eyed, his breath so saturated with liquor Kandri could have ignited it, and he would not sheathe the mattoglin. Scores of onlookers, including many of their own camel drivers, watched from a prudent distance.

Prince Nirabha, arms crossed, studied Mektu with revulsion. "There is no haven in Urrath beyond this man's power to defile."

"What the hell happened?" said Chindilan. "He not much of a drinker. That's one weakness he's never had."

"Put the knife away, Mek," Kandri shouted, gripping his arm. "Away. In your belt. Are you listening?"

"I'll put it away in their intestines," said Mektu. "Lying shits. 'Come visit my family! We'll feast together, we'll roast a whole pig!' Where are they hiding? I'll give them something to roast."

"That is too much blood," said Stilts quietly, "for such minor wounds. It is not his alone."

The information was too much for Chindilan. "You Gods-forsaken miscreant!" he bellowed. "What the hell have you gone and done? We just finished swearing up and down that you were harmless!"

"Help me kill them," said Mektu.

The drivers soon told the story. They had discovered Mektu reeling in and out of a tavern across from the Lasting Joy brothel. A trio of men hung on his shoulders, dancing and capering, coaxing him to try one bottle after another. Eshett, seated apart on the tavern steps, had watched with amusement.

But the men were aware of her. Eventually one had urged Mektu to improvise an ode to her beauty. He had obliged, going down on one knee before her. Singing sweetly, making her laugh. Two of the strangers dropped beside him, trying to harmonize. And the third lifted the mattoglin from his belt.

It was so well done that even the watching drivers had missed the moment of theft. But Mektu knew, somehow, and in an instant he grasped the whole of the deception.

"He was struck with madness," said Kandri's friend with the clouded eye. "He knocked down the man who pilfered him and took back the mattoglin. He stomped on this man's chest and shoulders. And in addition, his face."

"Tell me he didn't kill anyone," begged Kandri.

"Not then and there, Mr. Kandri. But the other men leaped on him from behind and threw him down. They took the knife again and fled into the tavern, and Mr. Mektu chased them with the howling of a dog. Very soon he ran out again. Now he had the mattoglin and it was stained with blood. Seven men pursued him, and some were bleeding already, and then there was shouting about the Sartaph's guards. The men ran in all directions, and Mr. Mektu chased one screaming, promising death."

They had witnessed little more. Two women had ushered Eshett to safety in their dormitories, where she remained. Mektu himself had turned up in the stables, stumbling, demanding that someone lead him to Fish.

"We need to get him out of here," said Stilts. "If the Guard finds him blood-painted they'll have no choice but to haul him away."

Kandri applied himself once more to calming his brother, and after several minutes his efforts bore fruit. Mektu stopped lurching and twitching. A certain shame began to haunt his eyes. He made his way into a camel stall and cleaned the mattoglin on the beast's woolly rump. When he stepped out again he could not meet their glances.

"I'm not safe to have around," he said.

ᴄꙅ

Stilts made inquiries with the exorcist that very night. It took no more than a conversation with the matron of the boarding house to learn that Belac Bajamthal lived with his servants in an imposing stone house near the northwest wall. Stilts dashed off a letter to the household and sent it with the matron's son.

They sat down to a meal of yams, rice, and small, charred cuts of goat. Mektu did not join them: after submitting to a bucket-bath and vomiting twice in the courtyard, he had dropped insensate in his bunk.

The matron's son returned as they were washing down the meal with warm palm wine. The reply he brought was not encouraging: the exorcist was absorbed in some vital task and could not receive them for at least three days.

"Splendid!" said Nirabha, slapping the table. "Then for at least three days, we must perform the hourly miracle of keeping your brother out of mischief."

"And out of jail," said Talupéké, filling a plate for her grandmother.

"And," said Stilts, "we must persuade him to escort Kandri and Eshett to Bajamthal's house—without raising his suspicions. And we'll have to ensure that he's not barred for carrying a weapon. I'll send a second letter to Bajamthal on that point—and you must come along as well, Prince: you make us look respectable."

"I dare say," said Nirabha.

"But none of this will matter if we can't get the fool to show up." Stilts looked at Kandri. "Can I leave that in your hands?"

Kandri glanced toward the corridor leading to their rooms.

"If I ask him to go, he'll go," Kandri said. It was the only answer he could give: Mektu's life might depend on his visit to the exorcist. But Kandri hated the idea of deceiving him yet again.

"The trouble isn't getting him there," said Chindilan, "it's controlling what happens next. Mektu doesn't panic at the mention of yatras the way he used to, Ang be praised. But if he's forced at last to see that there's a creature in the knife and what it's doing to him—"

"He'll fall to pieces," said Kandri.

"Spectacularly," said the Prince.

"No he won't," said Stilts. "Not if you are at his side, Kandri, and he feels your love. You must start preparing for that moment now. Be his best friend. Remind him of the happy times in your Valley. Hell, let him take you to his charity whorehouse. You ought to go anyway, as long as Eshett is. We ought to make sure things with her are as rosy as they appear."

"That's the last thing I should do," said Kandri.

Everyone turned to him. Feeling ludicrous and exposed, Kandri stammered, "Mektu . . . has this notion that we're some sort of rivals—"

"Ha!" Talupéké leaned forward. "Where does he get these *crazy* ideas! It's not as if you and Eshett were, I don't know, sneaking off in the dark and—"

"*Jeshar*, Tal," said Kandri through his teeth.

Chindilan tried not to smile, but it was hopeless. His torso shook; laughter rose in him like water pumped from a well. Kandri's cheeks were on fire.

"Oh," said the Prince, eyebrows lifting. "I wasn't aware that—oh."

"Fawns," gasped Chindilan. "They looked like . . . little fawns in wet grass . . . tiptoeing."

Stilts turned and glared at Talupéké. "Gossip is a defect, niece."

"Yes, commander," said Talupéké.

Stilts nodded at her, frowning. Then he saw Kandri's struggle for dignity and collapsed.

Ꮳ

Despite their fears, the three days sped by quickly. More refugees arrived. The heat grew stronger. Yet keeping Mektu out of trouble was almost effortless: he was ashamed of his drunken performance, and swore to Kandri that he would not leave his side until they reached Kasralys.

"I won't hold you to that," said Kandri.

"I'll hold myself to it," said Mektu. "I've let you down."

He was as good as his word—so much so that Kandri soon felt smothered. It was hard enough to shoulder the task he had accepted: to boost Mektu's trust in him as much as possible before their visit to the exorcist. Now Mektu had become a kind of Ripheem. Even when Kandri visited the privy behind the boarding house, Mektu waited in the yard.

But he had no desire whatsoever to visit Belac Bajamthal. On this point he was obduracy itself. By the second evening, Kandri began to think that he would fail in his assignment. *And what the hell do we do then? Tie him up and carry him there?*

The brothers strolled the streets and gardens of Lupriz, Eshett between them, holding each by an arm. "Don't do it for me," Kandri said. "Do it for her, Mek. We owe her that much."

"Eshett doesn't need any curse-breaker," said Mektu. "She needs love and happiness and joy."

"Lasting Joy, you mean?"

"Precisely," said Mektu, "and she's not the only one. Uncle should be going there every Gods-damned day. And you, you're a wreck. We should go there together."

"The Letter of Cure doesn't need a steam bath."

"You can put it in the chest with the mattoglin," said Mektu. "Safe, locked, and never out of sight." With sudden excitement he turned to Kandri. "Let's go, just the three of us. Let's go right now."

"I hate brothels, Mek."

"You hate places like Aunty Boom-Boom's. This is different—it's clean, it's peaceful, the women are *in charge.* Misbehave and you're out in the street."

"Maybe after we see Bajamthal," said Kandri.

"*Harach*, what a mule you are. What do you have against happiness? When was the last time you felt a woman's touch?"

Kandri said nothing. Eshett's grip tightened on his arm.

"I can't make sense of you," said Mektu, exasperated. "If you think an exorcist can help her, take her yourself, or ask Uncle. Just leave me out of it. Those people scare me."

"What about your promise?"

"What about not holding me to it?"

In the end he was forced to bargain with Mektu: a visit to the exorcist, followed by one to Lasting Joy. Mektu argued and negotiated until Kandri felt like strangling him, but at last they shook hands.

"Just don't make any excuses after we see this Baja-Bekel, whoever he is," said Mektu. "You're going. And you'll thank me."

α

The summons came at last in the form of a letter for Stilts. The others crowded around the Naduman as he broke the oxblood seal and unfolded the paper. The message, in an impeccable calligraphic hand, was quite short:

BELAC BAJAMTHAL

FOE OF THE INFERNAL

FIRST SEER OF THE ORDER OF THE SHROUD

will be pleased to resolve your maladies
today at the thirteenth hour precisely.

OBSERVE:

Persons negotiated aforehand only.
No food for two hours preceding appointment.
No jewelry.

"That's forty minutes from now," said Chindilan. "Just as well Lupriz is a small place."

Mektu at once began to wolf down the slice of fire melon he had just procured from the cook. Kandri took it from his hand. "Ang's nipples, I'm just the escort!" Mektu protested. "He won't care about my bit of melon."

"Eat it later," said Kandri. "I don't want you stopped at the door again."

"It will spoil before we get back."

"Stop talking," said Kandri, "before I burst into tears."

Chindilan shook his head unhappily. "I'd feel a hell of a lot better if I were going along."

"I'd be glad of it too, smith," sad Stilts, "but five was the most I could bargain for, and even that took some persuading. Go and visit Kereqa. A chat with someone her age will do her good."

"I'll go," grumbled Chindilan, "but I'm not *that* old."

The five "negotiated" persons—Kandri, Mektu, Stilts, Eshett, and the Prince—set out minutes later. It was noon; the streets were blinding and deserted; the buildings throbbed with heat like the walls of a kiln. A few faces looked out from darkened windows. A street dog curled beneath a handcart watched them with one crusty eye.

They rounded the public baths and the gutted shell of the Palace of Justice—abandoned, like most of the large buildings of the former city, long centuries ago. The waters of the Faluvari snickered at them over the fence about the gardens. The refugees were still there, huddled under scarves and blankets against the onslaught of the sun.

Where the hell would they go?

"Here's the Palace Walk," said Stilts. "And will you look at that? Another crowd up ahead."

Eighty or ninety people—young, old, very old—stood lining both sides of the street two blocks away. Despite the heat they were orderly and still, but their eyes were searching eagerly for something.

"*They* don't look like refugees," said Mektu. "What's brought them all out in this heat?"

"Not our concern, lad, we're practically there," said Stilts, shading his eyes. "The matron said Bajamthal's house is two streets north of the Palace, which would put it—oh bowels of the saints."

A man up ahead was pointing at them. Ninety pairs of eyes snapped their way.

"Our appointment's no secret, apparently," said Stilts.

The crowd was clustered before a pair of iron gates set in a high stone wall. Now they surged forward; Kandri and his companions were engulfed. There was some jostling, but no shouts or arguments: indeed the crowd was remarkably courteous. They were at pains not to block the way forward, and made no sound but a low, singsong chant:

Kiyu korum tha Selulahi ya
Adu Jeshanu ji

"Thank them!" said Stilts. "They are invoking the Gift of Selulahi, for success in our venture. They will anoint us with wine next, if I recall the custom."

Murmuring thanks, the five moved through the crowd. Kandri had caught the name of Selulahi the Liberator, handmaiden of Ang, freer of the enslaved. As Stilts had predicted, a few onlookers dipped their fingers in clay vessels and flicked a cool, fragrant liquid on the travelers' faces. It was not unpleasant. Kandri wondered at this outpouring of goodwill. The crowd asked for nothing, not even with their eyes. But somehow he knew—by their determined postures, maybe—that they would still be waiting when they emerged.

Two servants in cinnamon-red cloaks opened the gates from within. Kandri saw that the wall enclosed a space much larger than he had thought. At its center was a grove of cedars, low to the ground but massive and twisted, and within the grove stood a tall stone mansion. Its whitewashed pillars were almost too bright to look at where they caught the sun. Above them in the pediment was a round window of scarlet glass segmented like an orange. A neat path ran straight to a pair of towering red doors.

The servants led them forward. Twenty feet from the mansion, a narrow watercourse flowed under the path in a stone culvert. Kandri saw that the water encircled the house, and broadened on one side into a tank where purple hyacinth bloomed and a tall gray heron stood upon one leg. The servants stopped at the culvert.

"You must enter alone," said one of them, barely above a whisper. "Remove your shoes once you are inside, then advance through the hall and climb the stairs. Master Bajamthal awaits you in the Upper Sanctum."

"You're staying here, in the yard?" asked Kandri.

"We shall not enter. Our quarters are behind the house."

"I told you he'd be strange," said Mektu.

Nirabha glanced at him. "Listen to the ocean speak of salt," he murmured.

"You may find us strange," said the other servant, "but the Master has sent us from his house with good reason. It is often thus: the fewer souls within the house, the better he can hear those who are troubled. He may ask some of you to step out into the garden. But first he would examine you all."

Mektu shook his head—*Not me*—but walked with the others over the culvert and up the marble stairs. The great red doors were counterweighted and immensely heavy, closing again on their heels as they slipped inside. After so much brilliant sun, Kandri caught only a brief glimpse of the interior—cabinets, statuary, dim distant candles—before they were plunged into total darkness.

There was a smell of smoke and bitter herbs. Water gurgled somewhere on his left. As his eyes adjusted, Kandri saw that the chamber was laid out like a temple, with dark benches to either side of a long central aisle. The candles burned straight and still in niches along the far wall. Between them opened a dim archway through which he could see stairs ascending.

"Shoes," said the Prince.

Barefoot, they walked down the central aisle, the stone floor cool against their feet. If the entrance hall had ever had windows they were now bricked over: there was no light whatsoever but the candles and the palest glow from the archway.

"Gods of Death," said Stilts.

Left and right, weird objects loomed from the shadows. Most were sculptures: a girl with eyes at her nipples and none on her face, two women embracing a serpent; a man besieged by small winged devils tearing at his flesh; a man with a crown of antlers having intercourse with a deer. There were also taxidermied animals—a raven, a leopard, a sloth—in lifelike poses; a chair with manacles at wrists and ankles; and a cabinet with human skulls arranged from large to shrew-small.

"Do not judge him by these eccentricities," said the Prince. "They were famous in Kasralys when he resided there. Each is a totem of remembrance of a man or woman who had lived in torment before Belac Bajamthal set them free."

Mektu twitched as he took in the ghoulish collection, and his hand fluttered near the hilt of the mattoglin. Eshett was even more upset. She leaned into Kandri, gripping his arm. For an instant her glance was more lucid than at any point since their parting in the hills. He half expected her to speak to him with her old, blunt affection, to chide him, to tell him something other than "Goose." But the moment of clarity passed. Her lips trembled in the darkness, and he thought, *I'll never kiss those lips again.*

One by one they stepped through the archway. The stairs beyond were dark, but the light grew as they climbed. Twenty steps brought them up into a chamber of the same length and width as the one below—built directly above it, Kandri saw—but brighter and devoid of ornaments. Long curtains hid the walls to left and right.

The Upper Sanctum. It was warm here, and the smell of herbs grew sharp. The floor was of lustrous black wood on which not a speck of dust seemed bold enough to settle. There was just one window: the round red window they had glimpsed from the yard. One beam of sunlight entered by it, so sharp and distinct it might have been a glass buttress supporting the wall. And at the spot where it touched the floor sat Belac Bajamthal, cross-legged, alone.

"Thank you for being punctual."

The voice crackled with age like tissue paper crushed in the hand. It came from beneath a black headscarf shadowing Bajamthal's face. His body too spoke of age—rounded shoulders, crooked wrists—but what struck Kandri instantly was its strength. The exorcist was nearly as large as Ripheem, but with none of the servant's lumps and asymmetries. He wore a dark sarong that left his arms bare, and they were muscled like a warrior's, although the skin was dry. Before him lay a fountain pen, a small blue inkwell, and a leather-clad book dark with age.

"I hope you will forgive these elaborate trappings," said Bajamthal. "Here in the desert they are pleased to call me Foe of the Infernal, but in Kasralys I was *Subyral Ossund*, the Breaker of Solitudes. I have earned such names through long years of labor and loss, and the objects below are how I remember. But my own solitude is nearly constant. Whether it be the Gods' joke or the devil's revenge, I find I must live quite alone to maintain my gifts."

"But you're not alone," said Mektu, nodding to the curtain on the left.

The exorcist gave a low chuckle. "And you have the eyes of an hawk, Mektu Hinjuman. No, not always. Come out, Lasúm, it is time."

A small boy parted the curtains and stepped out. His head was hairless, his skin deepest black. In his hand was a brass censer from which a wisp of smoke escaped. He did not glance at the newcomers. Ten feet from Bajamthal, he stopped and set the censer on the floor and drew from it a stick of blackened, smoking wood.

"Show them," said the exorcist.

The boy touched the end of the stick to the floor. Then he ran in a wide circle, keeping the stick against the floor as though drawing with chalk.

There was a burst of light. A line of red fire, sizzling and spitting sparks, leaped up behind the stick. It encircled boy and Master in a ring some fifteen feet wide, and when it was complete Bajamthal lifted the scarf from his head.

Kandri bit his lips to keep from gasping. The exorcist's face was covered with scars: long, livid scars, white and pink against his black skin. He looked like a man raked long ago by lions. The longest mark began at the crown of his bald head and swept down across his ear, which was split almost in two. But the damage had never marred his eyes—huge, lambent eyes, bright white surrounding brighter green—or the large, full mouth that smiled at the newcomers.

"Will you not approach?" he asked.

They approached. The boy lifted the censer and leaped nimbly over the spitting fire. He withdrew to the far wall and crouched beneath the window, hands about his knees.

"The fire will vanish presently," he said. "A parlor trick by appearance, but also very practical, for nothing unbodied may cross in or out of this circle without my consent."

"Nothing *unbodied*, sir?" said Kandri.

"All Urrath is flooded with spirits, Kandri Hinjuman," said Bajamthal. "They surround us like schools of fish—voiceless, watchful, nearly impossible to catch. Most are indifferent to human beings. Some wish us well. And despite what is told in markets, temples, and public houses, very few wish us harm. But those few are tireless. We cannot be too careful."

Kandri felt the hairs rising on his arms. Half a year ago he would have laughed at such talk. Never again, though. Not after Alibat S'Ang.

"We are in a bad way, Master Bajamthal," said Stilts. "As I wrote, our sister Eshett here has not been herself for many weeks. And we have reason to fear that Hinjuman here is afflicted with a tracking curse—or a kite curse, as we Nadumans say."

And Mektu, Mektu, Kandri chanted inside. But of course they could not speak of Mektu—his brother would panic, and bolt. He could only pray the man had read Stilts' letter with sufficient care. Of course, nothing prepared one for Mektu . . .

"Kandri Hinjuman is cursed," said Bajamthal, "as are all of you who travel with him. It is the Chiloto Prophet who curses you, with every tear she sheds for the blood of her son. Oh yes, you are cursed. You could scour not just Urrath but this whole world of Isp'rallal and find no more determined foe. And none more dangerous. All her dreams and plans are madness, but her powers are terribly real."

He closed his eyes. "Yes, Kandri, you trail a kite, and the thing you call the White Child can see it anywhere in Urrath. No matter. I will cut the string today."

Kandri felt a great wave of relief, even as a voice within him warned that it was too soon to feel it. *Please, Ang, let him be what he claims.*

"And the Child?" he asked. "What will happen to her?"

"She will find herself adrift in the desert, blind to the scent she followed. You will see her no more. But you were wise not to delay. A kite is one of the simpler demonic afflictions to resolve—there are several in Kasralys who would cut that string for you as easily as I shall." The exorcist opened his eyes, fixing Kandri with a piercing stare. "But I doubt you would have reached Kasralys. The White Child is close now, and the wrath of her mistress fills her soul."

"How do you *know* all this about us?" said Mektu suddenly, his voice a loud bray in the chamber.

"Hush, lad," said Stilts. "I wrote Master Bajamthal a letter. I told you."

"An eloquent and gracious letter," said Bajamthal, "as one would expect of the River Dragon's scribe."

Prince Nirabha's gasp echoed through the chamber. Stilts, staring motionless at Bajamthal, looked like a man stripped suddenly naked. The exorcist's words meant nothing to Kandri—but clearly they meant a great deal to the Prince, who gazed at Stilts with wonder, as though seeing him for the first time.

"The River Dragon?" he said. "Are we speaking of—"

"Yes," said Stilts. "I was scribe to Therel Agathar of the Scarlet Kingdom. But that was long ago, Master Bajamthal."

"Long ago, but green within you," said the exorcist, "and I speak of it now because it concerns you all. The River Dragon is stirring, Naduman. He has been pricked and prodded by lesser men, and at last they have prevailed. The Dragon will once more go to war."

"And who will Therel Agathar make war on?" cried Prince Nirabha. He eyes shone with hurt and accusation. "You served the Magnus General of Shôlupur, our greatest enemy. How could you hide this from us? And what more is there to learn? Are you making for Kasralys to be his spy, his agent?"

"I'm making for it," said Stilts, "at my general's orders. General *Tebassa's* orders. Agathar, your great enemy, was only a colonel when I kept his books."

"All this," said Kandri dubiously, "*and* the circus?"

"I've lived a long life, Hinjuman," said Stilts. "If you're born in a circus it's what you run away *from*, not to, when you come of age. I ran all the way to Shôlupur, and joined a cause I believed in. When that cause failed, I came back."

"A long life," said Bajamthal, "and a long road of conscience. Do not let the truth break your friendship—now least of all." He pointed suddenly at the Prince. "Your city will have need of *every* ally soon, Nirabha Ilasfarel. You dare not squander one."

Nirabha looked at him in horror. For the first time in weeks, Kandri was reminded of how young he was. "What are you telling me?" asked the Prince.

The exorcist sighed and lowered his arm. "That three thousand years are nothing," he said. "That is my message, though it gives me no joy to speak it. That is why I dwell here in the desert, and no more in Kasralys, jewel of Urrath, where I have been most happy in this world. It is the Time of Madness, the Darsunuk. It is the year of the Pilgrim's return. And in this time of ultimate danger, the Fortress City cannot yet even name her enemy. You fear the name of the Dragon, Agathar, and that is wise in its way. But Therel Agathar is a creature of the daylight: he wears his own face and no other. You should fear the darkness that surrounds him, and the enemies that darkness conceals. Kasralys is sleeping, Prince Nirabha—sleeping through the tremors that should warn her of the earthquake to come. You must hurry and wake her, if you can."

With a last sizzle the fire went out. But on the floor where it had burned, something remained: a red line, bright and throbbing, like a wire heated in a forge.

"Step into the circle, Prince," said the exorcist. "And you as well, Master Stilts."

The two men hesitated, glancing awkwardly at each other. Then the Prince held out his hand, and Stilts took it and rose to his feet. Far across the room, the small boy sat up, suddenly alert.

Stilts and Nirabha stepped with care over the glowing line. As they did so, Bajamthal cocked his head, as if listening to some slight noise. Then he beckoned to the two men, and they sat down before him.

The exorcist leaned forward, placing his hands flat on the floor between them. Eyes closed once more, he drew several deep breaths. A sudden draft swept through the room, rustling the curtains. Stilts and Nirabha looked suddenly agitated: the Prince raised a hand to his temples. Stilts shook his head as though his ears were ringing.

"There, that was easy," said Bajamthal, sitting up. "You are fortunate. The spells upon you were no more than cobwebs, and they are gone. Neither of you has been singled out for malediction, by the Prophet or any other. But your deepest wounds—" He sighed. "—they are not to be healed by my arts, or any arts, save those you learn yourselves. Do not ignore them. And please, do not inflict them where there is no need. It is easy to descend into the chasm of bitterness, much harder to climb out again into the light."

Blinking and abashed, Stilts and Nirabha rose to their feet. "Do not leave the circle," said Bajamthal, "only draw back a little, if you please." He crooked a finger at Eshett. "Come here, daughter of the sands."

Eshett's face was suddenly wild with alarm. Her nails dug into Kandri's wrist. "No, no, I don't want to!" she said.

Joy exploded in Kandri's mind. She had understood Bajamthal perfectly, *and she had answered him. With words.* Kandri saw the same hope and wonder in Mektu's eyes. "Don't be afraid, darling," Mektu whispered. "I didn't want to come here either. But Stilts and Kandri were right. We can trust him. We have to."

His words—or perhaps just the sound of his voice—appeared to soothe Eshett slightly. Her gaze moved to Kandri, and he nodded. "I think he's on our side," he said.

Bajamthal smiled, and the scars on his face crisscrossed. "Take her hands and come with her, both of you," he said. "Do not worry if she touches the spirit-wire; it will not harm her. But take care: she will be dizzy. You must not let her fall."

Kandri couldn't help but admire Bajamthal's tactics. He had let Stilts and Nirabha demonstrate how simple a curse-breaking could be. And now— bless his wise, ugly head—he had given Mektu someone to focus on besides himself. Mek might be free of the yatra before it ever occurred to him that Bajamthal was freeing him.

They led Eshett forward. Despite Bajamthal's assurances, Kandri was glad to see Eshett step over the glowing line without touching it. *She knows what she's doing. Ang's love, she's going to be all right.*

But as they stepped into the circle the exorcist's reaction was much stronger. He jumped, and for a moment his serenity was gone.

"Morolosc!" he said. "Back with the Pilgrim, are you? I should have guessed."

"Morolosc?" said Kandri.

The exorcist smiled; he was quite recovered. "All in good time. Lower her gently; she will soon be asleep."

Mektu turned to Bajamthal, frowning. "Why asleep? What are you going to—"

Eshett pitched forward.

Kandri gasped and seized her waist—all at once she was made of lead—as Mektu leaped in front of her, just in time. Her head fell on his shoulder; he caught her in his arms.

And Bajamthal pounced like a cat.

He had struck already and was out of the circle before they realized he had moved at all. But in that instant he had torn the mattoglin from Mektu's belt.

An animal snarl burst from Mektu. He dropped Eshett—Kandri staggered with the sudden weight—and sprang for the exorcist. But as he tried to cross the glowing line, the fire sprang up, brighter than ever, and Mektu stopped as though he had collided with a wall.

It was the same for all of them: they were trapped, as though a fishbowl had been inverted atop the circle of flames. Mektu leaped up and attacked the barrier again with a shriek of madness. The others were shouting too—all save Bajamthal, who might as well have been alone.

His eyes gleamed like a serpent's, fierce and blue. With a look of deepest satisfaction he raised the mattoglin above his head: one hand on the sheath, the other on the jewel-studded grip. He pulled the two apart, exposing an inch of golden blade.

"Idiot," he said.

And died.

ൽ

The fire went out. The exorcist crumpled atop the knife. In a moment all of them wished they could unsee, something invisible had seized his head and turned it—with a sound like a bottle uncorked—one hundred eighty degrees, so that his face was where the back of his skull should have been. His eyes had burst like two blisters, and the blood was trickling across the floor.

The small boy stood like a statue beneath the window.

Eshett's eyes fluttered open. She looked around, bewildered. "Kandri?" she said.

The fire was gone, but the bright red line remained, and so did the unseen barrier. They beat at it, they kicked. No use. The barrier did not so much as tremble.

Nirabha, almost green with horror, pointed at the exorcist. Bajamthal's mutilated face was smiling at them. His jaw moved; his tongue emerged and licked his swelling lips.

"I have dreamed so many deaths for you."

The voice was not Bajamthal's. Nor any human voice. It was the hiss of coals in a furnace, the winter wind on Candle Mountain, the devil's nails scratching a door.

"Across the whole of the Sumuridath Jal," said the voice. "So many tortures, so many deaths. But now I think I shall merely leave you there to suffocate. Unless the little one finds you first."

The mouth went slack. The eyes bled on. Kandri turned away, knowing he was close to being ill.

"We're dead men," said Mektu.

No one, for once, told him to be quiet. But he was quiet; the whole great chamber grew quiet as they stared at the carnage before them.

At last Stilts called out to the boy by the window. "This was not our doing, lad. Nor his. A fiend killed your master, as it has tried to kill us. You must run now. Run and tell the servants."

The child did not move.

"Do you hear me, lad? They will want to know. And we need their help to escape this circle."

As if in a dream, the boy walked to the corpse. He knelt and placed a hand on his master's shoulder. Kandri thought he was praying. But when he rose a moment later the mattoglin was in his hand.

Once more, all of them were shouting—screaming, really, an undignified barrage. *Drop it, drop it, it will kill you, there's a demon inside.*

The boy tugged the headscarf from his master's broken neck and wound it about the mattoglin. He looked at them, indifferent, as their howls of warning reached a fever pitch. He ran to the stairwell and was gone.

"Fuck," said Mektu.

Like a sleepwalker, Eshett rose and brushed the barrier with her fingertips. "I can't believe it," she whispered. "He was dead."

"*Was?*" said Kandri, trying to turn her away from Bajamthal's corpse. "Eshett, he is dead. Very dead."

"Not him, Kandri. That one." She pointed at Stilts, who was leafing through the exorcist's book. "How can he be here? I saw him fall from a cliff."

☙

The red-robed servants came first—timidly, until they heard the prisoners' cries for help. By then a good hour had passed: an hour of shouting and fear. "What the hell kept you?" Nirabha demanded.

"Master Bajamthal made us swear on the Well of Fire," they pleaded. "We were never to enter the house until he called us. Never to ask questions. Never to intrude."

"The boy," said Mektu through his teeth. "That bald little shit. Do you know where he went?"

"Away to his family behind the lemon grove, I would guess," said one of the servants. "Poor child. He was so terribly distraught."

"Fetch him back here! He's a thief!"

Some time later the Sartaph arrived with a great entourage—elders, scholars, seers, witches, priests of the many temples of Lupriz. The servants had wrapped Bajamthal in a shroud and mopped the floor. The monarch of the oasis looked a long time at the swaddled corpse; when she turned to the prisoners her gaze was an explosive mixture of wonder, pity, and rage.

"I felt when you arrived," she said, "that you would bring us loss and ruin. I was correct. Disasters swarm to you like flies to meat."

The barrier was not a dome—this was among the first discoveries—but a sphere which passed through the floor, making escape by saws and picks from below impossible. The seers consulted ancient books, scrolls, engravings, and even a stone codex, unthinkably ancient, that had been saved from the looting of the old city museum centuries before. The priests rang bells and chanted prayers. A great hulk of a man appeared with mallet and chisel, but his attack on the barrier only succeeded in hurting his arms.

The prisoners stood about like zoo animals, watching these efforts. Only Stilts sat alone, reading the exorcist's book in the fading light.

The air grew stale. Bajamthal's body was carried from the chamber. The wise folk of Lupriz began shaking their heads.

The Sartaph stepped close to the unseen wall. She looked more rigid than when she had entered, and her gaze more sharp.

"Your companions are outside," she said. "I will give them leave to enter as I depart."

The Prince bowed his head. "We shall be glad to see them, Your Grace."

"Before *we* depart," muttered Mektu.

The Sartaph made a point of not looking at him; she spoke to Kandri directly. "All this began with recklessness," she said. "Your recklessness. If you wound a foe as deadly as your Prophet, it had best be a mortal wound, and of that you were not capable. I fear there may be worse to come."

"Of course there's worse to come," said Mektu. "We're suffocating."

"And when you have, what then?" cried the Sartaph. "Am I to leave you here forever in the heart of Lupriz, a horror under glass? Or shall I have the whole mansion demolished, and the city gates as well, and this magic sphere with your putrid corpses rolled through the streets and out into the desert?"

"How can we make this up to you?" said Mektu.

"Insolent dog!" said the Sartaph. "I wish none of you had set foot in Lupriz! Why do you stare at me? Why is that fool Naduman reading a book? Say something intelligent, one of you!"

"Have you spoken to Ifimar Jód?" asked Eshett. "Maybe *he* can get us out of here."

The Sartaph gaped at Eshett. A small sound of anguish escaped her throat. If she had been able to reach Eshett she might well have slapped her.

Footsteps, clattering wildly up the stairs. The Sartaph turned on her heel. Omzal, the suzein who had brought them to the palace, burst into the chamber with two armed men at his sides. They bowed hastily and began to whisper in the Sartaph's ear.

The Sartaph grew very still. When she had heard them out, she said, "Double the force on the wall, and wake the captain of the day guard. We may need him before sunrise."

Something in her voice chilled Kandri's heart. "What's happening, Your Grace?" he called out.

"A creature has appeared at our gates," she said. "A child, a waif of a girl, but with the eyes of a demon from the Pits. And white, they say. White as sun-bleached bones."

She narrowed her eyes, and Kandri knew his face had betrayed him. "It's you," she said. "This thing has come looking for you."

If only he could deny it. If only he could offer some reason why she shouldn't wish them dead.

"Flies to meat," said the Sartaph. "I have never seen the like."

She stalked from the chamber, seers and servants trailing in her wake. None of them ever saw her again.

ଡଃ

"The girl's just standing there," said Chindilan, "sixty feet from the gate where we entered. She hasn't harmed anyone. But when she looks up with those unholy eyes, no one can face her. The guards cringe; some are ill, others start weeping. A few have fled their posts."

He had come with Talupéké and Ulren. The three were helplessly pacing the chamber—lightless now, save for a lamp left by servants. For the five in Bajamthal's trap it was growing distinctly hard to breathe. Like the others (save for Stilts, still poring over his book), Kandri was trying desperately to think, to imagine some means of escape they had not yet tested. To keep his breath slow and shallow. To keep his mind away from the question of how long they had left.

"Is she so horrible to behold?" asked the Prince.

"Yes," said Talupéké. "She's the worst thing I've ever laid eyes on. I'd rather fight ten Rasanga on sandcats. And they say she's talking to herself."

"Master Ifimar saw her a second time, you know," said Ulren. "She was standing on that hill overlooking the Crescent Palmeries, after we sent your Prophet's army off on its wild goose chase. He didn't want the drivers to panic, but he sent Spalak up the hill to investigate. The man came back . . . changed. I think that was the moment he made his choice."

"His choice?" said Kandri.

"You know what I'm saying," said Ulren. "His choice of the Prophet over his brother. His choice to condemn us all to the Pits for helping you."

"Well he's going to get his wish at last," said Mektu. "He can come and see us, when Her Grace rolls our 'putrid corpses' out in the desert. He can laugh at us."

"No one in Lupriz is laughing," said Chindilan. "In fact they're scared to death. The ones who've seen the Child are saying the whole settlement's going to die."

"But tell me that's not rubbish," said Ulren. "There's three thousand souls in Lupriz. What's one little girlie going to do to them?"

"You didn't see the elephant," said Mektu. His voice was slow and slurred. A jolt of fear went through Kandri. He leaned over and pinched Mektu savagely on the arm.

"Ouch," said Mektu softly. With a great effort he raised his head, and opened his eyes wide. "We're going to die in front of you. Ang's tits. We're going to pass out and not wake up."

"No," said Stilts, closing the book and rising, "we're going to walk right out of here. Now get to your feet, everyone, and step away from the barrier. Come on, quickly."

He stood up, waving them away from the invisible wall.

"Don't bother, Mr. Stilts," said Mektu. "You couldn't throw yourself at it any harder than I did. I nearly broke my skull."

"Be quiet, and get up," said Stilts. "I won't say it again."

"I will confess," said the Prince, "that I am too tired to—"

Stilts kicked him in the buttocks.

The Prince got up, and the rest followed his lead. Stilts pulled them all to the center of the circle.

"Face inward, and cover your eyes. And you—" He gestured at the three outside the trap. "—get well away from us. Away from that window, too, for good measure."

"What's this about, Stilts?" said Kandri.

"Hide your eyes, I say!"

They stood and waited, dumbfounded, huddled like athletes praying for victory before a match. Two minutes passed. Mektu fidgeted. Kandri swayed. Pressed together it was even harder to breathe. Four minutes passed.

A distant, mournful sound met their ears: the priests of Ebirid had rung the midnight bell.

"Uncle!" shouted Talupéké from across the room, "this is the dumbest fucking thing I've ever seen you—"

An explosion ripped through the chamber, shaking them right off their feet. Like the sandstorm, Kandri thought, in that instant before he blacked out: wind like a tidal wave, a roar as if the earth itself were dying, sand driven with furious violence against his flesh.

But all of it—the wind, and whatever had felt so much like sand—was the next instant gone without a trace. Kandri's ears popped, and he gasped with joy. *Fresh air!*

"It's done," said Stilts. "By the Gods, that man understood his limits! I think we'd best—"

The room convulsed. The walls bowed; plaster fell from the ceiling; floorboards parted and cracked. The orange-slice window burst as though struck by a hurricane.

Right beneath their feet, the floor was listing. Breaking. About to fail.

They fled toward the walls, Kandri holding fast to Eshett's arm. No sooner had they moved than a round section of the floor fell away to dangle by a last brave beam over the chamber below. It was the exact outline of the magic barrier, its edges charred and smoking. In its destruction the sphere had burned through the floor.

The house groaned in agony. Through the hole, even stranger sounds reached them: voices, human and animal, raised in a mad ecstasy of howls and laughs and screeches, the mingled noises of a demented zoo.

"Should have guessed, the whole mansion's affected!" cried Stilts. "Run, run and stop for nothing!"

They ran. The stairs bucked and twisted beneath their feet. Kandri held tight to Eshett. Whirling lights below them. Something burning. Stark terror in Mektu's eyes.

They spilled out into the exorcist's museum—and a scene that rocked Kandri's senses. Balls of green and yellow light raced above them like schools of fish. The taxidermied animals were running, flapping, braying. The skulls in the glass case chattered in unison. The iron chair crab-walked across the floor.

Every last sculpture had sprung to life. The winged devils tore real flesh from the body of their howling victim; the antlered man gripped and thrust into the deer, the two women rode their serpent around the chamber like a horse.

"They weren't keepsakes, they were cages," said Stilts. "Prisons for the fiends he tore from human souls. And now the prison doors are open. Run!"

No one needed persuading. They charged through the hall, groped at by the nightmare beasts. Kandri leaped over a coil of the great snake, felt the boy with eyes at his nipples snatch at his shirt, beat away the raven when it dove at Eshett's face. The curtains burned; the bookshelves burned. They smashed through the great red doors and flung themselves down the stairs.

The nightmare beings flooded out behind them—hooting, screeching, snarling. By the open gates, a crowd of onlookers turned and fled with a collective scream. Bajamthal's servants, much closer to the building, flung themselves down in despair. But as the night breeze washed over the creatures, something changed. They were thinning, fading even as they radiated from the mansion. And as they flew or stepped or slithered over the encircling watercourse they vanished altogether. Within seconds the mansion grounds were empty, save for the eight travelers and Bajamthal's devastated servants.

"Well, well." Stilts held up the exorcist's book. "It's all there, in fancy Naduman," he said. "'*My works of binding and holding shall not outlive me. At the stroke of midnight on my night of death they shall shatter like crystal, unless before that night I master the most ancient of the caging arts.*' Doesn't appear he succeeded. Lucky for us."

"You could have said something," said Kandri.

Stilts smiled. "I found the passage at three minutes to midnight. Had to pray I'd understood it."

The mansion groaned and trembled. From the round window, smoke belched like a chimney.

Now the servants approached, looking like survivors of a shipwreck. The eldest among them held out his hand to Stilts.

"Give me the book," he said. "It is part of our Master's estate."

"This book *is* your Master's estate," said Stilts, "unless he's got a second home hidden away somewhere. And as I see it—"

Mektu snatched the book from his hand.

"To hell with your master," he said. "That hairless thief took my mattoglin, and it's worth more than all his dead animals and dancing chairs put together. Find that boy, return *my* property, and then we'll talk about a book."

"Listen to me for a moment, brother," said Kandri carefully. "I didn't expect it to happen this way, but that mattoglin—"

"Is *mine*," snapped Mektu, whirling on him. "I fought for it. I killed Woeden Surk with it."

"Stole it from your own friends too, didn't you now?" said Ulren.

"You lied to us, Mek," said Kandri, "but it's not your fault. That thing, that yatra inside the blade—it's growing stronger the closer we get to Kasralys. I don't know why. I don't know what its game is, but you're just one more person it's using to get its way."

"I don't obey the yatra," said Mektu. He was speaking softly now, but with more desperation than ever. "I'm not in its power. Never was. Never will be. You can't understand."

He retreated a step. The others were drawing around him in a circle.

"Here's what I understand," said Stilts. "That knife has brought us nothing but misery. From the start. I dare say the Prophet's son never imagined Kandri was entering that shack to stop him raping a child."

"No," said Kandri, "He thought I was there for the mattoglin. He was a mad beast."

"I'm not a beast," said Mektu.

"You will be," said Kandri, "if you don't give it up."

Chindilan stepped closer to Mektu. "This whole disaster that's engulfed our family comes back to the mattoglin," he said. "You, for example: you're a true, loving Hinjuman, whatever else you are. But that blade's driven you to acts that will shame you to your dying day. There's only one question: are you still yourself, deep down? Or has it broken you already?"

Mektu stood at bay, flame crackling behind him. "You don't understand," he said again. "I fought one of those creatures when I was six. I beat it. Your exorcist died before his chin hit the ground."

"Not the same creature," said Kandri.

"I'm the only one strong enough to control it," said Mektu. "You'll see, Kandri. When I get it back I'll prove it to you, I'll—"

"Mektu," said Eshett, "forget the mattoglin. It's gone."

She took his hand. Her voice was strict, but her eyes were full of warmth. Once more, gratitude brought Kandri to the brink of tears. *That's her, that's our Eshett.*

"I carried it much longer than you did," she told Mektu. "Its teeth sank deeper into me. It turned me into an animal. I barely survived."

"I'm stronger than you," said Mektu, his voice almost pleading.

"No," said Eshett, "but you're precious to me."

"But I need it, Eshett, I need—"

Eshett seized his face in both hands and kissed him fiercely.

"I need you—" She kissed him again. "—to be strong enough—" A third kiss. "—to let it go."

The fourth kiss went on until Mektu's eyes bulged with wonder. His arms went nervously around her. And Kandri, watching serenity steal into their faces, knew that whatever part of Eshett's memory had returned or might yet return could not change what he was seeing. She loved his brother. And he, Kandri, could only hold his tongue.

But how safe was either of them? How sound were their minds? Eshett had been lost inside herself for eight weeks, not responding even to her name. And Mektu had deceived her before—deceived all of them, when the mattoglin crooned his name.

Finally their lips parted; Mektu stood there beaming. "You shut him up!" said Ulren. "You're a miracle worker, girlie."

"Call me 'girlie' again and I'll kick your balls so hard they'll pop out your ears," said Eshett.

Stilts' mouth twitched in a smile. "You've been spending time with my niece," he said.

He plucked the book back from Mektu's hands and turned to the servants. "The Sartaph is not likely to grant another audience—indeed I expect she'll want to see the back of us. So it falls to you to see that she understands. That boy ran off with an object far deadlier than anything in your late Master's collection. A yatra dwells in it."

"A yatra!" cried the servants. "Then you are to blame! You should have warned our Master! He might still be alive!"

"Of course I warned him; I'm not a fool," snapped Stilts. "Your Master simply chose not to listen. He may have been intrigued by the very art of the yatra's imprisonment—for whoever chained the yatra inside the knife used a spell that has lasted centuries. Maybe he saw in that spell what he was never able to accomplish with his stuffed animals and statuary."

"He cried 'Idiot!' before he died," said Nirabha. "Perhaps the word was directed at himself."

"Whatever his reasons," said Stilts, "he must have tried to cast the yatra out of the mattoglin, as he had cast so many spirits out of human souls."

"Did he manage, do you think?" said Ulren.

"No," said Eshett.

"No," agreed Stilts, "but he opened a brief window through which the beast could strike with all its power."

"We saw that power unleashed once before," said Chindilan to the servants. "It wasn't pretty. That boy's in terrible danger."

"The Sartaph must lock the mattoglin away in some vault beyond sight or temptation," said Stilts. "Or better yet, give it to the ghouls in Jekka's Grave."

"We will take the book, though," said the servant, holding out his hand. "What use can you make of it, after all?"

"We'll find out." Stilts tucked the volume under his arm. "Your Master placed us in a deathtrap, sir. I'll consider this a small compensation."

With a *whoosh* and a spasm of fire, the roof of the mansion collapsed.

"A most gifted man," said Stilts, "but wanting, as my general would say, in the matter of business ethics. Right, then: who's buying my drinks?"

29. THE EYES OF THE CHILD

YOU ARRIVE WITH THE DEATH OF IFIMAR JÓD, OUR PARTICULAR FRIEND.
YOU SPILL BLOOD IN OUR TAVERNS.
YOU SEEK THE AID OF OUR MOST REVERED AND FAMOUS CITIZEN AND
LEAVE HIM DEAD.
YOU REDUCE HIS HOME, A LANDMARK OF LUPRIZ, TO SMOKING RUINS.
NOW, HAVING DEPRIVED US OF OUR EXORCIST, YOU DRAW A DEVIL TO
OUR SETTLEMENT TO WORK AN EVIL AS YET UNKNOWN.
NOT SINCE THE FASINDAR PURGES HAVE ANY VISITORS INFLICTED SUCH
INJURY AND EVIL WITHIN OUR WALLS, NOR IN ANY AGE SO SWIFTLY.
THEREFORE—

"We're banished," said Kandri, looking up from the silver-edged parchment. "We've got forty-eight hours to quit Lupriz."

"Don't leave out the best part," said Talupéké, pointing.

. . . FOREVER AND WITHOUT EXCEPTION, AND A SWIFT DEATH ONLY SHALL
GREET YOUR RETURN.

Kandri passed the edict to Mektu and rubbed his eyes. Dry, gritty eyes. It was early morning and he was already exhausted. He had slept little. Or perhaps not at all. The horrors of the night before—and the deeper horror outside the oasis—had flooded his thoughts as soon as he crawled into bed.

The matron was clearing their breakfast plates with an almost feral eagerness: she too wanted them gone. "Hardly a boarding house in Lupriz with any beds left to fill," she'd announced that morning, "but somehow I've got a number."

Kandri finished his coffee before she could snatch it. Like everyone in Lupriz, her other guests had heard about Bajamthal, the fire, the flood of escaping spirits. By the time Kandri had risen that morning, they had all cleared out.

Suzein Omzal, who had brought the edict from the palace, stood near him, worrying his hands. "Her Grace is in earnest, brothers and sisters," he said.

"You don't need to tell us," said Eshett. "I'm surprised she hasn't *already* ordered our execution, the way she looked at us last night."

"Sister, you do not know what you are saying!" cried Omzal. "Her Grace does not hate you. On the contrary: she is on your side in spite of everything."

"This," said Kandri, lifting the parchment, "is 'on our side'?"

"Yes!" The suzein winced at his own shrill voice. More quietly, he said, "The Sartaph's power is not absolute. She has rivals. One or two would gladly depose her, given the chance. She has indeed resisted calls to deal with you as criminals, as enemies of Lupriz. Many demanded it. This banishment was a compromise—a very mild, even-handed compromise, if I may say so."

"That's her, Madame Mild," said Mektu. "After all, she's only banishing the two of us."

"The loony boys," said Talupéké. "The Twin Abominations. Not the loony soldiers who are supposed to keep them safe, or their uncle, or the Prince. They're all free to stay. Even rat-faced Ulren and his drivers are free to stay. I wonder what he told her about Ifimar Jód?"

"The truth," said Kandri, "at least as much as he knows."

"Meaning what?"

She looked at him; Kandri dodged her eye. Who could he stand to be honest with? What would become of these friendships, these lifelines he cherished, if they knew?

As always, more immediate questions crowded such thoughts to one side. They were banished—but how were they to leave? He did not think the Sartaph meant to drive them through the gates into the arms of the White Child. They could scamper down a rope under cover of darkness on the opposite side of Lupriz. But what then? Bolt into the desert? Better just to cut one's throat and be done with it. Without camels to carry water they were marooned here: sixty miles of desert still waited for them before the Ablasadur Mountains and the lush lands beyond.

In the mountains they might ditch the camels, true. There were streams; there were small mountain lakes. There were even shortcuts down into that green, serpentine lowland—the Sacred Plain, Nirabha called it—that lay at the feet of Kasralys City. Kandri could see it all, whenever he liked, in the strange mural of his heightened memory. He would not lose the path, but they still had to walk it.

Not for the first time, he found himself struggling to believe that they would ever travel again with the caravan. Why would the Mistajavs—battered, grieving, dirt-poor, terrified, vulnerable as hell—want to walk another mile with Kandri or his brother, or anyone attached to them? Jód had given them his protection, but Jód was dead. Ulren worshipped Jód, but he valued his own life even more. And no matter how much he had grown into his new role as Caravan Master, he still hated Chilotos.

Not that you have a drop of Chiloto blood.

Kandri surged to his feet, bumping the table.

"*Harach*," swore Chindilan as coffee spilled in his lap. "What's the matter, boy? You look like you want to slug someone."

"I want to see the Child," he said.

"Well fuck that up and down!" cried Mektu.

"Agreed," said Stilts.

"Agreed," said Omzal apologetically. "Up and down, so to speak."

"You said it yourself," said Talupéké. "You and Mektu should stay as far away from that thing as possible."

"Changed my mind," said Kandri. "She stood all night watching the gates, and she'll stand there right through the day's heat too, won't she?"

"Show her your face and she'll stand there till Doomsday," said Chind-ilan, "or at least until Lupriz is starving to death."

"Oh, we will not starve," said Omzal. "Summer is our time of hiberna-tion; we have filled our granaries, butchered animals, stocked our cellars with ground nuts and yams. And there are still the palm fruits to harvest. But all this is pointless. You no longer have the freedom of Lupriz, brother. You will not be permitted to climb the wall."

"I'll ask nicely," said Kandri.

"But *why?*" cried Omzal. "Why let her see you, if you and your brother are indeed her target?"

"She knows we're in Lupriz," said Kandri. "She didn't cross the whole of the desert on a hunch. She won't learn anything—but I might."

"You *might* learn what a stupid, stubborn mule you are," said Eshett, "but I doubt it."

"Stay here," said Kandri. "I'll be back before you miss me."

The others shook their heads, but argued no further. Something in Kan-dri's voice made it clear that he had decided: he was going to face the White Child. And just before he left the courtyard, Mektu, speechless with fear or anger, pulled on his sandals and fell in beside him.

❧

Fifteen minutes later they were nearing the South Gate. The morning rattle and roar of Lupriz was fading swiftly; the day's heat had begun. Kandri's hand sweated against the brass telescope.

Omzal trotted alongside the brothers, chattering as always; he was the only person Kandri had ever known who could fill the air with words as ceaselessly as Mektu. Something about the fallen city. Something about the fountains, the waterworks. *Quite spectacular—to think, we once could afford—locked away from the public—if all else fails I am authorized—utterly forgotten—even lifelong residents know nothing—as I said Her Grace wishes the best for you, though you are exiled, though if you return we must kill you without so much as—*

"Have they tried shooting her?" broke in Mektu.

"Shooting? Shooting who? The devil-girl, you mean?"

"No, that woman selling persimmons at the corner. Of course the devil-girl. With an arrow. Through the heart."

"Oh yes indeed," said the suzein. "Our two finest archers, with good Kasraji bows. Mind you, there was no *order* to shoot—for all that she is monstrous, she does resemble a small girl. If you should hear rumors that Her Grace commanded it in secret, I would ask that you not repeat, not circulate—"

"What happened?" asked Kandri.

"They turned the bows on each other. They let fly on the count of three."

Kandri sighed through his teeth, more from sadness than surprise. A part of him had expected it. He had seen the White Child face down armed men before.

"It was not effortless for the creature, they say," added Omzal. "She appeared out of breath. I suppose we may take some comfort there."

At the South Gate all was chaos. About twenty heavily armed guards were on hand: many bunched at the foot of the stair leading up onto the wall, others milling about the barracks just east of the road. Strangely, only three were on the wall itself. They were agitated, fingering their weapons, pacing with sharp, inhibited movements as though they longed to break into a run. Much farther along the wall he could see other guards; they looked tranquil by comparison, but they too had their eyes trained on the gate, or perhaps on something just beyond it in the desert.

The three guards here on the gate were not trying *not* to look at the desert, at least not directly. They glanced at it sideways, flinching, as though whatever lay beyond the great doors was too awful to contemplate for long.

"I thought you'd have more troops," said Mektu.

"In times of war, common citizens supplement the Guard," said Omzal, "but Her Grace has not yet made the declaration. We have enjoyed a reign of blessed peace these many years, and she is loath to declare it at an end."

Kandri glanced at him. *A note of disapproval, Suzein?*

"How many regulars, then?"

"Some three hundred at arms. But they are formidable soldiers, have no doubt."

Kandri did have doubts. The twenty on hand might be formidable, but what he saw most plainly was fear. Their commander was screaming at those on the stairs: "Up, up, and not another word! What's become of your honor? And your oath, eh? Was that just straw in the wind?"

He shoved at them, cursing. At last four of the soldiers shook him off and climbed together, like prisoners marching defiant to the gallows. But as they neared the wall that defiance was stripped from them. Feet slowed, faces hardened. They stepped onto the battlements as though entering a bitter wind.

Omzal went forward and spoke to the commander. The man shot hard glances at Kandri and Mektu. "Like hell I will!" he shouted. "Don't you know what's happening, suzein? This is the wall of Lupriz, not a viewing stand for every wandering sand rat! Take them away."

Omzal raised a warning finger. He did not raise his voice, however, and Kandri could not catch any of his rapid stream of words. But the commander heard them. He turned again to the brothers, slowly this time, and Kandri saw a change in his eyes. Then he nodded. At once Omzal beckoned them forward.

"Matters have grown worse overnight," he said. "I must return to the Sartaph, but I will not leave you here. If you still insist on this venture, make haste."

"What exactly do you mean, worse?" asked Mektu.

The commander glared at them. "Go see for yourselves." *And take a leap from the wall while you're at it*, said his eyes.

"Go, but do not linger," said Omzal. "And please—" He looked intently at Mektu. "—say nothing, do nothing to . . . aggravate the creature. Do not make us regret our lenience."

"I already regret it," said the commander.

The fear began as they climbed. Kandri took the lead but glanced back constantly at Mektu, lest he bolt. Never had a staircase felt steeper, or Kandri's legs more unwilling. The first and last time the Child had spoken to him he had also stood atop a wall. She had mistaken him for his father—for the man he had always known as his father. *Lantor, Lantor,* she had cooed from its foot, in that childish singsong more terrible than any scream, *I'll find you.*

Blood meant nothing to the White Child.

The guards atop the wall glanced at them with the same hostile doubt as their commander. Kandri stepped up among them. *Don't shy from her, don't show her your terror, don't wait.* He stepped between the two nearest guards and looked out.

She stood on a mound of earth a short stone's throw from Kandri with a man's severed head in her hand. Flies about her, black against her moon-white skin. Body slight as a heron's leg, lace gown limp and tattered.

All about her the jumbled stones, the cracked columns and fallen arches and ghostly outlines of structures great and small. Ruins of the vanished city. And the Child more still and stark and white than the stones themselves. Everywhere but her eyes.

Those black, oil-pool eyes found them instantly. The Child's lips formed a smile.

Mektu waved.

You stupid fuck. Kandri jerked down his arm. He could feel Mektu's fear like bottled lightning; the wave had been in lieu of something cowardly or unhinged.

All the same it had provoked her. The guards drew back from them. The Child let the severed head slip from her fingers; it rolled down the earthen mound and lay leering at the sky. The Child raised a spindle-thin hand and pointed—not at Mektu but Kandri. In the absolute stillness her voice carried thin and clear.

"Lantor," she said, "I've missed you."

Her black eyes held him, windows on an abyss. And with a sudden feeling of deliverance Kandri knew that what he wanted was to surrender, to be no more hunted but caught, captured, the hare finally at rest in the teeth of the hound. For months and months he had got it backward, imagining that he had no choice but flight, endless flight, a life forever one step ahead of the servants of the Prophet, a life of infinite exhaustion and fear.

Her smile grew. How could he have missed the obvious? All he needed to escape these tortures was to die. Simply die. And death would never be more effortless. It was his for the asking. Right here. Right now.

She raised her arms, welcoming him. Two steps. No one could prevent it. No one could blame him, after all he had suffered.

Then, so quietly that he almost missed it, another sound rose within him. It came and went like a dying echo, a hawk's cry over endless mountains. But it was no hawk. It was a woman's voice, and Kandri knew it had escaped from the most private, armored part of himself. The sound was a laugh, Ari's softest laugh, a noise she made sometimes with her face pressed to his chest, or when they curled together in the meadows above Blind Stream. No message, no hidden meaning. And yet it was so precious to him that he had guarded the sound in vaults within vaults, safe from the desert and the army and the Prophet and the killing and the faith, all those sick blooms, those weeds that had sprouted in the space she left behind.

Ariqina. Fiasul had claimed that she was alive. And if that was true—if there was any *chance*—then no, he could never seek death. Any world she might be found in was the one where he belonged.

He raised his head. The black eyes blinked. The White Child let her arms fall to her sides. And in that moment the whole force of her terror diminished. Mektu and the guards shook themselves and staggered, as though waking from a dream. They had experienced something very different, he thought: a blankness rather than a call. Whatever the Child had just attempted had been focused on Kandri.

It had cost her, too, and now she was enraged. Her lips were parted, slack. Her waif's hands closed to fists, flexed open, closed to fists again.

"Gods of Death, what have you done?" It was the commander, bounding up onto the wall.

"This fool waved," said a guard, pointing at Mektu, "and *this* one locked eyes with her, same as Onesh did." He flicked a glance at the Kandri, then pointed at the severed head. "That's Onesh," he said.

The White Child had begun to sway side to side, as though feeling out the rhythm of a music only she could hear. Very faintly, she began to sing.

"You stupid bastards, you've baited her," said the commander. "Whatever happens now is on your heads."

"*Harach*, you babies, nothing's going to happen," said Mektu. "Not to you anyway. Not inside this wall."

The guards' reaction disturbed Kandri almost as much as his first glimpse of the Child. They laughed. Wretched, despairing laughs. Omzal's words echoed in Kandri's mind. "How exactly," he asked the commander, "have things grown worse?"

But the commander ignored him. He and his soldiers—and even the White Child herself—were all gazing into the west.

Kandri looked. At first he saw only the ruins of Old Lupriz. No shadows, no life, Then, three or four miles out, he caught a glimpse of movement. A living figure, walking upright.

Mektu squinted. "What the hell is *that?*"

Kandri raised the telescope to his eye. After a few moments' struggle the thing swam into focus. It was not human. Its enormous body was covered in rough slabs of skin like the hide of a rhinoceros. It was cadaverous, hollow-bellied, and yet unnaturally wide in the chest. It was naked save for a tattered loincloth, and it carried nothing but a kind of war hammer, long-handled and huge.

Merciful Ang, help your children.

He could not tell just how large the creature was—there was nothing but stony debris to judge it against—but its every footfall raised a cloud of dust.

"We know that beast," said the commander. "He's a legend. He's the dark mascot of Lupriz."

"Mascot?"

"Old Slag, we call him, because his skin's like the clinker you scrape out of a forge. He's an ogre, the last living spawn of Septhru the Executioner. That makes Slag about the oldest living creature you'll ever see on two feet. He can't run any more, though he's as strong as ten rhinos. He lives among the ghouls in Jekka's Grave. Sometimes he crawls out onto a hilltop and just gazes west into the desert. For days. But he never approaches. Never ever, until today.

"At dawn, we spotted him out there. For hours he didn't so much as scratch his arse. Now he's coming for us." The commander shot them a venomous glance. "Can't imagine why."

"Don't forget the ghouls, sir," said another guard.

"Ah no, I shan't," said the commander through his teeth. "A pair of ghouls came racing out of the west last night on the heels of the devil-girl. Some hours later, four more appeared. She's calling them, like she called Old Slag, from their burrows in Jekka's Grave."

Kandri nodded. "We won't bother you again. Let's go, Mek."

The brothers turned to leave, but the commander grabbed Kandri's arm.

"They can climb like lizards, these crater ghouls. And that's just what they attempted. Threw themselves at this wall like mad things, they did. Gibbering, crooning for our blood. We got lucky. We shot them dead."

"Glad to hear it," said Kandri.

"But just before dawn eight more appeared, and this time our luck didn't hold. Three of them gained the wall. Their poisoned reek felled one of my soldiers before she could draw her sword. It pounced; it tore open her throat. Another man lost his balance and fell to his death. And a third took a bite to the arm. Do you know what ghoul slaver does to human flesh?"

"He does," said Mektu. "He's seen it."

"We hoped he'd lose no more than his arm," said the commander. "We were wrong."

"I'm sorry," said Kandri.

The commander looked at his troops. "This man's sorry," he said. "*Good* and sorry. Ain't that a relief?"

Kandri caught Mektu's eye, and a silent message passed between them. His brother was rigid, eyes wide, arms drawn up close to his chest. Ready for violence, if it came to that.

"We'll see no ghouls by daylight, Ang willing," said the commander, "but what do you suppose the night will bring? Another doubling, and another after that? Where will it end, I ask you? There are many hundreds of ghouls in Jekka's Grave. And Slag will be here long before dark. What do you have to say to that?"

Mektu had one foot on the stairs already. But several guards now blocked Kandri's path.

"Toss him," hissed the nearest. "It's him the devil-girl wants. Go on, toss him, save the settlement. No one would blame you, sir."

The commander did not move.

A second guard murmured, "No one would even *know*."

Kandri tugged his arm free and pushed through the soldiers, feeling certain it was their last instant of hesitation. They descended. A guard hacked; spittle struck Kandri's cheek. A stone whizzed by his shoulder. They kept moving. Twenty to one would not do. Omzal saw the latent disaster in their faces and drew them swiftly away.

"I told you this was pointless," he said.

In Kandri's mind, a silent howl. Three more down. Three more souls beloved to someone. Three more deaths, never to be forgotten or atoned for or made right.

"Will you listen to me now?" asked the suzein.

Blood from one end of Urrath to another. Blood wherever they rested, wherever they paused. Gushing like the fountains of the Faluvari. Pooled and sloshing at their feet.

"Will you at least *discuss* the matter with your friends?"

His friends. Luckless drifters. Some had died already. How long before he doomed the rest?

"Mr. Kandri, you are not even listening!" cried the suzein in despair.

Kandri stopped in the street. "What were their names?" he demanded.

"Their names? Whose names?"

"The archers who shot each other. Who were they? What were they called? What did they plan to do with their Gods-damned lives?"

Omzal sputtered: "I'm not clear who—we have several—"

"You palace clown," said Kandri. "You're right, I wasn't listening. I don't care about your history, your fountains, your fucking waterworks. I care about the ones who keep dying for us. I care about getting away from here before we do more harm."

Omzal, he learned suddenly, was not immune to offense. His plump hands closed in fists. He brought his face very close to Kandri's own.

"What in the bowels of hell," he asked, "do you think we've been discussing?"

℣

It was true: Kandri had heard it all as they approached the gate to begin with. Heard and not heard: in his fear and impatience he had closed his mind to Omzal's chatter.

Mektu, who had walked a few paces ahead, had absorbed even less. "You're joking," he said.

"I am serious by nature," said Omzal.

"A *what* beneath the fountains?"

"A canal. Yes, we once had water in such abundance that we could move goods in and out of the city by barge. Of course the canal is bone-dry today."

"And you use it as an escape tunnel?"

"It is maintained for that purpose."

"But why dig it underground in the first place?" asked Mektu.

"Why do you suppose?" asked Omzal. "The Kasraj beggared us with taxes. We could not throw off the yoke of empire, small as we are. But we could resist."

"How many in Lupriz know of this tunnel?" asked Kandri.

Omzal sighed. "Brother traveler, this is no time for idle questions."

Kandri nodded, the man was right. They went on, nearly running down the empty streets. If what Omzal said was true there was a glimmer of hope—for the travelers and the oasis alike. Belac Bajamthal had never cut the "kite string." If the brothers slipped away, the White Child would sense it and follow them, as she had done from the start. And whatever creatures she could call to her service would be set to the same task. Lupriz would be spared.

He thanked the Gods for the White Child's slowness. For that, and for the safest refuge in Urrath, ten days ahead.

If Kasralys lets you in, said the voice of doubt. But Kandri dared not dwell on that particular *If.*

"Stilts won't join us, will he?" said Mektu.

"I hope not," said Kandri. "You heard what he said: Kereqa needed at least a week in bed. That was four days ago now. A few more, and Ulren will have the drivers back on their feet, and the camels ready for the trail. Don't worry. They'll reach the city a fortnight behind us."

"We're not going to stroll away from that Slag bastard," said Mektu. "Everyone who leaves today will have to ride."

"I know, I know."

They reached the boarding house. Kandri put a hand on the door—and paused, turning to Omzal.

"There will be some yelling," he said. "I'd appreciate it if you didn't say a word."

The suzein looked at him with surprise. "They will have questions, just as you did. Why should I not answer them?"

Several replies swirled about in Kandri's mouth. After a moment he settled on honesty. "I don't know," he said. "It's just a feeling, like an itch. But every time I've ignored that itch—"

Omzal raised a hand. "Explain no further," he said. "I will visit the stables and begin the preparations. How many will travel with you, do you think?"

The brothers glanced at each other. "Uncle and Eshett," said Kandri, "and the Prince, since he's as conspicuous as we are. That's five, counting us."

"Stilts won't like this one bit," said Mektu. "He'll want to send Tebassa's soldiers along."

"He will," Kandri agreed. "All of them, except for Kereqa."

"Five of you and six soldiers besides?" asked Omzal, dubious.

"What's the matter?" asked Mektu. "Is that too many to smuggle out of Lupriz?"

Omzal shook his head. "The trouble is camels, rather. All who leave must ride, not walk, or you will never escape the ghouls. And in this heat, you will need water-camels as well: one beast for every three persons, I should think.

Thus, fifteen camels, or fourteen if you cut your water margin to the very bone. Do you wish to deprive your loyal drivers of so many?"

"No," said Mektu.

"No," said Kandri, "and you've just given us our answer when Stilts presses us to take them all." He thought for a moment. "Speed is what counts, now, isn't it? We might be better off with none. But let's say we agree to take one of Tebassa's fighters, if only to keep Stilts from bellyaching."

"Then you will be six, and will require eight camels in total."

"We can leave a purse for the drivers, to cover any goods they have to abandon," said Kandri.

"They need abandon nothing; the merchants of Lupriz will happily buy their goods—" Omzal bobbed his head. "—at a certain discount. Leave the purse all the same, if you would treat them justly. And I will see that eight camels are readied for the trail."

Kandri looked at Omzal with sudden affection. "Thank you," he said. "You didn't have to be this . . . decent to us. We're total strangers."

Omzal's smile broadened, but his voice when he spoke was fierce. "What I have done is mere common sense," he said. "I love the Font of Lupriz and its people. There is nothing I would not do to keep them safe."

He swept off down the street. Mektu watched him with wary eyes. "Why didn't you want him to speak?" he asked quietly. "Don't you trust him?"

Kandri was startled. "Why wouldn't I trust him? Yes, I trust him. I think."

"Glad we're cleared that up."

"I don't think he's lying," said Kandri, frowning. "Something's just . . . not right."

"About this plan?"

Kandri nodded. "I don't have words for it yet."

Mektu pulled open the boarding house door. "Let me know when that changes."

The common room was deserted and cool and smelled of pipe smoke and bread. For a moment it seemed altogether too good for the world, a little doll's house of comforts. Then the matron's son stomped in from the kitchen.

576

"There you are!" he said. "Your friends were starting to worry."

"Where is everyone?" asked Kandri.

"Mum's gone for persimmons. You have to buy them before the flies lay their eggs."

"Fascinating," said Mektu. "How about our friends?"

The boy's answer was cut off by a sudden noise: a sharp, low *boom* that rumbled through the very building and made the glassware tremble on the shelves. The brothers jumped; the boy actually yelped.

"What was that?" he cried. "An earthquake?"

It had not been an earthquake. It had more resembled an explosion—or perhaps the deep thud in the floorboards when something enormous falls in an adjoining room.

"Go on, go on," said Mektu. "Where are our friends?"

The boy, stammering a little with fear, explained that some had gone to the hospital, for "your granny"—he meant Kereqa—was at last up and about. But Chindilan had gone looking for them at the South Gate. And Eshett—

The boy turned and gestured at the doorway to the courtyard, which stood open as usual. His eyes widened. "That's funny. She was right there in the corner."

Kandri did not find it funny in the least: Eshett had become herself again just twelve hours ago after two months of madness.

Boom came the noise again. Voices across the settlement cried out in its wake.

There was no need to speak: finding Eshett overrode all other plans. The dormitories proved deserted, and the privy. They looked up and down the blazing street. *Boom*, came the sound a third time.

They stormed back into the common room. "Someone's been fucking careless," said Kandri. "What if she has a relapse?"

"Don't say that," said Mektu. "She's fine."

"Fine, is it? She was a madwoman until last night!"

"Where could she have gone, Kandri?"

"Hell if I know. If she's lost her reason again, they could lock her up somewhere, or take advantage of her. Damn to hell whoever left her alone!"

His brother was shaking, eyes swimming with panic and misery. Kandri knew suddenly that he had gone too far.

"Get a hold of yourself, we'll find her," he said, his impatience calculated to reassure. "We'll start at the hospital. Ten to one we'll find she's with the others, cheering Old Kereqa on."

They cut behind the farrier and the Temple of Ebarid, then walked along the side of the orange grove behind its wrought-iron fence. The orange season was over; the whole grove smelled like honey and sour rinds.

Boom.

This time, as certainly as if the noise had declared itself in words, Kandri knew what he was hearing. "That's the ogre," he said. "Old Slag. He's using that weapon of his against the gates, or the wall."

Understanding bloomed gradually across Mektu's face. "Do you think he's strong enough? Those gates look like they could hold back a river."

"The sound's been moving," said Kandri. "Moving along the wall, maybe. I think he's looking for a weak spot."

"And in this broken-down place—"

"He'll find one," said Kandri, "sooner or later." He turned, peering among the orange trees. "There's our uncle," he said.

Chindilan was walking swiftly up the street on the far side of the grove, passing through bars of blinding sun and dark tree-shadow. The contrast was so powerful that the hefty man seemed almost to be blinking in and out of existence.

Kandri felt a stab of gratitude for the man—his tenacity, his steadfast love. He thought of the night on Ravashandul's Wall: the lame camel, the shouting that had almost come to blows. *You owe me obedience, boy. I promised your father—*

He wanted to call out to Chindilan—nothing could be simpler; it was a matter of thirty yards. *Here we are. Come with us.* He stood silent. There was a painful tightness in his chest.

"Where's he off to in such a hurry?" Mektu wondered aloud.

"Looking for us, of course," said Kandri. "Don't call to him, Mektu."

Mektu turned to him, wary. "That feeling again?"

"Yes, that itch."

578

Chindilan rounded the corner of the grove. He wiped the sweat from his brow, then turned into an alley and was gone.

Blink.

Kandri felt suddenly hollow. The itch was growing stronger by the minute. They left the grove behind, walked another block in silence. Ahead loomed the old city hospital.

Like the Palace of Justice, it was mostly a great ruin, with a crumbled facade, a cracked onion dome, corbeled turrets from which bricks had fallen into the street. But the nearest corner of the structure was in fine repair. The great doors were brightly painted and stood open as if in welcome. The tall lancet windows sparkled in the sun.

Just outside the doors, back turned to them, stood Prince Nirabha. He stood hunched, his head bent low over his hands as though he were lighting a cheroot. An object in the Prince's hand winked in the sunlight. It was a silver box, smaller than a deck of cards.

"That's odd," said Mektu. "He doesn't smoke."

Suddenly the Prince threw his head back and gave a great, deep-chested sniff. A great spasm passed through his body. A second followed, causing him to stumble.

"That sneaky little fox," said Mektu.

The Prince recovered himself almost instantly. He straightened, hid the box away, and reentered the hospital.

"He's got a habit of some kind, that's clear enough," said Kandri. "What was that red snuff the pikemen were always getting caught with? Monkey something?"

"Monkeyshine," said Mektu. "I tried it. Horrible stuff. Three hits and it claims you for life, they say."

Kandri glanced at him. "How many did you take?"

"Two. And yes, it can make you twitch like that. Like being tickled, and at the same time stung by bees. Our Prince is a shiner, I'll bet you."

"He must have been craving it across the whole of the desert."

Kandri laid a hand on Mektu's arm. "I know you two don't get along, but you can't talk about this. You can't even hint."

"Of course not," said Mektu. "We have no idea what he's going through. If that's monkeyshine, it could be the worst thing that's ever happened to him."

"All right then."

"Which is why I'll only tease him a little."

"The hell you will."

"I'll just wrinkle my nose."

"Mektu!"

"*Harach*, brother, I'm kidding."

They started for the doors. But they had not gone twenty feet when Mektu stopped before the first of the narrow windows. Something within had caught his eye.

Kandri looked. Through the heavy glass he saw a clean ward of perhaps a dozen beds, old iron frames, grass-stuffed mattresses that might have been spirited across the whole of Urrath straight from Ariqina's clinic. Motionless patients lay in several of these. And along the central passage between the beds moved Kereqa—creeping, smiling, gaunt—wrapped in a hospital gown, so strange upon the warrior that she seemed another person entirely. Holding her elbows were Stilts and Talupéké. They too were smiling, but Kandri knew in an instant that the smiles were feigned.

"She's better," said Mektu, "but not much better." He shook his head. "What are we going to do?"

Kandri said nothing. The woman was not going anywhere. Not today.

"I don't see Eshett," said Mektu.

"That's because she's not here."

Boom. The brothers looked at each other, and Kandri felt something pass between them. Without a word, they turned away from the hospital.

"She could have gone to visit the camel drivers," said Kandri. "The women love her. I suppose she could might be at your charity brothel too."

"If it's us she's looking for."

"Who else?" said Kandri. "But the gates are most likely of all."

"You don't know what's *likely*," said Mektu bitterly. "Nobody does. She could be lying in a ditch."

"Have you seen any ditches in Lupriz?"

They retraced their steps, bickering all the way. Only close to the boarding house did they reach a fragile accord: Mektu would check the gates, Kandri the drivers' dormitories. They would rendezvous at the stables, where Omzal was already waiting.

The boarding house door sprang open.

It was the matron's boy, some new fear in his eyes, although he was clearly glad to see them. He put a finger to his lips, then beckoned them inside.

They followed him across the common room. Once more the boy pointed at the courtyard. Kandri looked: there were the benches, the thickets of flowers and greenery, the little table where Talupéké had roundly thrashed his uncle at Babaturri—

—and Eshett, seated peacefully against the left-hand wall. She was in deep green shadows, arms wrapped about her knees. A flame-orange ginger blossom dangled from her fingers. Her head was tilted to one side.

"She's asleep, just where I saw her before," whispered the boy. He looked up at Kandri, trembling. "But she wasn't there the whole time."

"What's bothering you, then?" asked Kandri. "We're not angry. It's not your job to watch our friend. And anyway it's all right. She went out and came back."

"No, sir, she didn't go out! She just went . . . away."

"What the hell's the difference?" said Mektu.

But the boy's fear was rising. He kissed the back of his hand and blew across it for luck, as Kandri had seen many do in Lupriz. Duty done and conscious soothed, he fled the room.

The brothers crossed to Eshett in silence. Once more came the ominous *boom*, and as it rolled through the courtyard they saw her eyebrows furrow and her fingers twitch, so that the flower slipped from them to the stone. But she did not wake. Kandri had never seen her look more peaceful, unless it was in Tebassa's stronghold, the night they first made love. Mere months ago, a lifetime. He had refused her at first, for Ari's sake or Mektu's or both. At last Eshett had taunted him: *You have ideas about Parthans, maybe. Our bad blood, our smell.*

What would she say now? If blood meant anything, he was as much a Parthan as anyone in Urrath.

"I want to marry her, brother," said Mektu.

"Ask her, then," said Kandri.

He was shocked by his own words. Mektu, married? The idea was obscene. Marrying him would be like chaining yourself to a boar; Kandri could not wish it on anyone. Of course it was horrible, horrible, to have such thoughts about your brother—

The devil take him, whispered Spalak in his mind. *He's not your brother.*

"If you're going to do it," said Kandri, "you should get down on your knees, like Uncle says. I'll be outside."

He turned to go, but Mektu touched his arm. His eyes were moist.

"Not here," he said. "Not yet."

Something gave way in Kandri's mind. The itch he had felt all morning bloomed to devastating certainty. He knew what they must do. And he knew that Mektu, like so often before, had seen it first.

His closed his eyes, pressed a fist against his mouth. Fighting back against this new certainty. *Banish it, burn it, stomp it out.*

No use: it tugged at his hand, trying to unclench his fingers. Trying to steal away all that was left to him, everything that had brought him this far.

Everything, everyone.

But the knowledge would not be evicted. Sometimes, most times, you had to open your hand.

"All right, Mek," he whispered. "Just us."

30. THE LAST GAMBIT

Certain choices, once made, propel the chooser along a course as irresistible as a storm-swollen river thundering to the sea. A quick leap, the
shocking plunge, and then no further choice but to go where the river
takes you, or to drown.

So it was for Kandri and Mektu once they placed themselves in Omzal's
hands. The suzein was bewildered; he had readied nine camels. But he was
also quick to grasp their motives, and in short order they were leading Alahari and Fish and a third camel laden with faskas through the scorching
streets, around the Faluvari with its song of endless water, past the private
gardens of the Sartaph, the still-smoking ruin of the exorcist's abode. The
brothers asked him a few practical questions, but to each other they said not
a word. They were of one mind now. The dying for their sake was done.

The old waterworks building crouched in a locked garden overgrown
with sedge. The gate's fused and ancient hinges yielded to their combined
clawing with a shriek. Inside, the water-camel balked at the darkness of the
broken stair, but let itself be shamed by the calm example of the Sparaviths
until at last it descended spooked and timid between them.

Everything was as Omzal had described: a shaft straight as an arrow into
the darkness, bathtub-rounded at the base, devoid of ornament, a smuggler's

canal and nothing more. A tow path high on their left. Rats' eyes flaring in the light of their torches. Sand drifted into the canal over centuries, spits and splinters of daylight where the roof had cracked.

A mile of darkness. Abandoned boats, intersecting canals, old iron bollards along the path. Under the camels' feet the occasional snap of bones. Far away (and ever farther) the *boom* of the ogre's maul.

Then suddenly the terminus. An iron gate massively padlocked, a second stair, a round, ruined pump-house with a fallen roof but intact walls. Scurry of snakes and lizards. Barred windows, broken tanks, traces of ceramic pipes radiating from the building like the spokes of a wheel. The waters of Lupriz had once been ample enough to share with all its domain.

They mounted inside the pump-house, while Omzal removed more locks, bars, and chains from the single door. A small purse—half the rubies given them by Garatajik—pressed into Omzal's hands. Bows and blessings and awkward effusive thanks.

"Waterboy here's not a Sparavith," said Mektu, patting the third camel's neck. "Are we sure he can run?"

"I chose him myself," said Omzal. "He is strong and fit. The rest is in Ang's hands."

"Our friends will be angry," Kandri confessed. "The camel drivers may not understand at all. But Stilts will, once he reads my note, and he won't blame you. We would have tried to escape without your help, even if we had to scale the wall ourselves."

"We've managed that trick before," said Mektu with a cracked smile.

"Your friends will follow you, once the devil-girl withdraws," said Omzal, "but I do not think they will catch you before you reach Kasralys."

"They won't linger a day longer than they must," said Kandri. "They still have the heat to contend with."

"As do you," said Omzal. "Go now and think well of us. My mother was fond of saying that all Urrath is one spreading tree. The leaves may forget, but the branch remembers. And the trunk in the end nourishes us all."

He shouldered open the door, and they burst out into the sunlight. Before they could even take their bearings it slammed again; iron bars thumping down, thick chains rattling. Kandri twisted about in the saddle. There was Lupriz, there the distant mountains. And that speck, yes, that was the Child, still at her vulture-vigil by the gates.

And there, at a mile's distance: the long embankment of the desert road. His enchanted vision sketched it all before his eyes again. The road led northwest to Naduma, to bloodshed and war. But twenty miles this side of Naduma a lesser way branched off into the mountains. The road to Kasralys. The city felt near enough to touch. His journey would end as it began: running alone with Mektu, dodging and praying, all their hopes pinned on speed.

He touched the calfskin pouch against his chest, felt a quietness return to his heart. This had never been about the two of them alone.

He bent low over Alahari's withers, took a firm grip on the ruff of hair atop her neck.

"*Tarazed!*" he shouted, and as if expecting no lesser command she exploded into a gallop, drawing scandalized brays from Fish and the water camel. He glanced back: they were flying to catch up, the dust from their hooves rising behind them like a flag.

A noise from far behind them: the Child's scream, shrill and plaintive and chilling to the bone.

There came an answering roar, and then Old Slag was rounding the wall of Lupriz and charging them across the plain. The ogre had cast aside his maul; he was horrifically fast, devouring the space between them like a boulder crashing downhill. The shrill cries from the Child went on, furious and crackling with power.

The mile's gap shrank by half, then half again, and soon he could hear the groaning labors of the creature. No fight, no survivors if it closed. Mektu was only a few yards behind him now but the water-camel was foaming at the mouth; the poor creature was not a Sparavith; they were asking too much. The groans grew louder, and when Kandri dared another glance he saw that the ogre was within a hundred yards. It looked terrible, driven almost beyond endurance by the Child's power, its huge body built to crush and kill but not to run.

The camels, however, had decided exactly what they were built for. The gap held for another half-minute and then began to widen again. Kandri laughed through gritted teeth. *Sidewinders.* Ulren had not meant the nickname as a compliment, but it fit.

The Child gave a last long shriek. And with it, as though jabbed with knives, the ghouls spilled blinking from the holes and hovels where they had fled the sun. Mektu howled in rage and horror. Kandri looked left and right. They were everywhere, shading their eyes in misery but nevertheless loping toward the brothers, starting to run. It was not beyond ghouls to brave the daylight: it merely pained and frightened them. Kandri knew in an instant that the Child frightened them more.

He shouted to Mek over his shoulder: "One more mile! That's all we need!"

"Waterboy can't do this for a mile!"

Kandri glared: Waterboy had better. Like Slag, the ghouls were no match in speed for frightened camels. And most were far off, near the Child, gathered for their next assault on Lupriz. But six or eight had slept in warrens near the road, and they were flying along it now to cut the brothers off. Kandri cried to Alahari again, *Please, darling, a little more, just a little more.*

She gave it. All three of them did. Soon it was clear that no more than four ghouls from the pack on the road could hope to catch them. But it would take only one to break their stride, hobble them, let Old Slag close for the kill.

The embankment stood some eight feet higher than the plain. Omzal had said that the Sartaph maintained it for five miles outside of Lupriz. For those five miles it ran hard-packed and smooth. Once upon it they could run still faster.

Two more ghouls fell behind. That left only a gray-green monster with bulging eyes and another with the fanged underbite of an eel. Both were deep-chested and long of limb. He tried furiously to judge their speed: did the lead ghoul have the edge over him and Mektu? So close. Only a pace or two, if at all.

But a pace was plenty. The mere touch of a ghoul set a horse to bucking; if it got its arms around a horse's neck its miasmatic reek would fell the animal in short order. Did camels have some special immunity? Kandri wished he'd paid attention to the gossip of Eternity Camp.

Waterboy was foaming at the mouth.

They could break away, but in what direction? Not back toward Lupriz. Not toward the furnace of the Heart Basin without guide or magic to lead them to water. And not west—that was unthinkable. West lay Jekka's Grave.

The first ghoul had a gleam in its bug eyes. Where was Talupéké with her throwing daggers, Kereqa with her spear? Kandri had no plan for this. His plan had been to outrun everything. In that sense, too, nothing had changed.

Running. Always running. Are you man or fucking mouse?

Mouse, of course. But the thought was like sudden fever, and hardly knowing what he was doing Kandri snarled and drew his machete and turned Alahari straight into the path of the lead ghoul. Mektu howled at him but it was done, there was no turning, the ghoul's bug eyes widened as Alahari charged like a warhorse up the embankment. Kandri held his breath and leaned as low as he dared and the ghoul leaped and *There*, both clawed hands severed and flying and a section of the ghoul's scalp as well, and then he was crashing down the far side of the embankment and his camel was stumbling and slowing and the second ghoul was clawing at her hindquarters.

No, camels weren't immune. Alahari screamed deep in her gut and lashed out with both hind legs and crushed the ghoul's chest as though it were paper. But Kandri himself was nearly thrown, and in the seconds lost to scrambling back into the saddle he saw the gargantuan form of the ogre blotting out the sun.

The ogre was atop the embankment, wheezing and blowing like a whale. Near enough to step on him. Mouth like an oven. Bastard could bite a crocodile in two.

He should have stuck to the plan.

He brandished the machete (because why not) and the reek of ghoul blood and brains on the weapon made him vomit on his outstretched arm.

Not a good end. No dignity. He looked up and thought Old Slag was laughing, shaking in silent hysterics, great globular tears in its eyes. Kandri's rage flamed anew and he bellowed at it, *Come get me, finish it you worm in the devil's stool*, and then the ogre shuddered head to toe and gripped its chest and collapsed.

og

The sun crouched above the spot where the road met the horizon. It blinded and it scorched. It also likely saved their lives, for it was no easy thing for the remaining ghouls to charge straight at the lowering orb. Thirty minutes was all it took for the pack to vanish behind them, but Kandri kept them at a hard run for an hour, slowing only long enough to warn a band of scarred and limping refugees, Nadumans all, of what might greet them before they reached Lupriz. The Nadumans were so miserable with loss and fatigue they actually laughed—agonized laughs, laughs to crack the heart. All this, and ghouls by daylight.

"Leave the road if you see them coming," said Kandri, "and don't camp on it by night. It's not you they're after." The refugees stepped away from them at that, drawing scarves across their faces.

Darkness, of course, would revive the ghouls, but Kandri thought they could not possibly still be loping up the road. Surely there was some limit to how far the Child could project her will. She had not had ghouls or any other creatures in her service back in Mab Makkutin. But in the desert she had been attended by the man-spiders with the ropy hair.

Where had they come from? Had she pulled them from her terrible white ass? No, she must have chanced upon them, just as she had chanced upon these ghouls from Jekka's Grave, calling them from their slumber and making them obey.

It had not been an effort for her, like the spell she had cast on Kandri. And if the crumbling wall of Lupriz had stood against her, surely Kasralys had nothing whatsoever to fear?

Cheerful thoughts, but he knew better than to trust them. On they rode through the darkness, shouting warnings to refugees huddled about meager fires, terrifying them, setting off their dogs.

The road dwindled to a sand-swept path, and still they continued. Only well after midnight did Kandri permit them a nervous hour's rest. Mektu snored; the windblown sand collecting against him. Kandri watched the path. The Pilgrim Star throbbed like a blister in the east.

At dawn, Waterboy folded his legs beneath him and sat. In spite of everything, they laughed—"Don't think about it, Fish!" Mektu shouted—but their amusement soon turned to horror. The camel would not rise. They tugged and shoved in unison; they coaxed him with thatch, they slapped his hindquarters with machetes. Finally, desperate, they yoked Alahari and Fish to Waterboy's saddle and walked them forward.

The two Sparaviths dragged Waterboy for yards, ears flat in indignation, before he surrendered and rose to his own feet. Immediately he began to limp. The sight was pitiful, but they found no sign of wound or thorn or broken bone. "A cramp," said Mektu. "It happened sometimes with the Prophet's camels, remember? And it was cold last night."

"We'll move half the water to Alahari and Fish," said Kandri, and they did.

The operation relieved Waterboy's pain, but obliged the brothers to go on foot. *Won't do, won't do*, went the refrain in Kandri's head. Their pace had slowed after less than a day.

Midmorning the path began to climb. These were the foothills of the Ablasadur Sara, the jagged and disordered mountains whose name, a fleeing Naduman informed them, meant the Pallbearers' Range. The refugees, more numerous now, were appalled to see anyone fleeing west.

"Turn around," shouted a young woman, staggering toward Lupriz with three children in tow. "Naduma is on fire. Nothing awaits you there."

Her sarong was stained with sweat and dust and ashes. The three children walked barefoot. Even the smallest carried a bundle tied to her wishbone shoulders.

"We're not going to Naduma," said Kandri.

The woman nodded. "Kasralys, then. By the Sapphire Road. It is a savage path through the mountains, strangers."

"I know," said Kandri truthfully.

"Turn at the Customs House. You'll have company. Many Nadumans are bound that way, over the mountains to Perec Station, and the Sacred Plain beyond. Yes, many of us turned there. The strongest, the stupidest. The most afraid."

"My brother says it's the fastest way to the city," said Mektu, suddenly dubious.

"It is the *only* way," said the woman, "unless you return to the oasis and take the long east road to Twelve Hearts Valley."

The road the caravan would be taking. "Is that your plan?" Kandri asked. "The long east road?"

The woman shook her head. "We will shelter in Lupriz and pray that Kasralys comes to our aid. That they rally our warriors in the hills and drive out the Shôl invaders. We know they could do it. Some say there is no army in Urrath as great as Shôlupur's, but very few were sent, while all the might of Kasralys is on Naduma's doorstep. Chasing out the Shôl would be nothing for Kasralys. Like pinching out a candle. But maybe they cannot be bothered. Maybe they are afraid of a little burn."

℞

After their short midday rest the path grew steeper, the mountains frowning over them, snow glittering on the peaks. Many miles to the south, Kandri saw a vast, curving rift, and he knew he was once more looking at Jekka's Grave. A wonder that Lupriz could thrive so near that ghoul-infested crater.

Then again, look at the refugees. How many in this world were free to choose the spot they called home?

Late evening they came to the ruined Customs House that marked their turnoff: the old Sapphire Road, built by miners through the high Ablasadurs. They paused, dispirited by what they saw. The path had been steep enough for hours; now it became precipitous. Kandri tilted his head back. Far above them, small lights bobbed and flickered in the sky. Then he noticed the absence of stars and realized he was still facing a mountain. The lights were not some fairy-beings among the clouds; they were torches carried upon the road they were to climb.

"I'm *not* starting up that bastard in the dark," said Mektu. "Fish would never forgive me."

"The ghouls—"

"Have turned back by now, probably," said Mektu, "and even if they haven't, they won't catch up before dawn."

Kandri's resistance was token, especially when Mektu offered to take the first watch. The Customs House had no roof, but its sturdy walls blocked the wind. They tied the camels together in a corner, slid their burdens to the ground. Mektu settled down near the doorway with a good view of the crossroads. Almost before he could spread out his bedroll, Kandri was asleep.

A shrill cry ended his bliss. His eyes snapped open. It was a bird's cry, and unmistakable, though he had heard it just once in his life.

Safiru!

There she was, five feet away upon a fallen stone. Between her talons lay the carcass of a long-eared desert rat. *You came back*, thought Kandri. *Ulren was wrong about you.*

Was he, though? The man had declared that the owl would not return because he, Ulren, was not of Jód's bloodline. But Kandri was. Could the bird possibly have sensed what Kandri himself had never suspected?

Safiru's head turned like a wheel; she fixed her round eyes on Kandri.

Share my breakfast?

Kandri smiled at her. "It might come to that," he said.

He realized suddenly that the dawn was near. He'd served no watch; Mektu lay curled like an infant against the warm wall of Fish. Kandri's hand flew to the Letter of Cure, his thoughts back to Weeping Rock. But the Letter was safe. He rose and prodded Mektu with his foot.

"Ouch!"

"You didn't keep watch at all, did you?" said Kandri. "I should have asked the bird."

"Bird?"

"Get your lazy ass up. My next kick won't be a love tap."

The next calamity came after their meager breakfast: Waterboy again refused to rise.

This time nothing would oblige him: even dragged, the poor beast simply lay there, hide scraping across the ruined floor.

The brothers stood swearing. The day's first refugees passed up the trail with looks of concern. They transferred as much of the water as they dared to Alahari and Fish, but Waterboy remained on his side, calling their bluff.

"Water is not a Gods-damned luxury," said Mektu.

Kandri nodded. "I told him that yesterday."

"What the hell do we do? Leave him here to starve? Brain him to death?"

The sun was climbing, the cool of the night slipping away. In desperation they slung as many of the remaining faskas as they could over their own shoulders and lay the rest at the juncture of the paths. They removed Waterboy's saddle and left it just outside the Customs House door. "You're free to go," Kandri told him, but the beast did not move. He bent down and scratched his dusty cheek goodbye.

Forty minutes later, high above on the trail, they saw a group of Nadumans coax Waterboy to his feet, saddle him, and lead him downhill toward Lupriz. "That stupid fucker!" Mektu exploded. "Look at him, he's spry as a colt! He just didn't want to make the climb!"

"Call that stupid, do you?" Kandri asked.

ଔ

By the second morning they had drunk all the water they had slung on their backs, and there were still five days ahead in the mountains. Afternoons they roasted in the sun; at night they huddled freezing between the Alahari and Fish. They could rarely walk after dark: the path was too narrow, and the cliffs too sheer.

On the third day they faced a chasm of unthinkable depths. The road leaped over it by means of a stone bridge humped in the middle like a frightened cat. It was clearly ancient; littered with fragments of the crumbled guard-walls that now reached only to their knees. The wind in the chasm sang of mourning.

Two dozen refugees stood contemplating the bridge. Men stood with crossed arms, heads together, as though a show of unity might persuade the bridge to widen. Children wept. "This is bad," Kandri declared. "That bridge narrows as it goes. It can't be more than five feet wide at the center."

"And no rail," said Mektu. "Glowing piss of the Gods! We have to set free the camels, brother."

"We can't do that. We'll die of thirst."

"Most of them don't have animals."

"Yes," said Kandri, "and just look at them."

More refugees arrived. One family turned their mules around and started back down the trail, speaking of Lupriz. A young man crept halfway to the center of the bridge, bent very low, before hunching his shoulders and retreating. The wind, he kept saying. The wind.

When fifty or more refugees stood frightened and amazed before the chasm, an old woman hobbled up the trail. She had a game leg that made her rock with each step, but she rocked along swiftly, making straight for the bridge.

"Not this again," she shouted. "You're being cowardly, all of you. People have been crossing here for six hundred years. Animals as well. Come along!"

She climbed as far as the young man had dared, and then went on to the high, narrow hump at the bridge's center. Wind-whipped, she looked back at the motionless crowd.

"Did you forget how to walk," she shrieked, "or do you regularly fall over when the wind blows? Ninnies! People never fall from this bridge! It's the easy ones where we get clumsy. The easy way that hides our doom."

❧

They crossed without incident; the old woman was a genius, Mektu declared. But there were still worse bridges to come that tried her philosophy. The next day they walked a quarter mile on a walkway that was no more than old planks against a cliff, three hundred feet sprawling beneath them and no supports but beams hung from sockets in the stone. Later they encountered rockslides. The smaller ones they cleared by hand, working for hours alongside the refugees. The larger ones they crept over like ants.

One night they awoke to the echo of screams. Five or six voices, melded with distance, nothing certain but the pain they conveyed. Dawn brought vultures, spiraling down from the heavens, converging somewhere ahead. They reached the spot at midday: an eroded cavity in the trail, difficult even by daylight. Three hundred feet below, two bodies lay beneath the jostling carrion birds. A woman, a child. On the cliff wall, two names in charcoal, and a message: *Forgive us that we go on.*

The brothers passed that day in silence. The refugees were ever more numerous, strung along the switchbacks ahead and behind. Some were slowed by injury, others by hunger and despair. Kandri watched them as he had once watched the shuffling dead. Like the ghosts there was something removed from them, something taken by violence, never fully to be restored.

ℚ

That evening Mektu fell asleep before the light was gone. Kandri felt the cold washing over the mountains and knew he should cocoon himself against it, but instead he opened the calfskin pouch and drew out the letter from Chindilan.

Dead or lost to you, his uncle had said. Well, this was close enough. He unfolded the letter, gripping the pages tightly against the wind.

> *Kandri Lad,*
>
> *As I write, the sandstorm is raging like a demon army, Eshett is screaming and lunging in her chains, Mektu is in a corner fondling the mattoglin, and you are out cold with a blow to the head. Your uncle, meanwhile, is struggling for words. I grope for them at need, hopelessly, an old fool at the river's edge snatching at minnows.*
>
> *Our surgeon growls more than he talks, but when pressed he admits that he believes you'll pull through. I am certain of it. You're carrying the hope of this world strapped to your chest.*
>
> *And somehow or other you've become the hope of this caravan as well. None of us can explain it, but everyone's aware. Even Jód, who would rather be flayed than compliment a Hinjuman. You're the wick that keeps this candle burning. Therefore you can't be lost.*

Not so this old ironmonger. When my camel went lame atop the Wall, I realized at last that I might die without keeping my promise to your father—I mean Lantor, of course. Hence I'm obliged to write what ought to come from him. This will not be easy to hear.

That night on the trail I told you how Lantor met your birth-mother and brought her home out of the desert, with Jód's help. I disabused you of the notion that your birth was an accident, that they married because he'd gotten her pregnant.

All that is true. But love kept me from saying more, and now I must come out with it. Kandri, Lantor Hinjuman is your father in the ways that matter most, in his heart and soul and conscience. But he is not your father by blood, and I have never known who is. I can only—

Kandri closed his eyes, which were burning rather than watering. Too dry for tears.

Open your hand.

Chindilan had not known that Kandri's father was Spalak, but he had known from the start that Kandri was not his best friend's son.

Let the wind take these pages. It wants them. You don't.

How many other secrets had his uncle kept for Lantor? How much more was there to learn?

Open your hand. Let the words blow away.

He did not open his hand—only, with great effort, his eyes.

—suppose it was that same fanatic suitor who forced himself on your birth-mother, just as he had tried to force the Prophet down her throat. Which means that Uthé was not only saving herself from Orthodox Revelation, Kandri. She was saving you.

And it was to Uthé first that I promised to take this knowledge to my grave. She knew exactly who she wanted her child to think of when he heard the word "Father," and his name was Lantor Hinjuman.

Now you know as much about your origins as anyone. But all that is the past and must not imprison you. My grandfather liked to say that the past is a box of phantoms. Seal the box, lock it, bury it deep: no matter, they leak out eventually. But I say those phantoms are weightless. The only power they have is despair. Listen too long to their whispers and they may convince you to stop swimming. Don't let them. Life's in the reaching forward, not the harkening back. That's a lesson our family doesn't want to learn.

I always thought you were the exception. You pounced on life like a terrier when a certain girl appeared in the village. I was proud of you and Ariqina and the joy you found together. So was the Old Man, though he never showed it. His thoughts were dark in those days. He feared nothing so much as being exceptional—and Ari was exactly that. "Exceptional people get noticed," he whispered to me once, "and the Prophet notices more than anyone alive. Your life and your dreams are finished, brother, once she decides you're worth thinking about."

So he feared for you and Ari, but he was glad as well. Think of it: the Valley was falling to pieces. The war was on our doorstep, hunger was creeping back, schools were shuttered. Orthodox Revelation was spreading like a pox of the mind. But in the midst of it all were two lovers: our Kandri and the Nawhal girl, that sweet ethereal genius, and who could help but smile at that?

But there was one who didn't. Mektu could not bear it, could not bring himself to believe it. He had fallen for Ari himself, of course, though any fool could see her heart belonged to you. Even on the night of the chase, when I came out and said it blunt as a bugle-call, he managed not to hear. Perhaps only Ari herself could have made him believe.

Why did she forbid you to tell him? It has always struck me as a foolish choice. But above all I should like to know why she fled without a word.

That broke many hearts, of course: did you know that Lantor and your stepmother wept, as though it were their own child who had vanished? But you, Kandri: it cut you to pieces, like meat on the butcher's block. We feared for your sanity. It was almost a relief when you wound up in jail.

I am rambling. All the candles but my own have gone out.

You survived the loss of Ariqina, barely. And since then you've faced more horrors than a man ever should. But it's not all darkness, is it? Your new lover has come back to us—broken in mind, and your brother culpable, for the mattoglin he stole is at the heart of her madness. No one can say whether she will recover. But somehow I feel she will, just as I feel that you will soon open your eyes and rejoin us.

What then, Kandri? I say again that you must not let your past become your jailer. Ariqina left you. Eshett is real. And since I must choose or be damned for a vacillating coward, I will betray a further confidence, may Ang forgive me.

I spoke with Eshett the day you and Mektu fell into the pit. We were both wide open. We knew the pair of you might be stung to death, or buried, or impaled.

"Kandri loves his doctor-girl," she said. "He only makes love to me."

"Doesn't sound like the Kandri I know," I told her, "but what of your feelings?"

"I don't love him," she said.

It was too quick, however. She saw my doubt and became testy. "I was clear with him from the start," she said. "It was only anga, the needs of the body. It might have grown. We did not let it. And he's gone on loving a woman who spurned him and fled without saying goodbye. I won't be the fool who tries to come between him and a ghost."

"But if he gave up chasing that ghost?" I pressed. "Could you be happy with such a man as my nephew?"

She shrugged. "Why not? But that will never be his choice. He will seek his Ariqina to the ends of the earth. The Gods are cruel, don't you think? Mektu wants me, but only in the way a dog wants a treat—and I cannot be with Mektu, I'd rather hang. I want his brother, maybe, when I let myself think about it. And Kandri wants a mirage."

Then she poked me in the chest: "Repeat this to anyone and you'll curse the day you were born." Her words were harsh but her motive pure: like you and Ari back home, she did not wish to wound Mektu with the truth. Or to saddle you with obligation.

So much has changed since that cold morning. I think now that my silence would be a meaner thing than the breaking of my promises—to Uthé, to Lantor, and now to Eshett. Just as I have faith that you and Eshett will recover, I believe also that you will find Ariqina in Kasralys, or wherever she has gone. But once more I ask, What then?

You will beg for her hand, as I urged you to do before the madness of the fire-balls. But you have done that before. I was the soul witness to your first proposal, that night in Blind Stream. And I fancy little escaped me that night. Ariqina loved you. She longed to say yes. Something buried, something ghastly, made her say no.

What that something may be I cannot imagine. But refuse you she did, and the pain in your face that night is something I will recall to my dying day.

Which brings me at last to my commandments.

Listen, nephew: if you should find Ariqina, she will not be the girl you remember. Nothing holds still in a city, lives and hearts included. Ariqina may have found love in Kasralys. And though I urge you to find her—you will never be free of her ghost unless you do—you must face that prospect before you go down on your knees. Guard your heart, my boy. The second blow could land harder than the first.

That is my first commandment. The second is this: find help for your brother—and soon, before he grows too old to change. You're not doomed to spend the rest of your life caring for him. Better if you didn't, in fact. Once inside the city you can step away, live your own life, stop being his crutch. But find him a specialist first. A brain doctor. Someone who can bring out the man in him and banish the ape.

Now for my third and final order: be nothing short of saintly to Eshett, whether your love endures or not. As Jód says, she is the desert's daughter; in the city she will have no one but you. Treat her poorly and you'll answer to my ghost: a specter of wrath with hot poker in hand.

Uncle

"What the hell are you reading?"

Kandri started. It was almost dark. Mektu's eyes were open, but Kandri could not read his face.

"Nothing," he said, folding the letter hastily. "Something I picked up in Lupriz."

"Something you picked up."

"I mean wrote. I picked up Stilts' pen and wrote down some thoughts. Personal thoughts. Embarrassing, actually."

"It's a letter, isn't it?"

"No, Mek! Who in the Nine Pits would I be writing to?"

"You're not writing, you're reading. Who's it from?"

"I told you it's not a letter."

"Show me then."

"Mektu," said Kandri, "go back to sleep."

Cʒ

The next day Mektu gave a whole faska—their third to last—to a family felled by thirst. Two children and their parents, rasping for water under the meager shade of the woman's shawl. The sight of his brother squabbling with them—*First the kids, take it or leave it*—as he poured into mouths that strained upward like nestlings filled Kandri with clashing emotions. Pride in Mek. Shame that he had not done it himself. Anguish that they could not do it again.

When the faska was empty, the young mother reached beneath her hood and lifted free a necklace of ceramic beads, each beautifully painted in bright colors, tiny human figures alternating with animals. Mektu shook his head but she ignored him, placing it around his neck and whispering "*Sor kim rala, he rala Ushimni.* The heart most open is the most blessed."

In the nights that followed they huddled with the refugees in small folds in the cliffs, in shallow caves, in fortifications so old and broken they barely inconvenienced the wind. They lay close together, sleepless, shaking with cold.

"Why don't you show me that letter now?" said Mektu on the seventh night.

Kandri just shook his head. Mektu laughed as though he didn't care one way or another. "Be a prick, then. Just tell me this: what if she's right on our heels?"

"The Child?" said Kandri. "Then we'll fight her, I guess."

"You know we can't fight her. She kills with a touch."

"We'll find a way to beat her," said Kandri. "We just need time. Inside those walls we'll have time."

"They must have a dozen exorcists in Kasralys."

"A dozen?" said Kandri. "Mek, they'll have a hundred or more. And scholars to tell us what sort of devil she is, and her weaknesses."

"What I'd like," said Mektu, "is a catapult. Roll it up close to the wall. Choose a boulder, and—" His finger traced a parabola against the sky, ending with a smack of his palm against the earth. "Flat. Finished. No more White Child."

Kandri blinked at the stars. Mektu watched him a moment, then lay down and pulled his coat tight. "She'd never see it coming," he murmured. "Things would have been different if Lupriz had one of those."

"A catapult."

"Mmm . . ."

Kandri lay still. The wind in the peaks like the moans of a vanished city.

"Maybe fighting her's not the answer," said Kandri, but Mektu was already asleep.

C�

On the seventh day their own water ran out. On the eighth they clung to their camels like invalids, muscles starved for energy, weaker with every step. Their tongues stiff leather, their palates wood. Their dried food inedible without water to help it down.

On the ninth morning the old woman from the first bridge gave them the last two swallows from a nearly empty faska. Kandri gulped the water before his stealthy mind allowed him to wonder if the faska might be her last.

"Don't quit now, you pair of layabouts," she said. "Fah, you'd think these two had crossed the whole of the Sumuridath."

She hobbled around the next bend and was lost to sight. A quarter hour later they felt strong enough to rise and stagger on in her wake.

"There's no *air* up here," said Mektu. Kandri nodded. Ridiculous notion—there was nothing but air, a vast obliterating space—but also, somehow true. Mektu always saw them, those impossible truths.

That afternoon they found the old woman curled by the trailside, two of her countrymen kneeling beside her in prayer. They had covered her with a headscarf. Kandri and Mektu removed their own and stood with lowered eyes, swaying in the wind. No one knew the woman's name.

Another mile. Kandri's body was hollowing, becoming weightless, evaporating from the inside out. The sun slid below the mountains; a red-orange glow bathed the peaks.

The wind rose, sudden and icy. Kandri realized with a dull but absolute certainty that if he lay down in that wind there would be no rising. Then like the caravans of the dead, like all the souls who had followed him or passed unseeing, he would turn back to the desert and walk it forever, bereft and intangible, a shadow at midday, a whisper in a storm.

He found his brother's hand and gripped it a moment; the faint answering squeeze gave him strength. Another mile, and another after that.

ᘓ

In the last minutes of daylight they rounded a cliff and saw Perec Station, the border castle, not fifty paces ahead.

The castle was menacing at first glance: a sharp-cornered keep and looming black tower. Guards patrolled the ramparts, longbows in hand. But the gates stood open, and a lamp burned above the granite arch. Refugees, many of whom Kandri recognized, sat in the courtyard, drinking from cups and faskas.

Beside the trail stood a large plaque on stout wooden posts. The plaque was cast iron but painted in heavy enamel. It depicted a gray wolf atop a sentinel-stone, wearing a crown of golden leaves. The paint was peeling and faded, but the message beneath the wolf could still be read:

YOU ENTER HERE
THE SEVENTH ITERATION
OF THE SOVEREIGN DOMAIN OF THE KASRAJ

YOUR DREAM IS OUR DREAM
YOUR PATH SHALL BE OUR PATH
ONE SONG OF JOY SHALL OUR CHILDREN LEARN TOGETHER

NEVER AGAIN IN CONQUEST
FOREVER IN PEACE

BE WELCOME

Just beyond the castle, the land fell away as though carved with a trowel. Below spread the lush plain Kandri had glimpsed from the Night Queen's Pillar. The Sacred Plain. It was even more beautiful than he recalled.

"Look back," said Mektu.

Kandri turned. A second, smaller plaque was set into a rock by the trailside. This one faced east.

WITH YOUR NEXT STEP YOU ENTER

THE SUMURIDATH JAL

A LAND WITHOUT MERCY

GO WITH WISDOM
OR GO NOT

"Mek," said Kandri, "we just walked over the Great Gods-damned Desert of Urrath."

"Let's do it again sometime," said Mektu.

He gave Fish a tug and led her in through the gate. Figures in dark blue uniforms with green sashes milled in the courtyard. Beckoning, smiling. But Kandri, obeying an impulse he did not quite understand, walked Alahari past the gate and farther along the castle wall.

Fifty more steps, and he could see it: Kasralys, the Jewel Entire, vast and lovely and invincible and timeless. Guarded by the nine great Towers of Serenity he had seen from atop the Pillar, sunbeam-straight, otherworldly in size. Backed up to mountains twice the height of these that had almost killed him. Crouched above a lake like a small inland sea.

Kasralys, city of Ari's dreams.

The path became a road here, snaking down from Perec Station and darting across the Sacred Plain, skipping from village to village, pond to stream-side, farm to farm. At last, broad and tree-lined, it neared the gates of Kasralys. But the gates, like the whole of the city, stood high above the green heartland of the Kasraj atop the Nine-Mile Rift: that monstrous, magnificent plateau.

Connecting city to plain was a jaw-dropping structure: a slender bridge like an iron needle, suspended on piers as high as the plateau itself. The bridge rose first as a great iron ramp, then soared flat and straight for the city. It passed over the outer defenses—a black moat, three lesser walls—and ended at the massive gates of the city's great inner wall, the Ancestor Wall, hugging the plateau's sharp edge.

So that was how you entered the Fortress City. The way the Prophet declared she would enter her kingdom on the day of final victory. Heaven's Path. A road in the sky.

In fact many roads converged at the foot of the great bridge. There Kandri saw a fenced area like a great stockade, enclosing a mighty crowd. More people were approaching by every path across the Plain.

Kasralys. He felt the last of the Night Queen's spell tug him forward. *Hurry*, it whispered, *hurry, before—*

Before what? He could not say; the Queen had fallen silent. But as he stood there, nearly broken in body but rising within, Kandri's vision of the journey changed. They had not been lone travelers. Not a Gods-forsaken caravan lost in immensities. Not a collection of the uniquely damned. They were part of a multitude, drawn here from all over the continent, the blood in the veins of Urrath returning to the heart.

"The Flying Bridge," said a voice behind him. "A triumph of old Kasraji engineering—although the greatest marvel of its design we hope never to need."

It was one of the soldiers from the courtyard. The man offered him a cup.

"Blessings of Almighty Ang," said Kandri, taking it in thirst-shriveled fingers.

"We don't speak the Gods' names in my faith, Chiloto," said the man with a smile, "but never mind, it's a pleasure to be the one to break your water-fast. Also, your brother promised to stop talking if I brought you a cup."

"We'll need more. We can pay."

"Lucky for you, but we cannot sell," the man replied. "The Lady Chancellor would have our skins if we asked for money this time of year. That's snowmelt you're drinking. Plenty for all."

The man went back to his duties. Kandri drank slowly, carefully, moistening the withered prune of his throat. In his mind he heard Prince Nirabha, speaking to him after the burial of Ripheem.

You must judge for yourself if we are civilized, when you reach my city at last.

"Could this be it, Mek?" he said, although he knew no one could hear him. "Could this be home?"

೮೩

"We're going to catch a disease."

"Not that again."

"We're going to be knifed in our sleep, Kandri."

"*Harach*, you sound so ignorant."

"I am ignorant. And so are you."

Mektu turned his head this way and that. A multitude surrounded them. Some three thousand souls they'd estimated, fenced into an area better suited to three hundred. Every color of skin imaginable: coal black, ironwood-black, flinty goat's-hoof black, nutmeg-brown, caramel, olive, oak. The poor and the wealthy—or should that be the poor and the suddenly poor, the latter so conspicuously helpless, perplexed by suffering, their fine clothes turning to rags? The hale and the old and the bleary-eyed ancients. The young, the very young, the newborn. And their carts, camels, horses, donkeys, dogs. It was hard to sit down: the green turf beneath their feet was being trampled into mud. It was hard to breathe without choking on the smell of unwashed skin, or swallowing a fly. It was growing increasingly hard to think.

"What are they all *speaking?*" said Mektu. "I've heard Lañatu and Tohru and Solonj, and something that sounds like Talupéké's gibberish—"

"Lo'ac," said Kandri.

"Thank the Gods she spoke Common most of the time. *Khuh, buh, blurud!* That's not a talking, that's dry heaves."

"Not one word of the camel drivers' tongue. Mistajav."

"Not one word of ours, either," said Mektu. "I don't think they invited any Chilotos to this party. Except for us I mean."

Except for you, thought Kandri wretchedly.

"You! Urchin!" cried Mektu suddenly. "Did I warn you, or not?"

He kicked at a boy who had ducked under Fish. The boy started to wail.

"Oh stop that, he'll piss on your head," said Mektu. "Or bite. He loves biting. Or he'll step on you and your guts will squirt out like a jelly roll."

Other children—those who understood the Common Tongue, maybe—started to laugh. "Jell-y, jell-y, jell-y-roll!" they chanted. The boy Mektu had kicked chose to laugh as well.

"Go on, get out of here," said Kandri. All day long, children had been sneaking under the camels: there was room there, and shade.

Mektu's mood collapsed again as soon as the children dispersed. He fingered the bright beads of the necklace, the young mother's gift. He had worn it day and night.

"We've crossed the Ravenous Lands," he said. "We've crossed the whole Gods-damned *continent*. And we're right back where we started. Locked in a prison camp. Why the hell did we leave?"

"This isn't prison," said Kandri. "We can leave any time." And that was true: the guards had made it clear that they were free to leave when they liked—by the same gate they had entered by. But to do so would be to abandon their petition for entry altogether.

"You know why we left," he added, "so stop carping. Prince Nirabha warned us things were rough in the city."

"We're not *in* the city," said Mektu. "We're caged. Like swine."

Kandri bit his lips. Even yesterday he might have argued with Mektu's choice of words. It was not that bad: the Kasrajis had provided food and water, thatch for the camels, blankets for elders and children. The latrines they had dug were no fouler than those at Eternity Camp.

But this morning made a week—a week!—since he and Mektu had come down from Perec Station, crossed the Sacred Plain, and joined the mob of refugees at the foot of the Flying Bridge. Each day the crowd had grown, sometimes doubling by sunset.

"Not swine, even," said Mektu. "They let pigs into the city. Those bearded fuckers with the dogs must have had two hundred."

"Offer yourself up to be eaten," said Kandri.

"What did I tell you about trying to be funny?"

The city's massive, many-towered wall loomed over them, sweeping away into the distance, hugging the rim of the Nine-Mile Rift. All day long they heard temple bells ringing the hour, some close and clear, some faint as echoes in the mountains. Occasionally they heard voices from the city: a guard's shout, or a foreman's. One windless morning they had heard a children's choir.

The stockade, constructed of nine-foot iron fences, inevitably did bring farm animals to mind. It was actually three vast enclosures, human holding pens the size of the largest drill yards at Eternity Camp, bursting with desperate souls. Outside the pens were still more fences, enclosing the guard barracks, a viewing platform, and the great iron ramp ascending to the bridge.

All the refugees entered through a western gate, after which they were herded, seemingly at random, into one of the three enclosures. Kandri and Mektu had spent the week in the middle pen. Each of the three had a heavily guarded gate letting into the yard at the foot of the ramp. The ramp itself narrowed like a funnel as it climbed to the bridge.

No one since their arrival had left this pen, or the pens to either side. The stockade looked new and somewhat thrown together, but it was serving its purpose. It had frozen the refugees in place.

Not their dreams, however. Diverse as it was, the mob shared a single faith: that all of this was an error, a misunderstanding. Soon the guards would remove these fences, these humiliations, and they would climb the ramp and walk the Flying Bridge into Kasralys, and a better life. Work, food, health, safety, new homes, new loves. All there, all waiting for them. The mob lived this faith, voiced it, repeated it, breathed it in and out. They had all made journeys of loss and terror, violence and tears. What else were they to cling to? What other ending could make sense of such pain?

"What's happened to devil-girl?" Mektu asked suddenly. "Why hasn't she come for us?"

Kandri flinched at the mention of the Child. "I can venture a guess, if you like."

"Venture away."

"You saw how she faded," said Kandri. "Flickered, like, after she tried to magic me on the wall of Lupriz. That cost her; she was angry when it failed. And I'll bet it cost her ten times over to force Old Slag to run like that, until his heart burst. She has her limits, Ang be praised."

"Limits?" said Mektu. "She killed an elephant with her finger. What limits?"

"She was close to the Prophet then," said Kandri. "Now they're hundreds of miles apart. If the Child's power is tied to the Prophet's own, maybe it can only stretch so far."

"Like toffee candy."

"Uh-huh."

"So maybe the Child's heart burst too."

Kandri shook his head. "Believe that if you want," he said. "I'm just hoping she's weak. As in smack-down exhausted. Too exhausted to follow us over the mountain, at least for awhile."

"Keep watching the pass, all the same."

"Thought I might," said Kandri.

With the aid of the telescope he could easily study the castle at Perec Station, and the road by which they had come. He did it now, recalling the moment there that had felt like triumph, while behind him somewhere a child burst into tears. *Mama, Mama, where is Mama, is she dead?* A man's voice tried to soothe her. Kandri's hand felt for the calfskin pouch.

Only the Cure made sense of it all. Lost, regained, sand-blasted, blood-defiled. Carried over a continent. Soon to be surrendered to Ariqina's hero, the great Dr. Tsireem. He closed his eyes. The mob's voice like the swell of the sea. They were right to have faith. The gates would open, Kasralys would receive them. Just one possible ending, for no other could be borne.

☙

The city was not, of course, closed to everyone. Day and night the bridge conducted two narrow streams: one entering the city, the other departing. People, horses, camels, cattle, sheep. But none of those entering Kasralys had come from these holding pens. No, they were citizens of the Realm—that or trading convoys and caravans, known and sanctioned by the city. All such persons carried ornate passkeys of polished bronze, or stamped letters from some registry in the city center.

The mob watched these persons come and go, bearing their talismans that worked a magic upon the guards. Most were not even questioned. Some were greeted by the guards with recognition, smiles, jokes.

"You should give it another shot," said Mektu. "With the guards I mean, and the letter."

"Right," said Kandri, "because it went so well the first two times. I'd say we've nearly won them over."

On their first afternoon in the stockade, they had fought their way to the corner of their particular enclosure nearest the viewing platform. Any outer fence was prize territory, for only there could the waiting thousands breathe clean air, or gaze at the exquisite landscape of the Sacred Plain. This particular corner was the most prized of all because of the view it offered of those who would decide their fate. Day and night, soldiers passed within a few yards of the spot, along with others whose tasks and rank were a mystery. Sometimes the refugees called out to them with pleas or promises, or even bribes. Most stood in melancholy silence.

Once a day, however, soldiers approached the fence themselves, shouting instructions:

"If you're holding a passkey, you don't belong in there! A passkey or a stamped petition. Hold 'em up where we can see."

"Is that a lamp, Uncle? Don't light it. Can't risk a fire."

"I said *stamped*, madam, no exceptions."

"Any children traveling alone? Truly alone now—don't get clever. Nudge 'em forward if you please."

That first day, Kandri attempted to speak with the guards. He had extracted a promise from Mektu not to say a word. As they drew near, the words he had prepared tumbled about his mind in disorder.

"Officers!"

Keep it calm hurry make it urgent don't sound mad.

"We're not refugees, not really. And we *are* carrying a letter. We were sent here on—business."

The pair of guards (older man, younger woman) paused for a weary instant. Kandri tore open his shirt. "This," he said, raising the calfskin pouch, "is a message from Lord Garatajik, son of Her Radiance the Prophet. The Chiloto Prophet—you've heard of her? I don't worship her, I'm different. I've carried this letter all the way from the west, over the whole of the desert. It's for your Dr. Tsireem."

At the mention of the famous doctor, the young woman turned to Kandri, and for a precious moment he was seen. A person, not a texture. A man, not a facet of the mob.

"Tsireem Fessjamu? The hero, paladin of the realm?"

"That's her, that's her, exactly!"

The woman raised an eyebrow. "Original," she said.

The man sighed like a buffalo, and the pair walked on. And Kandri, who had told himself to expect no better, was blindsided by despair. What had seemed like a noble commingling of needy souls when he looked down from Perec Station now felt like mere helplessness. Like erasure. All they had lost, regained, wept for, fought for, overcome: it was nothing, it was invisible. A lifted eyebrow. A mocking sigh.

"That was horrible," said Mektu.

"Thanks."

"*I don't worship her, I'm different.*' What the hell were you thinking? You didn't even mention the Plague."

Kandri rubbed his jaw: it felt brittle, beneath his three-week beard. As if his clenching might break it. A vision arose of them safe within the city, the Letter delivered and Ariqina found—and a new life, as his uncle had hinted, removed from daily contact with the ape. This brother who sneered and struck him. Who never noticed when his words became knives.

The next morning Kandri returned to the fence alone. After four hours, the same pair of guards passed along it, asking the same questions. When they drew near, Kandri caught the woman's eye.

"This letter," he said, "describes a cure for the World Plague. An absolute cure. It's going to change the world."

The two guards stopped and looked at him, as if they could not help themselves. Kandri's heart lifted.

"This bone," cried a man beside him with sun-crazed eyes, holding up a drumstick chewed utterly clean, "is a relic of Saint Buiri the Lawgiver. Anyone who touches it—"

"Shut up," said the young woman, expressionless. Her eyes had not left Kandri. "A cure for the Plague, is it?" she said.

"I swear on my honor," said Kandri. "I tried to tell you yesterday. Lord Garatajik developed the Cure, and he put it all down here for your Dr. Tsireem. It's the only copy in existence."

"Listen to this one!" guffed a man somewhere behind him. "He's a savior, like."

"Many people," said Kandri, eyes locked on the guards, "have died to help me get here. The Cure is real."

The older man pursed his lips. "So this Gabarachik finds a cure for the World Plague," he said, "and then—what? He made *a single copy*, and gave it to you? Why in seven hells would he do that?"

"I don't quite understand myself." *Because it's impossible to understand, because it makes no fucking—*

"Have you read this letter?"

"It's not for me," said Kandri. "And besides, it's sealed against the weather. And most of it's in a language I don't speak."

"You're lying," said the man with the drumstick. "How d'ye *know* what language it's in, if it's sealed? This bone, now—"

"My letter's from the Grand Illim himself," said a youth on Kandri's right.

The older guard turned the youth a scorching look. "You realize," he growled, "what a crime it is to forge the hand of the Lord of Kasralys?"

"Not *from!*" stammered the youth. "I meant to say *for* him, for His Lordship! But I must deliver it in person. He's sure to be angry if I—"

"Scoundrels!" boomed a third man. "Read my petition! Don't tell me about stamps. Can't get it stamped in here, can I?"

"This bone—"

"*Damn it, I am telling the Gods' own truth!*" Kandri bellowed, pressing his face against the fence. "Trust me, please, just look at the letter! I'm not a crackpot. The letter's real, the Cure is real. Why else would we fight our way through storms and spiders and flying jellyfish—forget the jellyfish—I swear on my mother and father—"

"I've got the runs," screamed an old woman, and the guards moved on.

ಆ

"I keep seeing faces," said Mektu. "Faces we know, that is. Always deep in the crowd."

Kandri nodded. "I've seen the Old Man, and our sisters, and the woman who gave us shelter in Mab Makkutin. I turn and look and they're always strangers. It's infuriating."

"The others could be here by now."

"We didn't sneak away to save time," said Kandri. "We did it to save Lupriz and everyone in it from the Child."

Mektu's eyes swept the crowd. "I'll bet Ulren's had one of those fucking pass-keys from the start. They'll march right in, camels and all. They'll never see us."

"We'll see them. Eighty camels are hard to miss. Stop worrying; you'll just make yourself sick."

"What if they split up?" Mektu demanded. "What if Uncle and Eshett and the soldiers took the mountain path like we did?"

Kandri's teeth were on edge. There was no escaping his brother here, no stroll to restore his patience. They would end up strangling each other.

He pointed at Alahari. "Every day," he said slowly, as though addressing a child, "I've stood on her back and looked around. Every single day, like a Gods-damned stork. I might not have seen them among so many people, but they'd sure as hell have seen me. They're not here yet. Relax."

"I saw Captain Utarif," said Mektu. "I saw Ifimar Jód."

Kandri eyes widened. Once more, he wondered if his brother meant it literally. *Do you see the dead, Mektu? Have you seen them from the start, like me?* But Kandri knew better than to ask such questions aloud. There was no telling what would become of them if Mektu panicked in this place.

"I could be wrong about the captain," said Mektu. "It was dark then, I can't be sure. But I'm sure about Jód. I saw him; he was watching us. He was right over there." Mektu gestured at the adjacent pen.

"With a great bloody hole in his stomach?"

"Kandri," said Mektu, "I'm disappointed in that remark."

But Kandri had stopped listening: there was commotion at the bridge. Mektu looked up and whistled. Six riders on magnificent horses were descending the ramp. Four carried spears; all six wore swords on their belts. They wore uniforms of the same pattern as the guards, but these were gray with gold sashes, rather than the soldiers' black and green.

Behind the riders came four muscular drays hauling an extraordinary carriage. It was armored, its heavy wooden frame clad in sheets of beaten brass. The doors were brass plate, the windows barred, and even the high seat for the driver was defended by cocooning iron shields so that only his hands and a central sliver of his body could be seen.

At the head of the riders, on the tallest, blackest horse Kandri had ever seen, rode a woman some ten years older than himself. "That's her!" whispered several voices. "That's the Lady Chancellor!" Kandri was fascinated: she had a dignity and presence that riveted the eye. She belonged, he thought, to some clan he had never glimpsed even in pictures. Her dark caramel skin had a glow like polished wood, and her hair hung straight as a horse's tail. Her oval face revealed no particular emotion, but her large eyes, tapered like raindrops at the corners, never seemed to blink.

Kandri felt at once that he was looking at a person of tremendous kindness. Then he wondered if he should trust his impressions at all. *That face*, he thought, *shows what she wants it to show. Nothing more, nothing less.*

The whole entourage passed slowly by the brothers' stockade, then the one where Mektu had hallucinated Ifimar Jód, and halted at last by the viewing platform. The woman and one companion, a rough-faced man with a gray moustache, slid from their horses and climbed the ladder bolted to the stand.

Once atop the platform, the woman raised a hand over the crowd—not with command but with gentle entreaty, and yet the effect was the same. Dead silence fell over the crowd.

"What has happened here," she shouted into the hot, still air, "should not have been. It is not Kasralys, and I apologize on behalf of the city. There was no need to keep you ignorant, wondering why you risked famine and heat and violence only to be held in these—enclosures."

Somehow Kandri knew that she had nearly said *cages*. The nearest soldiers glanced at each other. The woman's words pleased some and angered others, but it left none of them indifferent.

"I am Kosuda Sarika Serr, Chancellor of Kasralys," she shouted. "We have failed the test of courtesy, but I would have you know that your confinement is not a whim. We seek peace with all lands, but the Scarlet Kingdom is preparing for war. I for one do not expect an open war, which could only bring despair to all the clans of the north. But a shadow-war has begun already. The most vicious killers, hands stained with the blood of countless innocents, have been enlisted. Already they are at work in Kasralys, within the city and without." She paused, then added with reluctance: "Some fear these enemies are among you."

Cries and whispers raced through the mob. But in her hesitation Kandri heard a very different message. *Some believe it. You don't. And you want us all to understand that. Why?*

If such was the Chancellor's wish, she had failed. The crowd was simmering now with fear and suspicion. The refugees began to struggle, impossibly, to separate from one another. The Chancellor again raised her hand.

"One level of safety you have attained already. The ground where you stand is also Kasralys. We defend the realm as surely as the city, as our enemies have learned throughout history, to their cost. No killers from abroad shall find you here."

The sounds of approval were tepid, and Kandri wondered why. *No killers from abroad . . .*

"Next year marks three hundred since the fall of the Empire of the Kasraj. We shall observe it not with mourning but joy. For we have built a fairer, fonder home in these three centuries than ever we attained as the rulers of Urrath."

Movement below: it appeared that someone in the carriage had signaled the riders, for one had dismounted and approached the carriage door. The latter opened a few inches. The rider stood listening and nodding. All of this went unseen by the Chancellor.

Whoever was addressing the rider passed her an object. It was a short white rod with inlays of colored stone. The rider held it with both hands, like something fragile or priceless. She looked up at the Chancellor. The door snapped shut.

"You have heard it said," cried the Chancellor, "that the cornerstone of the Seventh Realm is kindness. So it must ever be. The past is gone. A dead hand on the rudder. A cry on the wind. And we Kasrajis who would not be judged forever by our ancient sins—how shall we judge you who wish only to join us, to grow with us, to start anew? You have come fleeing terror and death, but you shall find hope here—hope and welcome. That is the promise of Kasralys, and I—"

She broke off. The rider had scaled the ladder and appeared at her side. Among the refugees some cautious cheering had already begun; now once more all fell silent. Making the same bow she had offered the occupant of the carriage, the rider presented the rod.

The Chancellor was clearly astonished. She did not take it, but looked swiftly over her shoulder at the mountains in the north. The rider leaned closer, speaking swiftly. Kandri could see that she hated the message she was obliged to relay.

Who in Jekka's Hell was in that carriage?

The Chancellor's hands tightened to fists. She questioned the rider sharply. The rider nodded again and again, clearly miserable. At last the Chancellor stood motionless, gazing at nothing. Kandri almost expected her to storm down the ladder, fling open the carriage door, and drag whoever lurked there out into the sunlight and the fullness of her rage.

But her composure held. Turning back to the crowd, she slowly crossed her fists over her breast, eyes lowered as though in prayer.

"I am obliged to tell you," she shouted, not raising her eyes, "that any who have tired of this . . . process, may depart by the western gate, the same by which you came here. You will then be—" Her mouth worked, as though the words burned her tongue. "—escorted, to a labor colony in the Nightfire Range, or by river barge to the Thrukkun."

She lowered her arms, turned on her heel. As she left the platform the crowd came to life in a collective howl of dismay. *Labor camps! In the mountains, or the marsh? Better if we'd stayed and died at home! M'lady, wait, m'lady!*

The Chancellor did not address them again. She mounted her horse and turned it in a prancing circle. As soon as the horse found a gap it exploded forward, galloping up the ramp, bearing the Chancellor back alone upon the Flying Bridge.

The other riders looked at each other, stunned. The wailing went on. At last the Chancellor's deputy, the man with the gray moustache, walked to the platform's edge and called down an order. The riders formed a line. The armored carriage moved away from the stockade in search of room to turn around.

As it returned, the man with the gray moustache descended to his horse. Just before he left the platform, his eyes swept over the multitude. A look of sadness and apprehension. A look of a man who wished to cry out a warning but could not.

CR

"Kandri? Are you still awake?"

". . ."

"Asleep, then?"

". . ."

"You're asleep?"

"I hate you, Mek. I simply—"

"What do you think she wanted to tell us? The Chancellor, I mean, before they cut her off?"

". . ."

"She was going to tell us we'd be allowed into the city, wasn't she?"

"I think so. Yes."

"Did you notice how she glanced over her shoulder?"

"I noticed it."

"She was looking at the mountains, Kandri. The northern mountains, not the ones we crossed."

"The Nightfire Range."

"The Nightfires. Did you think she was afraid, brother?"

"I thought she was angry. Whoever was in the carriage outranked her."

"Why do good people always have someone above them who's a shit? We'd be slaughtered in here if anyone attacked us."

"That's not going to happen, Mek. Kasralys is still one of the strongest lands in Urrath, and we're right at the heart of it. Enemies don't drop from the sky."

"That's what you said about fireballs."

"I didn't say anything about the fireballs. That was Uncle."

"And is Uncle the one who wrote that letter to you?"

". . ."

"Let me read it, Kandri. I have a right to know what it says."

"The fuck you do, if it's addressed to me."

"So you admit it's a letter."

"Stop talking. Go to sleep."

"If you let me read I will, Kandri."

"If you don't shut up, I'll feed the damn thing to Fish."

∛

Mektu said no more that night, but he snored at a volume that made sleep impossible for anyone in the vicinity. At first the refugees grumbled; later they threw pebbles and clods of dirt.

His snoring ended at last, only to be replaced by children waking from nightmares with howls to freeze the blood. Three woke in rapid succession, as though the dreams were contagious. By the time the last child had been soothed, Kandri glanced east, expecting the dawn. But no, it was still dark. He sent a prayer of thanks to Yarasht, Mistress of Silence. If he were a mighty sartaph he would build temples to Yarasht: bells to strike with cottoned mallets, domes of the serenest blue.

He woke with a start. The dawn had come; the mob was rising with groggy sighs. Mektu was gone, to the latrines no doubt. The pocket owl peeped drowsy-eyed from the folds of Kandri's cloak.

He sat up. The bird departed as always, but there was an uneasy quality to its movements. As it rose it gave a high, sharp screech that made the refugees jump.

Something was off. Something that brought a frown to Kandri's face before his mind could sift for a reason. He tried to peer beyond the crowd: were the guards more restless, more numerous than on other mornings? He could not be sure. Then he glanced down and forgot the guards altogether.

"Oh flaming shit."

The Letter of Cure lay at his feet. He pounced on it and mouthed his second prayer of the last few hours, this one to Ang All-Merciful. The waxed envelope was muddy but unharmed. His hand flew to the calfskin pouch on his chest: unbuckled, empty.

Hands shaking—correction, whole body shaking—he cleaned and dried the Letter of Cure and secured it back inside the pouch. He squatted there on his haunches, one hand resting on the pouch, trying to still his heart.

Then he looked up and saw Mektu between the camels, holding Chindilan's letter. His eyes were hollow, and his voice, when it came, bereft.

"The ape," he said. "That's what you call me, the ape? That's what *Uncle* calls me?"

Kandri stood, his hand still pressed to the pouch. He took a step toward his brother. "Do you know what you did? Do you know what I just found *lying in the mud?*"

"I don't even know who the hell you are," said Mektu.

"What?"

"If the Old Man's not your father, who is?"

Kandri's chest was too tight to breathe. Mektu raised a hand and pointed at him, trembling. "Who's your father?" he hissed. "Don't you lie to me again."

Kandri looked up at the mountains. *Do lie, absolutely lie.* Lying would be better for everyone. As for the truth, it could go drown itself. It could crawl back to the desert, dry up and blow away.

"What, is it another secret?" said Mektu. "Between you and Uncle, maybe? Or you and Eshett? Something to laugh about behind my back?"

Kandri walked forward and ducked under Alahari's chin. When he straightened his face was inches from Mektu's. "Nobody's laughing," he said. "I'm your brother. Nothing has changed."

"Eshett loves you, hates me—she'd rather *hang*—"

Kandri shook his head. "You've got it backward. She loves you, now, not me."

"But nothing's changed, eh?" Mektu's eyes were moist. "Lie after fucking lie."

Kandri closed his eyes. They stood so close he could feel Mektu's breath against his face, and yet they were like two people calling to each other across a canyon, across a void.

"She hated you at first. You bought a night with her at the brothel and then forgot you'd ever lain eyes on her. To say nothing of the rest of you. But now—"

"What about Ariqina?" said Mektu.

The old anger flared in Kandri's chest. Mektu had good reason to ask him about Eshett. But not her. Never her.

"Ariqina," he said, "is all that's kept me alive and walking and fighting and breathing these last three years."

"I have as much right to her as—"

"Who gave me this?" Kandri held up the thumb with the copper ring.

"Hell if I know."

"You do know. You know everything. She was my lover, Mek."

"Liar."

Kandri wanted to strike him, a harder blow than the one Mektu had landed on his jaw back in the desert. He wanted to break something—their bond, Mektu's denial, Mektu's teeth.

"You knew," he repeated. "All that talk about sleeping with her yourself, about how clumsy she was, how bad at sucking you off."

"Everyone's bad at *something*."

"*You're still at it!*"

"Sorry."

"There's nothing you won't say, is there? For fuck's sake, you claimed the two of you were engaged to be married."

"All right!" Mektu was breaking, suddenly, fighting the urge to hide his face in his elbow. "I'm sorry. The marriage part was a lie."

"Every part was a lie," said Kandri. "You didn't sleep with Ariqina. It was all to bait me, to punish me for having someone."

"You already had someone!" Mektu's jaw was quivering. "You and me, Kan, that's what I knew. Since the day the Old Man brought you down from the mountain. I can still see you, hiding behind him, a hayseed with patches on your shirt. Dug from that burrow of yours up on the mountain, scared out of your mind. I knew before Papa spoke. A brother, my age, a best friend. I knew the minute you arrived."

"Come off it," said Kandri. "You resented me the minute I arrived."

Mektu shook his head. "Loved you," he said.

It was like a blow to the chest. Kandri felt shamed and diminished, though he did not know just how he had failed. Mektu lifted his hands, trembling, and stopped with his fingertips just inches from Kandri's face.

"Listen." Kandri swallowed. "Those things Uncle wrote, about me leaving you in Kasralys, I never—I mean I don't have any—"

"Spalak."

Kandri went rigid. Mektu's eyes had filled with some new and terrible light. He lowered his hands, and it was as though he were lowering a mask from Kandri's face.

"Your father is Dothor Spalak."

"Yes," said Kandri, "but who cares? It doesn't change a thing. Does it?"

"That holy lunatic who tried to kill us all." Mektu retreated a step. "Who whispered in your ear every chance he got. The fool, he called me. The jackal, the slovenly ape. Spalak thought of me the same way Uncle does—*and the way you do*, isn't that right?"

"No, Mek, no."

The letter slipped from Mektu's fingers. "Spalak, who wanted to save you by pinning everything on me. That monster. He's your dad."

"Just in the one way," said Kandri.

"Spalak," said Mektu, "who put a spear through his brother's heart."

ଓ

Mektu turned and vanished into the crowd.

Kandri was relieved, at first, to see him go. Only time and distance ever resolved his fights with Mektu. This was a bad one, perhaps the worst since Ariqina's disappearance. But the pattern would hold.

He waited, watching the guards (yes, they were nervous: like the Chancellor, their eyes drifted north), the children, the merchants who came and went upon the bridge—and through the telescope, the pass from Perec Station. No ghouls, no White Child. He would have liked to watch for the approach of the caravan, but from their enclosure he could see nothing of the West Road. Mektu was right: if any of them had gone ahead of the camel train they might already be here, locked in an adjacent pen.

Hours passed. He fed the camels, stroked the owl when it alighted, mere seconds only, on his arm. He shouted his brother's name into the multitude but received no answer. The morning clouds burned away and the day grew hot.

The bastard. The absolute prick.

Kandri knelt Alahari and climbed into the saddle. He coaxed her back to standing, and gasped.

The crowd was so large now that even the vast stockade could not contain it. The guards were no longer admitting refugees into the three holding pens, but those outside could have easily filled a fourth. Kandri had seen larger crowds greet the Prophet, at her great war-musters and sermons. But those people had come seeking wonder and revelation. These were only hoping to survive.

He stood in the saddle, feeling a fool as always. Slim chance of spotting his brother in that crushed-together mob, but he would try. He would give Mektu a chance to look up and see him trying.

He stared; the mob stared back. It was dizzy work, locking his eyes on face after face. Bemused, bored, irritated. Sympathetic, spiteful. A wrinkled old man like a human candle stub. A fat baby boy with an amputated hand. Two girls so still and hollow-eyed that he shuddered to imagine what they had passed through.

And as always, the mind-game. The impossible familiar faces. There was his baby brother, Perch. There was his old schoolmaster, arrested for heresy when Kandri was sixteen. The priest from Bittermoon who stared at boys. The willowy prostitute who worked the gates of Eternity Camp. One of the amber-yellow Xavasindrans from—

His eyes snapped back. A *Xavasindran*, of all absurdities? An Outworlder, one of the missionary doctors from across the forbidden oceans, hiding out in this ragged mob?

Utter nonsense. Trick of the light. He could not even find the face he thought he'd spotted. More to the point, there could be no Xavasindrans outside the clinics, or under heavy military escort, like the few who had visited Eternity Camp. Kandri had never expected to glimpse another Xavasindran after those few eerie hours in the clinic at Mab Makkutin. The day the Outworlder doctor had cured his brother's festering wound.

But what Kandri had just seen—or imagined—was stranger still. Not just a Xavasindran face, but a face he knew.

Which was even more ridiculous. How many Xavasindrans had he glimpsed in his entire life? One surgeon: the severe, tall Dr. Skarrys. One nurse at his side, one woman guarding the clinic door. And of course, the silent ones: those eight observers, staring ghoulish through a wall of heavy glass as Mektu, around a corner from Kandri, went under the knife. Were they apprentice doctors, students? And what had they seen done to his brother?

Kandri slid to the ground, angry with himself now as much as Mektu. *Whatever they saw,* you *saw nothing, fool. No Xavasindran, familiar or otherwise. Keep this up and it won't matter if they open the gates. Step through, and they'll lock you up again. In a madhouse.*

ᙣ

The sun was setting. Mektu had not returned. Troops bearing the evening meal (pea porridge, hard rolls) shouldered their way into the designated corners of the holding pens. The mob contorted itself into a snaking queue, but Kandri could not join it without abandoning the camels.

Mektu's in that queue right now, he told himself. *Getting food for us both.*

But Mektu did not appear. At last, in desperation, Kandri begged an older Naduman to watch the camels for a quarter hour. The man was just finishing his meal.

"They'll be no trouble, I promise," Kandri said. "I doubt they'll even stand up."

"Glad to help, *boyan*," said the man. "Take all the time you need."

"You don't mind, Uncle?"

The man gave him a bleak smile. "No plans this evening. You're in luck."

But no more good luck came Kandri's way. His brother was not in the food line, nor at the latrines, nor along the fence where the guards passed on their rounds. Darkness fell swiftly. Kandri swore, quietly, ceaselessly, the oaths passing from his lips like smoke. He must have looked crazy, but what did he care? Everyone looked crazy, their faces melting into shadows. No lamps or even candles permitted. No idea how this would end.

It took him an hour of groping and stumbling to find his way back. The old Naduman was seated with his back to Alahari, true to his word. But when Kandri returned he stood up with a guilty air.

"I'm sorry," he said. "I tried to talk to him. I told him to wait."

"Here? My brother came back *here*?"

"Barely a minute after you left," said the Naduman. "Must have been watching you, waiting for his chance."

Mektu had not responded to any of his entreaties, added the Naduman. He had simply gone to the saddlebags and taken what he wanted. A shoulder pack. A machete. Clothing and food and faskas. Then he had tossed the man a coin and told him not to tell Kandri about his visit.

"You take it," said the old man, holding up the coin. "I didn't agree to hold my tongue."

It was Kasraji true gold, one of the sovereigns from Lord Garatajik. "Your brother went that way, for what it's worth," he added, gesturing east.

He lay down to sleep among his meager belongings, pocketing the coin Kandri insisted that he keep. Kandri stood beside the camels, peering into the night. He was hungry, and finally afraid.

East: toward the gate that faced the Flying Bridge, the gate that never opened. What for? Did Mektu imagine he could talk the guards into welcoming the refugees? Or that he could burrow under the fence like a human mole?

Fuck him. Let him try. Kandri spread a blanket and lay down. The red eye of the Pilgrim rose above the wall of Kasralys, so bright now it outshone the yellow crescent of the familiar moon. He told himself that his brother was somewhere close at hand. Exceptionally close, closer than their house had stood to the little dry-goods shop, where Lantor Hinjuman would send them for nails or cleats or creosote. If they ran they could make it back before the Old Man forgot what he had sent them for, or grew impatient. *That's your only problem, Kandri: patience.* Mektu was trapped here, like everyone. Sooner or later rationality would slink back into his mind, like a repentant drunk sidling into a temple for morning prayers.

Not a thing to be done until that happened. Except to rehearse, lying here on your back under that demonic star, what you will say when it's time to take your uncle's advice. To live apart from Mektu. To start over with Ariqina, somewhere in that city that loomed in the dark. And soon, he resolved. Yes, as soon as it could possibly be arranged.

CR

He was still awake when the screams began.

He leaped up. Thousands around him were doing the same. He found his knife and his machete and turned in a circle. A faint glow near the horizon: dawn was near.

"Mektu?"

His brother was nowhere to be seen. The camels had risen, and they were terrified, nickering deep in their throats. The screams were coming from the north pen. Hundreds of voices: high shrieks of children, men's bellows and roars, women's cries full of deadly rage. Kandri could not see much: it was still too dark, and he was too far from the north pen. But he could tell that the throng it enclosed was churning with panic.

"A raid!" shouted a man in the darkness. "It's the Shôl come from Naduma to finish us off!"

"Impossible!" cried another. "That little force, marching over the Sacred Plain? Straight through the army of the Kasraj?"

"Well *someone's* bloody out there!"

That much was certain. The guards were howling orders, blowing whistles, lighting lamps. Their voices all but lost in the uproar. And it was not just the refugees who were drowning them out. Other voices were shouting beyond the stockades, and they were not pleading for mercy. They were furious. They were the voices of men on the attack.

The camels hauled at their stakes. Kandri fought to control them, still trying to look north. The new mob was enormous and undisciplined. It had torn through a section of fence and was gushing into the north pen, flailing at the refugees with clubs, axes, pitchforks, scythes.

Ang's mercy. They've come here to kill.

Bodies were already falling. The attackers drove deep into the pen. The refugees who were able to climb were hurling themselves over the fences, screaming for aid. And now there were fires—sudden hungry fires in a dozen places. The refugees' shelters and belongings were being doused with some sort of oil, and torched. Then Kandri heard the attackers' cry.

Beggars out! Kasralys for Kasrajis!

It was a raid, but not by the Shôl or any other invader. They were being slaughtered by Kasrajis. The very people into whose arms they had fled.

Some of the refugees fought like tigers: they had far more to lose than the attackers had to win. But many were driven from the pen and out onto the chilly plain.

To the river! the attackers were shouting. *Don't let 'em steal so much as an apple, boys! Don't let 'em stop!*

Then Kandri understood: the attackers had not come from the city. They were villagers from the Kasraji heartland, those pleasant farms and dales through which they passed on the way to the gates.

Again he shouted for Mektu; again no answer came. All around him people were pulling their children close, stuffing their possessions into sacks and slings.

The voices around him suddenly spiked in pitch. Not just fear: those were cries of pain.

He whirled and saw that the attackers had reached the fence between the north pen and Kandri's own. They were flinging stones into the latter, hooting and jeering. Makeshift spears and sharp stakes jabbed through the iron links. Masses of refugees ran in terror from the fence line, shoving, squeezing, impossibly crowded.

Where are those Gods-forsaken troops?

The old Naduman appeared out of nowhere. "Ang save us, they're cutting the fence!"

He pointed. Two thick-chested men in the hostile mob were attacking the fence with metal shears. Already a small rent had been opened.

"Those beasts," said the Naduman. "If they get inside, you know we'll all be—*ah!*"

He staggered: a stone had struck him in the ribs. At the same Kandri's mind was filled with white fire. He knew what it meant even before he registered the pain: another stone had struck his head.

Momentary blankness, followed by a snap of clarity in which he knew he had made some irrevocable decision. He was sprinting toward the fence. Abandoning the camels, leaping the fallen, screaming defiance of the attacking mob. As he closed he brought his machete down with both hands and shattered two wooden spears. A third, iron-tipped, narrowly grazed his side but that was perfect, he dropped the machete, caught the spear and *wrenched* and it was his.

They would not be getting it back.

Jab, pull, jab, pull. Short strokes are what you wanted, numbskulls. Leather punch. Needle and thread. Blood on the shaft, blood spraying him through the fence. The metal shears clattering to the ground. Fucking peasants. Same story everywhere. No good at killing.

Jab, pull, twist, jab.

Gods, but he hated what he was good at.

Refugees lay against the fence, bleeding, weeping. The attackers screamed for Kandri's blood. Then one of them gave a warning cry—"They're here! They've come!"—and suddenly Kandri had no one to fight. The attackers were fleeing, many of them hurling away their arms. One glance to the north told Kandri why: Kasraji soldiers, their discipline restored, were flooding the pen in numbers that could not be resisted.

But for many of the refugees it was too late. Their dark forms lay twisted and moaning beside the fence. How many would die before aid reached them, a few inches from safety, a few inches from Kandri's feet?

"You."

A man's voice, faint with pain and exhaustion.

"It *is* you. Twenty-seven!"

Kandri could make no sense of the remark. But that accent: where had he heard it before? Kandri squinted. The figure was leaning against the fence, one hand clutching like a vine to the iron links.

"Wait for the soldiers," said Kandri. "I can't help you from here."

"You are twenty-seven!"

"Younger, actually." Kandri turned away.

"Not age, not that!" wheezed the man. "You were brother escort to *patient* twenty-seven! Come, be honest. I know it is you."

Patient twenty-seven! Suddenly it all came back. The accent, the oddly formal speech: he had heard them both before—in the Xavasindran clinic. And the Outworlders, for reasons of their own, had never used the brothers' names. They referred to Mektu as a number, Kandri as "brother escort." It was strange and disconcerting, but so was everything in the clinic, and the Outworlders themselves most of all. Like actors playing the part of doctors and nurses, or children forbidden to laugh.

And Mektu's number had indeed been twenty-seven. Kandri turned to face the man, struggling with a shapeless dread.

He was short and plump and mobbed by flies. Kandri crouched down, and the man raised a shaking hand and pushed back his hood. A bloodied amber-yellow face looked at Kandri through the fence.

"You *were* there, in the crowd this afternoon," said Kandri. "I saw you. I thought I'd lost my mind."

"They beat me," wheezed the Xavasindran. "For nothing. For spite."

"Who the hell *are* you?"

"No one, anymore. But I was almost a doctor. My studies were behind me. I had the highest, the highest marks—"

He coughed. More gurgling. When at last he recovered, he said, "I just needed this mission. Three years, then home with every honor, and a good post awaiting me. Money enough to feed my children, to keep the creditors from seizing our home."

The man's hair was tied in a single thick braid. And at the sight of that braid, Kandri suddenly knew him. This was one of the observers in the Xavasindran clinic, the silent ones who had watched Mektu's surgery with such unsettling coldness.

All but this man. He had squirmed, clearly appalled by what he saw. And before the procedure ended, he had slipped away.

Now he lifted his head (sharp winces of agony) and met Kandri's gaze. "Twenty-seven. I have prayed for you, soldier."

"Well . . . thank you." Kandri wondered if the man was dying.

"We're the same, you and I," said the Xavasindran.

"Because we're runaways?"

"Because we're ex-believers. Running from our faiths. Your Prophet's war, my mission in this land. Do you think history will condemn us? How were we to know we'd swallowed lies?"

"I haven't had time to worry about that. My Prophet's trying to kill me."

"As I said, we're the same." The man looked vaguely over his shoulder. "They're encamped there, across the Súl. My comrades. The Realm allows them as far as the river bank, but no closer."

Kandri nodded. "I'd heard the Xavasindrans were barred from Kasralys. Why do you think that is?"

"Because they suspect our motives, and know that bribes always come at a cost. No other power in Urrath held out for long, when they saw what we could offer."

A vision danced before Kandri's eyes—the wonders he had seen in the clinic, beyond anything his father Lantor had ever invented. Glass that could not be broken, light that could not be traced to any flame. And the deadly spore arrows: those too had been Xavasindran gifts.

"I know the kind of bribes you could offer," he said, "but what's the cost? What would Kasralys have to give up?"

The Xavasindran waved with his fingers. "At first? Not so much. Only the pride of her best thinkers. Her own science, her own medicine. Her freedom to seek the truth." He brought his face close to Kandri's, forehead pressed to the fence. "That is what frightens, what terrifies my comrades," he hissed. "The truth. That is why they will do *anything* to conceal."

He began to cough again. "You sound awful," said Kandri. "What's the matter with your lungs?"

"Consumption," said the Xavasindran. "I hid in the marshes when I fled the mission camp. Nine days, soaked and shivering. At last I could stand it no longer, and crept across the plain by night. I hoped these crowds would keep me safe. But how can they, when they are not safe themselves?"

He touched a spot on his temple, winced again. "I am sorry, man of Urrath. No one told us, you see. Not on the ship, not on arrival. They keep us ignorant through the whole of our training."

"You've lost me, friend," said Kandri. "Ignorant of what?"

"This sinful project. This game that cost your brother's life."

"See, that's where you're wrong," said Kandri. "My brother was dying of an infected arrow wound. The doctor in your clinic *saved* his life."

The man sighed. "But for how long? A week, a month?"

"Don't you start too," said Kandri. "Every damn place we go, someone tells us we're finished."

"*Tells?*" The man bolted upright, his pain seemingly forgotten. "You cannot be saying that he is alive?"

"I believe I can. Unless someone's brained the fool in the night."

"Alive!" cried the Xavasindran, shaking the fence with both hands. "It worked! Usthe my Protector, the operation finally *worked!*"

"You don't sound too happy about it," said Kandri. "Did you want my brother to die?"

The man hauled himself to standing. His breath was ragged and his face drenched in sweat. Looking at Kandri but not appearing to see him, he shrieked with astonishing force.

"The vermin! The vermin!"

His cry had two effects. It caught the attention of the advancing soldiers, a large number of whom turned and charged in the Xavasindran's direction. And it plunged the man himself into his worst coughing fit yet.

"What vermin?" said Kandri, gripping the fence in turn now. "What the hell are you saying?"

The other wounded, in a rising chorus, began to scream for aid. But the Xavasindran collapsed. His coughing fit went on and on, and Kandri saw the gleam of blood upon the hands he pressed to his face.

"Tell me!" Kandri begged as the soldiers drew near.

"The others—died." The man squeezed out the words. *"All* the others. Keep him—"

The soldiers pounced. "Survivors to the aid station!" shouted the officer in the vanguard, waving his troops at clusters of the fallen. "Not a soul still breathing is to be left behind, do you hear? Look sharp: *this* one's barely able to breathe at all. Get him to safety!"

A stretcher appeared as if by magic, and in seconds the Xavasindran was upon it and being carried away. Kandri bellowed after him: "Tell me! Keep him *what?*"

"Quiet, there!" barked the officer. "Can't you see he's coughing up his lungs?"

"But that man, he's—"

Kandri stopped himself. What did he intend to say? That the man was an Outworlder? They would learn that soon enough, when they beheld his skin by lamp or torchlight. And the man obviously *did* need aid. Shouting out his secret now might delay it long enough to kill him.

"He's what?" demanded the officer. "Your friend, your brother?"

"Insane?" said Kandri, defeated. It seemed a plausible answer. *The vermin, the vermin.*

"Ah, you're a great help," snapped the officer. "Get to the Bridge, if you don't want to lose your chance."

His gestured, and Kandri turned. His own vast pen was emptying of people. Someone had opened the east gate, and the refugees were stampeding through it—straight onto the ramp that climbed to the Flying Bridge.

One person, however, was hobbling toward Kandri with a heavy burden. It was the kind old Naduman, the man who had watched his camels.

"*Boyan*," he said, "I thought they'd killed you."

"What's happening, uncle? Are they letting us into the city?"

"Don't know. Don't care. The bridge is a damn good start. Here, these are yours."

The old man thrust something against Kandri's chest. Alahari's saddle-bags. With his telescope, his money, everything that remained to him in this world.

"Your camels are running loose," said the Naduman. "I grabbed those before they tore free. It was all I could salvage."

"You're a hero," said Kandri, squeezing his arm.

The old man laughed. "Come on then. Before the Kasrajis change their fickle minds."

He followed the Naduman toward the Bridge. The light was growing. Jackdaws flitted above them, crying *How, how, how?* Already more than half the pen was empty. *Mektu! Damn your hurt feelings. We're out of time.*

He shouted his brother's name again and again. What had the Outworlder tried to say? Keep Mektu warm? Keep him tranquil? Keep him from licking his wound like a dog?

From the third pen, still tightly sealed, countless refugees were shouting, pleading for access to the Bridge themselves. But in the northern pen the battle was over. The attackers, glad to beat and stab at road-weary families, had no appetite for battle with the forces of the realm. Some knelt in surrender. Most turned tail and ran.

"Kasrajis, clan of kings," said the Naduman bitterly.

The sun broke above the horizon in a sliver of fire—and there by the south fence, as though stepping from a dream, walked Alahari, dragging a tether and a stake.

"Oh Gods." Kandri squeezed the Naduman's shoulder, a last gesture of thanks. Then he ran for his camel, calling her name.

Alahari turned and saw him, and her ecstatic bray turned heads across the plain. She bolted for Kandri, eager as a puppy. When they came together, she rubbed her head against his chest with such force that he fell, laughing, to the ground.

"Where's Fish, girl?" he cried, bounding up again. "What's happened to his fool of a keeper?"

There was no sign of Mektu or Fish, but scores of animals had been swept toward the ramp along with the crowd. Kandri and Alahari stood alone in the vast, empty space. There were not even bodies: the violence had never reached the middle pen.

Which meant that Mektu was in the crowd ahead, squeezing onto the ramp. Nothing else was possible. The ground had not swallowed him up.

Kandri grabbed the broken end of Alahari's tether and ran with her toward the gate.

A lone figure in uniform stood there, beckoning impatiently. "Come on, lad, hurry!" the figure shouted. "Why were you dawdling back there?"

It was the Chancellor's deputy, the tall man with the gray moustache. The man was powerfully built and stern of bearing, his voice military-loud but in no way cruel. One large hand beckoned Kandri; the other gripped an enormous ring of keys.

Scores of guards were milling about the foot of the ramp, including some in the gray-and-gold uniform that appeared to mark the company of the Chancellor. "We have you to thank, don't we?" Kandri said as he arrived. "For opening that gate. For letting us in."

One expression chased another across the man's rugged face: surprise that this indigent was addressing him so boldly, exhaustion, suspicion—and strangest of all, amusement.

"Say it a little louder," he murmured. "There's still a chance I won't be sacked."

"*Harach*, sir, forgive me."

"Too soon to celebrate, anyway," said the tall man. "Yes, I opened this first gate: Lady Kosuda gave me that much discretion. But the Sky Gate, the main portal into the city at the end of the Bridge, remains closed to you, and I have no authority there. Now move along."

Kandri led Alahari forward. But as they passed out of the pen, the man stopped him with a hand on his arm. The move was calm but uncontestable.

Kandri did not breathe. The Chancellor's aide had locked eyes with him. *Don't look guilty, don't look away, this man knows nothing about you.* But did he know about the Prophet's eyestain? Did he know how to spot a soldier of the Army of Revelation?

"You alone, boy?" asked the tall man.

Kandri started. The tall man narrowed his eyes.

"The enclosure's empty, First Marshal Lisrand," said one of his underlings. "This one was the last."

"I said," repeated the tall man, "are you alone?"

What answer would save him? Or see him jailed, or worse? What answer was even true?

"Not while I have my princess," he said, patting Alahari's neck.

The man was a very long time in smiling. But at last he did, a twitch at one corner of his mouth, barely visible beneath the moustache. "Get on, then, you and your Sparavith. Lovely animal, by the way."

Kandri floated through the gate. He was at the very back of the multitude, which was all but running up the iron ramp, as though they still could not quite believe their good fortune. Behind Kandri and Alahari came a detachment of twenty guards, their shoulders heaped with great lengths of chain.

The ramp was slick with mud and morning dew, but it was not steep: carts and carriages had to manage it, after all. He saw now that it was constructed of three iron spans, each well over a hundred feet long and supported at the junctures by piers as solid as those of the bridge itself. The crowd's progress slowed as the ramp narrowed, but it never stopped. And as Kandri rose, the aftermath of the battle came into view. The soldiers—cheered on by the watching refugees—had corralled the villagers who surrendered into a corner of the north pen. Others were treating the wounded on both sides. The dead still lay where they had fallen, wounds steaming in the chilly morning air.

Kandri looked beyond the stockade, and horror flooded his mind.

A truly enormous crowd had appeared there—swarmed there, it appeared, from all over the Sacred Plain. They were still coming, by the thousands, running along the roads, thrashing through the new-planted fields. Like the first Kasrajis, they had come with arms.

Devil's prick, they'll sweep the guards away.

But the refugees went on cheering. Then Kandri noticed the cluster of attackers who had escaped the guards. They had been met by the vast crowd of newcomers and surrounded, stopped in their tracks. The newcomers were roaring, pointing at the ground.

And over Kandri swept a feeling he had no name for, darker and deeper than joy. The newcomers, like those who had come to kill in the night, were common folk. Villagers, farmers, workers of the land. They had come too late to prevent the attack. But there were more of them, so many more. And by their cries and gestures Kandri knew that they were appalled by what their fellow Kasrajis had done.

The fight went out of the attackers; in one swift act, they threw down their arms. Kandri saw other villagers approaching the bridge, escorting the refugees who had been stampeded toward the river. Even the guards behind Kandri cheered. "*That's* my country," one of them said, wiping his eye. "That's Kasralys, not shameful deeds in the night."

"Both are Kasralys," said a voice Kandri knew. It was the tall officer, whose troops had called him Lisrand. "That is what my lady would tell you, were she here. One's the country we long to inhabit, and some days get lucky enough to see. The other's the country that will rise like bile if we ignore it, leave it to fester, pretend it does not exist."

&

The man's words drove Kandri to a choice. Minutes later, when the whole crowd stood stretched along the Flying Bridge, nearly two hundred feet above the plain, he turned Alahari about and nudged his way closer to Lisrand. The crowd slowed him, even here at the back. The other soldiers had plenty of time to step between him and the mustachioed First Marshal.

"Hold him there!" snapped Lisrand over his shoulder. He and several others were securing the chains they had borne to iron posts on either side of the bridge, just beyond the last section of ramp. When the chain was made fast he brushed off his hands and lumbered toward Kandri. He was not really looking at him, though: his gaze flickered across his troops, the crowd, the scene below.

"What's the matter, lad? Change your mind?"

"My brother has disappeared," said Kandri.

The flickering ceased. The man worked his jaw, eyes locked on Kandri. "You lied," he said, "right to my face."

"I'm sorry. Yes, I lied. I was afraid you'd stop me. That I'd never see him—"

The man lunged. Before Kandri knew what was happening Lisrand's rough hand seized him by the jaw. He did not resist. The surrounding troops had drawn their swords.

Lisrand turned Kandri's face to the morning sun. "Don't squint," he said. "Open your eyes."

Kandri knew he was seeing the Prophet's mark. "I was a soldier in the Army of Revelation," he whispered. "I deserted months ago, with my brother."

The man was enraged—at Kandri, and perhaps at himself. He leaned so close that his moustache grazed Kandri's ear. "You," he hissed, "are the brother assassins. The ones she's sworn to kill. The ones who have turned the West into a flaming hornet-hive."

Frustration, fury. Even here the story had raced ahead of them. Even here they could not start anew. "Close enough," Kandri said through gritted teeth.

"You're coming to the Chancellery," said Lisrand. "You and your brother alike. Where is he, damn you?"

"Weren't you listening? He stormed off yesterday at sunrise. We . . . don't always get along."

The First Marshal's eyes widened. He let go of Kandri's chin and took a fistful of his shirt. "Are you telling me that your brother—the *other* most wanted man in Urrath—could be anywhere in this blasted crowd?"

"Where else could he be?"

The man turned Kandri roughly about, sweeping an arm over the Sacred Plain. "Where could he *not* be, my blood-soaked friend? You know we allow people to leave, to give up on entering the city. Hundreds do so every day, and who can blame them? Those pens are atrocious sties."

"Mektu wouldn't have given up. Not after all we've been through, all we've survived."

"What have you survived?"

Kandri looked up at the man. His mouth opened, and a dispassionate part of him waited curiously to learn what would tumble out. A torrent of stories, a broken laugh.

Or as luck would have it, nothing at all. Yet somehow the man saw it, saw him, and Kandri's unspoken answer brushed the worst of his suspicions aside.

"Right," he said. "No more questions until the Chancellor's present. But I suggest you keep an open mind, lad. Your brother might have made an impulsive decision, especially if you'd been fighting."

His gaze snapped up. A deep, strange sound, like thunder inside a mountain, rolled over them. The iron bridge trembled. The crowd closest to the city let out a cheer:

"The Sky Gate! The Sky Gate is opening!"

"Lady Kosuda's right on time," said Lisrand with a smile. "Company Twelve, you know the procedure. And you, Chiloto—" He shot Kandri a warning look. "I'm not going to bind your hands—you'll need them to lead your camel-princess. But once we pass into the city, you stop in your tracks and wait for me. Try to slip off alone, and I'll make you wish you *had* fallen into the Prophet's hands. That clear?"

What was clear to Kandri was how little this man knew of the Prophet. All the same he nodded.

"Then run," said Lisrand, "before they slam that gate in our faces."

Kandri saw now that there were soldiers stationed all along the bridge. All began to shout the same warning: *Run! Hurry!* And like a river when the dam has burst, the thousand refugees bolted for the city. They were desperate but not thoughtless. The strong were aiding the weak. The strongest of all carried children or elders or the wounded on their backs.

Kandri soon found himself part of that number, scooping up a young boy whose mother, alone, was struggling with a smaller child. He held tight to Alahari's reins, wishing he could toss the boy up into the saddle. The mother gasped out effusive thanks as she ran. The little boy on his back planted sticky kisses on his headscarf.

The bridge soared over the city's outer defenses (low wall, dark moat, higher wall) and soldiers stationed there gawked up at them, pointing. Kandri touched the calfskin pouch and felt a catch in his throat. To hell with the Prophet. When he handed over the Cure, he would have achieved something that no one—not even the Enlightened One and her torturers—could ever strike from his soul.

And here at last was the plateau on which the city was built, and the monstrous, final wall that hugged its edge. The Ancestor Wall, sheer and dizzying, its turrets like castles in their own right. No cracks, no seams. The only opening was directly before them: an arch of glittering blue-black stone, so wide it could have spanned the whole of Blind Stream Village with room to spare.

The Sky Gate itself was of this same curious stone reinforced with bands of steel. It was really three gates, half-recessed into slots in the arch. They were not on hinges; no, they rode on rails. Built not to rise or fall but to slide. Kandri thought of the White Child and nearly laughed aloud: nothing in Urrath could assail those doors, or the wall they were part of. What did Kasralys have to fear?

Under the blue arch gushed the thousand refugees. Some flung their arms high in praise or ecstasy. When his turn came Kandri did laugh, with a joy he had not felt in ages—

We did it, brother, we escaped her. We did what no one's ever done before.

—and then the Forward Keep of Kasralys swallowed them like a mountain, blotting out their voices, and oh the scale, the wonder, a flock of black-birds wheeling above them as if through empty sky. Cast iron, chiseled stone, mosaics sprawling over floor, walls, pillars, distant ceiling. Figures in marble and turquoise and porphyry and jade. Heroes and monsters, horses, serpents, Gods. He'd heard stories, but nothing could have prepared his peasant mind. This opulence, this brilliance of built things. His father Lantor would have wept. *Did you pass this way, Old Man? Is this where your learning started? Did you look up at that ceiling and want more, and more, and more?*

He was through the Keep. Dazzling sunlight. A vast round plaza and wide boulevards like spokes of a wheel and high elegant halls with bridges between them and glass stained green and scarlet and sapphire and high balconies and groves of gnarled, weeping trees. Throngs of Kasrajis—well-healed, hard-bitten, curious, bemused. And at the heart of the plaza, perfectly centered, a bronze wolf large as an elephant, reclined on a black rock and crowned with leaves of gold.

Under the wolf, a thousand souls huddled together as if for warmth, although in fact the cold had not come with them through the Gate. Bright eyes, cautious smiles. A goat bleating. A child's shout of joy.

31. CATHQIMAR HOUSE

Something—a phantom net, a smothering, invisible shroud—had been torn away at last.

Kandri had entered the city, and could breathe freely for the first time since the killing of Ojulan. He crouched down; the boy slid from his back and ran to his mother, and her eyes swam with emotion as she mouthed a silent *Thank you.* Kandri smiled at her and rose.

A thousand refugees surrounding a wolf, singing a song of deliverance. Many were embracing. An old couple dropped to their knees and kissed the paving stones.

My brother is hiding in that crowd, Kandri thought. *He is watching me, and will put his pain aside and step forward. Because he feels this too. Don't you, Mek? We've done it. We've beaten them all.*

"No Chancellor." Lisrand's sigh lifted the edges of his moustache. "My lady planned to be here, with the reception corps. God of my naming, the *chaos* of this day. Company Twelve!"

The soldiers snapped into a line. "Sort out the wounded," said Lisrand. "There's a ward set aside at Bathuldashik, and extra doctors on call: my lady's seen to all that."

Doctors, thought Kandri, and his last whiff of patience evaporated. "First Marshal, there's a famous doctor, Fessjamu—"

"*The* famous doctor," he said, eyes busy elsewhere. "What do you want with Tsireem Fessjamu?"

How to begin? With his heart, or the world? This time Kandri's heart prevailed.

"Does she have assistants? Other doctors who work for her?"

"Dozens, I should think. She's the dean of Kasraji medicine—and just about the most beloved person in this city. She aspires to cure the World Plague, no less."

"I might know one of her assistants."

"Yes, and I might—*Corporal!* Tell the gawkers on that balcony to show a bit of respect: these are families, not zoo animals." He stepped away from Kandri, snapping out orders. "Ask our citizens to move along. Then start a list: missing children, missing parents. And where's the drinking water Lady Kosuda ordered? Six barrels. Find out where they went. And by all that's holy—" He whirled and pointed. "—find this man's brother."

For a moment all eyes were on Kandri. "He's about your age, I gather?" asked Lisrand.

Kandri nodded. "He's *exactly* my age, but—"

"Take that camel." Lisrand gestured at Alahari. "Feed and water the beast. Don't worry, boy; she'll be in good hands. But you and I must find the Chancellor. Private, fetch us a horse."

He gestured across the plaza at a long, cream-yellow building. At its center was a plain rectangular opening in the shape of a door. A small sign dangled beside it.

"Bring the horse round to Cathqimar House, saddled and ready. Quick as you can, private."

A soldier saluted and dashed away. The First Marshal led Kandri around the refugees, making for the cream-colored building. "I saw you," said Lisrand, "helping that mother with her pair of brats. That was a kindness."

"She looked—it was just—listen, sir, about those doctors—"

"Who helped *you*, by the way? Across the desert I mean."

Kandri wanted scream at him: *Not now!* But he had this man's goodwill, and that was precious; what would happen if it were withdrawn? "So many helped us," he said. "So many died. We joined a caravan in the distant west, near the Arig Hills. But we . . . had to leave them. For all I know they could be in the city by now."

"You have a lot of missing persons in your life," said Lisrand. "Never fear: there are only so many places equipped to receive a camel train. Less than fifty, anyway."

"*Fifty?*"

"Kasralys is a big place, boy."

Kandri took a deep breath. "Your Dr. Fessjamu," he began again. "Does she have someone named—"

"Sergeant Burlizar! Are you daydreaming or just thick? Tell that brute there we'll clap him in jail, refugee or not, if he throws that bottle. Who in Ang's tight britches gave them wine? Keep order, there, sergeant, that's your job. Now boy, what is it?"

"Dr. Fessjamu—"

"Yes, yes, what *about* her? Be quick; seems I'm indispensable today."

"Ariqina Nawhal!" he blurted. "Does she work for Fessjamu?"

"For her, with her, how should I know? Same hospital anyway. Ah, but of course, she's a Chiloto too, and there's a handful more in town if you're lonely, that expensive butcher, that slob of a—boy! Boy! What's the matter with you?"

03

He had never in his life broken down in tears before a stranger. Before anyone, save Fiasul and his stepmother. Now the tears claimed him entirely, no more visions, no wishful thinking, love was a flood in which you drowned but did not perish, he tried to explain but mouth and mind were swamped with it, and anyway after a moment Lisrand grasped it all without Kandri speaking a word, Great Gods boy he said, you're just one mad thing after another.

Last Interlude

Well, my host: you have done it. Or rather, *we* have done it, for as a yatra I am not given to affectations of humility. All of us, human and otherwise. We are on the cusp of changing the world.

Of course, the world is not waiting for us. When you stood atop the Pillar of the Night Queen you could not see it yet, despite the enchantment she lent your eyes. But you saw it from that higher vantage—that dark, star-lidded pasture from which even beings like myself are excluded. You saw it from the Mountain of the Gods. The world convulsed. The Prophet rampant, and the Pilgrim Moon waxing bright. The Time of Madness, dawning. I fear it is very close to the dawn.

Still, rejoice while you can. Life is the aria sung by the universe in defiance of solitude, and you have won a round for life. Provided you don't lose that blessed Cure between this plaza and the School of Medicine, that is, and that Fessjamu's genius lets her decipher it.

Then find your Ariqina, if yours she remains. Find her quickly. Never again leave her side. I confess I hope she does not break your heart. I am a poor judge, perhaps, but I think it is a good heart, pumping sanity drop by humble drop into a world deprived.

As for me, I am packing my bags. I have scarred you already, and will not compound my sins. Deliver the letter. Then I depart. I must choose some outbound traveler, some healthy nomad, packed and ready for the road. There are too many of my kind here, in drowsy oblivious hosts. Too many bound to aid in my capture, and my punishment. Bound by our immutable law.

Peace and long life, Kandri Hinjuman. I shall never interfere with you again.

But I find myself hoping—for what reason I cannot imagine—that you stay well clear of Cathqimar House.

He stood up, wiped his eyes with his sleeve. Well well, Lisrand was saying. Kosuda is going to be astonished in more ways than one.

"How do you mean?" asked Kandri.

"We won't discuss that now," said Lisrand firmly. He gestured with his chin at the doorway ahead. "Go on ahead of me. Just give me your word."

"Given," said Kandri. "I won't move from the spot until I see you. But there's one last thing." *One last, world-changing thing.* He tapped the Letter of Cure beneath his shirt. "You're not going to believe me—"

"Then save it for the Chancellor, Hinjuman. We can disbelieve you together."

"But Marshal—"

"No, I say! You need a fresh shirt and a bucket-bath. Tell the tavern staff you're Emberi's friend. They'll sort you out."

"Emberi?"

"That's me, Emberi Lisrand. The ninth of that name; we're sentimental. Go, boy! Cathqimar's glorious." He narrowed his eyes. "You like coffee?"

"Do I like—sweet love of Ang my Redeemer—"

"Ha!" laughed the Marshal. "An assassin with taste. They say no one whose visit to the city begins at Cathqimar House ever wants to leave. Fine smokes, too. Won't be long."

He started away, eyes turned to the refugees. But after two steps he stopped and faced Kandri once more.

"Why did you do it?" he asked. "We've been wondering for months, my lady and I. Why kill your Prophet's firstborn?"

"Ojulan was her thirdborn, in fact."

"I stand corrected. Why?"

"Because he was raping a little girl."

Lisrand grew still. Doubt and confusion shone in his eyes. "You weren't chosen, you weren't groomed for that suicide task? You weren't part of a team, some secret resistance?"

"We weren't anything at all. He was hurting her; she was bleeding. What would you have done?"

"The very same, I hope." His face looked so deeply troubled that Kandri wished he'd not asked his question. Then, with effort, Lisrand smiled and clapped him warmly on the arm.

"Someone must say it, or our good name will be tarnished. Welcome to—"

ↄ𝕘

The last word had no chance. For once again—the sound had grown all too familiar—the refugees howled in fear.

A company of riders was thundering toward the plaza from a side avenue. There were hundreds, all in silver mail, wielding pole axes and spears. The refugees, convulsed with horror, bolted for other ways out of the plaza—any other way, save the Gate itself. Bags, packs, carts hauled for days or weeks lay abandoned about the feet of the black wolf. Lisrand's twenty soldiers looked on helplessly, ignored by riders and refugees alike.

The First Marshal shouted a florid oath. He began to sprint toward the oncoming riders, checked himself, and whirled to face Kandri again.

"Keep well out of this! Wait here as you promised."

"What's happening?" Kandri asked.

"Someone has betrayed my lady," said the First Marshal, and with that he was gone.

Kandri set off at a run for the doorway. But what was this? A figure, a child, darting back into the passage, no sooner glimpsed than gone. Caught in the act of gaping at the foreigner, or more likely at the horses. Kandri reached the doorway. The neat little sign bore words in crimson:

Cathqimar House
Pipes Meats
Spirits

The passage itself was dark and surprisingly long, but far ahead it opened on a sunny courtyard with a suggestion of greenery. The child had vanished. Kandri took a few steps into the passage and turned to face the plaza again.

The riders had divided into several parties. Some were pursuing the refugees, weapons aloft, jeering and threatening. Others had formed a galloping circle around those who remained by the wolf statue, walling them in. Kandri felt sick; he was reminded of the Slaughterhouse Clowns.

Lisrand was blowing a whistle, waving vehemently for the riders to desist. They did not desist, but stormed past the doorway, making Kandri glad of the shadows he stood within. When they were gone he looked out and saw a thickset officer with medals on his chest bellowing at Lisrand from atop his charger, sword in hand. Other riders were shouting beneath the windows of the turrets to either side of the Sky Gate. Still others were trampling the goods the refugees had left behind.

Again they swept by Kandri's doorway. This time the pounding hooves seemed to blend with a deeper thunder that continued after they passed. Now when he looked out Kandri saw vast gears turning in the windows of the turrets—and the Sky Gate starting to grind shut again.

Betrayed. None of those desperate souls still out on the plain would find shelter here. No more giving. No more hope.

It could have been us. A later start, a different holding pen. A guard pointing left instead of right.

The stone slabs met with a colossal *boom*. Dust like a breaking wave swept the plaza; Kandri coughed and shut his eyes. When he looked again all was bedlam, refugees kneeling, Kasrajis driven indoors, the riders cheering as though some great victory had been won.

And there in the midst of it stood the Chancellor herself, Lady Kosuda, more proud and splendid than she had seemed when Kandri glimpsed her from the pens.

She was fearless, and he felt her kindness again, but this time as a certainty. He trusted her as he trusted his Uncle, as he trusted Ari herself, instantly and without reservation. Nothing, nothing, could diminish this woman. Not the rope binding her hands behind her back. Not the sight of her deputy, Lisrand, forced to his knees like the refugees he had tried to protect. Not even that slap, a brutal one, delivered by the officer with the medals. Kosuda's face merely absorbed it, and despite the blood on her lips, remained itself, unchanged.

ೞ

Twenty minutes later the silence was profound. The riders had taken no lives, nor even any prisoners save the Chancellor and First Marshal. Their main objective, it seemed, had been the re-closing of the gate. But what of the ragged thousand Kosuda and Lisrand had helped inside? The children who had played under Fish, laughing at Mektu, the old Naduman, the boy Kandri had carried on his back? Had the riders driven them out onto the plain to fend for themselves? Or had terrorizing them been enough?

If so, they had succeeded. Lisrand's small company had remained loyal to him but had been helplessly outnumbered. They had scattered, pursuing the refugees down the splendid avenues, begging for their trust. But none of the refugees had returned to the plaza, and who could blame them? Would they be attacked again, or clapped in irons? Perhaps flung over the wall? What good was a promise of safety, or the word of Company Twelve?

The final stragglers were hobbling away when Kandri emerged. Debris littered the plaza. Windows were shuttered. Not a soul looked out.

"Excuse me," he said to the last soldier in the plaza—one of Lisrand's, by her uniform. "The First Marshal told me to wait for him here. Will he be back, do you think?"

The young woman was salvaging items abandoned by the refugees. She turned to him, eyes bright with more than just the early sun.

"First Marshal Lisrand is on his way to prison," she said, "along with the Lady Kosuda."

"What crime are they charged with?"

"Crime?" she snapped. "If anyone committed a crime it was the colonel who struck my lady, and took her and the Marshal away. Having a conscience, that was their crime. That and believing in the dream."

"The dream?"

"Of the Seventh Realm. *This* realm, this time around. A Kasralys wiser—" She averted her gaze, scowling, then mastered herself. "—wiser and better than we once were. When we ruled this world but did not love it."

"'One song of joy shall our children learn together.'"

She nodded, desolate. "You read the old sign. At Perec Station."

He saw that she was heaping the sturdier objects—a leather vest, a wooden toolbox, a trumpet—onto a woolen blanket. "What will become of them, sister?" Kandri asked.

"Those two?" She flicked a hand, as though the question were a trifle. "My lady and the First Marshal will be free within the hour. If the laws of the Realm still count for something, that is. If they still exist."

She toed at a blue parrot, hand-woven and soft, a child's plaything. Her eyes lifted to Kandri—not really seeing him, he thought.

"What about my city, though? What if Kasralys is never the same?"

Something cracked beneath Kandri's heel. He glanced down, sliding his foot aside, and grew very still. He had stepped on a necklace of brightly painted beads.

Kandri's breath caught in his throat. One of the beads was shattered but the rest were unharmed. He bent and closed his hand about the necklace, shaking.

"Pretty," said the soldier. "I expect you're going to tell me that it's yours."

Kandri shook his head. "My brother's," he said. "It was . . . a gift."

"'Course it was," said the soldier. She tossed the parrot onto the mound. "Help me?"

They lifted the blanket by the corners, tumbling the objects together, and made for the edge of the plaza and a waiting handcart. Kandri had forgotten what he wanted to ask her. He was thinking of a winter night last year, bearing another blanket with the woman who became his lover, a blanket enclosing the body of the Prophet's Thirdborn. The running had started minutes after he and Eshett had disposed of the corpse. It had only ended here.

They heaved the blanket into the handcart. The soldier nodded her thanks, eyes on the necklace. Kandri placed it in his pocket.

"Tell me something," he said. "What do you have against the Outworlders?"

"Not a thing," said the soldier. "I've never lain eyes on one."

"What does *Kasralys* have against them?"

"That's another matter. Could be we don't think people who won't tell us a thing about their own country should learn all the secrets of ours. Could be we even suspect their intentions. Not that we're paranoid."

"'Course you're not," said Kandri.

"There are only a hundred in all of Urrath, you know."

Kandri nodded. "So I've heard."

"And those terrible stories, we don't listen to them. That they're secret cannibals. That they smoke children like hams and ship them back across the ocean. That they stitch up wounds with vermin inside."

A needle of cold touched Kandri's spine. "What did you say? Vermin?"

"It's nonsense," said the soldier. "There was wild talk of Xavasindran doctors placing the eggs of some giant insects inside the wounds they healed in their clinics. Wounds on the bodies of those making for Kasralys." She looked at him, bemused. "The eggs would hatch, you see, and burst from the body, and multiply out of control. And if we had let the poor sap in, well, the city would be overrun with monsters."

"Oh Gods. Oh Ang's sweet mercy."

"Only it never worked. The eggs hatched too soon, or spoiled into poison; the hosts just died. But it's a good story, you have to admit. *Hazat*, what's wrong with you?"

Kandri started away, turned back, revolved helplessly in a circle. The words of the Xavasindran runaway throbbed in his head.

The others died. All the others.

But not Mektu. He was here in the city, and he carried a weapon in his flesh that could destroy it. And the surgeon, what had he said? *A symphony of pain, and a filthy death to follow.* It was all true, and every step they had taken toward Kasralys had brought it nearer.

The soldier, as though she could stand no more hysterics from anyone that morning, was wheeling her cart swiftly from the plaza. Kandri shook himself. The news was hideous, unspeakable. But his path was clear.

"Wait, please!" he shouted. The soldier turned to him with clear reluctance. "I need a doctor."

"You should have followed my mates to hospital, fool."

"No, no—I'm not sick. I need Doctor Fessjamu. I—I have something for her."

The soldier lowered the cart, turned to look at him squarely. "Tsireem Fessjamu?" she asked.

Kandri sighed. "That's the one."

"You're a strange man," she said, "or at least, you have strange luck."

"You have absolutely no idea."

"Dr. Fessjamu died today. Fell from her balcony, at sunrise. We're to observe three days of mourning, by order of the Grand Illim."

Kandri looked at her, his mind in open revolt. As though he might smack the knowledge back across the plaza and down her windpipe, make her change her story, make it untrue.

"Sunrise?"

"Any time now, there should be—"

Bells. She cocked her head at him. Near and far they began their tolling: sad single notes from all the towers, temples, schools, guild-halls, armories, keeps, and convents of the endless city. Each note a hammer to Kandri's chest. He had scarcely passed an hour in this city, knew nothing about her. But he knew with dreadful certainty that Dr. Fessjamu had not simply fallen from her balcony.

The Outworlders feared Kasralys, the little surgeon had told him. Enough to want it destroyed, obliterated, erased from the map. Enough to make weapons of the very patients whose lives they saved in their clinics, if those patients were bound for the city.

Enough to goad the great clans of Urrath into war.

And the Outworlders, too, had ordered the surgeon to stop the caravan from arriving, but not because it carried a secret weapon. Because it carried the Cure. In a letter addressed to a doctor of genius. A doctor who had just, conveniently, died.

The Xavasindrans were not in Urrath to seek a cure for the World Plague. They were in Urrath to be sure a cure was never discovered.

He clasped his hands before his face. The soldier blinked at him, and he thought she would ask why the news distressed him so particularly. But she said nothing, and at last moved away. The bells rang on. Kandri stood alone in the shadow of the great Kasraji wolf.

And yet not alone. *My brother's here. Ariqina is here.* The spark inside him had been buffeted and battered and spat upon and savaged, yet it burned on all the same.

He put Mektu's beads around his neck and made for Cathqimar House. A coffee. That was what he needed. A coffee, and a different world.

ભ

The child was peering from the doorway again—and again it fled back into the darkness at Kandri's first glance. This time, when Kandri reached the passage, he could see the child, a boy he decided, flying toward the sunny courtyard as fast as his short legs could run.

"*Harach*, I'm not a cannibal," Kandri called after him. But the boy ran on, a living shadow framed in light.

Something in the apparition—short hair, manic urgency—produced a surge of feeling in Kandri. It was a view through the wrong end of a telescope. There in the distance was someone he knew, his childhood self or Mektu, light-footed, listening to no one, running headlong toward a future blinding with promise.

Or simply blinding. Kandri followed him. In the passage, the cool and darkness of the night seemed to linger, as though he were wading a few hours backward in time. When he reached the sunny courtyard his eyes were dazzled again.

It was a scene of peace and stillness. A quiet fountain, a flowering tree. Tables with crisp white linens set beneath other trees, dwarf conifers pruned into living parasols. Dark archways, far-off kitchen clatter. The bedlam in the plaza seemed to have left Cathqimar untouched.

Only two tables were occupied. Beside the fountain, a large man in a pale gray robe sat with his back to Kandri, drawing smoke through an elegant water-pipe by his foot. Under the flowering tree, a pair of ancient women with the bent shoulders of sloths turned from their card game to study him. Kandri gazed back, aware of the dry-blood blackness of his shirt. The women did not look alarmed.

Kandri moved across the courtyard. The red and green stones on the women's fingers were large as acorns, and their gaze seemed infused with a knowledge he needed, an accounting for life so much longer than his own. He was halfway to them when he felt the man with the water-pipe grip his arm.

He looked down into the eyes of Dothor Spalak.

"They are nearly blind," said the Submaster, "but the proprietors are not. I do not think they will seat you dressed like that, Kandradisurth. You had better join me."

Food covered a platter before him: cheese, sausage, apple slices, half a loaf of bread. "You're hungry," said Spalak. "Sit and eat, and cast that dread away. This is not a sacrament. I am not a priest."

The mourning bells seemed louder now, infiltrating the sanctuary. Kandri did not sit down. Never looking away from Spalak, he gripped the man's hand and forced it from his arm. Then he wiped his own hand on his bloody shirt.

The gesture was not lost on Spalak. He took a bubbling draw on the pipe, exhaled a rose-scented smoke.

"Fine beadwork," he said, nodding at Mektu's necklace, "but not as useful as what I carry." He reached into his shirt and drew out the blood-red pendant with its word of inlaid silver. "Kasralys has recognized the Athzimazl as one of its passkeys for centuries. You might have walked right into the city if you had taken my brother's rather than burning it with his corpse. We watched you from across the canyon, you know."

"You didn't have any water," said Kandri. "How many of those drivers who went with you died of thirst?"

Spalak pursed his lips but did not answer.

"You're alone in Kasralys, aren't you?" said Kandri. "Alone, like me?"

"As you define solitude, perhaps."

"Then this is your last chance to kill me," Kandri said. "Your Prophet is nothing here. No power, no temple, no worshippers."

"You reached that conclusion quickly."

"She threw everything she had at us," said Kandri, "but we made it all the same. Two nobodies, Spalak. Two farm dogs from Blind Stream Village, and she couldn't even kill *us*. The poor helpless fake. We beat her, and we brought *this*—" He slapped the calfskin pouch through his shirt. "—across the Sumuridath Jal. *This* is revelation, you sick fuck. A cure for the Plague, made without her, despite her. *This* is the message that will change the world."

"A cure for the World Plague? Truly?" Spalak raised his eyebrows. "How astonishing. My brother refused to tell me what you bore."

Clang, clang, went the mourning bells. The old women leaned together, whispering.

"Your brother had a soul," said Kandri. "All you had was a spear, and even that was stolen. Tell me: do you have a weapon now?"

Spalak gave Kandri a crafty smile. "I do, in fact."

"Then come out to the plaza and fight, if you truly love the Prophet. Or don't you think she'll give you strength enough to kill one of the Twin Abominations, man to man?"

Spalak's reaction was the last thing Kandri could have foreseen. He beamed at Kandri, face aglow with satisfaction. He looked for a moment like the bust of a saint.

"Kill you?" he said. "Have you not heard a thing? I had a thousand opportunities to kill you in the desert, child, but that was never my wish. On the contrary, I knew in my heart that you must live. The very instant you joined the caravan, I saw it. The Enlightened One made truth blossom in my sterile heart. You must live. I did not know why, but I obeyed. It is not for us to question revelation.

"But now the reason is plain, Kandradisurth. Her legions, her Rasanga, her white devil-child: all those had to fail. Their orders were to catch you, bear you back to Eternity Camp for torture and death. But does not Her Radiance teach us that Heaven's Path emerges from a shroud of mist? Only now do I begin to pierce it—and oh, the beauty of the path revealed! No one will bring you to the Prophet. You will bring the Prophet here."

This time the needle of cold reached Kandri's heart. He stepped back from the table. The mourning bells were calamitous now. Spalak's smile grew.

"You alone shall be the instrument of her triumph," he said. "No one in this sprawling husk of Empire, this city at war with itself, sees the danger—and you may go and tell them, scream it from the ramparts, and still they shall be deaf. She is coming. For she knows you are here, boy, and that Ojulan's blood is not avenged.

"I will never kill you, Kandri. But your brother: his head I will saw from his body and preserve in oil, until that happy hour when I lay it at the feet of Her Radiance."

"I won't let you near my brother," said Kandri. "Never again."

"You'll be lucky to catch a glimpse of him, before he comes of his own accord."

"He won't," said Kandri. "If you think he's an idiot, you've never understood him at all."

Clang, clang. Spalak pushed the platter of food away and lifted an object from his lap. It was a length of rough cloth, wound about an object some two feet long.

"Again, you have it backward. Your brother will find me. He will not be able to help himself."

"You're a madman," said Kandri.

"He will come," Spalak repeated, starting to unwind the cloth, "as surely as *she* will come. These things are certainties, older than the earth we walk upon, forged with the stars. The Prophet will crush the Kasraji army, throw down the Ancestor Wall. And when she takes her seat on the throne in the Great Tower of Eroqas, her sons arrayed in beauty before her, Urrath will have its new Empress, and the circle will be complete."

"None of that is going to happen," said Kandri. "I'll warn them. I'll denounce you all."

"Kandradisurth." Spalak waved as though shooing a fly. "You denounced the Prophet months ago, and only hastened this moment's arrival. Have you forgotten every word of scripture? For Her Radiance there can be no detours, no turning or being turned."

"Her feet walk Heaven's Path!"

The voice was shrill, but it rang with startling resolve. It was the boy Kandri had caught watching him, seated cross-legged by the kitchen door.

But now Kandri knew that he was looking at the same child who had served Belac Bajamthal in Lupriz. The little thief, Mektu had called him, but the truth was worse. And now the boy, his expression contorted by faith and fury, raised a trembling hand to point at Kandri.

"Abomination," he said.

"Yes," said Spalak, "but even an Abomination must play its part."

He unwound the last of the cloth, lifted the golden mattoglin in both hands to Kandri like a newborn, or a sacrifice, or a curse. In his eyes flickered that demonic blue yatra-fire that had burned out the eyes of the exorcist. But the fire went on burning, the eyes went on seeing, and Spalak rose slowly to his feet.

"Welcome to Kasralys, my son."

The Fire Sacraments is concluded in Book Three, *Siege*.

Robert V.S. Redick grew up in Iowa and Virginia; his father worked in nuclear nonproliferation and his mother as an electron microscopist. His novel *Master Assassins*, Book One of *The Five Sacraments* trilogy, was a finalist for the 2018 Booknest Award for best novel of the year. He is also the author of the critically acclaimed epic fantasy series *The Chathrand Voyage Quartet*, which begins with *The Red Wolf Conspiracy* and concludes with *The Night of the Swarm*. The books have been published in five languages and nominated for several major awards; *Locus* magazine calls the Quartet "one of the most distinctive and appealing epic fantasies of the last decade." Robert holds an MFA from the Program for Writers at Warren Wilson College and an MA in Tropical Conservation and Development from the University of Florida.

Robert's twin passions have always been storytelling and internationalism; previous employers include the antipoverty group Oxfam, the Stonecoast MFA Program for Writers, Hampshire College, and the Center for International Forestry Research. He has lived and worked in Indonesia, Argentina, Colombia, and the United Kingdom, and traveled extensively in Latin America, Asia, and Europe. Raised in Iowa and Virginia, he now lives in Western Massachusetts.

ACKNOWLEDGEMENTS

Novelists write alone. If they are very lucky, however, they are surrounded by people who make the work a little less than impossible. Some are directly involved with the book itself; others lift the writer's spirits, dispel their fatigue, forgive their myopia, remind them (often enough, but not too often) that there is a world beyond the laptop, a world outside the fictional dream.

I am especially grateful to my editor, Cory Allyn, for his tireless, cheerful engagement with this monster of a middle volume. Cory was both first and last reader of the manuscript, and his insights have made *Sidewinders* a much better book. I'm also indebted to my other early readers, Jan Redick and Stephen Klink, for their wise and timely remarks.

Matt Bialer, my agent, provided expert guidance at every stage. Heartfelt thanks as well to Elena Stokes and Brianna Robinson at Wunderkind PR, to the artists Thomas Rey and Mack Sztaba (for map and book cover respectively), and to my students in the Stonecoast MFA Program for their enthusiastic response to an early reading from the novel.

I'm deeply grateful to James Heflin, David Anthony Durham, Claire Cooney, Carlos Hernandez, Patrick Rothfuss, Mark Lawrence, Mira Bartók, Stephen Deas, Michaela Deas, Will Stanton, Julie C. Day, Bruce Hemmer, and Brendan Plapp for so many forms of encouragement and understanding. You sustained me throughout a long campaign.

To my large and beautiful family: all my thanks and love. Special thanks to my parents, John and Jan Redick, for always encouraging me to dream.

To my *compañera*, Kiran Asher: thank you, dearest heart, for holding me together, for your love, for your faith.